Cogs Tyrannic

John Arden

COGS TYRANNIC

Four Stories

Methuen

First published in Great Britain in 1991
by Methuen London
Michelin House, 81 Fulham Road, London SW3 6RB

Copyright © 1991 John Arden
The author has asserted his moral rights

A CIP catalogue record for this book
is available from the British Library
ISBN 0 413 64400 6

Photoset by Deltatype Ltd, Ellesmere Port, Cheshire
Printed and bound in Great Britain by
St Edmundsbury Press, Bury St Edmunds, Suffolk

Dedicated to

the poets, musicians, singers, controversialists
and talkers of Women's Scéal Radio
and Radio Pirate-Woman (Galway, Ireland)

whose impertinent exploration of a
government-inhibited Technique has cheered
their immediate listeners and enlivened
others' imaginations well beyond the
limited range of their Subversively Inexpensive
and Courageously Unlicensed Transmitters.

Some fix'd the anvil, some the loom erected, some the plow
And harrow form'd & fram'd the harness of silver & ivory,
The golden compasses, the quadrant, and the rule and balance . . .

303 In human forms distinct they stood round Urizen, Prince of Light,
Petrifying all the Human Imagination into rock & sand.

                        . . . cruel Works
Of many Wheels I view, wheel without wheel, with cogs tyrannic
Moving by compulsion each other, not as those in Eden, which,
Wheel within Wheel, in freedom revolve in harmony & peace.

                       William Blake (1757–1827)

Table of Contents

Introduction

These stories are set in very different periods of history, but are linked by one theme – the essential fallibility of the human being as a tool-making tool-using animal. We are (and, I suspect, have been for as long as we have walked on two legs) obsessed by technical *progress* of some sort, whether mechanical or theoretical, even during such reputedly conservative epochs of civilisation as Ancient Egypt (*cf* my first tale). But practical inventiveness always seems to have had the utmost difficulty in walking in step with moral and social responsibility. The more spectacular the invention, the greater its supposed benefits, and the more terrifying the perils of its widespread exploitation. Children these days can learn at primary school to handle computers, while their leaders and teachers, elder statesmen and women with silver in their hair and the pride of sovereignty in their rhetoric, still demonstrate a code of public conduct that has not improved since the most primitive ages. Cain in the Hebrew myth had only an ass's jawbone as a weapon for his hatred. But he had worked out how to use it, so he used it and denied culpability: 'Am I my brother's keeper?' He invented more than Armed Conflict, he was also the innovator of Disinformative War Propaganda. Has our *progress* taught us anything beyond building upon his discoveries?

While I write this, Baghdad is being bombarded by aircraft and missiles of what used to be called Christendom (temporarily presented as the 'United Nations', with a few Muslim clients roped-in to authenticise the assumption). Three days ago I spent a Christmas book-token on Steven Runciman's *A History of the Crusades*, but the immediacy of the twentieth-century playback is so dreadful that I have not yet been able to open the volume and reacquaint myself with the prophetic imbecilities of the middle ages. For the last six months or so the news-media have puffed their excitable notions of high-tech war, state-of-the-art electronics for mass-murder, super-industrial 'surgical' destruction, all allegedly in the interests of the freedom of a small nation, Kuwait. Very lately, the same media, with decorous embarrassment, have slipped us the hint that their reports from the Persian Gulf will naturally accommodate a military censorship.

At the same time (approximately) the British government reopens diplomatic contacts with Iran, all the better to isolate Iraq, whereas my fellow-writer Salman Rushdie is assured by Iranian theocrats that the death-sentence against him for blasphemy still holds. Which death-sentence of course caused the breach of relations in the first place. Oh yes, and the Christian Vatican reviled *The Satanic Verses*, presumably in a spirit of professional solidarity.

At the same time, an unarmed crowd of Lithuanian civilians, demonstrating on behalf of the freedom of their small nation, is fired at by riflemen and run over by tanks. Soldiers and civilians alike belonging to that once-hailed 'new species' of the modern evolutionary revolutionary era, Soviet Socialist Man.

At the same time, a young citizen in the north of Ireland is also shot dead, at a checkpoint, and who can tell how? – apparently because he was known by the 'security forces' to sell a newspaper (*An Phoblacht/ Republican News*) that campaigns every week for the freedom of his small nation.

At the same time, six Irishmen from Birmingham remain in gaol for their seventeenth Christmas, even though nobody of repute now dares argue that they could conceivably have planted the bombs for which they were sentenced. The difficulties of exploring archives and analysing an enormity of contradictory documents have been offered as an excuse for the delay in setting them free.

At the same time, an antique suburban railway train runs into the buffers of a London terminus, kills two passengers and injures two hundred more. A managerial person from British Rail tells the media that all possible safety precautions are constantly being taken, therefore the train was safe, despite its age – and if it wasn't, then it will be, as soon as new rolling-stock is provided, which is of course a matter of funding, which is of course a *political* matter and out of his hands. The political matter of the Middle East, its oilfields, its socio-religious furies, its flailing, conniving, connived-at, authoritarian post-colonial and neo-colonial regimes, must already have cost the British government more money in one half-year than would have served to put an entire national transport system right for the next whole century.

At the same time – what else? Or should I ask, what else *not*?

I don't think I am a deeply cynical crusted reactionary. I am as glad as anyone to see new things, to learn new ideas, and to hope for them and with them. I am writing this book on a word-processor, and managing very nicely, thank you. Last month I attended the general election count at a polling station in reunited Germany and noticed with pleasure that only one forlorn vote had been cast for the neo-Nazi candidate. And 'catholic obscurantist' Ireland has a new president, a liberal secularist lawyer with an excellent record on civil liberties, a woman.

I just wish, though, that the human race was not quite so often trapped by its own versatility.

J.A. (*Galway, Ireland: 17 Jan 1991*)

Twelfth Century (before Christ)

SLOW JOURNEY,
SWIFT WRITING

Slow Journey,
Swift Writing

I found lying open upon his board certain books of
Cosmography, with a universal Map; he seeing me
somewhat curious in the view thereof, began to instruct
my ignorance, by showing me the division of the earth
into three parts after the old account; he pointed with
his wand to all the known seas, gulfs, bays, straits,
capes, rivers, empires, kingdoms, dukedoms and
territories of each part, with declaration also of their
special commodities, and particular wants, which by the
benefit of traffic, and intercourse of merchants, are
plentifully supplied.

By degrees I read over whatsoever printed or written
discoveries I found extant either in the Greek, Latin,
Italian, Spanish, Portuguese, French or English
languages, to the singular pleasure, and general
contentment of my auditory in my public lectures.

I call the work a burden, in consideration that these
voyages lay so dispersed, scattered and hidden in several
hucksters' hands, that I now wonder at myself, to see
how I was able to endure the delays, curiosity, and
backwardness of many from whom I was to receive the
originals.

Richard Hakluyt (d. 1616): *Voyages and Discoveries*

ONE

Most of the scribes who served Pharaoh's government used only the
government hieroglyphs; sometimes in the relaxed cursive form, but
always inhibitingly conventional; restrictive of phrase and feeling.

The man of this story despised such practitioners. His name was Harkhuf, a senior in his department, well-known for his versatile skill, scion of a famous dynasty of accomplished scribal ancestors. He saw his contemporary colleagues equipped to express little beyond the recognised thoughts of unchangeable Egypt and Egypt's understanding of diverse but unchangeable god; thereby indeed they kept clear of error (political error as well as religious, twin evils writhing each within the other like copulating demons). But Harkhuf, entirely sure of his intellectual correctitude, did not need such protection; he knew his talents were from god; and one of the many aspects of god would look after their continued integrity.

He had a script of his own invention, extremely flexible, and unintelligible to anyone else (a device not unknown among his rivals, but he had developed it to an unusual degree of efficiency). It marked single sounds instead of the syllables and idea-symbols of the official writings. He exploited it most happily in conjunction with a sort of shorthand. When conducting and recording interviews, for example, he jotted shorthand notes into wax, no more than the main heads of the discourse he was hearing. Meanwhile his well-trained memory stored the detailed responses to his questions, which then he could draft upon papyrus, in his personal script, more or less verbatim. No better way to catch the full *flavour* of the spoken word and convey its shades of meaning. Through the words of men you knew men, and only through men could you know truth – and what was correct government but truth-in-action throughout an entire population?

Afterwards he must transcribe into official script, formalising, simplifying (sometimes, alas, almost to the point of missing the whole point), *straightening out*, for the archive and the eyes of his superiors. Even so, he insisted, his hieroglyphic final versions were more delicately precise to the full intention of what he recorded than could ever have been possible without his particular process. A compromise, necessarily; but he made shift to live with it, for of course he never doubted that the official script was a sacred work, as essential to Egypt's sacred identity as the life-giving river itself.

Sometimes, when a little in drink with trusted friends, he had launched large assertions about his invention: he could (he said) set down speech with no more than twenty-five, twenty-six, or twenty-eight specific signs (the number varied from one cup of wine to the next) and perhaps half-a-score of pen-jabs and squiggles to modify them; and moreover these signs could as easily be employed for the Syrian and Chaldean tongues as for the Egyptian, indeed for any recognisable language of day-to-day international acquaintance, not excluding Hittite, or Libyan, or even the barbarisms of the northern islands. There were those of his fellow scribes who believed him and made fruitless efforts to discover his secret, although most thought he was only boasting – the profession as a whole was extremely prone to displays of unprovable brag: what else could be expected from a trade so congenitally mysterious?

It was possible that one day he would pass on his invention to a pupil: but certainly not just yet. He expected, after all, to live many more years – he was only thirty-two, an age at which it would be the height of folly to raise up rivals in his own workshop. Out of sheer malicious mischief he had once tried, after a quarrel with an elder cousin, Chief Scribe to the Department of Granaries, to teach a proportion of his twenty-five (or six? – or eight?) signs to a slave-girl, Mira, just enough to enable her to write her own name and his. She had proved quite adept at it: in fact, too adept. To shame an arrogant kinsman by means of her skill was a good joke, but not if it might establish an irregular caste of trained scribes among the servile population. He hastily discontinued the lessons and warned the child (on pain of a week's daily whippings by the women's-eunuch of his household) never to speak of them to anyone. Nor did he display Mira's talent at his cousin's birthday supper as had been his original intention.

He thought this disappointed her; so he bought her an exceptionally sly and graceful kitten to be her personal goddess, an extravagance that angered his wife. The latter sprang round at him with the amazing energy of sudden spite (as he lovingly trickled water over her in the marital bathroom) crying that it was one thing for him to be allowed a slave-concubine, but altogether something else to traffic with her in true-lovers' gifts like a licentious courtier from the palace: and did he not know that several licentious courtiers had been tempting his wife's fidelity with just such a style of gift, and in vain, over several years? – if he did *not* know, he knew now, so let him forthwith take heed of his manners. A water-jar was broken and one of the potsherds cut his neck.

Since this painful episode Harkhuf had been most careful to avoid all description of his invention, even very loose accounts of it designed to mislead, even when tipsy, even with friends. A highly-placed devotee of an important craft-mystery ought not, in any case, to permit himself the indulgence of friends, or at any rate not drinking-friends in the same line of business: the gods alone knew the damage that might be done.

Historians, rarely so sure of the facts of history as they would like us to think them, give the third year of the hectic reign of the third Pharaoh Ramses as 1195 BC (according to Christendom's reckoning) in one book, and 1184 BC in another. An unwholesome measure of doubt is thereby sprinkled over events of that year. To attempt a persuasive account of even a few of them will inevitably involve conjecture, and conjecture inevitably must be seen as unpersuasive.

However, it *was* that year, whichever year-of-modern-certainties it
might in fact have been, when Harkhuf was sent by boat, downriver, from
splendid Thebes to small unkempt Rakotis on the coast. He himself was
very well aware of the date, he had his own immaculate reckoning; he also
knew the season, indisputably winter, with persistent squalls of northerly
wind and rain, as he was rowed through the unsheltered mudflats of the
delta: but concerning Rakotis – what kind of horrid place it was; what kind
of feckless people he would find there; how far those people themselves,
out of ignorance or remoteness from the centre of affairs, had *confected* the
awkward problem he was sent to solve on behalf of the Department of
Barbarian Affairs (Commercial and Maritime) – upon all this he had
practically no information. He did not like the sound of any that he did
have; and the doubts across his mind were considerably more than
sprinklings – indeed he felt himself quite soaked in them; an unusual
occurrence for a rising official personage so positive and correct.

After all, was he not named after his distinguished forebear Harkhuf,
who had served the Pharaoh Pepi thirty-four generations ago (the family
records had kept very careful count), and whose diplomatic triumph had
been to open to Egyptian trade the southern end of the Red Sea and the
Arabian coasts? The descendant of such a man could scarcely afford a
diminution of self-confidence, or of faith in the powers of his calling.

Had the younger Harkhuf known, as our historians now positively state
they do know, that Rakotis, in another eight hundred and sixty years (give
or take the odd decade), was to be augmented by conquering foreigners
until it became the great and un-Egyptian city of Alexandria, he would
have brushed the knowledge aside as *incorrect*, an abuse of prophetic
powers. At least, at the start of his mission. By the end of it, it is probable he
would have accepted the doom of history as being exactly the sort of
malevolent nonsense divine wisdom might well have in store. For, from
then until his death, his doubts and himself were to be all of a piece, an
unhappy disaffected air-breathing *nothing*, that called itself an Egyptian,
and yet (in its secret heart) belonged nowhere, present or future.

To begin with all he had to go on, all there was to provoke doubt, was a
letter from Rakotis written by the beachmaster-collector there, the only
royal magistrate along that stretch of coast. It baldly announced that a
strange ship's company had arrived at the little port with a very strange
story, a most unlikely story, probably criminal, just possibly dangerously
subversive. So would higher authority please come and make an
authoritative assessment because the beachmaster did not claim to be
competent?

If the beachmaster reported the truth, then included within the truth was a blasphemous statement quite contrary to religious belief. Religious belief was established by the priesthood, most notably by the priesthood of the dual godhead Supreme Amun-Ra. The Lord Pharaoh Ramses – his dynastic title secured by sacred intermarriage between fathers and daughters, brothers and sisters – was the incarnation upon earth of Amun-Ra, so the god's priests were Pharaoh's priests; if their doctrine should be contradicted, Pharaoh's right to rule over the empire of the Two Egypts (Upper and Lower) was likewise contradicted, it stood to reason. Therefore the sailors' tale could not be true. Harkhuf's superiors in Thebes had at once assumed, as had Harkhuf himself, that if the tale had been told at all (and the beachmaster's letter was not very clear upon details), then it must be a lie. The scribe's mission was thus to establish the truth behind the lie, the purposes for which it had been perpetrated, and to discover how far it should be seen as a serious threat to the security of the state.

The blasphemy was simple, so simple as to be enormous. The men from the strange ship, whoever they were (their identity was another thing about which the beachmaster had not been clear), alleged themselves to have set sail from the east coast of Upper Egypt, the shore of the Red Sea, several years previously, and now to have returned by way of the Middle Sea, through its western gates. In itself the wildest, most inordinate assertion; but not quite impious, not beyond possibility. It was known that the Stream of Ocean surrounded the lands of human habitation; put a ship in it, and with good luck and the blessing of heaven, you might conceivably make the voyage. But these men had gone on to offer what they apparently thought a most natural and casual piece of news – as they might perhaps have said that in Ocean tide-waters it was hard to row against the current, or the like – they had 'happened to mention' that for a great part of their journey *the sun had shone from the north*.

Now the divine Unconquered Sun was Almighty Lord Ra, as a conjoint person of Supreme Amun-Ra he contained the person of Lord Pharaoh, he moved solemnly and irrevocably from east to west, to the *south* of the entire world: the priests said so, they were sure of it, had charted his progress every hour of every day for more than two thousand years, noting his variations (summer and winter), relating them to the movements of stars, planets and moon; relating them to the bountiful annual flooding of the river, relating them to the destiny (after worldly death) of the soul of superior lineage, relating them to the total system of human government and social degree without which the Two Egypts could never have existed as the central system of all systems. And these sacred charts were constructed by means of writing and ciphering, divine activities, infallible, the scribe himself had professional share in them: were they proved to be incorrect, he himself must be incorrect, his conscientious adult life from its very beginning must be shown to be utterly futile.

Even a pack of transparent lies (spread by sufficient people among people who might believe them) could cast so much doubt upon the established truths as to cause *all* truth to be doubted: if a scribe let that happen, why, barbarians from the world's margin might just as well take over the world.

Harkhuf was deeply conscious of the peril inherent: and yet the whole affair could easily be nothing but nonsense, an absurd misunderstanding. He wished that government had not so swiftly taken the view that it *was* a misunderstanding, for otherwise they might have allowed him a state-barge to bring him to the coast. But that was the view they took; he had to find his own transport at his own cost. River boats chartered exclusively all the way from Thebes were not cheap. He restricted himself therefore to only four personal slaves for the expedition, two men and a boy and the girl Mira. The accommodation, even so, was cramped; and protection from the weather inadequate. Long before they reached Rakotis on its sand-spit between the inland lake and the Middle Sea, the scribe realised he had failed to equip himself with anything like sufficient clothing.

His slaves, used to undemanding domestic work in the sun-flooded courtyards of an elegant town house, had practically no clothes at all. They shivered and moaned unceasingly, neglecting or making a muddle of their simplest duties, driving him mad with irritation: and he could not express it because if he did the hired boatmen would be witnesses to loss of dignity, they would question official judgement in choosing such a petulant snarler as Pharaoh's messenger to the coast; such a question, even unspoken, would of itself be impious and treasonable. He must permit no pretext for it. At the exorbitant price of a whole goatskin of wine (out of several brought on purpose for his own refreshment), he purchased blankets from a bedouin on the riverbank, wrapped his people in them, refused one himself as deleterious to dignity, and continued to shiver in his white linen shawl and kilt, crouched away from the rain under the very skimpy awning, pretending to be calm and cheerful; pretending that his authority (which was Pharaoh's authority in miniature and thus divine) remained, as ever, unalterable, impregnable. Already he was beginning to wonder if it really did.

For the nearer Harkhuf came to his destination, the more the sullen landscape unsettled him, and the greater grew his distress at the overheard conversations of commercial men and small officials in the riverside rest-houses. As a matter of professional principle he kept himself aloof from garrulous fellow travellers, but he could not order their silence while he ate.

Every evening he found himself listening, with increasing gloom, to gloomy and continuous talk of continuous frontier trouble. He had not realised, until this journey, how Rakotis – according to the archive, well inside the Two Kingdoms' territories – had imperceptibly become an endangered frontier port. It was now the last town on the coast westward: beyond it, along the shore, spread anarchic hostile Libya; while across the bay, only one mile out to sea, the Free Island of Pharos sat on the water, anomalous, scowling into Egypt, the lurking-place of strangers' gods, impregnate with their eccentric power, directing unharnessed malice against the peace of Amun-Ra and his incarnation Lord Ramses (who nonetheless had not been willing, perhaps had not even been able, to pay for a state-barge).

In the days of the truly great rulers all these things would have been very different. Treasonable and impious doubt. Not to be countenanced. But how to put it out of one's mind?

TWO

The town, when they reached it at dawn after a dreadful night of seasickness on the turbulent lake, proved as shabby and forlorn as the scribe had feared: a deserted and half-ruined fort, its broken gate banging in the gale; a long low-lying straggle of adobe huts crouched among dunes of wet sand; intermittent and scrawny palm trees; a dozen fishing boats drawn up on the beach. About a hundred paces from the boats lay a single sea-going ship (the object of his journey, he supposed), an odd-looking clumsy craft in very bad repair that seemed to have been built and rigged by village carpenters rather than shipwrights. An attempt had been made to pull it higher up the strand upon rollers, but this had been blocked by an outcrop of rocks. The stern was still in the water and the waves were breaking over it.

At the north-eastern end of the irregular street stood the statue of some ancient Pharaoh, so weather-scoured that his engraved name had become illegible under the frettings of sand and salt, his hawknosed profile now blurred into the outline of a cabbage. There were indeed cabbage leaves blown between his feet – or maybe deliberately swept there – fish-heads, potsherds, withered palm fronds, fragments of worn-out cloth, market rubbish of all sorts. A literate person (and therefore, presumably, an influential local dissident who ought rigorously to be detected) had painted an insulting message in coarsely-formed hieroglyphs on the statue's left buttock, to the rough effect that dead kings were as dead as dead fishermen and there was no carnal congress beyond the grave for any of them.

Harkhuf shuddered at the implied atheism. It rhymed uncomfortably with the refrain of his visit here. But the inscription was old, it could not have resulted from the coming of the strange ship. Had it to do, though, with the proximity of the Free Island?

He looked around for someone to ask about it, but saw only the impoverished men and boys who had carried up his baggage from the lakeside wharf. He was not at all sure they were even Egyptians (although they chattered the language importunately enough). Some had thick beards like barbarians from Asia, most were as dark as deep-desert Libyans; and there were two pale young men with *red* hair, which was very outlandish indeed.

Beside the statue was the only house in Rakotis that could properly be

called a house. It must belong to the beachmaster-collector: but where was
he? And where were his guards who ought to be securing Rakotis against
pirates, smugglers, desert raiders, and the men of the threatening island?

The scribe decided that his dignity left him but one course of action: he
could not wait in the street to be received, he must enter the house and take
control of it. He climbed some steps onto the seaward-facing verandah
(fully exposed to the rain and wind), and ordered his people to break open
a locked door that gave access to the interior. As they did so, he heard
women and children squealing inside. The door fell back, he strode in over
the threshold, and caught a quick glimpse of flying skirts and long hair
disappearing through a second room beyond the lobby and thence across
the internal courtyard.

They had left behind a charcoal brazier which offered some heat to the
meanly appointed room. Harkhuf told his slaves to bring a stool out onto
the verandah for him, he would wait there in full sight and dignity until his
arrival was officially recognised; in the meantime they could clean the
room, make it habitable, and gain what comfort they could from the
brazier. Let them also cook some food on it. His girl-slave must cross the
courtyard to the beachmaster's women and explain things to them; he had
no wish to put the man's family in fear. It was, after all, the beachmaster's
own letter that had brought him all this way. No doubt a dutiful officer,
though clearly not as *prudent* as he might be.

Settled, then, on the porch, with his writing materials in their basket
beside him as a sign of his status, the scribe folded hands upon lap and
considered the prospect. A small but growing group of ragged townspeople
stood below him in the street, at an appropriately awe-struck distance, and
considered *him*.

Looking out over their heads he could see only the beach and the island
and the tossing grey waves of the sea. There was no indication of the sun
this dismal morning: ill augury, almost a rebuke from Lord Ra, on whose
behalf, after all, he had travelled all this way. Was the god trying to tell him
something?

No sun; because of clouds. Clouds; because of wind. A wind that blew
from Cyprus and beyond Cyprus, from the mainland hills of the Hittites,
and beyond them from the mountains that uninformed people believed to
be the absolute rim of the world; but which the scribe knew were only the
barrier between the real world and its immeasurable margin, the huge
wastes of Scythia where there were indeed men, but where it was so cold
that they must wear beast skins in order to live at all as they drove their
herds hither and thither, thousands of miles at a journey, in desperate
search of pasture, little convoys of men-of-nothing, knowing no gods in

that immense wilderness except the anger of the freezing clouds, wondering what could have happened that they were created so eternally outcast, so ignorant of the sun's true nature, so ignorant of the world's centre. It was *their* wind, the Scythian wind, the wind of utter nothing, that now beat upon this coast: and before it hit the coast it was surging among the trees of the island, look at them in their thick green cluster, scores and hundreds of palm heads all bending together, the dark mass of their closely planted trunks concealing what wickedness from the watcher on the mainland shore?

So: to the island the absent sun was directing Harkhuf's attention. Already men in rest-houses and rude words upon a statue had put this island into his mind, whereas his instructions hardly mentioned the place at all. He had to turn his head a little to the left to get a good view of it; and he did so very carefully, determined not to show himself to the gapers below him as just another curious gaper no better than themselves.

The island must be important. And its importance, however he came to interpret it over the next few days, could be a crucial element of the report he must make to Pharaoh's minister; and eventually, if he achieved any results of significance, to Pharaoh himself. Along the east strand of the island, and therefore directly facing him, he could see a greyish-red line of stonework, a quay and projecting piers, backed by a number of white-washed buildings. In the archive it was alleged that these harbour-works had been destroyed by earthquake and tidal wave several Pharaohs' reigns ago: it would appear that the archive was not up-to-date. Repairs had been made, even at this distance he could see that. He could also see ships moored to the quay there – not many of them, this was the storm season, the barbarians who used the island as a trade depot had for the most part returned home with their vessels to the distant places where they lived – or rather, from which they *swarmed* – the Hittite and Syrian seaboard; Crete; the archipelago behind Crete and the mainland behind the archipelago (later to be called the home of the Greeks, although Harkhuf thought of them only as disparate predatory tribes with something like a common language, Achaeans, Danaans, Myrmidons); to say nothing of the little-known corners of the further west. Altogether *too* little was known of these people; of their gods, of their plans, of their real reasons for establishing themselves by ancient treaty with Egypt so very very close to the Two Kingdoms, so suspiciously close to the Libyan land.

They were vaguely designated as the People of the Sea, a ridiculous description – they could not live in the sea itself. The name suggested a degree of confederacy, but who could say how close it was? Were the interests of all the diverse ships and their owners always the same, however many places they hailed from? The barbarians who had raided Egypt so unmercifully a generation since had also been called 'Sea Peoples'. Were they the same nations as the Free Island traders of today, or some of the same, or totally different? The archive was uncertain about this. And the eventual repulse of the raiders had not involved the troops of the then Pharaoh in any operations against the island; nor had the treaty been repudiated.

It *was* known that for the past few years there had been great movement of tribes all over the northern mainland, disrupting the Hittite realms, and thence into the hills of Canaan by way of the Syrian coast. Without doubt it had begun from Scythia, the cloud gods were assembling distress for the sunlit world, perhaps the north wind from now on was fated to blow continuously and all Egypt would have to wear woollen blankets, all Egypt might even have to wrap themselves in beast-skins; and then, while they shivered, demoralised, the Sea Peoples would come again and in greater numbers than ever before and this time they would not be repulsed . . .

The scribe took a wax tablet, tried to scratch down a few of these thoughts, rejected them as incorrect, reproached himself for disloyal impropriety and obliterated the markings with his thumb; he snapped like a dog over his shoulder, three sharp words towards his slaves who made too much frivolous noise just behind him in the house.

When she heard him, his girl crept out to him with her timid smile. It was more than a decade now since some king of her homeland of Hindustan was defeated in some war and his people put on the market. Mira had been fetched to a Red Sea slave-port in her mother's fettered arms: the scribe bought the pair of them when he first set up house with his wife. But in less than a year the mother was dead. Of fever. Or of sorrow? In any event, he had brought up Mira (as one might say, or as *he* often said) just as though she were his own daughter.

It was the girl's normal duty to stand at his back while he worked, and to cool him with a fan of feathers.

Now she was faced with the opposite task, keeping him warm. She was intelligent enough to realise that, but had no experience of how to do it. However, she had a dry shawl for him, and exchanged it for the one he was wearing; and she put the thickest wig from his baggage onto his shaven head, which was thoughtful of her.

'Oh sir, you are very cold: if your work must keep you out-of-doors, shall you not embrace me?' she said, folding back her blanket to reveal her sweet little copper-coloured breasts. Thoughtful, yes indeed, and good-hearted as well: Harkhuf prided himself upon his ability to arouse affection among his household. But no, he could not think after all that this child was intelligent. It was quite out of the question that he and she should embrace on a raised verandah across the middle of his writing in front of half the town. This was not Thebes. No sensuous elegance, no charming variations of flirtation, in a place like this. Old formalities must be rigidly adhered to, official persons must not be seen to have commonplace desires, Pharaoh's man must be of adamant, unmockable, unattainable. The riff-raff of Rakotis must tremble before it was permitted to grin.

The girl had something else to say to him. She understood that her tenderness was inappropriate to the situation, she pulled the blanket tight again round her shoulders, but she did not leave: instead she bowed her head, put the palms of her hands together, and appeared to wait to be asked what she was waiting for. The scribe was annoyed and he showed it, his tetchy fingers closed and unclosed.

'*Well?*'

She flinched and lost her smile. 'Sir,' she faltered, 'oh sir, they said I must tell you, there is a eunuch with the women in the back of the house, he is very afraid of you, and he asked me to tell you: he dare not leave the women to come out and speak with strangers, not even with very great strangers, because the women are his trust and the beachmaster would hold him to blame if anything went wrong. If strangers harmed the women, the eunuch's honour would be destroyed. He says he has lost his manhood and his honour is all that he has left, he would die for it, he says. He says, sir, please wait for the beachmaster: he cannot be far away, he thinks he went no further than the shrine of the Lady Neith – she is the lady of this town –'

'Is she indeed? They told you that? Did they tell you she's a lady of Libya as well as of Egypt?' The scribe was frowning. A frontier town ought not to be under the patronage of a goddess worshipped across the border, particularly when the town's name was so auspiciously prefixed by the divine (and unimpeachably Egyptian) syllable of the great god Ra. An unnerving ambiguity, government should look into it.

'Of Libya? Oh sir, no sir, no, I did not know.' The girl was a fool. 'But he said, the eunuch said, that her shrine is beside the shrine of Almighty Amun-Ra, they are quite near, over the sandhills, there to the east, and the beachmaster went to them early this morning, just before our arrival, sir, and he took all his men with him with their spears – the eunuch does not know why.'

'Go back to him and tell him to send a message to his master.'

'Sir, he says his master will already have heard. The houseboy was sent – through the back door, he says, as you came in at the porch.'

She gulped, nervously wiped back her strands of hair, stooped to kiss Harkhuf's foot, and began to creep away. He stopped her with a pressure of his hand on her arm, lifted her up, kissed her mouth, gently, briefly; he preferred not to let her think his annoyance had been more than momentary. Though indeed it still continued. She should have given him this important piece of news before she started fiddling with his shawls. But the girl was scarcely more than fourteen years old, he needed to feel that she was confident in his benevolence; a permanently frightened child would be no use at all for any purpose of service, and would only shame him when he looked at her. When she grew into a wide-hipped woman, she would hate him moreover; and that would be highly dangerous. He gestured dismissal, but a kind dismissal: she went away.

As she passed into the house and before she shut the door he could hear his boy-slave say something to her, something mischievous; he heard her laugh. Light-minded, after all: on the whole a good quality, despite its inconveniences. She was not the sort of slave that a man wanted to have to sell.

He thought he could just distinguish little figures of people, moving about in the distance upon the quays of the island. Did they know, over there, that he was expected in Rakotis? He supposed the local fishermen would be going backwards and forwards in their boats, bringing their catch for sale, bringing news. Oh what in the name of Isis had possessed that long-dead Pharaoh who allowed the intruders to settle there?

And why had no subsequent government made any effort to bring them under obedience?

And what about the Libyans?

At least there could have been established some better official presence here in Rakotis, a regular military governor to replace this inept beach-master; or certainly a regular priesthood, in charge of a well-endowed temple, instead of a miserable pair of shrines, to counteract the doubtful cult that obtained (did it not?) upon the island. Harkhuf searched his memory: he had once read in some religious schedule that an oracle of sorts was kept there, hidden deep in the palm groves; the 'Old Man of the Sea' who gave prophecies to barbarian sailors, directing their voyages, whether speciously for trade or – more realistically – piracy: was there in fact an old man? How many priests did he have? Or were they priestesses? Sacred harlots; or not so sacred, for the amenities of the port? All this ought to have been discovered from the archive in Thebes before he set out: it was not entirely his own fault, the men who prepared his instructions should have thought of it. No, *he* should have thought of it. He was at fault. But even had it crossed his mind, he suspected he would have found little information of any current value. In all likelihood the documents relating to the island's original charter had been pigeon-holed, neglected for centuries; many of them, no doubt, irremediably mislaid.

He made more notes on his tablet, obliterated them, sat chewing his thumb.

This unseemly posture was at once corrected by the sudden arrival of the beachmaster, a short plump anxious man, hurrying from over the dunes with an undisciplined bunch of spearmen all disorderly behind him. He pushed through the townspeople, fussing at them with the palms of his hands to get them to clear a way for him, he sprang upon his own doorstep; and then sprang back again, in nervous awareness it was now become the judgement seat of that 'higher authority' he had been pleading for. His formal wig, that should have been crisp and glossy black, was besmirched with sand, out-of-curl, askew on his sweating head. Despite the cold wind the perspiration ran down his jowls onto his collar-of-office and his bare shoulders.

The scribe said, 'You are late.'

The scribe said, 'That does not matter, except that you left the entire town without a master or even a master's servant to supervise the Pharaoh's peace. Please explain.'

The beachmaster was already doing his best, but most of his words had been lost under the chill venom of the scribe's rebuke. Nor was the scribe about to *let* him explain, not just yet: the initiative in this conversation was not to be surrendered; it must be put to immediate use.

'The Free Island!' he snapped. The beachmaster was surprised, he looked foolish in his surprise. The scribe pointed grimly across the bay: 'I said, the Free Island. The island of the Sea People. The island of barbarians. How often do you go there?'

'How – how often? But, sir – never!' Taken aback by the unexpected question, the beachmaster could only stammer a discursive account of how government forbade him – or anyone else from Rakotis – to have any dealings with the island, while the islandmen themselves forbade access from Rakotis. 'They are most fierce over there to – to protect their – their independence. Oh no, sir, they have nothing to do with Egypt at all.'

'But are they not there to trade with Egypt? If not, then what?'

'Ah yes, sir, yes, of course, I quite see what you mean.' It seemed that barbarian ships brought cargoes to the island, which were then fetched along the coast to the nearest main mouth of the Nile; the crews of the trans-shipment vessels were Egyptians, to be sure, but not from Rakotis, nor did the islandmen allow those crews out of the boats onto the island itself. The quays were patrolled with armed men, and savage dogs; the island-slaves to load the boats were all foreigners, of foreign tongues from far-off parts. Oh, the island was well protected. 'In fact, I may say, sir – ' (he expanded himself, complacently)' – I may say, in point of fact, that all affairs of the island are outside my jurisdiction: and I express myself most thankful for it. They are fierce and dangerous people, not wanted in Rakotis, not at all.'

'Do Libyans go to the island?'

'They are not a seafaring people; but they do have some boats. Yes, sir, I think they do. But for reasons I have told you, it is not easy to know.'

'Do they come to Rakotis?'

'Nomads, now and then by land, once a month, once a week sometimes. They make a market. They behave quietly. We do not give them strong drink: most strictly prohibited indeed. Perhaps once a year, twice a year, their chariot chiefs will perpetrate a raid of robbery, burn and loot, take slaves from our people; sir, it is very terrible, when they do, I have to fight them. My coastguard is insufficient. Sir, it is so insufficient that I must urgently request government to –'

'We know all about that. It is under consideration.' Which was not true; but Harkhuf could not allow complaints against government upon military matters at this stage. Not his department; he had his own complaint to deal with first. As the beachmaster well knew: he was still sweating.

'You were to tell me for what reason you were not here when I arrived?'

The beachmaster stammered again. 'Sir – sir, it was the strangers, the crew of the outlandish ship. Have you seen the outlandish ship? She is pulled up there onto the strand. I had, as I wrote to Pharaoh – or at least to Pharaoh's House – I had ordered these men to be employed, in bonds and under the whip, carrying stones for government. We were building, or attempting to build, a breakwater at the turn of the bay to shelter our boats when the wind blows as it does now; you can see the commencement of the work, over there, beyond the ship. There were women and children with the men when they arrived: I thought it best to separate them, distribute them, as domestics and field-slaves, among the better house-holds of the district, to people prepared to pay an appropriate sum for them into the treasury of the port. Which was done, which was done: but now the men chose to rebel. We do not know their language but they made trouble at the shrine last night and the servants of the shrine were terrified, they sent for me and I had to go, to restore order with all my guards. Sir, please understand, these men are very big, despite their famished condition when they came here; big and strong and very black, and they were most violent to regain their women, I had to take all my coastguards and two of the black men were killed. Also I have a guard with a broken head and another with a broken leg. Oh sir, it was extremely serious.'

'Is the rebellion quenched?'

'Praise the gods, it is finally quenched.'

'How many black men?'

'Twelve, sir, and the two dead, fourteen altogether.'

'How many women?'

'Eight, and ten children. They too have been violent: there have been complaints from nearly every house where they were placed. It is hard, oh very hard, to know what ought to be done. Look, sir, at my spearmen, almost every one of them has a gash or a great bruise, or a hidden injury to his gut, I had a hard time preventing them from killing all of the slaves: I said repeatedly, "Government property, if you destroy it, you will be liable," and at last I was listened to, was I not, captain?'

The captain of the guard, a sullen stupid-looking man, grunted a wordless acquiescence. He had blood on his mouth, and a missing tooth. He kept spitting blood onto the sand.

'Why in the shrine?'

'It is the only building here made of stone and not in ruins, there are storehouses behind it strong enough to use as a prison for men of such strength. But the priestess did not like too many of my guards within the precinct, I was foolish enough to pay heed to her, now she wishes she had kept silence, there was very nearly desecration of the Lady Neith's sanctuary, very nearly; thank Our Lady, not. And what a mercy the ship-captain was not with his men. Had *he* broken loose, he would have massacred the town, he and his big woman, oh terrible malefactors, terrible.'

'Where was he?'

'Oh, at the shrine also, but in a different building. I could not use *him* for carrying stone. Sir, you will see, if you will only be patient, you will see him very speedily, in a very few minutes. Oh sir, please forgive me, I do understand all is not as you would have wished. But I did take good care that none of the townspeople were told what is going on. See, they are astonished at the condition of my spearmen, they regret not having known about it, but they are fools, bazaar sweepings, beachcombing rascals, they are too late to laugh at government, all is secure. I have always a difficulty here in obtaining sufficient respect. I am not myself a local man: and these are not proper Egyptians. Captain, drive them away.'

The scribe wondered how much of a 'proper Egyptian' the beachmaster was: his features were degradingly irregular, and his language seemed not to have been learned absolutely at his mother's knee. He might be a Canaanite, a man of Israel, or perhaps Moab, there were many such in the coastwise regions. Nonetheless he was an accredited officer and did require respect. But something had to be said about his careless governance. Apart from whatever had happened last night at the shrine, there was a blatant example of it right alongside this very portico.

Waiting until the captain had dispersed the giggling crowd, Harkhuf considered how most delicately to put his question. He must be careful not to make an enemy of the beachmaster before the enquiry had fully opened.

'I suppose,' he said at last, 'I suppose those indecent words written up on the sacred statue are the sort of thing you have to deal with here, repeatedly, I suppose?'

'Ah, the words. We tried our best, sir, to get rid of them, but they are scrawled there in boat-builder's pitch, very very difficult to scrub away. But no one in the town is able to read them, except myself and my scribe, a most trustworthy young man, unfortunately very ill; also of course the priestess, who never leaves her shrine, and the old priest at the other shrine who is in any case blind. I did not think they would do much harm.'

'If no one can read them, who wrote them?'

'Some jocular miscreant out of a foreign ship: he was gone before we discovered them.'

'He must have been an Egyptian miscreant. The signs are very accurately presented.'

'Unhappily, sir, that seems to be the case.'

'Are you sure it was not a man who had dealings with the island? You bring me here to examine blasphemy; the very first thing I see is blasphemy, before even I see *you*.'

'As I say, sir, I can only guess; we do not know the man who did it. But I am sure he cannot have come to do it directly from the island, he would have been –'

'Prohibited. As you have told me.' Little point in pursuing the matter: if the fellow did not know, he did not know. 'Try again to scrape them off. They deny the immortality of the noble human soul, the soul of status that has taken pains, laid out expense, to take order for its future life; they are an offence to the gods of the Hidden World: if they were true we would none of us have reason to furnish our tombs, all our years upon this earth would be pointless. Ever since I came to manhood I have been preparing my tomb and its grave-gods, I have put aside goods and gear continually from my earnings to the loss of my daily comfort: and so ought you if you were the man of sense I took you for, when first I read your letter.'

'Oh I have, I have, I do. I have a most commodious tomb, very nearly

complete, secure against thieves, moreover I am able to afford embalmers
from some city of the Delta for when I die, I have most certainly put aside
enough treasure for such a purpose, witness the poor state of my house;
you may think it squalor, but no, sir, it is frugal piety – oh sir, I do beg you,
do not think I am an atheist, or a mere peasant to be thrown at death into
the water without even a shroud round me: oh no, sir, most very sincerely,
I am a religious man!'

At this point in the conversation the squall of wind ceased, the rain blew
away; the sun broke out as the clouds fled, causing the sand of the beach to
gleam and the waves of the sea to glitter – the scribe felt it was almost, once
again, Egypt. He watched the rising steam from the soaked ground and he
rejoiced: a confession of religion from a mud-minded lukewarm man and
an outburst of sunshine all at the same moment, here was an augury! Lord
Ra was displaying himself, confirming his unconquerable power,
encouraging his servant who was here for no other purpose than to defend
the almighty name.

Harkhuf stepped forward and gave the astonished beachmaster a formal
embrace, a kiss of greeting; a declaration, as it were, of his knowledge of the
man's worth, a recognition that this little officer was no less Pharaoh's child
than he himself.

Even as he did so, a curious procession appeared over the dunes to the
east; a half-dozen coastguards as escort to two groups of four men,
shaven-headed slaves of priestly service, each group trotting under the
burden of a sort of dark swaying palanquin, borne on their shoulders by
carrying-poles. Not by any means palanquins-of-state such as might
convey lords and governors, nor fashionable litters for the indulgence of
shimmering ladies. The shapes were all wrong. The scribe had the sun in his
eyes, he had to blink at the strange sight from under the end of the
verandah.

The beachmaster observed his puzzlement, and was pleased with
himself. 'Ah, there, sir, you see, you shall see the ship-captain, see also the
big woman: now you shall enquire of them all you need to know, and you
shall do so in comfort in my house. It would be better perhaps if we went
through into the courtyard, the townspeople should not be witnesses
perhaps, not just yet?'

THREE

With more of his fuss and more of his sweat, and angry contradictory instructions, the beachmaster produced a regular judgement-chair for the scribe, had it placed in the shade of a corner of the courtyard, and refreshments set upon a table within reach, along with the scribe's writing equipment. Mira at last had employment for her fan; and without her woollen blanket, for the heat of the sun was now perceptible. Her fellow slaves (the ink-and-writing-tablet boy, the travelling steward, the cook) disposed themselves smartly beside her as a proper background to their proprietor's business. The beachmaster screamed to his womenfolk to be silent in their wing of the house – they had been calling out to him from behind the lattice windows – and bustled his eunuch onto the verandah to organise the arrival of the palanquins.

These were carried in, one behind the other, and deposited by their bearers in the full brightness of the sun, symmetrically opposite the scribe. The carrying poles were slid out of their sockets and taken away to one side of the yard. The six coastguard soldiers stood about, tensing their muscles, in what they thought was a posture of attention. They were swordsmen, so they pulled their weapons from their belts and held them forward fiercely, to impress Harkhuf. He was but moderately impressed: the matter had been handled far too clumsily; but swiftly, he had to admit, in spite of last night's emergency. The soldiers resisted all temptation to chatter; and the beachmaster, he felt, now felt an affectionate loyalty towards him.

He sat quietly, in well-cultivated calm, looking carefully at the palanquins, and with growing abhorrence. Around each one hung a buzzing miasma of flies, and they gave off a stench that turned the air in the hot courtyard as oppressive as the fumes from a sacred beast pen. They were in fact cages that might have been brought to such a beast pen in procession of flute music and dance, live hyenas or jackals inside them to be worshipped as manifestations of God: but these acrid coops were for the carriage of men, indeed for the *keeping* of men, and certainly with no thought of worship.

They were narrow upright containers, about a handspan less in height than a normal person's stature, and barely two foot-lengths square, pegged together from strong scantlings and laths with papyrus stems interwoven to form a mesh, only partially concealing the occupants.

The one to his right was a heavily built woman, very black-skinned, almost purple. She was not young, but extremely muscular, with pendulous breasts and what had once been a generous fat belly and buttocks but were now a sad sight of fallen folds of half-starved flesh. She hunched, immoveable, totally filling her cruel box, her wide eyes glaring out at the scribe from between the bars; strong shattered teeth, brilliant white, delivered him a saurian snarl.

In the opposite coop, a man, elderly, pale-skinned, stocky and short; bald head, ragged white beard. He tried to shift himself continually, agonisingly, by inches, moaning from the pain of his confinement and not ashamed to be heard. But his eyes were as wild as the woman's, and as dangerous.

Both of them were quite naked, both had their hands clamped in heavy wooden manacles; and Harkhuf saw with contempt that both bore the unmistakeable signs of utter barbarism. The man, for example, seemed never to have shaved his bodily hair (indeed he was covered in it, white-flecked, tawny, like a species of ape), nor was he circumcised, a disgusting thing to have to contemplate. The woman's skin on her cheekbones and round the top of her thighs was thickly ridged with ritual scars into which some blue tattoo pigment had been infused. She had other wounds as well, new ones, unhealed, in her wide underlip, the lobes of her ears, her left nostril, where pieces of jewellery had no doubt been torn away by her captors. All such valuables were now government property, the beach-master must give an account of them: Harkhuf took his tablet from the boy and made a note.

No attempt had been made to clean out the cages. Puddled filth hung in crusts against the bars and was oozing from the lower gaps of the basketwork. It was obvious, at any rate, that the prisoners had been fed. The scribe held a hand to his nostrils.

'Oh yes, they have been well fed.' The beachmaster was self-congratulatory. 'Porridge and broth through the slots of the cages by means of a funnel, sometimes also goat-milk; the woman tried to refuse, but after many days we prised it into her, observe how it broke her teeth: oh no, sir, I could not allow Pharaoh's captives to fail in health, not until instructions came, not until my orders were changed, perhaps today?'

'Take them out of the cages, wash them, find a garment for each of them. I am to talk to these two creatures, they will not answer me like this; why, look at the way they are looking at me, look!'

'Take them out? Oh but, sir, you do not know, they will be ferocious, I must protect you –'

'You have more than sufficient guards, and of course you can leave them manacled, but they *must* have some scope to move their limbs and live a little – or else how can they think? I need to hear their brains speak, not only the rage of their pain. They have a story that is to be sifted: of course by continued torment I could obtain a mere denial of its truth, but I need to hear the voices of whatever demons so possessed them that they dreamed of so vast an imposture, I need to *understand*!

'Beachmaster, please do what I tell you. Take plenty of time, take if you like until sunset: I need them both rested and exercised, and fed once again if need be. I too require rest and food; and so I suppose do you, after your experience at the shrine. I will lie down in one of your rooms for an hour, with my girl; and then I will hear your full statement of the ship and its arrival. The others of my people will meanwhile prepare my dinner; please see that they have what they call for.'

FOUR

Harkhuf lay on a wide string-bed in the beachmaster's own sleeping room, limply stretched out, seeking sleep, never quite finding it. At first he had Mira stand beside him and fan him, but the thick insalubrious heat that now succeeded the earlier sunshine was not amenable to her exhausted flappings. He took pity on her and told her that she was idle and stupid, why not leave the fan alone and lie down beside him? Which she did, displaying neither natural relief nor any awareness, even unwilling, of amorous preparation. Dumb submission only: of course, she was as tired as he was.

Mosquitoes came in, from the marshes at the edge of the lake, to trouble the two tired bodies. It appeared that the girl was troubled in her mind as well, probably by what she had seen in the courtyard – she was always very pitiful for beasts or people in pain; on the whole a good quality, despite its inconveniences.

Harkhuf made a start at caressing her, her sweet little copper-coloured breasts; but he himself was unaccountably troubled, and he found he must take his hands away from her, laying them quietly along his thighs. For an hour or more he held himself thus, still and quiet upon his back, sweating heavily, frowning at the mildewed plaster of the upper walls, the tattered reeds of the unplastered ceiling, now and then taking a swipe at an insect.

He could not rid his thoughts of the two tortured pairs of eyes in those cages, rolling at him, accusing him, taking note of him, defying him. The gods knew he was no enemy of strangers simply as strangers – and whatever the true history of their arrival, those two had surely made a remarkable and dangerous voyage, one look at their ramshackle ship had been enough to convince him of that – but he was here to investigate, he must do so in proper sequence, he had to follow the prescribed form, it was his function, he had no choice.

Mira lay curled up, her face buried in her arms, hurt, and vulnerable to further hurt, had he cared to turn himself and look at her: but he didn't.

At length the beachmaster's eunuch tapped softly on the door: his master was quite ready to give his excellency a full account; moreover the meal was ready, and the two prisoners were on their feet, able (more or less) to walk, clean, clothed, available for questioning, would his excellency wish to commence business? The scribe sat straight up from inharmonious half-sleep, put his feet on the floor, crouched to pass water into the vase held for him by Mira, stood to allow Mira to wrap his kilt around his loins, stooped so that she could array him in his collar-of-office and set his wig in place: and then, correctly embellished, he walked smartly out into the courtyard to his dinner (for which at last he found an appetite); and thereafter to his duty – which might very well last all day and then all night.

In fact it was not until three full days later that he felt able to begin to construct the draft of his report, for which he would employ his personal secret script.

He commenced, however, with a few lines of traditional hieroglyphs: an invocation to the demigod patron of scribes, the Lord Imhotep, who had been but a mortal man over a thousand years ago: scribe, magician, physician, famous architect (he'd invented, and built, the first pyramid), precise administrator, devout searcher after the truth of this world and of all the other worlds:

LORD! YOUR FAITHFUL SERVANT, PROFOUND- TASK-BURDENED, THOUGHT-HEAVY, NEEDS WISDOM, HAVING NONE; AND SKILL, HAVING SOME, WHEREOF PRIDE AND HUMILITY ALIKE TEACH HIM THAT NO SKILL SHALL AVAIL WITHOUT YOUR FAVOUR, O GRACIOUS LORD. GUIDE MIND THEREFORE TOWARD TRUTH THAT SHALL LIVE UPON TIP OF PEN, EVEN AS *YOUR* OWN TRUTH LIVES FOR EVER WITHIN HEARTS OF YOUR SERVANTS. LORD IMHOTEP, BLESS MY PEN.

Which was easy enough to write; he had composed something like it many times before, although every time with a fresh emotion. He added his name and status; and then drew a line, very exactly, in an elegant curved flourish around the whole paragraph, making of it, as it were, a dedicatory label at the beginning of his scroll. And now: proceed straight to the beachmaster's statement. Which needed some thought: and he was distracted.

It was raining again, he must have privacy to write, the verandah was no good because of the wind, the rooms were no good because of the bad light; so he sat in the courtyard under an awning the beachmaster had had rigged for him, and wished it were as rainproof as the beachmaster claimed it to be. His cook and his steward squatted in front, one to the left, one to the right, at a discreet distance, a pair of outposts to protect him from the intrusions of the beachmaster's household – particularly from the children, who cropped up noisily everywhere now that the first fright of the scribe's arrival in their home had worn off.

His writing boy was at his knee, alert, with all his materials. Mira passed softly in and out of the house, face averted, no timid smile, bringing him refreshments, making sure he was warm enough, warding off the beachmaster's cats when they slid past the male slaves and came rubbing themselves against his legs. He was attractive to cats, and as a rule *they* pleased *him*: but their purring affection was inimical to careful writing. He was sourly aware that Mira smiled upon the cats. Forget the girl: begin!

To summarise the incoherent and self-serving narration of the beachmaster-collector –

Annoyance with the beachmaster because of the dirt, disrepair and confusion of his house. Also, sweet copper-breasted Mira had been accursedly irresponsive to his sensual needs ever since he had been in the accursed man's curse of a house. Also his sensual needs had been irresponsive to himself, or should that be the other way round? Also the weather. Rakotis upset him.

Malevolence toward the beachmaster was an easily attained recompense. Avoid it! Start again.

The beachmaster-collector has told me that the ship washed ashore upon the beach of Rakotis two nights before the last full moon –

He inserted the requisite astronomical and astrological details to fix the date and its auspices: the department's priests would need to know.

– was blown here, despite the efforts of its crew, upon a strong and sudden northerly squall. Their captain alleged that until the final day of their voyage (during which they rowed the ship with great difficulty across the wind eastward, following the last miles of the barren coast of Libya) they had been out of sight of land for twenty days, driven hither and thither by arbitrary winds. Their intention had been to make harbour along the quays of the so-called 'Free Island' of Pharos, but they were emaciated from heavy toil in the open sea, their water and provisions were exhausted, their mast and sail had gone overboard in the tempest, and a good third of their oar-looms were shattered. They missed the island altogether, unable to alter the course of their labouring vessel as they were swept past its easternmost point.

The beachmaster and his troop of coastguards intercepted them on the strand as they were struggling to re-launch and make across the bay to the island. Even for so perfunctory a landing at Rakotis, they owed harbour dues to our Lord Pharaoh: immediate collection was mandatory; as was their immediate arrest when they proved unable to pay, either in treasure or proportion of cargo.

He paused. So far, a reasonable summary. What was now to be inserted would be his own comment. He ought to mark it (and all such subsequent personal interventions) with a marginal mnemonic. If he retained it in the final draft, he would have to make its subjective nature perfectly clear, quite separate from all recital of undisputed fact. He drew a zigzag line down the margin of the column.

This eventual landfall, so very near to Pharos – indeed Pharos exactly, had the weather been hospitable – must be attributed to the courage and skill of the ship's master in defiance of divine displeasure. However, he claims a miracle at the hands of a god. Impertinent! and requiring meticulous refutation.

(Now back to the report proper.)

The ship was built for eighteen oars, two men at each oar. By the time she reached Egypt she had no more than twenty-two rowers left to her, and that included eight women. I have inspected the hull, where it lies upon the beach. Although as large as many a deep-sea ship in Pharaoh's own service, she can never have been a well-found craft: her structure consists of a huge log of some unknown wood, hollowed out by fire, with outriggers and a rudimentary deck fixed onto it at the sides and above. The timbers have not been properly shaped, but are lashed and pegged into place much as they came from the tree, in many cases with the bark still on them. The surviving oars are similar, mere sapling trunks with leaves and branches rudely hewn away.

The only tools found in the vessel were a couple of adzes and an axe, all badly blunted and hacked. There was no whetstone. I noted that these implements, despite their ruinous condition, are of good iron, rare and expensive, of excellent manufacture. I believe them to be Egyptian in origin.

I should mention an unusual item in the structure of this unusual ship: a damaged figurehead, lashed to the sternpost, which clearly once belonged to another, more civilised vessel, Egyptian or Phoenician; in fact a portrayal of the goddess Neith.

The beachmaster was resisted when he attempted the arrest, but succeeded in detaining all the ship-people without loss of any of their lives. They are of African race, Nubian or Ethiop, but speaking no language known to the beachmaster or to anyone in Rakotis, where of course the usual longshore facility with divers tongues is prevalent. Nor could the ship-people understand anything the beachmaster said to them, although he and his men and his neighbours (including the learned priest and priestess from the local shrines) tried them with every possibility and permutation of the aforesaid divers tongues.

The exception to all this was the ship-captain, an apparent islander from the far side of the Middle Sea. He spoke comprehensibly, and exceedingly volubly, in bad camp-Egyptian, mingled with Syrian, mingled with an Achaean dialect of the archipelago; in short he is a typical seafarer of these waters, and had he not made such outrageous claims, calling government to witness their truth, it is likely that the beachmaster would have released him and all his crew into an ordinary house-arrest until the financial demands of government were satisfied (or, if they remained unsatisfied, he would have sold the entire company on behalf of government to a slave-dealer, and would not have found it necessary to make any special report).

(Another subjective passage:)

'The beachmaster was resisted.' Oh yes, indeed he was, and had only eighteen of his coastguard to gather the whole shipload in. If the newcomers had not been three-parts drowned and four-parts starved they might well have seized the town. There is a fort in Rakotis and nobody lives in it. The coastguard is supposed to live in it, but for years has been billeted up and down the beach with wives and families, living not as Pharaoh's soldiers but as fishermen scraping a living among all the other indigent fishermen of the district.

I suspect the coastguard captain himself is neither more nor less than a smuggler nine days out of ten: on the tenth he puts on his uniform kilt and takes up spear and sword and performs his official duty with a very poor grace.

The beachmaster admits this sorry tale without prevarication. 'What is to be done?' says he, 'the only pay these fellows get is a proportion of the contraband they seize: and of late it has been an ill season for contraband.' – which no doubt is the excuse for the reduction in their strength, though no excuse for the abuses it has led to.

'There was a time,' says the beachmaster, 'in the days of my predecessors, when the garrison of the fort numbered more than four score commanded by a nobleman, they drew a regular wage every turn of the moon, they were not permitted marriage until expiry of fifteen years' service; they even manned a guardship, rowing twelve oars a side, to patrol the coast a day's sail in each direction.'

Says he, 'I tell you this, so that you may tell government.' So I do, seeing that the beachmaster did not dare put it into his letter; which was natural enough, though not to be commended.

Harkhuf paused again. So far nothing he had written conflicted in any way with the presumed intentions of those who had sent him to Rakotis. But what was to come next was a different matter. The ship-captain had said things, first to the beachmaster, and then later to Harkhuf, that would need immense care in their recording. Harkhuf's worth in the estimation of his superiors might be damaged if he wrote too much: if too little, he would degrade himself in his *own* estimation.

He had always been proud to complete reports with but one preliminary draft, which he hardly ever had to amend before engrossing the final document. But today, he uncomfortably realised, he must revise this habit of work. A preliminary draft of unusual length could not be avoided. He must write out every word of what he had been told throughout all of two days and a night, and of what he had witnessed (which was normal); but also he must write (and this was unprecedented) his own immediate opinions of it, before he could decide whether he even understood it, and (if he did understand it) how far he dared allow himself to *judge* it; and how should a man dare write what he might not dare to read?

He could only proceed by degrees. When he finished his first draft he would read it over and thoroughly edit it, another unprecedented task, even more fraught with peril than the writing; and thence make a second draft, testing every implication against correct understanding by converting his own script into regular archival cursive. That awkward exigency of his craft, potential contradiction between the truths of two different species of script, with which he had hitherto 'made shift to live', had now become an absolute *dilemma*; but he absolutely had to go through with it. The second draft, in due course, must be the basis of the final document.

He would not make the final document until he was back again at Thebes, and had used his second draft to sound out a few men in the department. But in any case he could not write it in Rakotis: it must be beautifully engrossed in official hieroglyphs upon the most expensive papyrus, which of course he had not brought with him – too many risks upon a long boat journey for material of such value.

These meditations settled his mind a little, gave him scope. He would write now, with freedom: and afterwards take the decisions. A routine that he was used to; but today's decisions would be more crucial than any he had ever confronted. They would not necessarily be ruinous. He was allowing himself plenty of time. No need to excite himself.

The ship-master made his prodigious claim (that he had sailed right
around the lands of Africa) as soon as the beachmaster demanded the
harbour dues, before even the ship was properly salvaged and all the
people brought safe ashore. He repeated it again and again. He had set
sail more than seven years ago with three deep-sea ships from a port
on the Red Sea, the port nearest to broad Ocean, though he claimed
he had forgotten its Egyptian name (he knew it only by a sailors'
nickname, an indecency against our towns of empire that I scorn to
record). He had followed, so he reiterated, the African coast south,
into the Stream of Ocean, and so on and on, and then north, and so
through a narrow gateway on and on east, and here he was at last,
returned alive, a *circumnavigator!* – he had made the word himself for
he was the first of the sort ever known, as far as he knew – he had
found, as he had been ordered to find, how the Stream of Ocean runs
uninterruptedly right around the bulk of Africa, and again and again
he repeated it, his voyage had been made at the orders of Pharaoh,
therefore he himself (although barbarian) was an accredited officer of
government.

The beachmaster demanded proof.

No proof was forthcoming, neither sign, seal, nor document.

'Explain,' demanded the beachmaster, 'how, if you are such an
officer, you sail straight for the island of Pharos instead of one of
Pharaoh's ports?' A cogent question; but the man had his answer. He
needed urgent replenishment of food and water, which he knew
Pharos could supply. He did not know whether Rakotis was still an
Egyptian port: there were rumours along the coast to the west that
the Libyans had seized the place. His destination, he insisted, was
Memphis, upriver; which city he intended to reach by means of one
of the main mouths of the Nile. But he *must* replenish first; so,
therefore, the Free Island. He continued to assert his status with
violent oaths, and then with violence of his body, until restrained: yet
amidst his assertions was also an admission: that the ruler who had
sent him sailing was in no wise a legitimate predecessor of our present
Lord Ramses. Indeed, he loosely named that immigrant Syrian
opportunist (to a devout subject unnameable) who usurped the
throne and ruled from Memphis for a short space of time in defiance
of the laws of Egypt and of the justice of god, until righteously
overthrown by our lord's sacred father.

Mention of this traitor's name immediately caused the beachmaster to give order for the preparation of the felon cages: a most correct decision, I set it down here to his credit.

Note: the ship-captain had not at this stage made any mention whatever of the position of the sun over southern Africa.

He did, however, assert (even as they thrust him into his cage) that this usurper seven years ago was the only apparent Pharaoh, deemed legitimately so by all. How could any man be blamed for dutifully serving him? He asserted furthermore that as he himself had been upon Ocean throughout all the seven years, he could not possibly be expected to know what the beachmaster was now telling him: how our Lord Ramses' sacred father had arisen from his worthy obscurity at the call of Lord God Amun-Ra, had called together all the good men of Both the Egypts, had put the presumptuous foreigner to flight and to death (and all his miscreant politicians with him), had splendidly restored the throne, and had brought peace and good order to the realm; for which Amun-Ra and all the gods be praised now and for evermore.

Here was the scribe's first difficulty.

The fact was that Lord Ramses was the son of a man who had raised a revolt in the army at a time of political and dynastic chaos, with the laudable aim of ridding Egypt of a whole series of concurrent usurpers. But of course he had had to be a usurper himself in order to do it.

The original legitimate dynasty, which had succumbed to the period of chaos, seemed to have left no representatives – although there was still talk about one or two unhappy princes, and some royal ladies, held captive in remote forts far to the south in the Nubian regions, or possibly put to death there in secret; or possibly (in the case of the ladies) married off with a change of name to unknown individuals who would adulterate their wombs with low-caste offspring.

A barbarian sailor who wished to fabricate a claim to official recognition by government might well choose to base it upon the act of a discredited usurper, which would not be easy to check. And the 'Syrian opportunist' (if Syrian was what he was – he had several different tales about himself) had indeed been the sort of immigrant to keep personal connections with maritime adventurers; to commission (for example) a barbarian to carry out a voyage-of-search, maybe search for barbarian alliance; for the good, maybe, of Egypt? Or for her permanent degradation?

Thus the ship-captain's explanation, unprovable as it seemed, did suggest he might be telling the truth; even though it also very strongly indicated the possibility of a calculated lie. How much of the usurper's history might this barbarian know? For instance, was he aware how the scoundrel's name and titles were struck from the record in abhorrence of his presumptuous *blasphemy*?

For blasphemy, more than anything, had brought about his downfall. While he had been reigning, of course, *while he had been reigning*, army and navy, scribes, and the priests of most of the cults, had obeyed him without question. It was finally the priests of Amun who had stirred Ramses' father to the act of rebellion. The Syrian had had an outlandish allegorical god of his own – a thornbush, on fire, with neither face, feet, nor genital organs, a perfectly ridiculous entity! – and was commencing to impose it as a superior cult, a most ill-advised attempt that failed as soon as it was discerned.

Harkhuf had now to decide, was it politic, was it even desirable, to request a search in the archive for any reference to this voyage among acts-and-deeds of the usurper's years? He knew that at Thebes there would be nothing: he himself had played some considerable part in purging the documents there as soon as Ramses's father seized power. If there had been anything remotely relevant, it would first have been amended (to remove declarations of the usurper's sovereignty and laudations of his work); then retained by the department, as a necessary record of recent barbarian affairs. And Harkhuf would have remembered it.

But the usurper had ruled chiefly from Memphis in Lower Egypt; the Memphis archive therefore was the most likely place for any such search. A few months ago the scribe had sent an underling to Memphis to enquire for another document, from the reign of a legitimate Pharaoh. It ought to have presented no problem at all. The messenger discovered, to his horror, and to Harkhuf's horror when it was reported, an appalling confusion.

Ramses' father was on the throne for no more than three years, and spent them in warfare within his own boundaries, securing his position. He had to eliminate the usurpers' most zealous officials; documents were lost; the memories of the men who had compiled them were lost, in traitors' graves or in distant slave barracks. (Harkhuf's own rapid promotion derived directly from this nerve-racking 'redistribution' among servants of the state.) After Ramses succeeded his father there was a vigorous attempt to rationalise and restore the records: in Memphis even today it was not nearly complete. The curators were still endeavouring to correct and collate and transfer the archive to Thebes, and all at the same time, so that most of the scrolls and tablets were either heaped into travelling-baskets, largely undocketed, or spilling all over the shelves and writing tables with all the dockets misplaced. The department in Thebes had been disgusted.

To probe the records, then, seemed fruitless. And even if it were not, it would only breed suspicion. No official could rummage at random among usurpers' acts and deeds so soon after the years of anarchy, without some jealous colleague dropping the hint in superior quarters; was a coup in preparation? A legalistic claim to the throne by a faction who supported yet another potential usurper? A prospective rehabilitation of one or other of the dead usurpers? A most dangerous line of enquiry. And besides, there was no-one to desire it to succeed; for success meant the ship-captain's tale was already half-proven. Far better altogether to say, 'No documents: the man is a liar: he was never commanded by any Pharaoh good or bad to make any such voyage, and that's final!'

Far better for all concerned. Except, perhaps, for a conscientious scribe who could not bear to ignore possible records, because *all* records, their making and keeping, had been always the very blood of his life.

He wrote all this down, worrying over it desperately; but came to no conclusions. In due course, no doubt. At the proper time.

Of course the beachmaster questioned the captain about the details of his supposed voyage; and questioned him sceptically, of course. He received a floodtide of answer, which totally bewildered him; the beachmaster is not a man of developed imagination, and had no idea whether the narrative he heard was plausible or nonsensical.

He was told that for every year of the voyage, at the onset of bad weather, the crews landed, built a settlement (where possible, making friends with the local nations; where necessary, fighting them for a secure beachhead), tilled the soil, planted crops, subsisted until the harvest, and then sailed on. The length of the voyage amazed all of them.

Tales of disagreement, privations, disaffection, mutiny; tales of warfare and casualties, tales of shipwreck, of inconceivable courage and comradeship, innumerable marvels.

By the commencement of the fourth year two ships had been lost: a year later the third ship, overcrowded, was cast ashore in heavy surf and broke up. This happened upon a coast facing west, in a district of huge forests.

As the beachmaster heard of this shipwreck, he also heard the blasphemy.

The coast faced west. And the ship, blown towards it, was heading north-east when gulped under by the great seas: the captain chose to aver that *the sun was in his eyes*, he standing at the helm in mid-morning, and because it was in his eyes he must lift his head to shade

them or he could not see his course; and that was how the steering oar
was dragged out from his grasp.

It seems to have taken a few minutes for the dull beachmaster to fully
understand what had been said.

When he did understand it, he did not know what to do, except
immediately to consult the local priest of Amun-Ra, 'Whose shrine being
the house of the two mightiest of the gods, must of course contain double
the power of either god worshipped alone.' (I quote him directly: his
religious understanding is crude, but basically correct.) He feared there
might have been some cosmic eschatological sign ('Lord Ra, sir, as it were,
re-arranging himself during the past few years, though not over Egypt, or
I'd have seen it, yes?'); perhaps revealed only to the keepers of mystery and
hidden – of divine purpose – from unlearned men such as himself. The
priest, longtime blind, had not personally observed the heavens: but was
certain no known prophecy suggested any untoward activities that *might*
have been observed there during the current cycle of celestial movement.

Our Lord Ramses, affirmed the priest, is a dutiful representative of
Amun-Ra: his reign therefore will not be disturbed by prodigies, unless
he himself were to show himself apostate, an impossible hypothesis.

Hearing this, the beachmaster – with agreement of the priest – at once
knew that the ship-captain's story must be a fabrication. He could
imagine no motive for it: but the drawing-in of the Syrian usurper
already seemed to indicate Offences-against-the-State, either contem-
plated or in active preparation. He now had the man in a felon cage, the
man's woman gave him so much trouble that he ordered the same
treatment for *her*; his next step (very properly) was to write his letter to
Thebes. Government received it, sent me; here I am.

The scribe had a thought at this point. A troubling thought, even more so
than his previous reflections upon the usurper and the archives. He wrote
it tremulously. He was sure his private script was safe from any interloper;
but could he be *quite* sure? If what he wrote was to be read, by so much as
one pair of eyes, *trusted* eyes, a friend's eyes, it could nonetheless cost him
his life.

*I think the beachmaster had not understood (while the priest understood very
well, but did not tell him) what very high matters of state might conceivably
be involved in the ship-captain's blasphemy.*

*It is only two hundred years since a legitimate Pharaoh, the fourth Amun-
hotep, apparently beloved of Amun-Ra, did indeed show himself apostate,
and upon no other matter than the identity of the sun. Acts and deeds of his
reign have of course been struck out of the record; although I break no secrecy*

if I suggest that there are *records, kept in the innermost sanctuaries by priests of undoubted integrity, that adequately delineate the monstrous events of those days, far worse than the iniquities of the recent short-lived Syrian. This fourth Amun-hotep, changed his title to Akh-n-aten, he changed the name of the sun from Ra to Aten, he abolished Amun and all the other gods and their cults, declaring that all Egypt must worship this Aten alone, 'There was but one true god, Aten, and Akh-n-aten was his dearly beloved son upon earth in whom he was well pleased'! He did not just* try *to abolish: he enforced his decree and perverted the entire realm.*

It took no less than three subsequent reigns for the banished gods to be re-established: some say the Kingdoms of Egypt have never quite recovered from this outburst of impiety. Certainly the bounds of empire have observably contracted – witness the deplorable state of frontier enforcement at Rakotis, but I need write no more upon that subject. Nor indeed any more about reviled Amun-hotep. If my report is read in the proper quarters, the implications will be well enough understood, without my having to allude to him by name. Only here, I do write it, for the clarity of my own whirling mind.

Finish with it.

Get on to the final item from the beachmaster's statement.

The woman of the ship-captain.

The beachmaster was not at all clear as to the reason for her presence in the ship. His alarm at the blasphemy put an end to any rational questioning. But he had gathered already she is an alleged native of western Africa, an exile of sorts from her nation there. The ship-captain maintained it is the nation upon whose coast his third ship was wrecked, and also implied she had prevailed upon him to build a new ship and sail onward with a new crew, some of her own people, wives and children, for exactly what purpose the beachmaster did not discover.

The Rakotis priestess of Our Lady Neith seems to have had communication with her while she guarded her, caged behind the shrine. How, in what language? The beachmaster did not know. I found this holy old lady enigmatic and equivocal and at this stage learned little from her.

In my opinion the priestess despises my function, regarding all men of government as fools who exalt gods above goddesses for the augmentation of their professional status.

(My remonstrance, that the craft of hieroglyph was first devised and has since been divinely administered by the immortal Lady Seshat of the Stars, fell

on deaf ears: the priestess cruelly dismissed it, saying, 'You don't give a piss on a midden for Our Lady Seshat. Imhotep and no one else, yes? a slyboots of an innovator. And all the other innovators call him ''lord'' – you don't really think he is?')

I have never, throughout my career, been able to take a satisfactory statement from a priestess: the holier they are, the more satirical they become. This one affected to believe I was in Rakotis for no other purpose but to share her bed, and when I tried to turn the conversation she made further sexual mockery of me in front of her three young female acolytes.

FIVE

All the above was in my mind, and well enough assimilated, when I commenced interrogation. I began with the ship-captain.

Amazing recovery, for a man so old and ill-treated. The whole of his life, I was to find, had been one such recovery after another. Relieved from the cage torture, filled up with wine, he took courage and began to talk to me with intense hilarious freedom, at such a speed it was hard work to catch and hold his flow of words. He evaded questions with the same rapidity; sometimes he gave what seemed a forthright answer, until you realised it was nothing of the sort but a crafty slither; the whipping-away of a snake from under threat of a sudden footstep.

I asked his name.

A difficulty here. Even in my personal script these foreign names are scarcely possible. Transferred into the official script they are quite out of the question. I must do what I can with the symbols available to me.

He said he was Od-diss, 'To be sure it's a short name and they all call me by it for short, if I ever had a longer one I've forgotten it.' Idiocy. I knew better, I knew (though he did not at this stage know that I knew) a quite copious vocabulary of the island tongues; and I knew that 'od-diss', or something like it, was a common usage, meaning 'nobody'. He might very well have so described himself, or been so nicknamed, among his unscrupulous compatriots: it would have been perfectly appropriate to his character as he later outlined it to me. When I told him I saw his game, he laughed immoderately and at once corrected himself:

'Of course I *did* have a longer one. Now you mention it, I *do* remember it. But *you* must remember I have been for many days in a great deal of pain, and it does things to a man's brain, oh gods what a pain in that cage!'

Then he said he was Od-uss-isis, son of La'ar-tesh, father of Tel-emma-kossa, an Achaean of course, and a king. King of what?

'Ah,' he said, 'you'll not have heard of it, an island, that is all. Ith-kaa, in the western sea.'

In fact, I had heard of it. I learned the names of all the islands as part of my professional training. Names, produce, natural features. *Ithkaa*. Goats. Pigs. Small. Stony. Inhabitants scant; supposed aboriginal. Hearsay description only. Never, so far as is known, visited by any Egyptian. Evidently (after our archive was compiled) Achaeans had conquered it, and given it a little king of their own blood. Here he was. At my feet. With his wrists clamped.

'I was king and am no longer. Nor is my son. My son is dead. Do you have a son?'

I told him, yes; two sons and three daughters. Abruptly he stopped laughing and wept.

'Are they alive?'

I told him, yes; all alive, but of course they are not yet grown.

'When my son was not yet grown I left him, cried good-bye to him, to go seafaring and warfaring, one season, that was all. Would you believe, when I saw him next, he was a tall sword-wearing man with a great beard on his face?' Then all the tears were gone, in an instant.

Upon first hearing his whimperings in his felon's-coop-of-little-ease, I thought him decrepit and done for: but seated in front of me, on a low stool, managing a wine cup with dexterity despite his manacles, kicking his feet up and down to show his ten toes they still lived, tumbling about from one haunch to the other to comfort the remains of his cramps, he wept and laughed; and then caught my eye, and laughed again, head twisted round, allusive, collusive, as though to tell me that none of his previous humiliation had ever in fact happened, or – if it had – it had all been a kind of joke played by me and him between us to deceive the beachmaster and Rakotis underlings, jacks-in-office, contemptible fellows, he and I after all knew much better!

He kept on laughing as he talked to me. Yet I do not think his laughter was any more truthful of his real self than were his tears or had been his moans and curses: he is a man who presents himself with a crafty calculation in accordance with his audience, in accordance with the place where he finds himself, in accordance with his conception of how a man in certain circumstances ought to behave toward those circumstances (and toward any witnesses of them) if he is to obtain the best advantage.

The purpose of my interrogation: first, to prove him a liar; second, to elicit the reasons for his lies. From the very beginning, therefore, I was up against difficulty. For clearly he *is* a liar, does not even deny it, takes a gorgeous pride in it indeed. When you catch him out, he changes his lie to another one and defies you to catch him again. Two hundred years ago or more, when the empire of Crete was Egypt's largest neighbour in the area of the Middle Sea and the Sea Peoples no more than a few vexatious (but scarcely dangerous) island communities of barbarians intermittently in rebellion against Crete, an enigmatic axiom was current among officers of the department – I came across a version of it in an old memorandum in our archive, an agenda for a trade conference:

> *Our resident advisor upon Cretan affairs says all the Cretan delegates are liars, but he himself is a Cretan; so whom is Egypt to believe?*

My predicament exactly.

Except: I did find an area of discourse (quite early in our talk) where it seemed to me the man might be tied down to truth. I had begun by asking some questions as to his notions of the gods – essential, if I were to discover whether *blasphemy* was indeed part of his process of thought, for with barbarians one can never be sure. Quite apart from his immediate peril as Pharaoh's caged prisoner, he is of an age to foresee death: indeed death (as he said to me) walks daily, hourly, right behind him, an imitative monkey with its long finger crooked into the fork of his buttocks. But his religion (yes, he calls it a 'religion') does not admit of a future life, except the most miserable shadow-show – 'squeaking ghosts,' he said, 'gossiping eternally of how lively they were on earth and now look at them, dead leaves, blowing hither and thither through the twilight with neither present nor future to occupy their minds, only endless memories and regrets, that is all . . . Don't I know? I have been there and seen them . . . Oh yes, if you like, in a dream. Oh yes, if you like, these past days here in your cage.'

Whereupon he offered me his intentions for this hopeless death-realm.

For him, the short space that remains of his life on earth is to be filled, if he can contrive it, with the ordering of his own memories, so that when he joins the squeaking ghosts he will be able to squeak to some purpose with them, better than most of them, he told me, and he rocked upon his hams with self- applauding glee:

'By the gods I will be a *bard* amongst them, they will cluster around me down there from thousands of generations back, to hear me declare who I have been!'

His laughter stopped directly, his face stiffened with despair. 'Rustling and squeaking, crowding upon me, in through the cage bars; oh gods, I was not alone there. They *knew* who I was!'

I think he did wish to try, for once in his rascal life, to express

something like the truth. To speak to me was, as it were, rehearsal for
the land of the shades. But then, a *bard's* rehearsal? When did a
barbarian bard ever sing upon oath?

He was glaring at me like a lion.

'So my son was never a child for me. But by the gods he was a
man. And a beard like a lion. And now he is a squeaking ghost. Oh
gods, the pointless gossip he and I will shortly have.'

Once again into his laughter, not loud bellows but a most woeful
sideways titter, as though he were a ghost himself. I wondered if he
thought at moments he had died already, in that cage? Later, I was to
find he thought he was long dead before they put him there: but he
did not think so all the time. That was the difficulty. Little serpent
under a footstep, he slithered away even from himself.

So far, as we talked about the gods, our conversation was easy, very
nearly friendly: I did not contradict him, although I did find him
quite ignorant on the subject. Nor did I think he at all understood the
nature of divinity, its all- embracing transcendence. To him the
Sublime Personages were augmented variations of kings and
chieftains such as he might have dealings with every day in his
piratical goings-on; and no more scrupulous. He told brutal and
salacious jokes about them.

I thought the easiness had gone far enough.

I said suddenly, 'You never sailed round Africa. But this much I
will grant: you may well have left the Middle Sea, westward through
the gates of Ocean, and made raids along the African coast. That
woman and the other blacks are of quite a different race from the
Nubians as we know them in Egypt. If you tell me they are western, I
see no present reason to doubt it.'

'Good,' says he, with insolence, 'you are wise not to find reason to
doubt what is truth. But raids? Do you think they're my slaves? That
I *stole* them from the African coast? Why can you not accept that they
might have stolen *me*?' A sharp point: whatever they were, they
could not have been his captives, for what companions had he with
him to guard them?

But it led me to my next question. 'I did not say you stole them.
But I know what you *did* steal. You have the Lady Neith, goddess of
Egypt, goddess of Libya, as your figurehead. You sank an Egyptian
ship and took her as trophy. Or the Libyans had already taken her
(she is not shaped in their crude manner of carving) and you took her

from them. Or else did they give her to you? Tell me directly, no more lies: you and the Libyans, what is between you?'

'Libya? A very wild place. Nothing to do with it at all.' He slid from the question, which did not surprise me. But I was surprised indeed when he at once denied that his figurehead was what I knew it to be; and denied it quite forcefully, a rebuke, if you please, to *my* ignorance. 'Neith? Nonsense, man, how can she be Neith? She is Pa-lassa-'thnai, virgin goddess of my people, lady of wisdom, lady of craftwork, lady of victorious war, close friend to Od-uss-isis: did you not see her goatskin cloak: the bow and arrows in her hand? Though more usually she has a spear. But she *was* made by an Egyptian, so of course she has an Egypt shape. You say I never sailed round Africa? She can prove that I did. She was carved by the shipwright who made me my ship, on your *east* coast, I tell you, *east*: she went with me the entire voyage, moved with me from wrecked ship to new one; and here she is, come home again. Pa-lassa-'thnai, she kept me alive every day of my journey.'

'None the less, she is Neith. She is worshipped all over Egypt. All Egyptians know her portrait and tokens. *I* know her portrait and tokens. D'you think I am blind? Goatskin and bow and the weaver's shuttle upon her head.'

'Weaver's shuttle? Is that what it is? I thought some fool Egyptian had made buggery out of carving a helmet.' And he laughed. I was exasperated; which he saw, and seemed sorry for, because he most maddeningly mended his manners and began to agree with me. 'Suppose we say then that poets have told us that your Neith and our Pa-lassa-'thnai are one and the same? Would that solve your difficulty? Tell me, if I find the way around all of your problems thus, you'll let the goddess who fetched me from shipwreck fetch me out of these damned manacles too?'

I controlled my anger. 'We shall see. For the time being you will endure them. If I release you, I must have the guard with us, which will prevent us speaking freely. You are a tighter thewed man than I would have thought, even though you are white-haired: no, I will not trust you, not just yet.'

He rolled his eyes toward my slave girl (she and the writing boy were the only others in the room where we sat). 'Tell me, would *you* trust me, little lady, a poor old beggarman that has come here with a joking virgin for his goddess friend? Aha, you see, she smiles at me. I am trusted by none but children.'

Happily, I do not think the girl understood his mixtures of

language; but his tone was unmistakeable, and angered me further.
'You will not speak to my slaves. They are mine and I am Pharaoh's: I
am the man who is talking to you.' He laughed again and rolled his
eyes. He had the scar of an old wound running all the way down his
thigh to his knee, it was itching him; he rubbed it vigorously.

I considered this business of his goddess.

'You say "virgin". Lady Neith can be called "virgin" insofar as her
virginity is ever-renewed and is seen as but one aspect of her most
fruitful divinity.But priests and poets call her "mother" as well.' I
enlarged upon the attributes of Neith, enlarging (I regret to say) upon
my own superior knowledge, not strictly germane to the
interrogation; but I did need to know his form of worship, as I have
said. Thence to the question: 'How many children has Pa-lassa-
'thnai?'

'Why, none, as far as I've heard. A swollen womb to stretch her
swordbelt in a most unsoldierly fashion? A yelping brat to scramble
between her and the clarity of her working thought? Oh no no, she'd
have no patience. Didn't I tell you, she's a sacker of cities?'

I was enraged that my careful theogony so amused him. He may
have called himself a king, but to all intent he was a rough ship-
master, a boisterous plain dealer toward his religion. Or was he? At
any rate, that was what he now studied to have me think: so that I'd
see his silly devotions as of no significance to anyone else, 'anyone
else' being an established priesthood, or a sacred government part-
and-parcel of such priesthood. I was not quite so gullible as he
thought.

'I am sure you understand very well what I mean,' I told him. 'And
very well what is legitimate speculation by inspired poets upon god or
goddess and their congress of immortal love. And also what is
blasphemy, the lewd mockery of that congress, the scorning of its
inevitable results. I am neither priest nor poet. It is my function to
write what I am told by wiser men; when I have written it, I bear it in
mind, I am trained. I tell you I bear *this* in mind: impiety to suggest
that the oldest of all the goddesses, Neith the ancient mother, has
closed up her thighs against the delight of all man-flesh and the
benison of parturition. How, if she were so unnatural, could she be
worshipped, as our wives worship her, for her passionate yet tender
guardianship of the marriage bed?'

It had occurred to me that if I could turn him into an argument
about exactly what was blasphemy, I might lead him toward opinions
upon Ra the Unconquered Sun (child of the Lady Neith); and thence

by degrees to an admission of his great lie. Perhaps he detected my tactic, for his only answer to my last question was an airy, 'How indeed?' and then off with a roar into his own question; not an absolute change of subject, but it slid him (or rather, *jerked* him) most adeptly from my projected course.

A terrifying poop-deck bellow that all but threw me from my stool: '*Why am I here, you bastard?* Why the cage, why the handcuffs? You filth-eating Egypt beetle, what have I done that you treat me like this? Tell me, can't you, tell me, what d'you think that I've buggering *done*!'

In response I was cold and cruel. 'Don't you know? You tell me.' He was tossing about in his fury, he hauled himself up onto his feet, but I was sure of the strength of the manacles, and his legs were still cramped and tottering; he stumbled and fell. I let him make his own heavy efforts to rise.

'Very well,' he growled, amid more curses, 'I had neither cargo nor treasure to be robbed of by that beachmaster: I take it that's the sum of it, and all else is invented to save the bugger's face. But I still am not told what *has* been invented. So are you going to let me know, or do we play priest-and-poet till the sun goes down out of the sky?'

As soon as I heard this chance phrase, I knew exactly how to deal with it; I caught him by his clasped wrists, gripping the wooden block with both of my hands, and dragged him, still half-kneeling, to the door. He struggled, but there was a coastguard outside; I called the man in, told him what I needed, and between us we pulled the prisoner (whom already I thought of, most justly, as 'King Nobody') out into the courtyard. We took no notice of the other guards and the beachmaster's people who were lounging about there, we went straight through to the verandah.

It was late afternoon, the sun long past his height; another half-hour and he would pitch faster and faster into his sunken nightly furnace the far side of Ocean. I turned Nobody directly westward, to face the red-gold glory.

'There!' I said, 'look at him! All day he has travelled above the southernmost eave of this house, and now, for it grows late, he conveys himself first west and so (by a little) north. Never any other course for him. He is a great god: he has laid his path: predetermined; irrevocable; setting all of our destinies in this world or the next by his own peregrination, eternally destined. Lord Ra, life of the Pharaoh; splendour of the splendour of Egypt; son and ruler of his mother

Neith! Do you think, you old rotten ship-rat, that such a one as he
can vary his majestic progress at the whim of your tricks and dodges?'

*I all but exceeded myself, I very nearly fell into the blasphemy of Akh-n-aten,
so determined I was to uphold the power of the Unconquered Sun. 'Ruler of
his mother' was altogether too strong: I should have said 'sovereign consort'.
Impossible to correct it without showing a weakness, alas. Spontaneous
sacerdotal rhetoric needs practice if one is to perform it unfaltering; my
profession does not often call for it. I have since said rotations of prayer to
Lady Neith, and made an offering (two gold ear-rings from my travelling
treasure box) to her Rakotis priestess, by way of propitiation. More offerings
to be made, upon my return to Thebes.*

I looked sharply enough, to see had he caught the error of my tongue:
but he was on his knees, without prompting, his head in the dust, his
bound arms flung out before him. 'He is,' he cried, 'a great god.' He
sprang to his feet, remarkably without needing assistance (I have
mentioned he is tight- thewed), and swung himself round to confront
me. 'Ah now,' says he, and a great grin as he uttered it, 'now do we
find the stabbed fish on the end of the trident! Such a fool you are to
suppose a grey sailorman of near threescore years upon the wave
would dream to tell lies about the *sun*! Such a fool to believe that *any*
of the sky-creatures – moon, stars, wind, birds, thunder or lightning –
could move a man like me to mockery! Don't you know they are my
living? And one word of them to the bad, they'd be my death. And
not even a purposeful word; a moment of error would drown me.
When did you last sail in a ship?'

I never had; and he guessed it. I saw the street outside the house
filling up with idle fellows, delighted that interrogation was taking
place just over their noses. I told the guard to bring him in again.
Now, at least, he knew the main ground of argument; if that was any
help to me, which I doubted. Indoors, he prowled about, rambling
disconnectedly about how the sun god had at one time put him into
the most terrible fear; how his virgin warrior Pa-lassa-'thnai had
shown him how to avoid the sun's anger; which led him on to tell
more about her, how she was not only no mother of children, but she
herself had no mother, only a father (Achaean substitute for Lord
Amun, I gathered), who made himself this girl-child all on his own in
a hole in his own brain instead of a woman's womb – a most
abominable perverted belief, if he really believed it. In fact a
blasphemy: and yet he did not sound as though he blasphemed; he
seemed, for the first time in my presence, to feel a real horror of

divine power, an awe-struck comprehension of his own smallness set
against it.

I needed to know more of the reasons for this feeling; but I must
hear them in proper order. His current discourse was inchoate.

I began to think I had gone about things the wrong way. I was not,
after all, a skilled officer of Pharaoh's police, able to cross-question all
those set before me with inevitable hope of success. I was but what I
was, a recorder; then let me record. I should not have tried to pin
Nobody down to his essential lie at the very beginning. Far better to
allow him to tell his own tale (which the beachmaster, bear in mind,
had not let him finish); let him enjoy himself, if he wished, with all
his *inessential* lies – as for example, had he really been a king? And if
so, why 'no longer'? – for sure, the great falsehood would expose
itself when he came to it.

So I told him to tell me.

This report would need many rolls of papyrus. As Harkhuf filled each one,
he tossed it to the writing boy, who tied it up and hung onto it a tag of
coloured wool, a different colour for each roll, rainbow order, starting with
purple and ending with blue and then repeated with double tags and then
again with triple, and so on – that way a diligent slave would keep the
documents in correct succession and yet need not be taught to read. The
tagged rolls were stacked at one end of the writing basket, the unused ones
came from the other end.

A straightforward system, the boy understood it thoroughly, the work
went swiftly, without pause.

'Of course I was a king!' He answered my first question with an
assumption of command, straight-backed, beard bristling, from the
height of his humble stool. 'Can you look at me and doubt it?'

No reason in fact to doubt it. Among the People of the Sea kings are
hardly bigger than captains of but a single ship; although some of
them, from the great palaces, *have* possessed a certain grandeur. I
think none of the great palaces thrive any longer. Many invasions
from further north. The department's information is not all it ought to
be. King Nobody's story may assist in our understanding.

And he was glad of the chance to tell it. Bard-like, he rolled his
words, rolled his wild bright eyes, gestured grotesquely with his
fastened hands.

'Being a king, I required treasure, to bestow gifts and receive
honour, and receive treasure in return, from fellow kings and kingly
men. My island was small and not wealthy, my people did not live in

comfort, our young men must put to sea and myself with them, to prove ourselves at sack and pillage, to enhance our island and deter our neighbours who might otherwise take from us even that little which we possessed.

'My people had not lived in Ith-kaa very long, it is supposed we came to the place overland from the north, in extreme poverty, at a time of many seizures of land: whoever led us in those days cannot have been a chief of much penetration, he took what I suppose was the most miserable island he had ever seen, only because it was the only one he had ever seen; it was the first one he came to and he knew nothing to compare with it, and the adjacent mainland was even worse. His house ruled us for some generations until my father overthrew them and made himself king, to a far better advantage.

'He fell sick and retired from leadership, passing his sceptre, with the approval of the best of the people, to me. I negotiated for a wife, a woman of a mainland clan; Pen-el-alopa they called her. I needed her people for alliance, even though they were of backward customs, of the old secret-hearted tribes of that land before *our* people came there. A mistake. As I knew the very first day I had her, when it seemed she expected to live in her mother's house and myself with her, ruling Ith-kaa, I suppose, through a deputy. No nonsense: I seized her, sword out and chariot ready, had her down to the seashore and over the straits before any of the swarm of them could stop me.

'Upon the island she conducted herself fittingly; a precise weaver, with many other skills, a silent thinker of her own thoughts.

'I got her with child, and then looked about for warfare.

'As I told you, I required treasure. Big kings were making wars every year, back and forth, from big palaces on the mainland, against the other wider mainland the far side of the eastern islands, against the fringe of the Hittites, sometimes sacking cities, as often as not ruining themselves. I was too small either to join them as equal or oppose them on my own. So I hung upon the flanks, as it were, of their warfare: jackal rather than lion, oh I was no less crafty than my owl-eyed Pa-lassa-thnai. Her image then as now grinned always from the stern of my ship.

'I was useful to the kings, helping them to success, uncovering for them places of plunder and trophy; and then again (when they had scorned me) intercepting their scattered ships, raiding their outlying villages, always making sure they never knew it was I that had done it.

'So how did I make so sure? Swift and deadly attack-by-night, or attack in the foulest weather, unusual tactic and dangerous, I never fell upon a force so large as to contain any survivors afterwards.

'I thrived. My wife and son I barely saw, year upon year. The king who makes war in the storm season is not quite a king for his kingdom. I did not see that, not at the time: I was young; I was vainglorious; my kingdom was my shipmen and swordsmen. As for Ith-kaa – I sent home slaves, sent home treasure, trusted my wife. Perhaps I was right to do so. The island thrived; but not so greatly that anyone attacked it in my absences. Or else, they knew what I was, and did not dare to attack, *not even* in my absences.

'You're a long way from home yourself, I take it? And you'll put no lesser trust in *your* wife?'

He grinned at me, confidingly: it would have been pleasant if I had been able to give him a confident answer. I determined not to let him hold advantage over me thus. No, I would not *remove the manacles (he asked me once again), nor would I join in his dialogue. He was here to tell his story –*

'So tell it and no more delay! You were a king, now you're a castaway. How many years did it take?'

'How many years? How should I know how many? Each weary year became the next, oars in the water, keels on the corpse-littered beach, swords in the handgrasp.' As he sat there he slumped, neck bowed, shoulders stooping, an old man suffused with melancholy. 'All I can tell you; my child grew, my wife thought her thoughts, and I lived as a man who had neither wife nor child. Yet it was noted among the ships I wished always to be at home, and complained like a whingeing bard when I was not there, at my fireside, with my own people, respected, quiet, and prosperous. Was it true? Or rather, *which* was the truth? The insatiable sea-rover, the murderous double-dealer, voyaging anywhere at mere breeze of an intrigue? Or the free-handed heedful king trapped, hopeless, into everlasting warfare; warfare doomed onto us from frozen-topped mountains where if gods indeed inhabit they can be no more alive than snow-drifts – and all because of what? Because *we were men*?'

If he did not know the truth of himself it would be hard to establish when he lied about anything else. Yet nothing he had said was implausible. The department's archive will show us (though not in precise detail) the insanity of the barbarian wars among the islands and the northern coasts. Egypt's trade with those regions has collapsed almost entirely: not one single government across the Middle Sea with whom Pharaoh can exchange ambassadors.

I reminded King Nobody he was to speak of the anger of the sun god. I said, 'From what you are telling me, I would not think you

cared whether you offended one god or twenty. You yourself behaved
like a snow-drift god on a mountain, choosing whom to kill, whom to
betray, whom to incite to his own ruin?'

'And if I did, how strange do you find it? Does none of that happen
in Egypt? When Egyptians betray, they usurp a whole empire. Do you
blame me that *I* was granted but a ship or two at a time, a small fort
on a headland, a walled city now and again but scarcely larger than
this Rakotis? Oh I have been in your Thebes and your Memphis, I can
make the comparison. Size is the only difference: size; but not
ambition.'

I did not take him up about Egyptian usurpers. I was not quite sure which
ones he meant. But outrageous to assert there is no more to it than size? The
sovereignty of Pharaoh is heaven-bestowed: if it is seized by force (and held),
as upon occasions it has been, then the gods have disposed the transfer and lo!
it is legitimate. Whereas the Sea Peoples' petty dominions are stolen in despite
of god; and inevitably remain the guilt-ridden hoards of thieves, awaiting
only further thieves to come and steal them back again: and so it goes always
among barbarians – and so, he was to tell me, it eventually went with him.

He continued, still in his gloom, but a harsh anger grew out of the
gloom: 'The terror of the sun god; I did not know it for what it was
until long after it had fallen on me. And then almost too late.

'It was the year of the great disasters – one disaster among many,
but this one was the worst. A few of us took what we thought would
prove a rich golden city, Tru-ja, Il-juna (it had more than one name),
built hard upon the swift entry of the strait into the Scythian Sea –'

I write 'Scythian Sea', our official designation, significant in regard
to current barbarian developments. He called it in his own tongue the
'Hostile Sea' and then corrected it, in his own tongue and his own
superstition, to the 'Hospitable Sea'.

'We forced the city by no assault but a very wicked stratagem; *my*
stratagem, *my* treachery, nobody else's, and my confederates gave me
full credit for it. They gave me no credit at all for what we found
inside the gates. Why, the place was half in ruins (although its walls
from the outside had seemed well-enough maintained), it did not
even have a king, just a poor broken old fellow like an impoverished
village headman, with his wives and his sons, but what were they?
Coastwater pirates who stole sheep in fishing boats, and a miserable
handful of skin-coated horse copers.

'They had been stupid enough to take at rape and offer for ransom
the wife of a real king – they thought it would be the making of them,

turn them into kings themselves – which was why our attack was launched: but we were twice as stupid, assuming no one steals kings' wives unless they have the power to hold them, and if they have the power then of course they have the riches. That city had not been rich since the earthquake several years since, when the golden lords that lived in it lost everything and moved away; and then the ones we found there wandered in from the barren hills and set themselves up as walled people, housed people, for the very first time in their walkabout ragged lives. And of course I should have known. I think, do you know? I was deliberately misinformed by somebody's kinsman who held me secretly at feud, but I never found out whose.

'So for what little plunder we had there, we fought each other on that shore, ship's crew against ship's crew, and so sailed for home savagely, with empty hulls and men missing and men wounded and bleeding all over the bilge and a fatuous cargo of useless untalented ignorant slaves whom nobody anywhere would have the slightest wish to buy at the lowest price that could be asked!

'Add to which we set sail into the start of the storm season, a full month early that damned year, and it caught us and blew us everywhere, blew my ship and crew out from under me, and washed me up, a beggarman, upon the mercy of strangers' malice.

'Add to which, before that happened, my crew, desperate for food, took cattle from an island.

'How were we poor silly rovers to know it was a sanctuary island, the hidden and sacred precinct of the Unconquered Sun? Yes, I ask you, how *were* we?'

He looked at me, astonished (it seemed), as though he expected me to answer his question, as though for years he had been asking it without any success from everyone he met. But of course there was *no* answer: it is always perfectly obvious that a sacred precinct is what it is, unless you are a bloody pirate to whom nothing is sacred except your own bloody war goddess grinning from your bloodstained poop. I tried to get from him the orderly facts (the island might have been one of Egypt's oversea sanctuaries, and so recorded; we could check it): but all he said was –

'How should I know? Miles and miles away. The wind was taking us every way. Oh how the wind was taking us. And after the ox-slaughter we never saw the sun. Well, of course we wouldn't, would we? Ah gods, we were all well-cursed. And then, as I told you – wrecked. When I got back to Ith-kaa, I landed alone, so broken that nobody knew me.'

'You believe yourself still to be under this curse?' A crucial enquiry.
His reply to it was matter-of-fact and quite the reverse of what I expected.

'Not any more.'

'How do you know?'

He laughed. He saw my meaning. ' "Blasphemer against Lord Ra"?
All because Lord Ra has cursed him . . . No. The events are connected,
in that the one was to lead to the other; but the connection is not so
simple. We have a long way to go to unravel the loops of the knot. So
take your pen again, careful writing man, take your pen and tell my
story. I ought to have a bard to hear it, with a grape-nippled ivory-
necked muse lady beside him to tickle his cods and to stir up his warm
serpents of verse as he listens: but I haven't, so I tell it to a writing
man. I suppose your brown girl here, the one I must not talk to, I
suppose she will be muse toward *you*, in a manner of speaking? But,
as you say, she's yours, you are not hers; it does make a difference.'

*I could have put the girl out of the room; but even so he had already noticed
her, he would remember and refer to her again when he wished to irk me:
maicious ancient Nobody and twice my age. I needed to divert him; but
surprised myself by the way I did it.*

I called for a guard, I ordered the blocks taken away from his wrists. It
cost him some pain when the chisel was inserted between the wooden
manacles, forced in hard, and twisted, to crack the glue and split the
dowelling. I hoped the interruption to his foolery would not also have
interrupted his narrative mood – *which was in any case kindled by the
presence of my girl, so of course I could not put her out, could I?* Indeed it was
the mood of a bard who felt the stirrings, and *I* felt I was under no risk
from his free hands while it lasted. So I told the guard to leave us.
Maybe there *was* risk, of excessive credulity. But my attitude is
professional, I take such perils daily and I take them in my stride. His
hands free, he cried aloud at the intensity of the cramps he suffered,
cried aloud and walked about, shaking his arms and cursing me. Then
he sat again, laughed and wept, and so into the rest of his tale.

He told about his homecoming under the curse of the Unconquered
Sun.

He found he was reported dead, months and months before his
arrival, by some authentic-seeming bringer of news. He found his son
(Tel-emma-kossa) living in hiding in a mountain cave high up upon
his little island. He found his wife (Pen-el-alopa) great with child –
and who was the man, hey?

Craftily, he did not approach her and ask her. He roamed the island
unknown, vilely dressed as a beggarman, spying out the situation. At
least a dozen men possible; that was what he found. And she herself

would not know which. She had reverted in her widowhood (and for
sure she believed it *was* widowhood) to the customs of her own people,
whereby the island was now hers. She fetched her men from across the
straits to make fertile the succession. Tel-emma-kossa, being his father's
son, had no claim to it at all: and the new men had driven him out.

She had been led to this cruel course by certain maidservants from
her mother's house, one of them with magic powers of childbed
knowledge and other such dealings, Mel-n'th-o, an Ethiop, a
skin-and-bone fire-hearted length of black whipcord (her name in the
Achaean tongue means just that – 'black'), who had served Pen-el-
alopa since before she ever came to the island; part of the marriage
gift in fact, 'And a part I could well have dispensed with; why, she'd
lived in my hall all those years like a woodworm, gnawing holes in
the very pillars that held up my accursed rooftree!'

So why had Pen-el-alopa done what she had done? Congenital
infidelity? unappeasable lechery?

'Nonsense. Explanation far less simple, far less disreputable: by the
same token, far more dreadful.'

She had loved Tel-emma-kossa: but after a portent from her
mother's goddess (unnameable, deadly secret) she had recognised that
like his father he was a man-of-no-good-luck. Therefore when he fled
she had hardened her heart, even though she was well aware he was
almost mad with grief and rage.

'Let her heart be hard or not, it was surely torn out of her, though
she would never never admit it, not to him, nor indeed to me when
in the end I confronted her with myself alive and with the truth. I had
not discovered all the truth: in the end I had to extort it from that
wise woman, damned Mel- n'th-o. Before I did so, and *while* I did so,
oh I had my full revenge.'

Like a wild boar he showed his tusks at me. And then shook his
head from side to side, shutting his beard over his teeth and groaning.

'You'll remember, at my marriage, I had compelled my wife against
her will. Against the will of her people. A most ancient people, far
from trustworthy. Now against *my* will – no, my son's, I was dead,
wasn't I? – she brought both them and their goddess into the
kingdom of my inheritance. Suppose the men of Ith-kaa had offered
the goddess defiance? Well, the best of them were dead, having sailed
with their king, you see; and for the others, they believed my wife's
women, believed that they'd wither and die, that's what the portent
had said, that's how such divinities work; my wise wife believed it so
utterly she only smiled and never talked of it.'

As *he* talked of it, to *me*, his own old features creased into an unnerving quiet smile, pain and danger closely mixed: by the act of his remembering her, his wife's spirit had entered into him.

He said, 'Perhaps it is better I speak only to a meagre writing man. A bard at this point would tend to diverge from truth; make a quite different story. Hate my wife and call her she-demon; or by contrary exalt her, as jewel-eyed, dutiful, faithful (even to a husband she believed dead), prevaricating with those who wooed her, smiling toward her loom, waiting for deliverance. Bards are soft, truth is hard. Truth not being paid for by good dinners at noblemen's tables; more commonly by beggary, by beatings and nakedness, cages, filth, and handcuffs, yes?'

Writing these words, Harkhuf shook, unavoidably, with recollection of his own wife, of the broken bathroom jar, of all the licentious noblemen with whom she had prevaricated and prevaricated again (or had she?) while he squatted at his important work and never thought of her at all. In Thebes there were no barbarous 'bards', but a swarm of clever poets, licking honey, stinging like hornets, delighting in mendacious wives.

These doubts were not appropriate: the report must be completed. Let him write, and keep on writing.

At his elbow an abrupt turmoil, breaking into his concentration; this very particular moment, the worst moment possible for such trivial but infuriating disturbance. And the worst moment possible for it to have been caused by the one who caused it. The girl Mira had become bored by the repetitive necessity of shooing away the cats: instead she had taken to playing with one of them; and all of a sudden it scratched her, she dropped it, it gave a yowl and leapt panic-struck across the scribe's feet.

His writing board fell to the ground; his inkwell rolled away from him, splattering the white hem of his kilt, shooting dark wet streaks along the courtyard pavement. Mira lunged, to try to catch the unfortunate animal; Harkhuf too lunged out and caught *her*. Without regard to time or place or how many might be watching, he hauled her in his rage upside down across his knee, whipped up her flimsy skirt with one hand, pulled off his sandal with the other, and leathered her slender haunches until she screamed. He let her fall, she rolled away from him, he ordered her out of his sight.

It took an enormous effort for him to sit himself up straight again and dispose himself as though nothing had happened. Immeasurably trivial: but the blood inside his ears was roaring like a cataract; and he did not wish to ask himself why. His boy replaced the inkpot, re-ordered the writing board, Harkhuf's fingers blindly searched for the pen.

Write: and keep on writing!

SIX

Once he knew the full problem posed him by Pen-el-alopa's conduct, King Nobody, to be brief about it, had seen but two solutions, had assessed them in three days, made his decisions, acted. He could take his son from the island and go. Or take his son down to his own house, and kill: and then take his chance as to whether his son, later on, would kill *him*.

He accepted the second course (well-advised, he said, by Pa-lassa-'thnai); he succeeded, by wicked stratagems; murdered (with blade and bow) all the intruding chieftains who might or might not have been sucked into his wife's thighs; murdered (with strangler's noose) all the slave women who might or might not have connived with them: and then, did he murder his wife?

Strange to say, he did not want to. Strange to say – or not so strange, because I know how he must have been – I have *seen* him as he must have been – her smile became *his* smile, and he offered her a compromise. He suggested she plead rape, that the men he killed had been her violators. She stayed silent, refused his suggestion. But he ignored her refusal, made his suggestion into a public announcement, sent her back home to her mother's land – what else could he do?

'A sort of wild conclusion that gave no great pleasure to anyone, but no one could complain about it – or not much.

'So it was over and done with; and yet not finished. I had to think about how I would live. I had very very slowly, through a year and more of misfortune, come to understand the curse of the sun god. But now there were two curses: the second one, my island blood-guilt. For the chieftains' murder, no urgent trouble. My son paid compensation, according to our custom, to the houses of their outland kin, and for the time averted feud as far as *he* was concerned. As for *me*, my son informed me (he being a man now, a lion-beard, yes?) that he absolutely refused all blood-guilt for any of his mother's slave women, that he had never insisted they should be hanged for doing their duty, and did I not know that even a slave had a dangerous ghost, if she happened to be a wise woman? – yes, he meant Mel-n'th-o whom not only had I hanged but savagely put to question; and now she was haunting me, my son said he could see her upon me hourly, a black bat with its claws in my hair.

'Which meant I must go to some very distant sacred place to be rid
of her and cleansed. Which meant that Tel-emma-kossa must be left
alone in his own right to rule over Ith-kaa, and very gladly I let him
do it. Those kinsmen of the dead chieftains were not going to stay
quiet, no matter about the compensation: if my son were a true lion,
then lion-like he would survive. If not, then not. And in fact, not. He
was dead within the year, and I was very well out of his
neighbourhood. He ought not to have been so gleeful when he told
me of the wise woman's ghost.'

'Would it astonish you to hear that the sacred place I chose for my
cleansing was the Island of Pharos, our Sea People's oracle-shrine,
haunt of ships, haunt of sailormen, haunt of Pa-lassa-'thnai's
dishonest strategists? Pa-lassa-'thnai herself put it into my mind. I
took a spear tasselled with goat-hair, as being her emblem, rowed a
night and a day into deep water, and laid it upon the sea to observe
which way it would point while the weight of the blade dragged it
down. The current seemed to direct it upon what would be a course
for Egypt; so I followed that course. No better destination: here I
came!'

The Old Man of the Sea, it appears, is not an old man at all, but a
woman, wearing a seaweed beard and no clothes but a sort of shawl
of sealskin; she is painted all over blue-green and the Sea People
hugely revere her. She is said to be the sea god, who was once a sea
goddess, until differences arose among the pirates who frequent
Pharos. Those sailing there from the north-west required a male deity,
but the shrine was in female hands, and the crews from the north-
east (having been some centuries longer in these waters) insisted that
it so remain. Solution: either war or compromise. They were all on
edge to have war; but the great tidal wave frightened the lot of them,
so they settled for the present compromise 'between fucker and
fucked' (the characteristic ship-captain words of the ship-captain).

The 'old man' must be always of nubile years and an accomplished
swimmer; once she is past child-bearing she is replaced by a young
acolyte. She then joins her ageing predecessors in the direction and
administration of the oracle. All these women are close kin, when not
practising their sacred craft they control the traffic of the Free Island, the
quays and the warehouses. They are jovial, ruthless, and very rich.

The whole business upon Pharos sounds most perilously barbarous,
it is totally new news to me and must be set down at once in the
archive.

I attempted to gain from Nobody a competent account of the rites of the oracle, with small success. To nearly every question I put to him, he replied, 'It is forbidden to speak of it.' It could be that he was at his lies; and when pressed, his invention failed him. It could also be that he has a genuine respect for the island's highly expensive magic, although his manner of describing what little he *did* describe fell very short of reverence.

He dropped certain *hints*, after the fashion of a sly adult questioned by a child upon how and why the engendering of babies. From which allusive bawdry (for it was nothing less) it is possible to make deductions, in the interest of national security.

First deduction, for what it is worth. The ritual includes a great deal of shape-shifting, whereby the 'old man' is perceived in successive disguises, each answerable to some heraldic property of the Sea Peoples' religion. Beasts of ferocious sort, and finally a 'rushing of water'. Her petitioner in turn must assume the appropriate adversary roles, as of another stronger beast, to grapple and win: upon the last metamorphosis he must give himself to the water; swim (if he can), or (if he can't) trust to the goodwill of the 'old man' to be rescued from drowning.

Second deduction: the danger of drowning is real; on the far side of the island lies a deep lagoon fed by sea waves, full of rocky holes, tangles of weed, swirls of current, safe enough in calm water but treacherous when the surf rushes in. The climax of the ceremony is a species of underwater orgasm. The 'old man' has swimming acolytes: King Nobody called them *mermaids*, dropping more of his hints about them, suggestive of bum-fumbling in a sailormen's pothouse rather than occult solemnities. Or did he joke with me deliberately, to throw me off the scent?

Perhaps not. He and his like do seem to inhabit a confused world of violent quarrelling, gross sensuality, and boisterous good-humour all mixed up together: his hints are at one with his way of life and, whether precisely true or not, must necessarily reflect the truth.

He did let me know that towards the end of the briny brawlings a divination of sorts was pronounced, putting into straightforward words the ecstatic cries already uttered by the 'old man' during her shape-shifts.

A formal statement to Nobody (as he lay on the strand exhausted, washed by the waves, lit by the sinking moon) that his guilt against Lord Ra could only be assuaged by his serving Lord Ra unreservedly for as long as the god desired. He would know when his time was up:

for he must carry an oar-blade with him everywhere until someone called it a winnowing fan. Which would mean he would have travelled so far from the sea as to be thoroughly removed from all thought or contagion of islands and of all the crime that went with them.

Third deduction, and I offer it with care: – I do not wish it to be understood as an irreligious mockery of the value of oracles, even barbarian ones – but might it not be said that the 'old man' had been tampered with by those Sea People kings and chiefs whom Nobody had so often betrayed, whom he had cheated so often of their spoil? He called them the 'big kings'; and in those days they *were* big; for all I know, they still are, though their power is now lodged among migrating warbands and upon shipboard rather than in palaces. They would be important to the wealth of Pharos; Nobody's exile, far from their sailing routes, would be important to *them*. For the very year of his visit to the oracle was the first year in all their history that the Sea Peoples found themselves with enough unity-of-command to contemplate a combined attack upon Egypt. None of them can have been prepared to trust the ship-captain any further: his mishandling of the Tru-ja raid appears to have become notorious; and some knowledge of what had happened upon Ith-kaa would already have been percolating among their fortresses, where the slain chieftains had both kinsmen and guest-friends. Despite – indeed, *because of* – his barbaric cunning (in our empire it might be termed his 'diplomatic skill'), they must have felt he was a threat to their new unity. Easy enough to pass on a quiet warning to the oracle.

Strangely, such a view of the matter did not seem to have crossed his mind. Let me repeat. I am not irreligious, but the department should consider the question: if the priestesses are 'very rich' it is because they handle stolen goods from all over the Middle Sea, and in all likelihood co-ordinate the thefts. I know of no previous document that has so starkly exposed the situation.

He chose to serve Ra by serving the then Pharaoh (Ra's incarnation) as a mercenary land soldier in our deep-desert war against the Blue Tuareg. A deliberate contradiction of his own nature and the nature of his race. He told me he did hear about the plan for raiding Egypt. Everyone in Pharos knew it. Did *anyone* know in Thebes or Memphis? Refer to the archive: those formidable landings of thousands of men took us entirely by surprise . . .

He was hard put to it to turn his back upon what was about to happen and to enlist (for day-wages and no plunder) with the destined victim: but he did.

After many seasons' intolerable despair of marching and fighting and counter-marching and fighting and garrison fatigues when the fighting died down, under the intolerable heat of Lord Ra at his most punitive, he did indeed hear, 'from some idiot of a Nubian, that "your winnowing fan, white comrade, is most surely a comical burden for the knapsack of an old soldier; why not contrive to have the poor oasis people thresh and sift your corn ration for you? They would do it most obligingly, willingly for such very small payment." '

Which sentence, he proudly told me, made him free, and all at a leap.

But not yet free from Mel-n'th-o. To find his ease away from *her* he had a far harder destiny, and even the Old Man of the Sea was unable to tell him how: except that the ghost would catch him when he thought she would have long forgotten, when he himself in fact would long have forgotten her; and then, and only then, would he know how to deal with her.

'And believe it or not, I did forget her. The appalling desert burnt her out of my mind. And because I cut my hair short the day I became a land soldier, she had nowhere to put her claws, you see, and year after year I never felt her, nor even heard her squeak.'

Once freed from Lord Ra's anger, he was at something of a loss what to do next. His desert warfare contract was over, he had attained some reputation in our foreign-enlisted regiments, and it was known to his commanders that he had previously been a seafarer. It was put to him that he should continue to serve Egypt as a captain in the Red Sea squadrons, escorting merchant vessels of the Ethiopian trade along the tidal coast of the Eastern Ocean. He was at first unwilling to accept such employment.

'I was nearly an old man. All my life I have *hated* the sea; and the sea has hated me! The only reason I ever went upon it was advantage of gain at the end of each voyage, but any voyage – as a voyage – in itself was mortal horror to me.

'Add to which, there had been some words, from the Old Man of the Sea. All of a sudden she'd bubbled verses at me in the tumbles of her lagoon, all of a sudden the swirl of lascivious waters had abated, desire of body (as yet unsatisfied) abated in my sudden terror: her still small voice, as still as death:

Oar is a winnowing fan, so it shall be
Nevermore dip tip down, never probe my wine-dark sea.

'Which meant surely more than "go to the desert"; it meant "no
more seafaring ever". And when she was sure I'd heard it, she
confirmed it with such love of my lust that I –'

He broke off, shut his eyes, turned his head from me, growled
sourly, 'Forbidden to speak of it.' Eyes open again, mood restored,
bold and savage as before, he said, 'I *can* tell you, that child-fool verse
of hers, it was all I understood of all her yelpings in the water, yet –
except for the winnowing fan – it was not repeated in the oracle's
findings they gave to me later. So I thought it not important. Now I
know it was, oh furies, the most important of all. Now I know – I
should always have known! – the true tongue of an oracle is forked.
You put it to me just now, had I thought that the "old man" might
have been suborned by my enemies? No! For this – this fork of malice
– has since proved to me it was a god that spoke. No seafaring ever;
and it meant what it said.'

To me it went far to prove the contrary. But did it not also prove
that he *had* been at the oracle? That he *did* indeed most strenuously
believe in the power of Ra, if he believed in the 'bubbles' of a shifty-
mouthed sea priestess? He went on to explain further how it failed to
deter his ship roving. 'Oh I did not quite forget it. I told the man when
he came to recruit me. He said to me, "*Wine-dark* is a Middle Sea
word: we of Egypt call the ocean the *Great Green*, the waters you'll sail
in are part of the ocean, a different element, tidal, and Pharos has no
power over it."

'I ought not to have believed him, but I made myself do so. Of
course he earned a commission for every sailor whose contract he
secured. And of course I had no home, no family, most of my Middle
Sea comrades were dead or broken; add to which, I had become most
shamefully accustomed to the regularity of empire, the discipline, the
system, the unfailing arrival of Pharaoh's half-yearly bullion chest to
fulfil our outstanding wages.'

Let me consider implications before I set down more of his story. If
the oracle is fraudulent, it could not have been a god that spoke. Nor
could he in fact have been made free of Lord Ra's curse; unless
divinity has chosen to recognise the pronouncements of corruption
and sets its seal upon them whether or no. I cannot believe it does. So
either way he was under the curse when he entered our naval

service: he had *never* been freed from it; or else he had been, but he breached his terms of agreement. Which is again to suppose that his tale of the curse is true. If it is not true, he has led me into a bardic romance of such complex and unprovable proportions as to render my interrogation absurd from its very commencement.

Short cut: I must assume that he told truth up to and including the years of his land service. Those can be checked. So let them be. The Department of Frontier Defence will know all about the Tuareg wars and should have kept muster-roll of at least the foremost chiefs among the foreign-enlisted regiments; I take it he would have been one such.

Similarly, check the naval records. If it is true he was given a ship, it leads directly to his alleged voyage of circumnavigation: but for that we are into the years of the usurpers, and the archive accordingly fails us. We have only the man's own word. As follows.

Thereafter, in the Red Sea squadrons, he attained some reputation.

And then lost it, all at a blow, when his congenital urge for piracy overcame him. Among other heinous outrages, he attempted rape of the chief wife of an influential young coastal sheikh, headman of an Arabian seaport under the protection of the queendom of Sheba, which in turn was in alliance with Egypt. Complaint was made, the old ruffian was arrested, his admiral condemned him to death.

'And for nothing. Oh true, I had hands on her, and laid her down, and chewed at her mouth and grappled her breasts, but that was *all* I could do, all; I pulled myself off her and staggered away whining. "Nevermore dip tip down"? Nevermore thrust tip up! That envious foul "old man" had stolen my erotic power! My punishment, of course, for putting my brute-stupid feet once more upon a floating deck. And appropriate, no? To the time and place and goings-on, where the "old man" gave me my warning.

'Add to which, upon the day of the rape, we saw the sun three-quarters eclipsed: all my sailors were terrified, had at first refused to attack the seaport, so inauspicious the doings of heaven. But I told them Lord Ra and I were happily good friends once more, and his sign was a sign of the defeat of my chosen victims. The men of the squadron were foreign-enlisted, Syro-Phoenicians mostly; very glad to be assured that a mutiny against Egypt had the support of an Egyptian god. You see, we raided that Arabian town as a deliberate act of mutiny: our bullion chest for that season had not arrived – civil war (they excused themselves) downriver towards the Delta, to which we

at sea were expected to remain indifferent. Oh such turd-brained
nonsense! If you Egyptians could not agree upon who was your
Pharaoh, why should barbarians know any better?'

Now this matter of the eclipse does *not* require to be checked. I
remember it myself: it was observed all over Egypt. The official
interpretation at the time: the Syrian usurper had the blessing of
heaven in his seizure of the throne, eclipsing by his power the
discredited former dynasty. Interpretation afterwards: a warning to
the usurper that his coup was foredoomed; he arrogantly ignored it,
the eclipse was his *own*.

*Two interpretations; and both from the same set of priests? Viewed against the
jobbery upon Pharos, it does pose the question whether blasphemy from the
likes of King Nobody is quite the unnatural crime that this investigation
presumes. I put it no stronger. I doubt, in my final draft, if I dare put it at
all. But.*

'Why did I try to make a rape? We went into that town for food: no
bullion chest, no rations. So why rape?'

I would not have thought, given his character, the question
required answer; but he had an answer, it was germane.

'I had already taken note of a – of a cumulative shrinkage and fall. I
feared it was the chill of my own old age. But that day my blood was
hot with fighting Arabians to get at their storehouses, old age was of
no account; so therefore my blood must also be hot for a woman. So I
saw her, and seized her; I said, "This one is the test!" – and I failed it.
When she knew that I failed, she laughed at me. She threw herself
into the sea; for a wonder she could swim (almost as well as the "old
man"), so she swam, and she reached the far shore of the bay, and so
was able to tell her chieftains who it was that had burned the town. I
almost welcomed the rope at the admiral's yardarm.'

Like so many of his sort, I suppose he had lived for his pride of
lechery; the violent pikestaff, untrimmed and so abominably clustered
with hair, that lived in its own vile pride in the den of his groin.

For certain he deserved his death: and yet he was reprieved.
Because Pharaoh (so-styled and so very recently installed) was the
Syrian usurper; who found, in the court-martial record, an
unscrupulous filibuster, a barbarian after his own heart; he sent for
King Nobody, laughed and joked with him degradingly, and offered
him an alternative penalty. There might have been more to it; the
usurper in fact might have inspired the shipmen's mutiny? It won't be
in the archive; but there may be some sea commanders with personal

memories. All in all our Red Sea ports should be sifted for *anyone's* memories, both of that and of what follows, if the matter is held to deserve it.

What am I writing? It can only be held to deserve it – all the trouble and expense of enquiry through ships and harbours of the Eastern Ocean fleet? – if there is reason to believe it is true! How can I have allowed him to inveigle me to such extremity?

'He told me, this Pharaoh told me – and I call him the Pharaoh still, because I insist that is what he was to me, a fear-breeding angry potentate, but as kindly as my own father, though young enough to be my son – he told me there was but one way to keep a man like me obedient, and that was to give me a task no other man in his service dare contemplate, let alone attempt. He had such a task and all his admirals were taking fright at it. If I accepted, and carried it out, I would be granted an admiral's rank, and the status of nobility that goes with it. If I refused, or failed to complete it, then the yardarm as originally prescribed. So there it was, my choice. Years of further seafaring, for which already my manhood had been withered. Or the end of all hope of any sort of manhood, which (as I say) I'd almost welcomed; but *almost* is a wild long way from *done*. My choice? D'you suppose I had one?

'So I told him, three great ships, fifty oars each, supervise their building and fitting-out myself, with plenary power of requisition to evade the corruption and delay of your dirty dockyard officers and writing men. I must choose my own crews.

'He said, by all means, but he did not think I would find volunteers.

' "Very well," I said, "we'll press them. Defaulters, like myself. Achaeans, Syro-Phoenicians, Philistines; pirates in your gaols and slave-camps, do not tell me you have not hundreds of them."

'He said, by all means; gave me his signet: sent me off then to set myself to work.'

SEVEN

'And the purpose of the voyage? Why, no purpose at all; or a madman's purpose; or the purpose of a man who was more of a god than a man (which is what your Pharaohs say they are, though how many of them behave like it?): for there was no advantage of gain, I was to bring back no treasure, I was only to answer a question – which no one had ever asked until this mad usurping Pharaoh had suddenly thought of it, and yet you say he was not "legitimate"?

'He put the question to me, thus. "Egypt requires to know, *how far do possibilities extend*?

' "We have marched – *you* have marched – through the desert to the uttermost length of men marching away from their homes, from the water of their sacred river. And those marches have never reached any coast. We have however read the reports: they did reach the lands of men who knew other men who had heard that there *is* a coast, somewhere, deep deep in the south, an ocean coast to terminate the bounds that god has set for us."

'He said that when he said "god" he did not mean just the gods that we knew of, he himself came from outside Egypt and some people akin to *his* people had already found a god who –'

A god who burned eternally in an unconsumed bush, the great 'I AM' he called him. I write it only because I must, because the ship-captain told me, they are the words of the usurper – I do not think the ship-captain even yet understands what was said to him, the dreadful potential of the message he was sent out with, the message he has now brought back home.

Alleges he has brought back home. But if he does not understand it, how could he have invented it?

'In short, my instruction was to follow the Ocean shore until I came across men who have never known Egypt but who may perhaps know other men who have heard that there *is* an Egypt, somewhere, deep deep in the north, a land of power at the world's centre. Having found them, I was to remember them, to remember how I reached them, and everything about them; and so report it back to Pharaoh, and he in his own time would consider whether anything should be done about it.'

Note that: 'consider'. No immediate plan for advantage. Only knowledge. Lord Imhotep, O deified patron! would or would not such a design rejoice your noble heart? You alone, Lord, can answer that. You alone, Lord, can say what you would think of what Nobody said next. Which, once again, I write only because I must.

'This Pharaoh did nothing but ask the huge questions. Had he lived he would have been the greatest king of all your kings.

   'I embarked without hope. And yet knowing, as I've always known, that no hope often means more hope than you'd think possible: Pa-lassa-'thnai so many times had proven me the truth of that, Pa-lassa-'thnai against all likelihood might find me an advantage of gain; she might, even today, I can still think that she might.'

It took him all night to describe his voyage to me. I would not let him stop to sleep lest the interval break the spell, for spell it most certainly was. His faculty of recollection (or of creative improvisation, it could have been either) was amazing. Events of his narrative not always in the right order, but each event in isolation seen bright and clear as a shining star. Lengths of days of sail, directions of sail, accounts of landmarks and landfalls, accounts of peoples, their appearance, their ways of life and religious practices, astronomical observations (of which more later), nautical observations, currents, winds, birds, fishes, sea-beasts, he remembered it all.

   One difficulty: the man's tendency to imagine – and intermittently talk to – the barbarian bard who was not with us but ought to have been. Deep-set into and amongst the most apparently accurate of his memories was this awkward poetical strand: tales of one-eyed man-eating savages; of seagull-swift black girls laughing and singing in the surf, who murdered the men that jumped overboard to couple with them ('Not me,' he said, 'I was impervious, not the thickness-of-a-thumb of rigidity left to me at all!'); of dangerous narcotic foods proffered by seemingly hospitable tribes; of ship-grasping many-armed monsters; and sudden whirlpools in flat calm seas.

   I was careful not to tell him so, but I had heard most of them before, indeed at my nurse's knee (a woman of the Lebanon coast, herself brought up among ships). He was fetching them (deliberately?) from that great storehouse of mariners' fantasy that

exists in every seaport, and must have been in his own fantasy since
his own island childhood. Why did he do this? To *convince* me? Did he
suppose me so land-locked, so stuffed with priests' dogmas, that I
could not believe anything unless it was salted with marvel? He ran
huge risk, though he did not see it, of destroying his own case. And
yet, strangely, he strengthened it: for the marvel-tales were no more
marvellous than the things he retailed as new truths; and I was easily
able to separate the two.

My function to judge the latter. I have not yet fulfilled it. Is it possible I
cannot fulfil it? Are marvels in fact unjudgeable, without some exterior
evidence? As, for example, that you have heard them from your nurse, but
applied to a different voyage in quite different waters. They are either (of
themselves) persuasive; or they are not.

Plausible that the Syrian usurper should have failed to send a clear-
headed scribe with the expedition? The very fact that the ship-captain
says there was no scribe is suggestive of truth. Such a well-trained
recorder, with all his writing skill to hand, might surely be *too* well-
trained, might be tempted to bring every item of discovery into line
with official doctrine: only a pair of eyes unimpeded by received ideas
would have served the usurper, so greedy as he was for change, for
the total remaking of Egypt.

Do I say then that my writing skills are not *conducive to truth, when all my*
life I have proclaimed the contrary, in the face of boastful soldiers, fatuous
courtiers, intolerant barbarians, mud-minded obstructive officials? Lord
Imhotep, forgive your servant, for that is *what he thinks he is saying!*

I'll bring his story at once to what he told me about the sun. Perhaps
because he knew he had to tell it so as to be utterly convincing, he
introduced it by recounting, of all things, the felonious habit of his
crews.

    'You know they were as I was, my brothers-in-crime they could be
called, brave when they had to be, rank cowards when they preferred
it? I had had the utmost trouble, from the outset of the voyage,
withholding them from murder and pillage: their misconduct only
abated once they thoroughly understood that we were sailing on and
on indefinitely, that *I* would murder *them* if they refused (I was
desperate enough to die at their hands myself and they knew it), and
that therefore they would find no way to realise the value of their
plunder – which in any case was abominably scanty; we touched
upon no rich cities.

'I did have to kill a few of them, justly. They were ringleaders. And I admit I did appease the others by suggesting that once we were well on the way home, maybe a few diversions would be permissible, for a moderate plunder, provided we took care not to affront any of Egypt's friends. And I admit I did talk very large about Pharaoh's rewards, letting them imagine they would all be given collectorships, provincial governorships even, the full corruption of government gold would be theirs for the taking and spending!

'And then we found the sun day by day higher and higher overhead until at length he was right over the masts; and then, day by day, he rolled himself slowly aft, to ride at noon astern of us instead of leading our prow as you'd expect when you sail south. And of course the men were frightened. *I* was frightened. The more so as I deliberately had sought not to offend him by my choice of direction. We could have rounded Africa by sailing from the delta along by Libya to the Middle Sea gates – a few ship-captains from Egypt had already passed the gates to make factories-of-trade on the Western Ocean coast – but I considered that Lord Ra would be better pleased with me if I followed his *own* course, east to west. I had him very much in my mind when I made my plans.

'Perhaps there *was* a blasphemy? Perhaps it was outrageous to the god to see men follow his tracks as though we chased him with bailiffs to recover a debt? But we did it with the best intention; and Pharaoh had approved it. Bearing in mind who that Pharaoh was, it would have been better if he hadn't, yes? At any rate, I told the crew that the god was not yet *angry*; but he was showing us a marvel to correct our foul behaviour. Upon his very path we had presumed to act the pirate? Let them be warned; they were observed! A good device – they restrained what was left of their violence, and at the same time were released from the intensity of their fear. And very soon they got used to it.

'As they also got used to the stars shifting position and being exchanged for other stars, hitherto unknown. We could not try to steer by them: only by sight of the shoreline, most anxiously hoping we would not be blown away from it.

'Also the moon was all out of place, but I won't talk about *her*: she is, at the best of times, an uncanny disturbance for straightforward men. Pa-lassa-'thnai is a friend of hers; I trusted her to intercede. I think she did, for happily the moon's *phases* held fast to their usual intervals.

'Of course I told nobody of my old trouble with the Unconquered

Sun. I was assured the slain oxen were forgiven me. But of course I wondered – were they?'

So there it was. He had asserted what could not have been. He had moreover asserted it with a total plausibility. I have taken many statements from men sent abroad on all manner of foreign missions; when they have spoken to me as Nobody spoke I wrote their reports without a qualm. At times I have found lying, usually when some delegate has been bribed or intimidated by those he was sent to deal with. I think I know the signs of it. With this Achaean they were not there.

He asked me did I believe him? I refused to answer. For if he did lie there was a reason for it; and I had as yet no clue to what it might be. Perhaps the rest of his story would tell me. After all, he had not come to Rakotis alone. The people he was with might well have something to say about him. But first, *he* was to tell about *them*.

EIGHT

'I was beginning to be afraid we had sailed too far. The people of the southernmost territories were these little brown houseless men I have told you of, ignorant of metal working, timid, furtive, dangerous, impossible to catch. Pharaoh's government could have no use for them, nor for their great empty grasslands and deserts – at least, no use at such a distance.

'So we rounded the end of the world and slowly slowly picked our way north. The sun was now behind us, climbing daily toward our masthead. And then we were again skirting the shores of the forest country with seaside villages strongly built, palisades, timber huts, thick thatched roofs, and a host of seagoing canoes to flock around us. Hospitable people, savage enough, big and black like Nubians, great music makers, delighting in strangers. Every night, when we beached the ship to make camp and prepared to exchange gifts, they passed on the news of our progress, beating it on drums to the next village down the coast; so that when we got there the next day we found ourselves expected. And for the most part, expected with joy and acclamation; although our resource of gifts was expended, we must now give the people what we had been given by like people a hundred leagues back, nothing at all in the way of novelties, but they took it in good spirit; we laughed, embraced, clapped backs, shook hands and laughed again and sang.

'We even began to think that our voyage had become a safe one, that Pa-lassa-'thnai upon our sternpost was happily bringing us home. But we still met with nobody who could tell what "Egypt" meant. If home lay ahead of us, it was miles and miles and miles and months and months away.

'I have told you of two ships lost. Now I come to the third. Have I said the hull was rotting? I understood more of it then the men did. I ordered temporary repairs; I had just sufficient shipwright skill to know how temporary they were.

'I had come to no conclusion about this alarming state of affairs; and then the west wind reached one for me.

'Without warning, in broad forenoon, it rolled us suddenly over in the trough of two waves, about a mile from the shore, tearing out the mast and rigging, pulling planks, frame, and benches apart, forcing us all under foaming great rollers, dragging us toward a long white shelf of a beach where the outcrops of wicked rock were sharper than billhooks. Dragging us toward, ripping us back in the reverse current.

'I caught hold of one such rock and clung there. The fierce undertow hauled me off again: the skin from my hands was left in fragments upon the crag, like the pebbles that stick to the suckers of a cuttlefish wrenched from his hole.'

He repeated this last simile three times, with variations, relishing it, turning it in his mouth, as though he were his own bard in his own hall commissioned to construct the pathos of his heroism.

'Huge effort, and I swam sideways, just far enough for the next wave to bring me in onto sand and shingle. All of my senses left me. Or seemed to leave me, because I did not drown – not quite – I was thrown far up the beach, and still alive; while the ocean retreated to look for an easier prey. It found one and fetched her on top of me with the very next breaker; the corpse of a young woman, one of the wives my crew had carried with us from our previous season's encampment. She had her baby tight in her arms as dead as she was; she was black, the child was brown, I never saw her white sailorman again. Indeed I never saw any others of all our corpses, the current must have washed them from the shore: certainly I was the only one that lived upon that beach.

'Myself: and Pa-lassa-'thnai.

'The splintered sternpost, with my goddess still on it, stuck in the sand a little above me as though planted there on purpose as a grave-marker. There were other bits of wreckage too: a tool box burst open with most of its contents fallen out; some stoppered wineskins a quarter full of our drinking water, bouncing in on the waves like young porpoises; a gaudy strip of coloured cloth twisted sopping among sopping seaweed – I did not know what it was at first, then I recognised my admiral flag with the double crown of both the Egypts and the sun-disk of Lord Ra – sun in the north? *Sun bloody well half-drowned by the unbiddable Great Green!* (Oh yes, a different element.)

'I had been naked at the steering oar when the calamity fell upon us: to be at work without clothes is one thing, to face the whole of my future life in a deadly strange place with no accoutrements but an admiral flag is quite another. I tried and tried to reach that flag, I felt if I could but wrap myself in it I would be a man once again, almost capable of survival. It was not, after all, my first shipwreck; nor would it be my last, as you know.

'But my strength was insufficient. I just lay there, my arm stretched out, a stride or two short of the hapless flag, and that hapless dead girl's thighs and kneebones piled upon the small of my back.

'I will not describe the woman that walked out of the forest, down the beach, looking at us.

'You have her here, you have seen her. Even in her present humiliation she is an awe-inspiring sight, no? Gracious gods, you should have seen her curling the vigour of her ten long toes between the seashells of her own bright strand. I looked up at her, she was a mountain. Let me tell you what she wore.

'Upon her head a veil of some sort of vivid green rushes, hanging down before her face: her eyes and teeth looked out through it. Her cheeks and her bare arms were painted red and white. Her entire body down to the ankles was draped in – not a cloak, more of a curtain, or a pair of curtains, back and front, suspended from her wide shoulders, made of long interwoven strips of greenery from a living tree, with huge pale flowers shining between the leaves. She held a gourd rattle in each hand. Her lips, nose, ears, were plugged with gold (these people know gold, they know copper, they know tin, but nothing of alloyed bronze and nothing of iron).

'I heard her gourds clattering long before I could see her: and before I saw *her*, I saw the runners who made her path for her, young men and young women with clubs and spears, little drums hanging about their middles. They were a quite different people from any we had met on the voyage: I thought they were a dangerous people, I lay very still and hooded my eyes.

'She gave me and the dead girl one contemptuous glance; and then passed on to Pa-lassa-'thnai. The carved image seemed to surprise her; no, to *delight* her: she jumped, right up and around in the air, and all her greenery shook upwards, I could see the great cheeks of her arse. Round and round the image she pranced, she made a rhythm with her gourds, her young soldiers took it up on the drums. With a flick and click of one of her rattles she ordered a pair of them – strong-built girls with green feathers in their topknots – to run and stretch out the admiral flag so that she could see it to best advantage. She stopped her jumping, stared at it, you could count two hundred before she'd stared enough, then another flick and click; and they draped it around her shoulders.

'Then a pause, as though none of them quite knew what to do next.

'I was astonished to hear some of them giggle, their whole
proceedings until then had been so ominous-stately. They laughed a
bit, and they whispered, they came to a sort of decision: it was as
though they felt, all together, that what they'd found on the beach
required a ritual of some kind; but they knew of no precedent, they
had to search their minds, the necessity amused them.

Suddenly, as though they'd received an instruction from outside,
they all began, at once, to dance. The young ones, bare-bodied, swift
and elegant, capered around *her*, to a precise beat but with no proper
pattern of steps that I could see. She, in the middle, scarcely moved
her feet at all: but her great bulk under her draperies was swaying
and jerking with an increasing and terrible energy. She slowly edged
forward, sometimes sideways, sometimes even back, but little by little
I could see she was advancing, directly towards where I lay.

'Let me tell you, I was filled with fear; somehow I knew that she
knew now I was not dead.

'Somehow I knew that for some reason unexplained I *ought* to be
dead: and that this dance, without respite – it went on for at least an
hour – was the beginning of the process of killing me. I no longer kept
my eyes concealed, indeed it was impossible, oh I had to stare at her
as she was staring at me.'

'All the dancing and the drumming stopped, at once, without
warning. The same green-feathered pair that had picked up the flag
came running down to me, and picked *me* up, an angry tug that
jerked my blood onto the roughness of the beach. They held my
hands behind me, forced me to my knees in front of *her*, and then all
of them closed in to form a circle around us.

'She began to dance again, without the drum beats, only her
gourds, and this time she made a weird music in her throat. It was
altogether horrifying; to my Middle Sea ear completely unhuman, far
more so than the other musics of Africa which we had heard – and
some of *them* we had thought inconceivably strange. A long time
afterwards, I found out the words she used: if I tell you, will you
laugh that a frightened and battered and embittered old man should
have so misunderstood her?

> Little fish of no colour—

'She improvised, you see—

> Little fish of no colour
> With little hairs on your head

That have lost all their colour
(And so few) where you ought to have scales,
Little hairs on your little belly;
Why are they so unusually so yellow and red?
Big eyes in your big face;
Why are they so unusually so green and so blue?
Little fish of no colour
But here and there sun-colour burnt,
Wound-colour scarred,
Sea-colour soaked,
Sand-colour scraped and smeared,
Blood-colour cut;
How could you swim
In such waves and not drown?
Your fool woman drowned, your fool child,
Why not you?
If you don't know how to drown
Why don't you like my dancing,
Why don't you laugh and live,
Why don't you live and dance too?

'And so on. She was not killing me. She was attempting to bring me to life. Gracious gods, what a way to do it! The menace of her had all but choked my breath. And bear this in mind: I still saw it as menace when the next strange thing took place. As I tell you, I was kneeling helpless, my hands behind my back, and the glistening girls (who gripped them) scratching my back and shoulders, slowly and tirelessly up and down with dagger-like long fingernails; my mind upon death, which meant, in effect, my mind upon nothing: and out of nothing in my mind, right in front of this hideous woman, for the first time for seven years I felt the old red rudder standing up from the break of the poop like a cherry tree at full harvest! *I* felt, *she* saw. They held my hands behind my back: I was helpless to prevent, and no less helpless to have caused it; no, not by any fantasy nor exertion of deliberate will.'

I did not need to enquire what he meant by the *red rudder*. He laughed and he spluttered, slapped his crude hairy thighs, narrating for the next few hours all the arrogant love-conquest of the black woman over him, or of himself over the black woman, where they lay and how they lay, and who were the witnesses of it, for it seems a great deal of it was absolutely done in public, barbarian amongst

barbarian: until finally, for sheer lack of his bard, I suppose, he gave
over his prurient jargon and impudently asked me what I thought it
might have signified?

I did not deign to respond, I was sure he had an answer already
provided; indeed he had and he snarled it at me with fanatic intensity.

'She had cancelled,' he hissed, as he strode in swift circles all
around and around the pokey little room, his hands darting like a pair
of desert rats, 'she had cancelled the oracle of Pharos! More than that,
she had fulfilled it. For do you not see, writing man: within this huge
deep-forest black woman (although she was not aware of it, and Pa-
lassa-'thnai knows I was never such a fool as to put such a notion in
her head), grunted, shrieked, and sprang the unquenched ghost of
Mel-n'th-o, catching me when I least expected, and turning me there
and then in my very helplessness to her furious purpose?

'No, she was no longer concerned with revenge, but service, slave-
service, for Mel-n'th-o in her lifetime had been slave of my house:
and now I was the chattel of hers. And what could I do but what
Mel-n'th-o had done? – endure it. Endure, and enjoy, if I could; I did
my best. I am nothing if not adaptable. As you see here today. As you
see. Do you not?'

He put his knotted arm round the bare shoulders of my own slave
as he spoke, brother-and-sister in servitude, a quick glimpse of the
pair of them smiling and winking – my own slave girl, I saw her *wink*
at him! – and then he was away from her and her head turned away
from both of us.

*I forgot myself; I shouted; abused him. I roared that he was here to answer
my questions, not to make his vile comparisons: did he want, once again, the
cage? Let him tell me directly of his life with the black woman, if he wished
me to believe it, and I'd write it down and no more nonsense.*

*At once he was all apologies. 'Forgive, forgive,' he soothed, 'I only thought
that comparisons are the heart and soul of a story. Every poet I have known
will make them all the time.'*

I said he was not a poet but a criminal.

*He said he was not a writing man. He said he spoke only from memory,
which was the work of a poet, criminal or not. And his memory dredged up
comparisons: so was he to suppress it? He said he thought I wanted the truth.
The truth was, he said, slavery is slavery. I (the writing man) enjoyed my girl
as the black woman had enjoyed him. When the girl was greensick and
sluggish, did not the strength of my red rudder envigorate her hot spirit? Or
maybe did the nature of my trade (sitting day and night upon the itch of my*

*hairless arse, while I stuck little scribbles into the wax) defeat my manhood as
the curse of the Pharos priestess had quelled his? He said, 'What about your
wife?'*

*I said, 'What about my accursed wife? She is not here, you have not seen
her, you do not know her, how dare you even think of her!'*

*Apologies again, soothing, soothing, 'Forgive,' he whispered, 'forgive.' But
he insisted the comparison was important. My wife, he well knew, was no
wild barbarian: but his had been, and so was the black woman. And the
black woman in her far country lived just as Pen-el-alopa had wished to live;
he had learned to comprehend, from his place as her slave underneath her –
'Oh indeed underneath her, and look at the weight of her, ha!' – just how
Pen-el-alopa had induced service from the mainland men. It was perhaps a
little possible, no? that a writing man's wife, so far from her husband, had
many of the same thoughts; sometimes? He wanted only to show me that
between him and me, and thus between Egypt and Ith-kaa, between Egypt
and deep Africa of the north-rolling sun, there was so much of like-to-like
that the knowledge of it could only help me to understand his truth.*

*I had no words to reply to the insolence. All I could do was sit silent until
the squall had blown itself out, I mean the squall inside myself. Either I
waited for him to continue his tale; or I called the guard and lost thereby all
hope of getting more of it: impossible to leave it here, he had told me so much
that I must hear what came after or nothing would be understood.*

At last he did continue, very earnestly, no provocation. The black
woman was not, as he had first thought her, a queen (in the way that
he had once been a king), nor the priestess of a particular tribe; but a
sort of high queen, high priestess, the guardian of all the magics,
indeed the *incarnation* of all the magics of a whole nation of tribes
who lived dispersed across the forest over a matter of maybe one
hundred miles along that coast.

The young people who danced on the beach with her were her sons
and daughters. The girls were also priestesses. She mated with the
boys – 'A disgusting thing, we'd say in Achaea, but it happens in your
Pharaoh's house? – and also cast lots for their deaths, to *transform*
them, as she'd say, into a shape of the forest, beast, bird, or tree.'
Human sacrifice is abhorred in Egypt; but the Achaeans still use it, so
I was not astonished by the easy shrug he gave at mention of this
'transformation'.

I asked him the woman's name. He said she had at least three. He
did not know what they meant; and indeed I am not sure I have them
correctly, the pronunciation is most strange; clicks, coughs, grunts.

When she cast the Lots of Transformation, she was *Kur-kai*, and implacable.

When she chuckled and heaved her broad body with delight to see the *red rudder* growing hotly out from *his* body, then she was *Kal-p'so*, warm, loving commanding, and yet in her own way loveable.

And yet again she would be *N's-kaa*, making up songs at the ocean's edge, insatiably curious, as vain and as charming as any girl-child in Egypt.

She had expected the arrival of his ship. Drummers' nightly messages had reached her long in advance. She had been yearning above all things to see a boatload of strangers (pale-skinned, *of no colour*), to load them with gifts, to impress them with the generosity of her power; to show them all the virtues of the place where she lived, her shrine in its jungle glade (she called it THE CENTRE OF THE WORLD), and to send them home amazed. Far away home to their own rulers *of no colour* (whoever they might be) in disconsolate lands beyond the bounds of true humanity. But in the end there was only one stranger. She was not going to send *him* home.

He belonged in her shrine, with the rest of her trophies, for ever. Innumerable sacred objects piled up higgledy-piggledy, covered with baskets, hidden from uninitiated eyes; and among them was Lady Neith! A little image carved in wood with the same emblems as the sternpost of Nobody's ship. It had been there beyond memory, but she knew where it had come from. She did not say 'Egypt'; the name she used was 'Second-river': 'First-river' being the enormous stream that ran westward into the ocean a few days' journey from where she lived.

It had certainly not been brought by sea. Before the ship-captain's arrival the people of the coastal forest had never seen such a thing as a vessel of fifty oars. The nakedness *of no colour* of a man *of no colour* was equally strange to them all: even if he were no more than a waterlogged old ruin of a man needing a whole hour of magic to sufficiently stiffen his blood, he was considered well worthy of Kur-kai's fierce sovereignty, N's-kaa's eager questioning, Kal-p'so's unbridled pleasure (freely bestowed upon him as he bestowed his into her).

Slave-service? He assured me, vehemently, 'Yes indeed!' even though (apart from Kal-p'so's bed) he had had no duties, except to live. But he was totally unable to conceive of any stratagem to get himself out of there. Still less any stratagem to seize a profitable control of that country: Kur-kai was far too dangerous. Slavery, to him, meant inability to rule, combined with inability to move.

*

At one stage in his narrative, the ship-captain let slip another term for the woman's shrine: he called it THE WORLD'S NAVEL. He knew, and he knew I knew, that the world's navel is claimed by Achaeans to be a cleft in their mountains from which an oracle makes occasional utterance. Egyptian priests have visited it. Its power is authentic: but of course we do not recognise it as in any sense a *navel*. It is by no means centrally placed.

Now, had *he* ceased to recognise the claim of this oracle? Thereby blaspheming against his own gods as well as ours? I took him up on it, sharply. He said only, 'Whatever I say, there are somebody's gods upended, it would seem. How do *I* know where the world has its centre? I only tell you what I was shown. If it comes to that, how do *you* know? You only tell me what you were told. *Told* and *shown* are sometimes brothers. Fratricides. So let them fight.'

He shut his mouth and drooped his head, refusing to say any more. He was very very tired. He had talked incessantly for hours. For hours I had taken notes from his talking. My hand that held the stylus staggered and jabbed in all directions with weariness; I punctured my knee as often as the wax.

But I could not leave him, not now, no; not until I had heard—

'How did you get away?' When he told me that, I would be finished. I repeated it, 'How?'

And I found he did not know: somehow things had happened, that was all. Struggling with his words, he did manage to insist that he himself designed and built the strange improvised ship in which he had reached Rakotis. He had tools. Hadn't he said he had tools, they were salvaged from the wreck of his fifty-oar? He salvaged tools of course and built himself a ship.

All by himself? He said, yes.

I was incredulous: he then qualified it, tried to explain, broke down into a storm of weeping.

I asked him whose idea it had been; why was the black woman on the ship; who were the others on board?

He seemed again to attempt to explain, his tears overcame him in flood, I was lost among his evasions and digressions. Perhaps it was no more than his exhaustion, or maybe an old man's muddle: but surely some deeper reason? I could only find it out when I questioned the black woman. He had said he knew some of her language; he must be my interpreter; no simple matter, for her story was not his story, and I feared that the muddle would augment itself with every question. Perhaps between the pair of them they would augment it of set purpose. I had no choice but to try. Sleep first; and then fetch her.

NINE

I had the woman brought in to me very early the following day. I let
the ship-captain have a few hours' sleep to restore his faculties before
I was confronted with the two of them together; but I did not want
him so thoroughly relaxed as to allow him scope for strategies and
tactics. I made shift to master my own weariness. I had been able to
close my eyes for an hour or two, and after that I felt more in
command of myself. He was fetched first: I did not speak to him, but
let him stand just within my sight until the arrival of the woman. I
thought him on edge, apprehensive. He whistled between pursed lips
but otherwise kept silence, very watchful.

I saw immediately she was Kur-kai: she squatted herself down in
the furthest corner of the room, her wide mouth was dragged shut
across her face, her brows lowering heavily over her eyes; the eyes
themselves, dark and foreboding, peered between dark eyelids as
though from behind window shutters. They had put her into a white
linen shift that sagged from her big breasts like a half-hoisted
mainsail. In obedience to my instruction her manacles had been
removed. But she held up her hands below her chin as though they
were still fixed together in the grip of the wooden blocks, and she
squatted, and she waited for what came next. Her dreadful deliberate
silence was as violent in its implication as any massing of armed men.

I told the ship-captain to tell her she could speak freely to me. She
shot out an abrupt spit at him from the corner of her mouth;
remained otherwise immobile. The ship-captain smiled nervously: he
was twitching all over. I assumed he was afraid lest she refused to
confirm his story.

He said, 'She'll let you talk, I think. I don't think she'll answer.'

I asked her, through him, a few preliminary questions. She did not
answer.

I said if she kept silence I would have her handcuffed again,
whipped, put back into the cage. She did not answer.

I thought about it for a few minutes, and then sent my girl to tell
the beachmaster to send to Neith's shrine for the priestess. A difficult
message; the priestess never left the shrine. But I sent for her 'in
Pharaoh's name', and at last she agreed to come. We had to wait a

long time for her: throughout all that time I think none of us moved a muscle, except for King Nobody's twitching mouth.

I asked the priestess what she could suggest to get the black woman to talk. She replied that the black woman would certainly not talk to *me*: but she might talk to the Lady Neith's image, sister to sister; and she might allow me to overhear, if she (the priestess) remained in the room with us. It had been a great mistake, said the priestess gratuitously, to have put this woman in a cage; and worse, to put the cage into the storeroom of a holy shrine. Did the beachmaster know nothing about sacrilege? She knew the beachmaster, only too well: she shrugged off his clumsiness with a cackle of laughter. She did realise, she added winningly, that *I* was not the beachmaster. Just a foolish irresponsible gentleman whose ill manners deserved to be slapped: I did not know how to deal with ladies, but the ladies were fully capable of dealing with *me*. The first thing ladies liked was some stimulating drink. 'Drink before talk; talk before kisses: what are we waiting for?'

I had cups of wine fetched. The old priestess sipped hers with fastidious small gestures, ogling me and then hiding her kohl-rimmed eyes with her hand as a sign that she was, in theory, still in sanctuary in her shrine. The black woman gulped it all at a mouthful, dropped her cup to the floor, and continued to squat, immobile.

A medallion of Neith was centrally placed in a tangle of beads and jewels among the thick white powder on the priestess's withered bosom; as she breathed, and she breathed ardently, little puffs of this powder were disturbed by the jolting necklaces and hung about her gilded nipples like smoke. She fumbled with fragile fingers, tremulously detaching the medallion on its chain from the rest of her ornamentation. She held it out towards the black woman, who stared at it for a long time.

I said to the ship-captain, 'Tell her that Lady Neith wishes to know who she is, where from, how, why – everything. Tell her to tell her sister. Tell her pleasantly. We are all good friends.' He passed on the message, we waited.

Then, of a sudden the black woman became N's-kaa. An astonishing transformation. She did not move from her position; but she bent forward most gracefully despite her apparent grossness; despite the ugly wounds in her face, she smiled with the utmost confidence into the face on the medallion, chattering, confiding, bubbling with gaiety almost; sometimes tears in her eyes and a sob of sadness; sometimes a trilling laugh or a snatch of extraordinary song. She reached to touch the portrait, outlining its profile with incongruous delicacy, caressing it, *loving* it, I am able to say.

I am able to say, from precise observation, that she was beautiful; as she talked and talked. And the simple white shift was as flattering to her new beauty as a pearl-studded embroidered gown to the elegance of a great court lady.

Now and then among her words came angry flashes of Kur-kai; also slow sensual passages of indolent recollection, which must have been Kal-p'so: but once she was well into her rhythm of discourse, the interpolations did not at all affect its fluency. I listened, entirely fascinated, understanding nothing until the ship-captain caught up with her at breathless intervals, and shoved himself between us with his halting translations. A word-by-word record was impossible. To avoid undue distortion of her statement, I ordered him not to try to put it into Egyptian; I understood his Achaean well enough. But in fact, not altogether well enough. When he said what he thought she said, it sounded like this:

'All good forest, fish in river, beasts among trees, birds, fruit fruit; clear garden, grow corn – chop no tree until the lots fall, this tree or that tree? – when the lots tell us, chop no tree until we've asked her, may we chop? – so all trees still good friend, and then corn corn in garden, vegetable in garden, good to eat, fat gut, baby fat, mother fat, young men fat bollocks, fat gut, long cocks, good: more babies, more, good good good. Kal-p'so longtime happy, all done good and happy. Kal-p'so make warmth, breasts, cunt, belly, oh warm!'

From which rigmarole I deduced, and immediately made a note, that the life of her people had been highly prosperous, thanks to the favours of the forest spirits whom they had worshipped so correctly for so very many years.

Quite wrong, however, to think such primitive expression to be a fair representation of her words. The language she used (I could tell from her rhythms of speech) must have been most rich and complex, indeed poetical: My ignorance of it frustrated me greatly. The ship-captain's method of picking out here and there a few salient phrases was not quite useless, but very nearly so. As indeed, I do believe he intended it to be.

But whenever he stumbled in his interpreting, and it seemed as though he did so deliberately, she noticed it; and fixed him with a Kur-kai glare that immediately compelled him into better efforts. If he had learned her language from her, then obviously she had learned some of his from him: he was in no position to deceive her, and she was determined that her story was not to be mishandled.

I now understood the state of his nerves; and my comprehension startled me. Far from being afraid that she would give him the lie, his fears were all centred upon too much confirmation of his tale. Or, rather, of those parts of it he had chosen to hide from me. Nor had he hidden them from any politic calculation; but only because they disgraced him personally. For such a man, an extraordinary reason. He had boasted of rape and murder and ransack and treachery with the lightest of hearts, as though they advanced his quality (as no doubt they did, in the eyes of the bards whom he hoped would elaborate them). But his relation with this woman was something quite outside the normal intercourse of his life, and he did not want its progress told.

On the other hand, she wanted to tell it (to the goddess, not to me): and therefore used all efforts to have it rendered with accuracy.

So: she said her land was prosperous. She said that the prosperity had been threatened for years by the predatory king-god of another, larger nation to the east (she called him simply *King Savage*, as though she viewed her own people as unimprovably civilised). He had announced his intention of conquering the land and taking her, and her daughters; he would add them to his herd of wives, and thereby control all their magics. If he controlled the magics, he would clearly control the land and need no further warfare.

Then the ship-captain came. When asked where from, she replied simply, 'From where there is no sun.' Which could have meant he came from the south, if the sun, as he claimed, was northerly. But if the sun was *not* northerly, then could she not have been saying that he came from the north? She did say that her land faced the sun when it sank into the sea: so the west coast of Africa seemed confirmed. But nothing else does; and I nearly left off her interrogation at that point. The ship-captain's extreme uneasiness persuaded me to continue it. She was, after all, about to tell me about *him*.

He lived with her a year, she said, and all was well. He was her token of good luck, and all the people knew it. Then King Savage launched an attack. His army (surprisingly well-equipped with bronze and even iron weapons) was resisted at great cost and very nearly repulsed.

The ship-captain fought bravely against the invaders, using all his experience and skill: but then he was suddenly tempted to see an

occasion for one of his stratagems. He contrived to bargain secretly
with King Savage.

Even in the midst of his translation he tried furiously to deny it. He
shouted that he had been outrageously misunderstood, his stratagem
had been solely for the purpose of luring King Savage into a trap,
secret enemies of the black woman's magic had been working against
both himself and her from the very beginning, and so on and so
forth . . .

I cut him short: ordered him to let her speak. His denials caused
Kal-p'so to laugh – she knew these expostulations far too well, and
knew how to live with them and yet not stop loving him, for I am
sure that she *did* love him: nothing else would explain the absence, at
this unexpected moment, of punitive Kur-kai. She laughed, and went
on with all that she had to say.

If he had indeed played traitor, I do not know what he hoped to
gain from it; the woman herself was not quite certain. Clearly his
release from her thraldom. But would King Savage treat him any
better? Perhaps he simply liked the idea of a conquering king, felt
himself back (as it were) in his own old rapacious Sea People world;
he would know how to dispose himself to deal with brutal power, it
would not be very different from dealing with himself. And out of it,
if he survived, he might grapple some advantage, some sovereignty
even. He had a *hope*.

As a result of his action, whatever its exact nature, King Savage
broke in to THE CENTRE OF THE WORLD, looted the shrine, but
failed to lay hands on the women. This angered him, he blamed the
ship-captain; he had the ship-captain entangled among creepers of a
tree, hung him up there in a steaming deluge of rain to await slow
and well-merited death.

Then (I think) there was another battle, King Savage's troops
moved on through the forest. It seems that in their haste they forgot
about the ship-captain. The women (who must have fled) returned
and found him hanging there, half-mad.

Once again, as he told me that this was what she was telling, he
broke off his interpreting. He launched into a wild account of his
experience in the tree. He claimed that at the height of his pain, he
had been suddenly conveyed thence, aboard a swift ship with blue
cheeks, to the furthest bounds of Ocean, and marooned on a desolate
shore.

'Fog, twilight, and chill; dead bushes and thorns all decayed and
hung with fungus, thundering waters out of an icy cave: and a stark

livid grove of poplar trees, the only growth of any height in all that dire place. And squeaking and whimpering, thousands upon thousands, all the ghosts of all the dead that ever died on this earth. Mel-n'th-o, the foremost ghost. I tried to hear her speak, I could not, I only knew that what she meant was – was – was that I had been the very worst thing of all humanity, a slave that betrayed his mistress. Had I not hanged Mel-n'th-o for her act of betrayal of *me*? So for me, then, the very same, "very same", she squeaked (I could just catch those two words because she mouthed them so often), "very same, very same, very same . . ."

'But *my* hanging was not to finish me; no, my mistress came to the tree, and she pulled me down out of it, pulled me down before Mel-n'th-o could come close enough to grip hold of me, and thereafter my servitude was redoubled, it was trebled, *three-hundredfold* piled back upon me! Every day, every night since then, I have been again in the land of the dead: and still I could not truly hear them, not word by word to make good sense.

'Only through these last days, here, in your cage here, was I finally able to know what they said to me, only in your cage. They said *all* slaves betray: and of course it is true. They said, we must rejoice at it or die. They said; we must rejoice at it, and still we must die. Do you think they will have finished with me? Do you?'

He was screaming. And would never have stopped, if I had not called a guard in to strike him over the face.

Disregarding him entirely, save for a quiet laugh, sardonic and languid, delivered to the portrait-head of Neith, the black woman continued to tell how she and her daughters had rescued him. They demanded from him: had he betrayed them or not? The daughters swore he had, the mother was not so certain. He told all the lies he could think of, but his agonies had spoiled his cunning: none of his stories were consistent, he could not convince them.

Kal-p'so laughed again (at her own indulgently remembered foolishness, it seemed), and then told how the daughters swore that his coming had destroyed the nation for all of them, whereas the mother thought that had he *not* come, King Savage would still have invaded, and would already have been completely victorious. Only the ship-captain, she said, had saved her nation from defeat in those first crucial battles. But now they *were* defeated: they were refugees in their own forest, cut off from their own warriors, who themselves were broken up and hunted down by King Savage's men in every

direction. Either the ship-captain was their GOOD LUCK, or
absolutely their BAD: lots must be cast to discover which. But half the
sacred objects were missing, the lot-casting could only be botched, an
impromptu expedient. Nonetheless, they attempted it. It fell in favour
of the ship-captain. The daughters refused to accept it. They claimed
the procedure had been incorrect.

I saw that Kal-p'so was now shedding tears. Her hand went to the
ship-captain. He took it and held it and kissed it violently. He was her
slave, but did he *love* her? White-haired, scarred with old wounds,
untrustworthy, violent: I do believe he has no one else. He has now
come to realise that if she dies, he cannot live. He has surrendered his
pride to her affection, and at last he is no longer resenting it. His
confusion over what he did in regard to King Savage, and over what
happened afterwards, I do believe is the confusion of *shame.*

The first time he's ever felt it. It disrupts him, it dismantles his
heart, he tells (to me and to himself) more and more lies to conceal it;
and yet it is proclaimed with every lie that he tells.

She spoke on. He said that she said:

*'Lovely girls my children, lovely girls my enemies, love, hate, and drive
them away: so they went. There was me, him, our good forest, nowhere to
go, King Savage everyplace. I found women, their men, their babies, we came
together, where to go? Magic said: ''Shipman of no colour is GOOD LUCK.
We take him, make ship, we sail where he goes.'' No, he would not make
ship. Said he could not. Said he dare not. Magic said, ''Make it!'': and he
did.'*

That voice was Kur-kai: she *compelled* him to make the ship. With
only a few frightened peasant families to help him, an axe and two
adzes and no whetstone, and enemies all over the jungle: how did he
do it?

Well, it was done: however it was done, *wherever* it was done, the ship
is a FACT and I have seen it on Rakotis beach. There is no doubt that
its builder is a man of infinite contrivance. And somehow they sailed
here. Believe it.

What is known in our archive of the coasts of Africa to our west,
and then south into Ocean, does not conflict with King Nobody's
narrative. If he never put keel in those waters, then he has received
and remembered a very clear account of them from someone else
who did. He told the rest of his tale in a highly excited flurry, adding
to and contradicting the woman's statement until both of them were
yelling at each other and at me and at the medallion on the bosom of

the priestess. Contradictions of no great significance: small details as to who died when and why, arguments about the order in time of various landfalls, storms, fights, other incidents. A tale indeed most marvellous; but I'd say plausible.

The rage with which they told it was the rage of the events within it, and between the man and the woman during those events. I cannot deduce otherwise.

If it did indeed fall out as they say it did, it must have been the very hardest voyage ever completed in all the history of ships upon sea. They were lopsided, they were overloaded, the oarsmen had no experience of any craft larger than an eight-paddle canoe, their gear kept breaking under successive tempests, currents and winds were almost endlessly contrary (as had not been the case when he sailed with his original ships); the closer they approached the gateway of the Middle Sea, the more hostile became the coastal populations: and the ship-captain himself was infested with 'Furies' (his own name for them). Mere demons, sovereign goddesses, vengeful ghosts? – a little of all three, I daresay; but certainly female.

One anomaly, however: they ought surely to have touched now and then (in the later stages of the journey) upon certain beach-towns toward the Middle Sea gates where exists an Egyptian presence. They seem not to have known about these factories-of-trade at all, or, if they did, they did not recognise them when they reached them. They could have lied to me (the preferable explanation?): or they could have missed them altogether in the very violent weather they encountered: *or* – and it is *possible*, as discomfiting as it is far-fetched, yet I have to consider it! – our factories-of-trade in those parts are so degenerately assimilated among the native populations as no longer to be effectively *Egyptian*.

After the years of the usurpers, the troubles of their overthrow, and all the Sea People piracy, some of us in the department have noted a growing failure by resident representatives of our most distant enterprises to respond to government communication; almost nothing has been done about it. When did the last ship sail westward from the delta with a proper commission to inspect and report?

Whatever else about this affair, urgent action should be taken forthwith; or else a policy statement should be made at the highest level renouncing any further maintenance of redundant oversea establishments. Had it not been for the necessity of this, my present report, I suspect the whole matter might have been neglected indefinitely.

I have not been able to make out where they thought they were sailing to. The ship-captain drove the vessel, without plan of his own, only because the woman commanded him. Not until they neared Egypt did he begin again to recollect his prior commission: I suspect he would have preferred to have forgotten it. But he swears that once he recognised the Libyan shore to his starboard he could think of nothing else but Egypt and the Pharaoh who had sent him out. 'Reward, reward,' he cried, 'Reward was awaiting me! And all my burden was lifted, no Furies, no Kur-kai, only a crew of surly blackfellows fainting and failing at the oars; and I drove them and drove them and no longer listened to *her*!'

She swears, on the other hand, that 'Second-river' was not her goal. She had come, had she not? – with those families of her people, who accompanied her so faithfully with such an astonishing blind faith – from her lost CENTRE OF THE WORLD, to find somewhere upon the world's edge to replant her displaced magics. And every place through all the voyage was '*not right*'. Until they saw Libya. They put in to a Libyan haven. She admits it: he tried to deny it. Perhaps he tells truth, in that she does not say he himself set foot on Libyan shore. But *she* did: and Lady Neith had a house there, and she saw it, and 'gave love'.

A very confused translation. But whoever spoke with her at that place seem to have told her that in Egypt the goddess is consistently ill-treated. And that one day ('soon soon and why not now?') Neith's people from Libya must come to Egypt to *reclaim* the land for true worship. But they did not speak her language, nor she theirs. Messages, I know, can be brought without language. Tokens can be sent. Snatches of music, talking on the ends of fingers. All manner of devices to baffle all scribal training. Did she fetch from Libya a token for the priestess in Rakotis? Did she – or King Nobody – fetch a token to the Free Island, which in the end they could not deliver?

The Rakotis priestess evades all questions. Nor is it proper for me to threaten her. I merely state the conjunctive facts; the possibilities that they indicate.

Possibility number one. There was no voyage all round Ocean. Somehow a group of Africans (of a tribe we know nothing of) found themselves in Libya, and somehow they found an Achaean to bring them to the Free Island to concert some sort of subversion against the

Two Kingdoms. But why such a disastrous ship? The Libyans have vessels of their own, quite capable of making a short voyage along their own coast; and why send a parcel of foreigners?

Possibility number two. There was no voyage all round Ocean. The ship-captain is a slave-raider who ventured west through the Middle Sea gates, captured some Africans after an attack upon one of our (strangely silent) factories-of-trade, and was bringing them for sale among his islands. He ran into tempests, the slaves mutinied, killed all the crew save for himself, and ordered him to take them home again. But they were blown or drifted out of their course, lost their ship on a barbarous shore, were compelled to make a new one, and then again were blown, or drifted to Rakotis. He would be telling his great lie to conceal his attack upon Egyptian property.

And yet, what a lie! Why trouble to construct it? I can establish scarcely a flaw in it; but so long and wild a story, starting with his father as king of Ith-kaa, more than forty years ago? – it is absurd.

I can think of but one possibility *that is not of itself absurd. And that is the one that cannot be true: his circumnavigation. And the one part of that story which shows that it cannot be true is the blasphemy of the sun. It discredits his entire narrative; he does not retract it. Instead, he tells all about the island of sacred cattle and the oracle upon Pharos and his impotence with women for no other reason than to* confirm *his outrageous account. Lord Imhotep, what can I do?*

There is one thing I can do. I can talk to the man again; and I will. But before I send for him I will re-read all I have written, and sleep upon it, and pray. Already I have wasted a night and a day before I could bring myself to my present point of writing. But it cannot be helped. My task is defeating me. Believe it.

Lord Imhotep: to you, my prayer.

And what did the woman mean by the final words she said to me, the immeasurable sadness of little N's-kaa strayed from the warm bosom of her mother? She was on her way out of the beachmaster's house, between armed coastguards, returning temporarily to confinement in the shrine of Neith (though no longer handcuffed, no longer to be caged, I thought it best to allow the leniency to encourage further confidence).

The ship-captain for once translated into simple intelligible speech: 'You upon the world's edge do not know what the world is, and yet you want all of it. We in our forest thought we were the whole world and now we are not even the forest.'

TEN

Harkhuf stopped writing. His boy was all but asleep. His steward stood beside him holding a torch, for the light grew dim; in half an hour it would be quite dark. Mira should have held the torch, but she was driven away, was she not? The cook had gone too, not driven, but sent by the steward to prepare supper. The beachmaster's people had taken themselves indoors.

Harkhuf sat like a statue. He thought of all he had written, all the scrolls in the boy's basket. Re-read it? Sleep upon it? Pray? Was he mad to imagine he could so calmly conduct himself? To eat before he slept? And at his bed to soothe that distressful girl? *Tenderness*, of all things? Contemplation? When his whole mind was falling asunder because of what he had written? And yet he had written it so fully, so obsessively, solely in order to *contemplate*!

He wished he had never had such pride as to make himself a script that could thus toss his brain into danger. He must at once take pains to remove himself from its influence. So he sat like a statue, compelling himself rigid, because the *traditional* scripts and their stiff practice were always served statue-like; and he knew no other way to shape himself to think the traditional thoughts. If he let himself move he would never stop moving; god alone could say where his frenzied feet would tug him: they would race like his invented script and he dared not let them do it.

He snarled at the steward, without turning his head toward the man, 'Get the beachmaster, get the coastguards, get Nobody!'

'Get nobody, sir? You mean, *nobody*? Not the beachmaster, not the – ?' Mistaking of words, comical, what a silly pair of men; a week ago the scribe would have laughed, and explained, and the slave would have laughed too. Now the scribe's fingernails drove into the scribe's thighs, every sinew in his aching body tensed, his mouth tight to prevent a roar. But he sat; he could command himself.

He repeated quietly, carefully: 'The beachmaster. Tell him I want the ship-captain. Now. If asleep, wake him. Now is now. Go.'

Like a statue he waited; and at last the ship-captain came. The scribe said to the coastguards who brought him, 'Let him kneel. I am Pharaoh's man, I speak with the mouth of Pharaoh. On his knees, at my feet.'

The ship-captain was forced down; his face showed surprise and anger; but he saw that this was earnest. He grovelled, like a true suppliant. As he did so, the dim light finished and all was dark; until the beachmaster sent for more torches, and the steward with his own torch kindled them for the coastguards. Flames crackled and steamed in the drizzling rain; but the fire fought the water, they were not extinguished.

Harkhuf under his canopy: the ship-captain kneeling outside it; the tattered grey hairs of his beard ran little rivers down his hairy chest.

'For the last time, I put my questions. And I write down what you answer, as you answer it. Word upon word. We will go slowly.'

In the slow formal hieroglyphs of priestly authority, he recorded very precisely the ship-captain's replies.

THAT HE SAYS HE SAW SUN SHINE FROM NORTH AT NOONTIDE.

THAT HE SAYS THAT IF HE COULD SAY OTHERWISE ALL MEN WOULD BELIEVE ALL ELSE HE HAS HAD IN HIS DEEP HEART TO SAY: AND THAT HE KNOWS WELL THEY BELIEVE NONE OF IT.

THAT HE SAYS HE KNOWS LORD RA WILL CHASTISE ALL MEN FOR BLASPHEMY WHO DO NOT BELIEVE THAT HE HAS SHONE FROM NORTH. THAT NO ONE ELSE KNOWS THIS AND THAT LORD RA AND HIMSELF DO LAUGH FROM KNOT-OF-THEIR-BOWELS THAT NO ONE KNOWS IT. THAT LORD RA'S TRUTH IS ALL MEN'S FALSEHOOD AND HAS THUS BEEN MADE MANIFEST FOR TEST AND PURGE OF WHOLE WORLD WHEREVER IT LIVES, AT DEAD CENTRE OR UPON RIM.

THAT HE SAYS HE IS NOBODY WHICH IS FALSEHOOD AND YET IT IS TRUTH: FOR WAS HE NOT TWICE HANGED DEAD, BY KING SAVAGE IN THE FOREST AND AFORETIME BY PHARAOH; IN TRUTH, IF NOT IN FACT? AND IS NOT NOW THAT PHARAOH FALSE NOBODY TO ALL OF EGYPT: AND IF THEN *LORD PHARAOH NOBODY*, WHY NOT ALSO *SHIP-CAPTAIN NOBODY*, HIS HANGED CRIMINAL, WHO HAS WITNESSED TRUTH OF THAT PHARAOH AND THEREAFTER LORD RA'S TRUTH AND THEREFORE HE SHALL NOW BE CONDEMNED?

THAT HE SAYS IN THIS REALM OF EGYPT, WHERE GREAT PHARAOHS ARE MADE NOBODY, THERE CAN BE NO TRUTH. WORDS SPOKEN ARE AS SILENCE: WORDS WRIT ARE AS RAINPRINTS MADE IN SAND'S SOFTNESS, TO BE DRIED INTO DUST OF NOTHING BY LORD RA AND TO VANISH WHEN WIND SHALL BLOW. THEREFORE AGAINST FALSEHOOD OF EGYPT ALL HIS OWN FALSEHOODS SHINE AS TRUTH. SO HOW THEN SHOULD HE SAVE HIMSELF BY TELLING FALSEHOOD UPON FALSEHOOD UNTIL LORD RA'S TRUTH BECOMES ONE LIE? AT ALL OCCASION HE COULD HAVE DONE SO, SINCE QUESTION fiRST WAS PUT; SO WHY DID HE NOT? IF YOU CANNOT SEE WHY NOT, HE SAYS, GO STARE INTO SUN AT NOONTIDE: IN ALL TRUTH IT WILL MAKE YOU NO BLINDER THAN YOU ARE.

Harkhuf came to the end, laid down his pen, and was about to roll up the papyrus when he thought of one question more. He uttered it, and wrote the reply.

THAT HE SAYS CENTRE OF WORLD MUST BE WHERE IT IS FOUND TO BE, AND
NOT WHERE IT IS SAID TO BE, NOR YET WHERE IT IS SOUGHT.

He sat brooding over this for a considerable length of time. Then he slowly
raised his head, took the torch from the steward, and ordered everyone to
go away – except – 'Except the prisoner. Leave him alone with me. Leave
him still upon his knees. And let him *stay* upon his knees and hold this torch
to give us light; for he shall hear of life and death and he had best be very
ready for them, even as he says he once made himself ready for the
judgement of god's oracle.'

His voice was portentous, more so than he could ever remember it (and
he had played his part often in the highest ceremonial solemnities). The
ship-captain was properly impressed: he took the torch without a word,
without sceptical gesture, without even grimace.

All prevarications finished; all indecisions finished, between the scribe
and his written word (rainprints? rainprints? but the wind had *not yet*
blown). He had tried his own flexible script: it had failed him; out of it,
nothing but confusion. And now the hieratic; strong statement of eternity
as though graven upon stone: the result was exactly the same.

Or *seemed* the same. But not so. Graven statement was impregnable; its
end was predestined; its conclusion was now to be written: and he wrote it.
As he wrote, he spoke it aloud: the old man, kneeling, stared up at him in
the torchlight, and his eyes opened very wide.

OF HIS STORY: ONE PART ONLY WHICH WE FALSELY HAVE SUPPOSED FALSEHOOD,
NOW HARKHUF-SCRIBE SEES TO BE PROOF ALL PARTS ARE TRUE: THAT PART IS
THAT WHICH WE FALSELY HAVE SUPPOSED BLASPHEMY; NAMELY SUN-IN-NORTH.
EVEN AS SUN GOES DOWN, SO IT HAS BEEN SHOWN TO HARKHUF. LORD IMHOTEP
CONFIRMS SUCH SHOWING IN HEART OF HARKHUF; HARKHUF WRITES IT. ALL
TRUE AND GOD IS GOOD.

His eyes met the ship-captain's eyes. The ship-captain's eyes were
suddenly twinkling, the torch wavered: did this demon of a barbarian dare
to *laugh*?

Perhaps not. A trick of the flickering light. But he did dare to speak. He
said, in a curious collusive most wicked little whisper, 'So you'll send that
to your masters, and when they read it, you too are Nobody. Be welcome
then, writing man, to the land of the shades. I may return to my place at the
shrine?'

Without waiting for permission, he heaved himself up and limped
casually out of the courtyard. The torch lay where he left it, guttering in a
puddle.

ELEVEN

Harkhuf was no coarse recording instrument, he was no clerk taking dictation. As an official of consequence, he was expected to proffer advice, in effect to determine policy: most certainly to reach conclusions. Well, he *had* reached a conclusion, a most undesired conclusion; but what was he to do with it? How advise? And toward what conceivable policy?

The most sanguine recommendation would be, first, to welcome the ship-captain as a navigator of unprecedented achievement, and award him all the honours at Pharaoh's disposal; second, to welcome the black woman as an exiled foreign ruler, distinguished guest-friend in Pharaoh's house, and potentially valuable political contact when the ship-captain's new-found lands were exploited and colonised.

But surely this was no more than delirium of imperial fantasy! No one but a madman would extend Egypt's boundaries at this present time. The Lord Ramses was not mad, neither were his ministers. But they were bound to think the scribe was, if he gave them such advice.

A more moderate counsel; honour the ship-captain, lay all the facts in the archive, and postpone further action – how would that be any better? For it would most dangerously remind Egypt of the usurper who first thought of the voyage: at the same time it would uncover the very knowledge that the scribe was in Rakotis to hide. The blatant fallibility of the priesthood of Amun-Ra could only be divulged (even secretly, among senior ministers) if somehow it were to be balanced by very great practical gain, for Pharaoh himself, or the Two Kingdoms in general. And alas, there was no gain, no possible practicality; only the satisfaction of having an answer to a 'huge question'. Which might, or might not, have seemed a gain to the usurping Syrian – Pharaoh Nobody? But oh, to nobody else, oh no not now, least of all to the son of the usurper's supplanter!

So what *was* to be recommended?

Harkhuf should have done what he had written he would do: eaten, slept, tried to be calm. Once again he was unable. This time he did not sit. He strode out of the house and down to the beach and along the beach in the continuous rain, the waves crashing beside his feet, the wind whipping and tearing at his inadequate, drenched garments. Between the clouds a moon like a knucklebone, hurled upwards against the gale; beyond the surf the shapeless island, with here and there a light showing, diffused by rain, winking ill-wishes, tormenting the scribe's thought.

He had written what he had heard; and written that he believed it. Lord Imhotep, as he imagined, had smiled upon that belief. The reputation of the wise demigod had been always for generosity, kindliness, breadth of understanding. 'You too are Nobody!' – how *could* a diligent scribe be Nobody, if he followed Imhotep's way? And yet he would be, that was certain. 'Welcome to the land of the shades' – where else but to the *shades*, if he dared presume to question the earthly power of the Unconquered Sun? Question the Sun, or question Imhotep? No question about *that* question: the one was a high god whose high priests ruled Egypt's ruler; while the other, a mortal man who may have become immortal, was none the less obedient subject to the gods who were immortal always. He himself as scribe was Imhotep's sworn man. But as Egyptian, as officer of government, he was Pharaoh's man, Ra's man, and thereby drew his wages of silver. From Imhotep, no wages, no living, no status of life; only pride, skill, integrity; and now, 'the land of the shades'.

What right had Lord Imhotep to doom his servant thus?

What right had that beast Achaean to lead him to such a doom? Liar, pirate, murderer, friend of a ruthless goddess who denied her own mother, a man that would ravish distraught stranger-women for no other reason than to test his squalid *red rudder*! a man so vainglorious of his habit of crime that he could boast between him and the scribe the guilt-bond of 'like-to-like'?

Like-to-like; what did it mean? Here is a sea-rover sets his grip upon the breasts of a sheikh's wife in the midst of his rage of manslaughter. Here is a writing man so furiously fixed into his work that when a heedless girl intrudes on him, he sets his raging grip upon *her*, and throws her – and upturns her – and tears at her skirt – and – how much difference, after all? And neither of them, surely, had great joy from their deeds of outrage. But Harkhuf's deed (so reasoned Harkhuf) would never have been committed had not the words of his work been the words of the barbarian: *he was infected by the barbarian.* And thus his own barbarity. Salt water, roaring and pounding, to scour out the filthy plague!

A spring, a swing, a flop of his soft-jointed body, he turned his feet into the waves and pushed through them, till they broke against his waist, and then his chest, smothering his head with hard volleys of spray. Beyond them, the Free Island, with its thievish oracles to purge men's loins amid the rage of gripped bodies and volleys of spray. For him, an Egyptian, in the Egyptian surf, his own oracle. The relentless cold of the winter sea made clear to him what he must do.

Back to the house, into the room where his bed was, call for a lamp, call for his writing basket, and now he must be alone. Mira, of course, in the corner of the room (like the black woman before the priestess came) crouched in a lump against the wall as low as she could press herself, her eyes round and accusing, her cheeks puffed and darkly flushed, wet streaks upon them – tears? Very likely tears, and very properly; but this was no time to try to abate them. 'Out!' – and out she went.

He began, without more thought, hardly waiting even to dry himself; in his own script that made his thought as he wrote it, dashing the words across the scroll as though thunder and lightning would swallow them up before ink had left bottle. There was indeed a thunderstorm, it had come surging out of the sea, out from behind the island; if he took time to listen (which he did not) he could have heard the beachmaster's women yelping with fright inside their walls.

Contrary to precedent, I send this draft digest of my report ahead of me, without waiting to engross the fair copy. The subtended recommendations will explain why. I have been honoured, for the past year, by such high place in the department as allows me a certain discretion. Matters *unhelpful* to good government are at times, as it were, sifted, through me and my pen, before they are permitted to trouble great men with irrelevance. I have, upon this mission, been much troubled myself as to how far there *ought* to be sifting. To tell, or not to tell, all I have been told? I have been told a great deal: I shall not be thanked for laying the absurd burden upon encumbered backs of others who do not deserve to bear it.

Therefore I reduce the body of my report as follows:
    1) No credence need be placed in anything the ship-captain says of his voyage.
    2) Nor is it necessary for the state to discover from what place he has come here, except to understand that he touched upon the beaches of Libya before seeking to land at Pharos: I am quite sure of his subversive intent. He is an Achaean of the Sea People with a most violent history, a danger to our maritime commerce and the peace of our coastal regions.
    3) His companion, a woman of deep Africa, has associated herself with hostile elements in Libya, for purposes inimical to the security of the Two Kingdoms of Egypt.
    4) Further interrogation will not be efficacious. They are irresponsible adventurers acting as terrorist couriers for immediate advantage, but they know little of the larger workings of the

barbarian designs they have helped to promote. They only came to
government notice through demonstrably false blasphemy (which I
do not reiterate) against Lord Ra and Unconquered Sun. They
confected this wicked nonsense to divert enquiry from their real
doings, and at the same time to draw such attention to themselves as
might prevent the Rakotis beachmaster dealing with them summarily
(his original and most correct intention).

Recommendations.
For immediate action:
   1) The man and the woman should be returned to the beachmaster,
as pirates captured in the act, to be proceeded against by him
according to his powers of justice. I understand this means they shall
be put again in the cages, without food, drink, or clothing, and so
hoisted upon poles on the Rakotis strand (within sight of the Free
Island) as a mark to all seafarers: they shall remain there after death
for as many months or years as the beachmaster thinks fit.
   2) This penalty, however, should not be imposed, nor should any
word of it be uttered, even to the beachmaster, until a sufficient
contingent of regular soldiers be despatched to Rakotis. As the
priestess of Neith has developed a sympathy with the woman, it is to
be feared that government cannot be confident of her good faith:
hence the imperative of secrecy. Moreover the other blacks of the
ship's crew have been rebellious in servitude. To attempt justice
against their mistress in so small a community would provoke their
further disorder; the coastguard have shown themselves incapable of
sustained action: hence the imperative of reinforcement.
   3) Commercially unsound to put the other blacks to death. But they
ought not to remain among households, as they are now. They should
be sent under bonds in a slave-gang to the better safety of the royal
quarries: the day the troops arrive, but not until the two principals are
caged. Let the blacks see them caged.

For subsequent implementation (after consultation with appropriate
departments and as soon as circumstances of state permit):
   4) Send troops to capture the Free Island, abolish the oracle, and
kill all the priestesses.
   5) Strengthen the Libyan land frontier.
   6) Suppress the cult of the Goddess Neith in all places within five
days' journey of Libya.
   I despatch this report tonight: and will remain here myself, keeping
a close eye on the situation, until I receive an affirmative answer.

Memphis has authority to act on behalf of Thebes? Please be so good as to expedite.

There: it was done.

Without allowing himself further thought upon exactly what *had* been done, he began to copy his digest in a far more serene spirit, writing neatly in archival cursive. He read it over for any errors, rolled it, tied it, wrapped it; attached a department seal to the exterior package to authenticate the bearer; and then paused for reflection.

All the scrolls he had completed earlier? Quite unfit for other eyes. But other eyes could not read them; he could leave them as they were. Their impromptu hysterical postscript, however, beautiful sacred hieroglyphs (supposedly first used in the days of the greatest Pharaohs by none other than Imhotep himself): he could not leave *that*. It told too much of truth and falsehood. He tore it from the end of the scroll; held it, at arm's length, to the flame of the lamp; shuddered a little as it flared and then fell into ash.

He called for his steward, and gave him the sealed package; ordering him at once (without heed for distress of weather) to carry it across the lake in the boat they had already used, and then up the riverbank by post-chariot to Memphis as fast as he could persuade the drivers to take him: costs to be referred to Treasury. He thought he dared refer them, his report was sufficiently serious.

Thunderstorm was finished, rainstorm was finished, the waning moon shone unhindered into the beachmaster's yard. The beachmaster was not in bed but sitting over a brazier with his eunuch and a skin of wine. The scribe saw Mira flitting away somewhere in the shadows: he sent her to his baggage to fetch another wineskin. When she brought it he dismissed her, compassionately, to her sleep; and most jovially joined the beachmaster. He had made his decisions: he now desired to celebrate them.

The ship-captain's truth, after all was said and done, might just as well be left to the ship-captain's bards. The fellow's death would be no hardship, had he not said he was dead already? And as for Kur-kai/Kal-'pso/N's-kaa, she had so many times cast the Lots of Transformation, she could scarcely feel surprise that now they fell upon *her*?

By midnight both eunuch and beachmaster were totally fuddled. The scribe also was by no means sober; but he did not care, his work was done, he had justified his senior status.

He felt that tonight, the first time since he came to Rakotis, he would be able to take his full pleasure with Mira. She was in his room, waiting. She had offended him, she would be penitent. He was mellow, he would be forgiving. They would both forgive each other. He would let her drink some wine. It would all be very warm and sensual, and he was drunk enough to ignore the mosquitoes.

'Red rudder,' he murmured, and chuckled and belched a little, 'Red rudder at the break of the poop, heave-ho and we're all aboard . . .'

TWELVE

He lurched into the room, holding the wineskin in his swaying right hand, unclasping his kilt-waist with his left; and he discovered she was not there.

She could not have absconded, not permanently, not in Rakotis; for where on earth could she find to go from so isolated a backward place? She had taken upon herself to hide herself, against all sense of duty and discipline; it was truancy, childish pique, a wretched nuisance of a misdemeanour that demanded considerable punishment: he could not for the moment think of *what* punishment. Whatever he chose, he must eventually justify to his wife.

He felt cruel, but he did realise that open cruelty would not serve: the girl must be made ashamed, and then soothed into a mood of regretful affection. When she reappeared in the morning he would make up his mind what to do to her: hurt her tender body again? Deprive her foolish appetites? Or just ignore her till she begged for notice? Meanwhile, he was without her. If he went in search he would debase his dignity. He fell angrily, diagonally, across the bed, drank what was left of the wine, what ought to have been *her* wine; slept.

A creeping of grey daylight awoke him to sick stomach, swimming head, and a second discovery. Not only was Mira still absent, but the draft of his digest was spread open upon the floor. He had tied the scroll, he was sure of it, when he finished the fair copy, he had tied it and laid it in the basket. Beside it lay another papyrus, one upon which he had not written: but someone had. Who? What? The handwriting was ill-formed, messy beyond belief, but unmistakeably put together from his own invented sign system. His blurred eyes did their best to decipher it; he felt his heartbeats first quicken and then stop, quicken and stop and then surge in his breast, as though he were about to die.

'*Sir,*' he read, '*sir and master.*' The spelling was totally arbitrary, but he could make a sort of sense of it.

Sir and master, you are kind but not kind, not with that sandal when all saw. Not kind not at all because you said friends to sailorman and black woman and now you say in your writing which I can read you taught me some of it and I studied the rest without you, you say you send them again in cages, and death. Not kind. Your own fault. I can

write you taught me too and I studied the rest without you. Read it. Your
own fault and they have gone. I am Mira and gone too. Your fault. You
said often Egyptians are kind and Sea Peoples cruel. I liked that cat and
you beat me. I like Sea Peoples better. Better too for sailorman and black
woman. Ask the priestess. Now she must know now what I read you
wrote it about cages and quarries and death and about her. She is kind.
Dear sir and dear master, your fault.

He ran furiously to ask the priestess: and the priestess told him nothing. If
the prisoners, she said, were no longer in the shrine where they had been
put, he ought to ask the coastguards, who had sacrilegiously been given full
charge of the storerooms. The ship-captain was missing, the black woman
was missing, there were no stone-carrying black slaves in the storerooms.

The sun rose, red and glorious.

And then people came running to tell Harkhuf of an even worse thing.

The black women, the black children, distributed about the countryside
of Rakotis in the slave-huts of individual farmsteads, had all been fetched
away in the night. Horses and chariots had been heard, and seen, by
terrified families; locks had been smashed, doors broken, one or two
householders (trying to defend their property) had been seriously
wounded. An unpopular old fish-factor, who lived alone with his fish in a
miserly hovel, and had been allotted one of the women and two little girls
at a very high price, was found dead across the threshold, a spear wound in
his chest, his own gutting-knife deep in his throat. All agreed there had
been a raid by Libyans, overland, very swift and efficient; and nothing had
been taken but the slaves.

Somehow, it appeared, the coastguard had slept all night, all of them
including their captain: the captain said he thought the suppers had been
drugged. If he lied, it must be because he was bribed, or intimidated, by the
priestess. There was no proof of anything. The beachmaster knew nothing.
The beachmaster was still dead drunk.

A fishing boat was missing from the beach.

Between the beach and the Free Island a longship of Achaean build
rowed slowly up and down, as though upon patrol to prevent access to the
island. Armed men were clearly visible on its central gangway above the
oar-benches.

Harkhuf had no idea what to do. He must do *something* or lose his dignity.
He ordered the crapulous beachmaster to commandeer another fishing
boat. They were rowed out (against the breeze) until they came within hail
of the longship. A red-bearded man reared up aggressively on the

longship's poop, glittering in a horned helmet with white horsehair crest, ejaculating the rudest words of passable Egyptian:

'Go home, writing man, home! Fetch your false promises back home, promise safety to the splendid Thebes! Let you know you're going to need it! We have a king, we have a queen, we have a brave little princess; white, black, brown, we have all three of them safe and sound: the Old Man of the Sea will take them to her heart. And all their people have been taken to the true people of Pa-lassa-'thnai. Home at once or we'll kill you. Very soon we'll kill all of you. *Home!*'

The scribe had a fleeting thought: he had insulted his own patron, who was not only father of scribes but of every good man of science. Suppose the mild Imhotep were not after all so mild, nor so subordinate? And suppose his protection were extended to include *navigators*? In which case. . . ? In which case, it would be best not to pursue the thought: but to remember instead that Imhotep too had once served the state, assuredly by whatever means had seemed most needful in moments of peril.

He clutched desperately at the idea; even as he screamed to the boatmen to hoist their sail and no fooling and put back to Rakotis beach.

This lamentable end to his mission should have compromised Harkhuf's reputation irremediably: but it did not. His superiors were still deliberating, from department to department, when all was cut short by the outbreak of war.

A most dangerous Libyan invasion; followed by a vast incursion of the Sea Peoples, both overland through Canaan and ship-borne. Pharaoh Ramses' army and navy, at first taken by surprise, rallied their strength and skill and won a decisive succession of victories; they occupied Pharos, bloodily swept away the Old Man's oracle, and replaced it with a regular temple to Amun-Ra. The harbour quays were converted to the needs of the Egyptian fleet. The Libyan frontier was re-established and fortified; the Sea Peoples, their confederacy broken, scattered in confusion all over the Middle Sea. They seized and settled upon bits of land, where they could find them without serious fighting; where they could not find new land they succumbed to powerful intruders from the Scythian north.

After a few generations their bards began to remember the heroic past. They sang of the Age of the Great Destructions; and some of the tales they told bore some relation to the truth.

Because of the war it was not difficult for the priests of Amun-Ra to carry out the delicate task of down-grading the cult of Neith. Goddesses with barbarian associations were suspect at all levels of society.

The ship-captain, his African woman, and little Mira might or might not have been upon Pharos when it was sacked. At all events, Harkhuf heard not one word about any of them for the rest of his life. Nor did he take any pains to enquire.

For himself, the war fetched professional advantage and caused all his mistakes to be forgotten: he was careful to imply he had foreseen it in his 'digest', which hindsight now showed to be a unique and perspicacious document. Had it only been properly understood (men said) the invasions might well have been averted.

He received the praise, and the promotion that went with it, with what seemed to be modesty. But his reticence was no more than a heart-striking appalled silence; as he told himself again and again what the ship-captain had said ('*Lord Ra will chastise all men for blasphemy . . . for test and purge of whole world wherever it lives*'), and what *he* had said in response ('*ALL TRUE AND GOD IS GOOD*'), and what he had done with those statements. Purged? Tested? Chastised? Why, they had made him Chief Scribe! Had the gods no self-respect? Or were they indeed of inferior status to the Syrian god, the burning bush, I AM?

If '*words spoken are as silence*', then silence must be made of words; and the words of Harkhuf's silence most certainly were saying: 'The god who rewards where he ought to have punished was given his name by whom? By NOBODY: so there we are. So therefore . . . *I AM NOT?*'

Silence spread itself.

Harkhuf's wife, unable to forgive his loss of Mira, never spoke to him again except to meet some immediate need of household business. She claimed she had loved the girl more dearly than any of her own children.

From then on he avoided all sexual use of his slaves, and hardly ever had them beaten: nevertheless they hated him.

He remained a highly efficient royal servant, well regarded by priests and administrators, profoundly trusted by Pharaoh himself. His very coldness toward every aspect of humane sentiment was said by many to be the key to his excellence. Outside the requirements of service he was as taciturn among his colleagues as his wife was with him.

His public worship was always correct.

Upon his death his dutiful family placed him, with great ceremony, in his ornately furnished tomb. He had previously, and privately, made a small writing across the painted loins of the mummy case. If any of the morticians or mourners had seen it, they would not have understood it. The inscription was devised from his own invented sign system, which he had failed to pass on either to his pupils or his sons: but to be absolutely secure (and security throughout his career had been noted as his most positive quality) he pasted over it a varnished cloth embroidered with the image of Amun-Ra.

The words that the cloth concealed:

CENTRE OF WORLD must be where it is found to be:
Crouch naked in the cage, ask the dung-flies, 'Is it here?'
For sure you will be *THEIR* centre, that is all that they know.
My fault, or whose fault, or what is a fault?
Dead king, dead fisherman, dead scribe
After this, under this
Never to dip tip, never to thrust tip
Nevermore probe the wine-dark sea.

THE LITTLE
OLD WOMAN
AND HER
TWO BIG BOOKS

The Little Old Woman
and Her Two Big Books

Carlile the Bookseller has re-published Tom Paine and
many other works held in superstitious horror. After all
they are afraid to prosecute; they are afraid of his
defence; it would be published in all the papers all over
the Empire; they shudder at this; the trials would light a
flame they could not extinguish. Do you not think this
of great import?

John Keats (1795–1821): *Letters*

Cuchulainn beheld at this time a young woman of noble
figure. 'I am King Buan's daughter,' she said, 'and I
have brought you my treasure and cattle. I love you
because of the great tales I have heard.' 'You come at a
bad time.' 'But I might be a help.' 'It wasn't for a
woman's backside I took on this ordeal!' 'Then I'll
hinder,' she said. 'When you are busiest in the fight I'll
come against you. I'll get under your feet in the shape
of an eel and trip you in the ford.'

Táin Bó Cuailnge ('The Cattle-Raid of Cooley'): trans. T.
Kinsella

ONE

Christianity, like Judaism before it and Islam afterwards, is a *Religion of a
Book*. It is fair to say that for the greater part of its history most Christians
have not been fully literate; convenient at times for Church administrators,
enhancing their authority as guardians and interpreters of the Book.
Which in turn enhanced the Book's authority: it is easier to believe that
God's own hand wrote it if you cannot actually read it yourself. And from
the authority of the Book, a reflected glow (officially unrecognised) upon
all other books – whatever had been written *was written*, and people
remained in awe of it.

Invent printing, and the knowledge of books is extended; therefore, for a while, their authority. But extend printing, and there comes the danger that so many books will be produced on so many subjects, serious and trivial, that the authority of all of them will slacken. In the long run it is futile to scorn such a state of affairs as 'a climate of anti-intellectualism', or react with fundamentalist anger to 'the creeping disintegration of faith'; legitimate communal distrust has been born out of hard experience and will not easily fade away. People can be lied to once too often: they may turn sullen rather than rebel, but in either event authority pays the price.

Wisdom was once conveyed by the trained memories and the word-of-mouth of supposedly wise individuals. *Their* authority, when they possessed it, derived from their own characters, tested against circumstance and observed by their fellow creatures. Usually they expressed themselves in stories. Most of what they narrated has been inadvertently lost (after books became commonplace), or distorted while being transferred to the page. If they were women, *all* of their stories were deliberately lost, distorted, or suppressed.

Here is a woman's story, or at any rate the story of a woman; it tells also of two books, one lost, one kept, both printed; and yet the tale lived for nearly half a millenium without anybody putting it *into* a book: so, for all we know, it might be true.

A long long time ago and a very long time ago – when the Christian folk of Germany did not know whether they believed in God any more; or if they did, what kind of God; or, if they knew what kind of God, what kind of pastor they should be paying to order their orisons for them – in those days, which they called the *Luther Days*, and were to remember all their lives with a shudder of black fear and a throb of white delight, there lived an old witch-woman in a dark little house in the deep dark shadows of the forest.

Her name was Hulda; and without doubt she was a witch, because she had a black cat, and her house was full of spiders, and people had seen mice there living happily alongside the cat: and almost surely she kept a toad in the broken wall of the well behind the house, although no one had seen the toad. That is to say, not seen it so as to *recognise* it as a toad. But they *had* seen the old woman mumbling words of some sort as she painfully drew up her water-bucket: and to whom could she be talking, if it were not a familiar toad? Also she had no teeth to speak of. Also she had but one eye. Also her speech was not quite the speech of that country; and why would an outland wife (a widow, as was said, if in truth she were not a husband-killer) be living all alone in the forest unless she had come there to work some outlandish mischief?

Not that she had ever been known to do anyone any harm.

Indeed, the reverse. When the charcoal-burners, the trappers, the woodcutters of the forest (or their families), fell sick, or were hurt in one of the many types of accident so common under the gloom of the great fir trees, they sometimes found the wise women and bone-setters of their villages quite unable to help. Then they would go trembling to the witch's filthy house and clang the rusty bell that hung upon her doorpost; and call out to her, very loudly, because she was known to be deaf:

Hag Hulda, Hag Hulda, come to your door,
Blood rots and bone crumbles, I cry for a cure:
Name of Father, Son, and Holy Ghost, Amen!

Whereupon the old woman always answered from inside the house:

Name of what? I can't hear.
Cobwebs, cobwebs, in my ear!

Whereupon they had to shout again:

Name of sweet *Mary, Mother of the Son*!
Hag Hulda come cure me or my days will be done.

Whereupon she opened the door; but she kept it on a chain and never at this stage let anyone, man, woman or child, Christian or Jew or four-legged beast, put a foot across the threshold. Then the people told what was wrong with them, or showed her, if it could be shown. Sometimes they had to stand under the eaves of her tattered thatch and strip themselves of their clothes, even in rain or snowfall, to illustrate their maladies. Or she might make them lie on the doorstep, while she put her arms out through as much of a gap as the chained door permitted her and poked and prodded and stroked and handled their bodies until she was sure there was indeed some calamity under the skin.

Whereupon she shut her door and bolted it on the inside. The people would have to wait, sometimes as long as an abbey Mass with full choir and bishop's sermon, before she opened the door again. While they waited, even in snowfall or rain, huddled beneath the eaves, the black cat sat on a tree stump near the corner of the house, and watched them; green-eyed, wide-eyed, wild-eyed, very terrible to their peace of mind.

Then at last she would open the door. If the remedy was short and simple she would croak it out to them abruptly – 'Such and such a leafy herb, gather it by moonshine with this prayer or that, boil it in your soup, every day for forty days: if *that* don't give a cure, then Beelzebub's in your shit-pipe for all your wickedness under heaven and it's no good your coming to *me*!'

Whereupon the door was slammed: the consultation was completed. And more times than not, the cure was successful.

On other occasions, in particular when one came to her with a bodily injury, she would unhook her door-chain and let the patient in. There were two rooms in the hovel. No one ever saw the inner room. The outer one was very small, little larger than the bed that occupied it; but on cold days there was a fire upon the hearth, and strange sour-sweet smells from powders she cast into the flames. The patient must lie on the bed, while the witch carried out her treatments, anointing wounds, binding wounds, rubbing at muscles, jerking at bones, strapping and pummelling and, in the end, most marvellously soothing. And all the time telling prayers, or maybe curses, or magic charms; and who knew what language she used for them?

There were one or two hardy persons, encouraged by Hag Hulda's good care, who would ask her what they ought not to have asked: 'You don't *live* in this little room, it's no bigger than half-a-third of the house. So what's behind the inner door?'

Whereupon she would fix the fools with all the hatred of her single eye, and shoot out her three fang teeth at them:

Behind that door, my little dear,
Hag Hulda keeps her horror and fear,
Therein to pry and peer
You will never be so bold
Or all the pain I've pulled from you
Flies back five-hundredfold!

'So swear you will never go in, never try to go in, never ask never ask ever again!'

Whereupon they always swore. And not one of them broke oath. Until the day of Hag Hulda's death, when –

No: we must wait for that 'until'. There are other matters to be told about first.

TWO

We have said that Hulda was known to be an outland woman. What was not known was the region where she had lived before she made her masterless journey to the densest, emptiest heart of the Elector of Saxony's forest, there to set her home with neither good word nor bad in an old ruined hunt warden's hut among the woodlice and woodworm and spiders.

Shall we say Nuremberg?

Fifty leagues south of the forest, and as different from her present dwelling as honey bees are from horseflies. Perhaps five-and-forty years since, there *had* been a Hulda in Nuremberg – by no means Hag Hulda, but a brisk busy little woman, red-cheeked, small-waisted, wide-hipped and strong-armed, with all her teeth and two eyes; grey eyes as clear and quick as a pair of love-birds on a perch: and thick pale-gold hair the warm tint of the most costly parchment. The city's tradespeople would call her Parchment Hulda. They liked to guess, or some of them did (from admiration, and also malice you may be sure), how far down her hair would hang if any man could induce her to unwind the tight plait and let it fall in its full beauty. Some said to the waist, others preferred to think of it veiling her plump buttocks, while a few even insisted it would be bound to drag the flagstones like the train of a mantle. But Parchment Hulda was no sort of easy-body to loosen her locks for all and sundry.

Her father was a prosperous goldsmith and an alderman of the city council; she helped him with the business (she had prodigious facility with the ledgers in his counting house, and few could more speedily call in an outstanding debt); she was determined no man should own her before the counting house could own *him*. In other words, she looked for a merchant marriage that might bring gain into the ledgers, and custom and goodwill into the shop, and yet keep herself and her widowed father hen-and-cock of the whole roost: until she found the proper young fellow to suit such a proud plan, the market-place loiterers could break riddle-jests upon her hair as freely as they chose and they'd never find the answer.

Two reasons, in addition, for the nickname she was given. First, of course, all those ledgers: as she bent over them by candlelight, the clean bright pages seemed ready to unfold themselves upward, to embrace and kiss like sisters the coiled braids pinned so close over her ears.

And then, there was the strange nature of her father's second trade.

Behind his shop he had opened a printing house. There were very few such anywhere in the land in those years; and all knew that as a venture they were untried and perilous. But his goldsmith craft well equipped him for the intricate work of cutting type, casting it and setting it. As he said when he began, if *he* could not do it, who could? Carpenters? Haberdashers? Besides, had he not been to Mainz, some years before Hulda's birth? And there met the most ingenious craftmaster he could ever have hoped to talk with: Johann Gutenberg, lens-maker and lapidary, zealous uncoverer of the divine mystery of letter-print and perpetual book copies. That is to say, he'd uncovered it for himself and thereafter strove hard to keep it hidden from all others. No doubt he did not fully understand what he had made; he saw moneys coming in that hitherto would have gone to the workshops of the scribes, and that was all that he saw. But he printed God's Bible, and Hulda's father bought a copy. More regular to the eye, page upon page of it, than any scribe, however careful, might accomplish; and page upon page of it coming out of the shop with every excellence exactly repeated; not a colon, not a comma out of place.

Hulda's father said to Gutenberg in his quiet dry jewel-proving voice, 'Do you not see, sir, between these pages, the whole new shape of man's knowledge, enlightening and delighting the age? Praise Jesu and give thanks.'

But Gutenberg could only reply, 'New? Why surely not. This is the Vulgate of Saint Jerome, nothing in it that the Church has not already authorised. I hope next to make a Missal. Young priests often find the cost of manuscripts very heavy; and the Cardinal Archbishop desires each one to have his own book. I might print as many as twenty for him.'

Hulda's father said, 'If you printed two hundred the laity could buy them as well.'

'Ah no, sir, I scarcely think so. I doubt if the Cardinal would wish it; and there would be small point in making more copies than are asked for.' He politely but resolutely refused Hulda's father any access to the printing house.

There was a skilled journeyman who worked for Gutenberg, had indeed worked for years with him; had shared all the hazards of his invention; and was just then upon the point of deserting his master. Nor did this man scruple to tell Hulda's father why: 'At his craft there's no doubt our Johann's a right nonsuch, but for his cash he's all abroad, a miser and stupid with it; and as to credit he's stark dead. *I* know it, but he don't. Not yet: but for how much longer? Let me tell you, master, if Nuremberg has a place for good print, I'd be glad to go and squat in it and tell you all I've learned. *You* shovel the silver and *I'll* tickle the type.'

His name was Karl Grosskerl; and when in due course he brought himself to Nuremberg to set up, for Hulda's father, the first press ever seen in that city, he brought with him his newborn son Ulrich. Oh a very clever child; who was to read and write in High German at the age of four, in Latin at the age of ten, in Hebrew and Greek before he was fifteen.

Karl died, and the printing shop was from then on in the hands of Ulrich: and its ledgers in those of Hulda. Little by little her ageing father withdrew himself from the cares of business. More and more she concerned herself with the making of books (as well as the keeping of them) and took all the less interest in rings, brooches and gold chains; which was thought a strange prejudice for a girl. To be sure, the books were commonly printed upon paper rather than parchment; but now and then a special volume for a very special customer would be produced in the richer material, and when such a work was finished, oh to see Parchment Hulda exult at it! No wonder they called her what they did.

You will not be surprised to hear that in the end it was Ulrich Grosskerl who was granted the most wonderful favour of letting down Hulda's long hair.

Hard to tell how far he did find it wonderful; he was not one of those men who make light of the secrets of the bedchamber to fetch themselves a lewd glory among wine-cellar companions. When the wedding took place he was almost, we would guess, thirty: Hulda perhaps four years younger. Both, indeed, quite old for the first breach of virginity. We suppose it *was* the first breach. Hulda's chastity for a decade had been matter of mark in Nuremberg; while Ulrich was so pale and stooped and shut within himself over books finished, books in the making, typefaces, ink and proofsheets (to say nothing of authors' manuscripts which nobody in the shop but himself could decipher), that he must have been either a most secret and mire-inhabiting Elagabalus, or in all truth a timid virgin: and nearly everyone said 'virgin'.

So we will say 'virgin'; and imagine, as we best may, how he and she stood alone between bed curtains and moon-shot casement, tentatively to touch hands, and then to grasp hands, and then, with a tremor of longing and a rose-thorn prick of fear, to let man's hands go to maiden's hairpins, and so round behind her to the ribbons of her plaits until all the white-gold shower was spread quite down her back, and she at the same moment was unhooking her bridal gown, unlacing stays, unclipping girdles and garters, unbuckling silver-trimmed shoes, dropping neck-chains and bracelets and ear-rings and great gathered petticoats in heaps across the floor – could it indeed have all been done with such a gentle stately poetry? He himself wore very tight boots, buttoned all the way to the thigh. There must have been some confusion, some tanglings, untutored awkwardness. But if there were, she had hoped for it otherwise: for she had strictly refused to be led to church as was always the custom, in her garlanded flowing hair. Hulda's man, once she chose him, would be the one to cause it to flow, and no one else. It was her promise, made in public over very many years. To be kept to the letter like all of her promises.

Moreover, the entire wedding had been so carefully arranged upon forms-of-contract, correctly notarised and signed and sealed, that we ought not to believe she expected or intended any slovenly unplanned accident to mar its concupiscent finish. *He* had read books, *she* had read books, poetry as well as homilies, that laid out very precisely the dangerous love that Christ's people need to learn through their sweet bodies one to another. They had read these books aloud and each had heard the other's reading. *Lustfrau* Venus and *Heilige Jungfrau* Maria must be at one in the bride's quiet linen, and all should be done to music. So the town band of Nuremberg was hired at great cost (woodwind and strings alone, neither raucous brass nor saracen drummings) to play under her window all night. We will not say the musicians' good labour was altogether lost.

But near upon six months afterwards, Hulda's father took suddenly to his sickbed and died: and the workshops were Ulrich's and hers. Or hers and Ulrich's. Which? In his will the old man left them to Hulda; with a codicil added at the time of the betrothal, stating that his intention remained 'exactly as stated above except insofar as it is modified by the marriage contract'. And gracious God, both will and contract were so strongly protective of Hulda that all should have been wide open and clear. But give such a parchment into the hand of a tight-hearted lawyer, and *anything* might be made of it. Of course there need be nothing made of it, if love and best intentions continue to put forth their warmth. Perhaps they did, but not so warm as to prevent the pale stooped Ulrich taking a copy of the marriage deed quite secretly one winter evening at the red hour of sunset to an attorney of his acquaintance, *Meister Rechtsanwalt* Dietrich Flechtmann, to ask him what he thought of it.

Dietrich Flechtmann said, '*Non'st bonum*, no good.' They talked easily in Latin, both of them very happy to be known as learned young men. Dietrich Flechtmann said, 'It's very difficult; but I do believe the lady claims far far more than she should.' Dietrich Flechtmann said, 'My dear sir, why don't you leave this in my hand? I will see what I can arrange. But I do warn, it is likely to take a very long time indeed; and I am afraid, a good deal of expense.'

Ulrich said, 'Just do it, *fac'hoc*. And the money will be paid.'

THREE

Back to his house through the snow crept devious Ulrich, dodging a glance now and then over his shoulder into shadows of doorways and buttresses, to make sure there was no one to see him and to ask him where he had been.

He stood still for a moment to look at the goldsmith shop from just across the narrow street; the shutters were up, the only light in the building was from the little upstairs window of his wife's private parlour – she had said she would be entertaining her uncle, Albertus Fortunatus the eccentric physician (in the vulgar tongue, *Herr Doktor* Albrecht Glueck), a man of so much more learning than Ulrich, so harsh with his learned refutations of Ulrich's opinions, that Hulda had felt no surprise when her husband pleaded 'business meeting' and left home upon the last course of supper.

The ginnel-entry next to the shop's doorpost had a large signboard nailed above its arch: a painting of a nymph lady in rare Grecian raiment watching over a German workman as he strove at the screw of a printing press; with the legend, '*Frau* Hulda in this House of Muses has Good Reading Books and Cheap for all! & if You Write them, She will Print them! SHE DELIGHTS AND ENLIGHTENS THE AGE! Christ & Mary Bless the Good Work.'

The varnish of the signboard was all a-sparkle with frost in the rays of the moon. Alongside it hung the gilded chalice that had for years proclaimed the trade of goldsmith. It seemed faded by comparison.

Ulrich's stare at his wife's new signboard might almost have blistered the paint.

Cat-like, he crossed the street, black footprints in the moon-bright white, let himself in, and went softly upstairs. He knocked at the parlour door, was bidden entry, came in gently, and bowed to the company. Strong heat from the gaily tiled stove; wine and sweet cakes on a side-table; Parchment Hulda in her best olive-green kirtle trimmed with leaf-green; her parchment hair wondrously rolled into a complexity of jewelled bands; and opposite her low stool, across from the stove, side by side on the carved settle, not only her shabby bespectacled old uncle with his gown out-at-elbows and three days' stubble on his chin, but a very precise full-bellied young man in a very glossy black robe, a great pile of neat paper on his fat glossy knees. Some of the pile was disarranged, loose sheets were held crumpled in the physician's grimy hands, others lay straight and crisp between Hulda's pudgy white fingers, while yet others were scattered among the wine glasses and cake platters.

Hulda said, abruptly, 'Husband Ulrich, you know my uncle; you don't know his son, my cousin Ludwig the law student, here he is: he has been helping good Uncle Albrecht to compile all his life-work –' she took a gulp to recollect the full schedule ' – of the physical science, the surgical craft and anatomy, childbirth and optics and brain-trepanning, the astronomical science, the astrology, the Arabian algebra, the extensions to Euclid, some excursions into the cabbalistic art and varieties of benign sorcery; the experiments, so far as they go, anent his search for the Philosopher's Stone.' Fortunatus and his son nodded their heads in concert, like a pair of wrought-iron clock puppets.

'Ludwig has taken my uncle's words out of Latin and Greek and – and divers other tongues of the ancients, he has put them into our German: we will print. I do think the greatest book we have ever had offered to us, though there is much to be done yet to correct it and shape it toward the common understanding.'

She paused. Eyes were alight, and teeth gleamed, she wore a smile of high triumph. Ulrich expected she would say further, 'What do you think, husband?' She did not. There was a long silence.

Knowing that Hulda did not know the language, Ulrich spoke in Latin, and at length, to the physician, of the huge honour conferred that the *Herr Doktor's* distinguished work should so confidingly be submitted to this house for publication.

Fortunatus snapped, in German, that Ulrich had misused a gerundive adjective, for which, were he still a schoolboy, he would require the most rigorous birch rod. And then he said, 'Submitted? I think *Frau* Hulda's understanding to be quite apart from that, quite.'

To which Cousin Ludwig added, 'Quite.' And Hulda said, 'Husband, did you not hear what I said? I said that we will print. I have decided. It is a very great book.'

Ulrich asked, would it sell? And then laughed and told lies about his evening, how he had talked in a tavern with several men of the Master-Singers who had a thought that their guild's songs might be committed to the press, words and music and sundry woodcuts of *Dichter* Orpheus and the like, for the 'enlightenment and delight of the –'

'Songs!' exploded Fortunatus, 'Oh your songs by all means! Oh your songs will at all costs sell, love songs and church songs and slight satires of the decay of manners. But when all humankind decays and not just its *superficies*, and neither brain nor body will serve any longer to fetch us from the abyss, of what use, little man, shall be music? Whereas God-given science – whereas thirteen hundred pages, folio, in divers languages, here they are – whereas the twelve hours' work *per diem* over six-and-fifty years, here it is, the cruel-gathered fruits of all my weary theory and practice – all this is at worst dismissed and at the very best *submitted?* God's bones, boy, who will judge it? *You?'*

He was on his feet and shaking with rage. Hulda hastened to calm him. 'Dear Uncle, I have said. And I am the mistress. No Master-Singers come between us. Besides, we have room for both books, and the slight one will pay for the greater. And besides, there is no doubt that all medicine books sell well; so how much faster will be the traffic of *yours*, when all shall know who has written it? Your name is a name of majesty in every land between Cracow and Paris.'

'For which reason,' suggested Ludwig, 'we should also print in the original tongues. I mean, the foreign universities—'

'In German first.' The old scholar was proudly decisive. 'The universities already have copies of my manuscripts. And, may I say, have done nothing with them. Why? Because I will not truckle to superstitious prejudice and accepted authority. Nor will I write what has not been, or cannot be, proved by Experiment! – unless it were some spells of the sorcery, against which expressly I caution my readers. To be sure, I have hearkened to many an old wives' tale: but thereupon I have *tried* it; if it worked, I set it down. Not so with the old priests' tales that hang upon dunces like Pliny (who draws many a moral from *natura divina*, but never an accurate diagram). At this present none of our people, the honest folk of workshop and tillage land, have word or inkling of what can be found to throw open their minds by diligent search and trial. So German! And then we shall see. Perhaps indeed, to gain their readership, we should even call it *The Old Wife Book*? Ah, but no; they would despise it, poor fools, they need learned authority. But if you print only in learned tongues, you nullify the blessings of the press. Enlighten and delight; yea, and *save*, both flesh and spirit!'

That night, within the bed curtains, Hulda demanded the deeds of love.

For the book of Fortunatus was a suddenly gathered treasure that would enfame her modest printing shop the length and breadth of all the Germanies; she stretched her round limbs and hung her swelling breasts around and above Ulrich to gather him in likewise to her glory. She was happy to forget how surly had been his mood when she gave him the news.

It was no news to her that husband and uncle distrusted each other's company, therefore she must deal between them, and she had dealt, and all was good.

Not so for Ulrich. He turned onto his belly and thrust his face into the pillow; until Hulda, from baulked passion, tore her nails into his shoulders and tried to drag his head round by the ears.

Ulrich was muttering: at first she did not hear him, but then she could not help but hear him; she abated her amorous frenzies to make some sense of what he would say.

'Why does the signboard have "*she* delights, *she* enlightens"? In the name of God, why not "*we*"? I told you, upon the day that the painter came to make it, that it ought to be "we"; but because I had to go to Munich Fair with two apprentices and our bookstall and goldworkstall and the hired swordsmen to guard the gold and so could not be here when he fastened up the sign, I never saw what he had written until already it was on the wall, and then you said if we were to take it down to change it we would both of us be made ridiculous and I let you say so too – but now I can tell you that every day that I see it I am more and more ridiculous; I am a married man and already withered, which is why I now lie on my face, and God's heart, it is already known to every lustful man in Nuremberg!

'He is a pimp, a fat pimp, your Cousin Ludwig, I saw his eyes; all the time that we talked I saw them searching your green bodice. So why did you never tell me Albrecht Glueck had a fat sweating son? And a lawyer moreover: does he scheme to get grip on your inheritance?'

Which made *her* see that brusque command was no way to arouse his desire; his ambitions and his griefs were too much at odds for that, she must find some softer gentler fashion. So she lay close beside him, and touched him lightly, and gave small kisses; and moreover gave small promises, and then larger ones (although upon her left hand, which did not touch him, she kept two fingers crooked in a cross).

She swore that the sign painter should be fetched again, yes tomorrow, if the man were not working elsewhere; and he should paint out 'she' and put in 'we', and where he had written '*Frau* Hulda' he should now give them 'Grosskerl and his *Frau*': and if that was not enough – (Ulrich mumbled that it was *not* enough) – then the muse lady should be granted a fair companion to stand beside her, no less poetical, and, if need be, to a larger scale, an Apollo or a Homer, or an Orpheus, would not that help?

In her heart she knew agreeably that the sign painter *was* working elsewhere, and would be for a very long time. In her heart, even more agreeably, she knew her cousin's bawdy eye-searchings had not much displeased her: she quite greedily looked forward to his frequenting the printing house, very possibly every day, to confer upon his father's book. And also in her heart she knew that Ulrich was not at all 'withered'; could she but get him now to turn himself, here, under her right arm, she would prove it to him and so could command him, as always before.

In *his* heart he knew the same thing. His anger at his wife had not drowned his body's yearnings for her, indeed it was nourishing them – and in ways that God might punish, if they were not kept close inside him. '*Vade retro, Sathanas*,' he murmured into the bolster, to avert the dirty demon. Squeezing his hand in between his fifth rib and the mattress, he crossed himself as though at Mass. His right hand, her left, two crosses in one bed, and each unaware of the other: do we not think that together they must have made but one sad crucifix?

For that night, at least, Ulrich did hold his demon tightly bound. We might suspect he could only do so because he allowed it a partial liberty, to sport among those bed-rites allowed by the Holy Church; by no means a sure preventive, as he and his wife were to discover.

But he must cause it to lie quiet; so quietly he let himself turn over onto his back, reaching out with both hands for Hulda's waist, whispering urgently of his sorrow for his ill-speakings; of how he would not enforce any change to the signboard until perhaps they had discussed it further; of how the book of Fortunatus must certainly make their *own* fortune and how acute she was to have found it out: and finally of Cousin Ludwig and what a trim young scholar he surely was, why did they not invite him to dine? His eyes ran with tears and Hulda licked them from his cheeks, while he kissed her dangling breasts and his hands slipped down her spine to the cleft of her rump and once again the white-gold shower spread wide and long to cover the pair of them.

(Outside the house the silent snow spread likewise to cover Nuremberg, the last fall of the season; and tomorrow it would melt to black mud.)

For that night, at least, he did not choose to turn his mind to *Rechtsanwalt* Flechtmann. He held him, we might say, bound; in the same dungeon as the dirty demon. Now and then, however, he (or the shameless other) rattled his chains there and Ulrich hearkened. His wedded lechery was given pause: he hoped Hulda did not notice. A brief shudder through his thin flesh, and then he kissed her again and again.

FOUR

Although Ulrich's tale of his meeting with the Master-Singers had been untrue as to time and place, he had in fact talked with those men, and they had placed an order for their singing book. So two difficult works were in progress together in the one shop and the craftsmen were heavily laden with them. To print music required a whole new system of laying out the page, rows of words letter-by-letter in the usual way, combined with block-cuts of lines and notations. The best workman from the goldsmith shop had to be brought in to make the blocks out of copper plate (wood was too coarse for Ulrich's standards); and, as metal-engraved printing was very much a new art, and transalpine, the man was Italian; and as an Italian he spoke little German; and as the song texts were largely in German there were continual errors in the setting of the words against the notes of music. Each proofsheet must be corrected, not only within the shop, but by one of the Master-Singers as well; it was not always the *same* Master-Singer; there were differences of opinion amounting at times almost to dagger-drawn quarrels: while the ornamental cuts of musicians and musical instruments (which the Italian was also asked to make) proved full of stark-naked pagans of lascivious sort, and the more senior Master-Singers were scandalised. Every picture had to be done again; the Italian refused to do them; they were given to a Nuremberger who cut them in wood, thereby marring the harmony of the page.

All of which maddened Ulrich. Hulda, who was more concerned with her uncle's huge volume, told him he made much out of little; and that the silly bloody song-book would have been in type weeks ago if he'd had half his father's wit and kept all his workmen in order.

She herself was finding her own difficulties. Cousin Ludwig's manuscript was, for certain, very neat and excellently clear to read. But his organisation of the doctor's matter was not at all clear. She kept explaining to him that optics and childbirth could not in truth be taken as themes for the one chapter: just because Fortunatus' scribbled notes on both subjects had chanced to be set down in the same notebook, it did not follow that that was how the printer must edit them. Ludwig said *he* was the editor, and the printer ought not to presume. He had kept his father's arrange-ment, which he admitted had been accidental, because he discerned an allegorical congruence: as the eyeballs peer out from their sockets at the world, rejoicing in God's Sense of Sight; so the child's round head emerges from its eye-shaped womb-socket to discover all Five Senses at once with a great cry of admiration. He incautiously pursued the notion, growing unduly familiar and grinning at it; until Hulda, who craved for a child, but alas had not yet been able to conceive, interrupted him to tell him that his allegory disgusted her, moreover it made no sense.

'If you, cousin, instead of debauching yourself all these years in the cloisters of Bologna, had found yourself a good wife to settle your nonsense, you might by now know that the entry to a woman's womb is no damned *eye*, even in poetry, even in ribaldry; nor is it a mouth, nor does it damned well have *teeth*: it pursues its own sacred function (made the more sacred by the Blessed Virgin Mary) and in my presence, if you please, you will show some respect for it!'

He thought she was unreasonable. He huffed and puffed that she mistook him entirely. But he had to take her point about the University of Bologna: he had consorted somewhat shamefully with harlots while he was there, about all he had ever learned of women (but how could she have known?); his experiences indeed had not induced respect. He apologised, she accepted the apology, he kissed her hand, there was warmth between them. She was pleased with him, it seemed, quite despite his overweening – we should even say, because of it: she could bring it down so very comically. Also, after nearly a twelvemonth married to the meagre Ulrich, she had her private thoughts about the beauty of well-fleshed and straight-standing men. They still wrangled daily, for there were many more flaws in his text and she kept finding them.

Apart from the flaws, there was the question of the pictures. When the Italian engraver declined to alter his work for the song book, Ulrich had sent him packing from the goldsmith shop as well as the printing house, and without any word to Hulda: who found out about it just in time, put the man to his bench and burin again, and gave him her uncle's scientific sketches and diagrams to be cut in copper at the fullest stretch of his artistry.

It is not known what she said to Ulrich; but his pinched features were quite filled with blood for several hours afterwards.

Those sketches, however, troubled her. They appeared to show that Fortunatus had been searching for his science among dead corpses; suppose they were Christian, then surely it must be a sin? And then there were sundry designs, purporting to be cabbalistic ciphers, which compelled her to look closely at the portion of text they adhered to. She asked Ludwig about it. He told her there was no need for fear: magic of many sorts was permitted to God's servants, provided only God's Spirits, rather than Satan's, were invoked. She said she could not know the difference. He replied, neither could he; but would she not trust her uncle? Fortunatus was not only learned, but most apparently a Soul in Grace, shriven every Saturday night, at Mass upon every Sunday; ask the priests.

'Ah yes,' she said, 'but which priests? And does he always confess all his sins? If he holds any of them back, then he is not only *not* in Grace but very deeply damned, and how much of it might be in his book?'

Ludwig said, 'Please trust,' holding both of her hands in his: and then their lips touched. She hastened away.

Did Ulrich chance to see and hear them? Their talk had taken place in her counting house, which lay between the goldsmith shop and the printing rooms; the door into the yard was ajar and Ulrich was in the yard, supervising an apprentice who carried bundles of new paper across to the store shed from the paper mill wagon just inside the back gate. She did not know this until she crossed the yard herself. But her husband, very busy, would not favour her with so much as a glance. She walked straight past him, under the nose of the paper miller's snorting horse, into the street, out of the city, along the fields speckled with snowdrop flowers beside the river.

FIVE

Her mind was troubled. Altogether too much trust. Trust Ludwig? Trust Fortunatus? She began to wonder, had she any grounds to do so? And on what grounds to trust Ulrich? He had submitted so very easily to her promises about the signboard. Above all, she began to ask, had she good grounds to trust *herself*? She thought about Ludwig's kiss; and wondered, was mere affection a strong enough excuse? If she were a Soul in Grace, she would know without having to wonder. For sure that was what the priest would tell her, if she knelt to him and asked about it. No, not *if*; but *when*: this would have to be confessed. But in confession, she knew too well, one thing led to another: she would also have to ask about *The All-Science Book of Fortunatus* (that was now its approved title). Suppose the priest denounced the book and ordered her not to print it? She counted moneys in her head, outlay upon paper, and on ink, and on workpeople's wages; to say nothing of the other printing orders they had had to refuse because this one took so much of their capacity.

To abandon the work now might very well mean ruin. The Goldsmiths' Guild would not support her: already there were men there, master-craftsmen always jealous of the prosperity her father had made, who had been listening to Ulrich, and now talked at large about how daughters ought not to be allowed to inherit their parents' trade; and everyone knew whom they meant. Also there was talk that Ulrich was canvassing admission to the inner order of city aldermen (even though he was of outland descent, which ought by right to have disqualified him). If his friends were to claim he was legal master of the shop, if the guild were to back the claim, he could declare himself not responsible for debts incurred by his wife, and that would be the end of her.

No, she would *not* confess the kiss. Or at any rate, not just yet. Of course it was mere affection. And if so, she could repeat it. If it grew to anything more – well, she would confess *that* – but all in God's good time – let her put all these things from her mind and work hard to finish making the great book. So she fell into damnation; it was the first day of the warmth of spring upon the soft green riverbank; she was aware of what she did; she strode home victorious over virtue.

She passed without a tremor a pair of peasant fornicators, bare-arsed and sweating in their love-couple beneath a thicket. Yesterday, had she seen them, she would have needed to feel amazed, she would have been awed by such a blatancy; her innards would have churned; but now she thought of them only as two friends unknown, in the same case as herself.

But after all, as it happened, Ludwig was gone when she reached the shop. He had left a message with a journeyman to say he had had sudden instructions to visit Frankfort. His father had heard of a rare copy of the great herbal of Dioscorides in the cathedral library there, with unique annotations; he needed Ludwig to study them and make notes – a matter of urgency.

Ulrich had gone out too, without telling anyone where.

She went to her parlour, taking with her a bunch of new proofsheets. She sat down with a sigh to look them over. There was much to be corrected. The compositor had made nonsense of the entire 'Discourse upon the Arabian algebra'. Indeed, she should not be having to do this: Ulrich had the proper learning, why was he not here? But even if he *were* here, he would refuse to work on her uncle's book. Ludwig could have helped; dared she wait for him to return from Frankfort? A hundred-mile journey, he might be away weeks. The book would be delayed intolerably. At least the words were German; though a very strange German that seemed always at the top of its voice. She must make the best of it she could.

If $a - 2a = x$

she read:

– how can we determine the magnitude of x? Do we say it is not possible? That $2a$, being so much greater than a, cannot therefore be taken from it? Man cannot, for example, take a jugful from a cupful, only the reverse? Despair not, good student, for by means of the algebra the impossible is achieved! *Al-Kashi of Samarkand* for this very reason has called it the Sorcerer's Science: and yet it is a sorcery that craves the raising-up of no uncanny spirits. By rule of equation (delineate on my previous page) $x = -a$ – and most assuredly! Is a then less than NOTHING?
Indeed and indeed! Out of NOTHING is the sorcery made: and lo! how I shall express it!
(*And thereby not only uphold* Abu al-Wafa *but confound* Aristotle; *and all those who have made him a demigod, holding our schools close prisoner, breaking our honest scholars upon the wheel!*)

Then there was an empty space in the manuscript, occupying a whole page, with nothing in it but a large O. (The compositor of course had muddled it, simply jamming in an ordinary capital O at the end of the paragraph and running the next paragraph straight on after it). Hulda stared at the big round meaningless shape with her mouth all unconsciously repeating it.

She had never heard the notion of *zero* properly explained; her work in the counting house had always been done upon an abacus, and when she wrote the results into her ledgers she used the roman numerals. She therefore could not grasp the climax of Fortunatus' thought – indeed did not even see that it *was* a climax.

And even if she had seen, what was to be made of all the exclamatory quirks that came before it? Yet another cause for her troubled mind in regard to this book – no longer the carved corpses, nor the cabbalism, nor Ulrich's jealousy, nor even Ludwig's carnal closeness: but her uncle's stern remark the day he brought it her. 'The honest folk of workshop and tillage land, none of them have one word or inkling.' Indeed they had not; but *would* they, once it was printed? No doubt the editing would make a difference. For instance, this particular 'discourse': it seemed to have been taken from dictation (no doubt by Ludwig, the 'good student') and she could not but feel the old man had been somewhat rambling, the problem of 'O' left entirely aside. Was Ludwig at all capable of sorting out wheat from chaff? Or more likely would he take offence that *any* of it be considered chaff?

Whereas most of the medical passages made very good common sense:

For a *jaundice*, no drug needful, nor for that matter efficacious. Howbeit, for the *lesser jaundice*, certain herbs are claimed as sovereign by such women as search out and apply them in traditionary manner – (refer to margin for these remedies' names; they vary much from region to region in accord with botanic diversity; some I have tried and found good, you shall find them printed in red).

ABOVE ALL, DO NOT LET BLOOD; blood must be cleansed; to diminish it is the work of a blockhead! Did Hercules *pull down* the stables of Augeus because of their filth? Lay your sick in soft bed, keep there days and months until the yellow shall abate and dark-tawny urine run pale and transparent as heretofore.

Feed only upon juices of fruit, at times the pulp thereof, horseradish very good, also carrot. Neither milk nor fat, nor fermented liquor, they are mortal, *strictly beware!*

And rub their skins with oil of mustard when they shall itch. So trust our good God and be patient.

Why, she could do all that herself, supposing Ludwig to be seized with a jaundice – no, she did *not* mean Ludwig, *Ulrich* was the man she would have to nurse, oh she knew how he detested carrots. She shuffled the pages again, found herself once more looking at the great O, once more yawned at the very sight of it: the warmth of her stove on such a warm evening was overcoming her, she shifted the cushions on her settle, laid her head back, put her feet up, and fell asleep.

SIX

She awoke suddenly, confused and cramped. She must have slept for at least two hours, for the room was in darkness – no, not complete darkness; there was a candle burning on the table, and it lit the large sagging face of a man she had never seen before. He was elderly and unhealthy-looking, with a shaven head half-buried in a vast black cowl, and under the cowl (and the black mantle to which it was attached) he wore a white habit, grubby and crumpled. A Dominican friar: who on God's earth could he be? For what reason did he stand there and prowl through her proofsheets? His smile showed an ingratiating mouthful of discoloured teeth.

'Gracious lady, I am so sorry to have disturbed your innocent rest, but we did feel we had no time to lose, we – '

We?

She blinked, attempting to pierce the blur of shadow behind the stove. Ah, so there he was, Ulrich, crouched absurdly on the sewing stool, nose cocked in impudent pretence that all was as it ought to be.

'Ulrich, what have you done? Is this some new custom for husbands in Nuremberg, to invite priests into a decent house to stare at your wife while she sleeps?'

Ulrich looked up at the friar, and the friar looked down upon Hulda. 'Now excuse me, gracious lady, there was no such intention, we had the candle already lit before we perceived your auspicious presence, and we did not wish to wake you, you must be so tired after all your work, pages and pages of it, and the script so small and closely printed.' The friar seemed flustered, he was at a disadvantage, his nail-bitten hairy hands moved uncertainly among the papers; no doubt Ulrich had let him think she would accept any outrage and never complain.

She always knew her husband desired to stand well with the clergy; no doubt he needed to prove himself master in his own house. If so, she would disappoint him. 'This is *my* room, I want you out of it. I want both of you, please, to leave, I mean this moment, I mean *now!*'

But Ulrich did not move. He bit his lips in agitation. He was as though fixed upon the stool, legs crossed, and eyes now downcast, not able after all to meet hers. He spoke more to his knees than to his wife: 'I met *Bruder* Herwald as it chanced, by pure chance, I was telling him, as it were in passing, of the difficulties of *The All-Science Book*, and I told him – and I told him – I told him there were certain passages which had caused me – ah – certain scruples, or at least when translated – in the learned languages doubtless there would be less cause for alarm – '

Alarm? And she *was* alarmed: the Dominicans had power, a most frightening power, some of them were officers of the Pope's Inquisition – *Domini Canes*, the 'Hounds of the Lord' – certainly they were able and willing to suppress books, suppress printers and authors for that matter, and in very dreadful fashion; and they needed no more than their own snarling opinion of what had been meant by the writings. This clumsy-looking offal bag of a foul-breathing cloister creeper had had time while she slept to have read nearly two-thirds of the proofsheets. She chased her memory for what was on them. The man was smiling again, still ingratiating, there was grey stubble on the loose skin over his hollow jaws and his complexion was a dirty yellow. She found she could not fasten thought upon the contents of the pages: except the one where she had read of the *soft bed . . . urine to run pale tawny . . . horseradish also carrot . . . so trust our good God and be patient;* for if ever she saw jaundice incipient, here was the flesh to carry it.

'I do hope, gracious lady—' (this friar dribbled as he spoke) '—you will not think "cause for alarm" means any alarm for *you*: your pious husband, extremely correctly, has sought immediate advice before he proceeds any further with his contract, and even were I to tell him that the book is – ah – *unsuitable*, then his good character and that of his printing house are already assured. Spiritual advice, obtained in good time, is sovereign answer to moral quandary, is it not?'

'I'm sure it is.' Hulda answered him very carefully now. This was no situation for defiance. (So trust our good God and be patient!) But let Ulrich not think she had failed to take note of '*his* printing house.'

'Have you – have you found then – any matters – "unsuitable"?'

'Yes, I fear I have – or rather I do not fear, I rejoice; because, you see, now I have found it, it is about to be rendered harmless, is it not? There is no need to keep it a secret between Holy Church and *Meister* Grosskerl, you as his helpmeet have a right to be informed. It commences on – ah – the fifty-fifth page of this batch.' He began to shuffle the disarranged papers in a rapid search for the fifty-fifth page.

She saw him leaf without hesitation through the engravings of carved corpses, murmuring only, 'I take it, not *baptised* cadavers? Turkish captives, he seems to imply; if so, no harm. But it ought to be positively stated.' She saw him leaf through the cabbalistic symbols. And there he did hesitate, but his comment reassured: 'I am in doubt about these perhaps; *Bruder*

Petrus-Maertyrer of our house would never combine the Signs of the
Zodiac together with the Pentacle for such a clairvoyance as your author
prognosticates here. And Petrus-Maertyrer is the acknowledged expert.
But I do not think that the error, if indeed it is an error – and in truth I ought
to consult *Bruder* Petrus-Maertyrer before pronouncing – no, I do not think
it shades into heresy or malevolent Judaism, the study of these arts is held
lawful provided their practice is eschewed – *vide* Paduanus, his *De
Quorundam Astrologorum Parvipendendis Indiciis* – though I do think they
should not be encouraged among the laity. In Latin, we would be quite
safe . . .

'I could have wished your author had not so greatly praised these infidel
sages, Abu al-Wafa, Al-Kashi, setting them higher than Aristotle; true,
Aristotle was a pagan, but (unlike the Saracen philosophers) he had not
had the inestimable opportunity of Christ's Gospel: they *did* have it, and
they rejected it – can we believe then their mathematic to be sound? Blind
yourself to one truth, you lose all the others in the mist of your own
darkness . . . Ah, here we are!'

The fifty-fifth page was part of the childbirth chapter. It was the most
recent print completed by the Italian, very precisely drawn, with tiny
words of medical commentary contained within the picture itself. A
pregnant woman, naked, observed from the side so as to present in full
profile her great belly. The outline of the unborn child was shown curled
up inside her as though her womb were of glass. An allegorical design,
religiously so: there were guardian angels and Our Lady supporting her
and looking down on her from heaven, with the sun and the moon and
stars; while a vicious devil-dragon coiled at her feet, to 'devour her child as
soon as it was born' perhaps, reminding the reader of St John's vision in
Apocalypse.

The friar had a magnifying-lens. He peered through it at the plate while
he talked. 'There can be no harm in demonstrating the Creator's enormous
charity, in that He provides so many times a safe deliverance for women in
travail, and has given certain signs to us whereby we might recognise what
is to be done for such a woman and how may her pains be eased: the
Christian physician fulfils a religious duty when he brings these signs to our
understanding. Much of this image before me (repellent though it
superficially may be) does in fact follow the said duty. But I do read with
some concern some of the notes that are engraved here. For example, this.'
He was no longer ingratiating, no longer flustered. He uttered Fortunatus'
words with emphatic disgust:

'If she be strong and in good daily posture of bone and muscle and has followed my diet as overleaf prescribed, and has moved her limbs daily for practice like an archer at his bow-drill (as overleaf prescribed), and has not been oppressed inordinately with taskwork (whether of the household or in the field), then oftentimes she may give birth avoiding almost all pain altogether.

Such fortunate wives have said to me that there is indeed a pleasure in their birth-labour, akin to the venereal. Pray God that it may be always thus with her that reads this page: it needs no more than skill and care, save when other ills intervene.

'Why, there *has* to be pain, it is commanded in *Genesis*, for chastisement of the sin of Eva. God's mercy if at times it be relieved; but gravest error to offer hope that relief may be "always", founded chiefly upon mortal "skill". No, for "skill" we must understand the physician's overweening pride: and when we understand it, condemn it. And what is this "venereal"? Dare he hint that the devil's ecstasy, such as fills impure women in the hot flood of their premeditated sin, be natural and desirable for a wife obeying her husband's behest? And then to look for it in holy childbed, to be rehearsed for – do I read it aright? – by means of idleness and diet and soldierly drills! Oh no no, this will not do: my dear children, how right you were to bring this book to my attention. How right, how very right. Oh no no, no no no . . .'

He tore the page into two and then into four and then into eight and with a flourish tossed the fragments over his shoulder.

Without so much as a word of courteous farewell, he surged from the parlour and down the stair. Ulrich followed him, with the candle, to let him out of the house (Hulda heard them briefly whispering at the street door), and then came back up again with a strange expression in his eyes: this time his eyes *did* meet hers.

'He says there is some chance the book may be permissible if your uncle can be persuaded to remove a number of passages, or change them. He will need the complete text as we work on it, and will confer with his brethren to see how it might be amended.'

'He will, will he?' Hulda was not about to rage. For a few fierce moments she had prepared to do so: left in the dark, however, during her husband's short absence, she found the calm and then the energy for a second thought. 'It is most indulgent of him.'

'Oh I can tell you old Herwald is, always has been, indulgent. Unlike some of them, I can tell you that. Not altogether stupid of me to choose *him* to speak to.'

'Oh, did you choose him? That was not stupid. I had assumed, I cannot say why, that you ran up against him in the street.'

His eyes shifted; he flushed. 'No, not quite.' Then he looked directly at her again. 'I put the question, Wife Hulda: will he or will he not be persuaded?'

'Herwald?'

'Oh God no, not Herwald; good God but you know what I mean! I mean your uncle, the sage Albertus, who's to talk to him, you or I?'

'You, if you dare. You're the one that went for the priest.'

'I went for him to *save* us. We are in a very considerable peril. I have tried for weeks to let you know of it, but always you have scorned me and laughed at me and ignored me and clenched yourself in idiot trust to that plumduff of a bloody Ludwig! I asked you, what do you think of it? Can we get the old man to agree?'

'Husband Ulrich, I will tell you; and what I tell you, you may believe. The sage Albertus, as you call him, has spent his entire life upon this book; wise words or rash, he will have all of them read by everyone. He said to me the night he came here: "We in Nuremberg are of a free and honourable imperial city, for enlightened scholarship and the noble arts we are like to be spoken of to the world's end, as was Athens of the olden time." He kept repeating it, "A free city": and then you came sliding home from your carousels with the Master-Singers and put an end to his evening's joy. No, he will never consent his book be stripped and plucked by fools; and most certainly not in Nuremberg! Why, he would rather cast every page with his own hand into the fire. Which means, I suppose, we cannot print. Which is, I suppose, what you have schemed for.'

SEVEN

Having said it, 'Which is what you have schemed for,' Hulda let fall her voice; a fading away of sorrowful resignation, a twist of the mouth, even a hint of self-mocking laughter. Certainly no challenge.

For now she understood the unusual expression on Ulrich's face: his eyes were alight, his teeth gleamed, he wore a smile of high triumph. She allowed him to believe himself, to be sure of himself, to *vaunt*; she took the candlestick, and lit his way for him downstairs to supper, at which he laughed and joked very pleasantly with the apprentices, putting riddles to them in Latin, catching them out over their mistakes in the grammar. And thereafter, submissive housewife and Christian helpmeet who knew no Latin and thus had remained silent throughout the meal, she lit him upstairs to their sleep.

That night, within the bed curtains, Ulrich demanded the deeds of love.

And she gave him what he wanted. The dirty demon remained fast bound, requiring no cross-on-the-heart to be kept there. True, Hulda did not offer to pretend any sort of ecstasy. Which hurt Ulrich's feelings, and he told her so. She reminded him of what *Bruder* Herwald had had to say upon the subject; to which Ulrich said, 'To hell with friars,' and Hulda laughingly agreed. Then he told her, as an amorous confidence, that *Bruder* Herwald had promised the printing house something very generous by way of compensation, if in the end *The All-Science Book* were not to be printed. No, he did not quite know what form the compensation would take. But he *did* know which way he desired Hulda to roll her body and move her hands, and the words he would have her breathe in his ear: he told her, and she did it, and so at length they were very merry; and continued so alone and in company all through the next few days.

Both agreed it would be best to wait until Ludwig was back in Nuremberg before they made any pronouncement about their intentions. It would, they said, be much the best to approach the old man through his son: otherwise, who could say? The bad news might be his death. In the meantime all work on *The All-Science Book* was laid aside, and everyone in the shop was put to completing the Master-Singers' contract.

Undoubtedly Hulda sent some sort of private message to her uncle; even slipped out of the house without Ulrich's knowledge and went to see him.

For when Ludwig came home, he discovered Fortunatus had heard all about the friar's opinions, and yet was not altogether in despair. 'These things are to be expected,' he said quietly. 'There are ways to overcome them, if we are patient, and think with strength. The world is full of ignorance and treacheries, we have always known it. But also we can meet with some very brave companions, loyal friends, enlivened minds. But no public talk about any of it, not just yet. And do not tell Grosskerl that I have said a word to you upon the matter. Go to see him, hear his arguments, and then offer him certain concessions.'

'Concessions? But, dear Father, you are not going to let them boast their victory, do not say that! Amending, distorting, your writings – I cannot believe it?'

'Believe what you choose, boy: but do what you're told. *My* book, *my* decision, no nonsense. Go to Grosskerl. Concessions are as follows – commit them to memory . . .' And he rapidly ran down a great list from his own memory, counting out with a snarl of scorn each item upon his fingers; and explaining how the list was to be introduced. Ludwig listened to him in silence, and (as puzzled as he was disappointed) made his way to the printing house.

When he got there, a distressed and compassionate Ulrich told him with tears what he already knew, repeating the words uttered previously to Hulda: 'There is, you see, some chance the book may be permissible, if your father can be persuaded to remove a number of passages, or change their meaning . . . But I don't suppose he can?'

'Alas, but I think he might,' replied Ludwig. He obeyed his father's orders without joy, and dutifully defamed his character: 'For he is not the man he was. He is thinking of the approach of death, the destination of his Christian soul. Already afraid of some portions of his own writing, from the very start he did suggest to me that this or that alteration might be made. If you are absolutely sure that the necessity is absolute?'

'Oh it's absolute,' Ulrich said. 'I'm afraid no doubt about it. But I truly do not know whether a few amendments will prove sufficient. God's dogs have got their teeth in.'

Hulda surprised both of them by cheerful bustle and a quite different view. 'Now, it is not so bad as that. No more than a few pages. Cousin Ludwig and I will sit carefully over proofs and manuscript and we will lay out all the problems in due order; then fetch the corrected text to the Dominican house and see what good kind Herwald has to say. He has offered his advice, we need it, and we seek it: if we accept it, no more trouble. Consider the thing, dear Ludwig, from *Bruder* Herwald's point of view (as I think, indeed, your father already has): here is a strange and learned book, the like of which has never been written in this land. Heretofore such scholarship was set down painfully by the pens of scribes, only the one copy at a time, and sent out amongst so very few readers, all near as learned as the author. But now it is to be *broad-cast* by the wagon-load over all the Germanies; God alone knows how many ignorant folk will get their hands on it. Worse than ignorant: *malicious*. We have a grave responsibility. We exist, as our signboard says, to enlighten and delight; heaven forbid we should corrupt! We are surely all agreed upon that?'

Ludwig, rather slowly, did seem to agree; but Ulrich was not so sure. The fact was, he had not expected these pre-arranged concessions, and was uncertain what to do about them. He tried to say that the matter was too important for Hulda to deal with; that it ought to be for Ludwig and himself to go through the text together, or else there'd be mistakes made. But Ludwig by now suspected there was something in the wind. He understood Hulda's hidden intentions, at a level of enraptured sympathy that owed little to spoken words; her message was very clear to him: 'Keep Ulrich out of this!' So he firmly demanded to work with her as before; she being already so familiar with the book, and what the devil was the point of wasting time?

Even as he spoke, he went up to her parlour with all the papers and herself and shut the door. Leaving Ulrich with half a mind to let his demon quite suddenly loose – 'Follow them in and murder them both!' – its voice grated urgently in his ear: but of course he could do nothing of the sort.

He hung about the stair-head, trying to listen through the thick planks of the door; but there were servants up and down the house, and then an apprentice came to tell him he was needed in the shop. His situation was degrading, he thought his people were covertly laughing at him; so he made as though he laughed at himself, breaking jokes with a married journeyman about wives wearing the breeches, and the like: while he argued with a succession of creditors, bullied a few debtors, and proudly showed the new song-book pictures to a delegation of Master-Singers who came in about midday to inspect them. These men were so pleased with what they saw that they invited him to feed at their tavern. They kept him boisterously to his great beermug all through the afternoon, compelling him to hear – and then to join in – one chorus after another. Not until long past sunset could he withdraw from their hospitality.

He cursed himself for having left Hulda and Ludwig alone together for so many hours. Entirely his own fault, indeed his own desire: for while he was with the Master-Singers he need not think of anything beyond their good fellowship, and in any case he enjoyed their songs – particularly the ones that made much tuneful noise and little sense, and had not been thought appropriate for inclusion in the book. One in particular appealed to him – a peremptory call for some girl with 'hefty backside' to minister to the revellers as they banged mugs upon table in unison and harmonised rhythmic syllables:

> *Hoch hoch, hoppla! Boom-da-rassa-saess!*
> *Ein, zwei, drei, vier,*
> *Maedchen, kommst'u hier?*
> *Ein, zwei, drei, das beschwerliches Gesaess!*

– and so on. He tumbled home through the ill-lit city, bumping into posts and tripping over cobblestones, while his raucous voice (by no means a credit to the Master-Singers as such) bounced and rebounded between the closely leaning gables of the thronged housefronts. Heads thrust out of windows to swear at him, but he took no notice. He was Ulrich Goldsmith-Printer and as great a man as any of them: if he chose to be drunken it was no one's affair but his own.

EIGHT

Not hard for us to guess that Ludwig and Hulda did in fact commit their first adultery that afternoon. Even easier when we consider what very small affection Hulda's employees had for Ulrich. Once it was known that he had yielded himself until day's end to the most notorious eaters and drinkers in Nuremberg, house servants and craftworkers became altogether knowing and discreet; we do not know what they might have been whispering among themselves, but none of them were so untimely as to approach the little upstairs parlour.

But supposing they had done so, and heard what they expected – the gentle moans, the sharp cries, the irrepressible bursts of laughter, of fallen creatures deep in sin – they would also have been bound to listen to much turning and shuffling of papers and a rapid flood of trade-talk, exceedingly practical, upon the present state of *The All-Science Book* and its future, page by page, word by word; for within the fevered room, before the reluctant end of the furtive and pagan devotion, conclusions were undoubtedly arrived at: indeed we might go further, we might assert that a plot was hatched.

The circumstances were all too conducive – hot stove, sweet wine, soft cushions laid out upon the thick Persian carpet (itself dragged from its proper place on the table-top and spread wantonly across the floor); and above all the happy comfort of two stout young bodies entwined among a careless cluster of unfastened and half-shed garments – what lovers at such a juncture would not have believed their plans infallible?

NINE

For the next weeks, to all appearance, nothing unusual took place in the printing house. Hulda busied herself with the accounts, as always; and spent much time supervising the work on her uncle's book. The typesetting of the pages not yet in forme was being completed, the engravings were being completed; Ludwig came constantly to make the amendments compelled upon them by *Bruder* Herwald, to change his mind about them, to think of new ones; he brought all manner of hectic messages from Fortunatus, most of which were to cancel those sent the previous day.

The amendments were worked out on the proofsheets, not the manuscript. Hulda explained to the workpeople that old Herwald's eyesight was very poor; it would be misery to him to have to study Ludwig's handwriting, with deletions and additions augmenting the hardship. Which might have been true (she had seen the friar with his lens): it was also the truth that Cousin Ludwig wrote a very clear Italian script, rather larger than the German typeface they were employing. If anyone noticed the anomaly, she did not encourage comment.

But some explanation was necessary: for this system meant that every folio had first to be set up in its orginal text; a proof of it printed and amended by hand, sent to the priory for Herwald's comments; then the type must be re-set to accommodate the amendments, sometimes several times over if the friar had second, third or fourth thoughts. To be on the safe side, as many as fifty proofs would be taken from the original text. Hulda explained that these extra sheets were needed for other clerics whom Herwald might wish to consult; also for workshop use, lest botched attempts at amendment marred the clarity of the first sheet. The original text was always to be assumed *unsuitable*: so the workpeople must take great care to gather up all spare proofs and hand them personally to Hulda, who was solely responsible for their safekeeping (or destruction): on no account must these questionable papers be allowed out of the shop to endanger the faith of Christian Germany.

Bruder Herwald was very slow in returning the amended proofs, and when at length they did arrive there was always a difficulty in interpreting them. Sometimes he made his own amendments on top of those already inserted by Ludwig, but more often he scrawled an acrid Latin commentary all across the folios, in between the lines, up and down the margins. Not always clear just how he wanted his views applied; it often seemed as though he desired the entire work reconstructed from the beginning according to a quite different argument. He was a very wordy old man (Hulda said he must be jealous he had written no such great book himself); he offered diffuse expostulations of the order of –

> Impossible for the upholder of true doctrine to accept such a diagnosis: why, it verges upon atheism to suggest that a man possessed of an evil spirit should in truth be laid low by surfeit and a bilious belly! If there is *any reason whatsoever* for diabolic interference to be so much as suspected, then an exorcist must *first* be called in. If he finds nothing, then of course the physician's opinion will be consulted: but a proper priority is mandatory. Let Fortunatus immediately look to it; and insert the needful warning in his text. *In the text*, mind: no footnotes!

Gradually, however, the comments became fewer and less vehement. The more Ludwig acceded to them, the more the friar was persuaded that all was going well and that an excellent orthodox book would at long last emerge from the press. Towards the end he even allowed himself short homilies of congratulation:

> Ah! how we rejoice that your excellent father should in his old age be content thus to show forth so meetly humble a countenance. It will assuredly be accredited him at the terrible, yet wonderful, and inevitable Judgement Seat. Of such a spirit are God's saints made!

All this business may have appeared very wasteful of time and labour. But the craftworkers were not inclined to look any further than the task that lay before them: why should they take interest in the content of their work – or in what the reader might eventually think of its content – so long as it was well printed, and they gained their due wage for what they did? And upon this job, the due wage, with all the printing and re-printing, was vastly increased by the extra hours worked. Strictly speaking, as day-labourers they had no contractual claim; but when they came in a body to make representations, Hulda most gladly gave them the money. 'If my uncle's rash theses are to cause me such trouble,' she would say, 'there's surely no reason why *you* need be discomforted.' Not every employer would have been so free-handed. She ensured a generous bonus for the apprentices too.

On the question of payment: of course Herwald was never so blunt as to attach his own little bill to any of the returned packages, but Ludwig understood what was expected. At weeks' ends a trusted apprentice would slip round to the priory with gold coins in an unassuming purse 'For the brethren to distribute to the poor, in gratitude for good counsel'; so everything went very smoothly.

Ulrich these days spent more and more time out of the house, drinking. He took no notice of *The All-Science Book*, nor asked any questions about it; and was never seen to check its costs in the ledgers. He left the final stages of the song-book almost entirely to the shop-foreman: the smaller contracts, handbills, ballad sheets, and so forth, more or less had to print themselves; although Hulda did her best to keep an eye upon what went on. Also upon what went on in the goldsmith shop, where the foreman was so experienced that she knew she had little to worry about; except possibly mistakes over money, and she was always most sharp to avoid *those*.

Her husband's increasing carelessness made her and Ludwig nearly as careless about the conduct of their Venus hours. Why, she would have him tup her anywhere, even in the store sheds when there were workmen back and forth across the yard; or the laundry, where the maids might come blundering in at any time with baskets of linen. Not that the two cousins were ever caught at their marriage-breaking: the household remained collusive. Parchment Hulda at last, they said, had dissolved into flesh-and-blood just like themselves; God love her, had she not a right to it while she still held her youth and beauty?

It could not of course go on forever, as both of them knew full well. But they never intended it should. God knows what they *did* intend. In a sense they had no goal to their doings; beyond the knowledge that once the amended version of *The All-Science Book* was finished and the bound copies put out for sale, some wonderful fate, or terrible, would appear writ for them on the wall as for wicked King Belshazzar, but their own burning fingers already had furnished the pen. Until then, what were they but Francesca-and-Paolo? or Isolde-and-Tristran? – or any other voluptuous pair from any other recollected poets. When of necessity they had to be apart, Ludwig in his father's house, Hulda in her parlour waiting for Ulrich to come home or in bed trying to withdraw herself from the sprawl of his beery sleep, they would dream themselves together as though they could *smell* each other's dear white limbs across the crowded breadth of Nuremberg.

If the amorous adventure seemed unending (and yet doomed to some imminent and profound change), they did have a precise goal for their dealings with the great book; and it was this that would finally determine the course of their love. No one knew it but themselves and the aged physician; but there were now *two* printed versions of Fortunatus' treatise in active preparation. The public one, as the friar had approved it; and another quite private text, with no amendments but those made by Fortunatus (at Hulda's insistence) solely to improve its clarity, all in loose sheets; at least two score unbound copies, carefully locked every night into Hulda's own strongbox which she kept beneath the settle in her parlour. She had never permitted Ulrich a key to this great box, she had never let him know what she kept in it, he had never dared demand.

And then the little cuckold found out.

Not possible to state just how far his drunken habits had been out of his control or deliberately assumed. In all likelihood a bit of both. In all likelihood he had at last found that one of Hulda's maids was corruptible, and he had covertly learned more about his wife's mishandling of his house than she or anyone could have suspected.

Somehow he discovered the hiding place of both the parlour key and the strongbox key (which lived by day upon Hulda's neck, and at night were tucked secretly into a hem of a bed curtain); he waited until he was certain she was asleep; he went soft-foot from bedchamber to parlour, into the parlour, into the box, saw what was there, closed the lid, locked up again behind him; and so back into bed, belching and grumbling (for Hulda's benefit, just in case she was awake) that the jakes was splattered with filth and if a man couldn't ease himself in decent order under his own roof he might just as well live in the street.

The next day was a day of vigorous business in the shop. Books and goldsmith-work were sold from the same counter; and upon it the first copies of *The All-Science Book*, having left the hands of the binders, were displayed in all their gleam of red leather and black, with gold-embossed letters on the spine. Hulda and Ludwig stood over them, recommending them to purchasers; and there were very many possible purchasers; the word had gone round that Albrecht Glueck at last had realised his high dream. Learned men from all over the city came to examine the volumes, and many of them bought. But there were also ungenerous comments, that the author had chosen to seek the requirements of the Church, and that more servility than true scholarship was likely to be found in his pages. Hulda kept her wary ears open for any such gossip, and her eyes upon the faces of those men who seemed to believe it and whom it seemed to disappoint.

To some of them (if she knew them) she murmured discreet hints from the side of her mouth: 'Perhaps, *mein herr*, there will be more for you to hear concerning that matter, at a more convenient time?' Ludwig, too, dropped his own hints. The secret plan was well afoot.

Fortunatus put in no appearance.

Neither was Ulrich to be seen. Hulda did ask an apprentice if he knew where he was: he thought the master had gone to the *Bloodred Boar* beer hall, or at any rate to some such place from which he would not emerge before nightfall. Seeing the crowd of browsers around the shop beginning to thin, she ordered the boy to replace her at the counter alongside the cudgelman who guarded the goldsmith-work, while she went upstairs to rest her bones. 'Rest my bones' was a secret phrase between herself and Ludwig; he heard it, and followed her a few minutes afterward.

And a few minutes after that, just long enough to give time for the tide of sin to be thoroughly flowing, Ulrich came out from behind a wall-hanging in the passage between shop front and living quarters, and soft-foot ascended the stairs. Two strong young ruffians crept after him, chuckers-out from the *Bloodred Boar*; very ready to oblige a regular customer for an extra *pfennig*. They had lurked in the yard for his signal, they were in shirtsleeves with their hobnailed boots wrapped in rags to deaden the noise, they sniggered over all the aspects of the job for which he had hired them.

Ulrich showed them the parlour door: they held a wooden baulk between them; they swung it; they broke the door.

When he saw what there was to see, Ulrich allowed his dirty demon to fly from captivity and do all it had a mind to.

The two louts threw Ludwig downstairs as it might have been a sack of coals. Body bare from calf to breastbone, the breech of his tight hose caught like gaol-irons round his ankles, his shirt up to his plump neck, there was nothing he could do to save himself. A wonder he was not killed; God knows what broken bones he sustained. His father was to spend months in the effort to heal him, and never altogether succeeded. Cousin Ludwig went on crutches for the rest of his life.

As for Hulda – she too was entangled in her clothes, spread out helpless and naked-legged among cushions and folds of carpet. Ulrich jumped upon her. He clawed at her. He let the *Bloodred Boar* boys claw at her and punish her with boots and fists. He stood and laughed to see them do it, he sang '*Hoch hoch hoppla!*' Then suddenly his manner changed, in a fury he roared at them, flung them their money, ordered them wildly away. He himself rushed down the stair and out, forcing himself past them, to drive the customers from the shop front; and then again indoors, yelling at the workpeople to take themselves home out of it, except for the apprentices who must put up the shutters at once and then go to their garret and stay there until he chose to call them. Everyone had heard Hulda screaming: there was terror throughout the house and all along the street.

Somebody thought to send for the archers of the watch. They took a full quarter-of-an-hour to arrive with their crossbows and clubs; when they did, there was nothing to see but a closed and silent house under the gaze of the astounded neighbourhood.

Ulrich came to the door, his contorted face livid as cheese and glittering slick with sweat. 'Yes,' he said. 'A woman screamed. She was my wife and her cousin *plundered* her. They have taken him home on a stretcher; he lives. She lives and I hold her here, because she was and is my wife. All she did has been well known, it seems, to everyone in Nuremberg but me. When I think fit, you will see her walking in the street. My good fellows, there has been no murder done. A husband's justice, that is all. If you are not here to mock me further, I would be glad for you to go.'

So they went.

Ulrich heaved himself up onto the bollard that protected his shop-entry, wrenched down the abhorrent signboard, threw it upon the cobblestones, and trampled it until the wood split. By the time he had finished, his stockinged feet were dark with blood.

TEN

Later that afternoon, Albertus Fortunatus came limping and jerking himself through the town in an unstoppable storm of rage, thundering on Ulrich's door with his heavy silver-knobbed walking stick, crying out toward the upper windows, 'Come down here and face me, you cowardly piece of *dreck!* You have destroyed my poor son, ah God, ah Sacrament, I despair of his life, and what have you done to my niece? Come down here and face me! Turn your bravoes onto *me* if you dare! Piece of *dreck!* Piece of *dreck!*'

Ulrich's haggard face appeared at a casement, which he opened just sufficiently to speak through. He seemed to be smiling, and his voice was subdued: 'I must ask you not to shout at me about what you think I may have done. For otherwise I shall feel impelled to shout back, and the whole quarter will hear of *your* doings. Would that be wise?'

The unstoppable storm was stopped. Fortunatus held his peace. The maid opened to him, and he passed in. He saw the girl red-eyed and quavering, tears upon her face. She asked him in a whisper to go upstairs to *Meister* Grosskerl's study: it was as though a coffin and mourners were awaiting him within.

The great-windowed house-place extended the width of the first floor; one corner was screened off to form the study, a room no larger than a large cupboard, crowded with books. Ulrich at his writing table. He touched his finger to his lip, enjoining quiet. The physician sat down in a chair placed ready opposite; he obeyed the gesture, continued to hold his peace, waited for what would be said. But he gripped the silver-knobbed stick poised for immediate use, and his bitter grey countenance was as grim as a casque-visor.

Ulrich was still smiling. 'Put the stick down, old trembler; and stay on your chair. So. I am not very strong; but as I guess, I am stronger than you. I have hurt *Frau* Hulda a little; she is going to need your art, you will be able to see her presently. I said, sir, *sit down*: I said, presently. In the meantime, you will kindly tell me what was it you intended to do with the irreligious book you have induced her to assemble in secret? Now please, do not pretend you know nothing of such a business. Look here, sir, look at this!' He swung himself up out of his seat, hauled open drawers under the bookshelves, showed them a-brim with printed papers. 'Two-score of six hundred pages, every page from your damnable volume, untouched by the good word of the priest! I do believe I could have you *burnt* for this.'

Ulrich's voice had sunk into so low and vindictive a growl, one might think he was talking to himself. 'I do believe that with this deception, she has betrayed me far more sorely than by a forty days' Lent-full of befoulments of my bed, even had she brought every journeyman in the shop, every labourer in the yard, to nuzzle the dirty liquors from off her crotch.

'So tell me, distinguished *Herr Doktor*, what is to be done to put things right? I am a scholarly man, of the utmost moderation. I need your help as to how to conduct myself. Be glad I ask *you* for it, before I send to *Bruder* Herwald.'

No doubt about it, the old man was greatly frightened; and for the time perfectly speechless. He sat like a church roof corbel-grotesque, neck bent, mouth open, goggling down at the open drawers. Ulrich took pleasure, leant forward smiling, close watch upon him as he goggled; a very snake-like little creature *Meister* Ulrich had become; he had his power, he knew what to do with it.

'Will you let me see my niece? I can speak nothing of all this until I see her – you must let me see her now!'

Ulrich kept him without an answer; until Fortunatus finally and most miserably said, 'Please?' The knobbed stick had slipped to the floor, and there it stayed.

'*Please*, you beg? So why *not* see her? I have a bed for her in her parlour; the lock on the door was broken, I have stapled a new padlock to replace it, I hold the key, moreover I have padlocked her window shutters: you would not expect me to leave her loose? She might just as well be in the city gaol; but she is not, because I married her.'

He led the way out across the house-place, up to the second-floor landing, and unfastened the parlour. Dimly in the dark room Fortunatus could see upturned furniture, ornaments and utensils knocked about all over the place, utter wreck of the bower of love; in the midst of it, Hulda, stretched upon a low truckle bed, very still, bandages over her eyes, dried blood around her mouth, vomit stains all down the rough blanket that covered her. She was but partly conscious, moaning and whimpering. Blood-soaked cloths lay in a bowl near the bed. Ulrich said, 'I will leave you with her. If you want to send for medicines and so forth, rap on the door for the maid; she will run any errand you require. When you wish to see me, rap on the door for the maid, I will be once again in the study.'

He went out of the parlour, making secure the door behind him, leaving uncle and niece locked in together.

Before he took to drinking, Ulrich had spent much time with his books; suddenly, this day, he was no longer at the beer tap, the books once again absorbed him. He sat and read for two hours in the study; it grew dark, he called for candles; then the maid fetched in Fortunatus, and Ulrich listened to his sombre words.

'She has in all likelihood lost the sight of her right eye for ever. She has lost half of her front teeth. She has also lost her child. Did you know about the child? Between one month and two.'

If Ulrich was startled by this, he did not show it. 'No, sir, I did not know. Nor do I know whose child it was. Except, for certain, not mine. For even though it be my seed, she has so *mashed* it together with others' that I refuse to acknowledge it. Let me assume, without reason, it would have been a boy: and if so, your great-nephew; your grandson, very possibly. But say a girl, and what difference? She still would have desired the nasty bastard to inherit my house,trade, reputation. If I had not taken steps, no doubt she'd have succeeded. However, I did take steps.

'How soon before she is fit for work? Do you think, when she recovers, it would be prudent to accord her her burgess-wife duties once again? I mean, those about the dwelling; under no consideration shall she enter my counting house. I mean, is she truly penitent?'

Fortunatus echoed 'penitent?' two or three times, trying to understand that Ulrich had really said it so harshly, so calmly. At last he compelled himself to make a considered reply. 'How can I tell "penitence"? I am not a shrift priest. She is *defeated*, that is all, that much I can tell. She swears she is done with Ludwig. *I* told her she must say that. I told her that if she swore it, you might – you *might* decide upon clemency? If not, I must take her from you. I am her only kin, I cannot leave her in this house. But – '

He had crumpled up in his chair, was weeping copiously, coughing and spitting, snuffling his nostril-rheum onto the back of his hand till all his sleeve was soaked. Ulrich snarled, 'But? Oh of course, *but!* In *your* house you have your Ludwig, some remnant of adultery is bound to continue, whatever her injuries and his. And you blame her, of course, for what has overtaken him. Ah no, she stays here; and admit you would prefer it?'

'You carry us,' whimpered the old man, 'in your belt like your own purse: expend us how you will.'

'First let's talk of Hulda. I must see her in my kitchen, I must see her in the sewing room, every day all day, and I must know – and all others must know – that the moneys she expends there upon the necessary provision are absolutely mine – '

'But they're not,' stuttered Fortunatus. 'According to her father's will, she – '

The objection was passed over; Ulrich's words swept on regardless: '– oh, and her hair is mine; every day all day she will wear it long and loose; token of her submission, token of repentance; an unusual one, but it pleases me. And you will tell all who ask about it just what I intend it to signify.

'As for you: I have your book. It was selling very well, until dinnertime today. I may have shut up shop, but not without checking the till. We will therefore, if you please, amend the contract – we'll not bother tonight, too late to send for a notary, but it's to be done before week's end – so that all the profits from the sales shall be mine and mine only. You did not sell the work outright to me; greedy crab that you are, you spread your claws to nip and gather three-fifths of all my takings; so we finish, no more of it.'

This time he *was* startled; the seemingly cowed Fortunatus suddenly sprang to his feet, his old nose jabbing forward as fierce as the spike of a unicorn: 'Oh no, that's not my book! *Herwald's*: and be damned to him. I withdraw every volume from sale. Their very existence shames me; they have cost me the life's joy of my son. Send a handcart to my house with all the unsold copies, and a notarised *affidavit* that you have dismantled the type, or broken the formes, or whatever you might call it. There is no more *All-Science Book*: that is all I have to say. Add to which, there is no contract. My contract was with *Hulda*, and *Hulda* even now in the toils of her agony has happily cancelled it! Get your notary to pettifog around *that* if he can!'

But Ulrich held the master card: 'Why, he has, he has already: would you look at these parchments?' They came out, in great handfuls, from the drawer above the drawers that contained the incriminating proofsheets. 'Advocate's briefs, counsel's opinion, statements of claim; my copies, at great expense, for the decisive putting-down of the learned Fortunatus, all furnished me week by week from the no-less-learned Flexuosus; stark death to your hope. And to hers.'

The weary doctor's brief attempt at reassertion fell away from him like flakes of old paint; out of this defeat nothing to salvage: he blinked through his spectacles at the documents, he understood what they must mean, the securing of all the business into Ulrich's hands alone, the revision of the father-in-law's will, the refusal of Nuremberg justice to allow wives to rear up over husbands; by now he knew Ulrich well enough to know 'death to your hope' was just that and no remedy. But he would not yield quite yet. ' "Flexuosus"? Dietrich Flechtmann, is that the shark you've been frequenting? I had not thought he would have Latinised himself so swiftly in his green years. If I were you, I'd put small trust in the experience of such a juvenile.'

'He's no younger than your son; three times as bloody crafty; *has full use of his brain and limbs –* ' (the last clause with so much malice, Flechtmann himself would have quailed to hear it) ' – when Dietrich sets snares, by God they're fetched home laden. Of course I can damn well trust him. And so can you, so no more words. The book is mine; it is on sale.' He rammed in the legal drawer and re-opened one of those with the proofsheets. 'Now, what is to be done with all this?'

Fortunatus tried to smile, a rotten-toothed unconvincing smirk. 'I hope if those pages are as irreligious as you say, you'll burn every folio forthwith. A moral danger to your maids and shop-boys; Lord Jesus, you have a drawer full of gunpowder!'

'Oh, well may you laugh, that's *exactly* what I've got: but you're the one, not me, to be burst open from windpipe to arse-bone. The very day, the very hour, that your niece turns her eyes and her tricky little fingers from the decency of her duties to anything or anyone else, these papers go direct to the house of the Hounds of God. And likewise if I hear of but one word against me from *you*, against my dignity as guildmaster, against my knowledge as a scholar, my capacity as a married man.'

And then, just as he seemed to be finishing, a roar of renewed brutality: 'No, and that's not all: I go further and you'll accept it! You're an alderman. Well. Next vacancy on the inner council, I want your public voice. "By Christ," you will say to them, "we'll have Grosskerl or nobody! And don't tell me he's no Nuremberger: his high marriage declares him eligible!" You know your influence, don't deny it: I expect it to advantage me. So make damn sure it does.'

The only sign from Fortunatus of the staggering impudence of this demand was a short flutter of his hands, a spit from the edge of his mouth, a smearing of his sleeve again across his watery face; and then he agreed to the terms. He asked might he tell Hulda?

Ulrich said, 'No, not today. *I'll* tell her, and let her brood on it. Then tomorrow – no, the day after – you can come with your physic and ointments, and see how she's taken her gruel. Do you know, I do imagine she'll have taken it very well.'

His voice was once more soft and even; he stooped his way to the stairhead, calling for the maid to show Fortunatus out, calling for a boy with a torch to light Fortunatus home, all with the utmost courtesy, as though two sober gentlemen had spent a quiet merry evening at the card table. Then he went back to his books. He read Roman writers until all hours (the lusts of Messalina, the *vindicta* of Claudius), and eventually fell asleep in his chair.

ELEVEN

When Hulda became well enough, she was once again seen in the living rooms, as had been agreed; but only in the living rooms. She never entered the workshops, never put herself before the craftspeople, never dealt with the customers; and as for the counting house, she did not even seem to remember where it was. Upon Sundays and holy days she went to Mass at the parish church with a maid – a new maid, an elderly gaol-wardress species of maid.

No one ever saw Hulda take Communion. When the Host was offered, she remained in her place behind a pillar, telling beads, bowed down to the flagstones. Ulrich attended a different Mass; he would not walk to church with her arm-in-arm, he would not walk *anywhere* with her arm-in-arm; indeed he would not let her walk at all, except to church.

As had been agreed, she wore her hair long; like a very young girl or a strumpet. It had lost all its freshness, it was beginning to fall out; she did not trouble to comb it; very soon it became matted and filthy and draggled down around her face. Her face was a ruin. She rarely raised her head to look at anyone or anything. Even less did she display her 'tricky little fingers': her fists seemed continually clenched; the fingers half-hidden by threadbare mittens, whatever the weather. She commonly walked with a stick, just like her uncle (who, by the way, was hardly ever seen abroad now: and Ludwig was *never* seen). Those who met her used to wonder, why did she not change her clothes? She wore the same gown she had been wearing the day of the beatings, a decent enough burgess wife's dress; if it had been washed while she lay sick, it was surely never washed again.

Ulrich showed no sort of interest in her appearance. He himself these days was as spruce as a Christmas robin. He assumed bright colours, scarlet, orange-tawny, and feathers in his hats, whereas his previous style had been deliberately sub-fusc, not shabby but by no means notable.

Hulda slept upon the floor of her parlour, its furnishings never put to rights; her truckle bed incongruous in their midst. At nightfall the gaoler-maid would lock her in, and in the morning release her. Now and again (but not very often) Ulrich came swaggering, to intercept the maid in the passage, take the key for himself, and enter the parlour to claim the use of Hulda's body. Not quite a rape; but as near to it as you can imagine. Nor did he take much pleasure from it; she was indeed far from desirable: we are to suppose he needed now and again to stake his territory. Perhaps when his fancy remembered how she had been at the time of their marriage, he went out upon the town to find a brothel house of harlots with long golden hair. Or perhaps not: he lived with his demon, his demon may well have sufficed him.

He also lived with much discomfort. The burgess wife duties that Hulda was supposed to be fulfilling were only done because the gaoler-maid did them: Hulda in the kitchen broke plates and burned food, in the sewing room she made but three stitches in an hour, in the laundry she put clean linen to boil and hung up the unwashed articles to dry. These derelictions were not, it would seem, deliberate; she was simply no longer capable. The new set of servants, whom Ulrich hired in place of those that had betrayed him, were quite as incompetent. What else, when their mistress would not (or could not) talk to them?

Hulda in the counting house was very sorely missed. Ulrich tried to take over the ledgers himself; but then he found that although the goldsmith work went on very well without him, his new employees in the printing shop needed him there all the time. Again, he had got rid of most of the previous workers because of their betrayal – he believed the business of the *All-Science* proofsheets must have been known in the shop, but for all his cross-questioning he could not find by whom. In the end he brought in a clerk to attend to the accounts. And then he suspected the man of dishonesty. And then he could not prove it. But the moneys were becoming confused, and business suffered as a result.

Among those dismissed was Josef the typefounder, a man of the utmost skill who immediately returned to his home city of Strassburg and set up his own business; no one to replace him. The house had cast type for every printer in Nuremberg since the days of Karl Grosskerl; that income was now lacking; against which loss, the new expense of importing all type from Munich. Ulrich had a poor opinion of the quality of Munich type as compared with that of Cologne. He was unable to afford Cologne. For obvious reasons he refused to consider Strassburg.

It was said throughout the city that Hulda was a true penitent. There were rumours of a hairshirt. She spent hours in the church after Mass, bowed over on her knees and guarded by her gaoler-maid. She seemed constantly to be waiting in the aisle for the priest to hear her confession, with the gaoler-maid rigid beside her: as soon as confession was over, the maid would step up to her and touch her on the elbow and bring her, almost with force, to the door. Could not Hulda be trusted to find her way out of church by herself?

And what did she confess?

There were great speculations. Of course, there must have been the adultery with her cousin. Her guilt for his maiming. Her pride in her parchment-gold hair. Her pride in her gowns and jewels. Her pride in her literacy. Her untoward skill with the ledgers, the sin of usury very probably. Her earlier pride in her virginity (or had that been but a sly dissembling, and therefore even more heinous?). It was also guessed that Ludwig was by no means her first paramour; names of apprentices, young craftsmen, the Italian Lorenzo in particular, were often hinted at: why else had Ulrich dismissed them all? He must surely have discovered immeasurable depravity, and for certain his wife now paid the price for it.

In fact, she confessed only one sin.

It was a very curious sin, not at all the sort of lapse that the priest was accustomed to dealing with: she bitterly condemned herself for being so helplessly *underneath Ludwig* when Ulrich and his bullies broke in, and thereby not enabled to fight for his rescue. She utterly refused to admit the adultery; and naturally, every time, the priest refused her absolution. Nor did she ever explain precisely *why* she so refused. The priest (it was always the same priest, a compassionate man, very troubled about her) began to believe she was out of her wits.

He would say to her, 'Dearest child, why cannot you understand that with a man who was not your husband – ?'

And then she would interrupt him: 'But they have broken so many bones he will never be *anyone's* good husband, and oh I am so sorry for it so sorry oh so sorry, they will never let me see him and if they did I would not dare.' And then always floods of tears, but never the sound of a sob, and so out into the church aisle, and the gaoler-maid as always to take her by the elbow.

Of this we may be assured: she never confessed *The All-Science Book*, her deception of *Bruder* Herwald, her attempt to outwit God's truth. Which is not to say she did not think about it.

Did Ludwig, or his father, confess it?

Here, too, we are on sure ground: they did not.

Fortunatus was so positive in his notion of the 'free city' that the ominous sword of St Michael himself would not have changed his mind for him: he *knew* he had done no wrong in writing his researched knowledge and trying his best to circulate it. He furiously believed that a 'Christian Inquisition' was an anti-Christian device. Of course he dared not say so. He began, for the first time in his otherwise impeccable life, to avoid the confessional altogether. Somehow, he feared, some nosey-parker priest might probe him too far and trap him into dangerous disclosures.

Ludwig, inspired by his father, had always held much the same views. But he had his own urgent reasons to crave for absolution. Hulda's screams still rang in his ears. He lay on his bed of pain day after day and thought of all the sins he had committed all his life and had not remembered to confess; drunkennesses, lecheries, from his student days; such misdeeds as led direct to his seduction of Hulda (for that is what he was convinced he had done); he kept recollecting more of them and sending out for clergymen to hear them at great length. And he had a most direful dream – or was it a *vision*? – recurrent: he saw Death standing alive between bed and window, and in unexpected shape; a squat ragged dirty young man with a spotted red kerchief round his head, waving a black horsetail, like a potboy chasing flies from the tables of a low beer house. Not that there were flies to be *seen* in the room. Only a constant buzz of them, all about Ludwig's pillow; and every time he heard them buzz, in and among Hulda's distant screaming (for the two sorts of noise continued horribly together), he saw the horsetail flick nearer and nearer.

One morning he told the priest about a greedy girl in Ferrara called Giulietta (or was she Giovannetta?). And then – for perhaps the twelfth time – of how he went that first day to Hulda's parlour knowing he meant to lie with her and how he told himself upon the staircase that he did not care if he was damned for it. And when the priest snapped back at him, 'You have already been forgiven that exceedingly wicked act; did you not find well-merited penance on those very same stairs?' Ludwig began to laugh.

Gasping and hiccoughing, he said, 'Ah but no, you don't see it, for God caused it, don't you see? For if only at that moment by God's miracle I'd dropped the papers and had to grovel on the stair to gather them, could not God have made sure the first one I lifted would be the one we'd had printed with huge letters of the upper-case, "ADAM'S SON, EVA'S DAUGHTER, TAKE YOU WARNING, THIS VENERY IS MORTAL!"'? For sure, when my father wrote it, he meant whorehouse ulcers, the rot in your secret parts; but there's more than one guise of mortality. I could have read it, had God helped me! And then bethought myself, and then – why, then, I'd never have *steered* her! Only love, crafty work upon proofsheets (d'you know what a proofsheet is?), O God I would never have *steered* her.'

The priest tightened his mouth at the coarseness of the word; and asked, quite uncomprehending, 'Proofsheets? Papers? To her privy parlour?'

Ludwig sharply realised (even through his delirium) that if he told any more of the truth, misprision-of-heresy would be instantly sniffed, his absolution would be deferred, the fiendish potboy and his phantom horsetail would become a fiend of a human interrogator with a wire-and-leather scourge; the phantom flies that maddened his ears would be gaol-flies, meat-flies, corpse-flies, to settle on him and suck his blood; and his blood would be drying all over him, from lacerations top to toe. He foresaw an earthly prison house far more vivid than the realms of hell; so immediate his understanding of it, he sought immediate escape, pretended deeper delirium, lay back and groaned, he muttered something about Hulda's ledgers and the paper-makers' invoices for his father's book; the priest thought little of it, and irritably took his leave. Ludwig did not send for him again.

Thus, as none of those who knew of the 'irreligious book' had spoken of it to anyone, even under seal of confessional, the proofsheets held by Ulrich were an even greater threat; chiefly, of course, to Fortunatus. For a long time the old man's pride, commingled with his fear, withheld him from any activity, good or bad, that might bring him to Ulrich's notice. But that was not enough. An alderman had died, a seat on the inner council was vacant; and nothing had been done. Ulrich became angry. Whatever his alleged right from his marital status, whatever all the earlier friendly talk, there were many who despised his candidacy; what, a young man scarce older than thirty, of ill mood and drunken habits (never mind his prosperity of trade), to set himself up against citizens with decades of public service to their names and thousands of guilders' worth of civic benefactions? Not to be thought of!

He needed Fortunatus, and by God he was going to get him: he wrote a most hectoring letter demanding instant fulfilment of their bargain, and allowing him but one week to show results. He gave it to the message boy to carry to Fortunatus' house. Hulda heard him from where she sat in the sewing room on a dark morning of raincloud and thunder, huddled over some botched needlework, the flame of an unshaded candle searing her one good eye till it trickled tears down her sunken jaw; a shrillness in his voice alerted her. She called down to the boy that she too had a note for him to deliver.

'He does mine first,' cried Ulrich, on his way into the printing house.

'Of course, Husband Ulrich, no question yours first: but mine is to Heydrich the tailor, your new gown for the guild procession, you must have it by Corpus Christi, there is no sign of its completion; oh agree with me, there is an urgency! Forgive me if I ask the child to take two letters to town's end for the cost in time of one, it advantages our trade, it proves I do my duty, it in no way spoils your dignity.'

She was coming down the stair in great haste.

'*What* dignity, you damned hag, and who do I thank for its loss but you?' Already out of sight beyond the corner of the lobby, Ulrich shouted over his shoulder: 'I need that damned gown for the banquet a whole week *before* Corpus! And you ought to have known it! Send what you choose to whom you choose; if Heydrich don't deliver I shall break him.'

He slammed a door and was gone; Hulda caught the boy by the arm. He was new to his service and in fear. She pulled him swiftly into the nearest room as being more private – as it happened, the counting house: the clerk was out upon some errand. She fixed the boy with her eye and showed her ravaged mouth at him. 'You heard that, Georg? Of course you did, the master is bloodshot angry against this man called Heydrich, of course the master wants him to get his letter first: what *can* be in the other letter that Gunther Heydrich's idle ways must wait for it? Give it me, let me see it: be afraid to obey Hag Hulda, boy, and she'll have her three strong teeth right into you quick-sharp.'

If she was to be 'hag', hag she would be: every day she learned lessons in the art of it from the maid her husband gave her.

She read the letter and sucked her gums. Then quickly, in a stumbling scribble (since the day of the beatings, her neat handwriting had all but collapsed), she wrote a peremptory note to Heydrich; and then, a vehement afterthought, scrawled a postscript upon Ulrich's letter – the only words that had passed between her and her uncle for God knew how many months. 'Now,' she said, 'take them. Heydrich first, then the doctor. And we don't tell *Meister* Grosskerl; because we know that *Frau* Grosskerl lives in the dreams of little liars and swallows up their man-things while they sleep. I'm sure yours is already big enough to make a mouthful for a hungry hag?' She darted out her crooked fingers like tiger-claws at the boy's codpiece. He had no reason not to believe her: there was a thick stench of hatred through all the rooms of this house, he tasted it with every breath he took there. Where a woman felt such rage, powers of evil were on call for her, between curtains, behind skirting boards. He knew it, and he fled as he was bid.

Hulda felt no scruples against speaking in such terms to him. Ulrich had tampered with the loyalty of her servant girl, so why should his half-wit boys be better served? Of course he had hired Georg because the child was so weak-spirited. Very well then; let him find out that weakness weakens everything, and not just where you want it to. She cast a quick glance up and down out of the half-open counting house door: no clerk coming, no gaoler-maid. She laughed to herself, hag-like, and rummaged through the ledgers; the only laugh to pass her lips for God knew how many months. She had suddenly discovered she was beginning once again to *think*.

TWELVE

When the note came to Fortunatus he was astonished to read the postscript: for a while he could not believe that Hulda could have written it, it must be some trick of Ulrich's. But the last few words convinced him. She would never ever have told such a thing to her husband. Before the day of the beatings she would have been too proud and confident; and afterwards too broken-down to share memories with him, of any kind, even those that made a fool of her.

> *Post-scriptum* (Hulda's word and I CAN WRITE IT!):
> Do what he says or don't do it. By week's end no need for it anyway. Cannot tell you further, ah God it will discover itself. Ah God does L. live? Do not try to answer. But I tell you all is changed. Hulda is changed, *today*. Pray for her, good uncle; as you prayed against penalty the time of the *blue bottle*.

Once, when she was about thirteen, she strayed into her uncle's dispensary and drank from a strange blue bottle: his fool of an apprentice, telling lies to impress her, had claimed it was Elixir of Loveliness, as first compounded in Samaria by Simon Magus the Hebrew Wizard, one draught of which would make a Helen of Troy out of the ugliest woman born. It made Hulda very very sick indeed; they called for Fortunatus, who happily had the antidote; and when her mother would have punished her, Fortunatus remonstrated: 'No!' It was Experiment, he said, and therefore greatly praiseworthy. 'It has carried its own warning, sister: the poor girl will not forget.' Nor did she. But had she profited from the warning? Had *he*?

Fortunatus understood two things from the cryptic message. First that Hulda was about to attempt something crucial but hazardous; and just as he had defended her over the blue bottle, so by the same token he must not deter her from this, whatever it might be. Second, that it was her secret, and therefore he ought not to write back to her or arrange any sort of consultation with her: the initiative was hers, he must be patient. He had grown far too old for such nerve-twisting tensions. She had told him to pray, so he prayed.

The very next evening some aldermen came, to know what he thought about Ulrich and the election. They were aware he had quarrelled with his nephew-in-law, but felt sure upon civic business he would nonetheless be impartial; and so he was. He sat for several minutes in trembling silence, wiping his spectacles, fidgeting with a urine vial; and then suddenly crossed his Rubicon. 'Grosskerl?' he snorted contemptuously: 'As alderman? Ha! Put a phoenix upon the fire, he comes back to life. Replace him with a dunghill cock, you have charred bones and feathers of ash.' They respected his judgement and returned to the *Rathaus*, determined instead to elect a master-mason of great integrity, an unimpeachable Nuremberger whose family had held office for years.

It was not long before rumour of this meeting reached Ulrich. He made no comment to the man who told him it, but turned dead pale and hurried home; he sprang up the stairs, crossed the hall, locked himself into his study, unlocked his drawer, took out all the proofsheets, wrapped them into bundles, tying yards and yards of twine around them in a frenzy of disordered haste; and sealed the knots. He dropped hot wax on his best red cordwain shoes and quite spoiled their gilt adornment; he did not even stop to notice it. He wrote a rapid letter to *Bruder* Herwald to accompany the parcels, explaining their whole history, only departing from truth in one particular: how he came to possess the proofsheets –

> – my false wife having connived with her degenerate stallion and his infidel father the physician Glueck, the three of them hid these papers under a loose flagstone in the floor of my jewel-house strongroom. I discovered them only this day, being occupied in gathering remnants of gold dust that had fallen from a burst bag. When I saw what they were, it was as though a great light had shined; so much of that foul adultery that had heretofore confounded me was now made most plain to my understanding. Reverend sir, I do declare to you, the Devil has dwelt in my house, and all unknowing I have suffered his residence. I beseech you, take what action seems best; forgiveness and leniency have but deepened the morass of sin!

He sent no silly boy to the priory; but the reliable gaoler-maid, with a labourer wheeling the parcels in a barrow, and a cudgelman to guard their important progress. It was the eve of a holy day, he shut his shop after dinner and sent the workpeople home; while the barrow was on its way he went into the strongroom with a crowbar, levered up a flagstone, spilt some gold dust (and damn the expense!); it was possible the Inquisition would need proof of his story.

In the event, he might have spared his effort.

The maid came back from *Bruder* Herwald with a verbal request for Ulrich to come to the priory at once. She seemed to be trying to tell him something else as well; but his obsession was so intense he could not listen. He ran to the Dominicans, and the woman ran behind him; he did not stop to ask her why. The friar was not in his cell but was expecting him in a hall of the guest-house, the packages before him on a table, partially opened, proofsheets spread all about. Two other friars, one a short square wedge of a man, the other amazingly tall and lean, stood impassively in a shadowed corner, their cowls concealing their faces. They were not introduced, and Ulrich thought they must be waiting for some visitor of their own.

Herwald at his most indulgent, brimming over with self-congratulatory Latin: 'My dear son, you have done so well to send me these upon the instant: but all is not quite as bad as you have feared. I knew of them already. *Habent sua fata libelli* – if books indeed have their destinies then surely this one has been guided from heaven – even though it shall cause us to cry with the Mantuan, *"Heu pietas! Heu prisca fides!"* – and also – '

Ulrich, alarmed and shocked, was in no mood for more quotations. He cut short a large piece of Tertullian even as Herwald commenced to roll his tongue around the first pungent consonants.

'What i'the Wounds d'you mean, you knew of them already! How could you have known! Why, I tell you *nobody* knew: they were hidden in my strongroom!'

A change had come over the friar's unwholesome features, his yellow skin was glistening, his wet lips protruded dangerously. 'Oh no, my dear son, they were not. They were locked into your study, and you kept them as a Damocles-blade to terrorise your soulsick wife. You lied to me in your letter, which was a lie to Christ's Church, and therefore a direct lie to Our Saviour Himself!'

A swift movement from the corner; the tall lean friar stepped forward, turning his cowl down onto his shoulders, revealing a face like a sheet of white flame: 'On your knees, man, say your orisons, say them earnestly, let me hear you sincerely plead. God is not mocked.'

No doubt about it, Ulrich's pleas were deeply sincere. He scrabbled on the floor-stones, weeping for forgiveness. Never mind now about being alderman, the best he could expect was a penitential parade through the jeering streets of Nuremberg, barefoot in a white sheet, carrying a candle; and the worst – he dared not think of the worst.

'Oh God, gracious God,' he blubbered, 'but how did you find out? In the malice of my heart I thought all was secure, how did it happen?'

Herwald answered him softly enough. 'It happened because *Frau* Hulda made up her mind to confess and to lay all open. Maybe she would not have done, had you not tortured her the way you did. So you see, your mortal sin brought her consciousness of hers. From which irony, we augur well. Grief and sorrow in both of your hearts, you grow together as God's children once more.'

'I trace something of a miraculous Providence in these extraordinary conjunctions,' put in the square friar from his corner; his voice was as hard-angled as his shoulders. 'This very day she came to our brother here, her guilt overweighting her, not an hour before your message, she groaned like you upon this floor, took oath to all that had passed, took gravest oath moreover how she and she alone had contrived the impudent plot, bedding the physician's son, misdirecting his father's dotage.'

'Here she is, if you would speak to her. Eva's semblance in her shame, sweetly conceals as it were her nakedness with God her Father's good green leaves.' Herwald opened a door in the wall behind him and pulled back a pair of curtains. Framed within them stood Hulda, supported crookedly by her stick, looking less perhaps like sorrowful Eve than Atropos Daughter of Night taking a prey (but then Herwald had his bad eyesight and a knowledge of women arrived at from a lifetime of sentimental prejudice). She had cut off all her hair, leaving her bony skull dotted over with macabre ragged tufts. The scissors were still in her hand.

'All *vanitas* departed with the sin-provoking curls,' commented the square friar in the tones of a connoisseur displaying a piece of sculpture. 'A new beauty of the spiritual; and do not deceive yourself, she did it of her own free will, nay she did it even now, as she stood beyond the door.' He clearly thought it a remarkable token of redemption. Ulrich, of course, knew different, but could hardly say so.

There was someone sweeping up the cut hair from the floor behind Hulda: with a shock of surprise Ulrich recognised the gaoler-maid. His penitence gave way to uncontrollable domestic outrage: 'I thought I gave order you were to go with her everywhere! Why did you not tell me you had let her loose to this place?'

The old woman was sure of herself: 'I did not let her loose, master. I brought her to church, as you said I might always do. Not *my* fault if for once she chose a different church, was it? She said she'd be here an hour, I had work to do in the house, I went back to do it, you gave me a message, the holy friar gave me another. I did try to tell you; God knows you would not listen. Not *my* fault, you see. Oh I'm naught if not dutiful.'

The lean friar blazed out again: 'Ah, mean-spirited to blame a servant! Blame only yourself, Son Grosskerl; as indeed you did, three minutes since. Be aware of what you've said already, and work not yourself into toils. So what is to be done?'

Ulrich could only say – or rather stammer – the first thing that came to his mind. 'There was one of you said "miraculous"? Seems to me the reverse. Seems to me we are bloody *bewitched*.' His snake's eyes met Hulda's rat's eye, and quailed at what they read there.

THIRTEEN

A long long time before this, and a very long time before – it might have been the very year Hulda's father returned from Mainz, and after him Karl Grosskerl, his little son Ulrich, and the secrets of the printers' mystery – two young black-friars of the Order of the Dominic toiled up a mountain valley in the south parts of Carinthia. They were weary and dusty from their struggle against the steep road, or rather track, fit only for goats. The place was hard of access, perched poverty-stricken in its high wilderness, the people hostile to outland comers, their religion suspected – of course they were supposed Christian, but what sort of Christian? Italy beyond the snow-topped peaks had been of Christ since Peter and Paul's days; Germany to the north succumbed near seven hundred years ago to the tense fervour of wandering Irishmen seeking God's truth in the lonely forests, and also, less happily, to the evangelical might of Charlemagne's armies: but the mountains were betwixt and between, no bishop made visitation, no schools of developed doctrine moulded the souls of the people. Even the language was doubtful; some of it seemed to be German, some of it a broken Latin (you could hardly call it Italian); and much of it a far older tongue, long forgotten by everyone else.

The two brethren were on foot, as became their humble status of Christ's poor visiting His poor with the Word and Deed of Salvation; they led their gear on the back of a mule, an unhandy ill-tempered beast well able to travel the precipitous ways but sulkily pretending otherwise. *Bruder* Jakob was long and swart; *Bruder* Heinrich blond and stocky. *Bruder* Heinrich came from the hill country of the Upper Rhine; the eastern Alps were new to him (although the people, he believed, could not differ greatly from the bloodyminded recalcitrants of his home district). *Bruder* Jakob was less of a stranger; he had known these regions all his life; the inhabitants disgusted him, the huge pure mountains exalted his heart. In a sense he was Heinrich's mentor here; although in fact this was the first time the two young men had been sent together to pursue the Lord's work without an older friar to keep them company.

In the village that clung to the top of the pass the solitary churchbell was tolling for a funeral. The people of the valley were gathered at the church. Poor goatherd folk, huntsmen, the carpenter, the blacksmith, the bowyer, the fletcher, the women who lived by distaff and needle, the women who churned the butter – they were proud of their skills, proud of their strength of life in this lonely fierce place: but look more closely at them, faces goitred and ill-nourished, mourning cloaks threadbare with age, the dead man's shroud was no better than a poor rag. His youthful corpse-face, uncovered, blistered and disfigured, yet had a dignity, a nobility; and the grief of the mourners was deep and filled with shock. They wept and kissed him, laid flowers between his crossed hands: the hands were black, charred to the bone.

The widow was supported by a group of women, comforting her and augmenting her keen with a formal chorus of their own: over and over in their strange dialect they sang out the tribute to the dead man and the valour of his death, how he of all of them was bravest and most glorious, he gave his life to save the children from the fire in the blazing house, God will reward him, the Queen of the Snow will reward him, young goat-horned King of the Peaks who offered himself thus for the Folk of the High Valley; nor did he need to have done so, the Queen had not yet called him, his courage was out of all measure and would never be forgotten, Christ-on-Cross was his brother and would fetch him to the lap of the Queen!

The village priest in his discoloured old surplice walked beside the bier, hearing these improper sentiments, but taking no notice. Why should he? He was himself a mountainy man; he read the Christian Office (as well as he could; he had a difficulty with Latin script and there was no one here who knew how to correct him), and he believed its virtue; he also believed in the Queen of the Snow, although – if pressed – he would have suggested that one of Her names should be Mary.

Bruder Jakob's lean face was distorted with scorn. He said, 'Listen to them! What did I tell you?'

'I do not understand them. Do they not invoke the Saints?'

'The Saints, Brother? Oh, they will say so. They will surely say so, if you force them to an answer. Let me tell you, their only Saints are the old dark devil-gods that held these mountains thousands of years since, before even the Caesar's legions came marching here and conquering. Out of that conquest little good: never any true control by Rome, and even less from the Rome of Christ.'

'Notwithstanding, we have our work. There is a priest here, of a sort, I see he has a book, there is a church, there must be some small money – they make a living, do they not, guiding travellers from more civil lands? And I suppose the travellers pay them?'

'Preach well enough, put the fear into them, they will pay us what they can.'

'If all of our house were sent into such regions we would never gain enough to rebuild our own church before the roof fell, or Judgement came. D'you suppose that the grey-friars have been here before us? They're making a new cloister in Klagenfurt, I hear. They'll have swept the valleys clean.'

'I think not: I think, Brother, that the little birds of Francis keep closer to their warm nests these days; they are not the men they used to be. *We are*, by the Grace of Mary; or if we aren't, we must prove different. Come, let us unbuckle. Devil's-botch, hold still there! Catch him, Brother, catch him — he'll be over the crag!'

A few moments' flurry and flounder with the mule (which hated the pair of them), and at last they had their baggage unfastened. There was a portable booth, framed on rods and decorated with little flags, each bearing a sacred monogram or the painted image of a saint. They erected this, and laid out on it their wares, Indulgences for Souls in Purgatory, devotional medals, bright coloured ribbons. By the time they had it set up, the dead man was in his grave, and the villagers very cautiously making their ways across the rocky churchyard to see who it might be had occupied this corner of it. There was nothing friendly about their slow advance; nor any great aggression. They saw two new men, and smelt at them, as it were, from a distance. They saw two superior new men, skin smooth, complexions glowing, habits and mantles (although travel-worn) of the very finest wool. When *Bruder* Jakob began to preach they heard something like their own dialect, refined and sharpened, now and then incomprehensibly mingled with High German and Schools Latin. Jakob disdained a total submersion of his doctrine into the speech of the mountains, which he claimed was quite unfitted for Christian truth; but he had to make some concession to the barbarism of the place.

He told them that all are sinners, that at death the Devil would burn them for their abominable lusts and depravities, their greed, pride and heresy, particularly heresy; and that this dead man they buried was of course no exception. He speculated cruelly upon the sins of the dead man. The village priest came to his elbow, trying perhaps to deflect him, to explain the nature of the young goatherd's death, and the deep feeling of the people concerning it; but *Bruder* Heinrich shook him off, bursting forth (in High German) with his own contribution: that only by the purchase of Indulgences and Holy Masses could any soul be fetched from Purgatory, and that this was what he and his Brother were here for, and how blessed a chance they had arrived when they did, when before their very eyes a mortal man went down to the pit – 'And here, my worthy friends, here in our hands, now, now today and not tomorrow, for the first time since how long in your lonely backwards place, you see the means to haul him out of it!' He clattered a feverish rhythm on a tambourine with little bells, and *Bruder* Jakob began to sing. His voice was harsh but very powerful:

> When your money in our box goes jingle-jing
> So the soul in Purgatory gives a spring
> And he jumps straight up to Heaven:
> From the Pope the power is given
> To accomplish here and now this marvellous thing!

Both of them together sang the last line over and over with musical variants:

> To accomplish here and now this marvellous thing!

And the mountain echoes doubled and redoubled it up and down the length of the valley.

'I will lift up mine eyes to the hills,' bellowed Jakob, 'from whence cometh my – ' He roared in Latin, forgetting himself; but it made no difference: the people had decided he was *not* going to tell them, in that or any language, just what was to come from the hills. There was a sudden surge, a gaunt, ravaged, grey-haired woman (the one who had led the keen) came pushing to the front, two other hag-like creatures immediately behind her. They were shouting and screaming something, words of fury which the friars, immersed in their showmanship, could not at once distinguish.

When they did, they were shaken to the soul; with anger, alarm and incredulity. 'Liars!' and again, 'Liars!' mouthed the women – and the others behind them took it up: 'Liars, you greasy young pups!' The first woman was declaiming louder than all of them. 'Liars, you filthy backbiters, here we have buried our loveliest and you stand and dare to tell us they will *damn* him where he goes? You be damned, you, your own greasy selves; get you back to where you came from; get you back with all your fuck-pickings; or God's Lady, we'll give you the crag!'

'Give them the crag! Give them the crag!' The surge had become a rush. In another minute the friars would indeed have been over the great cliff that bounded the churchyard: but Heinrich, with more presence of mind than his rapt brother, was already pulling down all the 'fuck-pickings' from the booth and cramming them under his mantle. They abandoned the booth itself, flung their bodies across the mule, and galloped higgledy-piggledy down the path, hard words and harder stones volleyed after them for a full half mile.

*

An hour or two afterwards they sat brooding beside an upland stream, eating what was left of their dinner (the bag that contained it had spilt in the confusion of flight), attempting to restore their composure. Jakob said, 'It was always so, I should have known it, I should have thought of it before we came.' His bread-and-cheese sat untouched in his hand.

'Thought of what, brother?'

'This is not the first time we have been received with contumely.'

'Oh, not the first, but by much over much the worst.' Heinrich bit into a cold mutton chop. He was still flushed with anger, but his spirits were reviving. 'I shall recommend a formal visit by Inquisitors, and before year's end.'

'Well enough, but that's not all. Who commenced it?'

'Why, she did, of course – the one with the flying grey hair – '

'Her hair is immaterial. Her name is immaterial. The only word you said that matters is *she*. Always a woman, and nearly always an old woman, at all events a woman with no man to control her. And yet, from pious widows, we continually have been told, the Church received her birth and growth. So what has gone wrong? How has the sweet grace of the Blessed Virgin been so perverted, and amongst Her own kind? Heresy indeed, but of a very special sort.'

Bruder Heinrich, with his mouth full, was crudely realistic. 'If the Holy Ghost could make entry into the Blessed Virgin's blessed womb, why wouldn't the Unholy Devil find his own route through an unguarded aperture? A wicked woman's water-gap? What in Rhineland we call ''hairy keyhole'' . . . through a score of them, through a thousand. It is revenge for the Incarnation, he impregnates them all over the world.'

Jakob stared at him, as though he had suddenly seen what he never saw before. 'Brother! Do you speak wildly? Or with analytical deliberation? Answer me, brother; it is a *crux*: a matter of crisis for the whole of mankind!'

'I confess I did speak wildly, and it was sinful of me to snigger.' Deeply struck by Jakob's question, he dropped his gnawed bone. 'Do you mean, I have revealed a truth?'

'I don't know. I don't know. I am too distressed to think clearly. And so are you. Our indignation, our outrage, is still turbulent in our brains. Brother, we will study this matter. It may take many years.'

'If it takes until death, I will pursue it that far. For if what you suggest is true – I mean, if it can be proved by precise theological dialectic – then our task is as great as Aquinas's! And I would say twice as exigent.' He rose painfully to his feet. 'Will you ride the mule or shall I? He'll carry the pair of us no further: would God the Natural Law had forbidden in good time the begetting of such hybrids. A horse now, or an ass, taken as it were *per se*, is a creature to some logical point – but this – this bad-hearted anomaly!' The mule brayed at him and kicked out its heels.

Jakob laughed. It was not a pleasant laugh, for it showed his new idea had taken a firm hold, and relieved him of the personal immediacy of his passion; from now on he would rage from principle, relentless. 'Ah Brother, offer it up! Poor quadruped, he knows not the weighty matters he must henceforth bear.' He threw his long leg across the animal's back and tried to urge it down the slope.

FOURTEEN

They had come far since Carinthia, the lean and the square; no chance they would meet with contumely now, whether they were publicly announced by name and office, or (as in this case) awesomely *incognito*.

They looked at one another and then looked at Herwald. Herwald beckoned to Hulda. She stepped very slowly from the inner room, halting heavily on her lame foot, and stood beside the kneeling Ulrich. Heavily and slowly she too went down upon her knees. Herwald was smiling, moving his hand in a vaguely benedictory fashion. Behind his chair the two strange friars were now authoritatively shoulder-to-shoulder, their hands folded in the sleeves of their habits, a formal trinity of black and white (its balance a little marred by the disparity in height between its standing components, but not at all incongruous); the Church Magisterial grouped ready to denounce the failure of humankind.

Herwald's gaze went up to the ceiling where brooding saints lurked in painted panels, and golden stars on a deep blue background gave promise of eternity. He spoke carefully, almost with embarrassment; the ears of the men behind him seemed to constrain his words. Were the two friars his superiors? And if they were, why did they stand while he sat?

'Witchcraft, yes.' He cleared his throat. 'In fact, not: there seems no evidence, not in this case, no.'

The lean friar murmured, 'Not in this case,' and the square friar doubtfully added, 'No?' The lean friar, between half-shut lips, then said something indistinct about there never being *any* case from which the suspicion could be excluded entirely. The square friar grunted agreement.

Herwald glanced round at them as though checking his cue; and continued. 'But remarkable that you mentioned it. Because out of witchcraft, that terrible perversion, comes today your one hope, son Ulrich, daughter Hulda, of restitution to Our Lord Christ and to His people for the hurt you have done them through your sin. You recollect I told you once that if *The All-Science Book* were not in the end to be published, we of Holy Dominic might find you another printing work no less voluminous, of our order's own writings, wherewith you might regain your lost profits. How competent are you to print in Latin, at great length, with scholars' precision? Your compositor, for example, your proof-reader, are they capable of the language?'

'Ah, yes,' gabbled Ulrich, 'yes indeed, we have often done the Latin work, I myself am adept, I would naturally in such a case correct the proofs myself; and at no extra charge. I have a trained compositor whom I personally instruct in the tongue, he would naturally be supplied with my constant supervision.' He was speaking of a fifteen-year-old apprentice who had just got past the ablative absolute; but proof-reading was the key, and Ulrich was confident. He was all of a sudden feeling a great deal of confidence, upon more than his grasp of Latin. Quite possible, even probable, that candle and shirt-tails of humiliation were no longer an immediate danger. His huckster's nostrils were beginning to tingle at the whiff of an 'arrangement'.

'Ah yes,' he repeated, 'yes indeed, so great an honour, setting commerce at the service of the Church, I am only too happy to – '

'That will do!' Herwald was severe, and Ulrich's temporary elation sagged. 'You will understand that at that time, before your duplicity was manifest, I spoke of profits monetary. There is of course little question of such a thing now.'

'Of course not,' murmured the lean and the square, in censorious chorus.

Herwald's thick underlip quivered with a hint of petulance. He spoke fast to avoid further interruption. 'On the other hand, profits spiritual, penitential, *restitutional*, are much to be desired and may well be available. You see,' – he spoke easily now, a practical tone of voice, not at all rotund or pulpit-like – 'these two brothers beside me have compiled a great book, an amazing compendium of all the witchcrafts in the world – I have already looked into it, amazing, amazing – it is to be sent to the Pope (which means its appearance must be impeccable, indeed I would say unusually beautiful), and also they will distribute it as widely as they may, through all our houses in Christendom and thence the universities, and thence – may we hope? – the shelves of the parish clergy, the secular lawyers and judges, and higher than that: princes, bishops, the Emperor even. A very costly venture. Who is to pay for it? Our order in Germany has of late been raising funds, but Christ's work brings such calls upon our purse, many and divers; not at all easy to reckon sufficient capital to dare to commence the project. Of course we do have our own modest presses in certain of our houses, but alas we do not think the brethren who serve them have as yet quite the skill for such a book as is envisaged. Therefore, this present affair, whereby we seek to restore you and your wife to a state of grace, whereby we – ah – we – ,'

He seemed to be losing his thread. To his confusion, and the obvious annoyance of the other two friars (though they did not deign to voice it),

Hulda unexpectedly struck in, harsh, almost humorous, sliding her eye sideways at Ulrich.

'He means they need a printer who will be the very best and will make them the book *gratis*; and take not a *pfennig* from the sales. In all of the Germanies no such a person, even though we are a heartland of Christ. They call it a religious duty, in fact it could be bankruptcy. I offered them *our* shop; its fullest craft-skill, its most willing services. We shall sacrifice our gold for the saving of our souls: if we do, not a word more of Fortunatus and his proofsheets. And oh, if we do, you'll need me once again at your ledgers, and all the more than ever before. Did you think I hadn't looked at them lately? Self-denial for salvation is not the same thing as cash into the pocket of a peculating clerk. For God's love, good husband, I hope you will thank me.' She turned her head away from all of them and looked between her fingers at the floor.

Ulrich was dumbfounded. '*Gratis*? You mean entirely so? *Non 'st bonum*, it's not possible! For such a vast book, the resources of the shop – I mean, all other contracts must go by the board – it was bad enough, that *All-Science* nonsense, it nearly did for me with the Master-Singers – but at least it was a *German* job – oh in Latin, quite impossible – I mean, I'd have to think about it – I mean – dear God she said *bankruptcy*!'

'Was she correct?' – the square friar, abruptly: his features blunt and uncompromising, his short blond-stubbled jaw thrust out as he flung his question. Ulrich nodded, helpless and miserable. He glared round at the trap that had caught him; he was seeing it (and he knew it) without remedy from the inside.

'Not quite correct,' put in the tall dark friar. 'Her account of your accounts, as given to *Bruder* Herwald, suggests that with her diligent management the moneys may be found to set up our project. Your completed Master-Singers book shows a profit, we know that; and I take it the acceptable version of the Fortunatus work still finds its purchasers? But even if she *were* correct, there is the obvious course available to you: you offer up your disaster of Mammon to God, and put trust in His mercy. He has promised it, He keeps his promises. So do you, sir, now keep yours. *I heard you swear upon your knees.*' He stooped suddenly forward, thrusting his words like a halberd across Herwald's shoulders into Ulrich's face; and then straightened again, arms folded. '*Bruder* Herwald, I believe, has not told you who we are. He did not want to over-influence you. But the knowledge will no doubt confirm your readiness to do what we ask.'

The square friar said, 'To do what your Lord and Saviour and His Blessed Mother require of you.'

A pause; so impressive that Herwald nearly failed to come in on time with his contribution to the fugue. Sweating and flustered, he recollected himself, and launched into a copious summary of the life-history of his two guests.

Clear beyond all doubt they were guests of the utmost consequence, more important indeed than any priest in Nuremberg, not excluding the bishop of the diocese.

Bruder Heinrich Kraemer was papal Inquisitor for the Tyrol, Salzburg, Bohemia and Moravia; Preacher-General of the Order of St Dominic; Master of Sacred Theology; Spiritual Director of the Dominican house of Salzburg. He was a pugnacious and famous preacher (Ulrich had heard of him, indeed) and a prolific theological writer. A long list of his learned books was reeled off by *Bruder* Herwald, all of them compiled for the refutation of monstrous heresies.

Jakob Sprenger had achieved the dignities of Inquisitor-General for Mainz, Trier and Cologne; and Dean of the Faculty of Theology at Cologne University. He had founded the Confraternity of the Most Holy Rosary (of which the Emperor himself was a member). *Bruder* Herwald again listed innumerable treatises, devotional and polemical, whereby *Bruder* Jakob had honoured Our Lord and Saviour (and also His Holy Mother), and given glory to the order of the black-friars.

They were well into middle age, but the athletic vitality of their contrasting frames gave an appearance of youth: neither had much grey in his hair, and neither appeared to have been seriously contradicted by any individual for a great many years.

Bruder Herwald was in some trouble with them, although all three did their best not to show it. He should have been able to have detected the malefaction over *The All-Science Book*, and he certainly ought to have referred its doubtful contents to a superior authority: Sprenger and Kraemer found nothing much amiss with his amendments (insofar as they had had time to study them); but they doubted his qualifications as a censor of such a learned work, and particularly disliked the way in which he had applied to his colleague Petrus-Maertyrer for assistance over the cabbalist chapter. Had he known that that imprudent Brother was himself under secret investigation, he would have conducted himself very differently.

However, as things stood, Herwald had done them both a great service. They were not disposed to be hard upon him. Nor would they be hard upon Fortunatus. A short visit at crack of dawn to his house, a brisk search of his papers, a lengthy and dismaying harangue, would probably be sufficient to cow him: it was scheduled for tomorrow. Ludwig, unhappy cripple, could be included in the intimidation. The wicked proofsheets, together with Fortunatus' original manuscript (packaged up amongst them), and also Hulda's foul hanks of hair, were burned then and there by *Bruder* Herwald in the stove of the guest hall; but not before he had secured an oath from Ulrich and Hulda that no other pages of the uncensored text remained in Nuremberg or anywhere else.

It was now most cordially assumed that all problems were solved, and that the work of printing the witchcraft book would proceed as soon as the manuscript was delivered to Ulrich's shop. *Bruder* Heinrich explained that this document was still in a very rough state: there were about twelve hundred pages of it; the finished volume would be refined down to perhaps half that length. It would not in fact be the *final* text, more of a 'digest'; one of the copies was to be sent to Rome together with a draft of a papal bull, which the Brothers hoped His Holiness would be induced to publish once he had thoroughly absorbed their reasoned arguments. They proposed another edition of the book, at a later stage, with many extra examples, analyses, and legal and theological precepts: the printing of this larger work might or might not be allotted to Ulrich. And he might or might not be allowed a 'monetary profit' from it. It would depend first upon how the Pope received the initial edition; second, upon how diligently Ulrich produced that edition. He held his future in his own hands, as *Bruder* Heinrich made very clear.

They then adjourned from the guest hall to a side-chapel of the priory church. *Bruder* Jakob concluded the meeting with a recital of eighty-one decades of the Rosary and a homily upon the graces and unutterable compassion and purity of Our Blessed Lady to whom they were addressed. Ulrich and Hulda endured this, for several hours, upon their knees, the gaoler-maid being called in to join them. They were instructed as to a severe rule of fasting and devotion which they must follow during the entire period of the printing of the book, and enjoin (as far as possible) upon all their workpeople.

After which, they were allowed to go home.

They walked the street in exhausted silence.

Ulrich chewed and chewed his lips. He was desperately searching his mind for something to say or do to Hulda that would crush her spirit once and for all; he had so clearly failed this first time. But every hope he conceived of a final revenge seemed blocked by the formidable image of Kraemer and Sprenger setting their feet upon his neck: he was as defeated as she had been (or as he thought she had been) after the day of the beatings.

Hulda kept her own thoughts well hidden, almost from herself. For if she were to let them free, she must turn her mind at once to the parcel of uncensored *All-Science* folios that she knew was in Fortunatus' possession. During his nightmare conversation with her, just after the beatings (she had all but obliterated it, and yet her mind returned to it), he had told her, had he not, of six hundred pages in proof? And had he not insisted that his folios were stowed, 'in exigency of great danger, in the teeth of the adversary', where no one could find them, 'except by magic power'? A vagueness; and a danger. Those two black-and-white magpies, as cunning as they come, might well deploy such power – why, their life-work was the study of it, they were the Hammer of the Witches; as was also their book, for that was what they'd said its Latin title meant. *Malleus Maleficarum*.

To 'enlighten and delight'?

More probably an immense tedium; after the pattern of all clergy books. Perhaps if this one had been put into German like the *All-Science*, it might have had some smack to it – for who did not believe in witchcraft? Who could prove it did not happen? Such tales of it everywhere, bestial-comic, hectic-frightening, lascivious as blood between the lips. She herself had recalled them, only that morning, to bend the fool boy to her will. What else could she recall?

She caught her breath, tried to recall nothing: oh had Ludwig used a witchcraft upon *her*, to take her hands and suck her mouth? 'Please trust'? Was it a spell? Or had *she* be-hexed *him*? Unknowable, even under torture, and she wished never to know it. Today she was *hag*; she gave her help to a hag-ridden book: every single piece of what had once been her money and now was claimed by demon Ulrich would be spent, and well spent, to cram the gizzards of those two magpies who had forced the little basilisk to his knees. And as for her 'state of grace'; keep her thought hid or let it brandish, she now knew with an utter certainty she would never be brought to grace by priest or friar of any sort: maybe God – maybe not God, but surely God's Mother? – would understand why not, and maybe Hulda might be saved. It cannot be said she worked at this with logic. Her brain baulked, she was not ready to understand herself at all. She wept, and she laughed, at the same time, and in silence; she limped behind her husband Grosskerl, looking neither to left nor right but fixedly upon pavement stones and gutter-muck.

The gaoler-maid walked at her elbow, grimly pleased with all she had witnessed. She loved priests, she despised Ulrich, she felt a cruel disgust for Hulda; her heart had leaped when she'd been called to help the noisome trollop get rid of that tangle of hair. Filthiness, hypocrisy, the craw-thumping corruption of gluttonous city fathers and their sensual selfish bitches. But God was not mocked! (As the righteous friar had said.) She marched proudly. Her decent gown left not an inch of her woman-flesh showing for the knaves of Nuremberg to pollute with their gaze.

FIFTEEN

If Hulda had known that Kraemer and Sprenger were in the city, would she have been so rash as to deliver herself to old Herwald? Even now she could not have realised by what a hair's-breadth she escaped calamity. The two Inquisitors were desperate for an immediate printer; and that was the only reason why they allowed her a breathing-space ('the interest of the greater good'; legitimate concept of moral theology). They had for years been a-chafe against restrictions upon their zeal, in particular in such places as Nuremberg. They were not permitted to work without diocesan approval, and a free city's government made great hindrance for any bishop. Sprenger and Kraemer intended the *Malleus* (or *Hammer* – they had learned to prefer vernacular in converse with the laity, more menacing, more direct), combined with a papal bull, to augment their own power and abolish all such hindrance. Let the Pope but be brought to see the huge peril of German witchcraft as imminent as *they* saw it, then surely he must grant them full freedom of action, answerable only to himself. Therefore lenience toward anybody could be no more than temporary; 'no bargaining with heretics' remained the essential principle. The predator magpies were hovering for the swoop.

But nothing of this was yet apparent. The *Hammer* manuscript was brought to the shop by a young Brother from the priory (Sprenger and Kraemer had left for Augsburg, to confer with the papal legate). His manner was most courteous, indeed deferential, towards Ulrich, the distinguished craftmaster. It was his duty, as literary and research assistant to the authors, to oversee the preliminary typesetting, to ensure that the abridgements of the text were properly understood, to approve the typefaces, brand of paper, and general layout of the work.

The printers were formally presented to him. Not Hulda, who remained in the counting house. Ulrich had grudgingly acquiesced in her resumption of work there. His ledgers were in a shocking state: he was in two minds whether or not to prosecute the clerk ('breach of trust'); for a charge of embezzlement there was no exact evidence. Hulda said there ought to be, she'd do her damnedest to find some; meanwhile the man was dismissed. She now had to discover the exact state of the business, gather in overdue payments, fend off creditors, and rearrange any other contracts that were not yet completed. There were several, all smallish items. They would be finished when and if Ulrich could squeeze them in between stages of the *Hammer* work, from now on the priority.

In the old days Hulda had passed frequently from counting house to workshop, and had personally supervised a great deal of the printing. She was well able to set type and operate the press. Now she was rarely seen away from her abacus; and when she did appear she was a disturbing intrusion, cropped head, unkempt clothes, dirty and foul-mouthed. She only entered the workshop to report to Ulrich about money, almost always ill reports, given to him loudly and bitterly with a sort of public glee. She made the most of the fact that the friars were paying nothing for the *Hammer*: this naturally troubled the workpeople – they wondered how long their jobs were secure. But somehow wages were got for them, often only after a vehement pretence that there was no cash in the strongbox. In fact the profits of the goldsmith shop were little by little being sucked into the void of the printing business; but they themselves were diminishing, for the Italian Lorenzo had left Nuremberg (after brooding for some time over the Master-Singers' censure of his designs), and no one had been found to replace him for the finest class of work. Ulrich's authority began to suffer. His sparkish clothes seemed less and less appropriate.

The full truth was not to be known, of course: strict orders from the Dominicans about that. As a result of the secrecy: rumours, among masters and workpeople of other craft-shops. Word went round that Ulrich had refused the friars' fee in return for their promise that they would get him appointed official printer to the archdiocese or even to the papal legation. If true, it would be illegitimate soliciting for monopoly rights, which meant trouble with the guilds. He was forced to make public denials. His reputation sank.

Hulda still slept alone in her wrecked parlour. But now she kept the key herself; her door was locked at night from the inside. Ulrich never tried to visit her. He was thought to have been seen quite often in bawdy-houses, or at least a masked man answering to his description was making himself unpopular there, mistreating the whores with a surly violence and on occasions being violently ejected. He drank heavily as well, no doubt, but also in discreet brothels; for the inns were too public and he had to remember the severe religious duties imposed on him by the friars. In church – usually the black-friars' church – he would make a parade of devout practice: his hungover hangdog appearance could plausibly be taken for the sad demeanour of inward piety, or so he tried to make it seem. He was altogether resentful and fearful, as well as furiously bored with the subordination of his life, unable to see any way out of it.

*

One day, quite soon after the *Hammer* had been begun, and before these detrimental circumstances were fully revealed, the young friar paid a visit by prior appointment. He wished to discuss the incidental decoration of the text, and Ulrich had all ready for him – a special display of the most sumptuous illustrated books the house had published over several years.

The friar was a man of keen taste, and gave much praise to the qualities of the work on show. Pictures were not required, he said, only small sacred monograms and the like, which might be useful for chapter-headings or page-fillers; he stipulated that all such items should be original: Sprenger and Kraemer would not wish re-used blocks to give their book a second-rate appearance. He was peering through a lens at some tiny flower patterns in a margin when Hulda erupted into the workshop. This was the first time he had seen her; she appeared not to see him (he was behind the printing press, in an alcove); he was appalled.

She banged her stick upon a table-top. 'Twenty guilders,' she screamed, 'twenty guilders astray from the Master-Singers' account! Jerking 'em out at the *Placket and Garter* – ' the name of a well-known bawdy-house – 'you dirty conniver; or did you spend 'em in sausage-and-cabbage and beer by the hogshead to fill the privies of the bullroarers who paid them to you in the first place? If these shave-heads call for woodcuts all over their pages, engravers'll need money, I mean gold, I mean silver, I don't mean your arsehole *credit*! So where's it to come from?' At which point she affected to notice the friar. She dropped her stick and fell on her knees, sobbing and begging his pardon; and then she laughed wildly, scrambled to her feet, and planted a hideous kiss upon Ulrich's mouth.

'Ah look at us, reverend sir! And who am *I* to talk of shave-heads? But if you wade into the sties of Mammon, Mammon must be witnessed, and he splashes and grunts. Shite-stink in your nostrils, I know. You're a good man. Excuse it.'

Ulrich muttered something to the effect that he *had* had to entertain the Master-Singers, it was necessary to retain cordial contact with important citizens, an inevitable outlay; but of course there was sufficient capital for the employment of an engraver; the earnest Brother must not mistake *Frau* Grosskerl's robust manners – and so forth, but his voice failed. The earnest Brother, red-faced with surprise and embarrassment, was staring from husband to wife, wife to husband. The workpeople all bent industriously over their tasks, trying not to seem to know what was going on. There was a long silence. Uncertainly, the young friar resumed his discourse. He had been about to explain why no pictures were required in the book, and why therefore the expense of woodcuts would surely not be extreme. The authors' argument, he said, was too grave to be 'dressed-up' for frivolous tastes. He hoped that was understood, particularly by the gracious lady. He prepared to leave the shop, no doubt more quickly than he had intended. But Hulda stood in his way.

'I don't read Latin,' she announced. 'I asked him to teach me once, but he wouldn't. And quite right, I'd only have used it to compose filthy lecher-letters. But if I'm not to cause offence by breaking comments upon this job when all I know is the money of it (which God Above can see makes a madwoman of me!) then had you not best *tell* me the "argument"? *He* won't, I don't know why. I think he thinks that now he's in the confidence of the Church, he administers a damned confessional. But your Jakob and Heinrich said *I* was to be part of it; *my* sin was the sin to commence it – look at me, use your eyes, can't you tell it from the state that I'm in?' She began to weep once more, and clutched pathetically at the friar's mantle.

He felt the justice of her appeal, he wished to smooth relations between man and wife, he thought it anyway an opportunity to show off his own knowledge. He gave detailed tuition, there and then, in the printing shop, bringing all work for that morning to an end.

In sum, he declared, Sprenger and Kraemer had come to the conclusion that witchcraft was not at all what most people thought it, an aberrant misuse of natural powers by a small number of malicious deviants; nor was it mercenary conjuring; nor yet a rural cult surviving in ignorant places where true Christian teaching, for whatever reason, had failed to penetrate: it was a vast and growing conspiracy involving thousands of human souls, lost souls, apostate heretics, who deliberately sought to make Satan the world's master and thereby undo the entire New Testament.

To an extent this had been known before, he said: the Angelic Doctor, Saint Thomas Aquinas (that lodestar of the Dominican Order) had laid the groundwork for its understanding in his definitive theoretical work, *Summa Theologica*, wherein he made 'doctrinal system' of all the speculations of all the divines who had preceded him. Aquinas knew how witchcraft and soul-killing heresy were inextricably inter-organised, plaited strands of a hangman's rope: but the nature of his work, and the short span of his life, had prevented him from analysing it with that degree of rigorous detail he had given to the Kingdom of God. It was now time, pronounced the young friar, to build upon Aquinas, and similarly to make 'doctrinal system' of the Empire of Evil; and thence make 'investigative system' and 'judicial system' and 'graduated penal system' to deal with the Empire of Evil's adherents: this was what Kraemer and Sprenger had done.

'Now time? Nay, more than time, the emergency is acute. For the past two hundred years, heresy has been increasing, witness the Hussites in Bohemia, the Lollards in England; the Church has been sorely enfeebled by immorality and schism, witness the late division of the papacy between Avignon and Rome; we have fewer men and women of sanctity than ever before; and more wars and more fearful – plagues, famines, insurrections of the lower orders – than history hitherto has been able to number. While *manifestly conjoined to such imminent religious collapse* the witches swarm yearly to the high places of the land for their parliaments with insatiable Satan – he rears himself tumid yet icicle-cold atop the throng of his mortal concubines – more and more of them at every meeting, flying the stormclouds thousands of leagues. You have heard of the Brocken mountain, *Walpurgisnacht*, yes? Or did you think it a mere *fable* to fright children into peace and quiet? Why, the participants are more dangerous to us, because so covert and *in our midst*, than the ravaging janizaries of the Turk (who at least are overtly infidel and observable as they march, our soldiers may know where to fight them!); a witch to all appearance is a smug-mouthed loyal Christian, many of them of utmost regard, in bishops' palaces, courts of princes, city governments – *Bruder* Jakob has the names of five hundred and fifty-seven suspected witches, all connected with noble families in the German lands alone!'

Hulda seemed properly scandalised by the news. 'Does he list them in the book?' she asked eagerly.

'Ah no, it is too soon. When His Holiness has granted the bull to authorise full investigation, then the names will be released. Suspects cannot be denounced until good Christians understand the true nature of the suspicion, the correct form of denunciation. Also there are many aspects of witchcraft – the doings upon Brocken, for example – which we *know* about most firmly, but cannot yet exactly *prove*.'

He seemed not to relish having to admit this, his expression clouded a little. Then his eyes brightened again: the moment of doubt was brief, he knew how to overcome it.

'The authors,' he explained, 'are necessarily conscientious: until (after correct procedure) confession of an enormity has been extorted from its perpetrator, they will not write it down. Such reticence is not only honest but politic. For the Devil is deadly cunning; if he knew what we know before we can establish it, he would at once revise his strategy, all traces of proof would be gone.'

'Does he not know already? I thought he could spy everywhere?'

The young friar looked at her shrewdly; was there mockery, was there scepticism? Her scarred face was without expression. 'Gracious lady,' he replied, with care, '*Brueder* Jakob and Heinrich are so well fortified by orison and good words that the Enemy dare not approach them. Or at any rate, so we must hope, nay *trust*: Masses are said for their protection daily in every house of Saint Dominic, and a continual recitation of the Rosary is carried out in one cloister or another every hour of the twenty-four. And so it must be until the book is completed. And so, I hope, it will be with you. The utmost humility of conduct, from you and from everyone here. You walk in danger every hour. And yet you do not; for the very sanctity of your task will itself be a blessed shield to you. Fear only your own misconducts, lest through them Satan's self is inserted even here, between type and ink, between ink and paper. Correct yourselves accordingly; prayer, confession, sacraments and submission to your spiritual directors.'

There was a chuckle-headed journeyman, Hermann of Bamberg, who always said the wrong thing at the wrong time; and now he thought fit to interpose his views. 'My old grandma,' he offered, 'who was very well up in these affairs, *she* said there was no such a thing as witchcraft. Daft folk convinced theirselves they could work magic spells, broomsticks and that, and other daft folk believed 'em; and even if true, she'd say, they can't do no harm – a bit o' garlic or the sign of the cross'd always flight 'em; I mean God's more strong nor broomsticks, ent He? Even if Satan's broomsticks? Or why do we go to church? Stands to reason. What's all the push then?'

The friar's face darkened with anger, as much at the man's dismissive tone of voice as his retrograde stubborn opinion. 'Fellow, I can only hope you are speaking from ignorance; for if I thought you meant seriously those light-minded words of pride, I would be compelled to take action against them. I suppose you know what that would mean.'

Hermann shook his head. If ignorance was to be his excuse, he would show it at once, as he well knew how; stupid though he may have been, he had sense enough to see when he'd gone too far. 'Action, master? No I don't. Crave pardon, master, I said no more nor what I'd heard said; and a man must respect his grandma, like Lord Jesus with good Saint Anne.'

'There are grandmothers and grandmothers. And *some* of them merit respect. I'd say yours would deserve burning. What's her name? Where does she live? Indeed, *how* does she live? Answer directly, if you'd save yourself; answer me, man, don't dare to prevaricate!'

The friar, as we have said, was research assistant and no more. He had much to learn before he became Inquisitor; but research can be practical as well as academic. He thought he had here a first-class opportunity. His technique of interrogation was scarcely effective, and asked for the response it got. Hermann thickened his oafish countenance, answering indeed; but not so as to advance the friar's knowledge. 'Name? We just called her "Grandma". Live? Oh, rural parts, hither and yon, best call it the backside of Schweinfurt.' (He gave the town's name straightfaced, but the sound and sense of it seemed a personal insult.) 'Not that she does now: she's dead ten year. No I lie; it *will* be ten, All-Hallowstide, right? What was she? She was midwife. Owt wrong with birthing babies?'

The friar snorted and turned away. He regretted his own enthusiasm. He saw little point in pursuing the matter, little honour-of-God to be gained from it; and he thought he had heard a laugh from one of the apprentices. But he'd mention it to *Bruder* Heinrich. In all likelihood the old woman *had* been a witch, was it not the very ones who most scornfully denied the cult who were in fact its most cunning devotees? And yet there were clerics, some of them very senior, unaccountably prepared to support such denial.

No, he could *not* leave it at this: gaping mouths and round eyes all about him in the workshop; they had been frightened, of course, on behalf of the journeyman, but they had to be told just why 'Grandma' was so wrong.

So he told them: reading out to them great portions of the *Hammer's* opening chapter, first in the Latin and then improvising a German version. Kraemer and Sprenger here conclusively proved, by reference to Scripture, the Fathers, and Canon Law, that witches existed. It was intellectually disreputable to doubt it; and when the papal bull was issued, belief in their existence would be matter of official dogma. The close-woven translated prose was not the easiest reading.

If it be asked whether the movement of material objects from place to place by the Devil may be paralleled by the movement of the spheres, the answer is No . . . Wherefore, since the Canon makes explicit mention of certain women, but does not in so many words speak of witches; therefore they who understand the Canon only to speak of imaginary voyages utterly mistake the tenor of the Canon, and err most grossly . . .

Although women may imagine they are riding with Diana or Herodias, in truth they are riding with the Devil who throws a glamour before their eyes . . .

With reference to the last objection . . .

We may put forward the opinion of St Thomas Aquinas, his *Summa Contra Gentiles*, Book 3, c. 1 and 2, in part one, question 114, argument 4 . . .

Upon this point see Blessed Henry of Segusio, also Godfrey of Fontaines, and Saint Raymond of Penafort . . .

With reference to the last objection . . .

And the same argument applies . . .

This then is our proposition . . . *etcetera, etcetera* . . .

'So you see, do you not?' They said they did, all abashed, doing their best to look as though they had understood every word. The friar was not sure whether he had chosen his passages as cogently as might have been wished. He feared lest he be not quite ready yet to pronounce an exegesis of so learned a work to ink-stained men in leather aprons. But at all events there had been one sentence, somewhere at the start of his recital (although he'd muddled it a little, missing it out and then returning to it halfway through); 'Hammer of the Witches' indeed, it knocked the nail firmly on the head.

He sought it again; and repeated it with emphasis: '*Obstinately to maintain the opposite opinion manifestly savours of heresy.*'

And so he took his leave, avoiding Hulda's eye as he went past her. The woman was so uncanny, he thought, in her black sorrow for those sins that had destroyed her carnal body, might she be advancing toward sainthood? On the other hand, was it possible (O horror and nightmare!) she might herself be a – ? No, no no; *Bruder* Heinrich, *Bruder* Jakob, could never have allowed this house their book, if they thought. . . ? Or *could* they?

Did he dare to ask them?

SIXTEEN

In the course of one short morning, then, Hulda had done much.

She had left the friar uncertain as to Ulrich's sincerity (her casual reference to the *Placket and Garter* had not, she noticed, gone unnoticed); she had sown a huge bushel of fresh doubt over his pecuniary stability. It was all very well for the Hounds of God to accept work *gratis* as a self-mortification by a penitent printer, but if repentance went so far as to break the printing house in the middle of the job, the book would never get to the Vatican. As for the workpeople; they were thoroughly disturbed. Because the *Malleus* was in Latin, they had not even thought about its meaning. Now they knew it to be a most dangerous item, in all sorts of unexpected ways; diabolical, inquisitorial, financial. Finally, Ulrich had been made a fool of; for the last half-hour of the friar's visit he had failed to find one word to say for himself; his expostulations as the friar left – that all would be done to the best of the house's ability, that the excellent brethren could trust him to give them the utmost satisfaction (and so on and so forth) – had been far from convincing; she was sure the friar was not convinced; she was sure too that Ulrich knew he wasn't.

We must conclude she had done all this of set purpose; that she was constructing a revenge against the man who had killed her unborn child; that she played it – at any rate to begin with – as it were from day to day, not precisely to a plan, but letting herself seize each chance as it came.

She did not waste thought upon her own position. She was already a dead woman. Nothing the Inquisition or anyone else could do to her would be worse than what had been done in her own parlour: and that was that.

Throughout the next few weeks all went from bad to worse. The Latinist apprentice's typesetting was so irregular it would have been rejected by a street-vendor of ballad sheets. Ulrich had to do most of the boy's work for him; and then he had to read the proofs himself, an uncraftsmanlike practice – you do not see your own errors, simply because they *are* your own. Hulda, at odd intervals checking the work, found innumerable elementary mistakes: 'u' for 'n', 'ni' for 'm', 'f' for 's', and the like. Lines, even paragraphs, were overlooked and omitted; pages set in the wrong order, wrongly numbered. She was not able to judge the Latin grammar, but she did think that *Sanctus Ecclesia*, for example, could hardly be correct. Surely an *a*-noun did not match with an *us*-adjective? She looked at the manuscript, found she was right, told Ulrich within earshot of the apprentice; and laughed at his vicious oaths. She was quite prepared, these days, to endure another beating 'in the interests of the greater good': as it happened she did not have to, Ulrich's demon was now expending itself on fouling up the *Malleus* for him; and sooner or later he must confront the fact.

Half-shaped in her mind was the gloating and most marvellous vision of Ulrich so entangled in the snares she might weave for him that the only way he would finish the book would be with the help of her cousin. And for God's sake, why not? Whom else would he have to turn to? His competitors who believed he had schemed for monopoly, who knew he had tried to be alderman? Clergy or other scholars would have the Latin to come to his aid, but not the craft-skill; whereas Ludwig (after *The All-Science Book*) knew as much about printing-house work as – well, as she herself did! And if the plan succeeded, then Ulrich's great book would be the book of his wife's blind eye, the damned book of her beloved adulterer's twisted joints and shattered bones, *the book of her aborted womb*: by Christ she would *dance* upon it as it lay on the shop counter!

What did she think of the book itself?

She was in truth no longer interested; her suspicions that it would be pompous, priestly, logic-chopping and wordily disputatious, as well as acrimonious, had all been confirmed by the young friar's ill-chosen excerpts. She had, for a moment, thought something more stimulating might have emerged from his selection when he held forth upon women who rode 'abroad with Diana and Herodias'; but even that short glimpse of poetic colour was at once absorbed into an abstract dogmatic fog, as the authors chose to pontificate on the nature of illusion related to creation, on reality and phantasm, on how far God's creatures may be 'transformed' without God ordering it, and how far one might speculate on the matter without falling into theoretical error.

But then a day came to change her mind, and change it abruptly. She was sitting in the counting house, to enter figures in her ledgers and assess small change by piling coins into neat little heaps of twenty, when she heard furtive laughter in the lobby between her door and the printing shop. It distracted her: she pricked her ears. Ulrich, she knew, had gone out to a guild meeting to make more of his denials; his absence caused the usual lapse of discipline. A year ago she would have been swift to correct it; but now she could sit and listen, complacent and sardonic, letting carelessness take its course.

The apprentice compositor was airing his Latin, translating some part of the *Hammer* text for the benefit of Hermann; and the two of them seemed to find it unexpectedly amusing. So much so, in fact, that they had removed themselves from their fellows to guffaw over it, squatting cross-legged in a private corner. Hulda heard –

> Now the wickedness of women is spoken of in *Ecclesiasticus XXV*: all wickedness is but little compared to the wickedness of a woman . . . When a woman thinks alone, she thinks evil . . .

'Right,' sniggered Hermann, 'that's our Parchment, fair enough!'

> She is more carnal than a man, as is clear from her many carnal abominations.

The compositor had a breathy, throaty, salacious chuckle running under every word. 'Did y'ever hear what that Lorenzo chap is supposed to have said about her? When he used to do the cut-work, there's a story, y'know, she got him once to grave a picture in the bottom of a silver cup, one you couldn't see, y'know, till you'd drunk yourself ripe an'ready – d'you know what it showed?'

'Get away, that's an old tale, Lorenzo said there was no truth to it: nay, but you'd wonder though . . . Carry on, let's hear the rest of it, the old *amo-amas*: I always knew them monks was steaming underneath of their long gowns, but I didn't think they'd be quite that *ardent* to print it out in black-and-white.'

> It should be noted that there was a defect in the formation of the first woman, since she was formed of a bent rib, that is, rib of the breast, which is bent as it were in a contrary direction to a man. And through this defect she is an imperfect animal, she always deceives . . .
>   All witchcraft comes from carnal lust, in women insatiable. See *Proverbs XXX*: There are three things never satisfied, yea a fourth thing which says not, It is enough; that is, the mouth of the womb.

This time there was quite an explosion of smothered hilarity, Hermann's words spluttering out of it. 'Not now, not any more now – poor old hag, she's a dried-up culvert. Choked with dead nettles. Ten *pfennige* for the plumber that unblocks her – so who's a volunteer?'

Hulda came silently from her stool, into the doorway, and stood over them. They did not see her until she spoke, and then they were stricken as by a gorgon head. (Someone had told them, the foolish lumps, that their mistress had gone to church.) Her harsh voice like a distant wind in a very distant forest: 'Yes indeed, and our Parchment has indeed been *thinking alone.'* She brought her cane down with two fearful cracks that nearly split it, across the shoulders of them both, one after the other, quick as winking. They yelped and struggled away from her, but she had them in the corner; they flung up their arms to guard their heads and pressed themselves against the wainscot: she did not repeat the blows.

'Read on!' she grated, 'Read! I said *read*, you skiving bastards, let me hear what makes you laugh!' She banged her stick on the floorboards. The compositor boy made haste to obey her, stammering and gulping. He tried to turn to another proofsheet, but she slapped down the ferrule across the folds of the paper, compelling him to the chapter he had in his hand. She made him read all about bad women, how Kraemer and Sprenger could prove that a good woman, a steadfast woman, a woman to be loved and trusted, was as rare as the Virgin Mary herself (and She, after all, was protected so to speak by miracle); whereas Eve (who was not so protected) immediately fell prey to the Devil. The Devil, it was implied, did not venture to approach Adam directly; he feared lest he be repulsed, he knew that Eve would succumb, and so she did.

And in consequence of this, it is better called the heresy of witches than of wizards, since the name is taken from the more powerful party. And blessed be the Highest Who has so far preserved the male sex from so great a crime: for since He was willing to be born and to suffer for us, therefore He has granted to men this privilege.

'That's all there is, mistress – ' But it wasn't. She demanded more: she meant to hear all of it.

Three vices of wicked women: infidelity, ambition, and lust.
Since the last chiefly predominates, women being insatiable, etc., it follows that those among ambitious women are more deeply infected who are more hot to satisfy their filthy lusts; and such are adulteresses, fornicatresses, and the concubines of the Great. Seven methods by which they infect with witchcraft the venereal act and the conception of the womb –

'Never mind the seven methods, they don't apply to Hag Hulda: she's a dead woman, don't you know that? Dead ambition (save for one thing!), dead the rest of it, dried-up; in need of the plumber! *Don't you know that?*' She was beginning to scream. Ashen-faced, the two youths could not think whether 'Yes, mistress,' or 'No, mistress,' would be the more disastrous answer. 'Of course you do,' she said, more quietly. 'Back to your work,' she said in a whisper; they crawled away.

*

Ulrich gone to the *Rathaus*; the printing-shop people lounging about and tinkering at the job; the goldsmiths hard at it, under the strict eye of their foreman; the gaoler-maid (no longer able to domineer over her mistress) tyrannising the kitchen: Hulda wrapped herself like a beggarwoman into an old foul-weather cloak and left the house without a word to any of them. It was pouring with rain. She clacked rapidly on wooden pattens through the puddles and gutter-filth, not stopping till she reached her uncle's door. She had intended to go to him long since, but had always put it off; she was afraid of meeting Ludwig, even though her plans might demand it. But now everything was changed, she did not care whether she saw him or not.

Fortunatus opened to her, surprised and shocked (he had been told about her hair, but her hood falling off her peeled pate in front of his eyes was another thing altogether). He had the air of a hunted man, he let her in swiftly, closed and bolted the door behind her, led her into his surgery. 'You should not come here, miserable child; God's dogs have been already, and more than once, let me tell you, uprooting and growling and grovelling, let me tell you they found no bones. But for a medical man, it is bad. Many of my patients prefer to go elsewhere, my God they prefer *quacks!* Nay, I have no antidote for your *blue bottle* this time! I'm in fear it'll have poisoned all of us.'

Hulda grasped his shaking old hand between hers. She burst out: 'Sweet Uncle, you must help me, you must tell me what to do! I thought I had it clear, thought I knew where I was going, but Christ save me, all's upturned, and I don't know where I stand!'

He saw her distress; he must master his nerves; he must speak to her like a physician. 'Calmly now, patience; sit down, tell me everything. Tell it from the beginning, don't presume to know your symptoms till they're all laid out in front of me, and I have a chance to review them. "Objective": the word makes sense to you? I used it often enough in *The All-Science Book.*'

'Very well. From the beginning. But I don't know the beginning. I sent you that letter.'

'You did. You chose to reveal yourself and so destroy the hold *he* had on you – ' he would not dignify Ulrich with a name ' – and on me, and on my son. You now hold *him*. But it's tenuous. And there's a price. Are you come now to tell me you've found you've got to pay it?'

'Ah Christ but I made sure that when he printed this book for them, he'd do it so dreadful badly; and he has! How can I say why I made so sure? Just to jump on his dirty belly, same way that he jumped onto mine; oh I wanted him to bloody *wallow!*'

'Ah yes of course, most passionate daughter of your mother, never hurt without returning hurt, *nemo me impune lacessit*, well? *Vindicta splendida*, well? Revenge must brightly shine? For you are as you were made, alas. Need you search for a deeper motive?'

'No, but you see, I had to go further; put my own hands to Fortune's wheel and to spin it for myself, never mind *her*; she's a jealous bitch, blindfolded Fortune, she don't like it, never did; she breeds more malice than even *I* do – you told me her stories, often enough, of the fall of orgulous princes!'

Then she recounted all she had done; what she had hoped might come of it; her design in regard to Ludwig.

Fortunatus compelled himself to show no amazement; he considered the matter, physician-like, humming a low tune, and tapping his fingers together. 'No, the Dominicans very speedily would put a stop to *that* game, ill-conceived, dangerous . . . unless it were a *fait accompli*. It could still be a *fait accompli*. After Augsberg (I hear) those two to Prague. There are Hussite heretics yet in Prague, raising their refractory heads, Kraemer will have much to do there, and Sprenger will stay to help him, if the Bohemian king permits: which he ought not! There is a treaty, he gave his word he would *protect* his Hussite subjects. But whichever way, delay. Still time to fulfil your notion. So what has changed your mind? Is it Ludwig? Ah, my unhappy son, the crooked arrow in your quiver: are you sure he would have agreed?'

'I have not seen him since – since – not seen him for a very long time. I would have asked him, face to face, as *I* am, and as *he* is, ruined bodies, dead hearts, all of it. If he accepted, well and good. If not – oh if not – perhaps once again a *blue bottle*? And make damn sure to tell no one I'd drunk it till the venom fulfilled its work.' She bowed her head in her hands. He waited. 'But no!' she cried, all in a breath: 'that wasn't it, not Ludwig, not at all, oh I tell you I was ready for Ludwig. No: the book itself, the *Hammer*, what do you know of it?'

'Nothing. Except the name, which is not propitious.' And then suddenly, 'Sacrament, child! You have an insolence, to think to inveigle my son to give help to a book of that species! But who's to say I might not have let him, if only to laugh at their duncehood? What do *you* know of it? You can't read it?'

'No I can't, nor did I trouble myself. Until today. When I heard it read.' She told him just what she had heard, and how.

She said, 'They have gone mad. So mad with love for their Virgin Mary that they seek to be rid of all the women in the world who cannot match Her matchless obedience; they have written this book to tell pope, bishops, princes, judges, to catch and hold all women, and to torture us one by one until we all of us confess that as Eve's daughters we are the Devil's wives, and then with a clear conscience all the men in the world can burn us! This is the most terrible book ever written; and I have helped to bring it about. And did I plan to have *your son* help my help? God, what is to be done with me?'

Fortunatus was at a loss. He tried to tell her she hyperbolised, that all priests, being a eunuch tribe, necessarily slandered women; but to overmaster their chief arguments, one had to disregard it, a clot of gristle in a mouthful of meat, spit it out and keep chewing . . . *'Non'st bonum,'* he muttered, 'you don't believe what I'm saying to you; neither do I.' He changed his tack and tried to tell her that if in truth she had hit the true meaning of their book, then Kraemer and Sprenger were not only mad, but heretics; and as soon as their work was published the fact would be detected . . . *'Non'st bonum,'* once again; for even as he framed the words, he knew they were nonsense. How to assess the Inquisitors' heresy, they themselves being the authorised judges of it?

The most diabolical ravings, when written by such men, would be set out with such apparently irrefutable logic, such respect for theological system, that the labour of exposing it would throw into question the whole of that system from the very beginning, going back through Aquinas and all his learned predecessors to the earliest Fathers, to Saint Paul, even to Christ; or so it would seem. He did not think it could be done. Who dare attempt it? They'd be condemned before they so much as laid down their heads of argument.

He himself, with his own book, had made his modest attack upon the structures of superstition; and look what had happened. The fact was, the great men of church, state, philosophy, law, were all of them terrified; all their power was going rotten on them, they had abused it so many years, all they could do was to spread their terror; till the disaffected people became as frightened as the tyrants and huddled to the tyrants for protection, hating whatever 'enemy' the tyrants pointed out to them. Jews, infidels, heretics, *women*? It had happened often enough before. Yes, it was quite probable that Kraemer and Sprenger's inner intentions were exactly what Hulda said they were.

'Dear child, it is quite probable, but what is to be done?'

'With me? I am asking *you.*'

'You must answer for yourself, child. Or put the question to my broken son.' All at once he was cold and savage; he saw wolves between frozen pine trees racing to devour; out of his fear he would hurl anyone into their path to hasten his own escape. His compassion, for the moment, quenched; but his brain went tick-tock-tick. 'I meant, what is to be done with the witch-book. If it were no more than a manuscript, two or three copies, or even twenty, it would struggle in great men's libraries here and there with all their other books; and some would believe it, and some would call it mad; some would have it copied, others would take one look at it and cram it to oblivion in the cobwebs of their upper shelves. There would be harm done, but not great harm. As it is, it has been printed. Or will have been printed. To be repeated *ad infinitum*, until all the terrified men have read it, from Portugal to the Swedish north, have believed it, and will act upon it. My terror of them is even greater than theirs is of science. And I tell you, it cannot be stopped.'

'Oh it can, I can set the house on fire. Burn every damned page of the book, the book wants to burn *me*. Burn Grosskerl as well, why not?'

'And again the fool hyperbolises. Do you suppose the only manuscript is the one in your printing shop? They'll have had it copied as they wrote it, *they're* not the fools; it'll be locked in an iron strongbox in some stone-walled stone-vaulted priory – Nuremberg, Cologne, Salzburg, who knows where?' He rose from his chair and snarled at her, his fear was turning to hatred: '*To enlighten and delight the world*, your father's noble trade has begotten in you this minotaur, you bring it forth to its monstrous birth; and there is nothing to be done.'

She trod backwards from him in horror, feeling her way towards the door; an articulated skeleton hung from a ceiling beam, white, polished, ominous; it swayed as the edge of her cloak caught an arm, a rib, a projecting hip; jolted clear of its hook, it fell to the floor in a chaos of rattling bones. 'You yourself are Sprenger and Kraemer!' she cried. 'Oh now do I hear what you say. It is the fault of Eve's daughter? Guilt of the woman? So root her out!'

She would have fled from that place altogether, to go wild about the world to her death very probably: but Ludwig prevented her.

He had heard the raised voices from his room at the back of the house. He knew it was Hulda; he fought with himself, to go to her or not? He knew it was Hulda, in extremity of despair; he knew that his father, for whatever reason, was failing her. He knew that he himself had failed her. Twisted upon two crutches, he compelled himself to the surgery, one leg bent inward, one leg out, his once fat fubsy neck all awry for ever and as scrawny as a plucked fowl's in the poulterer's.

Hard to tell, at that moment, what he thought of her, or she of him. All beauty, all desire, had gone: there was repulsion, there was remorse, hard anger at what each had inflicted upon the other. There must also have been love, or why else was he in the surgery, why had she stopped in the doorway the moment she heard his crutches shuffle and tap on the floorboards? But they did not touch, they spoke no greeting; old Fortunatus, staring hopelessly at them, could not see that their eyes even met. Ludwig demanded to be told what had been said. His father complied, no fudging, direct declaration; and added: 'She says *I* am Sprenger and Kraemer; she blames me that I blame her. Which is true; so I do. And not true; I blame *you* equally. And yet not true neither: you are wretched be-slimed organisms, the beast-with-two-backs split again into component duality! Blame you? Blame *Lustfrau* Venus who flung you together? Or *Strafefrau* Nemesis who tore you apart? I wrote once, "Out of NOTHING is the sorcery made." We go forward from the *zero*, we are driven back again behind it; *plus* and *minus* are equal entities; and no free will of our own can determine our current direction.'

'Why, Father, you used never to say so. You spoke always of our unconquerable mind.'

'So I did. But now no longer. For a few minutes, just now, the anger of my niece toward – toward *that man –* ' (again, he meant Ulrich, and again he would not name him) ' – her anger seemed to show me that she had not been conquered: but then she told me different. Seeking revenge, she fell to slavery; she is bondswoman to the crime of the witch book; and herself and you and me are dwelling irrevocably in the wasted dominion of *minus*.'

He stumbled past them, dragging his feet through his wrecked skeleton, out vaguely toward the kitchen, broken words in his throat about a hot drink to warm the chill, it was gripping his vitals; he tried to call for his housekeeper to see was the kettle boiled? And then the frost upon his heart caught tighter, he fell dead at the stair's foot.

Hulda stayed in her uncle's house until after the funeral; and neither she nor Ludwig gave a damn for the expostulations of the parish priest. Ulrich took no notice, or appeared to take no notice; which many people thought strange. But so few were now interested in Ulrich. He had become the black-friars' man, and pursued dealings with no one else. The day of Fortunatus' death he had had his final quarrel with the guildsmen at the *Rathaus*. He was still reckoned a city father, but none of his colleagues wished to talk to him. And he still had to finish the witchcraft book.

Fortunatus was buried with all the honour and solemnity that could be mustered. He had always been poor: the guilds paid for his requiem and attended it in ceremonial force (Ulrich of course did not); elaborate eulogies were spoken. He was described as a 'loyal son of the Church' by several successive clergymen, including *Bruder* Herwald who commended *The All-Science Book* as a great work of Christian scholarship. Hulda, in black veils at the back of the congregation, was ignored by everybody. Ludwig, beside her, returned no reply to the men and women who offered him condolence; and hobbled away with her home as soon as the earth was thrown into the grave. The guilds gave a funerary supper to which Ludwig was invited: he did not trouble to go.

SEVENTEEN

What was Ludwig doing while the city fathers drank their wine and swallowed their bakemeats? With Hulda to help him, and his crutches, he went upon the prowl through the empty house (Fortunatus' few servants had been paid off, except for the housekeeper who had her own place that evening at the lower end of the *Rathaus* banquet); together, hotly and fiercely, they searched upstairs and down, in cupboards and drawers and strongboxes and medicine jars and between the leaves of books, for some clue to the hiding place of the unexpurgated *All-Science* folios. Why? They had hardly spoken since the death of the old man, except to say one thing, upon which they were both agreed: 'Free will is unconquerable: believe otherwise and a free city is impossible here or anywhere.' Ludwig said it first, Hulda repeated it. To find the folios would prove it true. The Inquisitors had sent men to make their own vain search, men very well trained for it. Not surprising that Ludwig and Hulda were able to find nothing. The night grew dark; and still nothing. And then suddenly Hulda discovered. Her uncle's voice among her murkiest memories: 'In the teeth of the adversary'. Literally, 'the adversary' had meant Herwald, of course. Allegorically, usually Satan. But her uncle, a physician – what principal foe would *he* think of, if not Death? And must the teeth be allegorical too?

She forced open the ghastly mouth of the collapsed and dismembered skeleton; there it was! A small screw of paper (not at all notable, had she seen it in some more plausible place, she'd have tossed it aside), a receipted bill, '*Moneys due to Gerlach the Painter, being cost of the flower-pattern for* Herr Doktor *Albrecht on every wall of his house-place as ready lined with sized canvas*', so many hours' work, so many guilders, '*paid and given thanks for, God reward such early payment; upon this fifth day after Easter*, ann. dom. MCCCCLXXXIII'.

(Which had been the day before the publication-day of *The All-Science Book*. Ludwig remembered, how could he forget? He had had to go again to Frankfort, more library work for his father. Indeed the day of the beatings was the day after he came back, the first chance for full two weeks he and Hulda had found to 'rest their bones' with *Lustfrau* Venus, and hence their insensate carelessness. So all of Holy Week he was away: his father had a generous custom to let housekeeper, apprentice, and garden-boy home to their own kin through the sacred season. When Ludwig returned, he found the house-place – a room some twenty feet by fifteen – new-stencilled with snowdrop flowers, white speckles against green grass tufts, from floor to ceiling, and Gerlach wiping off his brushes ready to leave.)

'Those walls,' he now told Hulda, 'those walls had no canvas. Wainscot, and painted, red and blue, lozenge work. My father himself, alone in the house, must have lined and varnished every foot.'

And so he had. They ran for knives and tore at the snowdrops, pulling canvas away in strips. Under the canvas were sheets of print, pasted overlapping with flour-and-water in two layers face to the wall, hundreds of them. 'An entire copy of his book, every page, it's all here! For us to deal with as we will, if we can but get them down without hurt to them: warm water ought to do it. O God, it'll take hours. Let the housekeeper go to bed when she comes in, from her room she cannot hear us, we must work and work all night.'

They boiled water, found mops and a washtub and a couple of spatulas, made sure the shutters were tightly closed, lit more candles than was financially prudent; and did indeed work and work. They kindled a great fire in the stove and hung the sodden papers all about it to dry. They had hard trouble to separate them; many sheets were torn, but few irreversibly damaged. By morning, they had not finished. The housekeeper came down, found the door of the house-place bolted, knocked and called out in alarm. Hulda said, 'Let her in. I know her; she's a good woman; she'll only see what she needs to see.' Muck, mess and confusion: whether she needed or not, she could not help seeing it. She gaped in amazement. Ludwig turned upon her, light-headed, it seemed, with his grief: 'Did you not know, *Frau Haushaelterin*, how my father despised these damned snow-drops? He said Gerlach mocked him, laying symbols of verdant youth upon the walls of a sad old man! For his memory, his honour-in-death, they must all be scraped away! So we scrape.' The woman was a handsome widow no older than fifty; suspected of having consoled (now and again) Fortunatus' own widowed bed; she knew nothing of any such resentment against the snowdrops. Also, she too had been questioned by the Hounds of God. She thought Ludwig was a fool to try to deceive her.

'You're a fool, *Meister* Ludwig; and more than a fool, for you have not thought at all of what to do next! And you'll need to do *something*. That Herwald was at the funeral supper: he sought me out on purpose. Asked me did I know your intentions? Asked me did Cousin Hulda sleep in your room here, or in another? I gave him the truth, that you had in mind to undertake a legal practice, as they taught you at Bologna; but had not yet felt fit for it; also that you and she neither slept, ate, nor spoke together, as far as I could tell. But if I am asked it a second time I'll have to say you both strip walls: don't you think that will cause them to think? In my view she must depart. Depart today; and take these with her. I don't ask what they are. If you don't tell me, I can tell the priests they were rubbish papers to be sold to bookbinders for the making of pasteboard. Your father left so little money, you might just as well sell all the papers you can find. Poor old bastard, he was so brave; and so very very frightened.'

Her advice may have been good; but they were almost too long about taking it. While they argued how and why, wearily through the morning – where was Hulda to go, what was she to do with *The All-Science Book*, was it possible for Ludwig to help her? – they did not think (but perhaps should have done, if they'd had their wits about them) that Heinrich Kraemer might be back in town. And indeed he was at the printing house.

For he had never been to Prague at all; Fortunatus was misinformed. Sprenger had had to go straight from Augsburg to Cologne, and he left it to his colleague to revisit Nuremberg and inspect progress of work upon the book. The work was in a bad state and Kraemer said so; he was peremptory, indeed brutal. Ulrich excused himself no less brutally; he denounced his own wife as a witch.

Kraemer was not surprised. He had already been talking with the young amanuensis at the priory, and with Herwald. The evidences were clear, once you knew what you were looking for. Ambition, and lust, and malice, and secret-hearted treachery; what she had said to the boy Georg; her disgusting appearance (for witchcraft at length will show in the flesh, the Devil's features, as it were, ever-present under the delusive skin; seeming beautiful though the woman may once have been); her destruction of a husband after luring him to deeds of love in an unbearably ecstatic bed; her destruction of a lover (*ditto*); what she had said to Hermann and the compositor, and the cruel violence of her attack on them; her encouragement of her uncle to persist with his infidel writings; her present desertion of her lawful domicile: and most cogent of all, the malevolent skill with which she had consistently misdirected the great venture of the *Hammer* contract. 'Satan's self inserted, between type and ink, ink and paper.'

Had the Inquisitor been able to do all that he wished, he would have had Hulda stripped and chained within the hour, every inch of her body's hair shaved lest it conceal the devil's tokens, while the torture was made ready to extract her confession. He would have had every person from the printing house, and Fortunatus' house, into dungeons in the same space of time, awaiting their turns to testify, awaiting thumbscrews if their depositions were not strictly to the purpose. Inconveniently, this was

Nuremberg. He could not proceed without episcopal warrant, and episcopal warrant could not be executed until the secular power (the inner council of aldermen) had itself allowed the process. He did obtain a warrant from the *Rathaus* for the summoning of Hulda. But he had to wait for it until evening. The secular power had always been very good friends with Fortunatus, and still had sympathy for his niece. The secular power was not at all good friends with Ulrich. Not only did the secular power initiate delay; even worse, it put the word out.

Ludwig and Hulda received their warning, from an off-duty constable-of-the-watch, some time around noon. At sunset, when the summoner came, there was no one at home but Ludwig, hobbling on his crutches up and down the house-place, foolishly whitewashing and re-whitewashing the walls, weeping for the loss of his father and the failure of his handsome body. His housekeeper, he said, was in such grief he had sent her away to her own people. Hulda, he said, had indeed been with him a few days, compassion had compelled him, she had so loved Fortunatus; but he had had to turn her out; she was a remembrance of sin and he could not endure it. No doubt she was where she should be, under the roof of her husband?

In fact she was already out of the jurisdiction, hidden among casks and bales in a carrier's ox-wagon travelling north along jolting roads, its wheels mired to the axle. The carrier was a brother-in-law of Fortunatus' housekeeper. The physician had once healed his ulcerated leg when a barber-surgeon was about to cut it off: there was nothing he would not do for the safety of the niece. He was not to bring her very far; twenty-five miles at most. He had an aunt in a forest village between Erlangen and Bayreuth.

The housekeeper had said, 'No better place to stay than that clever woman's cottage; they thought *she* was a witch once, till she learned to hide her good sense, and moved to another district, which (thank God) she was rich enough to do. She knows well now what to avoid to keep the fools from talking. All her fault as a girl was, she showed opinions over-loud; said women should live with women; she refused to be wed. Add to which her gift with animals; why, she'll chat with them like human beings. She lives these days very quiet, never quarrels with anyone, gives money to the church, looks after her old friend, that deaf-and-dumb Johanna as queer as they come, and all her dogs and cats; they think in the village they're a pair of holy hermits (which very well may be, it's as likely as the other).'

Hulda could stay with her until word for good or bad might be brought again out of Nuremberg. Or so it was arranged: but in her heart Hulda wanted no news whatever from Nuremberg, not ever again; never to go back there, the city and its people had killed her. But where *could* she go?

And what would she do with the unbound tattered book that she carried in her sordid bundle?

What she did with it was to read it. She helped the aunt with the care of the animals, and sat in silence many hours, enduring the strange sweet silent smiles and caresses of Johanna, a fragile pale beautiful woman like a Palm Sunday frond, at least sixty years old, who never went out of the house. But whenever she had time to be private, and the light was sufficient despite continuous foul weather, Hulda pored over the physician's precepts with a kind of half-mad diligence. The aunt encouraged her. Johanna smiled sceptically and stroked Hulda's hands: encouragement, discouragement? It could have been either.

And then one day (to her huge surprise) she found herself able to cure a child in the village whose stomach pains brought it near death. But she made the mistake of letting folk discover she had found how to do it 'out of print-writing'. The parents mistrusted the cure, saying the child had never really been sick in the first place.

Great irony, Hulda told herself: how this printing of *The All-Science Book*, that should have sent its enlightening text end to end of the Germanies, had produced but a single parcel kept by one small terrified fugitive in a narrow backwards place; where its insufficient superstition caused the people to despise its value. Her uncle had been quite right in his first idea for its title; but alas it was now too late to be calling it *The Old Wife Book*; the damage had been done.

When the carrier came again his news was disconcerting. His sister-in-law, and Ludwig, all of a sudden had gone to prison. Kraemer, now joined again by Sprenger, had been tirelessly urging the city to follow up the affair; they had secured a strong support from the diocesan authorities, who in turn had used the imperial officials in the Castle to press the *Rathaus* to take action. Bail had at once been offered, and the prisoners were now free. No knowing for how long. The carrier himself had been questioned. Had it not been for a snowstorm, he might well have been followed today.

Oh yes, he added, another thing; that shitehouse Grosskerl was bankrupt. His book for the Hounds of God being just finished in nick of time, the buggers had forced him to pay to cover the costs of their finding *Frau* Hulda. House and business sold at auction; he'd had to shift his nasty carcass to the priory, a sort of lay brother, under wicked discipline. 'Good,' snarled Hulda, 'very good. But your brave sister, and my brave cousin! Ah no! They'll be *tortured*?'

'Ah no! the city council's never going to let them, at least it keeps saying not. And *Meister* Glueck has become a fierce lawyer, he whirls about him every word of the statutes like a broadsword fighter at a fair. No, I suppose they won't be tortured. But if they should be – '

'If they should be, I must guess they will tell. Ah Christ, it is dead winter, I have only my two feet.'

Johanna was making signs with her hands: the aunt interpreted. Hulda must go, snowstorm or not; but Johanna could tell her *where* to go. Johanna had her memories of curious friends in unusual places, Hulda knew that. She listened carefully to the names she was told.

EIGHTEEN

A long long time after that, and a very long time after that, Hag Hulda in her deep-forest hovel could perhaps remember how she got there, but as she never told anyone, no one could ever tell. It may be that she early decided: they hunted her for a witch, Johanna's old friends were called witches, so among witches she must move.

Where she found such people, what she said to them, what they said to her, and what they taught her, are questions as dark as the forest. You may be sure she did not discover much likeness between the truth of it and the great lies of the black-friars' book. Let us suppose she learned spells and incantations, methods of cure (both for mind and body); and curious understandings of God and of creation, of the earth, of the skies, of birds and beasts and fishes, of women and men, of the seasons of the year, that owed little to Christian priest-teaching: probably the Christian priest-teaching owed much to such lore but would never admit it. No doubt Christ, as the Son of His Mother, had been taught a great deal of it (although the books that described Him made sure that what He learned had long been forgotten or turned toward a quite different meaning).

If Hag Hulda found lovers, no one knew who they were (men or women), or whether in any sense they could have loved her in return. This was not because folk thought her hideous (which she was); no woman is so hideous there is not a beauty about her somewhere, and somewhere a lover to discover it. No: but another reason. Hulda had her secret; she was *a witch with a book*; it could be said to be a sort of witch book, so many old wives had gone into its making; but it was also, undeniably, a science book, and therefore might be thought to throw doubt upon her present life even as it doubted the priest-life of the churches. The very fact that she had it, closed her mouth and closed her heart among witch-people no less than if she lived in the church-world. If it enlightened and delighted her loneliness, it can scarcely have freed her from whatever sorrow she might have felt that there was no one to share with her its learning.

In the eighth year of the *Luther Days*, which to church-people was 1525 AD, the peasants of nearly all Germany ('honest folk of workshop and tillage land') rose in rebellion against their intolerable lords. The churches, both old and new (which is to say, of Rome and of Wittenberg), came together to withstand them: bishops threw holy water against them, pastors roared from pulpits, noblemen drove steel through so many hungry bodies that gold-braided right sleeves sopped with blood to the armpit. Wheels raised on poles lined roads and village playfields, with captured men across the spokes, and ravens eating the men. Soldiers stormed through the fens and forests.

There was a huntsman called Erwin. He lived about three miles from Hag Hulda's hut. When Gretchen his wife lost first one child unborn, and then another, and another, he had brought her to Hulda, who prepared her herbs and roots, and gave her news about what to do and what not to do with her body and limbs during the months of her swelling womb. Also she made her learn a number of rhymes, without which the woman would never have believed the other matters.

One blazing hot day, the forest alive with stinging insects, Erwin came up through the trees at a run; he called and cried for Hulda. The sweat of his running blackened his shirt, his hand flailed against the flies and mosquitoes, his breath surged in great gasps.

He shouted out that the length of his valley was filling with men in flight, a great battle had been lost by the peasants, the soldiers were after them and striking them down, like flies. 'They have ridden into the village, horse-troopers of the Elector, where never a man of ours went to the rebellion, there is a pastor with them, out of his wits; God, he will have them murder all the women of the village, to bind them, to burn them, my Gretchen, she is with child, he says she is to be the first! Ah God,' he groaned, 'ah Sacrament,' holding his heaving breast and staggering against a tree, 'are they tired of hunting rebels that they turn to the chase of witches? What man can have told them of your salvation for Gretchen's womb and how she told it to the other women? The pastor has his Latin book and all is printed out in it. He asks them this question and that, and the soldiers do his bidding with whips and with knives: I tell you, *Jungfrau* Hulda – ' (he was never one for discourtesy, he had always treated Hulda with more than respect) ' – before nightfall he'll have forced all the women to admit it! That they've all been a-flight to the Brocken to fill their clefts with Satan's seed! And if they don't admit, he damns them equally, for is not Satan the Father of their Lies?'

'He has a *book*!'

'He calls it his *hammer*, he says it is a papalist book, he says *Herr Doktor* Luther says the papalists only partly understand the work of the Devil but this book is the best part of their knowledge; God must have spoken direct to its writers, even though they wrote it for Rome. Can you come, can you help? Cast a spell and drive him out? I tried, with my crossbow, but God help me, the string broke: I think the Devil stretched his horn and cut it, all

I could do was run for you. If you cannot help then save yourself. They know who you are and where you are.' He sprawled on the grass, unable to speak further, unable to move.

Hulda plunged down through the forest, avoiding the usual path, as fast as she could go, catching her feet in briars and roots, slashing at ferns with her stick; she fell twice, wrenched her ankle, it took her near upon two hours. The village was in the bottom of a steep pine-shadowed gorge, not more than a half-dozen houses and a little church with no pastor, a very backwards place indeed. When she got there she was too late, for any good she could have done anyway.

The place was full of soldiers, bandaged and bloodstained and drunken. The corpses of rout-stricken men from the battle lay in blood all along the path. Villagers crouched in terror, they skirled like a flock of birds. A cottage was on fire, pouring thick smoke across the valley; and from within the flames a dreadful screaming; half of the roof crashed, the screaming ceased, a roar of vivid sparks went up into the smoke.

A white-faced young man in a black preacher's gown (he might have been Ulrich Grosskerl, if Ulrich Grosskerl had drunk from the Fountain of Youth) waved a great book in both his hands and howled out Latin words from it. When he put them into the German tongue, Hulda knew what words they were. She stood at the fringe of the forest, unnoticed by anyone there, seeing them all, hearing.

The young man closed his book, looked up through the smoke to the copper-coloured glaring sky, and brought his discourse to an end, thus: 'Now we have it, we comprehend, all is clear, we saw our duty. The mathematician said it, even though he was a pagan Greek, "*Quod erat demonstrandum, eureka, QED!*" The rebellion is a sin; all sin is from the Devil; the Devil's wives disperse his sin through the tainted *penetralia* of their womanhood; six women have confessed to carnal congress with the Devil; therefore these women did cause the rebellion; these women, oh most godly soldiers, did murder your slain comrades. You heard them confess it. Saw them burn in the burning house. And the Lord through His Glorious Mercy shall be praised for evermore.' He said 'Amen,' and so shook through the whole of his body that the book fell out of his hands.

Hag Hulda ran straight towards him, snatched the book from the ground, and hurled it into the heart of the fire. She gave hoarse voice to a few words, hardly heard, variously reported. The pastor, who was nearest her, said afterwards he thought them: '*My* book! No one's but mine; no making of it, but for me. No murder here, if not for me. Hulda's fire, she lit it herself; Hulda's book, and she burns beside it!' Whereupon, into the flames with a huge springing leap seeming impossible to one of her age; and the rest of the roof came tumbling and flaring down on her, covering her, covering her cries.

The pastor said afterwards that whatever her words meant they were a clear confession of devil worship, as clear as any of the other witches': he was told who she was, by one who had often been to her for treatment of his ailments. It was this man that denounced Erwin's Gretchen and the other five; and now he led pastor and soldiers up the forest to show them Hulda's hut that they might all find out her secret.

They found Erwin, and hanged him. They found the cat and thrust it squalling into a horse-trooper's knapsack. They burst the door of the inner room, and found nothing; except bunches of herbs, flasks of strange liquors, and a heap of *All-Science Book*, mildewed and falling to pieces, held together with twisted thongs.

It was wrapped between sheets of parchment, whitey-gold when it had been new, but now so discoloured it more resembled dead nettles in the slime of a dried-up drain.

The pastor looked through the pages. Of themselves they seemed no harm; but the place where he found them was a Temple of the Unholy, so therefore they must be a hell-book. He drowned them in the well, and the soldiers threw the cat down after them.

A month or two later, when the killing of the peasants throughout the Saxon lands and Thuringia was more or less finished, he made his way back to Wittenberg. Replacing the burned *Hammer* came hard upon his pocket. It had already cost him heavily to follow the Elector's colours, for he was not paid as a regular chaplain: he acted out of pure zeal against human anarchy; out of his great love for Christ's Church, now reformed.

But he soon found another copy; there were so many of them on sale, printed all over the Christian world.

Forty-one years earlier, a slovenly Pope bewildered by what he sensed were the frenzies and collapses of the Church beyond the reach of Rome, had casually accepted the labyrinthine thesis of Heinrich and Jakob. If the Devil was at large in Germany, then no doubt two holy Germans were the best men to know how to cage him? At all events, their book need not disturb nepotic complacency. So the Pope let loose his bull (or minotaur); and thought little more of the matter.

This story began by saying that books will lose authority as their numbers increase – 'in the long run', at any rate. *Malleus Maleficarum* had a long run of some two centuries.

Catholics accepted it, or *said* they did; although some were more poisoned by it than others.

The new Protestants accepted it; at first because they thought it proved how the augmentation of the Devil's Empire was inseparable from the growth of papal pretension; attack one and you're inevitably matched against the other.

Women frequently accepted it. Perhaps it gave them a strange comfort, this doctrine that told them they possessed the secret power of dismantling the good order of men. They even accepted year upon year the torture and murder of other women (particularly of masterless women who had skills that challenged the craft guilds); until the process became so natural that no one seemed to notice with what intensity it took place. It is said that when women who accepted it were arraigned in their own turn, they at first protested innocence but then (having been forced to confess) were perverted by their inquisitors into believing their own confessions; so their deaths in a sense appeared 'natural'. Of course, war upon all women is not a war that can be *won*; but it did change their nature, turning many of them willy-nilly into the bondswomen of *Malleus*; and to that extent the holocaust succeeded.

Often, too, it changed the nature of humane chroniclers who wrote (and had printed) well-attested books upon the wars of the world and the massacres, and did not think to mention this one. Nor did they think how, because of it, example could be taken; and all manner of other categories of 'Devil's people' devised and (year upon year) consigned for abolition.

Which is not to say it was never recounted anywhere, or this tale would not have been possible; but for all the world truly knows of it – meaning; *know*, so that we live with it always as we live with our own bowels and must void them or we die – the proofsheets of each printing of the terrible records might have been dropped into a well, or pasted to a wainscot and painted all over with snowdrops.

Nineteenth Century (after Christ)

USES OF IRON

Uses of Iron

Limping Hephaestus had a score of bellows blowing
  under his furnace to heat the crucibles: the flames
  leapt high, the metals melted. He set up his great
  anvil, took his tongs and heavy hammer, went to
  work. He forged a huge shield and embellished it with
  intricate devices.

He engraved upon it two prosperous towns.

The first was filled with weddings and festivities, complexity of dances to
  the music of flutes and lyres:
Also citizens crowding the market around the sacred place of justice.

The second town was besieged by enemies who could not decide
  whether to sack it directly, or permit it to surrender and thus ensure a
  more accurate division of captives and spoil; the craftsman-god
  engraved the shapes of Strife, and Tumult, and Death.
                        Homer: the *Iliad*, Book 18

ONE

They all saw at once the enormity of the innovation, but not many could be
sure just what was going to change and how. The first ever railway to run
regular trains for passengers, between Liverpool and Manchester (year
1830, King George IV just dead but liberty obstructed everywhere);
exciting and frightening, whether for good or for bad.

Joe Sandars, the Liverpool merchant who conceived the project, wished
only (at the start) to break the canal company's monopoly. His fellow
director Brandreth shared the intention but thought steam-engines should
not be used – 'Unnatural, unreliable – all Englishmen of worth know how
to handle horses!' – steam on such a scale involved a new type of citizen
whose specialised skill would be socially disruptive and inherently
undesirable – 'Uppity rogues, keep 'em out of it!'

William Huskisson, MP for Liverpool, carried the railway bill through
parliament as a contribution to reform. It helped him lose his place in the

Duke of Wellington's cabinet; when his old friends (still in office) reproached him for his zeal, he would sardonically point out that the trains were to run to Manchester – had they forgotten Peterloo, only eleven years before? Did they want it to happen again? Leave Manchester isolated, and it certainly *would*.

They replied (and the duke did not contradict them) that cheap mass-transport pandered to the unsettled instincts of a severely disturbed population.

The disturbed population had not altogether made up its mind what to think; like everyone else, its individuals were frightened and excited. Many were ready to believe almost anything, bad or good. In times of hunger, slump, repression, *all* change was in some sort to be welcomed, if only for the chance of a re-affirmation of protest.

George Stephenson, who built the railway, and ensured his son's firm would be building the locomotives for it, had by far the clearest notion of the consequence. He foresaw what he called (coining a vivid phrase and illustrating it with swift passes of his stubby fingers) 'A net-work of lines' all over the country, improving everyone's business, and particularly his own; he meant to be rich, he meant to be famous; why, he was to reshape England! From no education but a powerful intellect – *poetic* intellect, almost: he knew it, he needed it recognised.

The trains began running upon a day of disaster and mishap, of the ludicrous and the sinister: were the crowds who flocked to see them so affected by the experience that their lives would be changed for ever? Not really. Because most of them – invited magnates, local notables, independent sightseers, an actress or two (brought there to heighten an already theatrical spectacle), hostile demonstrators (among them enthusiastic socialists of an ideology as fresh as the railway itself) – had lives already filled to overflowing with priorities of their *own business*. So they offered the succession of untoward happenings little more than inattentive and divided emotions, distracted reflections, quirks of their privacy or prejudice.

The beginning of the railway occurred, it was experienced, it had been. In its own right, by rights, it was a never-before-known never-to-be-forgotten *astonishment*: in fact at the time people found it a dangerous muddle, assumed they'd get used to it, absorbed it into their daily preoccupations as it might be a new item of diet, and wondered had there not probably been a great deal of fuss over nothing?

And yet they were well aware it was by no means a nothing. Too much novelty all at once can deaden the expected responses, while at the same time heightening other ones, and only long afterwards surprising the memory.

*

It had chanced, eleven months earlier, that *Novelty* was the name given to one of the four locomotive engines put on public trial for the prize offered by the directors. She was the smallest of them, and without doubt the most beautiful. Beautiful, that is to say, to any gentleman who had studied the charms of scientific fitness and mechanical artistry from clock motions, distillers' apparatus, astronomers' telescopes, or the paraphernalia required to produce galvanic electricity. Moreover, to connoisseurs of the horse-carriage, she offered a pleasing reminder that the new modes of transport did not necessarily imply a complete breach with existing standards (possibly higher than had been known since the days of the Antonine emperors) of elegant and craftsmanlike construction. She was so compact that almost all her workings were able to be concealed beneath a flat light platform-frame of slender iron, royal blue with gold edging, gracefully set upon four generously proportioned royal-blue wheels, their spokes and fellies picked out with scarlet, and concentric gold circles to each hub; there was a gleaming brass handrail around the rim of the frame; and at its rear end, rising to about the height of a man's shoulders from the platform, a small vertical boiler cylinder of copper, polished no less brightly than the handrail.

The sight of two serious, closely shaved young enginemen strolling up and down the length of the vehicle in snow-white overalls, poising accurate shovels of coke in their gloved hands and periodically applying yet more polish to the brasswork, was at once to call to mind the impeccable quarter-deck of a king's ship made ready for review.

It was known that her designer was Swedish (although no one had seen him and she was certainly built in London): and to those few Englishmen familiar with the indefinably Lutheran austerity of Baltic craftwork, the information was bound to give comfort. That such superlative mechanisms should replace the warm-blooded horse was perhaps after all no great tragedy for the culture of civilisation.

The engine trials had more of the atmosphere of a race meeting than a crisis of engineering ideologies. Bets were being laid. Shrewd men in riding coats slapped *Novelty*'s brazen rump and looked, as it were, into her teeth. Gypsies told fortunes and beggars importunately begged. A sharper laying out his pea-and-thimble game for a gullible group of warehouse clerks (illicitly absent from work) informed them that he guessed the crowd at five thousand already, and like-as-not as many to come. The double line of new rail shot a mile in either direction through the flat misty countryside, straight as a spear and level as a well-aimed spear throw – indeed by the new surveyors' jargon this place was now termed the Rainhill Level, where

before it had been Coalpit Fields – and then dropped out of sight down the
inclines; westward some seven miles to Liverpool, east twenty-two into
Manchester.

Upon one of the tracks an extraordinary contraption had clattered into
motion; a flat wagon mounting a sort of treadmill; a sweating horse upon
the treadmill, held in by a wooden breastwork, whipped up to gallop
nowhere by a profane fellow in a postilion's outfit perched aloft behind the
beast's haunches. The treadmill was geared to the wheels; very slowly and
uncertainly it shuffled the wagon forward. This was *Cycloped*, otherwise
known as 'Brandreth's Wonder', the horse-loving director's notion of how
carriage trains could be pulled without total surrender to power-hungry
engineers. Joe Sandars had reminded Brandreth that the essential concept
of his device had already been found wanting by majority of votes upon the
Liverpool and Manchester Railway Company's board, there was no chance
at all of its reconsideration; but if he liked he could have it shunted up and
down for an hour or so at the beginning of the day to amuse the 'juvenile
element'.

The juvenile element was rowdy, it let out a jeering cheer: for
'Brandreth's Wonder' slowed and stopped, the slats of the treddle floor
choked with the morning's accumulation of horse dung, humiliating,
malodorous, adhesive, gears clogged, blows and swear-words alike useless.
The angry driver must climb from his high roost, reverse his whip, poke
and prod with its handle amidst hilarious abuse, flicking muck at his
tormentors, reviling them along with the incontinence of his steed,
smearing his mirror-glass boots, splattering his tight buff breeches.

Then a yell towards the frolicking youth: 'Get off of it, out of it, *get off
o't'bloody rail there!' Novelty* was on the move, they were in danger of being
run down.

Two men stood apart and watched her bullet-like rapidity, the hissing rattle
of her passage, with particular attention. One elderly and one young, in black
frock-coats and severe stovepipe hats. They shared a strong resemblance;
both faces appeared to have been cut out of timber and left only part-finished
by the carver. The elderly face hewn solely with an adze, the younger
improved somewhat with chisel and rasp, but neither had known sandpaper
or varnish. Stephensons of Tyneside, father and son. The obvious popularity
of the Swedish locomotive was threatening the family plan: they looked at
her, looked back at the grandstand with its fluttering flags and the money-
men of Liverpool *en bloc* there with their racing-glasses.

Mr Robert said, 'She's light and she's swift and she's damnably neatly
joined; but that boiler's not big enough to mash a cup o' tea, and look for
trouble with their flue-draught: lay a bet on it?'

'Keep wagers for wasters,' growled George. 'She's light and she's swift; she's naea guts.'

They laughed, in rude northern malice; watching *Novelty*, timing her run with stopwatches, snarling at their readings, chuckling on about the other competitors. Timothy Hackworth of Darlington had brought an engine (*Sans Pareil*) that both agreed would be bound to weigh-in too heavy and might well be disqualified; and Robert had just heard welcome news of the fourth entry, 'That Scotchman's job from Edinburgh – it's rolled off its dray at the very door o' the Green Dragon just this side of Prescot! I'd think we'll not see it at all. Smashed crank; and a dented firebox like a Blaydon jockey's skull after he tried to pull a race! Ha!'

They laughed again, very much at one today, although at times they could differ violently. Angry jealous blood, but they both knew their business. And better still, if they did not know it, they knew how to bluff. These few thousand gleaming yards of track, for example – beyond them was still a vast waste of ditch holes full of water, and peat-moss still swallowing every ballast-load tipped into it, nearly thirty miles altogether of what anyone else would call catastrophe: and the Stephensons claimed in public that all was ready save 'adjustments'. They were not quite dishonest: but their coats were well-buttoned; and their scruffily pencilled plans lay deep down in pocket-books in the recesses of their inner vests. Liverpool, even yet, was not sure what it had bought.

And then it was the end for *Novelty*.

The wind had shifted, sweeping the mist; thin cloud was flinging rain. Umbrellas went up, voices bawled for them to be furled; the view, at this crucial moment, must *not* be obstructed. A rush and a whoosh and a shudder, the little locomotive and her train of trucks was up to the grandstand, then beyond, hurtling onward, and still the velocity increased. Her white-clothed enginemen, as excited as anyone, despite earlier professional calm, broke for an instant from their tense concentration, waved their caps and screamed cheers against the cheering crowd; a blond man in shirtsleeves (he might have been the unknown Swede?), tall hat tilted back from his brow, stood high upon tiptoe on *Novelty*'s coke-wagon, both arms in the air for all the world like a victorious pugilist.

George Stephenson spat angrily through a gap in his teeth: 'Twenty-seven mile to an hour; a bit over, ca' it twenty-eight. If your *Rocket* canna match him, we're capped!'

'Ah but can he hold it?'

'Ah but that's to be seen. Aye, there's time yet though; time for the bugger to smash.'

'He won't smash, he might blow.'

'And by God, but he *has* blown! Woo-hoo, the bugger's capped! Woo-hoo, did we lay a bet?'

Flames and smoke and tumultuous steam, a skidding halt and shouting men leaping off onto the lineside; not half a mile along the track between the grandstand and the east end of the course. People in droves running to the stricken engine, her chagrined sponsors forcing their way down the tiers of the packed scaffold.

Mr Stephenson recollected his reputation for solid gravity; he held himself suddenly silent; glanced quickly left and right, hoping that his savage triumph had not been noticed by too many: he caught Robert's eye and winked.

Robert too was joyfully grave. 'No bet. I did offer. Your loss: and serve you right. End of *Novelty*, end of gimcrack, end of neat little gentlemen's bandboxes. Now for some engine work.'

'Darlington comes first, dim Tim Hackworth, or does he? Has he steam up?'

Rocket and *Sans Pareil* stood on a siding two hundred yards away; neither of them so sweetly ordered to the eye as *Novelty*, nor so suggestive of smart horse-drawn rig-outs. Both were encumbered with massive chimney stacks, and rods and pipes all over their external surfaces. But Robert's engine was the lighter and *crisper* of the pair, an effect well enhanced by her colours, white and buttercup yellow; while *Sans Pareil*'s dark green and black added a degree of gloomy bulk to what already seemed a behemoth, coarsely bolted and riveted together like the uncouth tackle of a colliery pump house. Squads of men swarmed about them, protected from the public by stretched tape and patrolling special constables with pickaxe handles. There was oiling and coking and general last-minute fuss.

Mr Sandars met the Stephensons, a stout man with a very splendid watch-chain: dignity prohibited his actually inspecting the wreck of *Novelty*, he was one who required his many underlings to report.

'All had seemed to go so well,' he breathed, shaking his several chins: 'And then, alas, on the first complete run! How are the mighty. . . and cetera. But I never did think them Swedes had quite grasped the – ah – what I might call, sir, the *index* of the company's requirements. Well.' He looked at his watch, and continued with quick annoyance. 'I told Hackworth to be moving, just this minute I gave him the word; we can't afford hanging about, this crowd could turn ugly; *all* crowds can turn ugly; if I said once I said a hundred times publicity's not public madness, but they *would* have a song-and-dance and now look at it! We ought to have had the yeomanry.'

He swung away from them toward the siding, to meet enraged gesticulation from the hammer-headed black-muzzled Hackworth; at the valve-taps upon Hackworth's engine three frantic mechanics twisted and banged. Filthy language fought for mastery with the augmenting roar of the steam.

'By God, but he's sprung a leak!' Exultant greedy George. 'Or has he cracked a cylinder?'

'Cracked a cylinder? Oh surely never!' Son's eye met father's blank innocence, almost sanctimony. 'He's bust a joint at one of his valves; and who's to say where else?'

'Ha' ye *Rocket* fit to run, lad? Let's go ready her into gear.'

But Sandars forestalled them, running over from Hackworth, waving and shouting to them to stop.

'No,' he cried, 'not now! We can't get *Rocket* out while *Sans Pareil*'s where she is, and the bloody fool can't shift her, and look at the state of the rain!'

'Yo'd nivver think to cancel trains on account of a drop o'rain?' Old George was truly shocked. 'Ha' some sense o'the duties of your trade!'

But Sandars was judicious, all his panic suddenly gone. 'No, Mr Stephenson, no: if your engine gets in difficulty and we're forced to reject its claims, you'll spend the rest of your life telling me, *and the public press*, sir, she was tried in unfair conditions, and I won't have it said, sir! No! We'll postpone until tomorrow.'

Postponement was the call all round. Turbulence of horses and carriages in the mud, collapsed bonnets and dripping hat-brims, hurrying footmen with umbrellas between grandstand and conveyances; Timothy Hackworth and his sodden men worked on under the downpour. Meanwhile the horse from slighted *Cycloped* was pressed into service to haul away *Novelty*'s trucks; and then *Novelty* herself, a sad remaindered relic.

By the middle of the following week all the Rainhill Trials were over. And at once the Liverpool ballad singers had their versions upon the street. One such, a disabled seaman, who felt a crossgrained sympathy with the Canal Company (as being to an extent *marine*), but yet despised its waterway for a mere tideless landlubbers' puddle, was at first at a loss how to deal with its railway rival. He expressed his mixed feelings in some of the stanzas of the resultant song:

It was bold Mr Sandars of Liverpool town
Fell in the canal and was bloody near drowned;
He swore to his good lady, 'That wet ditch no more
Shall rob my poor pocket and make my heart sore.

Your barges and narrow-boats and horse-groom tars aboard 'em
Must straightway give over their nautical whoredom,
And all on my rails' road shall ply a new trade,
So whistle up the eng-y-ines, let's see how strong they're made!'

On the second day of racing Mr Hackworth could never win,
His ugly eng-yne sparked but farts and a dribble from her chin;
While swift *Rocket*'s gorgeous tail shot thirty miles of fire an hour
Like them wild girls of Booble Alley (many a sailorman they do devour!).

Mr Hackworth he turned round to Mr Stephenson so proud:
'If I'd a-known you'd a-done it I'd have never allowed
That you in your old jealousies should ever have supplied
Such a rotten-bottomed pipe-iron that split itself so wide!'

It was, of course, quite true that Timothy Hackworth's cylinders had been
forged as a sub-contract in Robert Stephenson's workshop. It was also
perhaps true that one of them proved defective when *Sans Pareil* on the last
day of the trials came up once more for judgement. Certainly there was an
enormous waste of steam. But – as the Stephensons pointed out – to patch
a bad boot with good leather might well cause more trouble than it solved;
and if Hackworth was to allege deliberate malice then Hackworth must
damn well prove it; and he couldn't. With which the independent judges of
the competition all concurred. *Rocket*, they had to admit, was so much the
fastest locomotive, the most powerful, the most reliable, that not only did
her designer well merit the five-hundred-pound prize; but the case
(hitherto strongly argued by several directors of the railway company) for
doing without locomotives altogether and hauling the trains by cable from
a series of engine houses, was finally abandoned. Mr Brandreth alone
maintained total disagreement, and no one who had seen his horse-treddle
was inclined any more to listen to *him*.

At the celebratory banquet not even William Huskisson the politician
presumed to enquire just how far work on the line had progressed. But
despite all, it *did* progress. Somehow, the secretive Stephensons had got
themselves trusted. Somehow, embittered Hackworth had always known
they would.

So all you bold sailors that listen to my song;
Your boat-ways on land will not serve you long.
Geordie Stephenson, that crafty mole, has let out all your waters,
Fond par-i-ents try in vain to caulk the crack in their naughty
daughters.

NAY BUT CLEVER KNAVERY WON'T NEVER ABATE
AS ALL US POOR CHAPS CAN SEE AS WE KNOCK
UPO'T'WORKHOUSE GATE!

– the last two lines being the ballad man's signature, as it were: he added them to every song he composed and shouted them out with a lively pivot of his wooden leg and a skip and a stamp from his one whole foot.

TWO

Fanny Kemble had come to Liverpool to act, and make money for her father: she had no thought at all of the railway. Of course she had heard of it; with a simple but sceptical pleasure that her miserable journeys by stagecoach, month after month while on tour, might soon be as out-moded as the declamatory style of some of her colleagues in the theatre.

She was famous already, twenty-one years old, the daughter of actors, the niece of famous actors, the grand-daughter of actors: she loved her craft and she hated it. She stood for her cue in the wings of the Theatre Royal, and yet again cleared her mind for her night's work by reckless release of metaphorical fantasy –

she was a Christian captive of virtuous habit but, alas, libidinous nature, compelled as an odalisque into the seraglio *of the Grand Turk – drastic tearing of her spirit between outrage and exaltation, horror and sleek pride – who could say which emotions would in the long run prove the stronger?*

Always at this desperate moment she told herself something like this, but never told anyone else, not even her best friend, dear 'H' (Harriet St Leger, in Ireland), to whom she wrote with such intimate regularity as practically to furnish her a weekly newsletter of all the dreams and deeds of Kemble, private and public; but overt propriety nonetheless was a necessity of the age, not even stage-players were exempt; and *some* dreams were best left where they lay.

Tonight she was Juliet. Charles Kemble played Mercutio – not Romeo (and she gave thanks), as had at one time seemed only too likely. She distasted the very notion that she might simulate fresh young desire toward a tetchy middle-aged parent – a parent who had incontrovertibly been one of the best Romeos of his generation, until he assumed a manager's anxieties as well as an actor's and somehow lost the knack. Nowadays he had grown stilt-stalked and artificial when summoned to romantic transports by any shape of actress. He should leave such parts alone: but if he insisted, undoubtedly she would acquiesce. The only reason she was in the business was because he lost all his money, lost his control of Covent Garden, even lost his goods and gear to the broker's men – someone had to come to the rescue – she had volunteered, in trepidation; had submitted herself all untrained and unforeseen to audition, had found herself no less talented than any of her kin, had been rushed into Juliet after only three weeks' rehearsal: and immediately was *glorified*. Until finances balanced, she must act when and where he asked her, with whomever he hired to match her, before whatever perilous crowds or apathetic stragglings his hortatory playbills might be able to assemble. Nor was it only for her father – her elder brother John was an undergraduate at Cambridge, his bills had to be met – a scholar of such promise, a family comrade of such debonair delight – there was nothing (she had sworn romantically) she would not endure to see him fulfil his genius.

> *Held fast by fierce corsairs, she was thus borne unresisting into eunuchs' soft hands and thence into the bed of the sultan – whom she strongly suspected to be a* Bluebeard *of the old tale. Would she ever get out of it? And indeed did she want to? She had already been sprawling there for nearly a whole year.*

Every evening before curtain-rise she shivered and retched and compulsively sought her chamber pot; every night upon the boards she suddenly discovered how her skill could release intelligence, wit and passion upon a chain of precisely placed words across the pit, among the boxes, high up toward the gallery and the worshipping press of stupid faces glowing down at her from behind the bright tremor of the gasoliers.

Since childhood she had wished she might at length gain a living as a writer. This very summer, and in great haste, inspired by what she had heard from Paris of the storm-and-stress over Hugo's *Hernani*, she had all but completed an historical play in its image: doublet-and-hose kings and dukes, sacrificial fervency of love between brother and sister, imperilled honour of stately ladies, strange lusts and perverse ambition. Maybe – her father had told her – he would produce it one of these days; provided her heady text could be a little less interminable and a trifle more decorous in its sensual implications; and provided, of course, his affairs were sufficiently solvent. At one time she had expected that an appointment as a governess (of a superior sort, in some literary household, in France perhaps, where she had been educated) might be the best step toward such an ambition. Indeed she still thought it preferable to the stage, despite the well-known humiliations, even if the household were not quite literary, even if France were beyond any practical hope. But governesses earned only salaries, and at best the most meagre salaries, whereas actresses *sometimes*, and almost by accident, were able very rapidly to be rich. Just now, she must agree, was her very special *sometime*; she was a Kemble, she had a duty to the Kembles.

> *So she hugged the sultan tight and rejoiced to receive his lecheries.*

Fantasy only: and in secret. As an Englishwoman upon two legs, she stood no nonsense, permitted no impertinence. If the theatre must violate her, it was upon her own strict terms; they were not to be extended beyond the limits of the work. Let men indeed worship her Juliet, her Portia, as noisily as they would! When they chose to worship *Fanny*, she had nothing to say to them: awkward enough, for too well she understood what was expected. In London she had had letters of assignation from baronets, attorney's clerks and newspaper editors; and moreover from a duke. Each in turn re-sealed and politely returned. One of them was in her dressing room now. She had decided not even to open it, for she knew from whom it came. She recognised the handwriting; she had never met the writer.

Liverpool was no sanctuary against these degrading attempts. But in Liverpool at least she would be free from any awkwardness between fantasy and reality while in front of the audience. Here in this town it was fantasy altogether; for her new leading gentleman was a young woman, Miss Tree; by far the easiest Romeo that Fanny had yet experienced, sturdy, spare, strong-shouldered, husky-voiced, scarcely in need of the bandage across her bosom or loose jerkin-skirts round her thighs to fake the pretence of maleness. She could be *kissed*, without fear of any disturbing afterthoughts; although it did cross Fanny's mind that Miss Tree herself might have afterthoughts. She played so many male roles, she must surely be driven to do it by something more than the vigour of her stride?

Fanny thoroughly enjoyed, often adored, those frank young women deprecated by men as 'mannish' – 'H', for example, whom she had nicknamed 'the Irish Atalanta' (when she wasn't revering her in parody as a 'female Plato'), traversed the countryside of Meath and County Dublin in cropped hair and riding-breeches and refused to hunt side-saddle – whereas Ellen, offstage, could affect the mincing archness of any un-distinguished *soubrette*, an ambiguity almost repellent; one might say, dishonest. Fantasy and reality of the profession, once again; could it be they were sometimes reversed? But all that was Miss Tree's own business: the flowers she left in Fanny's dressing room (alongside the unopened letter) were acceptable as a generous token from one colleague to another. Miss Tree knew that Miss Kemble stood no nonsense, for everybody knew it. If generosity implied affection, affection need not mean passion, and certainly not possession.

Within the closed flats that backed the street-scene presently playing, stagehands made haste to place two stools and a table for Lady Capulet's garden; Lady Capulet was already about to settle herself upon one of the stools; and the Nurse (late as usual and altogether typical of the Theatre Royal's stock-company) was huffing and puffing herself down the

precipitous iron stair-spiral that led from the greenroom. She had a gin
bottle to tuck away into the folds of her seven shawls, and it hindered her
progress. The contents of the bottle hindered her *acting*, every night, and
most observably; it was high time someone observed: but never Charles
Kemble, for whom the reeks of gin and greasepaint inevitably mingled and
all might be excused provided neither he nor his daughter were upstaged
or interrupted – to give the Nurse her credit, she was not an interrupter and
was usually far too sodden to move herself upstage or down.

Beyond the front flats Miss Tree was now into the penultimate speech of
the scene. Romeo to Benvolio, refusing to accept the possibility of any girl
to surpass Rosaline:

One fairer than my love! the all-seeing sun
Ne'er saw her match since first the world begun.

She was making a quiet but very urgent sense out of each harsh-clipped
rapid word. Her script showed exclamation marks after nearly every
sentence, but they were not in her voice. There was something most
soldierly about her understated devotion. Just so the Iron Duke on his
horse above Hougoumont peering out through the gunsmoke and the
whistling balls to issue his calm orders – 'Hot work, gentlemen, yes; be so
good as to pay attention: colonel, fetch your fellows a little further to your
left, *there*; that should do very well . . .' and so forth.

True, Wellington won his battle; but Romeo was to forget Rosaline
within one brief minute of his arrival at the Capulets' party. So the sincerity
of such gruff diffidence (however much to Fanny's taste) was therefore
quite as suspect as Charles Kemble's ardent rant: so Fanny listened, and
learned, and thought about the manners of men and very nearly fell to
giggles that would have destroyed her first entrance if she had not
immediately *hated* herself. Hate herself, hate the theatre, hate the drunken
old basket that called herself the Nurse (and would muddle every cue she
was going to give) and above all hate the audience. That was how she
entered, always; that was how she found her strength; and once she had
found it, she was able to love. If the audience believed her, she had to
believe *them*, but every night their credulity amazed her.

Romeo and Benvolio were off (Miss Tree with a brisk touch of her hand
on Fanny's bare arm as she sprang past her into the shadows), the flats
slithered along their grooves to reveal the garden, *bang bang* went the front
wing-pieces as the stage-hands swopped painted cornerstones for painted
box-trees, and the Nurse's bleary voice shuffled already into her cry:

What, lamb! what, lady-bird!
God forbid! where's this girl? what, Juliet!

— no chance now for that chamber pot; Fanny at last was Juliet:

How now! Who calls?

— and no more trouble, she sped forward, she was *capable*.

In the last act she refused to have Miss Tree pick her up from the catafalque
and carry her bodily down to the footlights: the Romeo in London had
always done this, a monstrous sort of claptrap, absurdly implausible, but
hallowed by long stage practice. One night he nearly dropped her; and
then, only last month in another provincial theatre, a cocky young sprig
who belonged to the resident company and conceived himself an Edmund
Kean, had so indecently fumbled her as he wrapped his arm about her
hams (confident she was *as dead* and could not squirm) that she swore she
would never go through with it again. Miss Tree had believed the breach of
tradition to be a reflection upon her feminine strength, and had taken
some umbrage. Fanny feared no unseemly gropings from Miss Tree, but
she *did* doubt the question of strength: in the event she chose quite
different grounds for the defence of her decision.

'Now, Ellen,' she said gently (and her gentlest was always her firmest, at
least to begin with), 'if you lift me, I shall vigorously resist; and so destroy
your whole performance. That being understood, let me put it to you why.
Act five, scene three, and poor Juliet is about to die. Poor Romeo also. To
say nothing of poor Paris. So why not make four of 'em, lay Tradition in the
tomb as well? Don't you think it's all he's damned well fit for?' She knew as
she said it that her father would not like to have heard her. Nor was she
quite ready to allow him to hear.

End of the play: the Liverpool public roared and clapped and stamped its
feet, Juliet rose up to receive the longed-for tumult; receiving it, she was
Fanny again, she began at once to despise it, quivering from head to foot at
the inconsistency. She had Miss Tree's arm about her to lift her to her feet
and she felt she needed it. The roller-curtain fell with a crash. She kissed
Miss Tree quickly. Scrambling blind with tears to the dressing room, she
ignored the offered embrace of her proud father. But Charles was used to
such avoidance: the child, as he said, had the full *sensibility* of her aunt, Mrs
Siddons, 'nay, far fuller; she will often sob for a whole hour after the show,
and only then put out her faint little hand for porter and beefsteak. The
trick is to ensure she postpones it till the last act's over!' It is true that once

she had *not* postponed it: she had shrieked throughout the curtain-call, she remembered it with shame – God preserve her from any recurrence.

(She often prayed to God to resolve her contradictions; and at the same time condemned herself for superstition. She had enough real religion to be sure that God's ubiquity included, but could not be expected to be especially concerned with, the silly whims of a self-excited girl.)

Her dresser was waiting for her, to be as usual waved out of the room for at least fifteen minutes, twenty, before Fanny could bear to be pulled to pieces and reassembled – a whole hour was Charles Kemble's nonsense, the woman was never kept standing sentry outside for so long; most grossly unkind if she were. Fanny tried always to be kind. She fell upon the sofa and buried her face in a cushion. Not *sobs* exactly, but it was hard to take breath; at such times, to seem to smother herself was the best way of restoring the rhythm. After a while she looked up and behaved like a rational human. Her eye caught the letter, propped against the edge of the mirror. She intended not to open it.

What *could* he have to say to her that she had not already declined? 'Hot work, ma'am, yes of course; but soon you'll be cool as I am, and you know how cool I've been: your Miss Tree very competently recalled to you my peculiarities'. . . ? And very true, her Miss Tree had.

If Fanny were to invent incongruous contents for the letter, she might just as well discover the true ones. She defied herself; and broke the wax.

The Duke of Wellington has the honour to present his compliments to Miss Kemble and to trust that what may have been the indiscretion of his previous letter be generously overlooked? Fact is, ma'am (I lapse into the informal, but you may prefer it?) I am the sufferer in my gathering years of obloquy reaped by my insolent youth: no intent to treat you lightly, beauty and accomplishment demand respect. Shakespeare does not inspire me, but music does; and the music of your voice (quite confoundedly) refuses to leave my ears.

Public duty brings me to Liverpool, much against my wishes (but duty, we're aware, accedes to no man's wishes) upon the 15th–16th *prox*. I am let know that your engagement will still continue at the theatre there? A small supper with your devoted servant following your own evening's duty, upon the 15th, would commit you to nothing beyond two hours' quiet chat with an old soldier, to his chagrin turned statesman, sorely in need of a gentle word or so to relieve his preoccupations. I await, with *trepidation*, the privilege of a reply – to –

No. 10, Downing Street, Westminster
22 August 1830

Trepidation? From *him*? It was so obviously insincere, she was disgusted. He did seem to recognise that an actress these days might just possibly be a species of *lady*, and that any sort of approach to her, overtly amorous or not, might well be construed as 'insolent'. And yet he also felt she could not be quite like the ladies that would move in his own circles? But for all she knew of his circles, perhaps he wrote in the same vein to the daughters of the Countess of This or the Marchioness of That.

She did not know whom to ask for advice. She could put it all in her next letter to 'H'; there was probably time to receive an answer from Ireland; she knew already what the answer would be; not only would 'H' (twelve years her elder) laugh at her for her *naïveté* – insupportable! – she would also be bound to moralise, and even quote some of Fanny's own little religious solemnities against her; this was no occasion for inciting a caustic rebuke from a friend so notoriously impervious to male temptation. No: she must be dishonest; 'H' must never hear of any of it.

More conventionally: her mother? Her mother was in London, and even if she were not, this was not at all the sort of question she ought to be expected to deal with. One half of her – the regular-French half (for Marie Thérèse De Camp Kemble was French by birth and had sung and danced all over Europe as a child, with all that that implied) – could conceivably follow *tradition* and encourage her daughter to become mistress to the nation's hero, if such indeed was on offer here. But her other half, the English-wife half, that had lived faithfully married for a quarter of a century within a solid theatrical family of serious pretensions, would most certainly be horrified; even in the teeth of pecuniary necessity, she might snatch Fanny away altogether from the stage and all its dangers.

Internal clashes between her mother's two characters happened often enough, disagreeable for anyone within range (at times ill-natured gossip went so far as to imply that Mme De Camp's *mind was diseased*); clashes between mother and daughter were even more frequent and more unpleasant: to combine them was not to be thought of. Fanny knew her own temperament to be similarly divided; she felt toward her mother as to the theatre itself. Which meant she did not know *how* she felt; so best leave well alone.

While her father would be horrified without complication; the more so as his liberal principles abhorred the Iron Duke, chiefly as a politician, but even as a soldier – Charles's love for Marie Thérèse had been theatrically spurred by the fact that she was daughter of an officer of the French Revolutionary Army (even though she herself made little of that vivid history); and his views upon Napoleon were, for an Englishman, heterodox to the point almost of retrospective treason. He was perfectly capable of challenging the duke to a duel, and regarding it as a legitimate replay of Waterloo.

So: both comradely and parental counsel would oppose acceptance of the invitation. So: Fanny longed to accept it.

The fact was, she was deadly curious. She was as ready to sup peril with a perilous great man as she had been to play Juliet from no previous experience; and she dreaded her own temerity. She must answer that letter before she went to bed. If she left it until morning it would be left for the rest of her life.

A knock upon her door; the letter into her reticule; her call to 'come in': Charles Kemble on the threshold, and still in Mercutio's costume. 'Dear girl, your dresser said you weren't ready, I know, so I crave pardon; but then neither am I – ' He flourished his plumed hat down the length of his puffed, slashed, be-ribboned doublet, some such form of words as 'let me justify the incongruity of these my gorgeous weeds' implicit in the lavish gesture. 'To tell truth, I am forestalled by a most innovatory visitor; he has a message for *you*.' Her mind full of Wellington, Fanny turned pale; but no need. 'A Mr Sandars, of the dock-wharf; but also of the new rail-road, which neither you nor I have seen.' She grasped at the diversion, said she *longed* to see the rails, told herself she lied and then realised she did not; the rails were unprecedented; she was deadly curious. He went on: 'It appears the *grande première* is scheduled for the fifteenth of next month; very much as in our own business, they issue complimentary passes, they publicise with *éclat*. You and I and Miss Tree are the fortunate recipients; you have no objection to acceptance? The gentleman waits in the greenroom. Miss Tree is already with him.' Miss Tree, after the show, needed no time at all to recuperate; she had been acting for years. 'She is on fire, so she says, to travel to Manchester behind the fire-dragon, in two senses I might add, dragon-locomotive and dragon-dammit-*duke*!'

'*What*?' Now there was need to turn pale.

'How? You sway, exhausted! I am sorry, child, I am too abrupt; you are not yet composed after your splendid exertion, allow me to withdraw.'

'No, Papa, no: I should adore to ride the dragon. You said, duke?'

'Oh yes, the strenuous duke. Old Nosey, for God's sake; destroying the occasion with his reactionary presence. I always thought Huskisson a most reasonable man; how he can bear to have that lobster grabbing claws into his constituency I cannot imagine. I thought they had quarrelled altogether. I thought this fine city was claimed at last for Reform. But it seems not, he's going to be here; and he travels in the very first train. I very nearly said no; but I feared to disappoint Sandars, he was out front tonight, such a very good house indeed. Still, if *we're* all at the opening ceremony, I suppose no one will notice Wellington. To be sure *I* shall cut him dead.'

Her father's comic attitudes were the best things he did, particularly effective for the confrontation of bailiffs; and always irresistible: Fanny burst out laughing. She said, 'Tell him yes, tell him indeed yes! – I can't see him myself, I'm far too shaky – but do ask if there's any chance of a ride on the dragon itself, I mean, *on* it, not behind it, could he ever – ?'

Mercutio looked suddenly grave, as when imagining unwarlike Romeo doomed to death at Tybalt's sword; he shook his head. 'I scarcely think it would be thought suitable. You have to stand, I suspect, with grimy lads on a very small open platform and the wind beneath your nether garments. And it might be highly dangerous. I don't believe I'll pass that message.' Old Capulet now had taken over from Mercutio.

'Oh, Papa, I believe you will.' Her gentlest, and so her firmest.

'Ah, but your mother – '

'She's in London.'

Undressed for bed in her approximately clean but far from elegant Church Street lodgings, she wrote two acceptances. To Mr Sandars, nothing difficult: but Fanny liked to compose these things with care. She charmed her pen to be fresh and charming, with a becoming spice of girlishness – Juliet *de nos jours* in fact. She had seen, briefly, the railway projector on his way out of the theatre; had seen that he was fat and authoritative; she thought she guessed well what he would appreciate.

But to the duke, ironclad hero, potential *ogre*, embarrassing old fool – what possible form of words? Did she dare satire?

Miss Kemble to the Duke of Darkness: which is Shakespeare, tho' he inspires you not. Your strategy, Your Grace, succeeds; by feigned *trepidation* you have surprised my defence, and Miss Kemble's square is broken. As yours, I believe, never was. But if you enter it, horse or foot, I warn you beware of skirmishers; *guerrilleros*, were they not called in Spain? And recollect what they did to the Corsican. You will see I have taken pains to possess myself of military terms, do you do the same with theatrical. Our 'small supper' must needs be *offstage*; and yet not beyond *the call of the prompter*.

She was afraid it was arch (like Tree at her worst); but the right tone was not easy for a neophyte to hit; she inhibited, she hoped, as much as encouraged; let him make of it what he could. She supposed he must be sixty or more. Her father was five years younger, yet the thought of his Romeo had distressed her so irrationally . . .

She knelt and said her prayers and then climbed into bed, conscious of a dull pain in her side. *The* dull pain, in fact; she and it were old enemies; whenever her emotions were unseasonably engaged, it came crouching at her, pawing her, punching her like an ugly gloved fist. Absurdly, after particularly enthusiastic reviews in the newspapers; and now, because she had written a letter? But she would not accept it was to do with emotion: no, it was grumbling liver, she must look to her diet, already on this tour she had fallen into irregular habits of victuals and drink, so imprudent.

As she lay between the sheets she said her prayers for a second time over, attempting hypocritically to soothe her spirit; and then to let her body be soothed by the warm bed. With no great success, until she thought to enforce herself to think seriously of the railway, calling to mind what she had read in journals and seen in the aquatints already on sale in London. She was anxious to gain all she could from her promised experience. She tried to estimate the promethean labour – physical and mental – such a valorous undertaking involved. Surely far more important than doublet-and-hose kings, and its makers more alive than cocked-hat-and-epaulette dukes; her romanticism must not forever fling itself about through past ages, a wood-pigeon trapped in a bell-tower. Escape from inherited Tradition (slovenly stock-company, narrow lodgings, her maddening father like a madwoman's mad keeper) ought only to be escape *forward*, let her be curious of *that*, dream exclusively of *that*. Had not her father, after all, just now thrown it all open to her? and without even knowing what he'd done.

So she did dream: a long straight road of clangorous iron sweeping away and away across wet green fields until it dissolved into the distant mist. At the end of the road, mountains? But the mist was obscenely infested; *shadow-shapes of rutting Turks, absurd and lurid; not just one sultan, but two, and both silver-haired – all over.*

THREE

In a nearly completed genteel suburb, at the top of Mountpleasant on the eastern edge of Liverpool, stood Abercrombie Square; and in the square stood the solemnly new town house of Mr Sandars; and in the house sat a dinner party, a selected few from the railway board; William Huskisson guest of honour. Dessert and port were on the table and Mrs Sandars had led the ladies from the dining room to tea in the parlour – a less gloomy apartment, had not its mistress been imbued with the Methodist piety; from her grey-and-gold wallpaper, just above the seated sinners' eye-level an assortment of steel engravings bore menacing witness to old Judaic chastisement.

The hostess took post behind the tea-urn, in front of Noah's Flood: drowning malefactors swarmed in the surge over the top of her lace cap. She was as lean as her husband was corpulent, but equally authoritative (whenever she had the chance), and tonight she was quite angry with him: a careless remark during the fish course had revealed to her he had been at the Theatre Royal the previous evening; in itself a fleshly sin even had it not involved prevarication. He had let her believe (without actually stating the fact) that his late return home had been due to a board meeting. She now realised there was to be no such meeting until serious matters between certain directors and their parliament-man had been arranged at this very dinner party, a *fait accompli* to go before the board tomorrow. Exhausted by the strains of hospitality, she felt her resentment proportionately increased. But at last she could express it, among four or five ladies, nearly all of her own way of thinking, with replenishments of hot tea and great heaps of lard-mixed cake. She told them quietly and positively 'just exactly what she thought'.

A director's wife, shaped like a cottage loaf and crowned by Belshazzar's Feast, agreed with her, and doubted the morality of the railway itself. 'In my opinion, Mrs Sandars, if its business has incited your Joseph to the playhouse – ' (A parenthesis from Mrs Brandreth beneath the Orgy of the Golden Calf: 'The devil's temple – give it its name!') ' – to get the playactors onto the rail-train to make advertisement for him in the pages of the worldly newspapers – '

'Accomplice in their iniquity; his rail-road is corrupted by it; *he* becomes corrupted! It's not even as though he just popped in there to leave a letter;

oh no, he'd to buy a box-seat and sit through the entire performance: and *that* is what I can't forgive.' Mrs Sandars tightened her mouth upon a segment of condemnatory parkin.

Mrs Brandreth again: 'If it comes so soon for a man like Sandars, how swift will be the corruption when the workpeople grow hardened to it? Ignorant folk back and forth to Manchester at no more than two shilling a time? And Manchester folk coming in here? I always said our especial burden for Christianity in Liverpool was the seaport and the wickedness it brings; not only debauchery but popery; how many ships a day from Ireland? And another thing on top: as Brandreth still maintains, God's creature is the horse, strictly controlled in strength by unassailable divine design. The power of steam is beyond limit and therefore a blasphemy. It will be marked, oh marked against them at the dividing of the sheep and goats.'

A Mrs Cropper (sitting small with Jonah at Nineveh shouting above one ear, and Jezebel thrown down from the window directly towards the other) was moved to contempt. Her husband had been the chief advocate of cable-hauled trains; defeated at Rainhill, he had lain quiet for a while but was now engaged in a covert campaign of denigration against the Stephensons. His wife thought the Brandreths ought to support him and not fool away their energies with scriptural fads. She mingled horses, sheep and goats into a crabbed complex little joke, obscure in exact meaning, unmistakeable in tone, creating a spiteful silence.

Mrs Brandreth scented profane mockery; Mrs Sandars sniffed subversion against the better interests of the Liverpool and Manchester Railway Company, and wondered had she gone too far in her own comments upon her husband.

Sly change of subject from the Belshazzar woman: a succulent whisper of how this so-called Miss Kemble's father actually paraded the same stage as, and vaunted the charms of, his *very youthful* daughter: she thought (apologetically) that 'pimp' might be the word, if any of the ladies knew it?

From which arose allusive talk of the sailors' 'boarding houses' about Castle Street and Gibraltar Row. ('*Booble Alley*!' – a significant murmur from someone); much shaking of heads that the railway was to run in a surreptitious tunnel through the cellarages of the town into the midst of the dock district. Conveying, as it were, the worst elements of unspeakable Manchester to the very doorsteps of Liverpool's shame.

Mrs Cropper said, 'Liverpool's shame? That used to be the slave-trade. Now it's – the other thing. Well: I'd say, either road, none of us seem the poorer for it.' She was a vulgar woman, she sucked her tea through a lump of sugar as her cynicism again put the party to silence.

Mrs Sandars' morality was oppressive, but deeply felt; contradictions in it troubled her. She believed that her husband's projects (lay aside his flaws of character) accorded with the best principles of nineteenth-century enlightenment. But if it did damage to virtue, private or public, enlightenment ought not to be sought at all, whatever the social benefit that might otherwise accrue. An ethical dilemma requiring to be addressed.

'There is nothing about a railway that in itself need corrupt. I meant no more, ladies, than to say that for such a new adventure – and I'm sure Sandars's have never seen themselves as owt but highly adventurous where the nation's commerce was in question (*under God!*) – it behooves we should look sharp to be very very straight indeed and not be led astray by the sweets of expediency; and so I shall tell him. I'm only sorry dear Mrs Huskisson's not in Liverpool tonight to have come here with her good man: because if she had *she'd* surely arbitrate. She gives her husband, I do know, a very firm example; after all, wasn't he responsible among all that lot in parliament for getting us Dissenters emancipated?'

'He was out of office by then; it was the duke allowed the bill through.' Mrs Cropper was sure of her facts.

'Much against his deeper nature.' Mrs Sandars knew what she intended, let facts agree as they may.

Mrs Brandreth sniffed. 'Whichever one o'them it was, they did the same for the romanists too. I don't know as I can altogether give any credit to 'em at all. In my view they're all of 'em infidels; and that Huskisson's as clumsy as five.' During dinner the MP (who was indeed unhandy at any sort of precise physical activity) had all but emptied a gravy boat into her lap.

Mrs Sandars regarded him as an elderly *protégé*, more or less, and was very fond of his high-principled wife. But she would not stoop to defend him against mean-minded imputations, even though she knew the poor man to have developed such an arthritis at the Duke of York's funeral that he was now effectively paralysed all down one side. She said, merely, 'He walks with a stick; so would we if we suffered his troubles.'

Time for the next change of subject, which she initiated at once; setting to flow the words of others without further contribution from herself.

She followed her own disturbing thoughts: upon Huskisson and her husband and the reasons for the dinner. Why these particular guests to meet their member this particular night? What had they in common to distinguish them from those directors who had *not* been invited? Brandreth and Cropper, for instance, were regularly opposed to Sandars on nearly every commercial issue.

It occurred to her that the men at her table were either reform Tories or moderate Whigs; radicals and reactionaries had alike been excluded, and yet on the board there were examples of both, some of them very close to Sandars. A *political caucus*, at Mr Huskisson's special request? Not the sort of thing Sandars usually cared to meddle with, nor could she think he had much skill in that direction. Despite her admiration for the MP and his principles, she was unhappy he should use her house for party cabal, involving her husband in heaven knew what.

Nay, she felt *betrayed*.

She only hoped Joe Sandars would look very very sharp to what went on, and would not be outsmarted by slickjacks and cag-maggers.

Meanwhile the ladies about her talked of sermons, of preachers, of preachers' unsuitable wives, and had a high old malicious hour of it.

Mrs Sandars was wrong: it was not her Joe was to be outsmarted, but the guest of honour himself, and for very sound Liverpool reasons.

The dining room walls (crimson and deep purple, with mahogany panelled dado) carried no biblical pictures. Instead, frame against heavy frame, were dark oils of the Dutch school: landscapes, carousing peasants, piles of dead birds and fruit; together with sepia prospects of Merseyside buildings and shipping, Sandars property much in evidence. One un-expected intruder, gay-hued, incongruous, between ostentatious tiers of brand new (and riskily premature) railway prints over the black slate mantelpiece: a strapping young person quite unclothed, half-in half-out of a pond, furtively watched by a dirty man eating his lunch in a thicket. Mrs Sandars had accepted this costly keynote of her husband's taste only when assured that its painter, William Etty, was devout and the work allegorical: 'Infidelity envying the purity of Religious Truth'.

Mr Huskisson slumped over his port directly opposite the equivocal canvas, his wistful eye toward it while his fellow diners noisily wrangled – upon questions, did they not realise, that had nothing whatever to do with him. He was beginning to wonder why he had been invited. If Infidelity envied Religious Truth, *he* envied Infidelity: golden sunshine, a woodland glade, a round bud of a girl's pink bum to look at – his mind wandered to his youth, to the joyous use of all his limbs and his once carefree digestion. The young man in the picture ('Infidelity' nonsense! A randy gipsy; that's all that he was) had an apple to eat and cheese, and what looked like a bottle of cider. Whereas his own stomach had been shamefully routed by the massed battalion onslaught of the eight-course Sandars dinner.

He put out a hand to divert his neighbour's relentless advance of the decanter; hand joined with stomach in immediate mutiny, knocking over his unemptied glass, splashing wine across his shirt-front. He was sure the abstemious gesture would be construed as a drunken lunge; to correct the impression, he decided to speak; and by the Lord to be listened to, or else he must call for his carriage.

He said abruptly, 'This conversation is not to the purpose, Mr Brandreth. It is no longer necessary to dispute whether or no steam-power is required for the rail-road. And what, Mr Cropper, do you hold against the Stephensons? To be sure, George the father was no more than a Tyneside enginewright, barely able to write his name. And to be sure, he surveyed your road for you more by instinct than trigonometric erudition. But by heaven, sir, he did survey it; and somehow he built it; and somehow his literate, his mathematical, son is supplying you with first-rate locomotives! Yet you've spent the past half-hour whining hint after hint of their incompetence and their − not to put too fine a point upon it − their shiftiness, Mr Cropper: why?'

Cropper himself was shifty. Unable to deal with a practised parlia-mentary orator, he went red in the face and stumbled over his reply. He felt mortified to the soul to be so roundly *brought down* at this table, for he and Sandars were keen rivals in business dealings not germane to the railway.

Huskisson, brimming over with angry vain regrets for Etty's naked girl and the warm freedom of her deportment, trampled on without mercy across Cropper; while the others sat round and heard, in open-mouthed amazement. He accused him of jealousy in the face of genius and determination, of local snobbery in that the Stephensons were Northumbrians and brought the glory of their region to Liverpool instead of submitting to Liverpool's glory ('Why, I've heard it said there's a Northumbrian plot to run a monopoly of manpower on the railway! "Geordie's Geordies", the cant-phrase, is it not? Don't it occur to you, there's nobody *but* Northumbrians who've ever even seen a railway? Whom else would you expect Mr Stephenson to employ?'), and, finally, of *blindness to self-interest* ('Unforgiveable defect, sir, in a businessman, by the very standards of the business you profess!').

Even as he perorated, he wondered at himself. These at table had secured his election time and again to an unreformed House: if he seriously offended them he would cease to represent them. Did he *want* to leave politics? Allowing that against his will some part of him might so desire, surely it would be better to contrive it from a quarrel of principle with the duke and his reactionary friends rather than pique against these *new men* whose trusted champion he had been for − how long? Most of his life, he thought drearily: and never in all that time a bright girl by a bright pool in the green glow of a woodland glade.

But he knew, even as he wondered, that another matter altogether was fuelling his irritation. Before the conversation had entangled itself in the duckweed of this provincial backwater, a remark had been dropped that made him feel he was being *used*, indeed that all of them were being used; and now, he supposed, he was but fighting to prove he was his own man and no one else's. If he angered them by it, he might stir them to assert their own independence: could he once achieve that, then apologies all round, and their heartiness and his urbanity could run smoothly again together as always until today. He left Cropper, as it were, weltering in his gore; he returned directly to the main concern; he granted not a moment's pause for anyone to interrupt him.

'Exactly whose idea was it to invite the duke, will you tell me? He is known to be thoroughly hostile to constitutional reform: Liverpool has publicly, nay majestically, demanded reform throughout the decade. He is hostile to innovation: the rail-road is innovation. He is hostile to myself: he suspects me of wishing to defect to the Whigs, which is not true, but many think it. By all logical process, if you must invite a political leader, why not one of the Whigs? Nail your colours to the mast, *confirm* my threatened defection, secure popularity with your plebeian disfranchised element, avert riot and revolution in your streets; it's all so very clear, I don't know why you haven't done it. Why haven't you?'

'Ah,' said Mr Sandars, 'that was just what we wanted to explain, sir. Right.' He seemed relieved rather than angered that the point had been reached; perhaps it was only because he was not quite able to reach it on his own that he had allowed Cropper and Brandreth to talk their rubbish. 'First, we need this rail; and on account of depression of trade, we need it to make a right *fanfare*: now, this month, we need it! Of course the duke coming here might be seen by a few as an insult to your good self. Might be seen, like, as meaning a lack of confidence in you, on account you're no longer a minister. Might be seen as a sign the high-and-dry Tory class here is in summat of an ascendant. Not true. We need reform, and you've been the man to get it us. Never the Whigs – ' (a swift flick of Sandars' eye towards those present whom he knew to be Whigs, meaning *wait and see, you'll approve what I say when you hear it!*) ' – no, not the Whigs, all they can do is encourage radicals – like, riot, you said, revolution: why, look at France this very year! *That* came to 'em through *their* Whigs, and the multitude rampaged! Beyond all control of responsible men; and we know it, and we reckon as nowt but reform, Tory reform while this ministry's still in, can save us from the same thing here. But facts are facts, Mr Huskisson: we *have* had reform, not as much as we'd like – the mercantile and manufacturing classes are still short of a fair share in government – but we've had *some*; and we've had it sin' *you* went out of cabinet. I don't ask the duke's motives: I daresay they're devious – '

'Of course they are devious,' snapped Huskisson. 'I'm astonished you are taken in by them.'

'He's emancipated the Dissenters; he's emancipated the Catholics, which some might think dangerous. But if it helps to cure Ireland, then Liverpool'll no longer be flooded out by mouldy beggars thrust in thousands atween good Englishmen and honest employment. If that's what's being done, sir, then it's the duke as is doing it, unwilling or not: and we do have to show him we know! Moreover we've to show the people: disfranchised they may be; but their welfare is our trust.'

Another director, no less consequential: '*If* the duke comes – and he *says* he'll come, mark – then he'll see what we want of him – nay, of him and *you*, together! – why, maybe he'll change his line, I mean change it full-rudder and so swim the tideflow of *authentic* reform. Because if he don't, he'll lose the government. Our Tories here might lose the city government – oh I speak, sir, as a Whig – I know of a certainty that in such a case us Whigs'll be scuppered by radicals; and after that it's nowt better nor a pistol in your pocket for every man of solid property and watch out for your warehouses; for if you don't, no one else will! Don't you see the way we're thinking?'

'The duke is not popular.' Huskisson understated, but they nodded their heads wisely, they appreciated what was meant. 'How will you protect him?'

'Mobilise the militia; request, if it's necessary, a regiment of regulars; swear-in citizens of repute as deputy constables; let 'em do the same in Manchester; it ought to be sufficient.'

Huskisson nodded *his* head, not quite so wise but very gloomy: he knew what they were about, why they had him here tonight. He was expected to reconcile himself, during the ceremonies, with the duke, and to beg re-admission to cabinet: if he declined the opportunity, then Liverpool was finished with him. These Liverpool men were practical men, very little concerned with principle.

Why was he not anxious to comply? Their scheme, on the face of it, made good political sense. A young and vigorous ex-minister, with a full career before him, would avail himself of it with gusto. Huskisson *had* been vigorous, he *had* been young. Alas, he had also been proud. His pride had never left him; and now it refused him a refusal.

He blinked sad farewell to the lovely bare creature over the mantel; packed up, one might say, his picnic into his wallet. Far from enticing him, she'd never even noticed him; he was not any longer a gipsy but a working man bound down to his factory; his lunch-hour was over. 'Good,' he said, 'make your arrangements; only too happy to accommodate.'

His overloaded stomach heaved. He left the room in an awkward hurry. As he went he caught his toecap against the edge of the door and just prevented himself falling full length. Mr Cropper barked out a short laugh and was indignantly told to *hush* it.

FOUR

Covert and crab-wise designs, to turn the railway inauguration into a stroke of progressive politics, were of course not understood by local radicals. They saw only *one* design behind this minatory alliance of iron road and Iron Duke: black reaction bragging its strength in the districts that abhorred it most. Manchester was angrier even than Liverpool; and Edward Craig's garrulous pen had a great deal to write on the subject.

This most earnest young man was at odds with his grandfather, who was also his guardian and reluctant financial support. A strongly Protestant fustian manufacturer, the old fellow had found himself unable to bear continued iteration of the socialist doctrines of Robert Owen. So he had prevailed upon Neddy to shoulder his portmanteau and seek lodging elsewhere.

Elsewhere was a garret above the Manchester Co-operative Club, which in turn lay above the shop of one Bentham, a radical bookseller; and Neddy fell in love with Bentham's daughter Mary. As far as Neddy knew, he still featured in the fustian-maker's will, but he and Mary were agreed that they really must begin to earn some sort of an income between them before they announced a wedding – especially their intended Owenite secular wedding, with neither clergyman nor church, only mutual and equal affirmations of responsibility and self-respect.

Mary worked as a teacher in a Co-operative School in the slums, trying to persuade the children of impoverished mill-hands to read, write and cipher, and also (desperate hope) to understand the ways and means of co-operative socialism. She did earn a few pennies from this, while he contributed (with even less emolument) to a radical newspaper published by Mr Bentham. He was already making a name for himself as polemicist and theoretician.

Mary's glowing feminism (of Irish derivation; Mary Wollstonecraft and Anna Wheeler) and his own personal sense of honour kept them out of each other's beds until such time as they might both be self-sufficient. He read poetry to her, and she sang songs to him – Tom Moore's *Irish Melodies* were a particular favourite. They would walk in the country, whenever they found time, and hold hands, and talk socialism; they would kiss with great sweetness and trembling and a very great desire not to allow their desire to blemish true romance with bodily crudity.

Then Neddy received a most disturbing, exhilarating, letter; from no less a person than Robert Owen himself.

The great philosopher had been in correspondence with a cultivated Irish gentleman in County Clare. The latter's estate was so wasted by agrarian rancour that he saw but one solution: to convert his property and workpeople into a co-operative community, and whom could Mr Owen recommend as resident adviser and organiser? The individual appointed would be employed for a period of years upon (it was hoped) mutually satisfactory terms. Mr Owen had immediately thought of young Mr Craig, and now he wrote to tell him so.

The west of Ireland seemed as distant, and quite as exotic, as anywhere along the American frontier. Come to that, quite as dangerous. Whiteboy terrorists, thought Neddy, must have a great deal in common with the hostile Shawnee; and for much the same reason, the robbery of their birthright.

Mary hugged him tight and exhorted him to accept the offer. 'Such injustice to be put right!' she cried, 'and it is the land of Moore's music, of Anna Wheeler herself, so of course I'll go with you and set up a school, there *must* be a school in any complete co-operative, I am trained in all the principles, if the children don't speak English I shall learn the tongue of Ossian and teach them.' As an afterthought: 'Oh Neddy, whatever will your grandfather say?'

His grandfather said, simply: 'If you work among the papists, shall you organise a Protestant mission?'

'Indeed I won't, that's not the point of it: it's nowt at all to do with church. Agricultural co-operation. Folk's beliefs are their own business!'

'Mine aren't, nor should yours be. If you go, boy, then you go; and you're lost to God and me. That's the end of your inheritance.'

Robbery of birthright? he was now at one with the common folk of Ireland.

Mary said, 'It don't matter. You'll earn enough out there to snap fingers at any old grandad; and even if not, won't we be living *in community*, as we have always longed to live?'

It was while they were still waiting for the reply to Neddy's acceptance letter that the date was announced for the opening of the railway and the visit of the duke. The aristocratic, capitalist plot at once being detected, meetings were called throughout Manchester; the opposition began to organise.

A long lank choleric man, a country carrier whose wagon delivered goods among villages on and off the Liverpool road, was denouncing the railway to the crowded clubroom over old Bentham's shop. Bentham, from the chair of the meeting, called him to order several times: 'Nay, Harry, have a bit o'sense, and remember we've ladies present.' He meant, primarily, Mary; she had been quite shocked by the carrier's adjectives but she objected to being treated as shockable, and said so. Her father disregarded her. 'Highly necessary, citizens, to keep indignation within bounds. If these rail-trains do run roughshod over many of our livelihoods, we need patience to consider the implications from all sides. I'd request the citizen on his feet to put forward a resolution; that way we can further the meeting. Well, Harry?'

'Well, citizen chairman, I'd say, if I'm put to it, get hold of a cask o'blasting powder and blow their damned engines to – nay, it don't even need powder, lay a bloody great baulk o'timber in front of their wheels, chuck 'em off down Chat Moss bank and let 'em sink!'

'Right then.' Bentham remained unruffled. 'Motion before us: to engage ourselves in acts of material destruction for the purpose of preserving employment. Anyone second it?'

A fierce skinny woman with red wild eyes, a weaver's wife who always demanded the most melodramatic outrages of physical force (and sometimes got them) thrust up her hand and launched into a speech about Ned Ludd and how in her girlhood his gallant chaps had had the machine masters shaking in their very boots.

Neddy Craig stood to speak, knowledgeable but diffident, peering through wire spectacles to read from a paper of notes. 'Citizen chairman, the citizeness has evoked the memory of Ludd. But I don't think it'll do. Looms were broken, blood was shed, people were even killed: aye, and hanged, and transported. And yet today, look out of window: how many mill-chimneys? And nearly all of 'em smoking! I'd argue, for every hand-weaver that lost his job for machines, several hundred, maybe thousands, have come into Manchester and are working at those same machines. I don't say happily, or well-paid, I don't say their work is secure. But machines are our world and we live in it; as we find it, we must deal with it. Let me tell you how we deal. First, we give welcome to the possibilities of cheap swift travel, and consider how it will benefit our cause: next, we examine the conditions of that travel – I mean who's at work on the rail-road, what are they paid, how are they treated? From what I hear already there's a discipline to be imposed more like that in a despotic *gendarmerie*: uniforms, oppressive rules, a hierarchy of company officials. Maybe such rules are needful for safety: or maybe their purpose is to militarise the system? No coincidence the prime minister is only what he is because once he was a general-at-war. At all events the workmen were never consulted:

and *that's* a fair point for agitation. And according to this motion we're to hazard those workmen's lives? Nay, citizens, it's not good sense.'

'O'course it's not good sense.' (The chairman, quite improperly, growling his own comment into his grubby cravat; but Neddy's speech had not gone down at all well.) 'Afore we put it to the vote, anyone else got a contribution?' The red-eyed woman opened her mouth; but Bentham checked her. 'Nay, Mrs Scuffham, I think we all know where you stand; give someone else a chance. Mary – I mean, Citizeness Bentham?'

'I only want to say I think the chair is unfair to the citizeness. I happen to know Mr Scuffham has been unemployed for two years and from age and ill-health he's not capable of machine-weaving, which is far heavier toil and more degrading to the spirit than many care to contemplate; whereas he's well able for some degree of handloom work, but however is it possible for him to find it?' Mary was impassioned. Scuffham grandchildren came to the school, their ragged frocks and bare legs on a cold winter morning were an outrage to her soul. 'I don't agree we should wreck the trains, but I *do* think we should take note, *public* note, Father – ' she forgot correct protocol under the pressure of emotion ' – of the miseries inseparable from all these new inventions, fetched onto us only for profit; not *our* profit, not even Manchester's at large, but to the cash-boxes of directors and idle shareholders and – and – ' She had made her point, she stopped herself, she sat down abruptly: Neddy put his hand out to her but in a flush of irritation she brushed it aside.

Other people spoke, round and about the issue. It was growing dark, the little club-room was filling with noxious fumes; no amount of representation from the more fastidious members could prevent Manchester radicals from poisoning themselves with foul clay pipes, even some of the women were emulating the city's porcupine bristle of chimney stacks. Bentham got up to light the gas. The meeting was wedged at cross-purposes; he thought it might be time to send out for more gin-toddy (here too the puritanical element were in a marked minority). A mildewed old man by the door volunteered to go down to the public house at the corner, and all those who wished to drink dropped their pennies into his cap. Neddy ostentatiously refused; but Mary was not softened toward him.

She took advantage of the temporary confusion to hiss into his ear that he was far too *theoretical*: could he not have some regard for folk's instinctive feelings? Stung, he rose to speak as soon as the house was recalled to order.

He moved an amendment: in fact quite an imaginative one. The railway company, he said, were shifting heaven and earth to present themselves as a glorious triumph of modern enterprise, and the opening of the line would

be all pageantry from end to end. Very well then, let the people contribute
to the carnival. Why not set up a worker's handloom at the very edge of the
track, and have a poor handloom weaver – perhaps old Jack Scuffham
himself? – working away at his despised trade, in full view of all the nobs?
Posters and banners about him, of course, make a regular side-show of it! A
representative man in silent dignity, to challenge the inhuman machine.

Mrs Scuffham asked, who was to pay for the yarn?

A leery youth with a paisley-print neckerchief underneath his sallow
jaw offered to steal yarn from his place of work. He looked as though he
might be able to do so very efficiently: his suggestion was deprecated, but
no one actually forbade it. He seconded the amended resolution and it
passed with acclamation. The meeting, after all, was beginning to get a grip
on its business. Bright ideas came thick and fast. A march of protest to the
Manchester railway station, to meet the first train and show its passengers
what people thought of it. A special edition of Citizen Bentham's
newspaper with a special article by Citizen Craig. A letter to comrades in
Liverpool offering and requesting support for a joint petition or rally. A
unilateral rally of protest on either side of the line upon the outskirts of
Manchester to support the handloom *tableau* and to throw rotten fruit and
so forth at the trains as they passed. 'So long as it's only fruit,' muttered
Bentham. 'We want no more Peterloos.'

'*Why not?*' bawled the long carrier.

Neddy – who as a boy had been a terrified member of the St Peter's Fields
crowd, his dreams distorted for life by the sudden blood, the flashing of
sabres, the enormous trampling horse-hoofs – told him at once why not.
He pointed out that Manchester even yet had no proper city corporation,
nor member of parliament, nor serious police beyond the brutal yeomanry
(who were ready any day to do again what they did then). Let none present
here forget, constitutional reform was the first of their priorities, on behalf
– he stammered and coughed among the clouds of tobacco smoke, his
spectacles falling off – on behalf of a responsible citizenship, seeking only
their just right, as working men and women whose diligence and craft-skill
made their nation what it was! Discipline and determination: that was the
message this Iron Duke must take back to London; as a soldier he would
recognise it and quail.

'Formidable we must be, but on no account recklessly violent. I mean,
not a mob; above all, I mean, not Luddites!'

He ought to have stopped there, for he had the meeting largely with him.
But his own mention of Luddites sent him off on a different tack. He'd
found a chance, he said, to examine one of the train-engines: such a
marvellous piece of work, he was ashamed it was made in Newcastle, why

wasn't Manchester first? He gave the meeting a brief lecture, of how the valve-gear was connected to the pistons and the drive transmitted to the great wheels. He compared Mr Stephenson to Leonardo da Vinci.

Mary poked at the back of his thigh until he sat down. He blushed all over and took her hand; she did not rebuff him.

Even as he sat, the final point of his speech was thrown into doubt by the next speaker's embittered gloss upon it. A ferret-faced man wearing thick yellow whiskers who had said nothing all evening (but had drunk more than a few goes of the toddy) erupted with detailed statistics: there was no doubt about it, he proved, Geordie's Geordies were already at work upon this rail-road in every skilled trade of the schedule, not a Lancashire lad got a look in – except they chose to humble themselves sweating pick-and-shovel with a gang of damned Irishers; it was deliberate, it was malicious, it was just what you'd expect! Why wasn't Manchester first? Because Liverpool masters and Manchester masters together were in conspiracy to do down their own workforce. Let Citizen Craig think of *that* next time he felt high-falutin!

The meeting ended in xenophobic acrimony.

FIVE

Joe Sandars was no fool; he saw the dangers of the duke's coming, and set himself to outflank them. Before it could open, the railway must be made attractive and familiar to all. Pomposity about progress only went so far; folk needed *encouragement*, by down-to-earth jolly example. Which is how Fanny Kemble got her ride on a locomotive.

In the days prior to the ceremony, George Stephenson himself was taking *Rocket* for final test runs, after improvements to the valve-gear, with and without carriages, up and down the sixteen miles between Liverpool and Newton. Sandars notified the newspapers; brought visitors to sit in the carriages; persuaded George to allow them, at proper intervals, onto the footplate.

So of course he included the popular favourites from the Theatre Royal. Fanny was the only one of them actually to mount the engine. None of the gentlemen would do so, for they were all in white trousers as for a garden-party – delicious sunshine weather, the best possible for such an outing – and their attitude was decidedly 'garden-party', frivolous and foolish, Fanny thought, when there was so much to be absorbed and learned (although she herself was as merry as the others for all any of them could notice to the contrary). The ladies too refused the footplate; even Miss Tree, ashamed indeed of her lack of daring, so much in conflict with her stage *persona*; but, as she said, to combine a rocking engine-platform with her fashionable high-heeled boots was just the thing to break an ankle, and she owed it to her public to keep her bones in one piece.

Fanny was not at all sure what *she* owed to the public; at any rate, the Liverpool public. She found the city extremely depressing, and was puzzled to discover the reason. Worse than depressing, in fact; it seemed to her that there was a kind of *miasma* impregnating the whole place, streets, buildings, docksides, the ships in the river, the people. The pain in her side came daily, intermittently, at unpredictable times, and every night she had dreams. They were abominable.

Human faces, limbs, bodies, in abandoned and sordid contortions of pain: while she herself before their eyes – glaring, agonised, demonic eyes – was compelled to enact all the parts from her own play (Francis I) until her gestures failed through utter weariness and her throat was like hot sandpaper; and all the time they howled and howled, only to fall grimly silent when she ceased her performance and stood fainting before them for the applause they refused to render.

Every morning she knew these dreams had drained her; knew she had suffered them, but could not remember their content.

There was an old man in her lodgings, uncle of the landlady, a retired ship's-mate. In his youth he had sailed on slavers: he told Fanny cruel stories of that bad traffic. He said he was sorry for it. But the tone of his tales made her wonder whether he really was. She detected a *relish*; as an aged rake might vaunt his conquests and yet weep for the infections he had spread.

Also, her father thought fit to tell her a tale of his own; how thirty years ago George Frederick Cooke, a disreputable but powerful actor, sometime rival of the Kemble family, had been playing the same Theatre Royal. He was drunk, lost his lines, he was hissed, he hissed back; assuring the angry audience that insults from a town 'where every brick is cemented with an African's blood' were no hurt to an English artist, but rather a badge of honour. Charles offered the story as a local warning of the sort of indiscipline to be avoided by a sound professional, even when deeply pickled. Which it obviously was; but it moved Fanny intensely, and she could not quite say why.

Also, she had something new to hide from her father. A few days since, she'd received a letter, from Algeciras in Spain: her dearest John, her noble brother (noble, that was to say, to the point of imbecility) had slipped in secret across the sea, to enlist in an absurd rebellion – 'to fight in the cause of liberty' – when he ought to have been at his expensive studies for which *she* must work so hard. She knew nothing of Spanish politics, except that they contained *no* liberty. Would she ever see John again? The whole affair was surely a species of *opéra bouffe*; but even so, men could get killed. And how to tell Charles? who might upon the instant go chasing after his son, madcap for democracy (or more probably, family pride), and so become embroiled himself! Dismal conclusion: there was nothing she could do, but write about it to 'H' in the strictest confidence, and then try to forget it until the chance of further news.

The day of the private train-ride she was woken unusually early by some noise in the street; it broke into her dreams before the dream had attained its due end; her weary *Francis I* was still progressing and the anguished audience still howled. She sat up in bed with a start; now she realised, awake, all the images of her sleep.

Every face, every stark torso, every twisted leg and arm in that seething crowd

was jet black: she was giving her art to the cargo of a slave-deck, and (worse)
she could not tell whether she herself was a part of the cargo or of the ship's
crew that had battened it down.

Enormous relief, then, to be out in the countryside, upon the clean-cut
sweep of the rail-road, where all was new, free, rejuvenating. Relief, too,
among the railwaymen, as well as excitement; they had at last completed
what so many had foretold could never be put together; while if true
excitement lacked among her fellow visitors, *she* at least knew how they
were privileged before all England to ride these rails today. *Of course* she
must go on the engine! and disperse her dreams with one swift rush. The
slave-trade was ended, and slavery very nearly so; morbid fancy could not
live in the presence of this Stephenson, a natural democrat if ever she met
one.

(And her pain so suddenly gone – what had it felt like? where precisely
had she been feeling it? – forgotten, altogether.)

She repented having spoken of the engine as a terrible *dragon*. Instead
she now saw 'a snorting little animal which she felt rather inclined to pat' –
she wrote all this down that evening in a long laughing letter to 'H' – an
affectionate pretty animal, was what she described, in no way domineering
or contrary to a human scale, and very much the obliging friend of the very
human man who so gently induced it to go fast or go slow or pull hard or
run gaily alone.

She wrote of the man that she was 'horribly in love' with him – what did
she mean but that he was neither duke nor sultan, nor yet dyed-haired
Mercutio who would rather be a Romeo but no longer knew how to do it?
Nor was he a youth: it was not desire she felt but a sense of *pride* in his
nearness, that she shared his warm glee in the work he had accomplished.
For the first time in her life she met an imagination as powerful as hers, into
which she could not possibly enter. She asked him (at speed across the
height of a huge viaduct, her bonnet off, her dark hair flying) how exactly
had he come to see his road as it would be built, when no one before him
had ever conceived such a thing, except as a magical illusion?

He gave her his crooked smile: 'I never asked how it happened, it wor
there inside my head, I looked at it a-slantways, it seemed like good sense.'

And then he said, 'You're a playactor. How can *you* guess what to do to
show the folk in front of you you're naea Miss Kemble but a Miss Juliet and
want to wed wi'your young Eye-talian? You'd not get much time, stood
there upon stage-boards, to bide still and think it all out.'

She replied, rather foolishly, 'Well, we rehearse.'

He knew better. 'Aye: there'll be *work* to it; work and thought, o'course:

but I'll bet there's very many as might rehearse for months and months and nivver make a show. Timothy Hackworth built rail-roads; a few miles frae pit to keel-wharf; aye an' he hauled coals on 'em! But he didna build *this* *'un*; my God, he could nivver!' He spoke about Hackworth to himself rather than to Fanny, and the wind carried the words away; perhaps just as well, his emphasis was quite malignant.

And then he told her all about his engineering techniques, the practical difficulties of building the line, the more slippery political difficulties of making people understand how and why it should be built. He was astonished to discover that expounding these matters to Fanny was exactly like talking to another engineer. He need simplify nothing, her acute inquisitive eyes took every bit of it in. He too, for an hour or so, was 'horribly in love' with her. He did not choose to write about it to any old friend. His marriage was long-lasting and virtuous.

He had been in two minds about Sandars's zeal for publicity. He himself deserved a 'fanfare', no doubt about it; but better to keep it back until the official opening had taken place and all his trains were running to time. The heart of the railway must be daily reliability: when he'd made that, *then* he could swagger. And he had almost been too afraid of the traditional reputation of actresses to permit one onto his footplate. Now he knew otherwise. Of course they rehearsed, but it was 'there inside their head', she and he were of the same class. Even so, same meant different; so altogether different as to curtail (after an hour or so) his improper and hoar-headed fancies. He was in many ways a most traditional man; she utterly enchanted him; he had swaggered, and never wished he hadn't.

He told Robert during the evening that *Rocket* answered very well, but there was a deal more work and thought to be put into that valve-gear.

SIX

'I am not familiar with the northern cities. Don't wish to be. So why d'you have me go there?' The duke was beginning to examine his role in the reformists' intrigue: the more he perceived of it, the less he cared for it. 'Remember Joseph Bonaparte, going into Madrid when his brother made him King of Spain? They rose against him in the thoroughfares; and he had an entire army. What have *we* got, Peel?'

The home secretary admitted some doubts. 'Better, perhaps, to defer the visit till we incorporate police in Lancashire on the model of the metropolitan force; but then, your grace, the date of the railway – '

'Damn the railway. Why *me*? Don't like it at all. Bad enough that government must bank a commercial project with God knows how much of public funds. To insist on personal attendance is quite beyond the mark. Yet *you* insisted. Why?'

He confessedly failed to understand Peel; not altogether a gentleman and altogether too *political*; from Lancashire moreover, smoky, sooty, disturbed areas. Spain again in the duke's memory; just so must hapless 'King Joseph' have conferred with some Spanish official supposedly in collaboration with the occupying troops of France – but how would he have known for certain, how would he have trusted? *'Guerrilleros'*: he had just been reading the word in a very private little letter, and it stabbed at him.

Sir Robert Peel deployed politics. 'Your grace, it's a question of Huskisson. Catholic emancipation turned every High Tory against us – '

'I know; I didn't want it; had to have it; I must endure it.'

'But your government will not endure, unless you strengthen it at once. Which means Huskisson's support. Formal negotiation with him would appear a humiliation, far too overt, and the King would deeply distrust it. But you do have to talk with him. A social encounter between two gentlemen, as it were by accident, between Liverpool and Manchester – '

'Breaking our necks behind a damned steam-kettle? I don't like the word "accident".' The duke brooded. 'There was a fellow once tried to show me a new pattern of artillery rocket: it blew up in his face, damnably nearly in mine; we had fatigue parties collecting pieces of him for the rest of the afternoon.'

'*Rocket* is but one of their machines, I think; not the designation of a type.

But if it causes you concern, let me forward a memorandum: "pray submit for approval names of locomotive-engines for the official train." '

'Dammit, man, what are you talking about?' He stared at Peel, astonished; he knew nothing of engines' names. Peel stared back, thinking he *must* know and was concealing superstition. The two of them in government were rat and dog in the same basket.

When Peel was political, the duke turned abruptly military. 'Appreciate our dispositions. The enemy's too. So! If Huskisson's to be cultivated, then he'll urge me to more reform; and this time damned fundamental, erasing the very basis of the constitution. Abhorrent. Won't have it. Won't have a government either, if we can't persuade Huskisson. How can *I* be persuaded that *our* brand of reform would be less of a calamity than *reform*? Ha.'

'Ha' meant a sort of joke. The duke did not expect laughter, and Peel's laugh at best was an unconvincing gulp. Several moments of silence.

'Enemy dispositions. Desirable in a battle to know who your enemy *is*. Fact of the matter, Peel; I don't. High Tories, Liberal Tories, Whigs? I think I'm fighting in a fog.'

'For the purpose of this – ah, campaign – ' (as uneasy with the metaphor as he was with the man) – 'shall we say the immediate enemy is the Great Lancashire Unwashed? The *sans-culottes* of Peterloo.'

The duke glared. Was the sarcasm aimed at himself? Peterloo to cast its cloud on Waterloo? Nor did he like '*sans-culottes*'; French revolutionary levies had all but beaten all of Europe; was it possible again, and amongst Englishmen? In northern cities? Agrarian riots in the southern counties already – *Bastille stormed in Paris*, remember? *Blazing* châteaux *the length of the Loire* – enemy upon two fronts, classic horns of a strategic dilemma – or – *Bluecher's troops and his own, drawn together at glowering sunset, the last hour of the last hope of the Corsican irrevocably caught in the grip.*

Then his expression relaxed: 'Let's see your muster-rolls.'

Peel's dispatch case was full of documents, security precautions devised by the Home Office. The duke cast his eye down the lists, made his succinct amendments, scribbled 'approved, Wellington' across the file-cover, handed them back.

He sat and brooded. 'As far as I can determine, this railway notion is best suited to *sans-culottes* above all. Agitators, upon a steam-train, can move 'emselves at whim from one city to another. That is, if sprockets and pistonwork act as they tell me they should. Itinerant *guerrilleros*: at half-a-mile a minute, by God. I believe it a calamity; exactly like reform.'

His belief was firm; nonetheless he was too shrewd, too long in the tooth, wilfully to confront and reject either calamity outright. And thereby (*approved, Wellington*) he fixed the death-day of William Huskisson.

*

The duke did not travel directly to Liverpool; the less time he spent in that city the better. He was to stay in the mansion of one of the great Tory magnates, some miles from the industrial districts, in the hill-country of the south-western Pennines. Disagreeable excursions thence were already in prospect, one to a factory in Manchester, another to a town called Staleybridge – a hotbed of unrest (they unwillingly told him) where workpeople had refused duty in order to extort higher wages. The duke never refused *his* duty; once persuaded it was necessary to 'troop colours' in such places, he would troop them, and no malingering: a cool and commanding demeanour had in the past overawed disaffected battalions, maybe it would again.

And what of the little Kemble, his postal flirtation? To honour its intent he must stay for a night in the seaport, in some public hotel; undesirable, prejudicial to security. He had written to her so recklessly from his first knowledge of the need for his visit, without thinking at all of the dangers: good God, he'd been like a subaltern suddenly sent on a mission to Vienna! Why had they not told him, until it was almost too late, that the northern people hated him so much? Peel knew, Peel concealed the truth, Peel had been up to his tricks. The constabulary and military arrangements would be thought excessive in St Petersburg for a progress of the Tsar. The duke was never afraid for his own safety; but mob attacks on a prime minister imperilled the nation at large. Most galling to have involved a young woman in the vicious business. Duty demanded he withdraw from the rendezvous as chivalrously as possible. He'd send a note from Manchester. No doubt she'd be glad to be relieved of obligation to a debilitated pantaloon. Having decided, he expelled her, most competently, from his mind.

Somewhere along the road, in the ugly Black Country, which (he was assured) was if anything less black than Manchester, one of the springs of his carriage came adrift. He had to wait in a coaching inn (semi-*incognito*) until repairs could be concluded. His equerry ordered a private room; the duke went and sat there, alone at his own request, and grimly patient. Luncheon was provided. The inn was very busy, travellers in and out all day, great bustle and disturbance between house and yard. He was in the building, all told, for about an hour; in the course of that hour, a curious encounter with unexpected effect upon his subsequent conduct.

Was there something familiar about the maid who brought him tea after his meal? – something more than familiar – something scandalously well-known – and intimate.

'Good God, you're no waitress; you are Harriette Wilson, and you've laid me an ambush; why, dammit, in masquerade. Or *is* it a masquerade? Good God, child, don't tell me you are driven to this work for a living?'

'Child' was inappropriate; but he thought of her so, of course. Child more or less was what she had been when he last knew her, when he frequented her in Mayfair – the most impudent and delightful courtesan of the wartime years. Nor was 'frequented' quite appropriate either: two or three occasions only, upon quick visits to England to report to the War Office, while his ill-judged marriage was depressing his spirits, and the French (even to him) appeared unbeatable. She might have grown, had promised to grow, into a ripe and lovely mature woman: he looked at her now with care. He saw a haggard yet swollen face, one side of it all discoloured as though not long since it had met with a fist. Signs of drink, too: he had spent years detecting drink in the features of untrustworthy subordinates, he was not to be mistaken.

But his second question was absurd; she could never be a provincial waitress; without doubt it was a *ruse de guerre* to get her past his equerry. Had she followed him to this inn, or seen him by chance in the lobby and seized her opportunity?

She saw what he was thinking, and rippled into laughter. A slight forcing of tone as though her old gaiety must be quickly reconstructed from memory; but it was Harriette's laughter, well enough, and for a moment it went – well, not quite to his heart, but certainly, most surprisingly, to his loins. He had thought himself (aged one-and-sixty) to have reached that sad condition where he must tell his loins at length what he wished them to feel, rather than rely on them to leap unprompted into their own alertness and thus tell *him*. He did not welcome this sensation of surprise. Wilson was not Kemble. (And *Kemble* was supposed to be nowhere near his imagination.)

He was angry; he accused her. A year or two ago she had sent him a manuscript of her insolent memoirs and attempted to blackmail him. And here she had come to renew the performance?

She retorted with spirit: 'You defied me to publish, and yet you threw lawyers at me; you called the book *trash*, yet how could you know it trash if you did not trouble to read it? Ah, but one peek – I'm sure you gave one small peek – I *had* marked the pages, red ribbons just like a state-paper, I got it up so very neatly, I knew you liked everything neat, *tout à fait comme il faut pour monseigneur le maréchal*!' Again she was laughing; not only his loins but his fingers were a-prickle. To hit her? to caress her? why, he'd never hit a woman in his life.

She was standing very close to him, and all he seemed to see was her eyes, narrow-lidded, green, as tricky as they had ever been. Her mouth a tight little impish asymmetrical V-shape; he was keenly aware of it, how well he remembered! And yet he did not see it. Only the green eyes.

'Of course I threatened lawyers. You were in Paris, you made use of the diplomatic bag (I do not ask how) to despatch me your libels. I could not have sent a writ, not into France; I merely made sure you'd not pursue me in England. I appear to have miscalculated.'

'Pursue? Oh great duke, what a word from a lord excellency who so mournfully stood all night outside my house with the air of a rat-catcher, the pouring rain in rivulets down his excellent nose, when I had quite expressly warned I should not be at home!'

'*Assez de tes blagues, madame*: the incident never occurred.'

As a gentleman he ought not to notice the damage to her face. But as a gentleman he could not forget it. To his annoyance he felt deeply sorry for her.

'Why don't I sent for the constable? Fact is, ma'am, I don't think that for a blackmailer you've been much of a success. Fact is, you had your money from a good many gulls, but not for yourself. *Someone else* set you on to obtain it, *someone else* went and spent it, *someone else* (I do believe) in this inn at this moment awaits your report. If you return empty-handed he'll give you another of *these*?' So he stroked her marred cheek – her hair beside her cheek – he let his fingers linger, and then pulled them away. 'Rochfort, his name, yes? My position permits me informations not always very generally available. You met him a few years ago when you were washed-up on an awkward beach, he was convenient in your predicament; but, child, how could you allow him to behave to you like a slave-driver?'

'*Parce que, monseigneur, je brûle, et je souffre!* Oh godsake, Duke, I love the bloody man!' And he was sure she told him the truth.

'By God,' he said, 'you've given in; collapsed your front, broken square, very nearly a *sauve-qui-peut*. What's to be done with you?'

A pint of claret was on the table; he had drunk less than half of it. He remembered other bottles, such a long long time ago. 'A shame not to finish that. They only brought me one glass. No: there are more on the sideboard.' He rose and filled for them both. 'Among the nonsense in your book, which (as you know) I did not read, you had one anecdote almost correct. I came from Spain in the middle of the war, called upon you, found you ill, or so you seemed: in a scrape over a worthless fellow was *my* guess, but you wouldn't confirm it. You said I talked with you for three hours and wrote you a cheque.'

Their eyes met over the wine-glasses. His were very bleak. She did not know whether to say it or not; but as he remained silent, she took the risk: 'Do you mean to write another one?'

'Face-to-face is quite different from a letter-of-extortion posted in Paris. I'm in the book and you've published, I've no more to lose; so it's not quite a sign of weakness. Ha.' He had found pen and ink and was already making out the cheque. 'Tradition, y'see, most important, we should not forget friends, even when we thought there was no humbug about 'em and then alas there was. I don't mean your blackmail. No, the man who put you up to it, your feelings for him, slop and slush; damsilly novelette for boarding-school misses. *You* don't write like that, why credit it when someone else does?'

'You don't know what I write: except that it's *trash*.'

'My attorney's word, not mine. Point of fact, they made me laugh, your memoirs: lies, of course, but caustic; full of a strange good sense. So write me some more. Write for me, y'see, not *him*.'

Her skirt irresistibly up; and the cheque into the top of her stocking. Upon an impulse he thrust out his arm; he might have embraced her, but she twisted away. She seemed suddenly to have become bored with him. 'Ah, yes,' he muttered, baffled, 'anything else I can do for you, I – ah – '

She amazed him with her quick little whisper: 'Some other place or time I'd be pleasured if you'd kiss my cunt; sweetly, I mean, no ruffianism. Rochfort don't do it, not nearly as well as he might.' Her hand slid across the fork of his trouser, which amazed him again: and then she was gone like an eel.

'The devil!' he declared, to the door as it closed behind her. 'She used to say that and mean it, and I *did*; by God, there was no humbug. I wonder was the money all that she came for? God knows. I used to dream of her on the Spanish roads.'

He wasted no time in dreaming now. He wrote a short note, called his equerry, gave him orders: 'There's a man in this inn, describes himself as a Colonel Rochfort. He might look like a king's officer, in fact he's a swell-mobsman. Find him before he leaves. Detach him from his lady, bring him to an empty room, hold him. Discreet help from the landlord, two or three stout stable-lads sufficient for the business. If the lady has a cheque of mine, well and good. If she hasn't, then *he* has; get it from him and give it back to her. Put her in her post-chaise or whatever she came in, and tell her to go to blazes. Make sure she does go. Then let him out and give him a choice. He admits he's an extortionist and undertakes upon the instant to remove himself to France, signing this paper accordingly; or you send for the constable and charge him with – with picking your pocket. Sacrifice your watch as evidence. It's worth perjury a dozen times over. Once he's gaoled we can think of a stronger indictment. You suppose you can do it?'

'Security of the kingdom, your grace; or the lady's honour?'

'Does it matter?'

'It is a little cavalier; we may one day need to justify it.'

'Lady's honour, lady's safety; never mind about the kingdom. Get along with you. Do it now.' The young man went.

The duke thought again of his duty toward Kemble; and wondered, had he assessed it correctly? For him, an unusual doubt. But now he knew himself more than capable of her; knew the insolence of his youth to be as green as he could wish; and knew that to get her, he would blunder into any sort of risk – very well, *she'd* be at risk – very well, so were his regiments and he'd brought them through in the end, to glory and heroic memories for them, glory for him and a prosperous dukedom.

He continued the road north in this extraordinary state of mind (not that anyone could have detected it behind the frigid exterior); a kind of living and breathing caricature of his enemies' view of him; the inside-out of his always arrogant secret self, now become totally egotistical and well-nigh violently irresponsible; to tell truth he was as out-of-discipline as the most predatory proletarian rabble of his own worst imaginings. He was –

the frog who would a-wooing go
with his rowley-powley gammon and spinach –

and he was perfectly aware of it and didn't care.

SEVEN

From early morning of the fifteenth of September, the great day of the railway's inauguration, chaos began to infiltrate the programme. The company's publicity in fact had exceeded itself, crowds were too large, expectations too urgent, the opposition too strongly alerted.

An array of trains was to leave Liverpool at half-past ten; not from the extreme end of the line, the dockyard platforms (built for goods traffic), but high up above the town, almost out in the fields; Crown Street terminus, nucleus already of a fast-increasing 'railway suburb'. This station, or posting hall, or carriage yard, or train shed (people were not yet quite sure how exactly it should be called) was a long open-ended barn containing an alighting platform, offices, and a triple gradient of rail running steeply up and out into a tunnel.

The tracks were filled with strings of carriages, open and closed; eight trains in all, to fetch everyone of any importance out of their own city into Manchester; in the early gloom and sporadic gaslight every carriage gleamed and glittered with bright new brasswork and paint, yellow and black, blue, pale grey, like so many crack stage-coaches.

From before dawn the station filled with citizens as well as trains; by no means all of them ticket-holding passengers, although no one without a ticket was supposed to be allowed through the gates. Redcoat soldiers and specially recruited constables strove to keep control. Parts of the railway premises were more thronged with constables and soldiers than citizens, in other corners the private persons so outnumbered the official as to create minor whirlpools of *sotto voce* riot, heaving, pushing, toe-treading, under-bred threats and blasphemy. It was not clear that the law-and-order men entirely knew what they were doing; some of the soldiers had loaded their muskets, officers were bawling at them to keep the cartridges in their belts. Serjeants pushed among the squads, bulbous-eyed from their choking neck-stocks, parade-states pinned into notebooks; doing their best to keep a count of the men. Here and there a 'king's bad bargain' had had a drink dodged for him by a civilian friend: names were being taken, angry promises flew about of floggings at the triangle next day.

An army band occupied a large portion of the passengers' platform, furiously blaring; sublimities by Handel, breezy airs from Dibdin's sea-pieces. A huge black man, turban on head, gold-braided white tabard over scarlet tunic, dominated the ranks to jerk up and down his 'Turkish music' (a sort of brass-merchant's shop-sign on a pole suspended armfuls of clashing cymbals and bells) in time with the big drum; ragged boys nearby played copycat with broomsticks and curtain-rings. He was well-known as a barracks character: before he enlisted he had been cook on an illegal slave-ship, and before that he was a slave himself until the ship's master slipped him his freedom as the side-issue of some West Indian deal. He dubbed himself Sammy Jingles and wore out harlots by the score, if one were to believe all he said when he was drunk.

There were no locomotives at Crown Street. The carriages would be wound by cable up through the short tunnel into the second station at Edge Hill, a fearful place, mouth of Hades, deep-cut into the rock; where engines were stalled like Pluto's horses in dark caverns either side of the excavation, and two great Trajan-column chimneys reared up to pour out smoke from the cable-haul machinery. At the outer end of this Tartarus pit the rail-lines were spanned by a high horseshoe arch in the Mahometan mode, the only building upon the railway to display any stylish fantasy. George Stephenson had called it 'gingerbread work'; he resented its triviality, but the directors insisted. Mr Sandars, secret theatre-lover, said they needed a 'swank proscenium'; he'd seen just the thing in last season's *Ali Baba*, and the architect obligingly made contact with the stage-designer to secure a brief loan of his drawings.

High up beside the corner of this arch Jack Scuffham erected his handloom of protest. There had been a change of plan, when somebody in the Manchester club realised the inland end of the line held no command-ing site for the demonstration. Liverpool comrades were appealed to, and came up with a powerful suggestion: as soon as the engines were put upon the trains, they must all, one by one, process beneath the horseshoe; every passenger's head would assuredly be tilted to catch a glimpse of the ornate portico, why should they not see the 'representative man' as the first vital sight upon their pilgrimage?

Neddy Craig was there; also Mrs Scuffham and all the Scuffham family, in their everyday tatters and dirt. Craig had had trouble with this: the Scuffhams at the last minute decided to wear their few best clothes, and took a great deal of persuading that it would not be altogether appropriate. He kept saying, 'This is a theatre show, a pageant of unemployment: of course it's quite true, but it's *play-acting* an'all, y'know!' At last they had seen his point and grudgingly stifled self-respect. He himself was shabby but dapper, Parisian barricade-style; velveteen jacket, flowing necktie, a jaunty visored forage cap with a strip of second-hand gold braid. He kept his spectacles in pocket. His poor eyesight badly needed their help; but he feared they might be smashed by some gang of Tory bruisers, also he believed he looked much more revolutionary without them. He was highly excited, deadly determined, and very very nervous.

They had arrived as early as two in the morning to make sure of a good place. A 'Liverpool comrade' was supposed to be there to meet them and to help them select their position: he was of course late, coming hearty and unrepentant long after they'd fixed everything unaided. The loom had been brought from Manchester upon Harry the carrier's wagon, Craig and the Scuffhams crowding on top. They all stayed in the wagon wrapped in blankets (the children inevitably fretful) until daylight encouraged them to emerge. Neddy dispensed hot breakfast from a haybox entrusted him by Mary. It was a blustery sunrise, wind from the west, far-off promise of rain; but no more chilly than was seasonable. By five o'clock they were hemmed in by people, all sorts of people, ill-dressed, well-dressed, thrusting to the parapets, craning over to see the locomotives as the crews coked them up, kindled the furnaces, worked them out of the caves, filled the tender-barrels with water. Boys began to throw stones down; enginemen swore foully; constables lashed out at the boys; soldiers pushed forward to add strength to the constables.

These were not regular troops but the Lancashire Militia, a half-trained unserviceable corps. One of their hobbledehoy lieutenants came banging on the tailboard of the wagon: great cry and bluster to have the horses put into it, 'Get it out of the bloody road, can't you!' – indeed it was hampering the crowds. Harry cantankerously obeyed him. The wagon, when shifted, revealed the loom, perched right against one of the turrets of the bridge, and old Jack Scuffham stringing his warp. 'What o'God's name's all this? A bloody gallows to hang up a scarecrow?' The lieutenant was a useless son of an overbearing mill-owner; all his father's bad qualities and none of the good. He kicked at the loom's frame and began to tug the yarn off. Scuffham and his spitfire wife might well have gone for him, eyes and throat; but Neddy (quick as a panther) stepped in to prevent it.

'A statement of pride, captain, from the weavers of the county; their ancient craft shown forth *at behest of the railway directors* to celebrate the duke's passage and enhance his better knowledge of us. We're just waiting on a young lad with the patriotic flags to make a proper show of it.'

The officer (as well he might) stared in astonishment at the ragged Scuffhams. He could think of nothing more cogent to say than: 'Fucking shit-heap and fuck off!' He gave the loom a parting kick and moved away with his half-company.

The theatrical party, two Kembles and one Tree, arrived at Crown Street in a hackney-carriage a little before ten, startled and bewildered by the unexpected extent of the tumult. They should have been earlier, but Charles had taken a very long time to determine what he should wear. Contrary to popular prejudice, the young actresses had been fully attired at a most reasonable hour; but then neither of them was much spoiled by precocious success, and Ellen (indeed extremely fashionable) took her dressing so seriously that she always began it ages before she need. In the end, Charles decided that a modified modern Brutus was the role most fitting for his mood. Pearl-grey suit for unblemished integrity, dark-grey waistcoat for democratic fortitude, blood-red buttons and cravat for – well, allegorically, blood; and a low-crowned straw hat with a very wide brim for the hope that the hot summer would hold.

'This liberty-devouring duke,' he pronounced mournfully as he alighted, 'needs to be greeted with severe trappings.' (Fanny thought briefly of her brother and wondered what trappings *he* was wearing, among the Spanish *guerrilleros*, if indeed there were any, and he wasn't just sitting in a wine-shop in Gibraltar. Then she hated herself for not having recollected him until this moment. Then she firmly made the effort, hardened her longing heart against his callous irresponsibility, and forgot about him for the morning; he had, after all, gone there with his whole clique of Cambridge poets; they were so very puffed-up and silly.) 'But on the other hand,' Charles rattled on, 'we require light-heartedness to do justice to the novelty of science. I fancy I have selected as it were the *golden mean*? Good God, the crowd! Sandars couldn't have done better, he'll be sold out for weeks. What, not a single usher to lead us to the conveyances? Ah, he's slipped up there. I suppose if I *brandish* the tickets. . . ?' He fumbled in his pocket, looking keenly about him with the utmost assumption of dignity. But there was no dignity at all; the crowd hustled and heaved, tickets were waved in the air, shouting men demanded immediate attention, flustered porters disclaimed responsibility. The band for the fourteenth time played the march from *Rinaldo*; apt, for did it not recur in *The Beggar's Opera* as, 'Hark I hear the sound of coaches!'? But few could hear anything; the chaotic babel under the echoing barn roof all but quenched the strong beat of the music.

Sandars saw Ellen's ostrich plumes, and struggled perspiring to Charles's elbow, so elated and burdened all at the same time that he was barely able to speak. 'Ah, ha ha, Mr Kemble, dear ladies, my dears; very nearly too late! – they're mounting the folk already, get your seats, get your seats; pray, sir, don't ask me, *I* don't know where: didn't they give you a coloured ticket? Ah, right! That's it then, blue tickets, blue train, fourth train to leave, you'll find yourselves behind *Rocket* when we get you up to Edge Hill, blue rosettes on every coach doorhandle, we made sure there's no room for mistake!' Charles worked his gold-knobbed cane in front of him like Brutus's dagger; forcing passage onto the platform; dragging the two young women at his rear, hand-in-hand and helpless with laughter, as though a pair of Bo-peep's lambs had been caught at the brandy. At last, a firm cordon of soldiers: beyond them, comparative good order.

An inspector, irritably courteous, fingertip to hat-brim: 'Blue tickets, sir; very good, sir: cross t'track between them carriages there, please; *do* let your ladies watch out not to stumble. Carriages are made up into trains, sir, *not* separate, please note. Blue train, line two, top end o't'station. Choose your vehicle, open or closed.'

Charles of course, had to think about it: 'Open, d'you say? The prospect would be better; but – ah – do you not suppose it might rain?'

The inspector was no longer attentive; other passengers claimed his time. Fanny said, positively, 'Open!' Ellen was not so sure; but Fanny led the way, burrowing (so it seemed) down an endless narrow corridor between massive iron coach-wheels and dangerously projecting steps, until they discovered blue emblems on carriages to their right-hand side. They climbed one of the sets of steps, and pushed for places upon a long truck which (had it been horsedrawn) they might have called a *char-à-banc*; there was an awning overhead, so at least they would avoid an absolute drenching if the weather disappointed them.

The seats were not cushioned. Ellen said, 'You well may laugh at fashion, Fanny; but fashion today provides you with several good thicknesses of petticoat.'

'Thank God,' replied Fanny, profanely. She did not commonly invoke the deity; but her bonnet had been bashed by an elbow as she came up the steps, and she thought some bows of ribbon might have been knocked off. She was sweating, too, just like fat Sandars; she sat and mopped her face with the frankness of a washerwoman, staring around her at the curious sights. Strangest of all was another train, empty, immediately to the left of theirs: the foremost carriage (open to the sky) was built up in tiers in the manner of a concert platform. Behind it, almost within reach of her outstretched arm, a most glorious canopied chariot, all curlicues and arabesques and corded fringes of scarlet and gold with plush armchairs like thrones within carved gilded columns; a pair of outsize crowns or coronets upon the apex of its roof: a first-class practicable prop for a Christmas pantomime extravaganza, to be wheeled onstage perhaps with a chorus of *sultans*? Or perhaps – something else?

Miss Tree must have thought so too. She improvised a line from an imaginary sensation-drama: 'The hearse of death, gracious heaven! Incarnadine, uncanny hue; most weirdly refulgent!'

A serious old clergyman leaned forward to rebuke her: 'Madam, his grace the duke is to ride in that beautiful car. Mind you, though, I couldn't say what the lorry in front of it's supposed to be for.'

'For a pride of lions from the menagerie, *sejant regardant* at the feet of Europe's saviour?' Very easy for Ellen to break her coy jokes. Fanny's reflections upon Wellington were a good deal less *fluid*. Who'd have dreamed he'd be so close to her so soon in the day? Far better could she have thrust him to the back of her mind for the next few important hours. She had not yet thought of her response to the further letter he had had delivered last night to the stage door; and she would *have* to! Before this very evening, before she went upon stage. She busied herself, head averted, with repairs to her bonnet, biting her lip in annoyance: head averted was no way to receive all these unprecedented sensations.

Upon hearing the detested title, Charles Kemble had thrust out his chest and cocked his chin proudly above the rim of his stock. 'If and when *the man* arrives (for who can say whether he will dare?), and if he presumes to take cognisance of me, I shall know how to receive his advances!'

Even as he spoke, they heard a crescendo of noise from outside the station; cheering, apparently, but mingled with catcalls and boos. The band's rendition of 'Tom Bowling' stopped short in mid-bar; to be instantly replaced with 'See the Conquering Hero!'. The cheers were now inside the station; the catcalls continued outside. Angry cries as of violent conflict. Distant concussions of smashing glass. Nothing at all to be seen from the seats of the blue train. In haste, Fanny resumed her headgear.

Then, at ground level, beyond the sultanic chariot (or hearse) she suddenly descried movement; a cluster of tall hats, officers' shakoes, ladies' feather-fringed bonnets. As they came to a halt, one of the hats began to rise slowly upwards; its wearer was essaying the chariot steps. A short, trim, erect, elderly shape, swathed in a Spanish cavalryman's night-dark mantle; stern hawk-nosed countenance; unexpected appearance of (almost) hesitation when confronted by an insecure and (perhaps) distastefully lavish arrangement of seats. A younger man, brisker, more obviously assured, had jumped up behind the duke (for it must be the duke!) and now whispered in his master's ear, leading him to sit down in the very centre of the spectacular carriage. Thereafter the remaining hats, bonnets, shakoes, flooded up into the vehicle until every chair was filled.

Charles inspected his watch. 'Twenty-eight minutes past the hour, exactly to the second: who can say the old devil's not punctual?'

The old devil could have turned his head and talked with intimacy, had he wished, to Fanny; the two coaches were so close side-by-side. As it was, he faced mordantly forwards; a profile like the figurehead of a frigate. Charles's outraged glare offered silent invisible challenge to his as-yet unconscious adversary. But then, everyone was glaring – or at any rate, gazing; all along the blue train heads stuck out, hands waved, hats waved, flags, ecstasy of curiosity and idiotic hero-worship. The music had stopped; the band scrambled in awkward hurry aboard what the clergyman had called the *lorry*: the duke was to be heralded with sounding brass, drums, and woodwind all the thirty-odd miles to Manchester.

In horror Fanny saw her father jump white-faced to his feet, pull his hat down over his eyes, lay hand across heart, open lips to give utterance. Heaven knew what he would say! Despite the noise, he was sure to be heard! She plucked at his coat-hem; no use. He aimed his resonant mouth directly toward Wellington and portentously enunciated: 'Lord Duke!' Hawk-profile slowly revolved, vexation and offence in the very move-ment. Charles Kemble was no longer Brutus. But Caius Cassius, vindictive, of adamantine purpose:

Why, man, he doth bestride the narrow world
Like a Colossus; and we petty men
Walk under his huge legs – !

At which point he was interrupted. By no indignant shouts but a genteel flicker of clapping hands. Did none of those grandees realise how Cassius's speech was an incitement to murder? Apparently not. The duke lifted his hat and bowed toward the actor, recognition in his frosty eye. 'Why, Kemble! You too, made a parcel of, in the mechanical rattletrap? Damned glad to see you, sir. Oh, and hear you moreover. You've lost none of your power.' He was bowing a second time, several inches lower. 'Miss Kemble? We haven't met.'

Oh he could *not* have recognised Fanny; her bonnet-wings, she was certain, effectively hid her face?

'Fanny, my dear; the duke.' Why, how was her father behaving? Abominable! he stooped now, he kowtowed, positively gloated over his own servility. What could she do? She could do nothing: but reveal herself, blush, simper, pretend to curtsey from the absurd slatted hardwood of a rail-road carriage bench!

'Most delighted, Miss Kemble. Have a comfortable journey; *and back again*. Very good.' A third bow; to Ellen. Not the ghost of the smallest smile. Wellington's hat returned bolt upright to Wellington's upright head, Wellington's nose once again to the front. Wellington's train, without warning, began to slide out of the station; the only sounds of its passage the clumsy creak of pulleys and cables, the distant clank of the winding engine, affectedly affrighted *oohs* and *ahs* from self-dramatising patricians; until the bandsmen aboard the music-lorry (disappearing into the tunnel) magnificently struck up the 'Trumpet Voluntary'.

Father's eyes met daughter's; daughter's satirical, father's more than a little guilty. Ellen, not fully aware of the historic depth of Mr Kemble's political convictions, was puzzled and disquieted. Despite her irreverent jokes, she really did think the duke as battle-hero was thoroughly suited to civilian leadership; she would have made (Fanny once told her) an excellent loyal peasant in King John's guard at Runnymead. She was now so childish-proud of being granted a Wellingtonian salute, even a silent one, that she felt it best not to comment upon the incident at all.

The blue train had to wait at least twenty minutes before it could follow its three predecessors up to Edge Hill. At about the twelfth minute, Charles concluded he should speak. 'Fanny girl, you must understand, one distinguishes between the office and the man.'

'So one does, Father, of course. But I didn't quite know you *knew* the man. You've always talked of him as though he were some sort of graveyard bogey. But, goodness, wasn't he genial?' There was a warning in her own geniality, which he did not at once detect.

'Oh highly genial; yes, he can be. He was ambassador, you know, in Paris, just after the war. I had the honour to recite for him at an embassy picnic.'

'Honour?'

'And why not? He represented our country. So did I, upon the *artistic* plane. Greek, as it were, met Greek.'

'I always thought that little proverb implied mutual mistrust.'

'Yes, quite, exactly. I recited, he listened; we were *at arms' length*. He did not ask my opinion of government policy; I took care not to volunteer it.'

'You volunteered it just now.'

'Indeed I did.'

'And ambiguously, didn't you? You left out what Cassius meant:

Upon what meat doth this our Caesar feed
That he is grown so great? Age, thou art sham'd!

They all took what you were declaiming as a tribute. And then you stopped.'

'You know, child; you too ought to attempt a male role. I've never heard you try it before. Portia don't count. You and Miss Tree together, why not? Re-cast our *School for Scandal*, the Surface brothers!'

'Which of us for the rake, and which the hypocrite?' Sly question from minx Ellen, gladdened by the change of subject; she disliked domestic tensions.

'I fancy the hypocrite has already cast himself.' Fanny's tone was disagreeably acid. She repeated: 'You stopped. Was there a reason?'

'I *was stopped*, verb transitive. My public applauded. Even if they misinterpreted, I could not run counter to their expressed good opinion. A theatre artist does not *correct* the errors of an audience. Presumptuous. Unprofessional. Damned bad manners.'

'Damned bad.' (At which the eavesdropping clergyman behind her gave a scandalised cough.) 'And now you know why I tell you I do *not* enjoy the theatre.'

'But of course you enjoy it. You are *greedy* for it; don't dissemble!'

Charles's gesture clearly indicated that he had had the final word; the conversation was over. He sat sulking in silence until the train commenced its journey. Fanny too was silent; she *was* dissembling and knew it, not only about her ambivalence toward the theatre, nor upon the matter of her brother. A tiresome silly rigmarole came running into her brain; despite herself it formed itself into the sort of moral tale she had no desire to hear:

> Kemble dissembles
> Dissembling Kemble
> *Tonight at half-past ten*
> *Where will she be then?*
> Kemble dissemble
> Dissemble and
> Tremble
> And
> Tremble and
> Stumble
> And
> Stumble and
> CRUMBLE
> *And*
> *No more Kemble!*

And yet, for all his faults, her father *was* a superb actor (of the traditional sort): perhaps dissembling was an essential of the craft; inherited, like other skills; like, perhaps, a 'diseased mind'?

*

Neither sulks nor *les horreurs imprévues de l'amour futur* could survive the exhilarating reverberations of the gaslit tunnel and the brilliant emergence into Edge Hill's deep ravine. The other trains had gone on before; familiar little *Rocket*, spitting steam and all a-shudder with impatience, was more than ready to be coupled up; her sisters, *Dart*, *Arrow*, *Comet* and *Meteor*, waited in line for their own carriages below the cliff-face to one side; enthusiastic yardmen in clean shirts and new neckerchiefs (they had been promised a bonus on their wages if all went well) sprang to unhook the haulage cable and beckon the locomotive into place: smart bounce, backwards jerk, forward tug, and *crash*! A blank shot from a saluting cannon immediately above the tunnel-mouth – they were off, through the Moorish Arch!

The parapets overhead were crammed with faces; flags flew, ribbons streamed; Fanny, on her feet and stretching her neck like a mad swan to see what she could see beyond the edge of the awning, caught one quick glimpse of Jack Scuffham plying his shuttle, his family displaying their banner:

MUST MACHINES DO TORTURE-MURDER TO CRAFTWORKERS' RIGHTS?

Harry with a pasteboard placard:

EDGE HILL IS A KNACKER'S YARD!

– and Neddy Craig so downright fascinated by the belching swarm of steam-engines he was already near forgetting the true intention of his presence there.

That's all that she saw: in an instant the train was under and past the bridge, and so into the cutting beyond. She wondered, had the duke seen? She wondered, if he had, was he left with any notion what it meant? For herself, it brought tears to her eyes, and she wished she could ask him. If only for that opportunity, perhaps she *should* keep his tryst? She sighed, settled down in her seat, made up her mind to delight herself with the swift-unfolding landscape: not quite so swift, indeed, as upon her earlier rail trip; the leading train was under orders to proceed with deliberate care lest the ducal party be in any way shaken. Of necessity the trains behind it must trim their aspirations, even though they were now on the left-hand line while the duke's ran on the right.

She did not see (nor did she ever hear about) what happened beside the top of the Moorish Arch immediately *Rocket* had passed under it. The fifth train was being wound up through the tunnel, *Dart*'s driver had his hand on the regulator to move his engine out of the siding; the Lancashire Militia belatedly realised just what anarchy prevailed upon their beat. The lieutenant's negligence had allowed him to wander half-way down the stairs into the cutting to get a closer view of the trains; something caused him to look up; he saw the slogans, understood, recollected his duty, bawled for his idle men. Musket-stocks on to demonstrators' heads, boot-toes into their ribs; Scuffham grandchildren scattered screaming, Mrs Scuffham pinned spreadeagle under three raging redcoat louts, old Jack knocked down from his bench, Harry the carrier with a broken nose, young Craig flat on his back with his velveteen jacket ripped in two and blood pouring from a wound in his scalp. The loom was pulled to pieces; banner and placard tossed to the wind. Liverpool comrades had been drifting away, bored, from the Scuffhams' very personal demonstration; now they bethought themselves, rushed in to help; they were fended off with fixed bayonets.

'Good Christ, serjeant,' said the lieutenant, full of terror at his own incompetence, 'just think if they'd been Irishers! The bloody duke'd be dead already.'

No one was arrested. The magistrates had especially asked that such offenders (as far as possible) be kept out of the courts; the youthful reputation of the Liverpool and Manchester Railway Company had above all things to be considered.

The ducal train chugged along very happily for some seventeen miles; upon an average of one mile to every three-and-a-third minutes. George Stephenson himself was driving the engine, his son's best, *Northumbrian*; and had he wished he could have made nearly twice the speed. He was, however, perfectly satisfied to be constrained; he wanted everyone, in the coaches and on the lineside (where there were thousands), to admire not only the velocity of the trains but also their beauty and the smoothness of their movement. He thought, too, that the public should have a chance to observe the duke.

His own views on politics were conventional, which is to say sceptical: he had forged his own way in the world, he supposed other workingmen might do likewise if they had the energy; he believed politicians (on the whole) made it their business to frustrate that energy. Too much reform might increase their importance and thereby encourage their ignorance. On the other hand, the duke. Now: he had won the war, he deserved his fame for it, so once we've honoured *his* energy why not leave him to his peace? How was he prime minister? Because other folk surely needed a stalking-horse for their misdoings. Too many of such in the carriages behind; but the duke was good and visible in the red-and-gold car, and that was all that was wanted today.

George worked *Northumbrian* calmly, skilfully alert in his smartest black coat and glossy new stovepipe hat. He felt stiff and awkward; but formalities had to be followed. He would have liked once again to have had a young actress to chat with during the journey.

The duke did not chat, although the distinguished guests all about him twittered and gushed and carried on like the French. One of them was the Austrian ambassador, so a good deal of the talk was *in* French (of the diplomatic sort, for the most part very ill-accented). Sir Robert Peel sat at the duke's side; he feared his man's mood and did not try conversation.

Wellington today looked as though he hated everything; to be sure he had not abandoned his native conservatism, but morosity was also concealment. For his underlying mind streamed with erotic impatience, images of little Kemble re-enacting Harriette Wilson. (Crueller conceits, too: little Kemble not so pliable, himself quelling her stubbornness with a queer piece of news he'd only last night had from London. Dare he, for his honour, contemplate it any further?) And yet he was observant. Upon leaving Edge Hill he stared up at Jack Scuffham's loom, turned to Peel, said, 'Did you see that? No. You should have. Your job. It ought to have been put a stop to. These things are only a problem once somebody lets them start. Mind you, the other people along the verges seem jolly enough.'

A few miles further on: 'Is that damned band going to play all the way?'

'I really don't know; a matter for the railway people, I suppose.'

'First clarinet needs a new reed and the nigger with the jingles has lost the beat. Thrown about by the motion, I daresay. Not at all like a horse-carriage: it *excites*, quite unduly. Might drive a dirty schoolboy to spark off his pocket-pistol.' Peel flushed and looked away. The duke was rarely salacious; and indeed seemed to regret the remark, turning it swiftly aside. 'The music's getting tired. Send to the drum-major; he's to let 'em rest for half-an-hour.'

'I doubt if we can, there's no gangway onto their truck. I could perhaps make signs; call to them from the front of the carriage?'

'They'd think you were raving; or that *I* had had a fit: not at all the proper thing. No.'

After another mile: 'You did say "no gangway"? We're confined, absolutely?'

'It would seem so, your grace.'

'What about calls of nature? One of the ladies, for example?'

'I'm sure I don't know.'

'Could we stop the damned thing, at a thicket by the side of the road? You don't know that either?' Sniff of contempt from the great nose; and then: 'Of course, he was quite right, that tomfool on the parapet. It *is* a knacker's yard. No doubt he keeps horses. Poor fellow.'

Passing the tenth milepost: 'What happened to Huskisson? I expected to meet him. Why didn't I? Thought you told me he's the reason I'm here.'

'I think he's at the rear of the train.'

'Prefers the company of his Liverpool friends, h'm? Not a good beginning.'

'He says it's his bad leg; the draught in the open coach. And it's better for all parties you should meet in a more casual way. I did explain, I believe. The opportunity will be at Parkside.'

'Where?'

'We stop there very shortly. The engines must take on water. Then our train will wait; we watch the other trains file past.'

'What the devil for?'

'Well – ah – it's a show, your grace – a parade, a *review*.'

'Nonsense. One reviews troops, not coffee-pots lugging civilians. But if that's what the directors wish, I remain their humble servant.'

'The arrangements, your grace, have been arrived at after much discussion. There will be no peril of a mob at Parkside. The nearest place is Newton; only a village. One which you may have heard of. It returns two members; Tories, I do assure you. The Whigs are always going on about it; they say Manchester should have both seats and Newton be made part of the county constituency. It *is* an anomaly. I half-agree with them.'

'*I* don't. Reform, dammit, yet again! Only way to stop it is to make sure it never starts; look at France (I thought I saw a French tricolour hanging on that handloom); look at this damned rail-train.'

'After the review, we'll have the chance to dismount. And – ah – the ladies–'

'Thickets?'

'I believe, a special pavilion.'

'Glad to hear it.'

'So you see, you can *run up against* Huskisson.'

'Good God! While we're pissing?'

'Every possible forethought and care has gone into the arrangements.'

EIGHT

The halt at Parkside was the death of William Huskisson.

The wheels of *Rocket* were the death of Huskisson.

But chiefly it was brought about by the hidden manoeuvres of politics: which indeed may have caused *all* the misadventures, tragic and trivial, piling one upon the other through the length of the day.

First day of the first passenger rail-road; first locomotive to achieve individual fame; first known fatality of so terrifying a species. People were surely scared by the original abstract notion of the steam-bellied fire-lunged brazen-gutted iron-sinewed dragon racing them across country with neither rein nor apparent curb; but this morning (for seventeen careless miles) the ease of progress, the fine-weather comfort, had laughed away all doubts: and then! Shock, grief, anger, recriminations of post-poned fear at last atrociously fulfilled.

Those responsible never fully knew what they had done: but if they had not so pressed the member for Liverpool to seize the hour and subvert reaction, if Wellington had not been so cornered into coming north to be cornered by Huskisson, if the Wellington reputation had not given them the grandiose idea of a pseudo-military review, there would have been nothing to mar their Delight of Modern Transport; save perhaps some few small rallies of atavistic Luddism, futile, forlornly poignant, forgotten within the week.

As it was: the duke's train stopped; the second train (a few hundred yards behind on the other track) pulled in to its own watering-place; the six trains behind the second train followed example; scores of passengers opened the doors of their carriages and clambered out to stretch their legs. Many from the duke's train made straight for the canvas-sided pavilions-of-convenience. For the others, of lesser estate, no such luxury: there were, however, thickets.

Mr and Mrs Sandars shared a closed compartment in the rear of the train with the Huskissons. Mr Sandars said, 'We've got a pause. Good chance now, sir, to catch him.'

'Perhaps I'd do better to wait till we reach Manchester. More time for a proper talk.'

'Oh no, sir. There'll be a banquet; flunkeys, speeches, flummery. You could only talk to him there if we sat you right next him; and you see, we couldn't fix that aforehand, because – well, if he and you weren't to make it up together here this morning, it wouldn't be right to jam you at table elbow-to-elbow, d'you see what I mean? Everyone's getting out; *he'll* be getting out: walk along the line and meet him.'

Home secretary to prime minister: 'The gentlemen's pavilion to the right, your grace, if you feel the need?'

'I'll wait; filthy nuisance, with an ageing bladder. Peel! I am on duty, man, don't you know what that means? Can't go running off when under orders to take the salute.'

'But you might find your moment with Huskisson.'

'Damn Huskisson. Same applies: he must wait his turn. How long before parade commences?'

'I'll enquire.'

Sir Robert leaned out of the car, saw George Stephenson superintending the water-supply for his engine, called to him, enquired: received a blunt enough answer.

Turning again to the duke: 'Any minute now. As soon as you're ready, tell me; I'll tell Stephenson. By the by, you should meet him – after Huskisson of course – he's remarkable, I'd say a genius, inevitably crotchety, and why not? I think you'd like him.'

'Just so.' The duke once again suspected Peel's sarcasm.

'A knighthood has been suggested.'

'Out of the question.' The duke was spiteful. 'Knighthood's for valorous officers in arms against the king's enemies. Dammit, these days for political services.' (Peel flinched: his own *sir* was an inherited baronetcy, but his father had not been a soldier.) 'To an artisan, for doing his work? No! We waste time; call him to call the trains and get it over with.'

Whistle was blown, flag waved, railway guards ran up and down beseeching passengers to remount. Many did, many refused; they had met friends along the line and were deep into conversation, they found no reason to interrupt it when they could see the passing marvels very well from where they were.

Robert Stephenson, on the footplate of the first train to be reviewed, peered forward in some anxiety. 'Daft buggers all across the tracks: twenty seconds and then we go!' He pulled the cord for the engine whistle and it flung out its high-pitched scream. He pulled again and held it, as the pistons began their drive; locomotive *Phoenix* moved ponderously forward, howling like a banshee.

The military band, formed-up on the lineside, began playing 'The

Orange Lilly-o', unwise tribute to the duke's Irish Protestant heritage. A knot of immigrant platelayers, nursing their own heritage, felt aggrieved by the choice of tune. They had permission to watch the show as a reward for their efforts very early in the morning, packing sand between the rails to make a footway for the important guests. They barracked derisively, invoked Robert Emmet and Dan O'Connell, abused the Orange Order, abused the tithe-proctors of the Established Church, shouted, 'Up the Whiteboys!' Nothing could be done about them. Neither soldiers nor constables had been thought necessary at Parkside.

Firmly planted at the waist-high central door of his chariot, his hands behind his back (no nonsense about an actual salute), the duke narrowed his gaze upon the platelayers. He made rapid mental notes: 'Who hired those men? How long in England? Have O'Connell's people been organising here? Why wasn't I told?' *Phoenix* took him by surprise, arriving slowly enough indeed (a scatter of alarmed spectators dodging from in front of her buffers); but faster than the duke had expected. His survey of Irish intransigence was vehemently blotted out: enormous noise, shining bulk, prolonged and moving wall of coaches, gaping faces pressed toward him; and a cinder into his eye.

He had not quite extracted it when the next train came upon him and passed; he tried in vain to watch; he was still blinking and prodding with his handkerchief.

Huskisson and the Sandarses at the windows of their compartment, Mrs Huskisson behind them with her own thoughts; suddenly she pulled her husband to her and spoke; most passionately, but from the corner of her mouth; Sandars and wife must not hear. 'If your ideals mean nothing to you, William, let me tell you I too have a share in them; I shall not abandon it; you could be the next prime minister or you could throw it all away, so go, go this minute; see him *now*!' She was a strong woman. She knew that when her husband uncharacteristically postponed business he usually intended to cancel it. She feared that his body was failing; before it was too late, his spirit must be *driven*. She had married him for a dream of an enlightened Downing Street. It was still within his grasp.

He would not disappoint her. He humped his broad back, opened the door of the carriage, lowered himself painfully to the ground.

He limped along the side of the train, not fully aware of the difference between the adjacent tracks and the six-foot central gap. The Irishmen's trodden sand made the whole road look alike. In front of the ducal car stood gentlemen, at their ease and urbane, smoking cigars well away from the ladies. Some of them were members of parliament. They greeted him (with varying cordiality nicely adjusted to their political view of him), introduced him to the Austrian ambassador, asked after his leg. He looked up toward the duke; a bowed shoulder, a white handkerchief, he was not sure it was the duke's face they concealed. He stepped backward a few paces to see better.

In the distance: *Rocket*'s whistle, continuous, augmenting; the third train of the procession was on its way. Voices said, without urgency: 'Time to clear the road again!' Men began to move.

The duke's sleeve was touched by Peel: 'Huskisson, your grace; down there, by the ambassador. Not much time just now, but it would be useful to notice him.'

'Oh I suppose I have to; don't see him, where is he?' The duke lifted his head, peered over the edge of the half-door with the eye that was not weeping, recognised his old colleague, extended a hand. He could not quite reach, he opened the half-door and set a foot down on the step. Huskisson, awkwardly caught on one leg, attempted to convert backward movement into forward, staggered, fell away. His hand at the same time came out to seek the duke's, overbalancing him yet further.

'Clear the road!' These shouts *were* urgent. 'Get that bloody man into the train!' – George Stephenson, twenty yards away, forgetting himself in his fright.

'Get in, sir! Get in!' Everybody shouting now. Some of the cigar-smokers pressed themselves against the carriage, some of them scrambled in, the Austrian ambassador was *dragged* in by the brute strength of the duke's equerry.

Huskisson, confused by the confusion, tried to estimate *Rocket*'s speed. But judge a train as one would a post-chaise? Wrong size, wrong shape. The half-open half-door in front of the duke was swinging between him and the step; he had to calculate a detour to get round it.

His limbs no longer obeyed his brain.

Rocket's driver, Bob M'Cree, told those who later questioned him, that he reduced his speed when he saw folk on the line, then they cleared, he increased velocity to that specified by Mr Stephenson in the orders for the day. And then, he said, there was a gentleman; he was (like) dancing on the rail, he had his arms in the air and one foot, his walking-cane high over his head. White hair and a whiter face; his back was (like) turned, you see; but the face was twisted round: it must have been, it was that white, and how could a chap know, without he'd seen it full-face on?

Mechanically impossible to stop a train in so short a distance; no official person held the driver to blame. But there were many to remember he was one of Geordie's Geordies, what else could be expected?

Mrs Huskisson had been watching from her carriage for how her husband would manage with the duke. She saw everything. Screaming at full voice, she jumped down, she ran to him, arms outstretched, bonnet flying behind her on its strings. He lay mangled in the six-foot where the appalling train had left him. Mr and Mrs Sandars came following, with many others. Mrs Sandars pulled a devotional book from her reticule: she had a mad idea of reading from it there and then to Huskisson dying, to Mrs Huskisson almost a widow. Sandars caught it out of her hand: 'Don't be a fool, they don't want *that*!' She realised he spoke truth. They did not want it; but they needed it. Even so, she would not be so arrogant of her religion as to compel it in the heart of tragedy. Whereat she felt she denied God. She sat flat upon the sand and wept.

Mrs Huskisson all of a sudden looked up from her husband's blood; to the Sandarses, and to others of the directors who had gathered around, she uttered one wild sentence: 'You forced him into this, you would have ruined him if he hadn't done it, you have ended him, oh God, oh God.'

The accusation upset them worse than the pouring blood. Why, they'd forced nobody. They had simply hoped, having wit and craft to beget a rail-road, they could thence (all on their own) create another and far greater *new shape*, a government of their private choice to rule the entire country. Now they failed, they called it 'accident'.

NINE

Fanny, on the far side of her carriage, did not see what happened to Huskisson. It was in any case so very swift, all she remembered later was a series of broken images she was never entirely able to sort into their proper sequence: the unexpected unevenness of the train's speed, fast, slow, fast, then suddenly sharp to a stop; an abrupt dislocation of the wheels' movement; a jarring of all the buffers between all the carriages, throwing the passengers violently about (she saw or sensed immediately cuts and contusions over backs of seats and along the floor, shoes into armpits, flail of hands onto napes of neck); a glimpse of horrified open-mouthed faces in the duke's train across to her right; a glimpse of the duke himself, caught as it were in a spring-heeled agony between contemplative stillness and a Rumpelstiltskin leap; and behind it all, through it all, so rapid a rising-up of human cries, screams, shouts, swearwords (and then so rapidly gagged as the train shuddered to its halt too far off to be any longer within full earshot) – ah no! there was no logic, none of it had happened, it just *was*, and she could not remember it.

She did remember, with the greatest clarity, staring from the now-stationary train back up the railway line to see an ineffectual quickset of people bent about *something*, neither on the line nor off it; and suddenly this tight little crowd broke, from an impulse within itself; the black bandsman of the 'Turkish music' was forcing his way out. He cradled a drooped bundle in his vast arms, a white head hung loosely from his elbow-niche – (*her nightmare of the slave-ship, cargo taking its owner prisoner, cargo saving owner? – what? how?*) – where had he come from? All the other musicians were still across the way by the pavilion; enough time must have lapsed to allow Sammy Jingles to move himself thence, but when? How had she lost those seconds, minutes, half-an-hour? Perfectly clearly, she heard his voice: 'Empty the wagon, all the band-gear off of the music-truck! me and the doc, *we'll* take him, off of it, you bastards, get!' And simultaneous slither and scurry, plume-hatted redcoats running to the truck to pull music-books, music-stands, instrument cases to the ground; Sammy Jingles swarming from ground to truck, burden in both arms; and another man in a buff dustcoat (doctor?): a writhing striving grey-haired woman pitched herself in after them and no one with presence of mind enough to help her; she must have been Huskisson's wife.

*

If Sammy Jingles was the first to think of the bandwagon as an improvised ambulance, George Stephenson was the only one who knew what to do with it: he ordered its coupling unhitched from the ducal train, he jumped at once aboard *Northumbrian*, a quick word to his stoker, a quick message – *via*, of all people, the home secretary (only too glad to be of service as an errand-boy) – to his son, now hastening along the line toward him from *Phoenix* half-a-mile away; he opened the regulator, and plunged engine and bandwagon eastward at his fullest conceivable speed.

Mr Huskisson's condition was such (tourniquet around an all-but-severed leg, and so much blood now lost as to bring him to the very brink of death) that any notion of running him into the hubbub of unprepared Manchester was obviously absurd: he must be got straightway to Eccles, the next station of any size along the line, and there under some roof for whatever treatment might improve upon the first-aid already administered. Fifteen miles. *Northumbrian* covered it at an average of thirty-six miles per hour; between forty and fifty at her best moments of travel. An achievement of steam-in-emergency unforeseen even by Stephenson himself: during subsequent months he would make the very most of it. Indeed, as he went, he was already planning to make the most of it; he was not at all ashamed to check the mileposts against his watch and to crow his macabre glory as he calculated the readings.

Stranded beside his engineless train, the duke said to Robert Stephenson: 'Inappropriate to continue. You must bring us back to Liverpool.'

The home secretary concurred.

Protest at once from the chief dignitary of Manchester (who ought to have been mayor; civil government being unreformed, his rank was no higher than 'borough reeve', like the headman of a market town of perhaps one thousand persons): 'But all of Manchester will be at the train-sheds, they'll not know what's happened, they'll think we're all afraid of *mobs*! Already the race-course bookies are taking bets the duke'll cry off; if we can't show him in Manchester, the radicals'll ride all over us! I tell you they'll not leave us a sound square inch o'window-glass! Dear God, but we've got to go on.'

'I was well enough received there the other day,' said the duke sourly, 'in Staleybridge moreover. I daresay the populace is not as hot as you make out, sir.'

'Ah but the other day there was no advance notice. Save for respectable elements that we took pains to invite quite private. We fixed up a loyal crowd in one or two selected streets: altogether different today.

Some o'these damfool railroad directors ha'been *placarding* the bloody town.'

The duke thought about it. He was inclined to agree, the more so as he had now observed sufficient of railway practice to understand that if the trains returned the way they had come, their locomotives would have to push them in reverse, shuffling them into Edge Hill like rabbits dodging backwards after an imprudent half-sally from the burrow. Humiliating: he shook his head; looked at Peel. Peel said, 'Let's see the directors.'

Mr Sandars and colleagues summoned in quaking file like defaulters to orderly-room: 'But how can we get an engine across the line to the duke's train?' wailed Sandars, 'We've laid no points here at Parkside for swopping tracks! If we put him behind Mr Robert's loco, in an ordinary carriage with all his nobs, where to find room for the guests we must displace? I mean, it's all very well saying ambassadors and MPs and such have to have the priority, but there's very considerable men of consequence here from all parts of the north – oh aye, and their wives – we can't just leave 'em stood about in Parkside! Besides, that carnival-carriage cost us hundreds to rig up. They'll be *expecting* it in Manchester; all its embellishments were manufactured there! As it is, we've lost the bandwagon.'

The duke said, 'Manchester. Find a way. Get there.'

Which should have closed discussion: but certain directors nonetheless argued all round and about it for over an hour. He finally despaired of them; and went and sat in his chariot, a cloaked figure emblematic of, at least, resignation; more probably contempt.

Mr Brandreth was claiming to have been right all along about horses; he knew a farmer not far off who bred fine percherons, why not borrow a string of them and have them draw the train to Eccles, where (he caustically supposed) Mr Stephenson and his engine *might* (DV) be waiting? Mr Cropper was explaining how the cable-haul could so easily have been extended from Edge Hill, and if it had been, none of this need have happened. The reeve fretted that the longer the delay, the more ill-conditioned the crowd at Manchester would grow; by the time the duke arrived the railway offices would be looted and burned. Also it was beginning to rain.

Meanwhile Robert Stephenson (in consultation with his enginemen) organised the reversal of trains on the left-hand line, sufficient to bring his leading locomotive *Phoenix* and its rolling-stock to a position just ahead of the ducal car. He did not explain why he was doing this; and nobody took much notice of his proceedings, except this time all parties made very sure indeed to keep well out of the way of the wheels. The bandsmen were pressed into service as marshals; they enjoyed themselves ordering their betters to stand here and move there and eventually to climb back into the coaches. At last some of the Irishmen, who had been sent into Newton, returned loaded with sundry lengths of different calibre of strong chain, acquired from the local blacksmith. Robert set them to link the rear coupling of his own train across the six-foot to the front end of the duke's.

Charles Kemble had somehow evaded the authority of the drum-major; he stood gravely beside Robert Stephenson as though called in to give expert advice. '*Antony and Cleopatra* is not often presented,' he volunteered. 'I once had the honour to attempt it. To simplify the text, I began with a mobile *tableau*: Egypt's queen in her barge ascending the river of Cydnus. Athwart the stage, you understand me, sir? A host of slaves heaving a tow-rope, from PS to OP, third grooves. And then, at the end of the rope, second grooves, the practicable barge (upon castors) rolls on downstage of the slaves. The audience supposed to be viewing from the opposite bank of the stream, d'you take me?'

'No I don't. Who are you? What do you want?'

'Want? I want to tell you it didn't work; not at all. Rope at that angle, it just dragged the barge round to a halt, nose into the ground-row that purported to be the riverbank. Same's bound to happen here; you'll either pull the duke off the line, or jam his wheels against the rail so the friction prevents their revolving. Take the word of a practical man, sir.'

'Thank you for your help. Now pray have the goodness to get back into your seat. *At once*, sir, if you please.' Robert was a little less curt than his father, but stood interference no more gladly.

Very slowly, very cautiously, *Phoenix* was eased forward. It looked as though Charles might have been right. The sideways-stretched towing-chains were unable to transmit sufficient force to draw their load.

'Jesus Christ, but we'll *double* it! Couple *North Star* and her coaches to the back end of *Phoenix*'s, sling the chain from the duke's car to the rearmost coach of the lot, for God's sake look sharp, or we're bloody bedded down for the night!'

This time it *did* work; inch by inch the three linked trains crawled forward, two upon one track, one on the other. The remaining trains followed. Engines panted through the thickening rain.

It was well into the afternoon when they arrived at Eccles. *Northumbrian* and the bandwagon were waiting. The musicians (who had had to ride on the wet coal-tenders to the detriment of their uniforms) resumed their proper places; they were not asked to play. Four miles or so ahead, the ominous black smoke-cloud that hung always over Manchester mingled with the rain and offered nothing but general misery.

Wellington said to Peel, 'Upon the matter of the Irishmen; I want a proper report; the secret service fund to obtain it, if need be. We ought to have appreciated how the huge scope of these railway works would so – *re-distribute* the population. Did I hear someone say poor Huskisson was dead already?'

'No, your grace, not yet. They have him in Eccles vicarage, as comfortable as possible: he is not expected to live beyond evening.'

'God help his unhappy lady. She served his vitality so well.'

'He could as easily have slipped under a stage-coach in an inn yard.'

'No, Peel; you're wrong there. Not at all the same thing, no.'

Charles Kemble said to Fanny and Ellen, 'Back in Liverpool before curtain-up? Any bets, my dears? No. Three understudies in the major roles! The company will be lucky not to be pelted off the stage.' He found his own cause for joy in the very depth of his pessimism. Just then Fanny did not care whether she acted that night or not; nor any longer for what might happen (or fail to happen) after the play.

> *She took in nothing of the resumed journey: only continuous phantasms – pasted and wafted across flickering fields, shuddering treetops, crawling hedgerows, cloud-driven sky – of the dying man; the African giant who had swept him so strangely aloft; the red hearse that was not to be a hearse after all, the black man's bandwagon having been chosen (by the black man himself) to usurp its mournful function. Or not? For was not the duke as he sat there (wrapped in silence, wrapped in his night-dark covering, Duke of Darkness indeed) already more dead than Huskisson? Therefore conveyed to the end and beyond the end of his fore-ordained course of imperium?*

Her sense of grief was apparent to Ellen, who did not quite comprehend it but held her friend's hand and did her best to be a presence.

> *How did it happen that the hearse-car upon its rails had left its rails and sailed the sea? where it met a great tattered ship, with the people aboard casting slave-chains into the water; and high-pitched ululation, 'We are free!'; amongst them another corpse, laid out abaft the bowsprit; Fanny thought the ship's flag was Spanish but pouring weather and blown spray dimmed her vision, she could not be sure.*

Ellen had a pretty little summer-day parasol with which she tried to protect the three of them from the vicious gusts of rain, until the wind caught hold of it and blew it inside-out.

TEN

The subsequent mess at Manchester was the direct result of the Parkside delays.

Mary Bentham and her father had gone early to the railway station. An enormous demonstration against the duke, and very well-organised: political clubs and workpeople's associations from all over the cotton districts; to lobby for reform, to demand reform, to extort reform, to oppose machines; to denounce the cotton-masters, the military and the special constabulary, child-labour in the factories, the corn laws; to advocate the freedom of Ireland, the freedom of slaves in the West Indies; to remember Peterloo, to incite revolution, to cry for republicanism, simply to revile a hide-bound soldier who dared govern a free people, and – even more simply – to roar as at a prize-fight for Manchester against London. The behaviour of the demonstrators varied with their aspirations; savage or phlegmatic, carefree or angry.

Most of those who had not been angry changed their mood when they found the streets about the new station so dense with redcoat ranks they could not get near the place. The trains, they had been told, should arrive between twelve-thirty and one o'clock: the distinguished visitors would eat luncheon in a warehouse on the rail-road premises; after which, it now appeared, they were to re-embark for Liverpool without anyone beyond those premises being afforded a single sight of them. This revised *coda* to the ceremonial schedule angered the loyal crowd as much as it did the dissidents. For there *was* a loyal crowd, ready to cheer for church and state and the victor of Waterloo: many had not known (until it was too late) about the duke's hugger-mugger visit of a day or two earlier, and were anxious this morning to make up for their disappointment.

Mary was in charge of a dozen older children from her school; they had made their own placards with affecting inscriptions (not all of them suggested by Mary):

DUKE, KEEP MY DAD OUT OF THE WARS, KEEP ME OUT OF THE MILL!
BECAUSE YOU KILLED FRENCHMEN YOU DON'T HAVE TO KILL *US*!
MY DOG GINGER BITES DUKES' LEGS!
TEACHER SAYS *GO HOME*, SALLY ANNE SAYS SO TOO!

– and so forth. The day wore on and nothing happened, save for the lugubrious onset of rain. She began to worry about the children, badly clothed, hungry, pressed upon and endangered by men with clubs and gin bottles who made quarrels all around her (for loyalism just here over-lapped and clashed with protest). No way out of the throng to bring the little ones safely home.

Oh why were the trains delayed? She was becoming afraid for Neddy – could events in Liverpool have grown so ugly that the duke had never started? Could a massacre have taken place there? She had quite lost sight of her father. She hoped for some protection from a self-disciplined group of old soldiers who had gathered (in what was left of their Peninsular and Waterloo uniforms) to tell the duke they had won his victories and all their reward was black penury. One of them said, 'You'll be all right, love, if you get in behind us wi'them kids up into t'snicket there; there's an old woman sells hot pies i't'furthest cellar; hang on, don't *you* go trying to shove yourself through – Josiah'll fetch the pies for you, won't you, Josiah? You're nearest. O'course he will.'

But Josiah was not listening; he wore faded corporal's stripes on an ancient green rifle-tunic and was suddenly impregnate with a tactical idea: 'Why ha'n't none on us thought on it? We're not bound to bide for ever crammed up the arseholes o'that shower of a militia! Round and over t'bridge, lads, stop the damn train afore it gets in – come on, come on, at the double! Over t'bridge an' bloody outflank 'em! Run, you skivers, *run!*' His parade-ground bellow could be heard the full length of the compacted street, other people took it up, a surge of excited movement – round the corner *away* from the station, down a cobbled hill, over a humpbacked stone bridge now dominated by the much taller arches of the rail-road, up a squalid suburban lane, through gaps in a broken wall between derelict cottages, into and across a muddy field – and there at their feet, the railway line, quite empty in its raw new cutting; they flowed into it, hundreds of them: Mary and her children had been caught up in the undammable tide, the wicked imps would not heed her cries, they hurled themselves ahead of her among adult legs, yelling with glee out of all control. She herself was carried forward to the very brink, and barely stopped the little wretches running down onto the track itself.

Terrible yet basely exhilarating to see *Northumbrian* come pounding, barking, whistling under the downpour, no faster than a man on foot, into the mass of soaked people; stones and turf and bottles in flight through the air, to bounce off boiler-plates and the sides of carriages – astonishing that no one aboard was hurt – George Stephenson on the footplate, and his stoker, crouched almost into the firebox door to avoid the missiles;

bandsmen lay flat on their lorry; passengers flat in the coaches; only the duke remained as he had been (as he had ever been, in India, Spain, France and Flanders) bolt upright and oblivious to the fall of shot.

Astonishing, also, there was no repetition of the Huskisson accident. It was not that the demonstrators lacked foolhardiness: but old George had understood just what was going forward the minute he drove into the cutting. He kept the speed very low; but he *kept* it; and trusted Lancashire good sense to get itself clear in the nick of time. At least the buggers hadn't thought to block the line with a pile of sleepers, or any of that!

Once the duke had gone through, the succeeding seven trains (whatever the impressive novelty of their appearance) interested the crowd less and less. The day was too wet, the ground too slippery, the menace of the grinding pistons too blatant for even the most angry-hearted. Iron locomotives were not factory masters' flash curricles to be stopped and overturned at random. The place now to be was back at the station; beset it, besiege it, let none of the arrogant cormorants set foot into a Manchester street! Once again people ran.

Mary called for the children, counted them, found them (thank God) all together and undamaged. She was relieved and disappointed that at this wild exciting moment she must lead them away out of it; no question, it was high time. Not possible now to reach the pie shop near the station; but other places, yes! She promised sweetstuff as well as meat-pie; she promised lemon-and-ginger and hot water; and if she added a dash of rum to deter the pneumonia, who was to tell her she shouldn't? She thought the duke was so brave, but hateful; she hoped desperately that his men had done no harm to Neddy.

Maybe eight thousand people in the station. And, at last, eight trains; protected to an extent by the haggard line of troops surrounding them, backs to the coaches, bayonets to threaten the crowd. Large notices among the rafters of the platform shelter announced GALA LUNCHEON THIS WAY, TICKET-HOLDERS ONLY; cheerful arrows insanely pointed into the thick of the mob. Already nearly four o'clock; it was luncheon now or starve; for who could say when or where the 'ticket-holders' would find their supper? It was starve in the carriages or be torn and trampled by the furious multitude.

Most of the loyalists had reached the station first, to be sure, and acted as a kind of extra protection between the militia and the protestors; but they were by now so frustrated, so determined to indulge their sense of proprietorship over the nation's great men, that trampling and tearing came as naturally to them as it did to their rivals. And many of them had luncheon tickets; they scrummaged up against the buffet, abusing the waiters. The latter withheld all wine glasses, all plates of cold fowl, until prime minister or borough reeve came to table; such being their instructions from the borough reeve himself, impossible to countermand if he could not make his way through to them. He might perhaps have attempted it, but that the duke refused to do so; he could not in all conscience abandon the duke.

'Surely, your grace, with a few soldiers tight around us, we could make shift to press forward? The civic buffet's in the warehouse there.'

'How far?'

'Not more than – across the goods yard and along – not more than – say, three hundred yards.'

'No *no*! they'll perceive us as prisoners under escort.'

The Wellington temper was about to snap. He was confronting enraged enemies, was altogether unschooled in the operations of a railway, was totally at the mercy of panic-struck jackasses; his battle skills were useless. Until the butcher-blow at Parkside, he had regarded the day's events as a vexatious tohu-bohu he must live through as well as he could, they were the price of his actress tonight. Now in all likelihood he must resign himself to *no* actress: and moreover upon the edge of a grave.

The reeve still besought him: 'But how are we going to *eat*?'

'Manage without. What d'you expect on active service? For that's what it is. You could have ordered haversack rations: you didn't think, man, *did* you? Have a constable tell your people to feed whomever can get there. *I* don't propose to stir from this car. Nor should you: you hold public office; sustain its dignity. You'll not be coming back to Liverpool with us, I take it? Cram your belly in your own home once we've left. Godsake, madam, furl it, be so good!' (A party of ardent ladies had broken through the cordon and were flourishing their union jack right into his carriage; a reverential offering perhaps.) 'Government funds allow me a sufficiency of bunting.'

Word slowly went round the trains that the luncheon was after all served and people could attempt it at their own risk. Conveniences for calls-of-nature were to be found there, adjacent. For the one cause or the other several passengers dared to dismount, among them Charles Kemble. 'Still a chance they might get us to the theatre in time! But if we've not ate since breakfast, we'll collapse into the footlights. Come, my dears, arms together; professional responsibility, the forlorn hope of prancing Thespis!' He with his cane, Ellen with her broken parasol, Fanny in between, closed up as a phalanx of three and inserted themselves into the crowd. To reach the warehouse they must first pass across the tracks round the front of the duke's train; if possible, within the cordon. This station was not provided with an overall roof like Liverpool's; as soon as they left the coach they were under rain and upon mud.

Shunting had already begun, to bring the engines to the turntables, and thence out of the station upon a parallel track to the rear of their trains for the return journey. But because the half-finished facilities at Manchester did not yet include watering points, locomotives must be driven in batches to Eccles to fill their tanks. (*Northumbrian* had filled already, during the delivery there of Huskisson.) These novel, complex and thunderous operations added confusion to confusion; they would have inspired romantic horror in imaginations not surfeited by the real horror of the past few hours.

A scalding jet of steam from *Northumbrian*'s cylinder, almost into Charles's earhole; dodging away, he wrenched his arm out of his daughter's grasp. At the same moment Ellen was blocked; a foul-mouthed immoveable militiaman thrust his bayonet toward her stomach. By the time she had dealt with him (surprising herself by her reversion to stage-type in a moment of stress – Romeo raging into the street-fight – '*fire-ey'd fury be my conduct now!*') she too had lost hold of Fanny.

Fanny tried to keep moving; she did not even notice her friend George Stephenson on the engine (although he noticed her; for all his preoccupation, he grinned at her and tapped his nose); people shoved past her; she was almost off her balance; she put a hand out to steady herself against the step of a carriage: it was the duke's. Above her, a bitter small voice: 'Miss Kemble!' he was looking down, slightly sideways, directly into her face. Two very bright eyes in a drawn grey countenance and a certain – scarcely a smile, not at all a smile – but a *twitch* of indecipherable emotion on his narrow lips. 'You never answered my last note.'

'No,' she said, 'No.' Good God, what sort of time was this for him to be thinking of *her*? And would not others overhear? Probably not: he had his back to his travelling companions, hers were swept from her in the hubbub, and *Northumbrian*'s whistle was shrieking and shrieking no more than a few yards away. In her waking dream of shock she had seen him as a dead man. And since then she had been carried, as it were in his *cortège*, between the hideous cat-calling stone-throwing crowds along the cutting: her shock had not left her. How to answer him? How?

'I – I would not have expected, sir, you'd expect – I mean, under the circumstances – poor tragic Mrs Huskisson – surely you don't mean–?'

'Oh yes, ma'am, I do. I must. God knows I've paid respects, written letters of consolation, to widows enough in my time, hundreds of them, in batches, d'you think I don't know what's involved? In fact, the very reason; you and I, *tonight*! These things must be talked about, if nothing more. In whom else can I confide?' A jab of his fingers toward the flustered public men in his carriage, their weeping and berating womenfolk – the smallest possible gesture but absolutely dismissive. Suddenly she knew what he meant.

'Why, yes,' she said, so quietly she was not sure he could hear her. But he could, his eyes told her so. Gratitude in them, or *vainglory*? 'But where shall we be? I might not even reach the theatre.'

'Indeed. Quite out of my hands. But we don't assume all's lost till we *know* it. Same time, place, as I stated. Convenient? Of course.' Someone behind him was attracting his attention. He bowed to Fanny, replaced his hat, turned angrily away to deal with nonsense.

She had no appetite for the luncheon, even supposing she could gain entry; but call-of-nature was imperative. As she thrust through to the yard she made up her mind she could keep this duke-business to herself no longer. Oh if only 'H' were here, but she wasn't; it would have to be Ellen. She could not fathom how much experience, or wisdom, the ambiguous Ellen might possess – sympathy, surely, or those flowers in the dressing-room meant nothing. But until she told her, the evening's burden was far greater than she could carry alone.

Lavender, town-constable of Manchester, a bullying person in top-boots, was always very positive of the truth of his opinions. But now he was beginning to fear they might not be as well-founded as he thought. He had sworn to the borough reeve there would be no trouble that day beyond the scope of routine management – 'Just a bit of a shout,' he had predicted, 'from an unrepresentative minority of extremists.' The reeve had told this to the duke. Early in the day the duke had been inclined to believe it; upon hearing the reeve again at Parkside he was not quite so certain; after the events of the past hour he was downright incredulous.

Lavender hung abjectly upon the side of the ducal carriage, pleading with the home secretary, for the duke would not trouble himself to deal with him. 'This train must leave now, Sir Robert; I mean *now*, this very minute, or I'm not answerable for the consequence! I mean, please, Sir Robert, speak to his grace, please tell him how I'm fixed! Them soldiers I called out, they've been at it since nine o'clock, they'll never take another bout of it. There's a new mob outside i't'streets there building up like a bonfire, half me deputies ha'shogged-off home; why, they quite lost heart afore midday!'

'We weren't here at midday.'

'I know you weren't but we were, all manner of abuse and nastiness. Look, I'm sure if the duke left and there was only the other passengers, there wouldn't be no more trouble. Oh please, Sir Robert, do!'

'We seem to have a locomotive "in steam", is that the phrase? I'll ask the duke to speak to Stephenson. I frankly don't know what his present intentions are, but I think what you say may have weight. Thank you, Mr Lavender.'

The duke sent for George, and George (fetched from his shunting and very worried) brought Sandars. Said George: 'Aye, we could take the train out. Problem is, we've four engines I've just sent ahead of us to get watered at Eccles. They could be on the up-line by now, they could be on the down, who's to ken? I've spoken afore about this, Mr Sandars: if the company canna bear to put its hand in its poke to pay for some system o'signals, we're intae this damn mess ilk aye time we run a train, and dean't tell me, man! *We are!* Ah God, Duke, we'll gie un a try! Ten minutes and I'm sided up.' The duke touched his hat, a gesture unnoticed by its intended recipient, who at once stumped off to his engine, the mud flying from under his boots.

'All-of-a-piece with this boorish locality,' said the duke, 'but I dare say a man of sense, a man of *bottom*.'

That, such as it was, was the only conversation ever known to take place between the pair of them.

Mr Sandars was a ruin. He smiled helplessly, pathetically. 'I'll just leave Mrs Sandars where she's put, and take the liberty of riding with you, your grace. If we get into more difficulties it'd be best to have a man beside you that can answer for them, I daresay.'

'No doubt. What time d'you estimate we reach Liverpool? Or perhaps you don't know?'

'No sir, I'm afraid I don't.'

'What about the other trains?'

'Oh sir – as for *them* – !'

'Tomorrow I am to receive the freedom of your city. Most sensible of the honour, of course, but under present circumstances – '

'Not *cancel* it, your grace?'

'Postpone.'

'Oh dear, your grace, what *will* the mayor say? Oh dear oh dear oh dear . . .'

The ladies' convenience, when Fanny at length reached it and nerved herself to submit to it, was in a nauseating state, used and misused by too many agitated people far too quickly; the elderly attendant had quite given up on her necessary tasks. Fanny made all haste and plunged out again into the rain. If detrimental matter had clung to her skirts, they were anyway so wet that it did not seem to signify. But she stopped nonetheless to examine them in a corner of the goods yard fairly free from the surge of the crowd. There was a small weather-boarded penthouse to shelter the freight-porters' trolleys; so she let it shelter *her*. Then she saw Ellen fighting her way out of the luncheon hall. Fanny called; they came together under the penthouse.

'Are you sure you won't eat?'

'I'd never get near the buffet, not now.'

'No you wouldn't and that's the truth; which is why I've brought you these.'

From a package under Ellen's shawl, ham and mustard, three pickled cucumbers, an amorphous honeycake, all wrapped together in a napkin.

'I don't know about drink.'

'I'd better not drink at all, it'll only mean having to go into *there* again. But Ellen, where on earth is dear papa?'

'Right up at the head of the table, would you believe? Absolutely sitting down to a leisurely gentleman's collation, and writing out free passes for the theatre for anyone who cares to ask!'

No appetite, but Fanny must eat; *professional responsibility*. She gobbled at the ham, trying to hurry the tiresome business, and choked. 'Oh God, Ellen, I'm disgusting. Oh, Ellen, I have something to tell you. I'm a damfool, I have to explain. Will you despise me?'

'I surely will if you keep swearing. It's all these lobsterback soldiers, they're everywhere today, and how speedily they have depraved you!'

'Oh they have.' She was serious and Ellen wondered at her. So serious as to quite trouble her friend. Fanny said, 'Lobsterback; yes. Oh, I ought to have asked you, but a month ago I didn't *know* you, so I didn't, couldn't, could I? Ellen, is it not degrading to maintain oneself impregnably – *maiden*? For no better reason than to fetch a higher price. Priced marriage is degrading. Have you read Anna Wheeler? – she's Irish, writes under the name of Thompson, she pretends to be a man – anyway, *she* says degrading. That's why she wrote her book. Have you heard how the chief eunuch procures his womanflesh for the Grand Turk?'

'*What*? Fanny, what are you talking about? Dearest Fanny, what have you done?'

Fanny told her.

'So what do you think? Ellen, you do think *something*? Or have I so *contradicted* myself – humble pride, orgulous servility – that you have nothing at all to say to me, neither today nor ever after? Ellen?'

Ellen's eyes upon Fanny were grave, and when she spoke she had altogether abandoned the spritely and irritating affectations of her normal

social discourse; her words were brisk and dry, abruptly *judicious*, the very
diction she so well deployed in her performances: 'I think I would like to
read that play of yours about King Francis.'

'You are laughing at me!'

'No: but what you write may be more lucid than what you speak. The
king lived three hundred years ago, Anna Wheeler's still alive (and yes, I
have heard of her): d'you live in *his* time or *hers*?'

Fanny felt shock. If Ellen was a minx, she was a minx of penetration,
intuitively to have hit upon the unresolved central crux (one of several, as
it happened) in that excitable convoluted script.

> *The chaste Françoise de Foix, yielding her virtue to King Francis (act
> of idealism, to save her brother from the scaffold), discovers, the next
> day, in guilty bewilderment, that she has pleased the king so deftly he
> begs to appoint her his* maîtresse-en-titre. *Situation broadly
> plagiarised from* Measure for Measure; *the louche boundaries
> between seduction and rape defined only insofar as the author's
> inexperience would allow.* Dénouement *of this plot still in rough
> draft. Is Françoise truly horrified by what the king has done to her? or
> by what she has learned* en passant *about her own self? Might she
> not, after all, accept the offered position. . . ?*

Charles had warned Fanny that her reversal of Shakespeare would be
possible for a modern audience only if the sullied maiden were to kill
herself. It might be necessary to accept his commercial logic. 'H', too, had
said something of the sort. 'H' could be very worldly at times, cautioning
Fanny against 'mistaking emotion for religion', which could also mean,
could it not? 'don't try to shape a private morality on the basis of your
fictional imagination'.

And out of that, a crippling thought! Had Fanny's fictions the power to
pre-construct the dilemmas of her *life*?

No choice but to pretend serenity, to answer Ellen's question with
judicial deliberation. 'I'd say, both. Anna Wheeler walked away from a
very brutal husband and of her own will made her home with Thompson
the philosopher: what does she care the world thinks her mad? Great
courtesans of Paris, however they were first seduced, chose to stay with
kings and lords of their own will, and walked away from them when they
chose. I think too it was like that no more than thirty-five years since,
when *he* was a young man. My mother was young then as well; if I had
been her I'd have been – just as she was, I suppose.'

'But your mother married your father. They could not be more
respectable.'

'Could they not? Ellen, for God's sake, look at him!'

Charles, loud and sanguine upon municipal champagne, held forth from the steps of the luncheon-hall, entertaining some fifty people with authentic reminiscences of Garrick (he was four years old when the great man died).

Just at that moment there were shoutings, pushings through the throng, shoutings again: the duke's train was about to start and all those that had places on it 'get to 'em, get into 'em, quick sharp and move it!'

Charles Kemble descried his young ladies: 'Prance, Thespis, prance! the train of the duke! Ours too will be off directly, oh hasten, ye nymphs, this way!' And he propelled them at once the wrong way.

The mistake discovered and corrected, they were again beside the ducal car; their train lay over *there*: but the platform bustle impeded them.

'Hold hard, you with the hand-signal!' The necessarily unpractised railway guard, whistle to mouth, green flag ready poised, stood stock-still in consternation. He knew that he and no one else was in charge of a loaded train: nothing had been said about prime ministers countermanding him. 'Kemble!' The duke's voice, raised, had as precisely pitched a clarity as the actor himself could have attained. Charles whipped off his sodden straw hat and swept a low and tottering bow. 'Kemble, they tell me there will be great delay for some of the trains. Which is yours?'

'Fourth, fifth, I scarcely know – ah, blue rosettes, blue, sir!'

'No good. You'll miss your play. Onto this one; find a carriage.'

The guard, offended, tried to assert himself: 'Ah no, milord, we're plumb chock-full!' For already too many people from the lesser trains had intruded upon the duke's. Rumour had leapt: there were no more engines fit to run, they'd all be stranded overnight in the rapine and riot of Manchester.

'Nonsense, get 'em in. Anywhere, they won't mind. Hardy vagabonds, all three of 'em.'

So they got in. Charles (his own tipsy impulse) upon the music-lorry, where the drum-major gave him a coal sack to wrap about his shoulders; he promptly fell asleep in the rain. Ellen and Fanny into the small private compartment (not much larger than a hackney-cab) previously occupied by the Huskissons. Out of respect, the guard had locked it, and put desolate Mrs Sandars elsewhere. Now, he thought, 'hardy vagabonds'; if they didn't mind, they needn't mind; but *he'd* never think to travel in the very heat of a dead corpse's cushions; perhaps best, though, not to tell 'em.

In fact, a fortunate choice. In no other part of the train would two young actresses have found the privacy for a prolonged and earnest talk of old

men and their lustful yearnings; to say nothing of their *own* yearnings,
lustful or not.

ELEVEN

It is to be admitted that Miss Tree's love for her younger colleague was now and then made acrid by a small pinch of jealousy; and how not? when tonight the play was *The Merchant of Venice*, with Miss Tree no more than Jessica, while Miss Kemble would be pouring Portia like treacle from backcloth to orchestra pit. Father's daughter, of course; and that's the way the business worked: but why Jessica? a good enough role for conventional sentiment; but without much humour, without *body*. True, Jessica (briefly) dresses as a boy, so Miss Tree's special talent was not ignored. But so does Nerissa; to far more striking effect, for her disguise has to deceive all the men on the stage at the time. Ah, but boy-Nerissa must partner (and *underplay*) man-Portia! – odious comparisons inevitably invoked. No wonder old Kemble arranged the casting as he did (all that about the Surface brothers this morning was only so much wind, for sure he'd never hold to it!)

These feelings were ignoble, as Ellen well knew; she tried to keep them subterranean. But they did influence her reception of *Fanny*'s feelings toward the duke.

Ellen shrank from all notions of carnal coupling. She expected, one day, to make a practical marriage; with an intellectual and temperate actor-manager, she hoped; for the general furtherance of her career and the improvement of the theatre; while her female friends would always remain her greatest private pleasure, and of that she was positive. From the marriage, of course, children; maybe an artistic dynasty that would rival the Kembles. The physical origin of the dynasty was not a process she cared to foresee. (She was not even too sure she had been told the full truth of it; her mother had been honest enough but reticent, her schoolmistress a frightened prude, her schoolfellows quite grossly fantastical.) Responsible self-respecting wives must submit themselves at intervals to the deed: it could not be entirely repellant. But, good heavens, to seek it out, for its own degrading sake! How could any woman be so untrue to herself?

This had little, if anything, to do with 'morality'. Sheer enjoyment of a man's bed seemed bizarre and unnatural, whether one was married to him or not, and quite unrelated to *love*. Although as an actress she had at times to present a woman of such a temperament, she always found it difficult; it was as though she undertook the role of some fabulous creature – human head, say, upon the body of a sea-beast. The cheerfully sensual Nerissa would not have been at all easy; jealousy alone induced her to desire the part. Playing a man was another matter altogether: men's physical desires were part and parcel of their strange physical structure; get the walk right, the voice, the stance, all the rest fell into place.

How curious, therefore, that Fanny should say 'degrading' when she intended the exact opposite of what Ellen meant by the word. *Maidenhood* degraded? If seen only as a calculated preparation for mercenary wedlock, perhaps it did. But how far was mercenary wedlock different from 'practical marriage'? Ellen resented being told that her own well-considered principles might offend against self-respect. Yet surely Fanny's implied criticism arose out of genuine innocence, and from no wish to provoke; at all events, Ellen hoped so.

Did Fanny really think to become a 'grand courtesan'? (There were less romantic phrases to define the type, some of them very filthy.) Out of sheer zeal for experiment, to present her virginity to the duke? If so, it was worse than degrading; it was utterly grotesque.

'*Lobsterback* indeed, Fanny! And so ancient and encrusted too; have you quite lost your wits?'

'He's not much older than Mark Antony; and just think what Cleopatra thought of *him*. As generals go, he's been far more successful.'

'As politicians go, you disapprove him altogether. Or else why were you so sharp against your father?'

'Don't you think I dare be sharp against a duke? If he sneers at people's liberty in my presence, I'll denounce him. But I'm sure he'd do so honestly: no one ever called him hypocrite.'

'They do call him a libertine. It used to be notorious. He has a wife, grown-up sons; and a very well-known mistress.'

'Mistress? I hadn't heard. Who is she?'

'A Mrs Arbuthnot, and her husband is his closest friend. Of course she's more than twenty.'

'So am I.'

'Not by much. I daresay it's possible he and the Arbuthnot never exactly – well, never – '

'A spiritual friendship?'

'A pair of old gossips, most probably. I don't know. When people are elderly, I really cannot imagine them – '

'Naked and wicked together, or on their own, or with someone of a different age? *I* can – often do; full of years can be full of beauty. Why, just now *you're* imagining me and him so, and don't shudder! You are, and I can tell. But, Ellen, there's no need. His Mrs A is not in Liverpool; he just seeks another gossip to fill her place: I'm a very good gossip, as you know.'

Ellen had tried hard to keep a Nerissa-like jocular ease, but Portia's confidences were never so bold. A good thing the part at the theatre had gone to someone else, for after this she would have found those mistress-maid scenes quite unplayable. She felt more like Joseph Surface about to be sanctimonious. It was very uncomfortable.

'I don't believe at all that's what he seeks,' she said, as lightly as possible, 'and I don't believe *you* believe it either. And my goodness, girl, I don't believe you can possibly think what you'd have me believe you've been thinking of! Because if you can – and if you have – and now you accuse *me* of it! – Frances Kemble, did I say "depraved"? I ought to have gone much further. *Diseased*, that's what you are.'

'I am not!' Fanny was almost in tears at the word, the sort of word she would never have heard from 'H' in such a connection; but she turned them to a laugh, and thence (shakily) to level-headed argument: 'Surely not. Do I not see it as plain good sense? I intend never to marry. So imagination needs not to be kept within bounds. If it extends to act and deed it won't deprive me of a husband. As I have said, Ellen, many times, I refuse to be slave to Tradition.'

'A great nobleman's actress-mistress is very very traditional, and most certainly a sort of slave. Look at Mrs Jordan. She lived with the king before he was king; and alas, where is she now?'

'If you must say "alas", I too can do the pathetics. *Alas!* In our business these days we have found a new tradition: or rather, a very old one, it comes straight from beastly Cromwell; the theatre is the pit of sin; we must try to pretend it isn't, even as we accept that it is. Hypocrisy! And I abhor it. I mean to leave the theatre as soon as I may; dear God, how I dread ending up like Aunt Sarah!' (Mrs Siddons, in her retirement: an exhausted husk of a woman, no roles to fulfil her imagination, no public to applaud them, no heart to her life nor joy in her past achievements.) 'And yet I'll never be respectable; the trade will *taint* me all my life. So let me take what advantage I can: wicked bits no less than the ideals. Oh Ellen, don't this train go abominable slow?'

Abominable slow indeed; it whistled every fifty yards. Somewhere up ahead were four locomotives, maybe on the same track; great danger of collision.

And they *were* on the same track, returning to Manchester, full up with the Eccles water. In fact no collision, George saw them, stopped *Northumbrian*, whistled continuously, they heard him, saw him, whistled, and stopped. All five drivers to the ground, intense conference, what to do?

If *Northumbrian* retreated, the duke would be brought back to the Manchester riots – out of the question. No, the four must run on westward, in front of *Northumbrian*, until crossover points could be reached; that meant all the way to Huyton, practically the suburbs of Liverpool. Ridiculous solution to a ridiculous predicament. Sulphurous words from every footplate as the slow and painful journey recommenced.

At Eccles, a brief stop; just sufficient to hear a man on the platform shouting out that Mr Huskisson still lived, but . . .

Fanny put her hands over her ears. All these images in her talk with Ellen about tricks and twists of mortal bodies; she had no desire to think of one so hacked, so torn as Huskisson's. But the conversation was not yet over.

Something about Fanny's posture, bent forward suddenly timorous, blocking out unwelcome news, piqued Ellen with a surprising hurt. This unwholesome little half-French Kemble, how sure of herself she pretended to be, how sure of her friend's sympathy! And yet how she *feared* to hear what she did not wish to hear. Very well; she must be indulged. If she wanted to be told to go alone to the old goat duke, then Ellen would gladly tell her: the more so because Ellen now realised she would *never* be at one with Fanny – not in a lifetime, no! – the girl's thoughts were no mere whimsies of inexperienced youth – she was actually made like that. Ellen's face went very red; she was nearly ashamed of what she was to do, and ashamed to be seen red-faced at it. Or was shame the only reason for her flushes?

It grew dark, no lamp in the carriage, heated cheeks could not be noticed. She laid a heated hand on Fanny's forearm. 'Oh but you are cold!'

'It's all that rain, I'll catch a fever.' Fanny was feeling the pain in her side.

'I'll snuggle you under my shawl, so; it's wider than yours, I think. I'll tell you truthfully, Fanny, I do *not* understand you. Therefore I cannot advise you. Therefore I can only tell you, you should follow your nature.'

'But how do I know what *is* my nature?'

'I suppose by your inheritance. Do as you would believe your mother might have done.'

'Ah. I didn't really want to hear that.'

'Yes you did, Fanny; or you'd have covered your ears.'

They sat silent, close together under the one warm shawl, while the train rumbled through the dusk over the drear waste of Chat Moss, the great peat-bog across which no railroad could ever be built; and yet it *was* built, and Tradition quite absurdly confounded.

A little kiss for the little Kemble; and then, a quasi-blessing: 'Do what you feel called to do; and, dear goodness, make yourself happy!'

Judas-kiss? No! For surely Ellen did not burn to *crucify* this creature (whom she thereupon kissed again); just to – to – bring her qualities closer to the best qualities of a close friend; which sometimes meant a little punishment. A libertine duke was surely punishment for a young romantic girl. He might be (indeed, was) a hero, he might or might not be 'wicked', but – naked? ugh! – so let Fanny find out!

And yet, if Tree and Kemble were never to be at one, punishment was gratuitous; must it not then be malicious? So therefore Tree *was* Judas; and as Judas she burned, once again red-ashamed, her boyish mouth drawn taut in a rigid (and quite aged) grimace.

Last effort to understand; to defeat shame, recapture love; final painful probe into the darkness of impossible Kemble: 'All that nonsense about the Grand Turk? – your Anna Wheeler, I suppose, overdoing her comparisons.'

'I don't think so.'

'No?' (and a third kiss) 'Ah, I have it! You saw that man in the band – '

'Yes I did.'

'– in a turban; he ran to lift up Mr Huskisson.'

'I did see him. Yes I saw. I did.'

'They always dress the jingles-player in something of a fancy costume; a military tradition, it don't signify.'

'Oh but it does,' whispered Fanny, 'and I saw him.' She refused to say more about it.

In dire disgust the duke said: 'A political defeat, Peel; not decisive, but undeniable. By God, sir, we flee from Manchester like Boney's *Grande Armée* out of Moscow. I arrived there with eight trains. I return with only one. *I thank you.*'

He was very nearly right. His train came into Liverpool at half-past seven. In Manchester at that hour the others were only just setting out. To begin with, there had been the hold-up for four engines to come back from Eccles; but of course they did not come back, they'd gone to Huyton and no one knew they'd gone to Huyton. Robert Stephenson, after a protracted wait, decided to take the remaining three locomotives to Eccles for their water; and for any news he could pick up. This was done; and he knew where he stood. He also knew upon which track to expect the returning Huyton engines; if he continued along to meet them, he must keep to that track (very cautiously, whistling all the way, with lanterns hung on chimney stacks and tail-bars), and he'd then have their help. But first he had to run back to Manchester and fetch out seven trains of coaches. The passengers were now so rebellious he did not dare keep them a single minute longer in the station.

But could three engines cope? The seemingly obvious expedient, to divide the rolling-stock among the engines, forming three separate ill-lit trains close behind one another in pitch dark and pouring rain, was a promise of outright disaster. But with all the coaches coupled together, and all the engines at their head? Disproportionate and clumsy, it might just be made to work; provided they could once get under way. Wet mud obliterated the rails; the driving wheels jerked and slipped; coupling chains broke and had to be replaced with lashings of rope; male passengers had to be asked to get out for a time and walk: but at last they were moving. And at last they met the other engines. And at last they came into Liverpool.

Ten o'clock at night, and half the city spreading rumours that the Stephensons must surely have killed them all.

Miss Tree and the Kembles had achieved the theatre just in time, for a most extraordinary *Merchant*: Shylock as hoarse as Noah's raven and nearly as drunk as Noah himself; Jessica quite violent – angry from beginning to end (even her tender '*In such a night did Thisbe fearfully o'ertrip the dew*' passages); and Portia unexpectedly tremulous, defending Antonio like a shabby-genteel attorney whose Petty Sessions client pled guilty to 'committing a nuisance'.

At curtain-call Mr Kemble begged the public's indulgence. His leading players, he said, had that day enjoyed a great and tragic adventure in the closest proximity to the kingdom's greatest man, they were smitten with the sheer *catharsis* of it, although nothing could prevent them nor ever would prevent them presenting their duties to their faithful audience. It is possible he would have continued with a full account of the railway excursion: but his voice gave out. He received tremendous applause.

As soon as he had removed his Jewish beard and gaberdine, Fanny sent him straight back to their lodgings, with his dresser to assist him, and a fresh bottle of brandy. He was in no state to ask why she did not come too. She knew that he would sleep until the middle at least of the next afternoon.

TWELVE

Fanny's allusive reply to the duke's invitation had been interpreted by him thus: a partially secluded alcove in the dining room of a town club for the Tory country gentlemen of Merseyside –

– who commonly don't invite ladies into their midst, but the chairman is said to be loyal and will stretch a point for me if I put it succinctly. Perfectly private and yet by no means *clandestine*; which is, I take it, the nub of your specification? If they insist, I must present you to them: tiresome, no doubt, but 'twill secure your propriety. They'll *know* you, of course, in one sense; is it a whole month you've enkindled their theatre? But I don't believe they'll insist. I do not desire public notice, and they're aware of it. On parade for the rail-train, on parade for the freedom of the city next day, my own evening in between. *Our* own evening. My young man will wait upon you at the stage door a full hour after the performance: sufficient time to accoutre yourself?

A full hour was far more than she needed. She had gone straight to the theatre from the railway, in clothes that were waterlogged rags, impossible to send for an evening gown from Church Street, her father was there, he might not have gone to bed. Only thing to do: find something out of stage-stock. Ruffs and puffs from the Shakespeares wouldn't do, but what about *The School for Scandal*? She had been Lady Teazle last week. Charles had wished to give the play some sense of period, it was over fifty years old, no longer plausible as contemporary satire. But not too archaic – 'Old Sherry was still active when I was a young fellow, let's take the styles from the start of the century?' – so light muslin, *décolleté*, without vestige of a corset (in itself an advantage, for Fanny loathed not being able to breathe upon stage). Lady Teazle for tonight, then; and add a gauze stole as a precaution, for when Old Sherry was still active Old Nosey must have been at his most libertine.

The equerry was punctual. And also apologetic: 'Miss Kemble, I'm afraid to say there has been a change of plan – ah, the peculiar circumstances of the day – if you'll enter the carriage I will explain what the duke has in mind.'

At this point she should have sent the messenger very firmly on his way without her. She had agreed to a particular proposal: which ought not to be amended, certainly not unilaterally. It was a hurtling gale-tossed rain-whipped night, she needed sleep, she felt distressed and unwell. She had had to drink brandy, nearly as deep as her father, to get herself onstage at all; she was almost sure her ensuing Portia had been ridiculous. But if the duke could survive, she could. Her deadly curiosity once again created courage; once again her absurd courage terrified her. She bent her bonnet under the equerry's scarce-manageable umbrella and stepped into the waiting carriage.

'The difficulty, Miss Kemble, is this: among the duke's own faction here, that is to say the chairman of the club, there's strong feeling that his grace ought not to have been at any sort of handshake with Mr Huskisson today, even tentative, even calamitous. While the other faction, I mean the "Peelites", are disappointed that the duke has postponed tomorrow's ceremony. They do see that Huskisson's death must make a difference – he *is* dead, by the by, we just had word from the rail-road – but they fear the duke has jettisoned a crucial political chance. And they're all very worried about the riots; not only in Manchester, disturbances all day in Liverpool. So gentlemen have recommended the duke should stay away from the club; or some of the members, in drink perhaps, might think fit to insult him. Which would do no good at all to government.'

'No club then; and no supper?'

'Oh certainly supper, but at a private house.'

'Whose?'

'It is a villa owned by Mr Sandars, it appears he lets it furnished and just at present it is vacant. He was – ah, prevailed upon, to lend it to the duke for tonight. It is not generally known that his grace is still in Liverpool. Mr Sandars understands that the misadventures upon the rail-road have – ah, put him in debt to the duke. He is most anxious, anonymously, to rehabilitate himself; rehabilitate the rail company and the city in general, I fancy.'

'This is very suspicious.'

'The duke said you'd say that, ma'am. He compares himself to Gaius Marius among the ruins of Carthage; but he's convinced you have the humour to see it through. Have you?'

'I haven't asked for the carriage to be stopped.'

The villa was upon Edge Hill, isolated, newly-built, in a windswept brand new street, the only completed building for several hundred yards. No light showed in the windows. An undeveloped garden of shrubs and builders' rubbish; the carriage drove straight round to the back door, which was opened immediately by a burly special-constable sort of man carrying a candlestick. He spoke to the equerry: 'I'd say it's all quiet, sir. No one knows we're here. Me other two chaps are i't'smoking room; they've brought pistols. Sorry about this, ma'am; needful security. You're to take t'lady straight upstairs, sir.'

Fanny declined to 'wash her hands': she had done so several times during her hour's wait at the theatre; now that her call was given her, she must stride forward through the wings at once or (shamefully unprofessionally) flee. Most of the house was under dust-sheets. The L-shaped room into which she was shown was large and similarly veiled; save for one candlelit firelit corner, where varnished paintings and vast mahogany made peculiarly Liverpool gloom; a small table laid for supper. A black-and-white, small, white-faced duke, strict rigour of his evening dress, old-fashioned knee-breeches, silk stockings, pumps. Had he worn trousers, she asked herself whirlingly, would they have concealed his famous *boots*? – to offer her, later on, the dreaded chance to find out? She would not think of it. She put forward a shaking hand, which he kissed as he bowed; the equerry withdrew. The duke seemed as nervous as she was. He *h'm'd* twice, and commenced to patter his gallantry.

'Dear lady of the thrilling voice, as courageous as the best of 'em; I was sure you would be here. And absolutely dressed like a gay little poem by that seditious little tomfool Byron!' (A vicious crackle in his voice there, instantly suppressed.) 'I do hope the man at the door was civil? Unfortunate, all the nonsense, but people are in a funny mood; so are the gentry. I'm made to understand I have to take precautions. Didn't alarm you, h'm?' *'H'm'* twice again, and he led her to a chair.

'He talked about pistols.'

'Unfortunate. Y'see, Sandars told me the rail company had employed a force of bruisers to protect their surveyors from attacks by disgruntled landlords; he was adamant Stephenson hunt up one or two of 'em, to look after me, or at any rate look after his property; they seem to know their business. The rooms are not cheerful, we must improvise, *bivouac*-fashion; sense of adventure, h'm? And pot-luck for the supper, I'm afraid. I have no cook with me, it's sent up in a cab from the club-kitchen and will almost certainly arrive cold. Still, we'll do our best. Are you happy to do your best? And you'll take a glass of wine with me to prove it?'

The wine was white and sparkling. She drank it thirstily; and wished she hadn't, after so much brandy and so little food. Spiced *hors d'oeuvres* to go with it; of an unfamiliar sort, they burnt her tongue:

'Madrassee kickshaws, I hope you like 'em. I asked for an Indian supper, *curree* and so forth; heat of the spices should outlast the mile-and-a-half trip from the kitchen. Oriental ingredients, abundant in these seaport towns.'

He talked jerkily about India, his service there, odd details of the native life. One of the bruisers carried in covered dishes: spicy indeed, so hot she had to gasp; it made it hard to converse. He laughed – oh yes, he could laugh – he was close to putting her at ease. But then an abrupt silence. Oh how to defeat his shyness, how to fulfil her boast? ('A very good gossip'?) Oh, *how*? He peered at her, profound stare, almost a glare, it was unnerving. The Grand Turk nursing his lust, she thought, the lobster's claws about to grip.

'The railway, your grace; what did you think of it?' Idiot girl! She *knew* what he thought of it: it had killed a man before his eyes.

But he answered her coolly, seriously, no more jerks, no sort of stress. 'At first, my dear, I thought it a subversive innovation, as most innovations are. But then I saw how Stephenson dealt with poor Huskisson, no stricken man ever delivered to the surgeon more efficaciously. Surgeon proved useless, but that's immaterial. By the same token, one might deliver a body of troops to put down sedition quite as fast as any move by any horde of insurrectionists. One might also use the system – provided it *is* a system, with ultimate control in the hands of government – to convey convicted felons, or suspects awaiting trial, in such numbers as may amount to battalion strength; one might also deport disaffected populations to wherever they will do the least harm.' (His expression was hard, decisive, relentless.) 'I look, of course, into the future – forebode, if you prefer the word – in the light of – of that pellmell in Manchester. Which need *not* be repeated. Faulty logistics, incorrect appreciation of the enemy's strength; worst of all, sorry to tell you, commercial directors playing the fool, playing politics, playing their wretched little games with *me*. Oh yes and they'll do it again!' (The vicious crackle once more.) 'I forebode; but let's keep our heads.'

The *enemy's* strength? And spoken so matter-of-fact! God, but her father had been absolutely right! (until he showed himself hypocrite). And no less right, her brother, volunteering so boldly for Spain, there was nothing John could do in Spain, nothing useful at all for liberty, except get himself out of there at once, he was wrong but he was right; he had chosen the experience.

Now, tonight, was *her* experience: to sup privately – no, clandestinely – with a take-it-for-granted tyrant. Question of conscience: to challenge, or not? She'd wanted to mention the ragged man at the handloom. But now she did not trust herself: a challenge no better argued than mere girlish denunciation would surely bring the evening to a premature end; the experience would go for nothing. She was, after all, an *artist*, experience her very life. Professional responsibility! Courage of her curiosity! As

against which, she gave thought to the courage of liberty. To Judith and
Holofernes. And then to Charlotte Corday. Holofernes drunk in bed,
repulsive Marat stretched stark in a bath. Wicked contexts, wicked blood.
Irrelevant contexts too; for his present line of talk seemed to muffle the
ogre's lust; should she let it continue, no challenge, simply listen?

She was not yet ready, if she would ever be ready, to discover what his
lust was like. Tension in her mind made tension in her neck; he was aware
of the strain of her posture.

He didn't tell her, for he feared it would be anaphrodisiac, that the 'little
games' he had detected, and their devastating consequence, had so
sickened him of government office that tomorrow he would write to the
king. Write, resign, and thereafter; let Peel do his damnedest. The reaction
of the local clubmen had convinced him the day's defeat *was* after all
decisive; and by God he'd always known when and where to cut losses.

Meanwhile, his compensation: the gentlemanly – or, if need be, knavish
– defloration of Fanny. (She behaved toward him like a virgin, but was
she? From her full-blooded vigour upon stage, he'd guessed otherwise; he
could be wrong; he would discover.)

Or perhaps not compensation; he should rather say, *revenge!* So
irrationally had it shifted its shape. Whether it could do any injury, let
alone prove anything, to his tormentors, he did not try to calculate: the
deed was required for its own sake. As with the late Bonaparte, his vulgar
urge for immediate conquest had now turned into Pursuit of Destiny:
despicably juvenile, and therefore most gratifying, one in the eye for that
fatbelly Sandars, one in the groin for jesuitical Peel. Because *he* would
know he'd done it; and *they* never would, no; and he'd gallop away from
them, grinning.

Meanwhile, he'd talk of Huskisson; he couldn't help it anyway, and it
looked as though it might produce results. Gentlemanly.

'Didn't like the man at all. Mistrusted his politics, his wife, his *intensity*, hers
as well. But he's dead, and a dreadful death. I do hope you didn't see it.'

She shook her head. The pelting tempest crashed all about the dark
house. Dreadful death; and she swilled wine.

'Good. *I* did. I thought, after Waterloo, no more of it, no more. I told
myself, live! Regard death from today forward as a quiet sleep, quietly
entered; burst flesh, severed bone, no longer a prerequisite. No longer the
knowledge they were *my* work, no one else's. Why, he and I had about the
same number of years; he should have gone on for a full score more; and
now so suddenly dead? – damme, child, I needed a young friend, no less

suddenly, a clever friend, a wicked friend, I can't do with a woman that's a fool – oh who else could show me, except someone like you, that death *as death* was not? Which I've needed to have proved, ever since they first told me the harsh duties of a gentleman don't on any account include devotion to music. I had a fiddle, which I loved; and I burned the bloody thing; since then I never played a single note. Which very much seemed to me, death.'

She saw his old eyes all swollen, little trickles down his cheeks. Without thinking what she did, she put out a hand to him. He grasped it, strongly; his touch dismayed her, excited her, she felt a thumbnail scratch deliberately at her palm. His expression became gently considerate, most grateful for her gentleness.

'Not very jolly, are we? You accuse my despotic politics, silently to be sure; but your profile betrayed you. I suspect you were employing the *guerrilleros* you wrote to me of. Whereupon I retort with a maudlin lament. My apologies, ma'am.'

'And mine, your grace.'

More wine, and unwisely. Her head swam, she was just able to judge that her judgement was gone. But the sweat was pouring off her from the *curree.* Muslin dress, even so thin, was altogether too hot. Stole stifled her.

'I meant to say earlier; don't call me "your grace". Obsequious, inappropriate.'

Nor would 'Arthur' do (did his wife call him 'Arthur', or Mrs Arbuthnot?); he was jolly and gallant, suggested 'Wellesley'; she laughed and offered 'Wesley' (aware it used to be his family name, doubtless there'd been fear of associations with plebeian enthusiasm); she was fuddled and dictatorial, refusing to be 'ma'am', and certainly not 'Fanny' ('Makes me sound like an actress!') – they were both very jolly, very *arch*, diffusedly genteel, until of a sudden she was able to recover her fleeing wits –

Françoise? *Françoise de Foix!* Why, her own play gave her her cue! Corday, Judith, nothing to the purpose! She had a *real* role to play here, most shameful she'd not thought of it sooner, when her head would have been cool, her slither of words precise.

Without preliminary she was blurting into a breathless, shockingly earnest, nearly tearful account of John's foray to Algeciras; 'Half-French romantic rhodomont,' so she described him and pled for him, he was entangled (and could have taken no forethought) with the devil only knew what cynical abusers of his good faith, if the cause of Spanish liberty were hopeless (and wasn't it?), what means by which a British prime minister could help? – to save an idealistic Englishman (half-French, just like herself) from the – the (she struggled for the phrase) – *the fatal corollary of his impetuous initiative?* – the phrase was too intricate, she stammered, slurred syllables, broke off with a gulp: had she, or hadn't she, made her story clear? and how about Françoise de Foix? affording the *quid-pro-quo* to the exortionate king? She, Françoise Kemble, must be craftier than that – unless already, unwittingly, she'd seemed (aha, horror!) to drop the hint her own favours were no less available. . . ? Dear heaven, this duke was grinning.

'Ah; Spain. Indeed.' (She could not fathom the grin, it was not at all jolly, not even sympathetic.) 'Foreign secretary has a full report. Our man in Madrid is far from pleased. My first reaction, had to be, was leave the troublesome jackanapes in their self-created blood-bucket, but dear Françoise, I don't know about blood-buckets, not any longer, what to think of 'em, what to do. It's been a very great shock; I mean Huskisson, a great shock.' (If he wandered from the point, he no doubt had reason; unfathomable; she *must* pay attention.) 'Your brother, in his insensate way – I suppose he's a reader of Byron – ?' (The grin had dissolved into a small twitch of a smile.) '– he's refused to "burn his fiddle"; so we can't call him dead, whatever the Spaniards do to him. You require discreet approaches to make sure they don't: I'll notify the Foreign Office.'

She was holding *his* hand with both of hers now; she swiftly disengaged, lest a surge of gratitude impel her to kiss it.

The smile no longer there, his expression quite blank; he had, it seemed, said all he had to say. Was it possible after all there need be no *quid-pro-quo*?

A long pause; he murmured: 'Mind you.' Haltingly, meticulously, one might think him as drunk as herself: 'Mind you; when I first wrote to you, I did have a different notion of what tonight was all about. I think, a different notion. Can't quite remember how I *did* think.'

He had said what he had to say, the subject of John must be closed, so what to say now? 'Music', he had spoken of; from music to her own art should have been the proper progress; yes, when he first wrote, that surely was his theme? Crafty enough, was she, to take *that* cue? Be safe, take it now, end the evening with polite exchanges, upon Shakespeare and maybe Mozart. But his damned wine took it for her; she betrayed herself, betrayed her own fatuous dissembling, broke again into laughter. 'I think you thought I'd – you might – that's to say, *we* might – God, Wesley, in a provincial club? Among decorous old Lancashire squires! How *would* you have got me – where?'

'These things can be managed. But if you're going to need to stop them, take care not to let 'em start. I used to be very good at it. Impertinent question; but are *you*?'

He was laughing with her, the wicked old devil (and she laughed with him), in a most wicked and reprobate intimacy.

'Good at it? No never. Never any such chance. I am – was – ought to be – a very proper person, very *pertinent* person, so now you know. Because I'm Juliet and so forth, young men love me. I haven't loved any of them. Haven't loved, except my brother, until they thought it was too perfervid; so they sent me to school in France, where of course (aged thirteen) I commenced to conceive *ideas*; I planned to elope with a beautiful young French lover; if I found one, but I never did; sad. Never more than his picture in my mind. Beautiful hair, beautiful clothes. And then – not the clothes. Apollyon, on a pederast – *Apollo*. Romantic classical and now I'm here. Pediment, I should have said. How. How, now I'm here, if I'd given you my fool encouragement, how d'you suppose you'd have *managed*? Oh don't tell me, let me discover!'

She swayed to her feet, disconcerting him, for he had his hand creeping gently up her arm; to tell truth, she had let her chair shift (of its own volition?) eighteen inches round the table nearer to his, and they were leaning together, one could call it close. Nonetheless, up onto her feet (a side-plate fell and broke), she said – to tell truth, she shouted – : 'Duke of Darkness, I mean to see what you have behind that door!'

The door was beside the fireplace, she swung toward it, the priapic duke on his own feet immediately behind her, stroking her bare neck, she thought, stroking her spine, as she fumbled with the handle, opening the door into a smaller, square room, a sort of study. Partly under dust-covers, but a fire burning low in the grate gave uneven jumping light. Dustsheet-swathed bookcases. A type of furniture she knew well from theatrical lodgings; sofa-bedstead, hinged open and ready made-up, clean sheets, blue-and-white patchwork quilt.

She was conscious of the duke behind her, a hand and forearm at her waist, or (surely not, but why not? it was all so very easy when you came to think of it) mercilessly fondling her *derrière*? His other hand higher up, fingers tripping about the shoulder-ribbons of her bodice. Somehow she no longer had the stole. And somehow the duke's quick, bird-like little movements – sweetly adroit, oddly courteous, no likeness at all to the snatches of lobster-claws – were as entertaining as a child's playtime; she wriggled and laughed and tried to seize hold of his fingers: it was as though she were once again on George Stephenson's speeding footplate, she knew that her adventure might now be thought very dangerous, she laughed to think others would think so, she was *La Kemble, fille de la belle Marie Thérèse*, inviolate at thirty-five miles an hour, she played his wicked catch-as-catch-can and exulted. (And he'd sworn he'd save her brother!)

He was whispering into her ear (had perhaps been whispering for a long time, because time for her had ceased to *work* according to its regular habit) sad and tender words of love, of extraordinary rapid diction; jumbled together with the most unbelievable indecencies – some of them even in French. Tribute to her motherland, or a baseless reflection upon it? She did not understand all their implications, or was *supposed* not to understand them; but they neither angered her nor frightened (all so very easy when you came to think of it) – comical – she mocked him for them – did she want him to kiss her *what*? Put his hand *where*? Put her own finger *how*? (And her brother would be safe, she had *done* it!)

This could not go on. Nor did it go on. She did not know, but her dress was already down to her waist – her uncorseted shift would have followed it, indeed half of it *had* followed – when she was abominably overcome, by the brandy, the wine, the unusual rich food, all the tensions of the day combined, drastic humiliating earthquake-threat of intestinal conturbation. She broke from the duke, she gasped to him to GO AWAY!, she fell about the room, frantic for the urgent vessel which ought surely to be somewhere, it must be, there was a bed, and whenever they made up a bed they surely set ready a – ? She was on her knees, scrabbling at a likely-looking door in some piece of unusual furniture, it seemed locked but the catch was weak, she wrenched it open: oh God no pot, only piles of written paper! Had they hidden it behind the papers? In any case she was going to need them, she forgot all else and pulled them out holus-bolus. And then everything happened at once to her overwrought body, she lay horribly heaving, befouling herself, like a poor little pig in a sty. The tears ran down her face at her mortal corruption, her vileness, the cruel crudity of it all.

The duke (unbuttoned but now far from priapic) sprang awkward and loose-belted to help her; struggled to extricate her from the clustering muddle, the sodden stinking *goulash* of heaped paper; he saw what was written across one of the leaves; sat plump on the bed, 'My God. God,' he could hardly sound the words, he was so shocked (his fingers forgot how to re-fasten his waistband), 'What have they done? God.'

Her first dire paroxysm was over; she looked up at him, eyes unfocussed, bowels lurching yet again. She saw him a-shake and white as quicklime, even sicker than she was. 'Do you know what they've done?' he was trying to say, and he mumbled like a grief-silly widow-woman. She did not care what they'd done. But he persevered; articulated, 'Ah God that villain Sandars; *he has put me into Huskisson's house.*'

Then again she spewed, and lost all knowledge, full-length on the defiled carpet, swirling hair, bare shoulders across the fender half-into the fire.

Lost all knowledge, that is to say, of anything but storm-driven dream, which came up out of her nothingness, and broke about her incoherent all hours of

the night until at length it settled down to wait with her and wait for the gale
to fall silent and the music to begin.

She lay stripped and spread out on the bed, not under the quilt but on top of
it, perfumed and oiled and bejewelled. The music was behind curtains,
unseen violin so heart-rending it seemed as though her own nerves were but
slender vibrations of catgut.

Her brother, impetuous in embroidered kaftan over silver sheen of his
chain-mail, clipped a final necklace around her throat, left her a last
worshipping kiss upon the tender inch of skin between ear-ring and upswept
hair, and so departed in glowing haste.

The curtains moved, the huge African stepped from between them as naked
as she was, save for Turkish turban, and heavy chains upon wrists and
ankles. He heaved a great bundle, wrapped in many-coloured silk; tipped it
out on the bed like a load of Covent Garden turnips.

He bent deferentially, chained hands pressed together, crept away. As he
went she caught sight of his back, bloody weals from his latest punishment
(which she gave to him herself, and now wept to consider its severity).

The crumpled thing he had dumped down began to stir and to roll, and
then to groan and stretch toward her. An aged man all bemired in the
doublet of Romeo, his face a distorted death's-head, his pleading hands black
muddy pulp, his left leg severed above the knee – torn ends of bone and
muscle exposed upon the quilt, blood spirting from the artery to wash over her
own legs in a flood of steaming scarlet.

To see how she desired him! She probed delicately, ruthlessly, knowingly,
into the flap of his trunkhose (no thought any more of her galliard brother),
seeking vigour, seeking iron! *And she found it.*

He buried the teeth of his rotten old phiz into the pungent gap of her
blood-stained thighs: proud as a Queen of Egypt, she caterwauled for the
pleasure she gave and received.

A grey-haired desperate widow stood and watched through the folds of the
curtains. Vengeance tautened every wrinkle of her terrier-bitch ugliness. She
ripped open her black robe, for a wonder her bared breasts were rosebuds,
young and lovely. She gave tongue, gross anger in French and English, she
had the quick harsh tones of Ellen Tree: 'You swore you would denounce
him; now we see how you do it. All our love has been despised. Mangeuse
de la merde, toi! Et fille du vieux mangeur, *foul cunt upon two legs that*
has eaten your own head and heart; and never in all this earth will its
fulfilments bring you anything but hatred.'

Which ought to have been the end of it, but was not.

Room suddenly empty and dead; nothing there but a bucket of water, scrubbed floor, scrubbed walls, Fanny's shivering nudity crouched in one corner (she could observe herself from outside herself); and the maddening squawk of her own voice, gabbling endlessly through the last four lines of the School for Scandal epilogue (wherein Lady Teazle denounces her past conduct and praises herself for having abandoned it):

> Blest were the fair like you; her faults who stopt,
> And closed her follies when the curtain dropt!
> No more in vice or error to engage,
> Or play the fool at large on life's great stage.

Repeated over and over, amidst steam-engine whistles and the rushing of wheels. Faster and faster, and for hours, until words were at one with mechanical uproar. Were there needles piercing her ear-drums?

THIRTEEN

Neddy Craig was the worst hurt of those at Jack Scuffham's loom. For a long time he lay stunned. Some Liverpool comrades, no doubt feeling guilty they had not immediately been there to give the protection they had promised, took humane (if not exactly competent) care of him. A donkey-cart belonging to somebody's brother-in-law was requisitioned from a nearby market garden, they laid him in it on a pile of cabbage leaves, and then wondered where they should take him.

They were footloose young fellows, attracted to insurrectionary politics by their very lack of domestic background, squatting in ruinous tenements, evading all rent; if any of them had any family, the connection (by mutual agreement) was contemptuously ignored. An injured companion was therefore a problem for them, if he needed – as Neddy appeared to need – intelligent nursing. One of them suggested the market-gardener's house: but that was not a good idea. The brother-in-law had not been about his yard when the cart was taken, his permission had been assumed rather than granted; as it was, they would have to return donkey and vehicle within less than an hour – 'If we don't want t'bloody traps after us! Hey-up though, I've got a notion: Kitty Brisket in Booble Alley! She owes me a turn for warning her when plug-uglies off o't' *Star o'Hoboken* came ashore wi'brass knuckles to smash every tart in her house. No better skirt nor Kitty's to swaddle a cully wi'a stove-in topside. Come on, me boys, shog!'

The donkey was lashed and anathematised at hilarious pace down through the city, a half-dozen responsible democrats whooping alongside the cart, revolutionary tricolour madly flying from the driver's whip; while the devastated Scuffhams and Harry were left almost upon their own to dismantle the heavy loom and fetch it painfully back to Manchester.

Thus, when Mary at the Manchester station was worrying herself sick about Neddy and his safety, he himself lay bandaged in a disgraceful sailors' knocking-shop, supping gruel at the hands of the proprietress. Her girls, in and out of their ragged shifts, uncombed and mid-morning frowsty, drifted one by one to the door of the room to take a peek at him. They agreed he was fresh and handsome – largely because he was pale and ill (and indeed without his spectacles); actively dogmatic he would hardly have been their choice of 'flash'; they were sad he could not answer their busybody gap-toothed grins after the spirit wherewith they were offered. The comrades who had brought him sat about in the grime of the parlour; they roistered and bragged derisively like cut-price buccaneers.

Some of them were still there, singing songs into the night, calling for drinks they could no longer pay for, when Kitty made up her mind she had had more than enough of them. She hocussed their last orders. They awoke well out to sea aboard no other ship than the *Star o' Hoboken*. The 'plug-uglies' (second mate and boatswain) had, as it happened, compounded their quarrel with her a good five or six days earlier, and she was supplying them her services as per usual.

Neddy himself had skipped it, just upon sunset. Once he'd realised where he was, he was in a mucksweat of fear. His knowledge of Liverpool, mythological rather than exact, included Booble Alley as the very sink of a latter-day Tophet. So when one of the more compassionate and daring of the girls whispered a word in his aching ear about the quirks of Kitty's character, and offered (for a kiss) to return his missing trousers and smuggle him 'out at t'backside', he lost no time in trusting her. Which was just about as clever as trusting Mrs Brisket herself; but of course he didn't think of that at the time. In fact she meant no more than she said; she was unused to his type; she thought he was a 'gentleman'; the entire incident was high romance and it fed her simple soul for years afterwards.

Of course, all the cash had disappeared from his pockets.

It was raining, the wind was fierce, he felt faint, he knew no one in town. He staggered crazily back up to Edge Hill; of course, Harry and his wagon were long gone.

There were everywhere signs of disorder, running groups of bothered constables, pickets of soldiers, streets here and there cordoned off, noises of fighting heard obscurely from dark entries beyond the cordons. He avoided these perilous symptoms, the city was large enough. But no doubt about it, he was frightened.

He leaned over the parapet, in the exact place where Jack's loom had stood, and looked down at the railway in its gorge. There were others alongside him, curious people who had ventured out despite tumults, despite the storm, to watch for the return of the trains; apprehensive speculation that they had not come back hours ago. Neddy sickly concluded there was trouble in Manchester. He was worrying about Mary just as she worried about him, but how on earth was he going to get to her?

He was in a fever of remorse for the events of the day. He feared he had led the Scuffhams into a very nasty trap, he had never thought the militia would have responded so barbarously to such a modest and straightforward display of dissidence. He had been badly misinformed about local support. The men who came to help were little better than a tearaway street-gang; he had allowed the contact to be made by one of old Bentham's cronies, upon clearly out-of-date information. There might indeed be a body somewhere of more serious activists in Liverpool, but exactly who they were was yet to be discovered. All in all, it was a *criminal* city, far better to have no more to do with it.

He had some wild idea of extemporising a *train trip* home, so he ought not to leave the neighbourhood of the tunnel-mouth. But there was nothing of any use to him down there at the moment; just a few tarpaulin caps and capes a-shine with rain, as little huddles of anxious railwaymen conferred. A hundred yards from the brim of the cutting he found a shed; the padlock was broken; inside were old packing-cases and straw, he plunged among them, fell down, passed out.

He awoke before dawn, very ill indeed; his head pounded like an engine, so much like an engine it took him several minutes to realise there were in fact engines pounding, hissing, clanking; and not at all far away. He crawled out of his shelter, and forced himself again to the parapet. The tracks beneath were alive with activity, torches a-flare in the gusts of wind, swinging lanterns, locomotives, carriages, wagons. Here, or nowhere, was his opportunity. Very carefully and in great fear, he descended the long stone stairs to the bottom. Or almost to the bottom; he fainted again, and sprawled helplessly.

It was not long before some Irishmen found him, yard-hands in the midst of their work. They took him for drunk and laughed and kicked at him. Then they saw his bandaged head and became at once sympathetic. He was able to tell them the militia had done it; they were more than sympathetic, they offered all sorts of practical help, drams of whiskey from their pocket-flasks which he had just sufficient sense to refuse. He said, 'Manchester, Manchester, I've been robbed, I must get to Manchester.' They assumed it was the militia who had robbed him, they discussed what could be done.

One of them said that *Seoirse Iarnaí* (by which he meant 'Iron George') was taking *Rocket* back to Manchester with a load of engineering equipment in little more than half-an-hour – 'For in that place are most sorrowful deficiencies of gear, would you believe, *Pádraig Óg*, not a chain in the city entirely, to bring two *fucking* cars together when the *coupling hooks* snapped asunder? And neither pipes nor well-caulked tanks to furnish water east of Eccles? *Seoirse Iarnaí* – come here till I tell you! – is an angry man whatever, for the treachery that is in it from the Manchester men of his venture, their incapability, their blackguard ignorance; nor do I mean his English, but the crowd of chancers from Donegal are after conniving themselves into his employ – unshapely truth, but the *fucking* nostrils of this ironroad are held open by the diligence of Liverpool alone! And yet he will not have it, he insults all his Irish in his rage; and damn his soul.' Which being said in Connemara Gaelic (except for 'coupling hooks' and 'fucking'), Neddy could follow none of it; he lay still and let his thoughts run upon Mary.

Another, in the same language, with much assumption of profundity: 'An angry man, surely, but I'd say he was a man of his name, and more power to him in the name of God. For who else after such a day would make another such journey without rest? And who else upon that murdering *Rocket*? For God knows it is a creature of blood.'

They discussed the death of Huskisson, greatly enjoying their verbal embellishment; and then, without more words, picked Neddy up between them, to bear him furtively to an open goodswagon that was standing ready-hooked to its train. They laid him very gently between two coils of rope and covered him over with tarpaulin, telling him (in whispered English): 'Manchester, me jewel, you'll be there, so you will, in nick o'time for your cabbage-and-bacon; now you don't shift a damn foot outa that, and God geld the bloody lobsterbacks!'

It was a fast journey, with only a few unloading stops – great need for haste – the first regular train with fare-paying passengers was to leave Liverpool as early as seven and could not be allowed to catch up. Neddy's wagon was undisturbed. Rain and gale abated mercifully as the feeble dawn light expanded. He was battered by the jolts of the wheels, he shook with fever, the pain in his head was continuous, his thoughts drifted all out of control. They were supposed to be about Mary; but the kiss he had had to give to the Booble Alley trollop came wantonly dancing amongst them. She had really been a most charming slut-child, of an unexpected delicacy – almost a *chastity!* – socially important to tell Mary all about her – was there nothing to be done for her? Of course there must be no taint of hypocritical moralism. By the time the train reached Manchester his adventure had become an Arabian magic-tale: abducted princess enslaved in the *bagnios* of Baghdad, sultan's son afire for her rescue with the aid of a convenient *djinni*.

No *djinni* flung open the side of the wagon: George Stephenson himself found Neddy bedded down among the rope. He might have been very rough with him; indeed he had been angry all night, but also he was jubilant, both with himself and with his railway – riots, confusions and a man's death notwithstanding. For every train had completed its journey, all passengers who *did what they'd been told* had (at length) been correctly carried from whence they were to whither they went. His entire life was therefore justified; he thought with friendliness of his rivals, even of directors (not one of whom had seen fit to thank him, not one of whom had understood what he'd done). One brief eruption of abuse; then he handed Neddy down from the wagon, a gesture fit to pleasure an actress; and told him, with weary gaiety, to be on his road and no more fart-arsing.

As he lurched across town toward his true-love it suddenly struck Neddy Craig: he knew who it was that had sworn at him! A year or two ago some friend had shown him Stephenson among merchants on the steps of the Exchange, oh how stupid to have forgotten! – and now he felt unaccountably proud. (Not at all so implausible to have thought of a *djinni*.) Something else came to his mind, a snatch of song from Booble Alley; he had heard it (but had not there and then registered it) floating in from beyond the window panes among all sorts of bestial cacophonies while he lay in Kitty Brisket's bed.

> Mr Stephenson, my praises are due to you, worthy sir,
> Iron Horse took Iron Duke all the way to Manches-*ter!*
> Now he's gone, you bright Mersey girls, sing clear as a soaring bird,
> You don't have to fear no more the great thrustings of his sword.

> But will old Geordie bring him back, and with what in his knapsack?
> All our liberties for Old England, oh *is* that a fact?
> Mr Stephenson, Mr Stephenson, you ought to ha'known better,
> For so smart a contriver you're as mad as a hatter.

> NAY BUT CLEVER KNAVERY WON'T NEVER ABATE
> AS ALL US POOR CHAPS CAN SEE AS WE KNOCK
> UPO'T'WORKHOUSE GATE!

In a strong effort to feel alert and alive, Neddy chanted the refrain all the way to the newsagent's shop. Mary was there alone; she'd sent a message to the school saying she could not possibly be at work; she was waiting and waiting for word of him. She grasped him into her arms; relief, laughter, joy, sorrow for his hurt, desire. She showed him a letter that had arrived that very morning. From a Mr Vandeleur of Ralahine, County Clare; he had received, and had been highly impressed by, Mr Owen's recommendation of Mr Craig. He would meet Mr Craig to settle matters, if convenient, in Manchester the very next time he (Mr Vandeleur) came over the Irish Sea – he hoped it would be no more than a question of a week or two!

Neddy told her about the Irishmen who had helped him out of Liverpool; he was certain – *she* was certain – that their kindness was the best of omens. And she too had had her own omen! Mr Vandeleur's letter spoke of a friend of his, William Thompson, Mrs Wheeler's distinguished collaborator; was it possible she herself might meet Mrs Wheeler in Ireland? Ah, to hug to her heart such a prospect of intellectual delight!

Neddy decided, best not to mention Booble Alley or any such details. Just as well; for her great love for him, her joy that he was safe, persuaded her there and then to shut up shop, never mind the customers. She led him (sick and dizzy, but what did he care?) into the little office behind the counter; she happily brought his hands to the fastening of her bodice; she let him kiss the daring tips of her bosom. She might even, such were their emotions, have granted him far more than that: but he knew his impecunious duty, and refrained. After which, she sent him lovingly to his garret.

FOURTEEN

Fanny lay stripped and cramped-up on the bed, not on top of the quilt but under it; except it had largely fallen off, or she had kicked it off; most of her was covered only by a sheet. She was cold, afraid, in pain. As though a carving-fork were lodged in her flank. Thin leakage of daylight through louvres in the shutters did damage to her closed eyes. She sensed a movement, and compelled herself to see what it was.

The duke, in his shirtsleeves at the bedside, sat watching her with the tired pessimism of a disillusioned medical man. A medical smell, too: carbolic, mixed with the fag-end of less sanitary aroma.

'My clothes?' she croaked. 'Where? Who took me out of them?' Unspeakable possibilities – *probabilities* – ah! If only she could have recollected but the smallest little thing of it, however degrading, she'd not have felt so utterly hopeless.

He could not have understood the sheer emptiness of her memory. 'I had no choice, ma'am, considering the – ah, state of affairs. My young man undertook to give 'em a wash. Deuced bad hand at it, I'm afraid to say. I confess I took over, *dhobi-wallah* for both you and myself.'

Surely last night, at some warm juncture, she had asked him not to call her 'ma'am'? She seemed to recall a great degree of intimacy. ('Françoise'?) Indeed, indeed, it *must* have been so; or else how came she as she was?

Had he – ? Had she – ? No doubt, *yes*: and now he regretted it. Pray to God that *she* would not need to regret. Lord Jesus, if she bore a child! And never to be aware of the nature of the deed that had caused it: elysian hosannas, as in the poets? or the grisly surmise of straitly-preserved virtue, a loathsomeness of worms among tangles of mandrakes? or nothing much of either, and a damned sight more likely than both? She had longed for Experience; had been granted her wish; and all of it, all, so utterly blotted out. She had not believed there could be such injustice. Unless it was *justice*. In which case she must bethink herself, and without any further delay.

But now what was he saying? Something else she should be aware of, but wasn't. 'Last night I was quite unmanned. I gather he did not really *live* here. Just a house for the odd occasion when constituency business called him to Liverpool and kept him late. He had a place in the country, and his lady tended to stay in it. That's where they both came from yesterday

morning; he'd not been beneath this roof for at least a month. I suppose it
should diminish the ghastliness. No doubt Sandars was at his wits' end. No
doubt all of us.'

It occurred to her his calm countenance was in fact dragged into a mask
of pain. She was not capable of enquiring why.

Two hours later she stirred again; discovered the room was empty;
discovered all her clothes, neat and damp beside the bed, murkily stained
in unfortunate places; quite useless any more for Lady Teazle. What
explanation to give her dresser? What explanation to give *herself*? She
began to stand up and at length succeeded. No carpet? Yes, it was there, it
was rolled up and lay by the skirting. Floorboards all wet as though recently
scrubbed.

She made sure there was no blood in the bed. Virginity, she had been
told, never *slipped* without blood. So maybe, after all – ? But memory said,
tried to say – blood? – spirtings? – how? She gave up.

Draped in stole and long shawl, matted snarls of hair crammed into her
bonnet, she felt again she was a woman upon two legs. (A *what* upon two
legs? The back of her mind flicked at memories, fins of a slimy sea-beast
against a net in dark water . . . would she ever dredge them up? More than
half of her hoped not; the rest of her said 'coward!')

She found the equerry; well-dressed, discreet, attentive. He showed her
what in fact he'd shown her the night before (oh why did she need to ask
again?); a small room with a *chaise-percée*, she used it copiously.

He was not much older than herself; it seemed likely he was in awe of
her. She might even take a high hand. Most knowing smile, most crafty-
experienced voice (*prance, Thespis, prance*): 'Sir, as a gentleman you will not
allow a lady, however enslaved to her own dear passions, to play the fool in
a false security. I mean, the duke, before I slept, how far he and I – ? *Quelque
chose – n'importe quoi*? – Oh sir – ?'

High hand was collapsing, if she persisted in its failure she too would
collapse; turn away, pretend it not said. But it *was* said; and he understood,
blushed and stammered, a gentle boy: 'Oh no, Miss Kemble, no! How could
he, given the – the state of affairs? Oh no, ma'am, how *could* he?'

She decided, no more questions. One day she would remember, if
indeed it was intended she should. If not intended, she was better without.

He was saying something else. 'The duke, ma'am, desired me to tell you,
that upon recollection, he is already assured of the life of your brother – the
democratical *coup d'état* was a failure, as expected; indeed it seems that at
least one Englishman was among those shot by firing-squad. But not Mr
John Kemble. He reached Gibraltar safely. His grace regrets he could not

inform you sooner; but dispatches from Whitehall have only just arrived, to confirm the intelligence.'

She sought to make sense of this. Was she really to believe the duke received dispatches, in *this* house, between night and morning? If not, then he knew the truth before he sent for his red-hot suppers! Oh, but she had been outrageously gulled, Françoise de Foix the willing victim of a most disgraceful three-card-trick! And yet perhaps not? She'd never find out for certain. But John, in Gibraltar: that, at least, must be true; let her be glad for it, thank God, and forget about how she heard it!

No more questions; she was consistent; she held her peace.

The young man brought her down through the back door to the closed carriage in the yard. She climbed in to find the duke already sitting there immobile, upright hat, Spanish cloak, face like the rout of a squadron. One of the bruisers was on the box, the equerry had mounted beside him; off they drove, and down into the city. At the turn of the street she saw the rail-road chimneys, babylonish twin giants vehemently erect above grey rooftops; it was a baleful grey mid-day, neither sun nor honest rain and still a great deal of wind; seagulls from the Mersey screamed and wheeled across the town in crabby agreement with the mood of the weather.

Just before they came near to Church Street, he cleared his throat and spoke. 'Miss Kemble, ma'am, some manner of an apology. What should have been a few bright hours of mutual delight were alas overtaken by what could not have been foreseen: a man of sense would have foreseen it. And now I return to my duty. Am I forgiven?'

She was unable to find a reply. He did not seriously expect one. His thoughts, in fact, were already beyond her. He was endeavouring to forgive *himself*.

Not for the ruin of Fanny's evening, nor for the possible ruin of Fanny, nor even for equivocation over John and the Spanish rebellion.

(He must, if put to it, accept that his conduct had smacked of the heinous – he had not behaved so ill towards a girl since his execrable days at Eton – but if ageing field-marshals were to be as subject as rude young cubs to the capricious savageries of sexual transport, then forgiveness was out of the question – a shell-blasted warhorse might as reasonably ask pardon for hurling his rider to the ground.)

The dereliction that so troubled him was a misdeed of different character; one well within his own control; one which, as a soldier, he had no right not to withstand. For he convicted himself of cowardice in the face of the foe, of contemplating desertion out of sheer debased petulance. Small excuse, indeed, that the desertion had been schemed for, a trap that had been laid to bring him to the north to confound him with Huskisson;

he couldn't prove it but he knew it. And by God it would have worked! Had his adversaries not been so foolish as to choose this one damned house for him to fuck in like a drunken dragoon, thus raising the ghost of the very man they had cozened to death, a ghost that sprayed filth and the stench of putrefaction. No man of sense believed in ghosts; but he thought he recollected an insidious Hindoo *swamee* telling him once, at Ahmednuggur (odoriferous town), how the unbelievable at times could be smelt without being seen, whereat the 'personage of interior spirit' would at once derive enlightenment. Last night in the duke's nostrils so startling and strange a reek as to recall to him on the instant exactly *who he was*: his king's man, no-one else's. His desires (strong or flaccid) were to be ordered accordingly. Well, he had *washed*, hadn't he? Scrubbed, pummelled, wrung.

He thought all this, and sniffed: the stink had gone, yet it stayed with him. Without doubt he had been warned. Most certainly he was to write no letter to Windsor today.

Meanwhile, the distress within the conscience of Fanny. A sort of ache of omission like the ache in her side, she could not accurately locate it – something over and beyond the ultimate cataclysms of last night – something not said that should have been said – at an earlier stage – before it *happened*. . . ?

Now or never was the time to *bethink herself*, dissembling Kemble, crumbled, despoiled and foiled, now she must stand to her amnesiac heart like – like boozy old George Cooke! She had a valiant little chin; she jerked it defiantly upwards.

'Yes,' abruptly, 'yes.' (She answered the duke's question a full minute after he'd posed it.) 'Forgiven: if you tell me straight out your fellow countryfolk are not your enemies: I fancy I remember that you said that they were. I fancy I let it pass; but I cannot let it pass. It was cruel and unworthy.' No ladylike reserve, no actressy archness, only pomposity: let him use it as he would. The motion of the ride was upsetting her stomach again.

'Ah,' said he, dry as a potsherd. 'I see. I do suppose we both made a mistake.'

The carriage came to a halt; he kissed her hand as she stepped to the pavement; not for a moment did he show he might wish to kiss her lips. With a shudder she tightened her shawl and walked away from him, most resolutely facing forward. Wheels and horsehoofs clattered behind her; the Iron Duke was on the road out of town.

It was to be a while before she cared to fix her thoughts upon the railway; apart from letters to Harriet St Leger, expressing the expected wonderment and fascination, implying falsehoods she was never to admit. Her chief (and private) emotion was in fact anger that she had allowed herself anywhere near a locomotive. Then she remembered more carefully, and was angry again: for having been so preoccupied – no ('tell the truth, girl!') obsessed – as to take such feeble note of the truth of history as it changed its shape. Then she decided she must venture once more upon the rail, and damned soon; lest for the rest of her life she'd be unable to dare.

As for him, and his 'calamity'; when he needed to travel, he'd use trains without a tremor, whenever it suited him.

FIFTEEN

So there and then the duke did not resign. But with Huskisson's death Peel had missed his last chance to turn the Tories (as led by Wellington) away from reaction; a new prime minister had to be found; and *was* found, within two months. The next government brought in a Reform Bill, pushed through after a great length of high crisis, and only after the whole country had prepared itself, *pro* or *con*, for revolution. The duke feared the bill would be the end of constitutional monarchy, he knew revolution *must* be the end of constitutional monarchy, coldly and laconically he gave up his political battle. This time upon principle and without self-reproach of cowardice, he having come to see that his squares were still intact while the enemy *guerrilleros* buzzed upon his flanks frustrated; for the bill gave the vote to about half the males of the middle class and to none of the working class, and most people (as usual) contrived to believe that somebody somehow had passed them short change. But while squares remain unbroken, *guerrilleros* do not disband. They scatter and lie in wait; their turn will come.

It was nearly a year before Edward Craig (now formally styling himself E. T. Craig, defying anybody but Mary to call him 'Neddy') made his second train trip, to Liverpool; on his way to Ralahine in Ireland. This time he rode the rails in quite a different style, he was setting out to do work as practically useful as it was theoretically sound: he enjoyed every furlong of the journey, writing into his notebook each device he observed for the mechanical improvement of travel.

Another year, and Mary (now his wife) had joined him in the socialist commune he had helped build, where all the members, men and women, possessed votes, and of which he was elected secretary. She taught in the commune school; they were exuberantly happy.

Ralahine was an astonishing success, in a country where such innovation could not (and some still say, cannot) be conceived possible; until an event that might have been the *coup de théâtre* of a sensation-drama. By miscalculation – or design? – the landlord Vandeleur never transferred the title-deeds of his land to the commune as a corporate democratic body. He was a gambler (as should have been guessed from his daring to set up a co-operative in the first place); one delirious damnable night in a gentlemen's hell in Dublin, during the autumn of 1833, he lost everything he owned upon the fall of a single card. His creditors seized the commune and evicted its eighty-one persons.

E.T.C. and Mary fetched themselves back to Liverpool, and yet again took the train for Manchester. They were quite without resources; one should say that (at least for a fortnight) they *despaired*.

But their optimism was as great as their naivety, their love even greater than their optimism. He lived until the age of ninety, she survived him by three years. They devoted their lives to the principles and practice of socialism and social equality, to education, to public health, to scientific innovation of all sorts. At their Owenite school in the town of Wisbech, Mary placed over the porch a stone plaque cut with the lines:

> *Of old things, all are over old,*
> *Of good things none are good enough,*
> *We'll try if we can help to mould*
> *A world of better stuff!*

Ellen Tree, true to her intentions, married Charles Kean, conscientious actor-manager and the son of farouche Edmund. He was a good deal younger than his wife. They acted and produced together for many successful and well-praised years. As Lady Macbeth her contempt for her vacillating thane was so grim that people said the grey mare of Cawdor was not only the better horse but king-stallion of the whole herd. After *Romeo and Juliet* she was to share neither stage nor shawl ever again with Fanny Kemble.

A mistake to imagine that Fanny's Liverpool adventure taught her the dangers of promiscuous Experience. Old Wellington and new railway came to mingle in her mind, not so much a hideous deterrent but rather a desperate narrow squeak that a brave woman should but laugh at and avoid the next time round.

She had sworn not to marry. And of course she kept her oath; with intensity, with troubled rage, through intolerable stresses of life and work and huddled-up theatrical companionship: all told, for *four years*.

No man, young or old, was (for certain) allowed to invade her independence, or (not so certain, but most probable) her virginity. If she still thought virginity degraded, she took care not to tell her friends. And then, aged twenty-five, on tour with Charles through the theatres of the United States, she staked all (like Vandeleur, like herself when she replied to the Duke of Darkness) upon a Philadelphia lawyer called Butler.

No doubt she was affectionately, sensually, *driven* – but remember, she had another oath, to leave the theatre as soon as she could; she was still an artist, she still needed to write; through marriage, maybe the chance; no Experience came without danger, to be faced and outfaced just as when she used to force herself, 'Onstage, Juliet, NOW!'

Idiot girl! This new *seraglio* was indeed a bluebeard closet and she only found it out once she passed between its stifling draperies.

Butler's main income was not from the law, but from plantations in Georgia worked by slaves.

When he told her this after the wedding, he told her also she could not judge until she experienced it herself. He cannot have known what he was saying, nor to whom he said it: he was compelled willy-nilly to take her there. She insisted upon living there. She experienced; she said what she thought; she *wrote* what she thought; she became a public abolitionist; incurred odium; left him; made up her mind to a divorce; eventually got one.

But already she had borne two daughters. He would not give them up (he was a lawyer) except under severe conditions: if she were to rear the girls, then she must undertake never to write, never to go back on the stage, never in fact to do anything that had made her Fanny Kemble. She had a *diseased mind*, she had brought him *into disrepute*, she had *unsexed herself*; he was more vindictive than any Grand Turk; he tried to bind her limb by limb. She dragged herself half-free. She did write. She did return to the stage.

Half-free, and that was it; he half-agreed to half-free, he exacted his penalty. One daughter she could keep; the other stayed with him. Civil war between the States, civil war in the family, Butler maintained a white-supremacist child, Fanny an abolitionist one. She died in London in 1893. She had continued her writing well into her old age. She was perhaps never quite sure whether she was English or French or American.

During her second theatrical career, even shorter than her first, she played Desdemona to Macready's tyrannical Othello: she hated it beyond reason, renewed dream of guilt and terror, revenge-death on the bluebeard-bed under the grip of huge black hands, degradation of loveliness, betrayal. Macready was jealous of her and showed it. Moreover, she was growing fat.

She took instead to public readings, entire plays, of her own choice, all the roles; and she rejoiced in every minute of every performance. So did her audiences. They claimed her readings established Shakespeare's rhythms and poetic structures with an emotional exactitude, a totality of dramatic truth, rarely if ever to be achieved in traditional stage production.

*

George Stephenson, by the way, was at last offered a knighthood; he refused it. Then he applied to join the Institution of Civil Engineers and *they* refused *him*, despising his rough origins, invidiously demanding that he send for their assessment full details of his qualifications supported by acceptable sponsors.

Afterwards, the better-educated Robert became President of the same Institution (having lived down an ambiguous scandal connecting his name with dishonest railway speculators). He was elected to parliament as a strong Tory, particularly opposed to free education for the working class. But he personally completed his father's most visionary enterprise, the east coast main-line from London to Edinburgh; they offered him a knighthood. He was contrary enough to refuse it: his reasons were *his own business*.

Twentieth Century (after Christ)

'LIKE A *DREAM* OF A GUN . . .'

'Like a *Dream* of a Gun . . .

Let us now praise famous men, and our fathers that
begat us. Such as found out musical tunes, and recited
verses in writing. There be of them, that have left a
name behind them, that their praises might be reported.

And some there be, which have no memorial; who are perished, as
though they had never been; and are become as though they had
never been born; and their children after them.

Ecclesiasticus, Chapter 44

ONE

Sigismund Clay, freelance investigative journalist (of Lord Eldon Crescent, Islington), specialised in the occult crimes of government and of the military-industrial complex. He began his career in the late 1970s, during the Callaghan premiership, with a biro, a notebook, a card-index and a shabby Raymond Chandler mackintosh; by the end of the '80s he was tolerably well-known; he still affected the mackintosh, but the card-index had given way to a computer. Only by means of this computer did he attain the very brink of what *could have been* his major success, the definitive exposure of a cultural conspiracy rooted deep in northern Irish counter-insurgency operations. The operations themselves were extensively computerised – 'So fight fire with fire,' said Clay, 'get it all upon disc and your microchips find you the answer!'

It is sometimes vaguely remarked that computers 'do our thinking for us'. They don't, of course; they extend our thinking, speed it up, develop its connections and organise its consequences; but the *thought* has to be there first. If it is a thoroughly stupid thought the computer may indeed expose its absurdity, throwing up some such abrupt message as –

DATA INCOMPLETE
WRONG FILE?   MAKE NEW SEARCH

or –

ABORT ABORT BALLS-UP

– injunctions in themselves an expression of the thought of the human being who has programmed them to appear. So they can be stupid too, and might be totally misleading. If the appliance then is able to complicate and elaborate stupidity, so also with lies, so also with neuroses. It may, in the long run, make madness even madder while speciously clarifying an appearance of sanity. And if it stumbles upon the truth and persuades its human being to recognise what it has found, the human being has still to persuade others to recognise it too, to look at what has been seen, to see what is being looked at. Very clever people have always had a difficulty here; for every Sherlock Holmes, a dull Watson, an impenetrable Lestrade; for every computer, an unresponsive (or worse, over-responsive) Holmes.

Holmes, it's as well to remember, looked at violent death and cruel fraud: whenever he got it wrong, devils were left at large.

And so with Clay: during the first months of 1990, just after his thirty-eighth birthday, his great investigation was to fizzle out, humiliated, under the ponderous vaults of the Law Courts in the Strand among wigs and gowns and obscure formalities, counsels' submissions, acrid rulings from the bench, smothered yawns from bored jurors. It had begun more than half-a-decade earlier, with a girl's face simpering on television; it ended with the loss of a civil suit for breach of copyright, and a wicked old judge telling Clay he was a worthless meddler. Which was all a dreadful pity, in itself an 'occult crime', for Clay and his microchips had really found out *something*: devils indeed had been loosed, and still roamed; everyone concerned in the case knew it.

My death –
said the evidence, or at any rate part of it, the crucial part, the angry nub of the defendants' rebuttal –

My death is an act of will against my will.
My act? Yeah but the death's not yours
Or hers or his, okay it's down to me.
Okay, my act.
Jesus Christ, I wish it wasn't.
Wish I could blame.
Wish I could condemn.

Wish I could (MP –
Or editor –
Or GHQ-spokesman-like)
Spout
Denounce my killers
Praise my mates
Say Cain versus Abel
And know which was which!
Ambiguity all to hell
And I can't, so fuck off.

Altogether about ten pages of it, in an obviously tentative style quite
appropriate to a young comprehensive-school educated poet who laid no
claim to be *professional*; and frankly no great shakes as a piece of literature,
exclamatory, embittered, uneven, and yet – by the end – obscurely heroic.
He did not want to die, and yet he knew his duty: if he had to be killed, then
for the general good he would face it, snarling at it certainly, but also
laughing. He was a good young soldier and he loved those that loved him.
He was very sad that they would be sad.

He would have been far sadder, said Mr Alaric Houndsditch QC, counsel
for the Ministry of Defence (defendants in the action), had he known that
for many days contending wigs and gowns would not only offer public
insults to the nature of his talent but would dispute his very existence. It
was a complex and almost *perverse* lawsuit, it ought to have been heard in
Belfast but was mysteriously transferred to London – Cabinet Office
pressure, if one was to credit irresponsible rumour.

Supported by sworn witnesses, the Ministry of Defence maintained the
poem's author was fully identified. He was (or had been) Lance-Corporal
Alfred Truethought, a clerk in the Royal Army Service Corps; not an outfit
conventionally alongside Uriah the Hittite in the forefront of the battle, but
there *were* occasions when its members must be thrust willy-nilly amongst
the murderous concomitance of the queen's uniform and her coercive
discipline. For no particular reason that anyone could discover – it was not
in his normal line of duty – Alfy Truethought had been sitting beside the
driver of a ration truck on a supposedly safe road in a loyalist district of
County Antrim in 1984, when the IRA blew off a landmine and blew him
and his companion, together with several hundred tins of curry-paste and
tuna-fish, most horribly and agonisingly into regimental history. The
deaths were swift, they were arbitrary, they would soon have been
forgotten – except, in England, by families and friends of the two young
men; in Ireland, by their immediate barrack comrades; and also by those

few officers of the army and the RUC who had to face prolonged enquiries as to how on earth the IRA came to plant explosive in an area where they were *known* to be incapable of operating.

In short, it was much of a muchness with scores of other soldiers' deaths: until a day or two later, when Alfy's poem turned up – in his barrack-locker, in an unsealed envelope, addressed enigmatically to 'Judy, who never wrote to me', endorsed 'send it if I'm killed'. The CO of the infantry battalion to which Truethought was attached found himself at something of a loss. 'Send', by all means, but to whom?

He would of course be writing a letter to the lance-corporal's declared next-of-kin, a great-aunt in Grimethorpe, Yorkshire; but her name was not Judy, and a good deal of the poem was outspokenly erotic to the point of obscenity – quite unsuitable, the CO thought, for a no doubt aged lady whose address read so uncompromisingly: 'c/o Lucknow Street Ebenezer Chapel (caretaker)'.

He did send her Alfy's hymn-book (inscribed 'from Auntie Dorcas, to keep you safe in the Valley of the Shadow'), a small volume that appeared never to have been opened since it left the hands of the bookseller; it was parcelled up and despatched to Grimethorpe with most of the rest of young Truethought's belongings. There was also a small collection of photographs of naked women; the CO did his usual with these, passing them to a Staff-Serjeant Hipkinson (his chief clerk) for such redistribution among the men as the staff-serjeant thought fit. But the poem remained in a pigeon-hole in the CO's office – a distressing little puzzle that perhaps one day he would have time to solve.

After the lapse of a month, Staff-Serjeant Hipkinson solved it for him.

'Excuse me, sir, them verses?'

'Yes?'

'I turned 'em out by accident when I was sorting the psychiatric sick-parade dockets. I hadn't had a chance before to look at 'em properly. Don't you think, sir, it'd be good for the unit if we made an effort to find that girl of his? I mean, public relations, sir, morale?'

The staff-serjeant was a conscientious man who felt that civilians in general did not understand the army's raw deal in the north-eastern counties of Ireland. Perhaps there was a chance here to put the squaddy's point of view, and to show the folks at home that soldiers *cared*. He had a soft heart, he did care for the unknown Judy, however badly she had treated young Truethought. If the poem could be got to her, she might be brazenly careless of it, but who knows? she might realise her loss and weep. The staff-serjeant thought she ought to be given the opportunity of weeping. If the bastards killed *him*, he would want to have a woman weep;

and Truethought after all had been a man of some steadiness, an asset to the unit. They owed him.

'If you'll excuse me, sir, I think we owe him.'

'Quite right, staff, I think we do. But how?'

'I'd say the press'd be glad to help, sir, if we got the right reporter, the right newspaper, what about the *Sun*?'

'I don't know about that, staff. Don't you think they'd make a meal of all the filth?'

'Not if it was put to 'em properly, sir. They're on our side, by and large. And when you think of it, it's not that filthy. He just had a good time with her, that's all: and then she fucked off. In a manner of speaking. That is, if you can believe anything that's wrote in verses; by my experience they mostly make it all up, these young wallies that go poetical; why, there may not be a Judy at all.'

'In which case the exercise would be pretty pointless, don't you think?'

'Ah, but on the other hand, sir; if there is, and if she turned out to be, well, a right cracker, what we call a *Page Three* – there's a lot could be made out of it – like, morale – ?'

'And public relations. Yes. I'll think about it. Thank you, staff, smart notion.

'Oh, staff – ' (as Hipkinson was on his way out of the room) 'just a moment. You said "go poetical". *Did* he? It's not very usual, and from what little I remember of him he never seemed to be in much trouble?'

'No sir, he'd a clean crime-sheet. Very reliable young NCO. But as I understand it, these versifyings are (like) a secret matter with the lads, when they happen to be caught by 'em. Like a disease, like. Like, you know sir, if *I* caught a clap, it'd be between me and the MO, highly confidential, if you'll pardon the analogy. Well, I mean, sir, their mail's not censored, so how'd we ever know?'

'How indeed. But it's always odd, when one turns up something like this. Shows how little we really know of the men.'

'Probably does, sir, yes. Will that be all, sir?'

'Yes. No. That is to say – staff-serjeant – ?'

'Sir?'

'Ah – *why* was he in the ration truck?'

'Oddity, sir. Still an oddity. No one seems to know. But he always showed initiative, I daresay he had his reasons.'

'Ah yes, I daresay. For God's sake just let's see it doesn't happen again . . . Thank you, staff-serjeant.'

As soon as he was alone, the CO took out the verses and had another look at them. He was not a man of literary discernment; but upon second

thoughts it struck him that the overtly sexual passages were not altogether
integral to the poem's general flow. Although the exact progress of the
lance-corporal's love affair was decidedly confused, there were a few lines
which did seem truly tender and in strong contrast to the harshness of the
rest. They reminded him somehow of his own departure, nearly twenty
years ago, to a very dangerous little business in Aden. He had been no
lance-corporal but a second-lieutenant, more reckless than scrupulous,
and desperate keen to make his name (he very nearly lost it, for ever). *Her*
name had been Cynthia, not Judy, and the locality, instead of a railway
station, was 'Daddy's place' in Eaton Square with a taxi at the door.
Nevertheless, the principle was the same. She had married a young
stockbroker before he (the CO) so much as achieved his first leave home, to
say nothing of his clearance by a court-of-enquiry over the unfortunate
deaths of certain Arabs. He allowed himself a nostalgic snuffle.

> Farewell my lovely, how much I loved and how much hated
> You hating that journey – like I told you I *had* to make it;
> You were right, I was wrong. Okay I did you wrong
> But I did right, didn't I? Why can't you think so, think so too?
> Lost you at King's Cross for a ride to sodding Catterick,
> Two hours and a half by rail, that was all. (Instead of, like, all night
> Sweet Judy-ride all night.) Just believe it to be no more.
> Your arms and you (all of you) could've enclosed two short hours?
> And a half? That was really all of it.

No, Hipkinson had talked good sense. Most assuredly this Judy must be
found.

And that was the position of the defendants.
    The plaintiff was Ms Bríd Ní Gairmleadhaigh, or Grimes, of Armagh.
Five-and-a-half years after Truethought's poem became public knowledge
and its supposed author a national celebrity, the evidence presented in
court by her counsel, Ms Naomi Lambert, also involved a poem – more
precisely, a sequence of poems.

> My death –

said one of them – and the jury had to pay a most careful attention to be
sure which stanzas were which: the lance-corporal's, or those earlier ones
claimed by the plaintiff to have supplied the lance-corporal's muse with
every crucial poetic ingredient –

My death is willed against my will:
By my own act of will? For good or ill
I was prepared to kill
Therefore to die. Why should I cry?
Why should I like a two-tongued bishop prate
Or (dog upon hind legs) orate
Like in Westminster a slick MP
Or in Dublin Dail a sly TD,
Or like a pig-Brit newshack spit
Convenient morality and shite
At bloody brother at the bloody throat of brother?
And never speak of chancer Abel's cheat,
And never howl for Cain's poor children's plight
Or mark the greedy rage of Abel's mother
That drove them both to their endless fight?
Fuck off then, friends, no word from me:
I die as silent as the swollen sea.

The plaintiff's claim continued as follows: not only were these super-ficially similar yet significantly different verses (together with others, both in English and Irish) the stolen originals of the Truethought poem, but the Truethought poem itself was not in fact by Alfred Truethought at all.

The real author would become apparent in the course of the evidence; but the original sequence was the creation of a deceased IRA volunteer called (formally, by himself and the Republican Movement) Tadhgh Ó Cuinn, or (by official sources) Thaddeus Quinn, or (by himself and friends, informally) Taddy Q. His work had been mendaciously published as the lance-corporal's in order to further military-intelligence psychological operations propaganda.

Ms Lambert's client, Ms Ní Gairmleadhaigh (unable to attend the first day of the court-hearing because she was held by the Stranraer police under the Prevention of Terrorism Act, a scandal to which Ms Lambert would return in due course), was the *de facto* literary executor of her dead common-law husband Ó Cuinn, and therefore entitled to substantial damages. Breach of copyright and blatant plagiarism.

As neither of the two putative poets was alive, the evidence to be presented was of necessity circumstantial, and the jury would be asked to hear a highly convoluted story which, Ms Lambert assured them, would nonetheless be conclusively established at every stage of the argument.

Mr Houndsditch, for the Ministry of Defence, asked the judge to strike out nearly all the evidence Ms Lambert wished to call, upon grounds either

of irrelevance or prejudice to national security. He implied that her client
had been induced by the Republican Movement to turn the court into a
propaganda field for unrestrained IRA bamboozlement. The judge rather
thought so too: but although by definition immensely learned and by
temperament fiercely anxious to uphold the honour of good government
(at the expense, if need be, of purely abstract conceptions of sentimental
public justice) he was also secretly frivolous and a congenital nosey-parker.
He could not bear to deprive himself and his court of all the outré notoriety
that seemed likely to ensue from the full development of this case; so he
decided, at least for the present, to refuse Mr Houndsditch's request.

'I think we shall soon know, Mr Houndsditch, whether the witnesses are
testifying of their own volition, or whether they have been, in some sense,
got at – *godfathered* – I'm sure you'll all understand what I mean? If the jury
cannot determine (and we are talking of events six years old, remember;
these affairs take their time coming into court), I shall use my best offices to
guide them. That's what I'm here for. Continue, pray, Mrs – ah, Miss? – '
(He seemed to begin some spurious little anti-feminist business over Naomi
Lambert's 'Ms', but cunningly let it die away.) 'Continue, madam.'

Ms Lambert began by 'proving' her first item of documentary evidence,
texts of Ó Cuinn's poetry. She showed the court a half-dozen sheets of
government-issue toilet paper, each of them covered with closely written
and almost illegible handwriting in two languages, in black ballpoint. The
jury was supplied with indistinct photocopies; with fair copies typed out on
a word-processor; with prose-versions in English of the Irish-language
texts. A typist (Ms Sally Noggin) from an independent agency gave
elaborate evidence to the effect that she had made the fair copies from the
originals and had had great difficulty in doing so. Dates and places were
exhaustively given. The typist successfully resisted a vehement cross-
examination from Mr Houndsditch, who sought to show that much of her
copying was no better than guesswork, indeed that interpretations of the
murky manuscripts had been 'fed' to her by tendentious persons from
outside – who these might have been was not clear, but the jury were
encouraged to imagine card-carrying (indeed *gun*-carrying) members of a
subversive organisation.

However, after three hours in the witness-box, Ms Noggin still insisted
that she had completed her work quite free from interference – except for
an independent handwriting-expert called in to advise her and a Gaelic
expert from London University who translated such of the verses as were
written in Irish. Both of these men were later brought to the witness-box to
support her account. She insisted, as well, that her own Irish-sounding
name was purely coincidental. ('No, sir, no! It's *not* a pseudonym, never

has been, and if you say it's the name of a suburb of Dublin, well I daresay you're right but nobody ever told *me!* I live in Bromley and always have. I am English; yes sir, really.')

'I suspect, Mr Houndsditch, *this cock will not fight.* May we accept that the young lady has made her point? she is English. No doubt the birth-certificate can be produced, if need be. Do you wish to have it produced?'

'I doubt, m'lud, if it will be necessary to occupy the time of the court.'

'Good. Because at this rate we shall be here till end of term. We'll consider the word-processing proved . . . Oh, Sallynoggin, Mr Houndsditch; is that really a district of Dublin?'

'I am reliably informed so, m'lud.'

'How extraordinary. Why do they call it that?'

'I am not in the confidence of the Dublin corporation, m'lud. Outside the jurisdiction.'

The judge, feeling the need to top counsel's small joke, muttered something about wishing that '*all* these people were outside the jurisdiction, or else properly within it and behaving themselves accordingly . . .' (*Laughter in court, from some of the few that heard him: one of the ushers, and a keen-eared reporter in the press-gallery.*)

'However, don't let me hold up your most interesting exposition of your case, Miss Lambert; continue. Pray continue.'

As had been intended, it was not easy for her to continue; she was not as fully experienced in her advocate's art as perhaps she should have been for a case so vulnerable to official subversion, but she did know how to counter this sort of nonsense, and eventually managed to put forward a good deal of her evidence.

It may be summed up, as follows:

In 1980 Ó Cuinn was convicted on charges of possessing weapons, handling explosives, taking part in armed attacks upon the security forces while a member of the IRA. He was sent to the Long Kesh concentration camp (or the Maze Prison – depending on your point of view: there was argument about this in court) for a long sentence, during which he wrote and smuggled out a large number of highly militant poems in English, as well as some more personal ones in Irish. He adopted a *nom-de-plume,* 'The Peelers' Goat', after a nineteenth-century ballad mocking the police. His writings were regularly collected by, or otherwise *reached,* the plaintiff, Bríd Ní Gairmleadhaigh.

Ms Lambert's case here suffered from the continued detention of the plaintiff in Stranraer. The Scottish police were far from obliging, sending affidavits up to London (at Ms Lambert's insistence, against recurrent objections by Mr Houndsditch and doubtful mutterings from the judge) to the general effect that enquiries were proceeding into various matters of serious crime. In short, they stonewalled, and for a while it looked as though Bríd could never be produced to give her essential evidence. When she did at length appear, it turned out that no charges whatever had been laid against her. Nonetheless she was stripped naked and bodily searched in the purlieus of the Law Courts. Ms Lambert made the mistake of making this public and complaining about it. Judge and jury, thus thoroughly fumigated by *smoke-without-fire*, received the Ní Gairmleadhaigh testimony with obvious scepticism. In addition to which, after desperately striving to use the Irish form of Bríd's name, Ms Lambert was forced to follow the judge's irritated direction and unworthily anglicise it.

Bríd (or Bridget) Grimes, the court heard, transcribed the Long Kesh writings in her home in Armagh – it had of course been Ó Cuinn's home too – and passed some of them (the demonstrably political ones) to a Republican journal in Belfast which intermittently printed them. It was thought that their authorship remained successfully concealed from authority.

In 1983 Ó Cuinn escaped from the Kesh in the celebrated mass breakout of that year, and immediately (it was later deduced) went to ground beyond the border. The British army came in search of him to the Armagh house, wrecking the premises as a matter of routine; but he was not there and there were no traces of him; neither did they find weapons or anything else of that sort. They did find typed copies of 'Peeler's Goat' verses. Bríd was arrested and then released: insufficient evidence to warrant a prosecution. The papers were confiscated and not returned to her for several months. Had the originals of the poems been uncovered, there might well have been charges of conspiring to breach prison security. But she hid the originals far too well. Under cross-examination from Mr Houndsditch she admitted – no, she *proudly proclaimed* in her accusatory Ulster accent (after first refusing to say anything about it at all) that she had wrapped them in clingfilm and stuck them with chewing-gum under a seat beside the bus-stops on the edge of the Mall, a loyalist part of town nicely placed between the Armagh courthouse and the women's prison. The indigenous insolence of this repository was lost on the London jury, but her red-haired surly defiance was not: it did no good to her own case, as the judge took pleasant pains to point out.

It was indeed only by accident that the fair copies were discovered: Bríd had been sorting them out for Belfast the evening before in her kitchen, and carelessly left typescripts of both sorts of poem (personal as well as public) in the flour-bin when she went to bed. She cursed herself for a fool and thought little more about it (the documents *were* restored to her, after all). She took the raid for just one of those many unpleasantnesses inseparable from her position as the irregular companion of a man on the run.

Shortly after his departure over the border to Donegal, Ó Cuinn was mysteriously shot dead on a lonely road; murdered, the IRA claimed later, by a hit-squad from the SAS covertly entering the Republic (in collusion with the *Garda Siochana*) to 'take him out'.

Ms Lambert's contention as to what had been happening in the meantime: while the fair copies were in the possession of the British army who seized them, or of the RUC who returned them, further copies were xeroxed to be perverted at leisure into a different class of poetry altogether, i.e.: verses suitable for dead soldiers to leave behind them, to draw tears from the media, and to nullify the popular voice if it cried over-loudly for British withdrawal from Ireland. Every dead soldier cumulatively en-livened the force of this voice, so as many dead soldiers as possible must be pressed into posthumous service to supply the cultural antidote.

Some soldiers might in fact have written genuine poems of their own; but too chancy to wait for one of these to turn up. By the same token it was far too chancy to look about for a true poet to confect verses from scratch out of his or her unaided imagination. Such people tended to possess hidden reserves of political independence and *integrity*; one never knew when even the most venal, the most servile of them might suddenly baulk at the implications of the task. Far easier to take existing poems (never mind that they expressed an apparently directly opposed point of view) and reconstruct them to suit the queen's fighting men rather than those of that allegorical personification of Irish struggle, the Lady Granuaile.

Ms Lambert attempted to show that this plan was given a code-name: *Operation Terrible Beauty.* It had been decided to start it off with an experimental foray, then to assess the consequence, and continue or discontinue in accordance with the assessment. Her witness for these dirty tricks was Sigismund Clay.

The judge objected strongly to the phrase 'dirty tricks'; Ms Lambert was compelled to withdraw it.

Clay suffered a barrage of Mr Houndsditch's personal innuendo, which left the jury with the idea that he had slept with Bríd Grimes on more than one occasion even though he was probably a homosexual. But he did contrive to give a general picture of how it might have been worked.

The ration truck explosion had caused a brief outcry – questions asked about it by an ex-army MP in the House – culpable incompetence alleged – the driver's father on television denouncing the army's Irish activities ('why the bloody hell are our lads over there anyway? in someone else's bloody country!') – no better occasion for a one-off tryout of the new scheme. Appropriate 'Peeler's Goat' poems, already adapted into a new collage, were secretly inserted among Truethought's possessions; for his CO to discover, and to deliver in all innocence wherever he thought best. The CO was a bit of a twit in matters not immediately germane to drilling and killing and 'having a smack at the terrorist'; unprompted, he might not handle the affair adeptly; but Staff-Serjeant Hipkinson (imperceptibly and plausibly suborned) could be trusted to put the word in at the right time.

The staff-serjeant was now retired from the army to a civilian job in the office of a Kettering security firm. He gave evidence for the defendants: he utterly denied having been approached at any time by any 'spooks', but agreed under cross-examination that he had upon one occasion had a drink in the serjeants' mess with an Intelligence Corps warrant-officer whom he had never seen before and who talked a good deal about the value of the fine arts to Britain's international reputation. 'A bit above my head, miss, but these I-corps bods are like that – no, I never saw him again – yes, it *was* just after Truethought's death. Point of fact, it might have been, yes, that very same evening . . .'

So thus it was done, implied Ms Lambert.

And thus, in the early months of 1990, the results lay before the court.

Results which (in 1984, at a time of some possible revulsion against the jingo excesses of the Falkland/Malvinas campaign) had proved briefly but discernibly beneficial to government.

Hipkinson's notion of the *Sun* was a good one, for it soared away at once with a boisterous front page:

'F—— OFF' TO PROVOS!'
Slain Hero's WILL and Testament!

– and lower down, beneath a photograph of 'a smiling Corporal Alfy in happier days';

WHERE'S JUDY?
Does She Know How He Loved Her?
A nationwide search is underway for the Bird who *Bonked and Bolted*.
Her soldier-lover pressed all his heartbreak into ringing verse less than a week before IRA thugs ambushed his truck on a lonely side-road in the bandit country of County Antrim. Did she jilt him because she so feared for his safety, in arms against the terrorists, that she could not bear to hold him to her heart?
Or was it just a one-night stand with a floozy?

*The Paper that Backs our Boys says NO, because thousands of you British
Birds say NO.*
'Right on, *Sun*,' you've all been telling us, 'go-n-get her!'

And indeed the *Sun* tried to; vigorously assisted and impeded by the rest
of the tabloid pack, once the story was generally released from the press
office at the Ministry of Defence. The latter refused to recognise the staff-
serjeant's exclusive Wapping contract (it was stated that he was acting
under orders from his CO when he contacted the newspaper, and had no
right to negotiate personal cash offers. Disciplinary action could not be
ruled out). For nearly a week the search for Judy went on, with artists'
impressions of how she might look in or out of her clothes, lady columnists'
meditations on 'The Girls They Leave Behind Them', reminiscences from
World War Two veterans about *their* last nights of leave before plunging
into the maelstrom of battle, clairvoyants' attempts to locate Judy by
fingering photocopies of the lance-corporal's poem, and so on and so forth.
'Top literary critics' were consulted, to find clues in the texture of the
verse as to the exact nature of the relationship. One of these pundits
burbled about John Donne, another thought of Burns, and a third (whose
views were not printed) became altogether too lah-di-dah for the *Daily
Mail*'s readership: he remembered Catullus' *I hate and I love*, but he wrote it
as *odi et amo*, and forgot to hint at the Roman poet's dirty bits. Excerpts from
Richard Lovelace's *To Lucasta, Going to the Wars* appeared in nearly all these
articles –

I could not love thee, Dear, so much,
Loved I not Honour more.

The most egregious, perhaps, of the baroque harkings-back occurred in
the *Daily Telegraph*: a stanza by Marvell originally addressed to Oliver
Cromwell; absurdly invoked as though Lance-Corporal Truethought,
instead of dying by a terrible blow out of the dark and without warning,
had destroyed the entire IRA single-handed.

And now the Irish are ashamed
To see themselves in one year tamed:
So much one man can do
That does both act and know.

The accompanying comment made the most of Marvell's imperialism
but deftly side-stopped his Republicanism –

. . . so many deaths in tormented Ulster. Sometimes it may need but
one to make a turning-point. *One man*, not only a courageous soldier

but also a sensitive poet, both *doing and knowing*, may be able to
'concentrate the mind' (in the solid words of Dr Johnson) of the volatile
British public. Can it be that Lance-Corporal Truethought – uncannily
appropriate name! – is to be that one? Are we at last to see a truly
effective national resurgence against the unholy forces that have for so
long embarrassed, intimidated, and enfeebled our will to resist?

For there is no doubt about Truethought's will:

> 'Call it off,' they squeak to us, 'pack it in, let's sneak off home . . .'
> I can't, I won't, no way; that goes for you, old son!
> Dead basic, cos we're HELD.
> By what we do, by what *they* do; by what's been bloody done.

The Times, anxious perhaps to distance itself from the over-the-top
blarings and *Sun*-burst of its Wapping stablemate, was more fastidious.
Two austere lines from Housman's *Epitaph on an Army of Mercenaries* did all
the literary business required by the leader-writer –

> What God abandon'd, these defended,
> And saved the sum of things for pay.

Mention of God introduced a magisterial criticism of one of His most
prominent Irish representatives, the Cardinal-Archbishop of Armagh: who
was sternly recommended, 'in the light of the lance-corporal's grand moral
simplicities, to manifest some humility and to disavow what right-thinking
people can only discern as an ambivalence, an *equivocation*, toward the
sinister ecumenism of terrorist mass-murder.' (The archbishop had lately
remarked unfavourably upon illegal activities by the security forces:
shoot-on-sight, shoot-to-kill, and suchlike.)

The Times picked up Truethought's Yorkshire origins:

> . . . encouraging, too, that this exemplary NCO should be a native of
> Grimethorpe, a village that has gained an unfortunate reputation in
> the miners' strike. Mr Scargill should take note. He has gravely
> misunderstood certain basic values of the colliery community.

The article avoided any suggestion (a) that Alfred Truethought's poem
was clumsily put together – just the sort of amateurish artwork indeed that
Times opinion-makers so objected to when it gained an Arts Council grant –
and (b) that its creator, hitching an unauthorised lift in a vehicle with
which he should have had nothing to do, had not exactly laid down his life
in 'exemplary' fashion (no doubt Truethought's clean crime-sheet provided pretext for the adjective).

Neither *The Times*, nor any other of the right-wing sheets, thought fit to compare Truethought with the active-service war poets of twentieth-century world conflicts. No accident: the Graves/Sassoon/Owen/Jones school of '14–'18 was perceived as too negative; while '39–'45 material tended to look inappropriately forward to an Attlee-led socialist future.

And yet, to some, the lance-corporal's 'grand moral simplicities' seemed almost as ambivalent as any Irish prelate's theological-political pronouncements. Only the *Guardian* (an expansive half-page feature in the book-section) was prepared to bite this particular bullet.

> I am the enemy you killed, my friend.
> I knew you in this dark; for so you frowned
> Yesterday through me as you jabbed and killed.
> I parried; but my hands were loath and cold.
> Let us sleep now . . .

Thus Wilfred Owen, who generously equipped his dead German adversary with an equally superb generosity of feeling. The same sympathy (albeit of lesser verbal accomplishment) can be found in the Truethought poem, notably extended beyond the concept of the uniformed servant of an enemy state to that of the 'civilian' terrorist with no valid popular mandate for his violence.

There is a strongly-defined stoical element about Truethought's contemplation of his own predicament: liable at any minute to be shot or blown-up by an unseen hand, he accepts responsibility for his duty and at the same time comprehends the need for the Irish nationalist to obey the behests of the IRA Army Council – a need that might be, *must* be, questioned by external observers committed to democracy – but nonetheless may appear self-evident to the man-on-the-ground –

> They sent you out, you bastard,
> With your gun in your fucking hand:
> They sent me out, the bastards,
> To clear you off the land!
> If I can or I can't, you faceless git,
> The grass grows green on the roadside yet.

Assuming Truethought's near-pacifism to be a tentative pointer, can we deduce that our young soldiers see their unenviable task with surprising clarity and honesty, true successors of Cobbett or George Orwell?

The search for Judy was no great preoccupation for the posh reporters.

They tended to accept her as a legitimate muse-figure highlighting the perils of the soldier's life, and left her flesh-and-blood reality to the hot speculation of the pops. They did make some use of Alfy's erotic passages. The CO had feared the *Sun* would exploit these, not understanding how the *Sun* would be sentimental and roguish while voyeuristic hunger for explicit sexuality chiefly characterised the intellectual drop-outs of what might once have been the officer-class. From the *Guardian* again:

> . . . Truethought struggling with his flies before making love to his fickle Judy is a profound image of male vulnerability, combined with ferocious aggression as he drags at the girl's jeans. And how predestinate the subsequent bathos:

> > Have 'em off, have it out, wet and red, have it in!
> > Hair scrubs against hair, pair of arses cold and bare,
> > Christ, let's hope Old Bill don't catch us at it
> > Till I've shafted the shit right out of her
> > Behind the trash-cans in the backyard
> > Of this shitty old Pentonville boozer!
> > Oh sod it, was that a footstep? And I've not even *come*, but
> > She's on her feet, her pants up, she's lighting her bloody fag
> > And me still all hanging out – Oi!
> > I can't tuck it in, it's as hard
> > And as long as a bastard copper's fucking truncheon.

> Arguably the most *realised* section of the poem; the military automaton unforgettably humanised. His partner, too, is allowed her own aggression – she is *lighting her bloody fag*, abruptly independent – life goes on even when 'love' is cruelly baulked amid a morass of obscenities.

The *Guardian* piece was in many respects the most appreciated by government. Diplomatic preliminaries to the Anglo-Irish Agreement being already under way amid much tension, the left-of-centre 'chattering classes' had to be brought into line behind them – strictly upon the terms of Westminster's perspective, rather than what might be thought to be Dublin's. The *Cobbett/Orwell* reference and *abruptly independent* must surely have clinched the matter. What more could be asked for?

The newspaper pieces were all meticulously researched by Naomi Lambert's instructing solicitor, collated, filed, docketed, produced in court, and 'proved'. Photocopies were distributed to the jury by direction of the judge. Similarly, recordings of all TV and radio programmes that had dealt with the Truethought poem were brought to court and demonstrated, on video or audio tape.

The electronic media had initially been a little less exuberant about the story than the press; but there was a fair amount of coverage to entertain the jury. It very obviously entertained the judge. He claimed he never watched the television, and rarely listened to the wireless because he was deaf (he did not explain how this was overcome when he sat on the bench); the recordings were therefore 'quite a treat' for him; perhaps a treat for the jury, if they could 'stomach the rubbish the broadcasting authorities are said to put out these days.' He made one of his semi-audible quips, about Charlie Chaplin; and came sharply down upon someone who laughed.

'These exhibitions have a most serious purpose. They are part of Miss Lambert's case.' If the judge sneered, it was only a fleeting sneer; maybe the jury did not notice it. 'Please give them your *fullest* attention, quite as much as you would give to a sworn witness in the witness-box. Very well: Mrs Lambert?'

They watched, and listened to, interviews with Truethought's CO, with Staff-Serjeant Hipkinson, with one or two cloddish or coltish other-ranks from the same unit, with sanctimonious bellicose members of parliament, with a psychological-warfare expert (very strong against IRA propaganda), with a politics-in-literature expert (the startlingly erudite R. M. Rance, head of the English Department at a Home Counties polytechnic, very strong against IRA propaganda, and obsessed by the way the Irish in general had, as it were, hi-jacked all the poetry in the world to favour the Republican cause), with the Grimethorpe nonconformist clergyman who conducted Truethought's funeral, and with Truethought's Auntie Dorcas. Nearly all of these people, if they had known the lance-corporal, agreed that they had not exactly known him to be a poet; but affirmed they were not really surprised. They all presented themselves as being very moved by some parts of the poem, not always by identical passages.

Auntie Dorcas, a large soft old lady with thick trembling lips, her pale eyeballs a-float in a pool of tears, told a BBC woman that the chapel minister had thought best to look at the poem before she did, and select some bits to read to her. He had heard things about it that he feared might distress her.

'He wor on about t'mucky words, I reckon; and taking the Lord's name in vain, and that. But I said to him, if our Alfy wrote it, he meant it. He meant it to be read. He worn't happy, our Alfy, not a happy lad at all. Afore he went for a soldier, he wor nowhere wi't'lasses in Grimethorpe. They'd laugh at him, tha knows; they'd call him *t'daft bugger*.

'So he's bahn off to t'regiments and never writes to me, not that I'd look for it – why, I don't think he ever wrote a word in all his life without t'schoolmaster stood over him. They say though he did write. Judy this, and Judy that, I daresay he did his best. He wor a good lad but a right misery, and now he's dead. Lord Jesus'll look after him, and no mucky talk up there. I keep crying and crying and I reckon I'll never give over.'

She had no idea who Judy might be.

She had no ill-feeling toward the Irish, but believed the government had to do something about them. Her late husband had been killed at El Alamein, and the government had had to do something about Hitler.

Her nephew, Alfy's father, had died in a pit accident. She thought that that and a battlefield were much the same thing. It was a wicked lie to say that our Alfy would ever have been a blackleg. He wasn't even at home when the strike began, he'd joined the army long before. Arthur Scargill was a daft bugger but knew what was right and wrong and she'd never hear a word against him (and the BBC woman changed the subject).

The video drew tears from the jury, as it had drawn tears from viewers when first shown. It proved nothing about the poem, except to indicate how the very fact of the poem's existence provoked exceedingly old-fashioned emotions; exactly the point Ms Lambert was concerned to make. 'Government has to do *summat* about them!': a sentence given haunting reprise at the very end of the interview, with Auntie Dorcas's face in close-up under her old black hat, behind her thick-lensed spectacles, against a background of children playing soldiers on a disused colliery railway-line.

A final piece of video, made nearly three weeks after the others, was from ITV's *TV-am*: an interview with Judy.

It was not the *discovery* of Judy. That had been achieved by the press. Neither the *Sun* nor any other of the national papers; but a small local 'free-sheet' published in north London, the *Muswell Hill Weekly Digest*, a journal unaccustomed to full-scale scoops, and quite overpowered by this one.

TWO

The *Digest* went to press every Thursday and was put through people's letter-boxes throughout the evening by underpaid after-school child labour. Friday mornings, therefore, were a pretty lazy time for the staff. On this particular Friday there was no one in the paper's office (above a tobacconist on Muswell Hill Broadway nearly opposite Woolworth's) except Miss Trevelyan, the elderly receptionist who also took the advertisements. She was reading the astrology in a women's magazine in the hope of some clue as to how to deal with her exorbitant landlord; he had yet again put up her rent and was *still* refusing to attend to the bathroom geyser.

> *Business relationships this week could prove tricky. Controversial argument may be inevitable but dangerous. Associates' good faith could be on a downturn.*

It did not sound too hopeful. If the wretched man were antagonised, he was quite capable of changing the lock on her door when she was at work and shutting her out of the house.

The astrologer's next sentence was more sanguine, if less probable:

> A surprise visitor may suddenly uplift you and do wonders for your self-image, but your reaction should be cautious: commonsense above all!

Even as she read this, Miss Trevelyan became aware of a person in the office. She had heard no footsteps on the stairs, nor had she noticed the door being opened. But the light from the window was suddenly blocked out – she looked up – there was a young woman, small and slight between desk and filing cabinet; sinuously posing herself, like a witch about to pounce, within a tent-like rag-bag of black clothes; drooping folds of tunics or blouses or curtains or whatever they were, over sloppy tights with holes torn in them; black high-heeled openwork shoes on dirty bare feet; thick black hair all tossed about (it resembled an angry jackdaw perched on top of her head); a gash of bright red lipstick; red fingernails holding a hand-rolled cigarette with a very peculiar smell. Also the girl wore dark glasses: their effect indoors was disturbing, almost deranged.

The unclean hand with the cigarette came uncertainly forward, describing an arc in the air toward Miss Trevelyan; it seemed to be hanging disjointed on the end of a very long, very skinny, bare arm which extended itself like a serpent from the bundle of black garments.

The dark glasses were aimed everywhere but at Miss Trevelyan's candid eyes.

The voice was thin and tentative, very much north London; although the girl did appear to be *foreign*. But that was not surprising, it was no more than consistent with the whole climate of Muswell Hill.

'Do you do, like, stories?'

'Stories?' Miss Trevelyan's mind was upon advertisements, the *Digest*'s main concern. Perhaps this unlovely creature thought 'stories' was a category, like 'personal', or 'accommodation'?

'Stories?' she repeated, and then became strict. 'Just what kind of an advertisement did you wish to place, please?'

'Ow no, no, hang about . . .' mumbled the girl. 'It's not ads . . . stories, like *news*, innit. . . ?'

'You want to see someone on the editorial side?'

'Yeah . . . thassit, editorial . . .'

'I am afraid there's nobody in just now. Ah, in conference, yes.'

'Ow . . . leave a message then?'

'I beg your pardon?' This ignorant mumbling was impossible.

'A message. I'll wait. Or . . . like, come back. Yeah.'

'Whom shall I say?'

'Thassit. Yeah. Tell 'em, Judy.'

'I beg your pardon?' Miss Trevelyan had been following the Truethought saga in various newspapers (every day in her lunch-hour she read widely, if briefly; she felt her semi-journalistic employment demanded it, and the public library was immediately round the corner). But for the moment she failed to connect. She had her pen poised to take down the girl's full name. 'Judy who? Is there a phone number?'

'Don't get it, do you? Here.'

From the interstices of her robes (no other word would really suit) the girl produced a torn-off front page of a recent *Daily Mirror*. The headline ran:

ALF'S JUDY A VICE-GIRL?
Police Probe King's Cross Sex-Haunts

Miss Trevelyan stared at it, incredulous. For a moment she was on fire with excited speculation – she herself, the obscure, even despised, front-office help, suddenly to file the sort of flaring blaring Top Story to rocket the nondescript *Digest* up to the heights of – ? Oh yes, yes, the surprise visitor! Reaction should be cautious: commonsense above all. Anyone could come sliding in and say they were Judy. No one should take such a nonsense on trust. And yet, and yet . . .

She put on her most unforthcoming face, an attempt to look like a TV detective receiving a confession to a complicated murder. '*You* are the missing Judy?'

'Yeah . . .' Flat uninterested answer; resentfully so, as though one had asked her did she ever do anything about her blackheads.

'*Are* you a vice-girl?' Miss Trevelyan could not resist that one, although it did seem a little rude.

'Nah . . . Like, not really. Bit of *letter-box strip*, know what I mean. . . ? Like in Soho, them booths where they put money in a slot to watch your nipples jerk for half-a-minute, then it cuts off just as you open your pussy. Just did it when I needed the bread, like. Dead drag and fucking cold . . . And that pub down Kentish Town, till the Old Bill stopped their licence . . . I'm a model, see. Straight. I need to be straight.'

She suddenly removed her dark glasses: such an action might illustrate straightness? There was, however, something indefinably odd about the uncovered eyes – almost *purple* in colour – Miss Trevelyan did not believe in them at all – 'Contact lenses?' she vaguely asked herself.

'Straight,' said the girl again: but the strange eyes refused to meet Miss Trevelyan's. 'That's why I come here. I want to make, like, an offer, do a deal, see what I mean. . . ?'

Another scrap of newsprint from out of her black draperies; just as crumpled, even dirtier than the first one. The *Digest* this time, a fortnight ago, the main news page. Miss Trevelyan remembered it well; the editor had been very pleased with his headline.

DRUG ORGIES IN MUSWELL HILL SQUAT?
Balfour Gardens Flat a 'Sink of Squalor': Neighbours
Police say, 'Hands Tied until Formal Complaint'
Ethnic Landlord Brands Locals as *Racial Bigots*

Mr Fred Das Gupta admitted to our reporter that the semi-derelict Balfour Gardens house taken over by Stonehenge-type multi-racial hippies ('local outrage', *MH Weekly Digest*, 25 June) is in fact owned by his Finsbury Park property company, but he denies having consented in any way to their presence there. 'I don't supply drugs,' an angry Mr Das Gupta told us, 'I totally refute that I put these people in the flat so they could drug-deal on my behalf. Anyone who says I did is motivated against me because I'm an Asian. You want to check your sources, it could be the National Front.'

Etcetera . . .

The girl's voice was still flat, infuriatingly offhand, but her words implied
a depth of rancour. *'Hands tied?* You're fucking joking. We been busted
twice by the fucking Bill since this was printed . . . and Leroy's still inside,
in'he? Gave him a going-over, know what I mean. So that's why I'm here
. . . I give you my story, you get the glory. I'm a poet and don't know it. Just
like Alfy, right? And then you print the truth about us. Like, apologise for
what you done to us . . . and what you done to Fred. Like, you owe us,
man. Print a correction . . .'

Miss Trevelyan understood she must now-or-never decide. Alone in the
office, *she* was now the newsdesk. If by chance this horrid young woman
was indeed the mysterious Judy, there would be no excuse for letting her
slip. But to commit the paper to repudiating its own very sound story about
Balfour Gardens, and then to discover it was all a low-class con-trick? Bird
in hand, birds in bush, did she dare? She played for time.

'I can't make *arrangements* without authority. But if you'll just tell me a
little more about yourself? You're not English, are you?'

'Yeah, of course I'm English. My old man though, he was Dutch, wasn't
he. . . ? Like, Moluccan Dutch, know what I mean?' (Ah, so the poor child
was a *half-caste*: which explained a great deal, and Miss Trevelyan softened
toward her.) 'We was never in Stonehenge. You'll have to change that for a
start.'

'What's your full name? Judy what?'

'Judy nothing. I'm Sandra. Sandra de Wit. He *called* me Judy, thassall,
"Judy Prudy", 'cos I wouldn't do it with him, no way, not when he first
asked. "Judy Prudy, Prudy Pricktease", he was a toerag, like the army are
. . . Afterwards was different . . . Hang about though, we've not made no
deal.'

'Ah: but that depends – ' Still she must play for time: and good gracious,
she nearly missed it. The girl turned on her heel and walked out of the
office.

Over her shoulder as she went: 'Fuck off then, I'll go to the *Mirror*.
They'll pay me fucking thousands.'

Of course, if the *Digest* was able to be first with the story, thousands
would still be paid, and the *Digest* would get oodles of it. If not the *Mirror*,
then the *Sun*: Miss Trevelyan must act at once. She rose to her feet.
Through the window she saw de Wit emerge from the door below and
dodge across the traffic to the 134 bus-stop: on her way no doubt to
Holborn, to the *Mirror* building, to fame and fortune. She must be stopped
and brought back. But leave the office just as the ads came in? There was a

man on the stairs already, *Second-hand Lawnmower for Sale, Good Condition* written all over his face. Miss Trevelyan pushed past him: she had made up her mind, no time to be lost, ignore the vociferous traffic, it was well worth a swift instant of danger: and thank heaven she caught de Wit before the 134 came in!

'Come back, come back, we'll *make your arrangement*, complete retraction of what we said about you, but you'll have to sign a contract – you know, we must be your agent, accredited – isn't that right? – for whatever we can get you from the nationals?' The last part sounded plausible: Miss Trevelyan only hoped it was fully professional and legally valid.

'Right on . . .' said de Wit, without a change of expression. 'Brilliant, okay . . . Let's go.'

So much for the personality of Sandra de Wit as expressed to Miss Trevelyan, who described it in her evidence for the plaintiff. Other testimony was heard from other people, mostly journalists, who had spoken to Sandra and made their assessments of her. None of these accounts were quite consistent one with the other. And none of them bore much resemblance to the Sandra self-portrayed upon *TV-am*. Most centrifugal of all was the very queer story told to the court by Clay. He, it transpired, had been 'approached by' de Wit many months, even years, *before* Lance-Corporal Truethought's death. When she appeared again as 'Judy' on his early-morning telly (he was in bed with a hangover, inattentively watching the box with no expectation at all of anything of any great interest), he did not at first recognise her. Only later – perhaps, he told the court, as much as five full days later – did he realise he could not get her face out of his mind; it clung there, because *he knew it*! And then he remembered.

And then, six years afterwards, judge and jury watched her too, on a large monitor-screen specially mounted in the darkened courtroom, amongst coughs, fidgets, giggles, whispers, and shocked ushers' admonitions to BE SILENT!

It was the usual sort of breakfast-time news roundup feature; bits and pieces of human interest relating to the events of the day, linked by two facetious commentators, a jocular man and a pert young woman, interspersed with advertisements (which caused the judge to snort), and exclamatory news headlines so incongruously out-of-date they might have dealt with the Sarajevo assassination and no one would have been surprised. Some press items on the lines of –

JUDY – the search continues!

– were read out, and then the great *Mirror* story (bought at such vast cost from the *Muswell Hill Weekly Digest*):

JUDY FOUND!!
AND SHE'S *SANDRA*!
Missing Model Tells of Doomed Romance
'*My loving kiss was kiss-of-death for him,*' she weeps!

And then Sandra herself was revealed, sitting on a studio sofa side-by-side with the pert woman. This was no witch-like sordid squatter-slag, no sideways creeping Balfour Gardens mumbler, but a very self-possessed young elegance, slightly Asiatic, slim and trim and carefully groomed, her hair cut and shaped into a glossy black casque with a hint of the gamine, her clothes precisely chosen to evoke that delicious little style of the fifties, sanitised Existential Parisienne. Tight black roll-neck sweater, skin-tight black trousers, gold neck-chain with Egyptian ankh pendant, gleaming ear-rings. One felt as one watched her that she could be picked up in the palm of the hand like a wounded sparrow and cherished – she might prick with her tiny claws and stab fretfully with her beak, but no harm! Her waist seemed as small as her wrist; her eyes no longer purple but languorous dark brown; and the TV woman's pertness appeared in contrast effusive and gushing.

It was never entirely established by what or whose means the transformation had taken place: between Muswell Hill and the *Daily Mirror*, and between the *Daily Mirror* and that newspaper's final authentication and publication of Sandra's story, four days altogether elapsed, and then another day between publication and *TV-am*. A *Mirror* journalist told the court that when she met Sandra the latter was much more 'together' than Miss Trevelyan's first impression suggested, and that afterwards the television 'brought her out enormously'. Mr Houndsditch wished Miss Trevelyan to say that the metamorphosis was unimportant and only natural, whereas Ms Lambert strove to make her admit that de Wit was an accomplished manipulator who chose her image to suit her audience with a total dishonesty. Miss Trevelyan accepted neither view, and she was perfectly stubborn about it: she had thoroughly distrusted Sandra, yet refused to assert upon oath that Sandra's story could not have been true.

In contrast to that hippy whinge which had so grated on Miss Trevelyan's ears, the televised de Wit voice was assured and articulate, emotional certainly, but crystalline, with just a colour of some continental intonation to modify its clear Thameside English.

'I knew he was a poet, as soon as I met him,' she enunciated. 'No, I wasn't fooled for a moment that he was no more than a thick squaddy. There were his mates that were with him – *they* were, and I told him so. I didn't care for them too much, you see; but you meet all sorts in these discos. "Right," he says, "we'll split. I don't have to stay with them all the weekend, do I?" And his eyes met with mine, I was up on a cloud, oh it wasn't really sexual, more of a dream – oh it's hard to tell you! Bloody hard – I have to say it, I was a fool, I should never have – '

She dabbed at a sparkle of tear with a minute scrap of handkerchief.

The TV woman waited, compassionately.

'The fact is, I was *lost*. We went back to where I lived – my flat-mate was away, you see – I made him spaghetti, we bought a bottle of wine at an off-licence, I lit candles and everything – he went through my music tapes till he found some Bob Dylan, we were brother-and-sister really, two kids, that's all it was.

'Oh yes, he stayed all through Saturday and all of the Sunday as well, till he had to go for his train.

'Yes, it *was* sexual, I suppose. I mean, we did – well, let's say we forgot where we'd left our clothes for forty-eight hours, or nearly that; and we did run a lot of bathwater. But it was all so very gentle – oh God, it's so hard to tell you!'

Another series of dabs, another compassionate pause.

'He said he'd call me Judy, because he was like Punch. Grunting and roaring and pretending to bang me with my little kitchen rolling-pin hooked into the crook of his elbows, he was clowning up his being a killer, you know, a soldier, a wild man bashing the terrorists.

'Just a game, he was never rough with me.

'The thing is, he didn't tell me his name. Wouldn't. "Alfy", he told me that, but not "Truethought". And I didn't ask. I thought it'd all come out one of these days, if it was meant to. If it wasn't, then that was that. They were sending him to Catterick, and Ireland after Catterick for his first ever tour of duty there, and oh God but I knew he was frightened. That's why he wouldn't tell me. He didn't want me to know, if anything – if anything happened to him.

'You see, I didn't tell him *my* name. For the same sort of reason. I couldn't bear that he should hear of me, or depend on me, while he was out there in all sorts of danger – because I'd only let him down, you see . . . In my job, we do have to do things, I mean *go with* people we wouldn't ordinarily want to.

'I was a sort of hostess in those days. I hadn't really got started on the modelling; and what bits of it I'd had, I didn't want to talk about, he could so easily think I was – well, I suppose you *could* call it porno. I never do it now, though. Never ever, no. I was only sixteen.

'It was terrible when he left. He told me I'd destroyed him. I'd given him life when all there was for him was death. Yes, it was true, sort of, about the "backyard of the boozer". I mean, we had a final drink in this pub near King's Cross, and then we slipped out, he pretended to go to the Gents and me to the Ladies, and we couldn't bear just to part, the yard was the only place where we'd be private. Just one more time. And not at all like in the poem; I mean, it wasn't *sordid*.

'But it *was* goodbye. And of course he felt it badly. Very badly. I realise now. I've read his poem. Oh I cried . . .

'It was the poem made it certain that it was written by the Alfy I knew. *Dead basic.* He says it three times in the verses: *Dead basic, cos we're HELD . . . Dead basic, I'm here because I'm here . . . Dead basic, it's gotta be done!* When he talked about the army to me, he kept saying the same two words in just the way he wrote them. I think he had a horror on him; and yet he was so truly brave.

'No, I don't think I let him down. I do think he thought I had. We were both of us so messed up. But that's what's wrong with all this terrorism. It messes up young people. I'd say we have a right to our lives, the way we want to lead them – oh why can't they leave us alone. . . ?'

The pert woman 'had to ask her'; why didn't she come forward, when all the press was looking for her? Or at any rate, why wait a whole fortnight?

'I was ashamed. I read the poem in the papers. It was me; and it hurt. Let's face it, what would *you* have done?'

The pert woman was too moved to find an immediate answer.

And then the screen filled up with little brown goblins hymning somebody-or-other's fatless yoghurt.

Clay was known in the trade as 'Muddy': blond-moustachioed, of insinuating manners, long-haired (where he was not bald), wearing the sort of characterless steel spectacles issued to military personnel as an article of uniform. He described himself as a freudian-marxist, which went down badly with the jury. But in the absence of Sandra he was Ms Lambert's strongest evidence, and she had to make the best of him.

His account on his first meeting with de Wit was gone over several times in response to Mr Houndsditch's dogged attempts to discredit it. The cross-examination did fault the story upon several details of places and dates. As Clay tetchily pointed out, it was eight years ago, and he had rather shrugged off the event when it happened – it only seemed significant in the light of later developments – he could scarcely be blamed for omitting his copious notes, he was not a policeman.

'No?' sneered Houndsditch. '*Not* a policeman. Just a detective, self-employed. After the model of the celebrated Mr Duncan Campbell, no doubt?'

'I admire Campbell, I do not *follow* him.'

'And if *he* had heard this strange tale, he would not have written it down?'

'I have explained, I wrote *parts* of it. I wrote down the girl's name, I wrote down the politician's name.' Clay was a British citizen, perhaps not by birth; his accent might have been Czech, or it might have been Serbo-Croat. Mr Houndsditch amused the jury by mimicking it in the course of his questions.

But just now he broke out strongly with undiluted Gray's Inn Oxbridge: 'Mr Clay, his ludship has warned you! You are not to introduce tendentious names! The court cannot listen.'

'I do not wish to speak to you again on this point, Mr Clay.' The judge was very menacing.

And yet the story was not quite absurd.

It was 1981 or '82, Clay thought; he had gone to a party in a studio-flat in Notting Hill, he thought his host was a novelist but he could not be sure – it was that sort of party, they had all come on from somewhere else, it was very late at night. *Substances* were being smoked and sniffed. In those days, he admitted, he dabbled in such things: but never to the point of mental impairment. He found himself in intimate conversation with this girl in a little bedroom-alcove tucked under the gallery stairs – the flat was split-level, he remembered that very clearly, people were eating pizzas and dancing downstairs, and upstairs they were . . . at all events, there was much noise; under the stairs was the only quiet; he himself had a bad headache. The girl was heavily stoned and half-undressed; when he entered the alcove she was there already, weeping on the bed.

'I know who you are,' she whispered to him, as he attempted to console her. 'They told me just now who you are. You write for the *Socialist Worker*?'

He said he did sometimes, and so what?

She said she had hoped he would follow her into the alcove (although he had certainly not done so wittingly); she said she had something to tell him that he ought to use in his articles; she said it was more than enough to destroy Mr ——— (the politician whose name the court must not hear). Mr ——— was an unreliable left-winger on the opposition Labour Party front bench, and authentic left-wingers (represented by the *Socialist Worker*) were abusing him as a seller-out of trade-unionists. She said she had been his mistress, had very recently had his abortion, he had been warned off her by MI5, he had treated her disgracefully, and now she was convinced that men were trying to kill her.

'She told you all this, Mr Clay – you, a sensational journalist – and *you rather shrugged it off?*'

'Not of course to start with. But the more of it she told me, the less I believed it. She was, as I say, stoned. She connected it somehow with the murder of Airey Neave, and then with the strange death of the Bulgarian assassinated by a poisoned umbrella-point, and then Gaitskell. I asked her deliberately, did it also have to do with Edward Kennedy and that car accident where a young woman drowned? When she said yes, and then obviously searched her mind to find some reason to have said so, I knew what I was dealing with. It is true, I discover plots: but they have to be probable ones.'

He assumed she was a pathological liar who would say anything to get attention. He met many such in the course of his work. She was very young, which did not in itself discredit what she said. It did deter him from carnal intercourse, for he chose not to exploit the sexuality of adolescents. (Mr Houndsditch was probing Clay's use of the word 'console'.) He agreed that she may have been seeking carnal intercourse, if indeed she had not been having it before he came in – yes, it *had been* that sort of party. For one so young, she was surprisingly well-informed about public affairs. But maybe not so surprising; in the circles where he moved there were children of all sorts of people, precocious, manipulative, fundamentally non-infantile.

She gave him a phone number, he rang it the next day, it did not exist. She gave him her name – Carlotta Wong. He did check it out against the politician's name on his card-index: but nothing turned up. He dismissed the encounter from his mind, until he saw de Wit on the box and then of course he remembered. Wong *was* de Wit. He was absolutely in no doubt of it.

'Even though you too were – *stoned?*'

'Even though. This Carlotta was in many ways quite different. She wore an evening gown, Latin-American cabaret, all flounces and naked shoulders. Someone had torn it at the bust; it was most *slinky*. Her hair was long and mounted-up in an array of sophisticated style, it had partly come down and hung about her neck: but not black, it was very fair, artificial against her dark skin. It was only when I was close to her I could understand how young she was. I don't remember the eyes. Dark, I would say: but they did have the Asian shape and I noticed those cheek-bones.'

As to her voice, it was notably foreign.

'As much so as your own?'

'Ah! The appeal to prejudice.'

A stern word from the judge: 'Answer counsel's questions without comment, if you please.'

'First, if I may, I will answer his *concealed* question. My father's name was Klaue, he was "displaced" out of Hungary, not himself a Hungarian, but a stateless refugee radical – if you were to approve of him, you would call him a "dissident". I am sorry for this, I do understand it impeaches my veracity.' (Ms Lambert winced, but the judge said nothing.) 'Okay, without comment: her accent was more foreign than mine. But the idiom was good.'

'You mean correct?'

'I mean, lively. She was street-wise, she swore like a Londoner. If she was not at school, she could have been of any profession; perhaps nursing-orderly, perhaps whore, perhaps the daughter of a duchess, perhaps movie-lab trainee, who could say? She might even have been typist in a barrister's chambers.'

'That is quite enough of *that.*' Clay's evidence had already gone on for a long time and there was much more to come; the judge was losing patience.

THREE

Media fuss over Truethought would in all likelihood have died a natural death had not Muddy Clay (with a headache in front of *TV-am*) begun to think there was something to investigate. The last thing he had in mind was a lawsuit; he foresaw only a series of provocative articles for the left-wing press, followed (if he were lucky) by a book; or, better still, a television documentary falling prosperously foul of government, a smart challenge to the undeclared censorship.

He was just then at a loose end, having completed the evisceration of a corrupt board of hospital governors in Wiltshire; tame enough target for his talents, despite his uncovering of the chairman's discreditable past – an army MO who had supervised torture techniques during Cyprus operations in the fifties.

Clay's mole-like burrowings now needed a new field: *TV-am* unexpectedly showed him where. A purely private enterprise, an opportunistic initiative, for general furtherance of his ideology and material benefit to his career.

First clue, indeed his only clue: De Wit and Wong were one and the same – what could this mean? 'Pathological liar' no longer covered the issue. He had learned too much about 'disinformation' in the two years since the Notting Hill party. Possibility – no, probability – perhaps indeed certainty; Carlotta/Judy/Sandra was a low-grade disinformation agent and he had damn well caught her out in a couple of separate jobs. Consider them both, and see what they led him to.

Easy to detect the general drift of the first one: to halt the advance of the strenuous Mr ——, acclaimed leftist, who in those days hoped to swing the bulk of the Labour Party toward him (was he groping for the leadership?) and at the same time swing himself somewhat nearer to its centre. Many left-wingers mistrusted him, as always when one of their own becomes admired outside sectarian cliques. They would be glad to see him punctured, but if the tories began it they would be honour-bound to come to his aid. So therefore the one to smear him must be a quasi-trotskyite journalist who 'may be a bit of a loony but God knows he's never been *bought!*'

Obsessive sex with a teenager struck exactly the right note. An adult call-girl or another man's wife would have been damaging but far from fatal. To be perfectly sure of it, add abandonment, abortion, and terrified paranoia about murderers.

Clay realised now how very well he was out of it. Had he fallen for her farrago, he'd have been his own second victim. In the long run the deceit would have been detected by somebody, perhaps even by Clay himself. It was his professional boast that he was never deceived; if once he were, where would he be?

In fact, as far as he knew, the girl's story failed to surface anywhere. Perhaps she was unable to trick others into believing her (she must have been new to the business); whoever might be running her cut losses and called her in.

But who *had* been running her? Extreme Conservatives on the fringe of neo-fascism? Or regular neo-fascists? (Either way they could be 'security services', no?) Ah but right-wing Labour elements were not beyond suspicion. *Nor were Clay's own fellow-trotskyites* – he allowed no illusions about marxist scrupulosity, but nonetheless the idea gave him pause. Suppose Carlotta's ploy had only apparently been directed against Mr ——, while its true target was Clay himself? He had his rivals among the comrades and some of them were vindictive. He thought of this one, thought of that one, thought of a gaggle of them all together, muttering and sniggering in a particular corner of a particular Mile End pub: such glee for those grotty ratbags had his career collapsed in ridicule!

It was this last possibility that made him so sure he must pursue the matter: he had been personally *got at* and that he could not forgive.

Hangover or not, he lurched in his underwear to his worktable, switched on his computer, opened a new file (access-codeword ORCHID – 'whore-kid', he enjoyed private word-games, very useful security- wise); he clutched his throbbing temples and tapped out his first entry:

CHRIST I'M GOING WILD, THE SWINE WERE OUT TO GET ME!
MIGRAINE-BLOODY-GUTCRAMPS, I AM *NOT* TO GO WILD!
WE CONSIDER THIS *RATIONALLY*. RATIONALLY. RIGHT.

Right. The Notting Hill purposes of Carlotta could only be determined in relation to her reappearance as Sandra. So (for argument's sake) assume the two incidents connected. Assume, assume, do not at this stage *assert*.

The crucial question: why Sandra?

More precisely, *why Judy?*

So take it from there.

*

The obvious reasons for Judy were to authenticate Truethought's poem, to keep it going in the public eye for a little bit longer, to soften the public heart toward the agony of the security forces as they struggled to contain subversion. How necessary was all this? Auntie Dorcas had already softened hearts across the nation. The verses declared the agony, and the press reception of them spread jam upon their butter. The search for Judy in itself extended the story many days beyond its natural cut-off point. Even had she never turned up, official propagandists might surely have been well satisfied? Her ultimate discovery could have added no more than a weekend, or so, to the general span of interest.

So what was left? Authentication. But why trouble to authenticate what nobody at that time appeared to be doubting? Not even Clay himself, when he read those crummy stanzas, had thought they might be the work of anyone other than some piles-in-the-arse orderly-room lance-jack with a longing for macho action and a nag at his scrotum that he never seemed to pull enough birds. 'Poor bloody Alfred, no?' he had in fact said to a friend at the *New Statesman*, 'all upon paper, nowhere *but* upon paper: and then the buggers hit him, and he never had time to know it!' He had toyed with the notion of publishing an analysis of the poem on those lines. No one else in the UK seemed to have thought of doing so, and the Irish papers, with one exception, were all as maudlin as the British; deeply moved by Truethought's courage, ashamed and guilty he had been killed by Irish people, anxious above everything to empathise with Grimethorpe, a community (the *Irish Times* pointed out) not altogether different from certain Irish haunts of industrial recession; Ballymun, say, or the Rahoon end of Galway city.

The exception, of course, was *An Phoblacht/Republican News* or (*AP/RN*, of Dublin and Belfast, the *Sinn Féin* weekly journal), where a vigorous demolition of the poem was merrily featured. Clay was sure that something similar on his own side of the water would have much-needed political impact. But he finally decided against.

His reasons were miserably personal. He too, from time to time, attempted verses – sexual licence mingled with revolutionist militancy –he was not very proud of the results, and felt an unwonted queasiness at doing unto Truethought what many might do unto Muddy.

He was uncomfortably aware he had been without a live-in lover since his wife walked out on him the previous year, he could count his one-night stands on the fingers of half a hand, his last young man had called him 'wormy-dick'.

He sometimes suffered from haemorrhoids.

He had to pluck up courage to go on any demonstration: he always made great play there with his press-card and avoided even the outer edge of a ruck with the police, to say nothing of the National Front.

And then, quite demeaningly for a ruthless freudian-marxist, he was sorry for Auntie Dorcas; he did not want her told that some four-eyed swankpot from London had been mocking her dead great-nephew in print. Had she not, in her own way, stood up for the NUM?

'A wicked lie to say that our Alfy wor a blackleg.' True to his class in Yorkshire, a class-enemy in County Antrim: the same old contradiction as in the doings of O. Cromwell, as in the writings of A. Marvell, contradiction inherent in the entire imperialist issue.

Imperialism had *required* those verses, to gloss over the contradiction. But imperialism must have feared that somehow, by somebody, they would be tested and found wanting.

Found wanting? They were a *fake*? Write down, at least, 'could be'. And if the fake was about to be suddenly exposed, then imperialism *required* Judy: and Judy at once was produced. So: if Truethought had not written the poem, who had? More to the point, who was on the verge of finding out about it, and how did imperialism know?

The satirical piece in *AP/RN* (cruel, chopping cat's meat out of Truethought and his scrawny Judy) seemed to have no doubts about the authenticity of the poem. And yet it also seemed to think the whole business had in some mysterious way been *pre-arranged*. Perennial Republican bias, granting no normal human motivation to a historically demonised enemy, or did the author (he called himself simply 'Druid') have reason to suspect there was more than met the eye? He used the phrase 'poetry-kick' – the Brits were on the poetry-kick because the Irish had taught them its value, and they didn't really know how to apply it.

Then followed an obscure reference to an event which the 'Druid' implied had happened a while earlier; he presented it *en passant* as an obvious illustration of the 'poetry-kick' and its incompetent handling:

> so a fusilier with a sub-machine gun, gabbling beatnik zen-speak to a woman whose house is ransacked by his chums, might be thereby supposed to win a whole new sexy friend for Anglo-Saxon art-and-culture; repeat the exercise everywhere; the troops, RUC, UDR, can move out; the Arts Council move in; Ireland's British Problem solved! At least give them so much credit – they're *trying*! Not their fault that four hundred years ago one of the top bards of their 'golden age' tried the same class of bollocks in the County Cork and made a hames of it.

The article wandered off into a derisive account of Edmund Spenser, comparing 'Truethought's Last Stand (of the Muses)' to *The Faerie Queene*, and deciding:

> Raunchy Alf perhaps has the edge over papist-baiting Eddy S., a more effortless troubadour, we incline to say – *ars est celare artem* ('the art is to conceal the art', or did the Christian Brothers never flog the Latin into yez?) – sure the art is to conceal the bloodshed till they have us all pressed together in a lethal little heap of love and creativity like a boxful of blind battery-hens . . .

Whatever about hens, the *fusilier* must be followed up. If the 'Druid' had made a connection, there might indeed *be* a connection; Clay ought to go to Dublin and talk to *AP/RN* personally. He knew a man on the editorial staff. Unwise to write in any detail from London to that particular paper's address, unless you wanted your letter first delivered to a Special Branch office (Irish or British, or both), and perhaps never delivered anywhere else after that. Much the same hazard applied to the telephone. He must travel to Dublin unannounced.

On a previous trip he had been held up for four hours by anti-terrorist police at Holyhead and missed his boat; this time he knew better. He clipped his moustache, thrust the superfluities of his long hair into a well-chosen county-gent's cap, wore collar and tie and a belted overcoat, kept his spectacles in his pocket; he was allowed through without question.

If there was a detective watching the down-at-heel Georgian building in Parnell Square that housed *AP/RN*, he did not interfere with Clay, and Clay did not detect him.

A scruffy room adorned with posters: the man he had come to see sat at table drinking coffee, mid-chat with a dark pointy-faced Spanishy-looking young woman in denim dungarees. Heaps of files and loose papers all over the floor spilling out of black plastic bags. An unsurprised greeting of minimum friendliness, overlaid with inhospitable irony: 'No, I don't think we want you. Fact is, the revolution's postponed; we're after finding out, you see, there's an army of occupation in the Six Counties that nobody bloody well noticed, least of all Leon Trotsky, and until we have them hammered there's nothing you can do for us. In other words, take your insurance and sell it to the next bloody house.'

Clay was used to this sort of thing; no more than another instalment of the everlasting *socialism v. national liberation* disputation he always had to have with the Irish. He ignored it, asked for some coffee, they showed him an electric kettle, he attended to his own needs and then came straight to the point.

'Your piece last month, signed "Druid" – the zen-speaking soldier: did it actually happen? Or did your contributor make it up?'

The Irishman shrugged. 'God knows, I asked about it myself. The contributor, as you call him – *I'd* call him a hollow-legged gurrier who thinks he's the new Myles na gCopaleen and never turns in anything unless it's "come to him on the breath of the malt" (and so it does, sometimes) – sure, he swore that it did happen and swore we printed it as a news item; would you believe, *two years ago*! We might have done, but who could remember? His cracks about Spenser were good, yeh? Not so sure, though, about his blackguarding the squaddy's poem. I believe the poor sod meant just what he said: he didn't want to fight us and yet he did want; and he fought. I can tell you the "Druid" never touched a gun in his life, by which token his sarcasm was just that much out-of-tune with the experience of too many of our readers, we'd have asked him to rewrite, but he sent it in late of course, we'd a gap in the end page, we had to print it as it came. I'd say we don't give enough attention to hard politics in the literary section, the bloody twists of the damn things and what they do to the twists and turns of our words. No, that's to be thought about; we never have the time: no, we'll have to get *organised*!' He slammed his fist on the table, to prove his determination.

The young woman laughed scornfully. 'Yeah?' she said. 'When?' Then they both laughed.

'I wonder . . .' Clay took it easy; if they wanted relaxation, he'd give them relaxation. 'I wonder . . . any chance, do you suppose . . . you could find that news-item for me?'

The man shrugged again. He waved his hand toward his Himalaya of plastic bags. 'Our files, as always, are open to you, as a comrade and a friend to Ireland . . . For Christ's sake, the bloody Branch was here, confiscating every document we've got. Back-numbers, stationers' bills, everything. You'd think they think the IRA mail their plans and their membership lists for us to spike as a matter-of-course and leave on the sub-editor's desk. If we *had* a sub-editor's desk. They're beginning to return what they took, this lot came in this morning. In the heel of the hunt we'll have 'em *all* back, next month, maybe next year. Meantime, Muddy, on your knees, boy: grovel!'

Clay grovelled, until the lunch-hour; with some help from the young woman, he finally found what he was looking for.

The news-item was short but bizarre.

It explained how Bríd Ní Gairmleadhaigh was a perfectly ordinary 31-year-old single-parent Catholic housewife; by implication, non-political. Her council house on the outskirts of Armagh had become the location for continuous security-force harassment; by implication, entirely arbitrary. Upon one of these occasions, in the small hours of a freezing cold morning, while soldiers were trampling and smashing about upstairs, she expressed herself so strongly against them that their officer ordered her held in the kitchen at gunpoint (shivering in her dressing-gown and clutching her terrified child) to wait for him to finish.

And then it went on to describe how gunpoint became *wordpoint* . . .

Clay read it several times, decided he did not at all understand its real significance, and said, 'I ought to go see this lady. Possible?'

The editorial man shrugged. 'She's well enough known, *I* know her, she's had a bad time. I don't think she'd want to see *you*.'

'Sod it that I never noticed this when first it appeared, I should have had it on my computer, but Christ I can't put everything every day onto disc from every single news sheet; even if I *did* read it, it just seemed not so important. But it could be.'

'Why?'

'Ah. Why. . . ? I don't know . . . I'm not sure . . . does it matter?'

'Begod it does, boy, if you know something we don't, and you bloody well want to rob us of it, why the hell have I been helping you? It's our country not yours; by the same token, *our stories*.'

'And so what? And I'll need *more* help; anything I find, I'll give you your share, give you an exclusive if it's worth an exclusive, oh I mean it: we should make a deal.'

'You've been straight with us before. Be sure you are this time. Okay then, a deal. Attracta, you hear the man? How to induce Biddy Grimes to have a private wee talk with an exclusive-hunting Brit?'

Attracta, brooding over a salad sandwich at her desk, was not at first very forthcoming. 'If he wants to *keep* it private, he'd do well not to go to Armagh, her place'll be under surveillance. They've not left her alone since Taddy was killed . . . He could meet her in Belfast, chance acquaintance when she's doing her shopping. A bar, café, bus-station even. I could fix it, Mr Muddy (or do you have some other name?); care for me to fix it? Better still, I'd go with you. I've to be there anyway the day after tomorrow. Sure, she'd be glad of me, and so ought you, a guarantee that you're bona-fidey: without it, she'll not tell you a thing.'

They both refused him further information until he had met Bríd. He did more grovelling in the plastic bags and turned up more short news-items, all apparently related, none of them adequately explained.

Next day: a frustrating chat with the 'hollow-legged gurrier', a sharp-nosed hump-backed disappointed literary malignant, who was indeed breathing the breath of the malt, who was very obnoxious in what appeared to be his personally rented corner of a bar near the north end of O'Connell Street, and who knew a Brit when he met a Brit even though the said Brit's 'haw-haw fucking accent' was deliberately concealed behind a 'fucking Hapsburg snuffle'. Clay mollified the 'Druid's' spite by disclosing his own (hitherto somnolent) contempt for both the English Elizabethans and the American Beat Generation. But there was little to learn. Bríd Ní Gairmleadhaigh's queer experience had stuck in the 'Druid's' mind only because he had read of it in *AP/RN*, and he knew less about its meaning than Clay himself had already deduced: 'It dealt with poetry, your man Truethought dealt with poetry, or so his sponsors maintain – and both within the manipulations of colonial military power – ha! subliminal, there's a word! I made *subliminal* connections which scratched with importunity against my imagination, so; and I used them, no one else did: care to argue?'

End of first line of enquiry, the fellow-journalists. Now for the second, vox-pop.

Clay and Attracta left for Belfast the following morning by the same train, but travelling separately. He met her at lunch-time in Kelly's Cellars, a city-centre pub with a splendid old spit-and-sawdust nineteenth-century atmosphere, except there was no actual sawdust.

But there was Ms Ní Gairmleadhaigh, and he confirmed what he had suspected. 'Housewife' she may have been, but 'perfectly ordinary'? Not on your life. To start with she was a graduate of Queen's University (history and sociology), and an ex-member (she *said* 'ex': Clay thought she might be telling the truth) of People's Democracy and Women Against Imperialism. When he asked her about *Sinn Féin*, she laughed and said, 'Do I look like it?' which could have meant anything; it clearly did mean his question was an impertinence, so he laughed too and submitted to a quarter of an hour of edgy repartee, part-feminist, part-Republican.

Not that she had any great *sexual* power over him. He had always found red hair and a freckled complexion emetic, evoking childhood recollections of horse-manure that steamed on a snow-covered road, of his squabby little younger sister (fair hair, *not* red) squalling in the bath after she had smeared herself and her cot-sheets with peanut butter. The freudian side of his ideology could never absolutely account for the crooked potency of this joint image, however much he applied his objective consideration to it . . . His main problem toward Bríd was much simpler: she seemed to know what he was thinking before he thought it;

and was damnably swift to disparage it, often with no more than a quick rabbit-like lift of her upper lip. She had green eyes, protuberant, contemptuous. Attracta's demeanour was similarly off-standing, to a lesser degree and modified by her humour, by her south-western slyness (she came from the Dingle Peninsula), by her youth (she was about eight years younger than Bríd); the two of them played him between them in a sort of scornful verbal ping-pong. Despite which, he was able to hear from Bríd's own mouth many very interesting details that *AP/RN* had not had space to print.

The full story emerged something like this.

The soldier left to guard her in her kitchen was a lean weasel-like old sweat with streaks of grey in his moustache and a serjeant's stripes, a winking grinning undersized fellow; he seemed disposed to make conversation. Bríd refused to talk to him; but he *would* talk. He roamed the room looking for subjects of discourse. He commented on her plastic floor-tiles, which were new and smart until that night; his colleagues had just been smashing them, and the concrete underneath them, in the hope she might have buried some contraband.

'Dead flashy,' he said, 'my wife's got some like it. Hate to see 'em wrecked, but you know how it is?' His eye shifted upwards, he looked along her shelves.

'Books?' he said, 'oho, no! we're not supposed to approve o'that. We're brutal and licentious, right? We only read comics and porn. All the rest is dead subversive. Specially poetry.' He had one of her volumes of poems in his hand as he spoke. Was he going to rip it to pieces, wrench pages away from cover, scatter it across her ruptured floor? He actually seemed to be absorbing it: 'Alan Ginsberg, well I never, here's a turn-up, wow! That sacred fucking man in a terrorist safe-house!'

He shot a collusive wink at her, perhaps he meant he did not quite mean such an incriminating accusation: she was unpersuaded, she stayed silent. He read some lines out aloud, more to himself than to her, he was twitching and hopping about in a sort of ecstasy.

> I came home and found a lion in my living room
> Rushed out on the fire-escape screaming Lion! Lion!

He winked at her a second time, trying to impel her to share his enjoyment of the lines' fitness to the situation. She stayed silent. 'He tells it like it is, don't he? Tells it like it is *tonight*!'

> Called up my old Reichian analyst
> who'd kicked me out of therapy for smoking marijuana

I ended masturbating in his jeep parked in the street moaning 'Lion'.

His mood changed, he became all dreamy, he held his sub-machine gun loosely between his thighs.

. . . that the vast Ray of Futurity enter my mouth to sound Thy
Creation Forever
Unborn, O Beauty invisible to my Century!

that I surpass desire for transcendency and enter the calm water of the
universe
that I ride out this wave, not drown forever in the flood of my
imagination
that I be not slain thru my own insane magic . . .

'Ah, wow,' he breathed, 'wow. . . ! Man, that is *out of sight* . . . You read this? You bet you do. Shit, man, o'course you do, no need to be so fucking scared. D'you write it as well?'
She stayed silent.
'*I* do, y'know. Oh yeah. Tell you what, give you a sample.'
Tucking his gun under his armpit in a most unsoldierly fashion, he fumbled in his trouser pocket and produced a little notebook, opening it with a single movement at a particularly dog-eared page.
'Here we are, Mrs Grimes,' he muttered, oddly ingratiating, '*The Serjeant's Dream*, "by one who was there".' And he actually did read to her eight lines of metrical something. Bríd recalled it very clearly, almost (she said) word-for-word:

On the roads of Ulster on my weary prowl
I had a vision of God and heard Him howl
I am your boots, He said, I am your uniform, I am your gun,
They can't forgive you what you done.
But I am you, He said,
I am your body and your weary head.
If they can't forgive you, then they can't forgive Me.
So how can I forgive them, don't you see?

He slid the notebook back into his pocket. 'So that's it, missus, there you are! God's everywhere and He hates us. But he's nowhere, and we're nothing. Like, we exist, man, until we've killed our own selves, and then at last all we are is the environment, that's all; we don't exist no longer because, simply *we are it*. DHARMA, you know? Greatest hate, greatest love. And this gun is like a – like a *dream* of a gun; if you don't believe it's there, then it's gone. You know, Buddha was trained in the Martial Arts when he was young? He gave them up; like, to meditate. But he never gave them up. They *were* his meditation. Peace.'

She stayed silent.

He seemed to grow angry. Angry teeth, lion's teeth, under his ragged moustache. He was very very frightening.

'*Peace.*' A sort of mantra, he hummed it and he hummed. 'WITH.' His hum rose, quavering. 'JUS. TICE.' A prolonged expectoratory horrible hiss.

So she too said, 'Peace.' Whispered it, smiled. At that point his officer appeared and beckoned him out: the search-detail left the house, empty-handed; giving Bríd a piece of paper acknowledging the damage they had done, explaining what her rights were as regards compensation.

She found it hard to believe it had all happened.

'Frightening? Aye,' she told Clay. 'Never so frightened in all my life. What he said to me was – well, at the time it seemed worse than shooting. But by daylight – Christ, by daylight I had to laugh, so I did. Do they come now to intimidate us by *verses*? Or d'you really suppose he thought, with his "peace" and his "dharma", *I'd* think he was – he was what Mao called a "paper tiger"? Paper *lion*, in point of fact . . . So the Republican people'd be taken off their guard? Was he trying out, d'you think, some oriental technique of disorientation? He was no damn good at it of course: but it could be that. It could be.'

'It could be,' said Clay, who seemed to be saying (or thinking) those three words rather frequently these days.

'I saw in the paper,' he suggested, 'some of the other back-numbers, that something of the same sort happened in other places, a month or two later?'

'So they tell me. And do *you* tell me it was the same old dog of a three-stripe bastard, or a different one every time?'

'Once in Derry, once in Coalisland, once in Andersonstown. On each occasion the poetical Brit was twice as old as any of his mates, but he wasn't a serjeant; and in Andersonstown he wore mufti, the man he talked to thought he was police. Nor was his poem the same. But he did talk in all three places about "peace", and Buddha, and dharma, and assorted sixties rubbish.'

'What d'you prefer then? One maniac, probably stoned, incredibly ubiquitous; or four separate clever wee butties, each one of them carefully briefed? I'll tell you what you prefer: same as I do, a bit o'both – one Brit, no way a maniac, carefully briefing *himself* into four different identities and trying it out four different ways. He was nut-house with *me*, slippery-smooth in Coalisland, gentle as a lamb in Derry where there was a woman in tears; and in Andytown he came on like an old-fashioned parish priest, hectoring the man of the house for presuming to uphold violence. It wasn't in the paper; but you see, I took pains to find out. Ah, you're sharp, Mr Clay: you're asking yourself, who is this woman, with her poetry books, her investigative neurosis, her part-time job in a solicitor's office, her totally nondescript council-house existence? You can discover my full history for yourself, so you can; I don't trust you beyond prudence. But I'll tell you one more thing, and make what you like of it: you *won't* have thought of this one, because I've no skill to imitate accents. But I can diagnose them when I hear them. The serjeant had two voices. Barrack-room cockney, and mid-atlantic hasheesh.'

'I did gather *that* much.'

'You did. But sure, I couldn't have made it clear to you that both of them were phoney. And I haven't made clear to myself what the man's *real* speech might be – if he has a real speech, which is very much open to doubt.'

'Something else you've not made clear to me – '

'Ah, sharp: didn't I tell him, Attracta? Well?'

' – you must,' Clay continued carefully (he was becoming more and more irritated by Bríd's assumption of superior insight), 'you must have come to some conclusion as to why he chose *your* house? Have you not thought, he must have been aware before he came there'd be poetry on the shelf? Are you known, in Armagh, for your cultural tastes? For that matter, the other three houses: how much could he have known about them?'

'Derry was a schoolteacher, Coalisland a student, Andersontown a wee man who purports to be a playwright. I took pains to find out. They didn't need to: they have all the nationalist houses computerised, didn't you know that?'

'What about the loyalist ones?'

'They *are* the bloody computer!' If it was a joke, she did not laugh at it.

Clay pressed his point: 'Yes, but your own house?'

Although the bar was half-empty and nobody seemed to be watching them, she took a cautious look around and hunched her shoulders over the table. Clay and Attracta followed suit. Bríd was now speaking more or less into the ashtray. Clay jolted it with his cigarette butt, idiotically wondering if pub ashtrays could be bugged. It slid across the table, he picked it up to replace it; he looked furtively underneath it, concluded it was harmless enough; hoped Bríd had not noticed his little movement.

'Attracta,' she whispered, 'seeing neither you nor anyone else in this country has had the titter of wit to see what there is to be seen in this business, and seeing that here at last is a stranger from God knows where, of apparent perspicacity; I'd feel an utterly stupid *amadhaun* if I failed to open my mind to him, and worse than stupid if I don't. Let's discuss what damage I can do myself if he's not what you say he is?'

To Clay's intense annoyance, the two women then muttered in rapid Irish about him, just as though he wasn't there. Five minutes or more of it: they were very serious, almost quarrelsome; until suddenly Bríd broke off, broke again into English, and addressed him with a bright smile: 'She says if you *are* a tout you're a paper tiger: there'll be nothing I know that you don't know already. And if I let you know I know it it'll make your employers think twice about – let's just say, about killing me. What I tell you goes on a tape-recorder, indeed it's already gone on one,' (She tapped her handbag: Clay winced; he had not actually thought that *she* would be bugging him.) 'And we don't do it here. It's too long to have to whisper it. Fergus's flat?'

She looked at Attracta. Attracta nodded. The women rose to their feet together and walked straight out of the bar without asking him to come with them. He had the sense to see he was expected to follow. He waited half-a-minute and did so. Outside, they were looking into a shop-window at the corner. When he emerged, they moved on. He strolled in their footsteps up and down a number of streets, until suddenly they disappeared into a doorway between a newsagent's and a shoe-shop.

On the doorpost he saw a panel of bells for four floors, and an intercom speaker; but before he could examine them the door was opened for him; the two women were just inside it; as soon as he entered and it swung shut-and-locked behind him, they started off upstairs with a gesture for him to come too. Several neglected landings, with the names of dusty companies pinned to the wainscot; and at last on the very top floor (in fact a garret under the mansard roof) was the open door to Fergus's flat and a man who doubtless was Fergus holding it open for the three of them. Throughout the ensuing conversation this man sat in anorak and dark glasses, on his hunkers against the skirting-board, and uttered neither good word nor bad: but he was a tense tough young man with a heavy moustache, he looked dangerous, he looked as though he might shoot Clay if Clay said the wrong thing.

(*Or maybe not: the commercial centre of Belfast was not after all a nationalist ghetto, let's not fall for bourgeois media-hype! A measure of play-acting was going on, nothing more. Nevertheless, Clay told himself, watch it.*)

The flat, sparsely furnished with a job-lot of secondhand pieces, was not very clean. A curtain was drawn across the single dormer-window. No pictures on the walls, no lampshade on the light; an apartment that exuded no personality whatever. Bed made up in an alcove; half of a lunch on the table – loaf, butter, an open tin of baked beans, a teapot. The man did not offer them any of it, nor did he attempt to finish his own eating while they were there.

Bríd took her tape-recorder out of her bag, switched it on, and laid it on the table. 'I am leaving this tape with Fergus,' she said. 'He will keep it securely. My insurance, in case of need. And you yourself will take no notes. Oh, you'd better first convince me that *you've* not got a tape-recorder.'

Fergus stood up, moved swiftly over to Clay, frisked him, found nothing, squatted down again.

'Now: first I should tell you that not quite all I said in Kelly's was altogether correct. When I said that that serjeant called me Mrs Grimes, I told a lie. The name he gave me was Mrs Quinn. "Is that a fact?" you're about to ask me. You're about to admit it means fuck-all to you, yeh?'

'Yeh.'

'Maybe so. But just think about it. You *have* heard of Taddy Quinn?'

Clay thought about it, scraping his memory. 'There was a funny sort of murder – ' he began.

'Aye. There was. Dead funny.'

'Over the border. Eighty-two, could it have been? Ah! Last year! Eighty-three?'

'It was.' Her hard round little freckled face had grown harder and tighter, her pursed puffy lips contracted to something that looked more like a navel than a mouth. The pallor of her cheeks seemed quite leprous under Fergus's unshaded bulb. 'My child is his child, and that'll do about that. You have heard of "The Peeler's Goat"?'

'Not for some time. I used to read the poems in *Republican News*.'

'You read about half of them. His best ones were never printed.'

'A sort of follow-on to Bobby Sands?' (Sands, before his death on hunger-strike, had smuggled a vast quantity of startling prose and poetry out of Long Kesh.) 'If they weren't his best, they were damn good. Not always as *doctrinaire* as you'd expect in such a paper. It's a while since they last appeared.'

She mimicked him, unkindly: '*Eighty-two, could it have been? Ah! Last year! Eighty-three?*'

'If you say so.'

'I do. And I've good reason.'

She then told him what Naomi Lambert was eventually to tell the court, how she received the poems from the Kesh, transcribed them, passed them on.

'We were confident no one knew who had written them, where they were coming from (except obviously from a POW); I was a long time connecting that dharma-pig with any knowledge of 'em: but I'm damned sure now I *was* suspected, and that was why they searched the house. His job was to test me on the issue, taunt me, soothe me, whatever he thought he could do to get me to reveal. Bear in mind, *Peace with Justice* is a Provo call, no one else's: all others that want Peace leave the Justice damn well out of it, are you ignorant enough to ask me why? In point of fact, he did none of what they'd hoped he'd do. In point of fact they found fuck-all. Later on, they *did* find.'

She told about the successful raid that had uncovered transcripts in her flour-bin.

'But that took place after, I mean immediately after I'd heard Taddy was on the run. It was so bad for me then, I was eating tranquillisers with sausage and bacon the way you'd serve fried eggs – and why not? At least in the Kesh I wouldn't expect him *dead*, I mean, not dead without some class of publicity, political opportunity. He could have been on the Hunger Strike, but thank God, no: I never had to face that horror, personal horror, *prolongation* of personal horror. Any better, though, to realise he was OUT, and at large; hunted, hounded! Where was he? *And I'm never told* – I couldn't sleep but I'd dream of him knocking and crying at my window in a storm of sleet and rain, his lips and nose all out of shape where he pressed them to the streaming glass, and how could I let him in, when I'd touts in the house and black bastards in the garden-shed, a pig-weasel with a grey tache digging up my kitchen floor and spirting Ginsberg bloody-at-me out of his arsehole? You'd say I should be glad of the escape, proud, a blow for freedom and against the Brits; and it was of course, and *I* was. With my good judgement all shot to pieces, and the transcripts lo-and-behold grinning up at the filthy buggers out of two pounds five ounces of health-conscious stoneground wholemeal.'

She sat silent for so long that Clay thought the interview was over. She switched off the tape-recorder, and then he was sure it was. Her pasty features were glaucous with tears, but if she did not sob aloud it was not for him to mention it. Neither of the others moved or said anything; so he sat there and kept his own silence.

Attracta looked from Clay to Bríd, and then from Bríd to Clay; her expression was contemptuous. 'I'd say that was enough for one lunch-time, but I wonder is it enough for Mr Clay? Sure you didn't come all this way from London just to watch a woman's grief, did you? If you did, you've done it briskly, and now you can go home. Write a sob-story; but what's the point?'

Bríd gave her head an angry jerk, ridding herself of her tears as a dog might shake its body after a soaking in a stream. 'The point is,' she said, 'Attracta; he came to make connections: he's just begun to make them, so shut up. Don't fuss about *me*, girl. Something useful's going on here, and if that rag of yours had been first with it and sent you to do the talking I'd have still have had the grief, sure I would, at this point; you could have blamed your own self instead of laying it all on a Brit.' Attracta was abashed.

'Okay, Mr Clay,' continued Bríd, short and businesslike: 'Let's hear what you've connected.'

The tape was running again.

Clay too was immediately businesslike. 'Judy.'

Judy had not yet been mentioned: they looked at him in some surprise. He related the Carlotta episode: their eyes were held, wide open. 'This is no less confidential than anything *you've* put on that tape,' he said – as brusquely as he could, lacking his own equivocal gunman to lurk on the floor behind him and impress people: his professionalism had to serve instead. 'I don't want *Republican News* spreading it all about, please. I said I'd share: I meant share it when it develops, not blow it prematurely. Understood?'

Attracta, her nose out of joint, nodded sulky acquiescence.

'Right: so that's *my* connection. The Brits have produced Judy because something made them, quite suddenly. What? Only one thing, as I can see: the "Druid" out of the blue recalls the raid on Bríd's house. *Republican News* was published on a Friday. Advanced copies no doubt available to Brit Intelligence over here on the Thursday evening? Right: a quick phonecall to London, and Judy turns up in Muswell Hill the following morning. She was not very well briefed. They had her in place okay, laying a trail of hash and havoc in that part of the world for a few weeks (which I take it was her own self-indulgent choice of cover): but they didn't expect to have to use her, and they didn't quite know how she'd be used. By the time they needed to call her, the *Mirror* had talked about vice-girls and the *Sun* had promised its readers true romantic heartbreak and no one-night floozies. So they were forced to switch her image, right? Not too much, but just enough, before the *Mirror* filled its first two pages and the first two pages filled the telly. Battle-of-Britain schmaltz, as updated Malvinas-style for the full-frontal eighties, that's what the public wanted; and that's what they had to have. "We were like kids" on the one hand; "we forgot where we left our clothes" on the other. And of course she admitted to *porno*. Make sense?'

Bríd sat sneering, rabbit-lip up, eyes opaque and unreadable.

Attracta's eyes however, had a very strange glint in them, a sort of challenge, invitation? – Clay did not understand it. She said, 'Jaysus, what a cute little Brit it is, I could put him in a pie and eat him. But *connection*? I don't see it. For what does it all add up to? Take it in the order it happened. The Brits became worried because Taddy used poems against them, they saw it as a Provie strategy they could steal to their advantage, they tried the atmosphere of the idea in various nationalist houses, and – and found out it was no damn good?'

'We don't know that,' said Clay. 'We know only those houses where it *proved* to be no damn good, because the people told the paper about it. Anyone's guess how many others.'

She shrugged. 'Okay; good enough for them to think they might shift it to a different scale, and across the water among their own. So then? So they *what*? Faked verses to suit their purpose and planted them on a dead lance-corporal? A *non-sequitur* somewhere, but for my life I can't see where.'

'Can't you, girl? She can't.' Sudden spite note from Bríd as though her pain had not left her as fast as she wished to pretend, and now she would terminate the meeting. 'Then I'll give it her begod, I'll give it now, for I'm sick and tired of this hedging-and-ditching! And directly I've told you, I'm for the Armagh bus at Victoria Street. My wee son, don't you understand! He is seven years old and with his auntie, I swore to him I'd be home for his tea: if I'm not he'll think again that I'm dead or in gaol – night after night again wetting the bed and roaring! If you want to follow it up, then find your own way of doing it: I'd prefer you never did. There's nothing can be proved, and even if there was, you'd need to take your time. And even when you've taken it, what good'll it do any of us?' She stood and pulled her coat about her shoulders.

Her next remark was a curt throwaway, but it utterly startled Clay, and yet it was so obvious; why had he not expected it?

'The *non-sequitur* is simply this – nobody told either of you that Truethought's poem was Taddy Q's. I've guessed it ever since I read it, but I couldn't see how it was done. Now I know. And now I know it, I'm – what's the word? – *responsible*. Aye. Mother o' God I wish I wasn't.'

She switched off her tape-recorder, dropped it into her bag, walked to the door. Attracta followed; although surely she was no less astonished than Clay she was able to dart him another quite unusual glance, no, dammit, triumphant wink. 'You never thought I'd have found *this* for you,' said the wink as clear as daylight, 'so now how do you think you will thank me?'

Fergus put a hand to a chair-back, eased himself to his feet, slid into the chair, took a spoon and resumed his baked beans.

FOUR

Clay did not like Bríd Ní Gairmleadhaigh, and he was convinced she did not like him. She had made her huge assertion (out of malice – was it possible? – just to baffle him?), had flatly said it could not be proved, had apparently decided to walk away from it and leave it flying. Clay could not leave it flying. If the connection between 'The Peeler's Goat' and Truethought had occurred to no one but Ní Gairmleadhaigh, then the unpublished poems must be crucial, and he *had* to have sight of them. How to persuade her?

The eventual persuasion did not go so far as the sexual seduction of Bríd by Clay or Clay by Bríd. Alaric Houndsditch, in court, was indeed to allege otherwise; his hints would have been more forceful had his instructing solicitors made enquiries about Attracta.

For what could Clay do, but cultivate Attracta? In fact, he had no choice. She lay in wait for him on the stairs of Fergus's flat, and caught his hand into hers, quite shockingly intimate. 'You go back to Dublin, this afternoon's train. I'll be in the north another two days. I know the b-&-b where you're staying, I'll give you a ring as soon as I'm south again. She's very upset, but she and I can be great together, I'd say I can probably manage her.'

After that, they were necessarily close. He was careful about it, and so was she. She was not a high-profile member of the Republican Movement; of course the police (north and south) were aware of her, but regarded her as no more than, perhaps, a tea-making secretary; they did not have the resources to keep her continually under observation. They may or may not have noticed her meetings with Clay: if they did, they saw nothing of sufficient significance to report to London solicitors when the case was being prepared for the Ministry of Defence; when detectives' memories, notebooks, floppy-discs, were anxiously searched for clues as to who had been finding out what from whom over a period of several months.

Clay had no moral qualms about bed with an informant, if thus he could attain his investigative ends. He needed to ensure that Attracta would keep her bargain and not privately use what she learned of his enquiries to serve her own newspaper. Nonetheless he did not at first make up his mind to make love to her. He had been exclusively gay since his wife found him that time with the reggae musician from Brixton, long, lithe and languorous, a man like a shining salamander. The excuse that he was 'uncovering police participation in the over-the-river drugs trade' had been of no avail. 'That's no bloody reason why *he* should uncover your cock!' cried Jennifer, and ran tragically out of the house. Quite true, no reason at all. The fact was, Clay realised he preferred it; and thereafter continued to do so.

At first in Dublin he was nonplussed, as it became so very clear that Attracta not only fancied him but was determined to have him. She declared outright she felt a 'nauseated mischievous tingle' at the thought of laying a British agent, even if he were operating on the Irish Republican side of the argument, even if he were not so very British – even if he were gay (as he warned her, to deter her: but it only seemed to excite her and she asked him embarrassing questions).

Moreover, Clay's declared atheism was a mighty incentive for her, putting to flight at one stroke such an ambush of complexities: for she was, of course a Catholic, by upbringing if not current practice; and so were the men with whom she normally came into contact. Her relationships with them had always gone rotten, almost from the first meeting of eyes. Accumulated mutual guilts, inhibitory reflexes; not in the least relieved by her daily work for the movement, that fearsomely self-conscious political élite with its yearning for its own virtue, its hectic atmosphere of imminent martyrdom, its sense of public duty inevitably destined to be misunderstood by the public.

And yet she was a most bawdy young woman: it was just that nobody had ever given her the chance to discover the fact.

With Clay she was able to be recklessly libidinous: from which he too made a discovery; that he was after all as bisexual as he once thought he was, and that Jennifer should perhaps have hung about a little longer. To be actively *desired* was something of a new experience for him; in the upshot he submitted to it with a high conceit, and felt no need for anxiety as to whether it would last. On the whole, he thought it shouldn't; provided he could keep it going until his present work was completed. It certainly secured his control over the help she was giving him: was not that the main thing?

She lived in the southern part of Dublin, in a leafy Victorian street between Ranelagh and Donnybrook. There was one other flat in the house, and it was just about to be vacated. The tenant, a man called McKeon, was a friend of Attracta's, a camera operator, that same week on his way to Germany for a series of TV films about Irish Euro-emigrants, and happy to leave her the key – on condition (he was altogether strict about this) that she did not bring in any of her felon-setting Provos (by which he meant determined characters who did not care whom they got into trouble) and their dangerous paraphernalia. She assured him she would not: Clay's paraphernalia consisted only of a notebook, where his entries were invariably in a shorthand code of his own devising. Even if the Branch raided her place, they would hardly connect her with the smooth bald Brit upstairs.

So there they were, very snug.

And she had wheedled all the poems for him, from that arbitrary woman in Armagh. Her Aphrodite tribute to his unsuspected magnetism? Or was it just that she was as ambitious as he was? 'There's nothing can be proved' – Bríd's statement was a challenge to both of them.

Clay said suddenly, 'Why are we doing this?'

Attracta, in outraged surprise, sat up from underneath McKeon's vast duvet, straight-backed as a mermaid breaking a crest of the surf. All she could see of Clay was the crown of his head on the pillow-heap somewhere below her elbow alongside the roll of her right buttock; pink hemisphere of skull, straggly yellow fringe above his nape, like the tonsure of a debauched Boccaccio monk – he was talking, as it were, *away from her*, looking out at floor-level across McKeon's miscellaneous mats and rugs and the litter that covered them – foetid ashtrays, heel-tapped tumblers, a cast condom, a copy of *The Joy of Sex* smuggled in through the republic's censorship, scattered typescript, shed garments, shoes – toward McKeon's roaring gas-fire at full blast and well it needed to be – mid-Sunday afternoon, wind and rain surged upon Dublin with angry malice and arctic darkness, no better place than bed, and now the bloody man asked her *why*?

'I thought,' she replied (if a reply was in fact needed, she wasn't sure whether he had known she was awake), 'I thought we did it because we liked it, at least *I* like it, I liked you even, till you started to act like a rat.'

'What? When? Rat? Nonsense . . .' Indeed *he* may not have been totally awake when he first spoke: but now she distressed him and he heaved himself round toward her. The duvet slid sideways as duvets do, to make them aware of debilitating nudity and (despite the gas-fire) chill – impossible to quarrel until they were covered up again – they worked together for a few seconds refurbishing the bed. Then he said, 'Oh God, are you always so quick to mistake people?'

Of course she was, always; that was always her trouble: once again she mistook him. She thought he implied by 'mistake' that this entire McKeon place was a mistake, *her* mistake – bed and gas-fire, and all that had been going with it for the best part of a week. She flung herself away from him and disrupted the duvet once more.

He had to get up and make her a cup of coffee before he was finally able
to persuade her of what he had meant.

'Start again,' he said patiently, 'I said, "Why are we doing this?" I meant
reading and re-reading Biddy Grimes's typed transcripts. Because we get
no further forward. Right: I can well believe that Grimes believes that
Truethought was assembled from Quinn. She had *lived* with these verses,
in her bed, holding her son; for as long as she could read them and say them
over and over to herself, Quinn was not in a filthy gaol but there-and-then
as he had been, HERS!'

Attracta fought down an irrelevant temptation to ask, 'Are you MINE?'

He continued, not noticing the little gulp in her throat and the swift drop
of her eyelashes: 'So of course she is bound to recognise them when they
turn up distorted elsewhere. But when she says no one else will, by God I'm
afraid she's right. See how we've broken them down! no one single line,
hardly even a couple of words, are repeated by pseudo-Truethought
exactly as first written. Don't you accept what I mean? Her *subjective
conviction*: and it's very very far short of proof.'

'So we publish what we think we know, say *we* believe it, Biddy believes
it, does it not look at least likely? We'd go some small way, so, to
undermine the Brit media.'

'We could. We could ask that "Druid" man to assert how Edmind
Spenser constructed *Epithalamion* on the model of some bardic ode which
he stole from a hanged rebel in Youghal; but *undermine?* They'd bloody
laugh at us.'

'Not Youghal. Smerwick. In Smerwick poet Spenser ordered his
murders. Poet Ralegh as well.' He was astonished at her matter-of-fact
vehemence: it was as though she were complaining to a policeman that she
had not been mugged in O'Connell Street, but round the corner on the
Quays, would the *Gardaí* please get their fingers out and catch the little
gougers! He knew about the Smerwick Massacre, six hundred Spanish
invaders and their Irish auxiliaries and their priests and their women all
chopped down by Queen Elizabeth's colonials, it was mentioned in the
"Druid's" article, it happened four hundred years ago almost to the
twelvemonth: why, shit, it was further back than Cromwell . . .

He supposed she had particular cause for finding it so contemporary. She
had: 'Wasn't I born within two miles of the killing-place? The Golden Fort
on the golden sand, you can still see the humps of its ramparts, between
green hills and a shipwreck ocean. I've sat there in my swimsuit on a hot
day of summer, swirls of mist came in from the sea, and would you believe
me? I heard screaming; shouting in English, screaming in Irish, hundreds
of voices crying out prayers in Latin and Spanish. For as long as ten minutes
I heard them. And *I know*.'

'Is that why you joined *Sinn Féin*?'

'If it was, 'twas eedjit romantic. I hope I've better purposes than that.' But she *was* idiot romantic: it pleased him, because he was not. His body wished once more to rejoice itself in hers, her glistening fronds of black hair, her taut tawny skin; but the nag of his mind was calling it to order, urging his hand out to take up a typescript.

'An example!' he said forcefully, he was resolute, he compelled himself. 'Just see what we're up against. Ó Cuinn wrote to Ní Gairmleadhaigh a love-rhyme in Irish. I've pencilled-in the English you gave me. He's on about her desolation when he left home to go to Crossmaglen for some job he wouldn't tell her of: she knew he was to meet a man with the gelignite, she knew he was afraid she'd never see him again.'

Wild mother of Liam my son, I love you like a man out of his wits
with anger at your anger that I travel the roads this night.
I know you have the right of it. I am a murderer in good standing
and I have the right of it too. Even though it is yourself (as well as the
            enemy)
that I murder; yourself and our small Liam,
accommodate my knowledge of your knowledge: and forgive.
Such a short ride to the cross, lovely white town made hideous
by strong strangers who befoul it with ordure of their khaki;
so short I will have reached it before you have turned in our half-
            empty bed
for second ease of sleep after your first tossing restlessness.
Then sleep, if you can, dear fire-headed Macha's daughter,
wrap the young man well into your grasp
who is not there, but will be: desire him there, he *is*.
No more to say: I have to go: last word upon paper, I'm gone.

            (*As I remember it from this prison:*
            two years ago in that house
            when I did not have the time or peace of mind to write it.)

'Ní Gairmleadhaigh says, and you say: no substantive change from *that* to *this* – ' He quoted the Truethought lines about King's Cross and the Catterick train. 'From one language to another, from guerrilla volunteer with his own house and a faithful mistress, to crop-headed wage-soldier between barracks and camp who must rummage his bints where he finds them, boozers' backyards and all of that? But it's the language itself, the identities themselves, that *are* the substantive change! Isn't that what poetry's for – to assert individual identity through language? I simply say what will be said.'

Attracta recollected some such definition from a literature lecturer at Galway University; she'd thought it a bit of a cop-out and still did. But she was also deeply moved by the 'wild mother' verses and not at all impressed by the Catterick piece: one-night stands disgusted her. If for Clay at this moment she was a 'one-night' (or at any rate a 'one-week'), then sure he could argue that the two pieces of writing had an equal but different inspiration. *She* could see only a strong poem of forlorn fidelity cynically parodied to make a girl-he-left-behind-him cliché – *Farewell my lovely*, indeed! Just the class of thing she could look to receive from Clay once he'd got himself back into England. But she must not hamper this crucial discussion with damned doubts of her lover's sincerity – she'd made the first pass, what else to expect? Only herself to blame; and the job had to be finished.

High time to leave poignancies alone, shift ground to a less painful area. Be more objective! select another two items, neither of which appealed to her. Pseudo-Truethought's blotch of smut about the 'backyard of the boozer' had a whole rake of imagery that *must* be directly lifted from a violent little satire by Quinn.

Written in English, the latter had never appeared in *AP/RN* but was included in a black-economy ballad tape widely circulated among Republicans and sung in their more macho clubs. Mere fiction of wish-fulfilment; hackwork, it could be called; but its raucous swing had been of value in the dark year of the Hunger Strike, when the nationalist ghettos day after day had gloom enough in all conscience.

The air was 'The Spanish Lady':

As I went down through Armagh city
Just at the hour of half-past three
What should I see but a bould Brit soljer
With his trousies down about his knees?
All in the rain so cold and early
And round at the rear of the public jakes
He'd this stout young screw of the queen's own prison
And her skirt was half-way up her back.
Whack fol the too-ra too-ra laddy
Whack fol the too-ra loo-ra lay!

'Stand where you are,' I told him softly,
'Stand where you are and don't dare twitch;
I've an Armalite with a full magazine, boy,

Ready to empty into your breech.'
I gently let him turn toward me,
He begged me allow him pull up his clothes:
What he couldn't get in he had to leave outa them,
Oh what a sight for the *News o 'the World!*

'Oh cunning young Fenian,' cried his lady,
'Terrible Teague, oh please forgive!
I never did more than do my duty,
All the girls in gaol I tried to love.'
Sweet deceiver, but who'd believe her?
I threw her a cig and away she flew:
In all my life I ne'er did spy
A maid so shy as the Armagh screw . . .

– and then several more stanzas, in the course of which the escaping
prison-officer is intercepted by a crowd of her recently released charges.
Vengeful young women, all a-cackle with pitiless laughter, their past
sufferings at her hands were described at some length. The strip-search had
been her particular pleasure, and the song told how appropriately they
repaid it.

Clay found it a brutal tale; and told Attracta so, instead of taking her
point about similarities with pseudo-Truethought's. 'What did our Biddy
think of it when first it was sent to her? Proud of it, was she?'

'She was in the gaol herself one time: she's no tenderness for the screws.
And satire has a right to be hurtful. True, there *is* a class of sexual violence
there, true. Any worse than in the strip-searching? Dare you tell me, any
worse?' Her voice rose.

'Eye for an eye? Rape cancels out rape? No: it won't do.'

She tried to be honest. 'The paper wouldn't print it, so. We needed
support from the middle-class in the Twenty-six Counties (for God's sake!)
for the Hunger Strike campaign. It was feared the poem would turn 'em off.
It would of course . . .' Having admitted this she could not leave it alone;
she tried to justify the ballad on literary grounds, declaring that it proposed
a significant negative image of hierarchised authority, demystification of
the queen's uniform and so forth. Galway's English Faculty for a moment
had hold of her tongue: she stammered and broke angrily free of it: 'Quinn
was on the blanket – have you forgotten? – when he wrote this! Beset by
uniforms, naked himself for months and years because he *refused* their
bloody uniform! And he lived in his own shit and so did the women in
Armagh! Jesus-sake, what kind of a poem d'you expect to come outa *that*?
We never claimed the man was Gandhi!'

Which had little to do with the Truethought question. Clay dragged her back to it, insisting that public exposure of persons' intimacies during the sex-act had for thousands of years been a staple of rough comedy, not surprising two authors should hit on it contemporaneously, both of them, why not? might be plagiarising Homer. He was learned about Hephaistos and Ares, and the net over Aphrodite's bed. 'I simply say what will be said.'

She sat and brooded (upon the bitter ethics of polemical verse, upon the last few days' light-hearted exposure of her own intimacies), arms tight about her chest, shoulders bowed, McKeon's duvet wrapped most carefully to conceal her. No more of her could be seen than hooded eyes that accused him without needing to look at him and sharp nose pointing away in the direction of the fireplace.

'Even so,' she said morosely, 'a man's poem, no doubt of it. He had a damned intruding nerve to interpret the Revenge of the Women.'

They could not sulk so for ever; they got dressed with very few words and sat awkwardly down in front of McKeon's telly, professing professional interest in the early-evening news.

Neither had bothered to look at the Sunday papers, so both were surprised to find yet another SAS shoot-to-kill outrage had taken place north of the border late on the previous day. The young man assassinated appeared to be no sort of terrorist whatever, but he never had the chance to say so; he was trapped between an unmarked car and a UDR road-block while driving from one Fermanagh village to another; no less than thirty-two bullets were put into him. A supercilious Englishman, politician from the Northern Ireland Secretariat, evaded questions and told obvious lies with the utmost candour: a glib Irishman, minister of the Dublin government, evaded questions but 'expressed concern' with the utmost ambivalence.

'Wouldn't you think,' Attracta said, ' that they'd know how false they sound?'

'They do know. They don't care. They can't be proved wrong until they're long out of office; and then it doesn't matter. Not to them, at any rate. That's why we *must* prove the Truethought deception as soon as we damn well can. Let's face it, and face it today: it can't be done by Lit Crit. Look how we've been trying, we don't even agree one with the other.'

'We don't indeed.' She was utterly scornful, of him, of herself. The more so because her afterthoughts upon the meaning of *The Armagh Screw* and the immediate impact of the liars on television had led her into a train of reflection she did not at all care to be following. Gradually, the TV news now replaced by some round-eyed fool who whooped and hooted over the

quiz-game he was in charge of, she began to feel sufficiently lonely to need
to talk to Clay about it.

'And when we do prove it, *if* we prove it, who's going to take it up?'

He replied with irritation: 'To start with, *Republican News.* I have
promised: I give you the story. Simultaneous with the *New Statesman* across
the water; but *NS* are more sceptical, they'll demand better chapter-and-
verse, I'd guess, than *AP/RN*. If they're difficult about it – *Socialist Worker*.
I'm not a party-member any longer, but I think they'd take an article. I told
you before, so why d'you ask?'

'We've gone on and bloody on poking and prodding at specific images,
fiddling little corners of meaning. The one thing we *haven't* argued is – is –
is what in the name of God is Quinn's poetry all about?'

She had only just realised the shape of her dilemma; she explained it in a
choking voice. How the published 'Peeler's Goats' had all been Celebra-
tions of Republicans in Struggle against Imperialism amidst Intolerable
Handicaps. (She *ranted* for several minutes as though Clay had never heard
of such a thing as a 32-county Irish Socialist Republic and the long and
filthy war to obtain it; then she bethought herself and continued quietly.)
How from these poems pseudo-Truethought stole his most 'positive' lines
and stanzas, his Celebration of the British Army in Struggle against
Terrorism amidst Intolerable Handicaps.

How the *handicaps* differed in detail but were the irreducible core of both
sets of verses; the emotions derived from them were very nearly exactly
the same; and as acceptable to *Sun* or *Telegraph* as they had been to
Republican News. 'Our brave lads', the chief burden of the song.

Whereas the *other* poems of Taddy Q, written solely, as Bríd had said, for
her own beloved self and in some cases for wee Liam – while they did not
directly contradict the public ones, they so dodgily displayed the tormented
contradictions within the mind of their author as to be worse than useless
to an insurrectionary party journal.

Pseudo-Truethought had found them of use: and here was the crucial
point. 'Strongly-defined stoical element'? 'Cobbett and Orwell'? *They sent
you out, you bastard?* – were not those angry lines an overt abbreviation,
even Clay had conceded it, of one of Quinn's most frustrated outbursts? In
translation:

Under orders which he cannot ignore, the despised Saxon ruffian
creeps green meadows, leafy lanes. (With bones watery as his leaking
piss
but his gun-barrel copulative-rigid.)
My nasty task is sluice him out of them:

in my own wetted pants, and under orders which I cannot ignore
from a ruffian I despise.
The grass grows there, spring and summer, whether or no I obey.
Good that the grass be let live longer
than us good men, the creeping killers?

'I'll put it briefly,' Attracta concluded. 'Internationally the Brits need
help with their democratic credentials; so they can afford a spice of
pacifism, a small pepper of disloyalty, cowardice, genuine revulsion at
Cain-against-Abel: we can't.'

Clay was shocked. 'Surely *that* "in the name of God is what Quinn's
poetry is all about" – a brave man with a mind of his own whose despair is
as fierce as his courage? If you can't afford that, you can't afford a free
country.'

She clamped her teeth on her cigarette so hard she bit off the filter-tip.
'What else am I trying to tell you? Sure there's more than myself at the
paper'd be only too glad to print all of Ó Cuinn, let him be read for what he
is. We do like to think we make an enlightened and enlightening weekly.
But we're no different from the rest of the press, political or commercial,
we've a proprietorial junta and a constituency of readers, and I know we'll
be in trouble with both. We'll be called upon to *lose* maybe half of the
poems. *Under orders*, take an example! *from a ruffian I despise* – don't think
no one'll know the name of the man who's meant. He'll not sue us for libel,
but . . . let's just say, he's of some importance; he's also in daily danger; if
he doesn't want it published, it won't be. That leaves only your English
papers to furnish the full argument. As it is, I'd to put ropes to Bríd to bring
her to *you*, and then only because you were working through *Republican
News*. She's well able to deny everything she's told you; and if you're to
hawk it around nowhere but England, she *will*. She left that tape with
Fergus. He'll erase it as soon as she asks him and clear her name from all of
it. He's an old friend of Taddy's, he helped her a lot when Taddy was killed.'

She paused, and then repeated: 'When Taddy was killed. Rumours
spread everywhere that his own people executed him; and d'you know,
they were believed? Fergus ensured denial, ensured an IRA funeral. But
once it had been said, it was said for ever, not forgotten. Last week I
persuaded Biddy to let a few things loose, but now it all comes back to her.'

Herself and Clay were one flesh.

Quinn and Grimes had been that and more: one spirit as well. Or so
Quinn's poems insisted (yet written far away from Grimes, from a brutally
wilful *abandonment* of Grimes, almost?); so, too, Grimes insisted, by her
rigorous guardianship of the poems (yet what had she really thought of

them when first she received them and read them, bed to be empty, arms empty, for God knew how many years?).

However it may have been, every line of those poems – insofar as they were love-poems – compelled Attracta to odious comparison. And moreover, very oddly for a political young woman, she was beginning to resent the exclusively political verses.

Clay asked her, 'So what's to be done?' He meant, about Bríd and the poems, nothing else.

'You tell me. You claim to be bisexual. If *this* one don't satisfy, rub yourself up against *that*. But what *that* ought to be . . . is for you to discover: I give up.'

She was utterly depressed, and he feared she would burst into tears. She left him then: to let him think about it further. Which he did; McKeon's cassette-recorder playing Elvis at the top of its voice, so much noise that in the middle of it he would be bound to find peace-and-quiet.

Her crack about him being bisexual. Right: so he was. And so he must move accordingly: turn the action, as it were, front-to-back. He now knew *what* had been done. Next, to find *how*; and to hope that maybe the discoveries would turn out a little more definitive. Forget Bríd and Quinn. He'd travelled away from them, the wrong direction. Reverse, then; pass them and leave them.

Don't examine any longer the end-product of a dirty trick and hope for clues as to who devised it. Rather re-examine all the dirty-tricks contacts he'd made through the past few years; ask, who among these might know who could have set this up?

That meant eventually London, and all his floppy-discs. But he'd have to prepare for it. He needed data, Irish data: before he left Ireland, he could get it. There was a man on the *Irish Times* who wrote intriguing articles: he covered the British army, at their Lisburn HQ. Right. Then another man in Belfast who'd had pieces in the *NS* and used to be a radical student at Queen's University. He knew both of them slightly. Both would be suspicious of him. 'Here's the bloody Muddy,' they'd say, 'on his rounds. Take care how we confide in him; he'll have us done under Official Secrets if he's given so much as a thumbnail.'

So: not to tell either of them why he wanted their brains picked; it would be difficult, they were dead sharp.

At all events, leave Dublin, go north, get them somehow to talk to him, talk to anyone else they were able to suggest, then take what they told him to London; and *analyse*.

So what about Attracta?

Start-to-finish, it had lasted eight days with her. Such lengthy anatomi-
cal forays, so little analytical loot, was he any further forward than before
she demanded his body?

If *Republican News* was going to fail her, then she was going to fail Clay, no
question. Best then to anticipate, and continue his work without. Besides,
their love-making had become neurotic. He felt he could not give it up: so
he *had* to give it up. An issue of self-respect.

Ah but.

Let's be adult. Let's give each other our needful freedom, independence,
each to our own concerns. To which end, a prolonged goodbye (not so
much *leb wohl* as *auf Wiederseh'n*, and why not?) would be something of an
agreeable investment. He'd go down now and tap on her door and entice
her up again, if he could, to prepare her for it. She might not mind.

So much for Sunday, early evening.

Thursday, early morning, he took the train again to Belfast.

FIVE

We need not follow Clay's subsequent investigation step by elaborate step. There were no episodes of violent action, nor (after Attracta) amorous innovation. He travelled Britain and Ireland without difficulties with the police; checked old contacts, made new ones, sucked as much from them as he could; spent hundreds of pounds upon overseas telephone calls (with experienced precautions against inevitable bugging); took planes to miscellaneous foreign destinations; put all his gathered fragments onto his computer and switched them about interminably; in short, he fitted together his jigsaw.

He was careful to bear in mind the recent notorious state trial of three fellow journalists in his own line of the business: they were accused of having infringed the Official Secrets Act by collecting and collating data from 'the public domain' and thence deducing far more about NATO Signals Intelligence than the authorities wished known. *Assembling pieces of jigsaw* was defined, by prosecutor and by anonymous secret-service witnesses, as in itself a crime. The jury thought otherwise: but upon the next occasion, maybe not?

He must be therefore most wary; take time; take time off, to meditate after each discovery; sharp eye always open for disinformation laid to destroy him – (his threatening vision and he never lost it: Carlotta in Notting Hill with the tip of one breast peeping out of her torn dress, weeping so winningly, so very very nearly bringing his arms around her shoulders and his mouth down onto her trembling lips) – he *smelt* disinformation in almost everything he found, until more than once he was on the point of abandoning the whole effort. Yet he could not disbelieve what he had checked and re-checked.

He was quite sure he had identified the creation of 'Truethought', in no widely incredible breakthrough but as the long-delayed culmination of immensely tedious process – he just had to be right, surely?

Every other day he was quite sure he was wrong; but the pieces of the jigsaw still came into his hand, and still he kept fitting them together.

One event, near the beginning, that *could* be called a breakthrough: a drunken night out with a disgraced ex-major of the Intelligence Corps.

Clay was put onto this man by his contact at the *Irish Times*, who told him casually that there had been some sort of scandal (apparently about officers' batmen moonlighting as rent-boys) in the Lisburn HQ, and that the major had 'gone a small piece of the road with it, at least to the extent of Conduct Unbecoming a Queen-of-England's Off'n'Gent.' He was now retired: 'Face-saving alternative to court-martial. Your peace-keepers in the north save more faces than lives, Muddy, but you know that of course.' He was thought to have held an admin post of a sort at Lisburn; it was not known whether he would have had any access to real secrets; but if Muddy wished to follow it up, the fellow was last heard of in Leeds in some grotty civilian job, having spread it about that the rent-boy affair was only a pretext to get rid of him. The *Irish Times* for a while showed interest but decided the story had to be a cul-de-sac; the major had dirtied his own record, was trying to find excuses, and that was all.

Clay hung about Leeds until he was able to strike up an accidental acquaintance with the ex-major in a saloon bar. He had to buy him countless drinks and listen for a great length of time to all the details of the grotty job before anything to Clay's purpose hiccoughed up through the broken torrent of repetitive narrative.

The unhappy man was now reduced to sifting coupons sent in, via a PO box number, for dubious competitions run by a publicity agency on behalf of local shops and newspapers – *Giant Bumper Prizes, up to £10,000!* He worked from his bedsitter and the pay was scandalously small even for a man already touched by scandal. He exhaustively explained the competition scheme to Clay, outlining the impossibility of anyone actually winning more than £27.54 (he had worked that out on a pocket calculator), and then he explained it again in case Clay had missed some cardinal point, and then he gave Clay a sort of viva-voce examination on the subject to make sure he had assimilated the full horror of it.

'Jew-boy firm, I'm afraid to say, chappie; or Pakis, or Armenians or Turks, don't actually know, never met the principals; I *do* know they're too bloody mean even to computerise; damned tacky situation. But what would you? I'm clapped-out. *Why* am I clapped-out? What profession are you in, chappie? Did you say you were s'licitor? S'licitors no damn good, been the rounds of the buggers already, washout. Fact is, I'm a whatnot, a scrapegoat, a – scrape? Shape? Ah, scape! A bloody goatscape. Yes I will have 'nother. Cheers. Did I totally explain this question of the cons'lationprize – ?'

Clay gradually steered him back on course.

'Still, y'see, I suit the little greasers, only too happy to have me.' He meandered on, chewing the cud of his employers' obliquity. 'They know where I come from. Dagoes they may be, but no worse than Command

Staff. Verb sap, *I've* seen it. "No such file exists, Major Haythornthwaite, you have seen no such a file dammit." Floppy-disc was on me desk for a week. Buggers tell me I never saw it. Wordtothewise, chappie; I didn't. Of course it's a comedown, got to be, from techno . . . techlon . . . techno-lonoligicality to Messrs Balchis Bros' cardboard folders, but. But it's alla samething, chappie: Rochdale Coupons, Wharfedale ditto, Humberside, *here!* Bags of bumf, collate, check, refer upwards for implementation. Londond'rry District PIRA suspects, East bloody Belfast UDA contacts, Larne/Ballymena RUC Liaison, Terrible Beauty Operatives, *there!* Bags of software, CCRU for implementation. Allasamething an' Haythornthwaite knows how to handle it! Get the point, chappie, do you?'

'Terrible Beauty? Don't follow.'

'No you wouldn't, you're only s'licitor. Quotation from the poets, chappie, the Paddy Poets; I looked it up. You ever been to Grimethorpe? A Terrible Beauty is Born in Grimethorpe. Filthy hole. Full of reds. In with the PIRA, wouldn't wonder. Wordtothewise, mustn't say so! Mustn't say anything about Terrible Beauty neither, no. I may be Psych'log'clly Incomp . . . In . . . Incomp't'nt but by Christ I'm bloody loyal! 'Fficial Secrets, sworn and signed.'

Major Haythornthwaite hazily tapped his crow-beak of a nose above a tache like a collier's thumbprint, winked an eye behind his half-moon lenses, accepted the offer of another drink.

'Cheers.' He had become unnerved, apparently, while Clay was at the bar; his tone was now apprehensive. 'Just as well to tell you, chappie, nothing at all that I said was ever said.'

He dropped his voice furtively. 'Damned unsafe, was then, is now. *I* never put it on me desk. Stoke Poges's fault, from Stat-tist-tics Branch.' (He worked his way beautifully round the syllables of 'Statistics'.) 'Was Poges on the carpet? He was not. My mistake, I asked 'em *why* not. One thing to see what you mustn't see 'cos it's not there; quitenotherthing to ask, when *they're* doing the telling. Draws attention, dam bad form. So they fitted me up with a crowd of filthy queers and booted me. Had to, y'see, one more question and I'd know too much: oh God they needn't have worried, I'm as loyal as the Duke of York.' He sobbed: and that was the end of his disclosures.

To Clay's hints that he should continue, he said only: 'Signed and sworn, chappie, 'fficialsecret, you're s'licitor, you oughterknow.'

Then suddenly he said, 'God's teeth, I don't like you. You're a Jew-boy yourself, I can tell by your accent, like all the useless lawyers in Leeds: washout.' And then he spied a drowsy-eyed youth with gilded hair, leather jacket, gleaming studs. He wove his way over to him, abused him for a filthy queer, apologised with tears and accompanied him out of the bar.

Would he have accompanied Clay if Clay had seemed to want it? No; for the boy with the studs was lovely to look at, of sweet and good-natured countenance underneath the flash-harry surface, it was a poem to watch him walk. The major, decayed or not, kept to his own demanding standards.

But the Terrible Beauty theme was already exhausted. Although the major may have known more than he told, he was very frightened: cornered, he would certainly swear there was indeed 'no such a file'.

Which left Clay with a rocky connection between Grimethorpe and a phrase from Yeats. A file of that title, sufficiently top secret to put an officer 'on the carpet' for unauthorised access? Sufficiently weird in content to allow the officer to think (or at any rate *claim*) he was being railroaded by spooks when he got onto a far nastier carpet over something totally different? Clay doubted there'd been any 'fitting up'. You'd only to look at Haythornthwaite to see the sort of trouble he'd fall into unaided. And if they really feared his knowledge they'd hardly ship him out to shoot his mouth off to all-and-sundry through the pothouses of Leeds.

But the major *had* found out something, perhaps more than his superiors suspected. He could not have predicted Grimethorpe, which was dependent upon Truethought, who had died only three or four months ago. So he had seen enough in the file to furnish an accurate guess as soon as Grimethorpe came into the news?

'Terrible Beauty': presumably an operational code-name. *The* operational code-name? At least it was a springboard for Clay's next set of enquiries. He checked dates in his notebook, which was already filling up: the rent-boy scandal belonged after the dharma-pig arrived in Bríd's house but before the next batch of searchers discovered the Q-poems. Useful to know; for what it was worth.

(Who, by the way, was Stoke Poges? Make a cryptic note – *Gray's Elegy? Computer-search, soonest.*)

He decided he'd not bother Haythornthwaite again, the poor man was too fragile and likely to run straight to the spooks. But there were other contacts for Clay to explore. Now he had a code-name to offer them, they might very well hook things onto it for him.

SIX

Clay's eventual narrative of *Operation Terrible Beauty* was in part put together from all sorts of informants, induced to talk by old acquaintance-ship, you-scratch-my-back-I'll-scratch-yours, flattery, bribery, or threats of exposure falling not far short of outright blackmail; in part from documentary sources, many of them classified, only accessible through lavish deployment of the same style of cunning.

He had reconstructed the hidden biographies of three ominous individuals. Unveiling these people limb by limb, he felt at times he could hear their voices, telling him – no, *singing* to him, over and over again – some terrible inaudible secret that would explain, if only he could distinguish the syllables, every enigma of forty years of otherwise unaccountable cultural history. What follows is a summary of his findings; necessarily a fiction, for he was never able to match it against those adversarial standards of British justice which alone are permitted to define in public life the boundaries of lies and truth.

> The girl 'Judy' was his starting-point: only through her was he able to discover the other two, indeed to discover that there were a couple of others to be hunted out and brought into view.
>
> He took the risk of seeking a lead from the politician whom she had tried (as Carlotta) to destabilise. As soon as her name was spoken, the man proved savage and revelatory – 'Emphatically off the record, unattributable, d'you hear!' – he strode up and down vituperating her, he told Clay a great deal of how he came to meet her, among what ignominious company, to what drastic hurt to his marriage, and with what advantage to his enemies, and so on and so (paranoiacally) forth. By his own estimate his enemies were numerous enough to provide lead after lead, really far too many, most of them useless, two or three unexpectedly valuable.
>
> Clay then took cross-bearings with a friend on the Daily Mirror and another who did research for TV-am. He also went to Muswell Hill and prowled around for a day or two. After that he went to the registries of births and deaths, he went to Somerset, he went to Scotland, he paid a visit to the Continent. He spent quite a time in Birmingham. He drove around the upper reaches of the Thames Valley and the hills of South Wales after components of the vagabond 'Peace Convoy' (in the course of which a farmer set dogs on him and he retired for a week to hospital).

As soon as he had gathered a fair outline of 'Judy', he computerised a
chronological order, continually making notes for further cross-reference,
although at this stage of his enquiry he kept all of these conscientiously tentative.
He was going back and back again in order once more to come forward. Major
Haythornthwaite was already in the picture: a fixed point that would have to be
returned to (as also Bríd's 'dharma-pig'), but only after circumambulation of
vast extent and apparent irrelevance. Clay was worried by the number of
'perhapses', 'possiblies', 'highly-likelies', 'it-does-look-as-thoughs', that
cropped up in his print-offs; he got rid of as many as he could, but a selection of
'perhapses' remained stubbornly undissolved. He decided in the end to be bold,
to let them in fact shape his narrative: more honest – so he hoped – and therefore
more compelling.

Going back, to come forward: 1949. Birth, not of 'Judy' herself, but her
mother. In Germany, near Cologne, in a house commandeered by the
occupying powers from its original Nazi owners. *Her* mother was Indo-
Chinese. Who was the father?

First *Perhaps*. The father was a British official of the Allied Control
Commission; a Captain Rance, no longer in uniform, a junior don from
Oxford, temporarily advising the Germans upon how to denazify and
rehabilitate their advanced education in the midst of post-war ruin.

He had been trawling the displaced persons' camps for academic
individuals with *bona-fide* democratic credentials, who might be salvaged
and given posts in universities and secondary schools. The Indo-Chinese
woman was not academic, neither did she speak German; but she was
desperate to emerge into civilised life, whomever she might sleep with to
get there.

Her history was obscure, and (as so often in such places at such a time)
not quite explicable. Rance was given to understand that she had come to
Marseilles on a neutral (Argentinian) ship, a stowaway refugee from the
Japanese absorption of her homeland. It was not clear what she had done
to be so frightened of the Japanese, but some sort of sexual vengeance
seemed to be indicated. After the occupation of the south of France by the
Germans, she was transported to the Rhineland, perhaps as a *Wehrmacht*
officer's mistress, perhaps as a conscript worker. The British army found
her close to death in a concentration camp and had no idea what to do with
her. Captain Rance had *his* idea: concubinage and domestic, all up and
down the British zone, until he realised she was pregnant.

Unable, or unwilling, to bring her into England, he somehow *did* fetch
her baby. Whether she asked him, or he stole it, is not material. She is
thought to have died shortly afterwards. Somehow he let the baby be

brought to Birmingham, eventually to the well-meaning but incompetent couple who adopted her there: a Mr and Mrs Herbert Flake. They called her Kitty, not knowing how her real mother had wished her named. They were incapable of understanding or influencing her.

Second *Perhaps*. A Dr Rance (who in 1965 gave a series of lectures at Birmingham University under the general title *Pop Art v. Top Art, a Pseudo-rivalry of Two Unmeanings*) was the same Rance, Kitty's father; and knew it. She did not, and neither did the Flakes.

Also in that city in 1965 was an unsavoury dwarfish priapus by the name of Martin Leo; by pseudonym, Big Chief Trotsky; by (temporary) calling, a 'performance poet'. He took a leading part in a 24-hour rock-rhythm-'n'-rhyme marathon, Brum's contribution to the Coming of the Age of Aquarius. Rance in his lectures had recommended this experience and was more or less a formal patron of it. Madly excited teenage girls pulled off their clothes and swarmed all over the stage and over the more charismatic of its male occupants. One such heedless chick was last seen being hoisted by young Leo aboard a mauve-and-yellow Volkswagen van, to speed out into the night with two guitarists, a drummer, six other female juveniles, and enough LSD to collapse the Bullring. She was Kitty, she was a free spirit, she had said goodbye to the Flakes for ever, and she did not give a damn.

Third *Perhaps*. Rance intended this to happen.

Kitty went to London with Martin and several of his associates and they all lived together in a filthy house, a commune of the sub-culture, at the north end of the Portobello Road. Enquiries being made by the police, Martin took her away to Swindon, and thence via Southampton to the West Country, changing his name, changing hers, playing his usual game of dossing, joint-rolling, incoherent 'creativity', along what had already become the usual drop-out route of crash-pads and foot-rot, sleeping-bags and psychedelic fuzz-evasion.

He put the seed of 'Judy' into her before the end of six weeks.

He was no longer with her when she gave birth to her baby girl (February 1966); an emergency caesarean in a Bristol hospital, after a panic-stricken call from a roadside phone-box near a rundown farmhouse in the Mendips. Three addled families of neo-peasants were devotedly and unwittingly neglecting goats there, starving poultry, stunting their own brood of children. These young people did not know who she was; she had arrived in their yard the day before with a haversack and a load of inconsistent but impressive talk about 'hidden forces' in the earth of Glastonbury and the 'womb-power' of the Cheddar caves. She went into labour almost at once: there was obviously something wrong: they could not deal with it. But they did do their busy best before they rang for help. Their 'creative responses to her nature-rhythms' had all but killed her on the spot, the ambulance crew said.

She told the hospital her name was Greenflower Dream. She called the baby Rainbow. After recovering from the operation she went back to the farmhouse. The local health services followed her up; only to find she and Rainbow had moved on.

In 1970 her current lover (a Gaelic-speaking traditional musician) found poor Greenflower dead of an overdose in his converted bus: they were camping miles from anywhere on Rannoch Muir in the Scots Highlands.

Rainbow was taken into care: a children's home near Fort William.

Greenflower's history was not difficult for Clay to search out. Her strongly-marked oriental beauty, her assertive enthusiastic personality, caused her to be well-remembered among hippy and peacenik survivors. The police, over a longer period, had failed to discover so much. They told the unhappy Flakes, distraught at the loss of their beloved child, that what had looked like an obvious trail turned out to lead nowhere and that was it.

Fourth *Perhaps*. The police bafflement was a lie. Someone with access to the highest official circles had put it about that 'security issues' were involved in Kitty's disappearance. The case, solved or not, was quietly closed: all reports of it were removed from the files.

By and by a plausible Dutchman, calling himself Jan Floss, arrived at Fort William and fetched Rainbow away. He said he was her father, once an avant-garde street-actor and now a minister of religion in Amsterdam, desperate to discover the daughter he had so shamelessly begotten during the 'years of his sin' in Britain. The phrase struck a chord with the devout Scots authorities; they asked very few questions. His documents were furnished through a highly respectable firm of Perth solicitors. Rainbow (at the age of seven) was taken to Holland.

Fifth *Perhaps*. Dr Rance, at that time on sabbatical at the University of Utrecht, was in some way responsible for the fraudulent documents.

Sixth *Perhaps*. The Jesus-gripped street-actor was Rance's son; born in Oxford in 1946, when Rance was known to have had a 'relationship' with Hendrickje Floss, an alcoholic Dutch historian at work upon a thesis about the drainage of the East Anglian fens. She failed to complete this because of her pregnancy, and because she became far too drunk; she lost her visitor's bursary at Somerville College; she went back home to Leyden; she was never heard of again.

Jan Floss (or Fooss, or Fluyssen, or van Fleyt) was only a clergyman when it suited him, when he needed the reversed collar to clinch an effective scam. Most of the time he was making a great deal of money in Amsterdam's red-light district. Various women in his service brought up Rainbow under conditions of moral nihilism that would have degraded the Borgias' Rome. By 1978 she was no longer a virgin. By 1980 she was notorious for her cunning, her hatred of men, her ability to dissemble, her taste for blackmail. A number of organisations, both criminal and political, sought employment of her talents.

In 1981 she was Carlotta, in London.

Seventh *Perhaps.* She had a controller, a ferociously anti-communist Czech émigré prepared to dangle (as it were) any number of human beings, no matter how pathetic, from his fingers – if thus he could help drag down *the miserable puppets of marxist totalitarianism.* By way of being a freelance, he executed commissions for reactionary European political groups, for the CIA, for a security department in Whitehall. He kept Rainbow docile by means of drugs when she did his bidding and physical violence when she did not.

Hints were dropped in the right places that she would make an ideal Judy for *Terrible Beauty,* if and when the incarnation was required. Military Intelligence (Northern Ireland) took her over from the Czech. She was not the most satisfactory acquisition. They began by doping her (and did not think to beat her up), so she wandered off and was only restored to the job after much expense and waste of time. And then she muddled her personae for the Muswell Hill/*Daily Mirror*/TV appearances.

Eighth *Perhaps*: and no more. She was the partially decomposed body found by picnickers in Ashdown Forest in 1987, strangled, clothes missing, features mutilated beyond recognition, fingertips cut off. Only clue to identity: the tattoo-mark underneath her pubic hair; no murderer would have found it unless he'd known of it already; a tiny green flower within the arc of what might have been meant for a rainbow.

The eighth *Perhaps* had not happened when Clay's report passed into the hands of Bríd Grimes's lawyers. They made expensive and time-consuming efforts to find Rainbow, but in vain; the defendants' representatives claimed loudly they had done likewise. So in the end, in the court, there they were, Lambert and Houndsditch, wigs on head and briefs in hand, the one trying to prove the girl a fraud and the other to insist she was genuine: and both of them unable to let the jury decide by the only true test, live inspection. Ms Lambert did call a Scotland Yard detective and examined him closely about the Ashdown Forest corpse. Despite all her probing, he refused to admit any definite identification. Cross-examined, he denied any *possible* identification. Another cock that wouldn't fight, in a case already brim-full of cowardly roosters. The judge made the best of his opportunity for sarcasm on behalf of the defendants.

> *Cross-references. From his findings upon Rainbow, Clay's research must extend to Rance, Martin Leo, the Dutchman, the Czech. The last two seemed only to have come into the affair at a late date and could be left on the long finger. Rance was a real problem, a vagueness, emerging from shadows and then again disappearing. And yet outside the specific case he was far from vague: quite the reverse, he was very well known; Clay at different times had read some of his books and heard more than one of his famous lectures. The man had actually pontificated upon television about Truethought: perhaps not coincidentally? Perhaps he was a key-figure? If so, best find out first if any more little threads could be followed up towards him. Try Leo.*
>
> *A clever guess: because in the end Clay came to know that Leo had been 'pseudo-Truethought'.*

> *How and why this exploitative mountebank should be the one who chose, or was chosen, to concoct such insidious poems (and on behalf of the very 'fuzz-system' he had done his best to outwit) made a long and difficult story, not to be explained until all of it proved explicable.*

Liverpool, 1942. Tallulah Leo, an ENSA artiste of questionable morals and a non-existent sense of responsibility, had a baby all of a sudden in a theatrical lodging-house. She called him 'Martin'. The same Martin? Not proven. But whether or no, he appeared to have been conceived during a garrison entertainment at Oswestry camp. For approximately three hours Tallulah had been 'close' to a young serjeant of the Army Education Corps who played a large part in organising the evening. She spent forty-five minutes of that space of time swinging her legs in the chorus upon stage while he stood in the wings and leered. After the show he took an hour and a half to thank her for her talents and to say good-night, somewhere in the dark between the camp auditorium and the guardroom.

Tallulah made an attempt to secure maintenance for her son from Second-Lieutenant Rance, still in the Education Corps and attached (following promotion) to the Eighth Army in North Africa and then Italy. He challenged her allegations of paternity. Through lawyers in England he caused her to admit that he was far from being the only possible father. Nevertheless, deductions from his pay were for a time passed on to her ('without prejudice'). He refused to correspond personally.

His gratuities ceased when he heard she had abandoned little Martin to a severe institution run by evangelical church-workers in Birkenhead. She

continued with her theatrical career, fetching the boy out of this
orphanage when he was fourteen. She then had him accompany her on
tour. Odd jobs were found for him about the theatres, none of which lasted
very long. She never told him exactly who his father might have been,
offering him at different times several different names, including General
Eisenhower, Tommy Handley and Knife Walley – a slippery fellow, tipster
and racecourse gangster, to be encountered at Aintree. She also mentioned
'something of an army schoolmaster, I think he was, dearie; so stupid of
me, I quite forget', a lukewarm social type that meant nothing to a young
boy who much preferred the glory or exciting sleaze of the other
possibilities.

In 1959 she had been at the gin in her dressing room between
performances at a Leicester theatre –

> *KNOCKITY KNOCK!*
> *The saucy show that was banned in Monkwearmouth!*
> *Nudest and rudest revue since RING-A-DING-DING!!*
> *ONE WEEK ONLY*

– she walked out onto the street to get a breath of air; a man shouted
'Watch it, you silly tart!'; she angrily watched *him* instead of the bus he had
seen coming; she died in hospital a week later. Martin at that time had
wandered back to Liverpool and was in business as a spiv's runner, in and
out of the docks for small smuggled goods and pilferage; and in and out of
the juvenile courts (although none of the charges proved serious). He was
acutely intelligent and picked up more than fragments of more than one
language upon the polyglot Mersey waterfront.

In 1960 a Martin Leo was conscripted for National Service, conning his
way into the Intelligence Corps by virtue of his linguistic quickness, quasi-
theatrical background, and quasi-criminal experience. He achieved two
stripes and then deserted.

He was in West Germany when he quit the army, and at once went out of
sight among the quasi-criminal quasi-theatrical bohemian sub-class of
post-war German anarchism. He shacked up with a young actress,
on-and-off adherent of a coarsely satirical 'underground' film-and-theatre
club in Munich. He and she explored the drugs scene and did deals with GIs
of the American garrison. But then he was approached by a persuasive
representative of the British secret service. This man made it clear that
Martin was marked as a deserter whose only hope of avoiding imprisonment in the glasshouse was to become an informant for MI whatever-it-
was.

The information wanted was against the American allies, and against

any British involvement in American racketeering, which by implication
led to involvement with Soviet-bloc espionage. Martin helped them,
without much in the way of solid results (except the unfortunate betrayal
of his actress and her confinement in a German gaol); until he began to be
seriously frightened by some of the very ruthless groups he was coming up
against in the central European underworld. He slipped away to the Irish
Republic, and thence into England, where he thought he had covered his
tracks.

An odd thing about his track-covering: he could never bear to dispense
altogether with the name 'Leo'. Perhaps it was all he had as an identity. For
he still used it as a Christian name, or suggested it by calling himself
'Tolstoy' or 'Bronstein' (even 'Trotsky', his poet-pseudonym), or 'Lyons',
or 'Cordelion'.

Throughout the tune-in turn-on impromptus of the later sixties he found
constant opportunity. He became a flower-power entrepreneur in many
legal and illegal ways. He was attached to (sometimes in control of)
alternative journals, alternative theatre groups, protest festivals, be-ins,
love-ins, fuck-ins, smoke-ins, acid-highs, pop-and-rock promotions,
Carnaby Street tat-shops. He shifted from anarcho-aesthetics toward
harder leftist politics as the situation shifted: it was the era of the Paris
revolt and the anti-Vietnam War movement.

He tried to join the International Socialists and the Socialist Labour
League. They told him to bugger off. He hung about the Spartacus League
and made himself useful with international contacts.

Just about the time (1970) that Greenflower Dawn lay dying in the back
of a beat-up bus in Scotland, Martin Leo went to Belfast and Derry. Thence
he wrote a series of hippy-style articles for an underground paper called
Sukkit. His theme was the essential psychedelia of the urban guerrilla,
whom he romanticised far beyond possibility of self-recognition by the
beleaguered council-house residents of the Bogside or Ardoyne. The
Official IRA thought he was an agent-provocateur (which in fact he was
not); they tipped off the RUC about him, just to see what would happen.

He was stopped by detectives at Belfast docks while about to board the
Liverpool ferry. He carried nothing incriminating. But his appearance was
suspicious: short, nervy, unhealthy-looking, with shoulder-length dark
hair, Zapata moustache, unduly large army-surplus parka, peaked cap like
a tugboat skipper's – an overall brigandish flavour, as of Ancient Pistol
following the column. Enough to infuriate any police anywhere at first
sight; how much more so when they were Protestant Ulstermen? They
held onto him pending further enquiries.

He had given them the name of Lo (or Leonard) Tino. They checked this through numerous files and through the new computer networks that were just then being established for counter-insurgency purposes. Somewhere along the name's archival progress 'Leo' was disconnected from Leonard and 'Mar' was experimentally added to Tino. It was put to him he was Martin Leo, it was put to him he was an army deserter, the military police were brought in to question him further, military intelligence were asked for advice. He could probably have brazened it all out if he had had the courage: but he collapsed, confessed, begged for another try at a deal (as previously in Germany), offered copious information about his contacts in the north of Ireland; and all to no avail.

Someone was determined to tear his balls off.

They forcibly re-incorporated him into the army, court-martialled him, sent him to military imprisonment. He spent a horrifying month in the glasshouse and nearly died (it seemed to him) from hard treatment. It seemed to him this treatment was specifically and personally directed; an impression confirmed when a colonel in mufti came to see him one day, to present exactly the sort of deal Martin had begged for in vain at the time of his arrest.

Concluding that the 'someone' had kept tabs upon Martin over very many years, Clay tapped in, on his word-processor:

RANCE?

– erased it, tapped it in again, added:

DON'T GO WILD!

ALL SORTS OF BLOODY MEN MUST HAVE HAD THEIR EYE ON HIM ALL THE TIME?

—and left it for further consideration. A marginal point of interest. Not essential to his argument that the supposition be formally asserted. But who at this stage could be sure of marginality? And then again, far from marginal, but all a-glow there, vivid green, dead-centre on his VDU:

M.L's FATHER, G'F.D's FATHER = R'B's GRANDFATHER – *BOTH SIDES!*

WHAT THE HELL *WAS* THIS?

OH NO NO I DON'T BELIEVE . . .

Disinformation! – or, more controllably, error in his cross-references – or he'd misread the archives – or had he been fed with leaks (by surprisingly well-trusted members of the establishment) so adulterated by gossip and malice as to be no better than a broth of poison?

Hidden history can contain anything: *which is why it has been hidden, and why he was thus compelled to track connections step by step. His accumulating data was a huge hound on a leash, dragging its master for a 'walk' of its own wanton choice.*

Martin's guilt as a deserter was by no means the strongest factor in his predicament; although in that respect, if he were to be released from the glasshouse upon suspension of sentence ('We're promising you nothing, you shitty little bastard; I only say *if . . .*') he would have to resume his army career for however many months he owed Her Majesty and still the sentence would hang over him as long as the authorities chose to allow, perhaps all the rest of his life. So the colonel said, anyway, and Martin was by now so beaten down, so cut off from the world into this ferocious little corner of unremitting and hysterical discipline, he was incapable of arguing against it.

But there were also charges in West Germany, for which he could be extradited – drugs and currency offences chiefly, against a tendentious background of 'associates revealed as student subversives suspected of terrorist conspiracy' (the Germans being most anxious to learn more about this background).

Scotland Yard, too, would very much like to hear what had happened to a large sum of money which had somehow dodged its way out of the books of a record-promotion company: a man called Dan de Leon was thought to have a certain knowledge of it, would Martin perhaps know de Leon?

And then what about that girl from Birmingham, 1965 was it not? And under-age, or could Martin prove different? Her parents were still searching; the police were still most interested.

He cringed as the list unfolded, wept, shuddered like a man with malaria, agreed to do whatever he was asked.

They brought him out of prison, signed him on for a three-year term of regular army service when the rump of his conscript service should be concluded, gave him a re-run of his old Intelligence Corps basic training; and then put him straight into *psyops* – Psychological Operations, a new science, of techniques devised to confuse the foreign enemy in world war, now adapted for counter-insurgency, applied against fellow citizens, and requiring new men of a quite unconventional type. Martin (they said) was ideal.

Indeed he was; and after the first shock of this totally illegal prolongation of his conscription, he found that he actually enjoyed it. He wore no uniform, did not drill, was soon promoted to serjeant, worked sensible office-hours in a parkland environment outside Salisbury with a considerable bonus over and above his regular pay. His private life was his own, always providing he kept out of trouble with the civilian authorities – and never ever flapped his mouth about his duties, which he absolutely did not dare do; the hold over him was never mentioned but he never forgot it: that glasshouse had scarred him utterly.

The duties themselves exerted their own hold. Once he was immersed in them and fully understood the depths of their opacity, he realised he might just as well have been recruited into Cosa Nostra; impossible to be free of his masters, so relax and become *part of them*.

When the three years were up, he was asked to enter into a contract to continue the same work as a 'civilian adviser': status as of captain's rank: an extra-legal right (not stated but in practice never questioned) to issue relevant directives to army personnel up to and including lieutenant-colonels. It did not occur to him to reject the offer. There was now nothing else he wished to do with his life.

Sometimes, usually in London, he ran up against old acquaintances (he had never possessed *friends*) from before 1970. Their own rackety lives had changed a great deal; either regulated into businesslike respectability or completely fallen to pieces. In his calculatedly informal getup (not quite rags-and-tatters, not quite Carnaby Street, now and again a raffish hint of Saville Row) and with his natural fluency for sliding without warning out of one characteristic speech-pattern into another, he found it easy to let the respectable believe he was a demoralised near-junkie, while to the broken men and women he showed himself so coolly confident they all thought he had it made on the stock-exchange – either way they left him alone.

The work at Salisbury was of a pioneering nature: perfecting theory; extending it to limited experimental practice; devising schemes for spreading lies among gullible journalists, for buying the less gullible ones, for planting stories of one's own composition in British and foreign media; inventing ways of causing strife between different factions of the queen's enemies. Most of it was concerned with the Irish affairs (Martin made several trips to the Six Counties), but there were also side-issues into which to intrude – useful practice grounds for the techniques – South Africa/Rhodesia, Chile, Israel/Palestine, collaborating with (and advantageously misleading) BOSS, the ANC, Mugabe, Allende, the CIA, Mossad, the PLO.

By the mid-seventies he was spending more time in Ireland than England. Aid towards the bloody split between the Official IRA and the IRSP. Acrimonious wedges driven between Paisleyite loyalists and less-extreme Unionists. Documentary evidence manufactured to show loyalist murder-groups just who among their Catholic neighbours might be considered to be IRA. The same, to show the IRA how many of their own might be touts for the RUC. The same, to show *Fianna Fáil* and the Irish electorate why Mr Haughey was quite the wrong man to lead either of them (not, as it turned out, one of psyops' better efforts). And much more.

All this was teamwork, and the longer they were at it the defter they became. Martin had also a few successes to his personal credit: he was proving most inventive in the genre.

For example: periodically he gave birth to 'the most wanted IRA man' (or woman), with appropriate nicknames, *Black Hawk*, the *Barracuda*, *Whiskey Deathwoman*, and so forth; spread their details all over the tabloids; and had good confiding citizens ringing the police from one end of Britain to the other to report every Irish accent they had heard on the local bus.

He created out of practically nothing an entire left-wing political tendency, devoted to two excitingly innovative marxist propositions: (a) British imperialism as regards Ireland was now a dead letter, for the true Imperialists were the southern Irish who sought to colonise the north; and (b) the 1916 revolutionary James Connolly, as both socialist and Nationalist, had been therefore a national-socialist, therefore a Nazi. This wreaked highly satisfactory devastation among the theoretic leftists of both islands. It cost Martin, by now a skilled pasticheur, no more than a month's work upon a well-researched 'seminal pamphlet'.

He came back into England for a change of air, attached himself to the collective of a naively radical theatre company, sketched the script of a 'troops-out' play for them; and then gently contrived to guide the collective's mandatory restructuring of it (they disapproved of individual playwrights, but could not do without them). All the sympathy of the audience was thus thrown toward the one character originally drafted as wholly contemptible, who cried, 'A plague o'both your houses,' and hopelessly abandoned every shred of anti-imperialist discourse – Martin took the role himself. As soon as the play opened, he telephoned anonymous bomb-threats to prospective venues, so that half of the tour was abandoned before it started. The Arts Council then withdrew the company's grant, upon solely aesthetic grounds: 'failure to achieve an adequate standard of excellence.' As Martin said, they weren't quite wrong.

Once again in Ireland, he secured his own flat; the Ormeau Road, Belfast, at a corner marking the boundary between a small Catholic area and a much larger Protestant section. A peculiar building, standing up amongst dereliction, a cracked tooth rotting alone in a bad mouth laid waste by the dentist. He was near the city centre, near the middle-class university district; he had all sorts of queer personal contacts readily available to meet in bars or even to bring home and set whispering in his upstairs apartment. His front door was round the back, facilitating furtive visitors. Downstairs was nothing but a boarded-up shopfront; its vainglorious old legend still gaudy along the fascia above a jungle of recent graffiti –

SAMMY'S WEE BARGAIN-HUTCH
SAMMY'S GONE MAD!
ALL PRICES CUT TO NOTHING!!

He kept his windows veiled day and night with seedy curtains, and allowed broken panes of glass to remain in situ – if the place looked three-quarters abandoned it was the less likely to attract dangerous attention. From this lair he ran a disingenuous private enterprise, mail-order sex-aids and pornography. He computerised his list of customers and stored quantities of information not solely derived from their carnal tastes. How many of the cheques that came in went to departmental funds and what proportion filled his own pocket remained secrets between him and his coded computer.

His landlord was a private company: a search for its directors (not easy: the trail was densely overgrown) might eventually have led to Lisburn and Command HQ Quartermaster's Branch. He never went near the Ormeau Road in any sort of uniform. The RUC were told enough about him to make very sure they left him alone. But occasionally he was unwise: he brought women back to the flat.

Attracta, on behalf of Clay, discovered one of these women, whose only political attribute was a most wholesome fear of any sort of political involvement. She was a Queen's University undergraduate (Eng Lit, what else?), from Kilbeggan, south of the border. She had met the 'small man – like Quilp, you know, Dickens?' in a student-pub near the WEE BARGAIN- HUTCH. Drink and his Brit/cosmopolitan streetcred overcame her rural caution. She remembered very little about the place - she wished she had forgotten all of it – for weeks afterwards the terror of pregnancy sat upon her like the giant roc on its nestful of talon-torn skeletons. She believed he had used a condom, but so what? had not the nuns at school said that condoms were not only sinful but manufactured for sordid profit from an unreliable class of fabric?

She had seen, she thought, a cluttered bedroom, a dirty mess of a kitchenette, an insanitary bathroom. She had been about to enter what she took to be the living-room, but the man had hauled her into the bedroom before she really observed. Yes, there was a computer; yes, well-ordered shelves of books and documents; yes, wall-charts in foreign alphabets (or ciphers); yes, it did seem as though it belonged to quite different premises. And yes, he talked round-and-about politics and asked her whom she knew. Her answers seemed of no use to him; he became bored, he rang a taxi, he put her out.

A month later she called at the door, to tell the man she was afraid she was missing her period (not true, thank God, as it transpired): no one answered,

and the door might never have been opened for years. He had called himself
Tolstoy, claimed to be writing a novel, claimed some undefined relationship
with the great Tolstoy – which set her laughing at him; and thereafter the
lamentable consequence. She felt she had defiled herself for life.

When she told this to Attracta she was more than a little in drink, she wept
helplessly on her shoulder. A Kerry shoulder in scary Belfast gave her great
comfort, she said.

When Bobby Sands, newly-elected to parliament, perished upon hunger-strike in 1981, the disastrous international impact caused something like a *sauve-qui-peut* among psyops: half-implemented operations were immediately brought to a halt, pilot projects sent straight back for radical reassessment, think-tanks and group-brainstorms urgently convened. Personnel rushed hither and thither to refresher courses, seminars, weekends of frantic role-playing. In a Buckinghamshire country house Martin and his colleagues were desperately assailed by expert civilian lecturers, British and foreign, psychologists, diplomats, editors, electronics engineers; to say nothing of academics, exultant at being thus invited to shove their querulous oars into torrents of power-consciousness, Charybdis-whirls of high security. One of them, a huge-headed liver-spotted yellow-faced old troll of an Eng. Lit. professor, his hair *en brosse* like guano-streaked pebbledash, his bushy great eyebrows the colour of burnt lentils, hacked and delved (as a man might clear a forest) at the vehement need for Untruth in the service of Ultimate Truth.

Undeterred by the presence of his most senior military sponsors, this spokesperson for the liberal arts *psyopped* the eager students of psyops itself; throwaway delivery, brutal common-mannish abhorrence of cant, sharp-sawing vinegar-tongue paradoxically tinged with north-of-Ireland gentility: 'Gentlemen (God knows why 'gentlemen', but gloved hands, as they say, are firmest on a pistol-butt), all this fucking high-intensity theory of *Low-intensity Operations* and the like! – to be sure it sounds the authentic note of precious civilisation at the delicate defensive, smooths down the flattered hackles of honey-licking demagogues.

'There's more ways of killing a cat than choking it with butter.

'Between ourselves, and we well know it, we're not just up against a vicious little knot of murderous cornerboys we can isolate like a typhoid victim and let die of their own damned virus. We're dealing with nothing less than an entire population of liars. The curse is that everyone believes 'em. And the blessing within the curse? Why, everyone believes that *we* are the liars. So if we are, where are we? In a position, my friends, to fix it that no one believes *anyone*: and then we can do what we like!

'Straight face and never waver.

'Bloody Sunday in Londonderry is the pointer for the way we go. All
those brasshats on the idiot-box swearing "My chaps were fired upon
first!" Who knows whether they were or weren't? Who cares? Fact is, *and
as a result*, for the next fifty years respected historians are going to tell us
how "confused circumstances, self-contradictory crowds, officers on the
spot to make instant decisions – even if PIRA marksmen had *not* started
shooting, understandable that individual soldiers should think that they
had," and boom-pah boom-pah the band plays on!'

Martin was entranced. He asked such intelligent questions and put so
many cogent points that the rebarbative scholar made a beeline for him at
coffee-break: a congratulatory private chat. (At least, that was the most
sanguine reading of the apparent cause-and-effect.)

Martin had not quite caught the man's name – everyone there seemed to
refer to him privately as Ranzo – Rats, was he? Rance? Ah, Rance, of
course, Rockingham Rance! Christ, Brum in the sixties, the whisking tits of
Kitty Flake! What else should he know about him?

It soon became clear that *he* knew a deal about Martin.

'I recall the face; recall the voice; poetry, am I right? *Trotsky on the Trot*:
miscellaneous obscenity howled-out rather than recited; fifteen years ago,
sixteen . . . Ring a bell? Ally Pally, was it? Or the Roundhouse? No it
wasn't, it was Birm – '

Martin dared not join in pursuit of so dangerous a detail. Parts of his past
could still sap his courage, Birmingham had been shatteringly recalled to
him in the glasshouse, the glasshouse was much nearer in time than Big
Chief Trotsky, his accent slipped out of control into an apprehensively
underdog whine. '*Trotsky with the Trots*,' he hastily, evasively, corrected, 'in
point of fact; yeah. Left it ambiguous as to whether it was me backing-
group or the state of me bowels or me political complexion, dead subtle,
yeah. I'd hoped no one would bring that up. Fucking rubbish, wasn't it?
Wanking.' He smirked and played mock-modest.

But Rance did not seem to wish to threaten him. 'Fucking rubbish? Oh
no. Disgracefully derivative; but it had – still has – its uses.'

Sigh of relief. 'Christ, you give me life and hope, man. Were you there?'

'Yes I was, Captain – ah – ? It *is* Captain?' (Nearly everyone in the room
wore civilian clothes.)

'Captain, yes, for present purposes, certainly, yes.' Officer-voice of a sort
(never entirely pukka) was coming back on stream.

'Captain what? You'd better tell me, we were not introduced.'

'For present purposes, Low. Matthew Low, Royal Artillery. Damn glad to
meet you, sir. Most stimulating lecture.'

'So I should hope. I'm well paid for it. They tell me you profess the drama? Agitprop, yes? Top hats for the villains, printed slogans hung on a stepladder. An accommodating pen, yours. Have you quite left verse behind you?'

'It's not been called for.'

'Ah but it has; I'm calling. You've grey in your hair already, don't delay till it's too late. Shit, boy, or slide off the pot.'

Rance was acute, conspiratorial, soft-voiced. He laid a hand, surprisingly warmly, on Martin's arm (Martin wondered, was the hideous old bastard gay? But we know different), and led him softly into a corner, behind the coffee-urn, behind the mess-waiter shuffling his teaspoons.

In a matter of five minutes *Operation Terrible Beauty* was suggested along its main outlines, and immediately accepted by the man who was to carry it out. Rance, or Ranzo (why Ranzo? Did these staff-college bullshitters detect a certain dago greasiness?), was genial and generous: 'Ways and means are for you, my friend, *Kamerad, compagnon, amigo, a chara*, what? I give you the general notion, let it breed. Any fuck-up in clearing it with the top brass, refer them to me. I'm a specialist, I *know*: the late Sands, MP, *he* knew too: as also this "Peeler's Goat": a very great mistake in the electronic age to underrate the power of verse. Archaic cultural survivals have direct dynamic input to inherited motivations. Positive? Negative? Entirely up to us. Wanking? Blockheads say "wanking": so? Isn't wanking a consummate pleasure, available to all? Only price a laundry-bill (if you're not bollock-naked like a felon on the blanket); no detrimental after-effects, bar the augmentation of the dreams that set it going. Supremely useless, what? So bloody well get out there, *use* it!'

He patted Martin's hand, turned from him all in the same gesture, and padded away to talk secrets with a brigadier.

'Clearing it with the top brass' was not quite as easy as Rance implied. The only top brass essential to approval, or veto, were the chiefs of military intelligence in Northern Ireland Command: it was not the department head, but an officer nonetheless of influence and personality, who took against it from the start. He thoroughly distrusted all forms of artistic expression as inimical to soldierly discipline, which makes him sound like a throwback to the Crimean war; but he did have his up-to-date reasons.

One in particular – Vietnam. 'Cannabis and sludge-music, and – what did they call it? – *rapping?* That shower of a so-called army chattered and sulked its way into every pinko newsrag, every bellyaching telly programme, till its will-to-win evaporated with the spit of its own logorrhoea. Poetry's no more than an extension of the same damned crap. Bloody confessional diaries upfront straight-up wide-open. Project's u/s from the start, drop it.'

His harsh realism met its match in the cynical grossness of Rance, and the operation was permitted to develop. But not before he had tried an inhibitory ploy.

Captain Stoke, Royal Army Ordnance Corps, a statistics officer with a repetitive bureaucratic job in the headquarters, received from Intelligence Branch a floppy-disc file (*Op. Terrible Beauty*, TOP SECRET) to be augmented by a numerical breakdown; the signature on the requisition was illegible.

POETRY APPRECIATION (inter-unit survey)
   Furnish soonest:
Tabular assessment of NCOs and other ranks in possession of
  1 O-level Eng Gram
  2 A-level Eng Lit
  3 3rd-level degrees/diplomas (state which) Eng. Lit.
  4 letters, rejection and/or acceptance, from publishers
  5 books, hard-cover, surplus to army-educational requirements
   NOT, repeat NOT of primarily sexual content
  6 ditto, of primarily sexual content NOT, repeat NOT hardcore
  7 ditto, paperback, all excl religious . . .
    (etcetera, for about 50 items.)

He had no idea how this absurd information was to be obtained, even by means of computer (the exam qualifications were already to his hand, but the rest of it. . . !); nor did he understand how he was expected to incorporate it with the totality of the file, which had no statistical structure whatever. He was a stickler for correct documentary structure. He suspected some clown in the press office of frivolous and offensive mickey-taking. But then again, maybe not. One never knew, with intelligence matters. He did what he thought best, referred it to the only officer in Intelligence Branch with whom he was on speaking terms, Bob Haythornthwaite.

Haythornthwaite was preoccupied with grievous private problems; the disc lingered among the accumulations of his pending-tray until psyops chased it up in a panic and played merry hell.

Why was Captain Stoke not put on the carpet like Haythornthwaite?

In fact, he was; but *unlike* Haythornthwaite he had the good sense to keep quiet. He began to realise he had been deliberately set up: he was meant to have sent in such an adverse report on the practicality of *Terrible Beauty*'s logistics that nothing more would be heard of the 'u/s from the start' operation. He strongly resented being used in this way, but the very thought of 'dirty-tricks merchants' suppressed his feelings there and then.

Whereas Haythornthwaite, we know, was less diplomatic; he *drew attention.*

> *Logical certainty; definitive return to the fixed point; and so consolidate. Unwise to approach Captain Stoke (still in the army); but the statistics officer's sealed-lips discretion was well recollected by a talkative ex-colleague as a notorious mess-table joke – 'He hated cloak-and-dagger merchants, spooks, special-operations goons – scared him worse than the PIRA – looked over his shoulder for 'em all the time – seems the buggers nearly broke him once, but he'd never tell us why.' Dates and places cohered; altogether too neatly; Stoke Poges' paranoia began to infect Clay; the shape of his jigsaw, three-quarters assembled, gave him nightmares.*

Terrible Beauty had false starts, indecision about aims and objects. For instance, the visits of Martin in various guises to selected houses on arms-search were not thought efficacious. They had been intended to be subliminal (psyops personnel attached great importance to the 'subliminal') but *Republican News* made a nonsense of all that by exposing and sneering at them.

> *Fixed point number two: the dharma-pig. No nightmares about him once he was properly observed in action; Bríd had experienced his antics as most dreadful and uncanny, but Clay's source had nothing but contempt for them. A pissed-off fusilier outraged by the way Martin handled his sub-machine gun – 'Called himself a fucking serjeant! Cordelion, did he call himself? Chinless fucking name, half-arsed bloody civvy, and who believed a word of it? What the fuck was he doing there anyway, giving orders to our own officer?'*

At long last, however, the main thrust of the operation was doggedly put into motion.

Ó Cuinn's poems had been secured – Bríd was quite right when she thought Martin knew she was receiving them from the Kesh – and their metamorphosis at Martin's hand was carefully completed. He took great pleasure in the task, giving his dramatic talents (such as they were) the broadest scope, and working amazingly quickly. Had he tried to construct *real* poems out of his own experience he might have been at it for weeks: he might even have been overcome by the blank horror of his disgusting life, and he knew it.

The next thing was to choose a suitable dead soldier upon whom to plant the verses. No great problem: the IRA were active enough. As soon as

London passed the word that Judy was in place, Lisburn need only wait for an incident. When it came, it presented a toss-up: Truethought or his companion the truck-driver? Martin decided on Truethought, because the driver's father had immediately made 'troops-out' noises on TV and might use some of the poem to fortify his subversive contention. Auntie Dorcas, when they researched her, seemed a far better bet. Her unfortunate little outburst about the NUM and scabs ought perhaps to have been foreseen and guarded against. But the research (computer networked) had to be started and finished overnight: Truethought's pathetic possessions would be got together almost at once. Martin must go to the barracks and pretend some dodgy bullshit about investigating a possibility that Truethought himself was a subversive (why, after all, was he on the truck?), and then temporarily take control of the contents of his locker. This was achieved with the connivance of the unit's intelligence officer: had the CO known about it, he would have blown a bloody gasket. Dodgy.

Nightmare compounded itself: the events in Truethought's barracks just after his death seemed to Clay so indeterminate, so muddled, *that perhaps – ? Alternative exegesis – ? More inevitably logical – ?*

Leo had conned Truethought onto the ration-truck ('Special orders, my son; intelligence mission, dead hush-hush, keep it dark!') – the murder was prearranged! *Had to be,* for the poem to be planted beforehand in the boy's locker and no complications or mistakes.

Uriah the Hittite? (Clay owed his atheism to the biblical naggings of his divorced mother, a dismal Calvinist; but he never forgot her stories.) Leo was no King David; a Joab at best: oh did it not make the strongest sense of all to postulate a key-figure, *savagely pragmatic, infallibly protected, to overcome all lower-rank nervousness and impose his exorbitant will?*
   Truth so sensational must needs be untrustworthy; without doubt the investigation had run into deep trouble.
   One simply did not mess with men like Rockingham Melchior Rance. Nonetheless . . . (Clay trembled as he carried on at his keyboard.)

This Rance had moved, for the best part of four decades, in an apparently unregulated individualistic manner among the career permutations of British and Irish academic life, with side-tracks to America, the European continent, as well as the countries of the socialist bloc. A progress like that of a knight on the chessboard; always a swift corner in it; he never reached the place to which he originally appeared to be pointing himself, but always somewhere else, and when he got there it was always as though he had planned for it all along.

Colleagues behind his back (if anyone ever knew where exactly his back was) called him Reuben Ranzo, after the man in the sea-shanty who was 'Ranzo dark and dirty / we should give'im five-an'-thirty!' and who created angry confusion upon every ship in which he sailed.

His scholastic speciality: the political determinants of literary structure and image-clusters, with particular attention to the Anglo-Irish writers.

Periodically he held chairs in various universities: but never for very long, and no one was quite sure (in any one case) why he resigned, or if indeed he *had* resigned and not been asked to leave. His lectures brimmed with queer minutiae of incontrovertible scholarship; invigorating, infuriating, cranky to the point of being very nearly crazy. His books likewise: where extensive footnotes challenging other scholars were masterpieces of hurtful derision. Almost definitive in their field: *Mussolini and Yeats; Clues to the Iconography of a Faustian Flirtation. The Patois of Synge and the Militarism of Spenser: a Comparative Study of Benevolent Exploitation. Le Fanu and the Satanic Threat of Sexual Democracy.*

He did not allow the political implications of his work to remain theoretical or even attached to literature. He was constantly at the elbow of one politician after another, never in the limelight, but always ready to urge some course of action which the politician was usually too timorous to have imagined independently, or too restricted by timorous associates to put into practice. In his earlier years Ranzo was thought to be a leftist, consulted (for example) by Harold Wilson's government over reform of education. But at much the same epoch he was invited to Djakarta to reconstruct the English department in the university there. Although he wrecked the department, the visit was not quite unfruitful: during his stay in the country he proved to be of great moral assistance to those Indonesian factions which just then were organising the massacre of thousands of supposed communists, many of them students and teachers of English.

The myth of his radical socialism lasted a long time. It had much to do with the obscurely profligate aroma of his private life. Some people said he was a bigamist. Certainly he once turned up at New York University with a wife who was not the Mrs Rance a couple of NYU academics had met the month before in Oxford. He was supposed to have fathered children, whom he did not rear at home, insofar as he had a home; nor did he talk about them or their mothers, except perhaps to his intimates, and who knew who his intimates were?

There was an ugly tale of a female student at Essex University during the late-sixties' campus disturbances. It was claimed she went out of her mind after an attempt at rape by Ranzo. Like so many impressionable youngsters she had worshipped him in the lecture-hall; and continued to worship him when he gave machiavellian support to the 'democratic expropriation of capitalist-élitist faculty buildings'. His only known comment came a year or two later: she was 'an unstable little bourgeois dolly – if she wasn't in the booby-hatch she'd be in jug with the Angry Brigade, so fuck that for a game of soldiers!'

There was less sexual scandal now than there had been; by the 1980s he was over sixty, his beetle-like physique had repulsively deteriorated. His undoubted personal magnetism bred resentment rather than yearning among young women of feminist ideas: he sensed this, resented it in turn, and became all the more flamboyantly reactionary.

There were other tales, of drunkenness. Not usually public drunkenness, though sometimes one heard of seminars disrupted while Ranzo flew into a wild rage and pitched books and water-carafes out of window (or a secretary out of window? But that was generally agreed to be pure legend). Many of his acquaintance knew of times when one went to his rooms to find him sprawled on the floor, helpless, or dancing like a dervish in his bathroom. Such bouts were intermittent and seemed never to interfere with his writing.

Nor did his work suffer from his occasional disappearances, often for so long as a month or more on end; although they did make it difficult for well-organised university departments to deal with him. Academia nowadays is less tolerant of eccentricity, as public money, governmental and commercial contracts, pressure from students' unions, combine to impose a discipline and a need for material results: perversely enough, Ranzo agreed with this need. Pure scholarship to him was anathema, delight in literature for its own sake despicable. 'Undergraduates,' he said, 'who don't know how to see themselves as nig-nog recruits in basic training for the war against liberal flab, should be shot out with the waste-fucking-paper!'

Students often shared his opinion. In the sixties, leftists, with Ranzo their Marcusan hero; after a lapse of twenty years the young sharks of the new right regarded him proudly as an aesthetic Milton Friedman. To both groups liberal flab was contemptibly inimical.

Indonesia may have started his political shift, but in those days he kept it for the Third World: not until '69 or '70 did he venture to bring it home, to coincide with growing trouble in the six counties of Ulster. This was not accidental. Ranzo was an Ulsterman.

By no means a conventional Ulsterman. He was once described (by someone who cannot have seen him in the flesh) as 'the acceptable face of the Orange Order', although he was never a member of it and scorned all those that were. But he did loathe nationalist Ulster Catholics, calling them 'mother-fixated stunted atavists' and sneering, in selected company, at their high birthrate and their supposedly swarthy 'bog-Celtic appearance'. Almost exactly his *own* appearance; but he angrily denied he was any sort of Celt. His mother, perhaps, was a Delagoa Portuguese, a papist? Sometimes he said yes, sometimes no: he liked to infuriate his allies. His father, Celt or not, had been a globe-trotting imperialist, journalist and colonial entrepreneur, very useful to the Protestant cause in Carson's time, 1914; a go-between with the Kaiser's war-office when German rifles were required to 'keep Ulster British'. Some said those German contacts continued throughout the First World War: but his father was never formally accused of double-dealing and the British government gave him a medal in the post-war honours list. No doubt he had been allowed a certain flexibility, the better to keep an eye upon the treasons of *Sinn Féin*.

When the Tories prevailed in the 1970 general election, Ranzo, behind the scenes, had more than a little to do with the abrupt change that at once took place in the role of the British army in Ireland. The troops were ostensibly there to protect nationalist civil rights from Orange violence. As soon as Heath was prime minister, GHQ imposed a stringently anti-Catholic curfew along the Falls Road: from then on the new battle-line was drawn – 'Our brave lads against IRA terrorism and no truckling to the *liberal flab*.'

Ranzo was in position (Trinity College, Dublin); ready at any time to pop up north. He gave advice to Brian Faulkner, Stormont prime minister, when internment was introduced.

At politico-military cocktail parties he made intellectual friends among the General Staff, and was always ready to justify 'disorientation techniques as an aid to interrogation'. He found quotations from Yeats, Carleton, Burke and Swift to support such ruthless practices. He was generally regarded as a *very helpful Irishman*, to which he replied with what he said the Irish-born Duke of Wellington had once said: 'A man's birth in a stable does not make him a horse.'

He wrote to members of the Conservative government, suggesting how best to abolish Stormont and impose direct rule.

He advised the Ulster Workers' Council over their political strike which destroyed the Sunningdale power-sharing system. When his intellectual friends among the General Staff were told by the Labour government to break the strike, and sought means of avoiding obedience without overtly committing a mutiny, Ranzo discussed various courses of action with them.

He recommended to the same government the criminalisation of political prisoners.

He stiffened the backs of Mrs Thatcher's ministers during the trauma of the Hunger Strike.

He secured for review (in pop-papers as well as academically respectable periodicals, at home and abroad) almost every new book about the Irish question. If the authors in any way hinted at any concession to nationalist claims, he demolished them with subtle yet peremptory scholarship. It was hard to dismiss him as a mere bigot: he put such quirky humour into his pronouncements that his angered opponents were all but disarmed, and uninformed readers most agreeably seduced. His influence as a critic was strongest in the Irish Republic, and could be measured there by the number of younger novelists, playwrights, poets and fellow reviewers whose humane denunciations of violence were now applied primarily or exclusively against the IRA.

He was the occasional associate of many individuals involved in undercover loyalism; but was never known to actually *advocate* the random murder of Catholics.

He was a horrid ignominious wretch; he had a finger in everywhere; and in psyops most of all.

A very clever general coined an axiom to the effect that 'Mao Tse-tung says guerrillas swim among the people like fishes in water. What to do? Pollute the water.' Ranzo took hold of this and went about repeating it until many came to think he had thought of it all on his own. He might just as well have done; for no one else was so ingenious in recipes for its application.

Clay was now in the midst of a maniacal Gothic nonsense, with very queer implications which all appeared to hang upon one individual – it would make sense to nobody until character and motivation were further elucidated. More time must therefore be taken, to look more closely at Ranzo's published work. And to hunt up, if possible, anything unpublished: *why, the old bugger was a swamp full of alligators, murderous gulping gullets under the waterweed everywhere!*

Asking around among his scholarly contacts, Clay was recommended to a young American woman at University College, Dublin, who had attacked Ranzo's views on Sheridan Le Fanu, a year or two since, in the TLS; *and had been savaged by him in return. She told of a series of papers by Ranzo on Irish matters, privately circulated among political associates, never issued to the public. Somehow she had obtained copies of some of them: she would be glad to pass them on. Clay read them, and began (obscurely) to understand.*

Ranzo had no religious fervour. Ulster Protestantism meant nothing to him except as a convenient moralisation of power. If certain persons preferred to believe their natural human urges were dictated to them by divine voice, he would not quarrel. His crucial test: 'What does this particular divine voice have to say on this particular issue, and does it say it with intellectual rigour?' He thought, in the case of Ulster, that it did.

He had no special enthusiasm for 'Britishness' as such. Again, in the Ulster context it was convenient, no more. It *stiffened backs*.

Nor was he exactly a racist. Through his father he had adopted a particular racial/cultural group, and it so chanced that another group (the Gaelic Catholics) coincided with that section of society which required to be dominated in the interests of – what? His own philosophy. An idiosyncratic mixture of Plato with Darwin with Nietzsche; but couched in the terminology of Marx. Despite the complex phrase-making by which he justified his ideas, they were simplistic to the point of insanity: the world must be controlled by *wise men*, and punished for not having accepted their rule already. Wise men were few; to secure hegemony they must deploy all available authoritarian forces: politics, law, armies, religion, wealth. But only as means to an end. Such forces of themselves did not transmit *wisdom*, and could indeed retard it if they were permitted to operate unchecked.

Did he in fact envisage an end? Ranzo, dictator? Not really: his delight was in the process: arrange and then rearrange, without anyone quite catching what he was up to. Above all, ensure the *checking* of one force against another. Always to be heeded, never seen.

So he nurtured his philosophy and it gave him a great deal to do.

But why *that* philosophy in particular?

Had he at some stage been slighted in his hopes for intellectual fame? Or was he dissatisfied with such fame as he already possessed? If so, his proceedings were not efficient. He desired to be known as more than a mere scholar; but did his pride nonetheless demand that he should not have it known that he was known?

He hid the answers to all these questions within (one might say) a curtained Elsinore alcove. Men of frustrated brain often think of themselves as Hamlet. Ranzo embraced the risk of combining the role with Polonius; and if Claudius came in as well, he wore plain clothes and no crown.

And what if Muddy Clay's pathological subconscious were making the whole thing up? Expecting to palm off upon our modern understandings the absurdly individualistic plot-and-character mechanism of Victorian fiction? Already a 'Quilp' was in the story, to say nothing of a sort of corrupted 'Little Nell'; were they to be joined by 'Count Fosca'? – or 'Frankenstein', for God's sake?

Ranzo as a baleful politico-cultural influence: okay.

But Ranzo as diabolical patriarch, a deliberate perverter of his own secret brood into incest and worse than incest, into hapless self-disintegration – what combination (random or inspired) of misleading informants each toting their own weird subconscious, and of a computer with no previously diagnosed inherent flaw, could have arrived at such a conclusion?

How far did available data attribute to Ranzo any theory of heredity?

Far enough.

Item: appendices to Ranzo's book upon Oscar Wilde and his unusual parents, Purposeless Pedigree.

Item: Ranzo's paper about Jonathan Swift's relationship with his suppositional sister 'Stella', originally written, at the time of Ranzo's first nervous breakdown, for the Dublin periodical The Bell; *and (after its rejection by the editor) reconstructed as an erotic Artaudesque scenario, an 'ithyphallic psychodrama'; it was eventually published, under the pseudonym 'Clodius Pulcher', by Olympia Press of Paris; Kenneth Tynan once thought of presenting it on the stage, but never got around to it.*

Item: Ranzo's assured statement in his notoriously extravagant 1959 Sorbonne lecture, Le Péché Mortel et Glorieux d'une Âme Introuvable *(or,* Le Violateur de la Comédie Bourgeoise)*, that Molière married his own daughter – this last being rather out of Ranzo's usual field, but his sources were unimpeachable and his deductions from them enraged the French (exactly as intended,* ça va sans dire?).

Analyse the documents, assess subsequent findings, print out the deductions – and dammit!

Ranzo had been *testing his genes to destruction* – a calculated private experiment – in the first place only to prove that his own very mixed ancestry (possibly including a black Bantu strain on his mother's side) could effectively master the acknowledged master-race of Protestant Ulster; and thereafter his mixed posterity could carry on where he left off? He was also concerned to make trial of heredity against environment, his children (as it were) being let slip into the most slippery social circumstances available to them, and then it was a question: would they reshape the circumstances or the circumstances them? Ranzo did not believe that his own role, with its alcove manipulations, invalidated the freedom of the experiment; he saw himself as no more than one of many factors that made up the circumstances; he chose to provide *free will* together with *predestination*, combined as only he knew how: let them go, call them in! checks, counter-checks, and coercion! deployed always toward his own main chance.

*

'Oh my God,' said Ms Lambert to Bríd Ní Gairmleadhaigh's solicitor (and part-time employer), 'does the client not realise none of this can be used in court?'

Mr Rory McCallion was proudly provincial, elderly, rough-edged, unimpressed by London attitudes, 'Of course she does, dear lady. And isn't that the whole point? If we can't get at the truth, at least we can achieve the considerable satisfaction of observing them hurtle to hide it. I'd say it was well worth the dubious pains certain dubious people have put in, gleaning our costs from we mustn't ask where.'

She made no comment on *that*. 'But you'd hoped for Irish counsel?'

'Not at all. My client, at the commencement, might have done. Once we found her cause was to be heard in London, she was glad to take a different line. No better men than the English for shovelling their own slurry in the splendour of their own High Court – indeed no better *women*, that's *her* view, she's a woman herself.'

'She *is*? And you don't approve?' (Naomi met his humour with her own brand of asperity.) 'And that's why Siggy Clay recommended me?'

'Ah, he has great respect for your commitment to civil liberties.'

'I've never before been committed in defence of the IRA.'

'Aye?' He squinted at her, wondering would she be about to moralise upon bloodshed? If so, perhaps she *was* the wrong choice. 'Where is the law to deny the IRA their right to their own poetry?'

No moralities; she was practical, with a harsh little laugh: 'Their own *war* is a different matter, and very well you know it. You don't have to be sly with *me*. Our client upholds the war. We can't afford to. Nor can we afford to denounce it. If we do she'll contradict us in open court and destroy her own case. War and poetry must be kept strictly apart: deeds and comment: quite separate issues. Our opponents will confuse them and smear us accordingly.'

'And why wouldn't they? Surely, aren't *we* smearing *them*?'

'I do hope so. I'm afraid that that's *all* we can do. Unless somehow we get these two beauties into the witness-box. The Leo man and – ah – Rainbow? What's the chances?'

'Of *him*? Oh dear me no. Even if he's let appear, they'll wrap him in a curtain or hide him behind a hoarding and call him Witness A or B and block four-fifths of your questions. "Security" rules all: if he's done what we claim he's done, he did it for government; they'll protect him to the hilt. I should say, protect *themselves*. My guess, he's out of the country already.'

'But the girl?'

'Where the hell is she? We do know she does exist – an agnostic might say she's more *real* than the Deity – for have we not seen her on telly! But now, ma'am, the jackpot question: are we to believe anything at all of what your man says he's found out about the luciferian activities of – this – this *crypto-mythical* professor?'

Naomi groaned and threw both hands through her mousey fuzz of wig-flustered hair, a despairing mime of tragi-comedy. 'Oh, Mr McCallion, you did believe enough of it to send me the brief! And it all seemed to hang together. But the more I go into it, the less I can hold to. I wonder, is Clay altogether in control of himself? I stayed awake throughout last night in utter despair.'

'There's no question but the plagiarism can be adequately proved.'

'Which ought to be all we need. But every time we look at the proof, all the rest of it comes clinging on like poison ivy – I'll tell you one thing, McCallion, we mustn't have the name of Rance even so much as mentioned! Agree that with your witness, or I throw up the case!'

'That's a pity, so it is. Oh what I would not give to have that Orange bastard take the oath!' He screwed his features, very cunning; dropped his voice. 'If only they'd call Rance as their expert on literature, to prove the one poem cannot possibly derive from the others! For if they did, you could *cross-examine.*'

'You *do* believe all that Clay says of him; even yet, you still believe! This is not your legal mind working, it's archaic Irish faction-fight, it simply will not do . . .' She was sitting on the edge of her desk, she suddenly swung her long legs about, jumped down to pace the office lino, and guffawed. 'Oh but it would be fun!' – she was like a schoolgirl. 'They won't call him, they're far too sharp. D'you suppose we might *lure* him? By God I think I dare!'

'Ha, I'd never curb a daring woman and "fun" is a powerful word. The only possible response, given the everlasting gobshites that have usurped the control of our lives.' He fell into a melancholy and frowned over the sheaf of papers. 'I sometimes think I'd have done better to have told your Mr Clay to publish all this as he first intended; and let *them* sue *him* for libel. But then, you see, the formidable Bríd: if there was to be litigation and she to be brought into it, then *her* litigation, no one else's, an Irish woman in an Irish cause, another one who dares, she had to *attack*: God help us, that's her.'

McCallion did not much care for the English. But he got on very well with Naomi – who was Jewish, he had casually supposed (her first name? Her political vigour? Her brooding silences and sudden raucous outbursts?) – therefore more like an American – he was always at ease with Americans.

She told him he was wrong there. She was sorry, she *was* English, old-fashioned 'middle English'; descended, she chose to believe, from General

Lambert, radical and regicide. 'A man of some strength, I don't know that I'd want to meet him, but he never recanted.'

'Good God,' spluttered the solicitor, 'a bloody Cromwellian.'

After that he got on with her better than ever.

SEVEN

By the time McCallion was calling her 'the formidable Bríd', Biddy Grimes had changed her attitude to one of unstoppable aggression, a furious invocation of Taddy Q's will. He'd made it in Long Kesh when he feared he might have to go on hunger-strike, leaving what little he possessed to her on behalf of their son. She never thought to mention the document earlier, not appreciating its significance; for it omitted any reference to poems. Natural enough: Taddy had not composed them for money and neither he nor Bríd had considered them in that light. But now she saw different. The poems were stolen; so therefore the thieves perceived them as embodying material worth, therefore she had to fight for them. The Irish (she declared), a long long time ago, saw but small material worth in their own paltry island, until a crowd of Anglo-Normans started out to rob them of it: and would you look what had happened since then!

She did not reach this position all on her own. She might never have reached it at all, had it not been for Attracta.

When Clay brought his high time with Attracta to what she knew was a non-negotiable end, she was distressed, frustrated, angry, filled with undirected hate. She hated Clay for using her, hated herself for using him, hated Ó Cuinn for using Bríd (such splendid flame-headed love quite wasted on his egotistical *warriorship!*) hated Bríd for her shilly-shally over the poems, hated the Republican Movement for its duplicity, hated (of course) the British power that produced this foul situation. She fetched in liquor and got drunk, for several nights on end; felt ill; maintained she was *really* ill; made her excuses to *Republican News* – she needed a break and would not be fit for work for – well, a week or two, a month or two, whatever. And so home to Kerry to sit about glooming on beaches; unsuitably ill-tempered for the very fine weather that came suddenly in along the Gulf Stream; troublesome and spiteful toward her family.

And then she had a phone-call from Bríd: 'I've got to see you, can you come up? And don't bring that bloody Brit with you!'

So she took a series of long-distance buses to Armagh, a deadly two-day journey on back-breaking cross-country roads: not to go to Bríd's house, which was unsafe, but McCallion's office where his assistant could talk to her visitor in privacy in an inner room.

Bríd said, 'Are you two still hoping the paper's going to print all that stuff?'

A delicate point: Bríd might not be pleased to know how much about her and Taddy had been confided to Clay. So – 'They haven't said they won't. I'm supposed to be still working on it. Working, hell. Waiting, that's all, for your man; bald-headed bastard, he fucked me and finished; my guess, he's already given up the whole damn thing as a no-go. We'll not hear another word from him. In the heel of the hunt, isn't that just what you want?'

'It would have been, a week since. Just now I don't know how to think of it.'

'Why?'

'Because I've been notified formally to drop it. And when you're back in Dublin, you'll be let know so too. And can you imagine the bloody reason?'

Attracta thought she could; but what Bríd told her was a new reason altogether – if anything, a worse one. 'Can you *imagine*!' Bríd was crying, 'Those poems, the word is out, were never written from the Kesh by Taddy at all, never! *I* wrote them, me, of my own unaided genius, to pass them off at the paper as *his* work – aye, a fraud to *heroise* him, when all he was doing was evading the hunger-strike and scheming to accept the prison uniform!'

Attracta could only stare and stammer. 'But – but – he wasn't and you wrote no poems, and everyone knows you didn't. What d'you mean, "the word is out"? Who put it out? The Brits?'

'I'd say so. Fergus is sure of it. Not that they've tumbled yet to what you've been up to; but they're closing the door against it on a well-guessed offchance. It was bloody Fergus brought the message. Strategical reasons, he said. Taddy Q, from now on, is a class of a non-person.'

'I thought Fergus was on your side.'

'On my side. Begod he'd like to be. Between me legs, for the matter o'that. Nonetheless, he brought the message. Even him, so he did. I threw him outa the house.'

She went on at some length, explaining what Attracta had not known, that just before his arrest Quinn had quarrelled with a faction in the IRA over an abominable error of military judgement: a bomb meant for the security forces had blown up a car with an elderly woman in it and two little girls, her nieces whom she was fetching from a birthday party; the atrocity reflected upon Quinn; he sought to have the men responsible expelled from the organisation; he was overruled; there was very bad blood; indeed a regular internal feud; not settled at the time of his death; not even settled now. 'Those three were never dealt with, they're more important today than ever they were, Fergus has to work with 'em: Christ, but I won't stand it!'

She shouted so loud that old McCallion put his head in to remind her he had clients in the next room – 'Naturally agitated by their business here, they look for a degree of *coolness* from the staff of a traditional attorney. Would ye have them walk out on me, saying "physician, heal thyself"?' The sight of him gave Attracta her idea. When he was gone, she put it to Bríd; startling herself by its simplicity.

Bríd too was startled, and shocked. To cut loose from correct Republican politics, abandon her natural base of support, appeal to law, to *British* law – 'You're out of your mind, girl, we'd not stand a chance in those courts; in the name o'God who's to pay for it?'

If money was already the worry, Bríd was halfway there without knowing it; this new news had made her so angry she was flailing around to do *something*; Attracta saw this and said so: 'No question but you'll redden their faces!'

' "Their"?' Bríd came in sharply, 'You don't say "our faces" and you don't mean the Brits? Already you feel like I do!'

'Maybe so. I don't like tricks. Neither Brit tricks nor genuine Irish. I'd say it was time we pulled some for ourselves; would you believe? the Revenge of the Women? We're in a lawyer's office. Why don't we ask? Now.'

Bríd looked at her, troubled. 'So he fucked you and finished. You're going to have to call him back. Is that a problem?'

'Of course it's a problem. I'll find a way out of it.'

But not immediately: her 'way out of it' arrived only by degrees. First she must ring Clay's London address several times with increasing self-arousal, increasing self-contempt, considerable relief that he was still vigorously engaged on his research, annoying doubt as to how much of it he would share with her even though he swore he 'most definitely' could use her help, some surprise that he did not condemn out-of-hand what she cautiously hinted-at as 'the legal solution' (no direct statement over the phone, sideways allusions only: 'security') – but her personal relationship with him remained totally unresolved. He was going again to Belfast, on a Tuesday, maybe for some time; had found a flat there, so he said, in the polite Malone Road; there were people he needed her to meet; give him a day or two to fix a few things up and then would she come there to confer with him – 'say, Friday?' She agreed, and like a madwoman took the train from Dublin on Wednesday morning. It arrived at 10.15 am, she went straight to the flat – which belonged to the university, Clay had negotiated an arrangement with an academic on sabbatical – and found her sometime lover not yet up, in dressing-gown and nothing else as he opened the front door, hand-towel and nothing else on the faun-faced young man who peeped out of the bedroom behind him. 'God, Siggy, that's no one for *me*, is it?' And then, all hot and giggly, 'Jaysus, pet, I beg your pardon, I thought for a minute you were me sister!'

Of course she had always accepted that Clay was bisexual, but of course had not *envisaged* it. Inside her clothes she felt she was shaking like dried peas in a bag; her lips went tight and blue as though marked on her face with a ballpoint.

Oh, but she was businesslike. She apologised and said she had come of course on business, a pity she was so early but things were very urgent, she sat down with the pair of them to coffee and croissants, waited until faun-face had made his departure, related in full what she had not dared explain on the telephone, and sharply argued the advantages of a lawsuit when Clay chose to harp on the difficulties – it might kill his 'scoop', but that was a long time hence at the rate he was presently going, and there would surely in the end be a *book* to be got out of it.

Then she flatly asked him what he wanted her to do.

That was all; no beastly emotings; much easier than she had thought; oh but she was a hard woman and creepy Clay could not meet her eye! (In fact he *did* meet her eye, he was offensively unperturbed; but she felt she had a right to compose her own scenario.) He told her something of Martin Leo. He proposed she should talk to any women who could be found who had a knowledge of SAMMY'S BARGAIN-HUTCH.

One of them, as we know, was the student from Kilbeggan. Attracta gave her the Kerry shoulder, to cry on, and why not? After an hour or so Attracta found with a surge of apprehensive beatitude that all her life and all unknown to herself she had in fact been lesbian, just like so many women she had read about in the feminist journals, and was it not wonderful; why on earth had she never accepted it before?

'Way out of it' at last: both for her, and (it might be hoped) for unhappy wee Kilbeggan.

The child's real name was Slattery, *Julia* Slattery after a faithful Roman slave-saint; 'Kilbeggan' by contrast had a good strong ring to it with no churchy subservience; and why wouldn't Attracta in turn be called 'Dingle'? They clasped hands and vowed fidelity: Attracta also vowed to wean Kilbeggan off the drink, but not just yet, sure there was time enough, so they each had another whiskey.

The problem of money was more easily set aside. Rory McCallion said effusively, 'Sure I'll not charge at all for the preliminaries of the case; if it troubles your conscience, Bríd, you can work it out in overtime. But there's abundance of funds lying untouched in America among the friends of Irish liberty and civil liberties in general, they'd leap at the notion!' He had a number of legal contacts in the United States, members of firms that had acted there for Irish Republicans on the run, and the like.

There was also the question of legal aid; he did not think it would be available for such an action, but dammit, they could always try – boldly carry the demand for it through to the highest courts in the Englishmen's realm! There were excellent precedents. He rolled his tongue around his phrases, giving the impression that an appeal to the House of Lords would be as good as three hot dinners to him.

And if the lords were so obstructive as to deny such a modest right, then – 'the European court, why not?'

He added, with obscure suggestiveness, 'What about your young man Fergus? I'm told *he* has a certain finger on mysterious sources, in the Free State and elsewhere?'

Fergus probably had. But they would be sources closely tied to Republican requirements. Unless Fergus could be brought round to outmanoeuvre a batch of factionalists, his finger must remain paralysed. Fergus, moreover, was Bríd's chief protection against any attempt from within the movement to use force to make her drop her lawsuit – a sanction she could not entirely discount, although she thought it unlikely.

She set herself to bring him round. Attracta did not ask how. It was unfortunate that Fergus had a wife already: but estranged, living in Edinburgh, so maybe in the long run matters might be harmoniously ordered. He was often to be found in the house at Armagh; and even baby-sat with wee Liam – an amazing development, given his macho personality. And then Clay's report was concluded, McCallion issued the writ, the lawsuit became public, and the security forces escalated the fruitless process of harassing and intimidating Bríd. Fergus now had to be more prudent; he could only meet her by stealth.

The defendants brought an American into court, Professor Katz of the University of California, as their chief literary witness. Rance was not going to appear; so Naomi endeavoured, without calling heavy attention to it, to build up from all possible testimony a subliminal mosaic-portrait of him that would colour the whole background of the case – and might even (fingers crossed!) *lure* him. But her main argument, in the final analysis her only argument, had to be drawn from the texts themselves.

As the judge was to pronounce in his summing-up: 'While an ordinary breach of copyright would be the unauthorised re-issue, word-for-word, of the versifications of the man Quinn – ' the judge scorned any *Mister* nonsense in regard to convicted criminals ' – this case is more difficult: it deals with the *essential structure* of a written work – a work of terrorism, you may think; but no matter – if you decide that such structure has, without acknowledgement, been fraudulently set forward as the invention of another, then there is plagiarism; an aspect of copyright has in fact been infringed. Alas, a subjective decision, but not entirely a literary one. For literary guidance, you have heard certain witnesses. But for final guidance you must rely upon your common-sense judgement of the value of evidence, as you consider the reputation and observed demeanour of those witnesses. You may think, for example, that Dr Cochrane has shown himself more than eager to extol a set of doggerels which avowedly hail the actions of men-of-violence in opposition to the Crown, and perhaps no less eager to denigrate the – the last testament, the posthumous utterance, of a – ah – a British soldier, a murdered British soldier, murdered . . .'

The judge had a difficulty here: he had been nauseated by certain aspects of the Truethought poem. But as government and media thought otherwise, he tried to affirm Truethought's loyal service and at the same time conceal his own cultural antipathies.

It is true that Dr Cochrane had not been Naomi's first choice as an expert witness. She had wanted some really impressive literary figure, whether creative writer or critic: but all those approached had found every conceivable reason for declining to testify. On McCallion's insistence, the northern Irish poets were tried before anyone else. One very well-known personality, whose published utterances in favour of social justice and against autocratic oppression were highly thought-of on both sides of the water, and who had indeed been mentioned more than once in connection with the Nobel Prize, failed altogether to reply to the solicitor's letters or to return his phone-calls. Another offered the excuse that he was by profession a civil servant and 'ought not to have public views, at least not in this sort of ambivalent context. You do understand what I mean?' A third was blunter: he refused on the ground that any recognition of an IRA man as poet would play into the hands of loyalist sectarianism and further divide the already riven community.

Southern Irish, McCallion thought, would do more harm than good in a British court: they would certainly run the risk of sneers over Dublin's extradition policies.

While English writers, when applied to, preferred on the whole to say they knew nothing about Irish affairs and it was best not to meddle where you didn't have a personal experience.

Jock Cochrane was from Glasgow, controversial proletarian, authority upon poetry and politics, one-time disciple of Rance and now his mortal opponent. He was Clay's idea; disastrous. A big man, dressed like a truck-

driver, with an adenoidal Clydeside accent and a forest of hairy chest
burgeoning above the rim of his T-shirt, he made excellent points about the
close parallels of imagery and phraseology in the poems and then
destroyed them altogether by take-it-or-leave-it social bias.

A sample of his technique: 'Lend a dekko for an instance to this
Cain-and-Abel construct of Quinn's – one brother kills another; aye but
who's to blame? Cain? Cain is Quinn, I don't need to tell you that, say the
names to yourselves, Cain-Quinn, Quinn-Cain, subliminal, aye you've got
it! Vernacular relish for ideological word-play in a repressive part-rural
part-urban residuarily oral culture – cross-reference Sean O'Casey – 'a
series of punning quotations from O'Casey, halted by the judge's
intervention ' – nae problem!

'So Cain-Quinn's no going to blame *himself!* – he's no such a silly
bugger–' (Another intervention from the bench.) ' – nae problem! a
vernacular polemic, let's get used to the vernacular.

'Cain-Quinn is a freedom-fighter; his freedom's been lost through the
aggression of Abel's mother. "Greedy rage!" Why, o'course! d'ye need me,
a Scot, to mark the coincidence of Abel's mother with Mother England –
Mother Thatcher, if ye seek the ephemeral referent – forcing the bloody
issue for eight hundred years – "endless" – aye and *rolling* in its
consequence?' (No intervention from the bench; just a slight smile
between the judge and Mr Houndsditch.) 'Now for the Truethought
version. Pay attention, ye've got your xerox-copies, it's the bottom of page
two.' (Reminded, for the fourth time, by a patient Naomi, of the difference
between a jury and a seminar-group of students). ' – nae problem!

'Line six and then skip: "Wish I could blame . . . blah blah blah . . . say
Cain versus Abel and know which was which!" He doesna know, he canna
tell, and why the hell not? Because he's no worked it out for himself, that's
why, he's no the initiator, he's the textual modifier, he's taken the
discourse as given: – aye, given him by "The Peeler's Goat"! – and now he's
to establish hegemony.' In other words, *to adapt from Quinn*, conformably to
the official view that the security forces were peacemakers keeping the
Irish from each other's throats.

'Dissolving class polarities so as to enhance bourgeois illusion, he
marginalises all commitment: "fuck off" – two words which he re-contexts
because they're there to his hand, but reverts them to minuscule from the
ur-magnitude of Quinn's.'

While Quinn's same two words, he roared, had intended no less than
'Fuck off Great Britain out of my Ireland, or I'll fight ye till I die!'

Naomi asked about Dr Rance's TV interview. He diagnosed Ranzo's
body-language on camera, the 'establishment stance' of the interviewer,

the 'status-quo positioning' of the camera itself – no doubt highly cogent
for an audience of semiological adepts. All Naomi had wanted was a brief
and withering reference to Orange-extremist propaganda links in Ranzo's
critical thought; Cochrane gave it all right but drowned it with everything
else, and Houndsditch of course encouraged him.

Professor Katz came confidently forward to ensure rebuttal of the
blundering Scot; complete contrast to the latter; a neat pale-suited pale-
faced smooth-cheeked precisian, thin and sharp and deceptively modest.
He was a computer-analyst of verbal patterns, currently in London to
demonstrate by his science that John Gower was the real author of certain
short poems hitherto attributed to Chaucer.

Mr Houndsditch led him gently to expound his techniques, with a few
choices examples from the Gower project. The judge watched the jury and
saw when their eyes glazed, 'No,' he said, 'Mr Houndsditch, your witness, I
fear, is assuming too much knowledge amongst us of the strange
vocabulary of the middle ages. ''To preyen hir on Crueltee m'awreke.''? Oh
dear. Can we not be convinced by some sentences from a more everyday
language? What do you say, professor?'

Katz was apologetic but firm. 'The very strangeness of the linguistic, your
honour – my lord – you must excuse me, I am not yet quite orientated to
the formalities of your protocol – ' (The judge purred indulgently.) ' – the
very strangeness of the linguistic is itself an indication. Computer knows
no difference between the fourteenth century and the twentieth; it
assimilates word-structures and grammatical idiosyncrasies, collates and
compares them, in a strictly objective tabulation. It would do just the same
for Egyptian hieroglyphics. It is all a matter of the frequency and order-of-
precedence of lines within the stanza, words within the line, letters within
the word. And thence it can calculate the mathematical probabilities. To
take, now, the transitive usage and the gallicising pronominal-infinitive
elision exemplified by ''preyen hir m'awreke''. By happenstance it does in
fact mean ''ask her to avenge me'': but that is not the importance of it as of
this current work-programme, where computer informs us that whereas it
is a comparatively uncommon Chaucerian phraseological phenomenon,
Gower in his total corpus employs related locutions upon no fewer
occasions than – if I am permitted to proportionately percentageize – ?' He
went briskly into statistics, relating Gower's earlier writings to his middle
period to his ultimate productions, numbering poems and stanzas and
'phraseological phenomena' with indefatigable dexterity.

The judge was amazed: 'Thank you, thank you, professor: I am sure we
are now very adequately persuaded of your scientific justification – unless
Miss Lambert wishes to challenge it?'

'I never challenge computers,' said Naomi quickly, 'Let's just hear, m'lud, how the professor interprets their findings on the matter in hand. Till then I leave him to my learned friend.'

So she left him for a whole morning; and then, after lunch, swept rapidly into her cross-examining stride: 'Come, come, professor, no more evasions. I am going to press you on this point. Listen carefully, if you please: "My death is willed against my will: by my own act of will." And, "My death is an act of will against my will, my act?" Do you absolutely refuse to see any trace of cause-and-effect between those two quotations?'

'Let me put it this way, ma'am; it is not what I *see*, but what computer has *read*.' The professor was unflurried. 'Computer, in Truethought-document, finds "act of will" contiguous to "my death" with only the pair of subordinated monosyllables to intervene. Quinn-document, however, appends "act of will" to the intensive pronominal qualification "my own", and removes it from the substantive context of "my death" by an entire enclosed predicate – "is willed against my will" – not to mention a colonic point.'

'You mean *colon*?'

'Whatever. Computer reads all punctuatory indicators as points, un-qualified; and then grants them adjectival attributes. Technological terminology; I'm afraid it's compulsive.' Katz's jargon was as bad as Cochrane's, but he had a winning habit (which gratified the judge) of seeming to deprecate it even as he spoke it. The general effect was of a genuinely scientific method, in all likelihood infallible; whereas Cochrane had appeared to take contemptuous pleasure in intellectualism for its own sake, brusquely *de haut en bas* until he lapsed into class-conscious rudery.

'Professor: I repeat my question. Cause-and-effect. None at all?'

'Computer doesn't read it so. Computer reads two totally different hands at work upon what might in subjective estimation be the same theme, but verbally speaking the two treatments of the theme are manifestly disparate.'

'But we know that, professor; we are not trying to show that the one man wrote both poems. I put it to you straight: the second man took the work of the first and *rewrote* it in his own idiom? Well?'

'No ma'am, I hazard not. Computer-wise there are variations linguistic-ally nonconcordant with direct derivation. Instance the pejorative imperative "fuck off". Quinn-document personalises this directly toward unspecified but clearly specifically limited "friends", Truethought-document presents it as a vocative to the world at large, a randomness of reference in direct contradiction to precise targetisation and carried through by means of line-lengths and detached subject substantives and omitted indefinite articles suggestive of a wholly original approach to the theme, insofar as "theme" is at any time a computer-compatible hypothesis.'

'Your distinction between the two "fuck-offs" seems to me (as far as I follow it) much the same as Dr Cochrane's; yet you draw from it an opposite conclusion – that the two poems have nothing whatever to do with each other? Oh really, professor!'

Katz addressed the judge directly, with an oddly contorted turn of words: 'As of this sworn oath and time, my lord, I *would* so hazard; *really*.' His clean features were blank and bland, his light eyes without expression. Naomi recognised she was blocked.

Time to change course, suddenly, without warning, swift as the tongue of a lizard.

'Computer can't read "theme"; "theme" does not interest you; linguistic statistics are the be-all and end-all; yes?' And then, before he had time even to nod his acquiescence: 'Five years ago at the Pentagon you sang quite a different song? You computerised, did you not, Professor Katz, a series of unpublished poems and short stories by young Nicaraguan writers? True or false?'

His poise was damaged, there could be no doubt of it. He twitched, and mumbled for an instant.

'Your pardon, professor, I can't hear you?'

'Yes, ma'am – I guess – true; I was – yes, I did, accept a consultancy – '

'In collaboration with Dr Rockingham Rance?'

' – yes, that is so, a joint consultancy in the interests of – uh – international – '

'International understanding?'

'Yes, ma'am.'

'To which your contribution was to programme an occult *theme* of stalinist totalitarianism to be run through all the works in the collection, a phrase here, a word there, now and again an entire sentence – ' Houndsditch was on his feet, the judge tried to make himself heard, but Naomi was at her most strident; the angry croaks went unheeded. ' – so that if and when the intercepted typescript proceeded on its way to its New York translator and publisher, the meaning of every item in it would have been subtly altered to fall in line with official anti-sandinista policy? True or false, Professor Katz?'

'It was an experiment only, it turned out to be non-viable, computer-wise it did not *marry*, it – uh – madam, you are asking me about a highly restricted category of governmental research, I am not in a position to proffer details! I appeal to your honour's bench, I appeal for protection here!'

'Thank you, professor: no more questions.' She sat.

The judge was glaring at her: 'Miss Lambert, your insistence upon an improper line of interrogation in the face of my disapproval is outrageous and presumptuous. It is well for you that you finished when you did. The jury will disregard both question and answer. My apologies, Professor Katz.'

Clay's Washington contacts had excelled themselves. But Rance was not to be lured; he came nowhere near the court, though it was believed he had a lawyer there, briefed to watch over his interests.

After Katz's discomfiture the judge became deeply malevolent. In his summing-up he commended the professor for his 'uncompromising and concrete rationality', explaining that 'I would hazard' need not be taken as in any way a half-hearted affirmation – it was in fact all the defendants needed to establish their case. 'The burden of proof lies solely with the challenger.' Apart from Dr Cochrane's intemperately expressed opinions, what proof had been offered?

'Various persons have been brought to testify to the activities of Martin Leo. It may be that a Mr Leo was in fact employed by government, for the necessary work of the security services; that does not make him a plagiarist of another man's verses. Any suggestion that it does is wildly circumstantial, based only upon the theories of the witness Clay (or Klaue), and very largely hearsay at that.'

The judge deprecated the unwholesome curiosity of scurrilous – indeed, *seditious* – pressmen who gloried in their breaches of the security of the state and pled the 'public interest' as justification. Let there be no mistake: the courts would decide what was or was not the public interest.

'As for the young woman called Rainbow Dawn: you heard a great deal about her eccentric career, you saw a face on television purporting to be hers, very little of it was proven, and none of it was at all to the purpose. The poems exist, whether she exists or not, and those are what you must judge. But no inference should be drawn from her failure to attend this court; women of her type have been known (for instance) to emigrate to the Commonwealth, to marry respectably, to settle down abroad in complete innocence of developments in England since their departure.

'Of the constant attempt by plaintiff's counsel to bring in the name of one of this country's most distinguished academic figures, I can only express my extreme disgust at what has amounted to little less than an abuse of the process of law, and I have a good mind to refer it to the Bar Council. You are

asked to assume that this – unblemished – personage conspired to plant
forged documents. But you cannot so assume until you have proved the
conspiracy; you cannot do that unless you know that the documents were
forged. Which returns us, ladies and gentlemen, to the magisterially
scientific Professor Katz – and of course, to Dr Cochrane.

'It only remains for me to say something of the plaintiff herself, Bridget
Grimes. You saw her in the witness-box, declaring her politics; you heard
in what newspaper she had her lover's rhymes published. When considering her sincerity in bringing this suit, you will doubtless bear all that in
mind. Incidentally, you may wonder why counsel made such an issue of
Miss Grimes's detention by the police at Stranraer, and again of her arrest
this morning just outside the precincts of the court, preparatory (we are
told) to a request for an exclusion order from the home secretary. Miss
Lambert seemed to think that these enforcements of the Prevention of
Terrorism Act should in some way arouse sympathy for her client. Of
course they should not, and I caution you very severely on that point – oh,
and neither should they prejudice you against her, that goes without
saying. The police have their job to do, and all good citizens, I am sure, are
wholeheartedly glad to hear of them doing it.'

Naomi felt that the summing-up alone was sufficient ground for an
immediate notice of appeal, but McCallion disagreed. He said, 'Dear lady,
don't let vexation deprive you of good sense. That judge was a conniving
hyena, but in law wasn't he correct? And the appeal court would have to
confirm it. Sure, we never found sufficient evidence; and we *knew* we'd
never find it, or have you forgotten? And consider Bríd herself: they've
already deported the poor woman, after arresting her twice and strip-
searching her God knows how many times. Do we want to make her
existence over the next three or four years one continuous hell of
harassment, for that's what it's bound to amount to? Let her marry her
bold Fergus and take her chances of a quiet life with him and his irredentist
friends. She did what she meant to do, break a nasty wee stink in the
sanctuary of the hallowed halls, and we helped her spread it, so we did,
with as much gumption as we could muster. What further could we ask?
Katz and Rance, I'm damn certain, are as discredited as they'll ever be on
every decent campus, east or west – which (behind me hand) is none too
many. Their brand of rascality is indispensable, not incidental, to the British
presence in Ireland; after this there'll be even more to recognise it; begod
but the word'll go round.'

Naomi was far less sanguine, indeed bitterly disappointed. And all her own

fault. How *could* she have placed such reliance on the investigations of Clay
– or rather on Clay's ability to stand by his findings in the witness-box? The
bloody man had been so positive, so ebullient, when she interviewed him;
why then in court was he ill at ease, touchy, tactically obtuse, at times
positively stupid?

She caught him, after the verdict, and asked. He blurted out that he
didn't know, he was very sorry, he'd fucked-up; and then immediately
made his escape, leaving Naomi wretchedly stuck there in the great gothic
foyer, wig all sideways, face drawn with frustration and weariness, angry
tears prickling at her eyelids.

But he did know. And he dared not tell her, dared not admit there was
anything to tell. He was in fact falling to pieces inside himself, dreadfully
dissolved with *fear*.

He had had a letter from Attracta just before the trial (which she knew
better than to attend – Prevention of Terrorism Act!). She was living in
Dublin with Kilbeggan, trying to start a women's journal, a sort of Irish
Spare Rib. The letter did not suggest an editor of poise and wide-ranging
experience; it gulped out panic in every line.

> Clay,
>
> *I haven't heard from you for months – years – nor you from me – which is
> what we said, isn't it? I don't want to hear from you but I have to, you Brit
> shit. With how many men did you play at buggery before you passed on your
> gleanings to me? Did you know about AIDS when you let me have you? I
> didn't, or not much, now I do and I'm shit-scared. Condoms or not, no one
> knows whether to be sure of them. I've got all your useless careless selfish
> bloody lying history creamed into my bloodstream – and not the courage to
> take a test – did you take a test yet? If you did,* TELL ME, TELL ME! – or
> don't, as it suits you –
>
> CLAY, I'VE GOT TO KNOW.
>
> *And oh Jesus, what about Kilbeggan? Can I have given it to her? No one
> in this church-blasted scumbag city seems able to tell me for sure.*

Nor did Clay have the courage to take a test. The letter put words to the
formlessness of his fear – perhaps it had already begun to shape itself a
little, when he felt the first doubts of his brain's ability to assess his own
research – but now he knew it every day and every hour of the night,
sleeping or waking; the letter gave him *guilt* as well. He wrote no reply. For
were he to attempt one, what could he say?

EIGHT

A month after the trial, another letter for Clay. Costa Rican stamp, no sender's address, on the flap of the envelope in red ink:
TIDINGS FROM THE LION AT LARGE!
A wad of word-processor print-offs, blotched with coffee-stains and sweaty fingerprints. It had been violently crumpled and smoothed out again – as though the writer, when he finished, could not make up his mind about posting it.

Friend Sig, Muddy isn't it? Yeah –
Saw London papers not long since, report of Grimes case, interesting.
Basically, you got most of it dead right at the trial.
Not quite right about Reuben Ranzo – Terrible Beauty *was mine – I put it up to the vicious old crab at that Bucks seminar, he put it up to top brass as his, and let them fuck-up with it to their hearts' content before foisting it back onto me. Judy for an instance – an Achilles heel if ever I tripped over one – Christ knows where he raked her out, had he been shafting her on the side or what? Like, she must have been worth shafting. I had a half-Asian chick once, never really forgot her.*
You never tumbled to it, did you? That we computerised 'The Peeler's Goat' to turn him into Truethought. One of Ranzo's Eng Lit brats (Peterhouse, Cantab, I think) helped me program the job style-wise – no leaving it to Leo's unaided creativity! – had-to-laff, didn't I? when Katz comes up so bright-n-shiny with his pentagonic re-computerising and lo-n-behold the right answer, spot on! But The Serjeant's Dream *was all mine and I meant it, every word.*
Basically, man, Ranzo was nothing. I guess you had to postulate him *to give yourself a datum-line, right? Psyops was and is pervasive, it's brilliant, it's how we live, it doesn't fucking need a mastermind. Look at me, blown because of* Terrible Beauty, *slung out of UK like a cockroach out of a kitchen, and getting old, man, old! – yet here I sit, brilliant tropics, swimming-pools, hammocks and slick brown greaser-girls, rum and coke, coke of the other sort (sniffs along the thin white line-o), same job, better pay, Brit interests saved from the Yanks, saved from the greasers, saved. Input vis-a-vis Noriega, Ortega, you name it. Ortega, for an instance – Washington had him dead set to win his election, Bush wanted him to win it*

*so he could stomp him Panama-style and enlarge his own wasp cojones –
what happened? Leo the Lion among other things, but how or why I'm not
telling. Use your paranoia, man, work it out. We're stuck-in in Belize, we
don't forget Grenada, nor Colombian drugs-barons, nor who it was who tried
to stop us wasting the Argies, work it out.*

Why am I writing you?

*Because I'm dead, man, fucking dead. Rum and coke and sweaty bitches in
their hammocks notwithstanding. If what I do down here is aborted like*
Terrible Beauty *(as well it might be, any day) they'll sling me out
(cockroach again!) to the Persian fucking Gulf, who needs to go there? to find
whisky/wog-women (*Inshallah!*) Sehr streng verboten! and sod-all else of
current interest – MoD's even sold all the desert uniforms to the Iraqs or Irans
or the Gyppos or somebody – oh I'm far too old, far too sick, to fucking cope.
Christ, man, I work for what they still call an* ARMY!

Let me tell you about ARMIES.

*Orphanage, Birkenhead, '52 or '3 or so – reproachful Jesus and cruel old
God and teeth-grinding Devil to scare the willy off you – but sometimes they'd
give us* culture. *Cecil Sharp's Olde Englysshe Folkesongs (expurgated), pretty
and sweet, unison singing, nice change from deadly hymns, but get a note
wrong or giggle and your pretty little bum-cheeks were pulped red by the
music-teacher's hairbrush. I took to giggling once, because we sang a number
called* Polly Oliver. *You know it, ever? End of seventeenth-cent., so they say
and that's scholarship.*

It's about this bint that joins the ARMY, *right?*

> One night Polly Oliver lay musing in bed,
> A comical fancy came into her head;
> 'Neither father nor mother shall make me false prove,
> I'll list for a soldier and follow my love.'

*—he being an officer, okay? So she puts on men's clothes, and off she goes,
marching and drilling and catching the officer's eye with her zeal-drive-
initiative yessir-nosir-three-bags-full-sir, Christ don't fucking tell me! He
wants her for his batman, she's to sleep in his room, and there it got dodgy,
didn't make much sense, somehow she's undressed and then dressed in her
own petticoats, he recognises her – WOW! they get married, end of song.*

*It struck me – aged nine or was it ten? – that this dressing and undressing
was what the song was all about – your mate Jock Cochrane might call it the
'thematic signifier' – so why wasn't it properly told? Because* psyops *had
sodding censored it, destabilised it, there's a turn-up! paranoia, man, think
of it. Yeah, I did think of it and got a really dirty giggle – and O! the crack of
that hairbrush!*

Now here, man, Muddy, Sig – here's the real story: Polly Oliver (in her own words) with her thematic signifier where it did have ought to be – not quite 'the real story of Thatcher's lies' (I followed your marx-farts often enough in the NS, Socialist Worker, *and similar) but the principle's the same and you ought to appreciate it. Call it the real story of King Billy's lies, and you're about right. I programmed it via* Fanny Hill *crossed with Bert Brecht, but I didn't have expert help, so maybe the style's skidded a bit?*

. . . being daughter to a tailor who made uniform for the king's regiments, I preserved my precious virtue from this young captain's importunities, affirming always my self-respect; albeit I loved him dearly, and well apprehended how contempt of my lowly station withheld him from offer of marriage. Now one day, while his roaming hands tried yet again to prevail against virginity, he chanced to make complaint of my coldness (as to both body and *heart*), with hyperbolical comparison: how sentinels' hands in winter weather would freeze to their musket-stocks – they were not issued with gloves nor could afford to buy them, the greater part of their pay sped heedless toward doxies and brandywine; a mighty unsoldierlike circumstance.

I thought upon it, yea deeply. Ah! let me once prove to him I was no mere trifle of flesh – I had a brain, and I *invented!*

Should greatcoat sleeves be made longer by the span of nine inches, folded back at cuff and buttoned, then in harshest cold might the buttons be loosed, flaps turned down, hands all a-muffle and warm. No augmentation of price were the cloth to be taken from surplus of the skirts, themselves by old custom cut too full for soldierlike smartness.

I made such a coat and showed it; the ARMY, strongly esteeming it, bespoke a host of others. I grew passing rich, until, verily, I could have *bought* the captain. Instead I was so fond I yielded myself and my treasure (irreplacable!) to his sheets; only to reveal him still of the same haughty mind, and no marriage. For brutal stanching of my petitionary tears he even boasted of gaudy ladies (half-a-hundred, more enticing than myself), who might be his at the click of his fingers.

I do think his insolence turned me mad; for in a frenzy I could see naught for't but to enlist as a man, to watch him, to follow him, to ensure hook-or-crook his disgraceful 'half-a-hundred' slip no stays, unlatch no garters, within reach of his sensibilities. The regiment at that time under orders for Ireland, to rid the land of King Popery James.

Strange to say, in the barrack-room I was safe against discovery, for it was ever bitter cold, and the men of such noisome habits that they went into their beds all clothed. Not a week had I been a soldier, without sight yet of the captain, and drilled by screaming serjeants to the tune of 'Lillibulero' 'til I was pretty nigh dead of it; and then I was warned for the guard-duty. It snowed. I had no gloves, not wishing to appear singular among my new companions. So what must I do but unbutton my flaps of greatcoat sleeves, to hold my musket warmly, as surely it was designed (by none other than myself) thus to be held?

The serjeant-major, with but one look at me, commenced his clamour: 'Improperly dressed!' Cuffs covering hands were NOT to be worn upon guard-mounting, idle and unsoldierlike! He said, 'Flogged.' Oh how I endeavoured (and in vain) to persuade him why sleeves were made as they were; he roared me to silence: the ARMY did with its clothing what it *chose* to do with its clothing, I had sorely broken discipline, nothing mitigated, I must be flogged. 'Have the drummer draw cat-o'-nine-tails from company stores.'

They marched me to the triangle in front of all the regiment. Am I to write of my lonely terror? Pray let me keep silence, in trust that the reader, already sufficient perceptive, shall not need nor desire circumlocutory pathos.

But yet was it e'en worse! for there on the parade-ground to oversee punishment – my captain-lover, aloof and cruel. 'Improperly dressed, and tried to argue? The man must learn, serjeant-major. He shall strip! for five-and-thirty, or as many more as may be thought due.'

Should I not, at this turn in my misfortunate tale, give account of my corporal appearance? Imagine, if you will, black curls and a slender form, lad-like, some said, not buxom, neither meagre, yet of a fragile symmetry, back and front, fit to inflame a gallant's –

(This must be the 'thematic signifier'; the programmed prose-style shifting from curt constructions of historical parable into voluptuous but detestable sadism, sweltering detail spread out over four-and-a-half pages. Clay's frame of mind deprived him of all interest in it. He noted only the captain's treachery upon recognising the naked Polly.)

. . . surveyed me through his quizzing-glass, skin, hair, teeth, armpits, toenails and delicious *etceteras*: ''Sblood, 'tis a wench! – and protests I know her? – never saw her before in my life – carry on, sarnt-major.'

(He skipped to the abrupt finish.)

. . . for if the captain, a man of honour, absolutely denied knowledge of me, who could I be? A French spy, concluded the colonel; other officers concurred.

They ordered her hanged. End of story. I don't like it.

Think about Polly Oliver, Sig, yea deeply; you might find you need a wank? And when you've had it, think this. She was fool enough to work a new technique, state-of-the-art, for an ARMY: and ARMY did for her with it. She exposed herself in front of all of them – even though unwillingly, even though compelled – it didn't save her. The reverse. Not my idea to natter Ginsberg and similar, round the Fenian households of Ulster. Ranzo's: and it exposed me before I was ready. Brasshat pressure on Ranzo to get his results, unsoldierlike to hang about; but Ranzo (take note, Sig) was never exposed. If he lives, he'll live for ever.

—as for Leo, dead basic; I'm fucking dead.

All of which, Clay venomously guessed, was yet another piece of disinformation. He must contrive to slot it in to his US/Latin-American files – no doubt some of the truth behind it would eventually emerge? On the other hand, the little liar had been remarkably casual in dismissing the Persian Gulf as a theatre of potential incident; so maybe the Middle East files?

HISTORICAL NOTES

Each of these stories contains a core of historical truth: all of them are invented. I leave it to my readers to determine, according to taste and prejudice, how far my inventions are probable. But I ought to give some indication of what is imaginary and what is not.

SLOW JOURNEY, SWIFT WRITING

According to Herodotus, a voyage round Africa was indeed carried out by a ship in the Egyptian service, but in the reign of Pharaoh Necho, six centuries after the date I have given. The crew's account of the sun shining from the north is mentioned by the Greek historian as a sailors' yarn unworthy of credence. The late Robert Graves, in one of his essays, suggests that the Egyptians (with their politically powerful cult of the sun-god) would have taken a much less relaxed view of the assertion. Herodotus reports a second and unsuccessful attempt at circumnavigation, which he says was enforced upon a delinquent nobleman by the Persian Emperor Xerxes as penalty for a rape. I have combined these features into the one story, shifting it back to the time of Ramses III in order to bring in the Sea Peoples and their Homeric associations.

The scribe's 'Egyptianised' versions of foreign names might make a difficulty for readers who do not have classical legend immediately on tap. Those who do will probably recognise *Odysseus* (and *Oudeis*, 'Nobody'), *Laertes, Telemachus, Ithaca, Pallas Athene, Penelope, Troy/Ilion, Melantho, Circe, Calypso, Nausicaa* . . .

Graves (in *The Greek Myths*) gives some variants of the Odysseus saga which Homer chose not to adopt; I have freely taken my pick of these. He is also my authority for the significance of Pharos as a Sea Peoples' oracle-shrine and entrepot: the *Odyssey*'s fairytale account of the goings-on there was compiled at a period when the island had long ceased to be a practical port-of-call for Aegean mariners.

THE LITTLE OLD WOMAN AND HER TWO BIG BOOKS

I have postulated a hitherto unknown Nuremberg first-edition of *Malleus Maleficarum*. Apart from that book's two witch-hunting authors (and of course, Johaan Gutenberg), all the characters are imaginary.

The Little Old Woman is in fact an expansion of an untitled short story

by Margaretta D'Arcy about the origins of the *Malleus*, which she wrote for
'Women's Scéal Radio' (see *dedication*) and read during one of the station's
programmes in 1988. I am very grateful for her permission to embody her
narrative within my own.

USES OF IRON

Most of what happens in this tale is a reasonably accurate account of what did
happen. The major characters are all from history. My principle invention is
the relationship between Fanny Kemble, for a long time one of my favourite
people in the story of the English theatre, and the Duke of Wellington, for
whom I have felt an ambivalent repulsion/attraction ever since I was a child
and used to look through the horrifying/exciting pages of a book of my
father's – *Great Battles of the British Army*, I think it was called, with some very
scary Victorian steel-engravings. When I discovered that actress and duke
were both present upon the chaotic opening-day of the Liverpool and
Manchester Railway, I felt determined to bring them together there, even if it
meant unashamedly doing violence to the details of the occasion as Fanny
herself describes it in her autobiographical *Record of a Girlhood*.

In fact, instead of being lodged in theatrical digs in Liverpool, she stayed
(with a slight but detectable sense of social presumption) at Heaton, the
Earl of Wilton's country house, where she was chaperoned by her mother.
Her mother also accompanied her on the railway-ride; and they had seats
in a carriage immediately behind the duke's triumphal car, not in the train
that ran over Huskisson. Fanny's performances that week were in
Manchester, the season at Liverpool having concluded; she did not have to
make the exhausting return journey; she slipped away directly from the
turbulence at Manchester station.

I have found no evidence that the duke ever met her face-to-face or even
wrote to her (although Charles Kemble had indeed given a private
recitation for him at an embassy picnic near Paris).

Nor any evidence that Harriette Wilson had an interview with the duke
in 1830.

Nor any information about how E. T. Craig responded to the railway's
inauguration, although he was certainly living in Manchester and would
have been bound to take an interest. His fiancée's surname is not to be
discovered; Craig in his Ralahine memoir calls her 'Miss B.', and other
records know her only by her married name of Mary Craig and describe
her as the daughter of a bookseller and newsagent: Margaretta D'Arcy
and myself decided on 'Bentham' in a radio play we wrote in 1984 about
the Ralahine Co-operative. There was a Bentham in Manchester at the
time, in the book-business, a radical, who *might* have been her father.

I'm afraid it would not have been possible for the duke to have been told about the fiasco of the Spanish rebellion of General Torrijos (and the survival of John Kemble) as early as September 1830; the doomed men were captured and executed late in the following year. But John's letter from Algeciras had in fact reached his sister while she was working in Liverpool.

And Ellen Tree did play Romeo to Fanny Kemble's Juliet, but only in London, as far as I can discover; so her Liverpool presence in *Uses of Iron* is as wilful on my part as the rest of my distortions of Fanny's experience.

'LIKE A *DREAM* OF A GUN . . .'
A few years ago a young British soldier was killed in the north of Ireland. A poem that he left behind him received a good deal of publicity, reporters being under the impression that he had written it himself. It then turned out that this was not so; he had apparently copied it from a printed source (ironically, I seem to recollect, an *Irish-American* nationalist source) simply because he liked it. I don't remember the exact date of the incident, or any details of the poem. '*Like a* Dream *of a Gun . . .'* is NOT based upon this distressing episode, except in so far as the media-exploitation provided the notion that Psychological Operations personnel could so easily have organised the whole thing from the start, had they thought of it. To judge from their known record, they would have been quite happy to do so.

No characters in the story are 'historical'.

I have used some real titles of newspapers (the *Muswell Hill Weekly Digest* is not one of them) and of television programmes, because it seemed absurd to invent an entire corpus of British and Irish media when everyone knows which particular organs would in real life be publishing what sort of news and comment. But the quotations attributed to them are of my own composition and do not reflect the work of any specific journalists or current-affairs presenters. Similarly I have used real universities and colleges to locate some highly fictional academic individuals.

One item has a foundation of fact – the behaviour of the 'poetical soldier' executing a house-search. This curious event – or something very like it – did take place, in Belfast. I owe the anecdote to Margaretta D'Arcy, who had it from a participant at a cultural gathering (*Duchas na Saoirse*) in that city in 1989.